"More than a novel about crooked cops, this is a book by a big cop who was on the take himself, and what a world he creates!"

—Norman Mailer

O'Neil paid for the drinks, waved to everyone around the bar like an ex-heavyweight champ, and walked outside with Jimmy. When they shook hands goodbye, Jimmy felt the nice feel of something green being pressed into his right hand.

Jimmy put his right hand with the money in it deep down in his pants pocket. He didn't dare look at it until he got on the Canal Street subway platform. Was it a five? A tenner? Twenty? Jesus, not a fifty? He walked to the front part of the station and lifted the bill out of his pocket and looked at it. *Holy Christ, a C-note! One hundred American dollars! You sweetheart, big Petey O'Neil, today you have made me a man. A man of stature, a man of wealth. See you in Gallagher's, Petey boy . . .*

ROYAL BLUE

JAMES REARDON

ST. MARTIN'S PRESS/NEW YORK

Royal Blue was previously published by Wyndham Books under the title *The Sweet Life of Jimmy Riley*.

Published by arrangement with the author

ROYAL BLUE

Copyright © 1980 by James Reardon.

Library of Congress Catalog Card Number: 80-24579

ISBN: 0-312-91053-3   Can. ISBN: 0-312-91054-1

Printed in the United States of America

Wyndham Books edition published 1980
First St. Martin's Press mass market edition/March 1989

10 9 8 7 6 5 4 3 2 1

To all the friends I made in the gambling world. With rare exceptions, they were all wonderful guys.

ROYAL BLUE

Foreword

THIS BOOK could be construed as either twenty-five percent fiction and seventy-five percent fact, or seventy-five percent fiction and twenty-five percent fact. It is undoubtedly very much autobiographical, as are many first novels, but I must admit I purposely did spice it up here and there to avoid anything resembling a documentary.

The main theme of the book is the Harry Gross bookmaking scandal of the early 1950s. The protagonist, Jimmy Riley, was an integral part of the scandal. He, of course, is in many ways a fictional character. He is a composite of a few policemen who suffered through many bad years as a result of the scandal.

Like all gambling probes, the unearthing of Harry Gross and his associates elicited from the media all the juiciest of clichés: Threatens the Fall of City Hall—Shakes New York City Police Department from Top to Bottom—Gross Case Tentacles Spreading Wildly. You name it, they wrote it or said it! As usual, the public ate it up.

As the scandal mushroomed, everybody wanted to get into the act. Except, of course, the poor cops and gamblers who were going to take the rap. The D.A. and his chief assistants were as implacable as Captain Javert in his pursuit of Jean Valjean. The judges, those paragons of virtue, could taste the blood of the crooked cops.

The amusing or amazing thing is, the same type of scandal erupts like clockwork every ten years or so. And it is not confined to New York City alone—it happens periodically in practically every big city in the country. Furthermore, if you counted the less publicized gambling scandals in the small cities and towns, I believe you would need a giant computer to program the alliances between cops and wise guys.

Perhaps "sad" is a much better adjective than "amusing" to describe these periodic bursts of scandal probing. Especially if you have ever been a victim of one of these holy crusades. Everyone who remembers the Brooklyn Dodgers knew that gambling was wide open around 1950. That includes newspaper and radio and television reporters; D.A.s, cops, and plenty of judges. Almost half the nation bet on horses and sports and still does. The whole system was a sham, and the investigative and judicial bodies knew it better than anyone else. If a bookmaker or numbers guy received a hundred-dollar fine after twenty arrests and maybe eight convictions, he wanted to kick the shit out of his lawyer. One poor bastard in five thousand went to jail, and then for perhaps thirty days, at most, ninety days.

In the Harry Gross scandal, the real target of the D.A. and the judges was that fine broth of a boy from the old country, Bill O'Dwyer. Yessir, the Pride of County Mayo, Bill O'Dwyer, the esteemed mayor of New York City. All the bullshit about Harry Gross, the kingpin of New York bookmakers, was exactly that— bullshit! There were twenty bookmakers in New York at the same time who could put Harry in their hip pocket, but for various reasons he appeared at the time to be the logical target—the means to topple the regime of Bill O'Dwyer. As the story unfolds, perhaps the reader will easily discern why Harry was the fall guy.

But what of the other fall guys? The poor bastards who couldn't stand the idea of disgrace and jail and wound up committing suicide? Then there were the guys who did end up in disgrace and who were packed off to jail for anywhere from one to five years. How about the homes broken up? The kids being tormented in school? The wives who split from their fallen husbands? Of course the law-and-order reader will rationalize that the cop who took gambling money would also take all types of crooked money. This is very possible, but the cancer of corruption in those days was the insipid, hypocritical gambling laws—the stupid, bluenose, bullshit gambling laws. We are finally coming out of the Dark Ages with the likes of offtrack betting parlors, state lotteries, and Las Vegas Nights. It is only a matter of a few years until gambling will be legalized throughout the United States.

Of course, the politicians and lawmakers in search of headlines will beat their breasts and scream that the mob will move in. Who the hell runs the oil companies and the big corporations but the white-collar mob? Just as they have the brains to make their operations successful, so has the mob the savvy to run the casinos. So long as government gets its percentage and there is more than a façade of supervision, so what? A prime example was in Freeport in the Bahamas. The wise guys ran a superlative casino in Lucayan Bay that attracted all the high rollers. It was honest, beautiful, and had everything Las Vegas offered the gambler, with the added virtues of balmy weather, lovely beaches, and a lush tropical atmosphere. Well, the headline hunters hounded Lucayan out of business, knocked the shit out of the Bahamian economy, and left them with one third-rate casino that resembles a big barn and draws flies to the tables.

The simple fact about gambling is that hardly anyone thinks it is illicit. Certainly the uniform and plainclothes cops of the late 1940s did not. The uniform cops practically depended for a living on the money they grabbed from the bookies on their post. The more the merrier, and the better the cop, the better the post he got. As for the vice cops, the anti-gambling squads that were supposed to enforce the gambling laws, forget about it. There are more lawyers and doctors whose fathers were police inspectors than you can shake a stick at. The vice cops formed friendships with wise guys and gamblers that were closer than with members of their own families.

But remember, ninety-nine percent of these uniform and vice cops had plenty of balls, and law and order reigned supreme in the more vital areas of crime. They did not get paid big salaries or overtime, or have fringe benefits. They stayed out all night, ever on the alert for a sneak ziginette game run by the Italians, a baboot game run by the Greeks, or the best score of all, a sneak crap game run by the Irish or the Jews. They patrolled all night, always on the lookout for a score, but God help the mugger or the thief they grabbed. Or the would-be tough guy that gave them any shit. You ever called a cop a pig in those days, you had better be prepared to take the shellacking of your life. Whenever the detectives took the stickup guy, rapist, or mugger into the abattoir called the squad room, even the cops in the station house felt pity for him.

One saying I'll never forget was attributed to our late, great mayor of New York City, Jimmy Walker. It seems the rank-and-file cops, the nucleus of The Job, long before police unions and overtime and such, were grumbling about a pay raise. "Gentlemen," Jimmy is supposed to have said, "show me a cop who wants a pay raise and I'll show you a bad fuckin' cop."

Thus, in the times I write about the cops received unbelievably low wages. As long as they thought they weren't doing anything terrible or really against the grain, making a buck was a way of life, a means of sustenance. So as the story unfolds, I hope the reader may find a little empathy for a cop like Jimmy Riley. He was a little bad, but not too bad—not too good, mind you, but not too bad.

Prologue

JIMMY RILEY stood nice and easy against the bar of his favorite restaurant, Jimmy Weston's. It was his kind of place: soft lights, well-dressed, good-looking women, the men in neckties and dark suits, the music sweet and low. Right off Park Avenue on East 54th Street in the heart of Manhattan, Jimmy Riley's own hometown. The first two Cutty and waters had filled his belly with a nice warm glow, and his eyes were bright with anticipation of a night on the town. Jimmy had a phrase for nights like this, "Let's go cabareting." As usual, his best pal, Tony, was right next to him, laying the charm on their two companions for the evening. And the companions were just Jimmy's and Tony's style, each about forty, career-woman types, and they dressed and talked right out of *Harper's Bazaar*. Beautiful, beautiful!

Jimmy kidded with Paddy the bartender, and when Paddy turned away to mix a drink Jimmy looked himself over pretty good in the mirror behind the bar. Not too bad, he said to himself. No, not too bad, Jimmy baby.

He had on a three-piece blue pinstripe Richard Bennett number, a high-collared white shirt, and a solid maroon tie. With a silent chuckle and the good Scotch whiskey in him—it was all he could do to keep from laughing out loud—he thought of his sweet mother and how, whenever she bought him something new when he was a kid, he would pose in front of a mirror and say, "Gee, Mom, Sister Loretta is going to flip when she sees me in this jacket." He smiled to himself. It's a good thing that none of the good sisters in Visitation School ever did flip, or there would have been a helluva commotion.

Tony kept holding the floor with the *Harper's Bazaar* ladies, and Jimmy shadowboxed the bar mirror a little more.

His hair was a little thinner but not too bad, his skin was tanned and good from all the golf and walking and swimming. He was tall and pretty wide, with a good carriage, and if he remembered to suck his stomach in just a bit, no one would even notice the little paunch. No, Riley, my good man, you don't look near your age. You're still here anyway, and life when you almost lost it becomes twice as sweet.

All in all, Jimmy was well pleased with his middle-aged image, and as the music of super Hazel Scott floated out of the dining area to the rear, he wondered if anyone ever played better piano than God Love Hazel. When she zipped into "Seems Like Old Times," he felt so good he almost burst into song. Instead he leaned into the ear of the girl on Tony's left—his girl, he hoped, as Tony seemed to have a lock on the other one—and gave his best sotto-voce imitation of Carmen Lombardo. "Dinner dates at seven, seems like old times, having you is heaven. I still get a thrill, the way I used to do, seems like old times being here with you."

"Oh, James, that was just lovely. I didn't know you sang."

Jimmy grinned his shy country-boy grin, laughed and said, "Come on, Nancy, cut it out. That's just the ham in me surfacing after a few Scotches."

Nancy laughed, and for the first time that night looked Riley over carefully. She seemed to like what she saw. She linked her arm through his and said, "I thought you were never going to join Marcia, Anthony, and me."

"Oh," Jimmy said with just the right touch of sarcasm to get Tony's ass, "I was so sure that Anthony's story was so utterly fascinating I hesitated to interrupt."

The girls both laughed, Tony silently mouthed "Up yours, Riley," and Jimmy stopped kidding with Paddy the bartender, stopped looking himself over in the mirror, and decided to get to the business at hand. His best pal, Tony, two fine-looking broads, great dinner waiting in the next room with fine wine and the super piano of God Love Hazel. Then on to Jimmy Ryan's for some great jazz and, as the *pièce de résistance,* when everyone had had enough Scotch and wine and music, Jimmy and Tony would go through their shaking-hands act—like they hated to part—and each would go his separate way with one of the *Harper's Bazaar* ladies on the road that spells Paradise Lane.

Jimmy was just about to ask the maître d', George the Greek, for their usual table when he felt a tap on his arm. He turned around, and a nicely dressed, well-built guy about thirty said, "Pardon me, are you Jimmy Riley?"

Jimmy shrugged, gave a slightly hesitant smile, and said, "That's me, my good man." No dope, Riley, even with a few Scotches in him, made the guy out for some sort of cop.

The young guy laughed and said, "I heard so much about you. I've wanted to meet you for a long time. My name is Johnny Tracey, and I'm a detective in Manhattan North."

Jimmy replied, "Why, that's real nice of you, John, to come over and introduce yourself this way. I'd love to buy you a drink, but I'm just about to go into dinner with some business friends of mine." He gestured toward Tony and the girls.

"But gee," Tracey persisted. "Would you mind, Mr. Riley? Only for a minute. I want you to meet my partner. We talk about you a lot and he's dying to say hello to you. His father came in The Job with you, and you can't believe how often we've discussed you."

Jimmy turned to Tony and the girls, winked, gave them his best Burt Reynolds "What's the use of denying it" look, and said, "Tony, tell George to get the table ready. I'll be back in a couple of minutes."

He followed Tracey to the far corner of the bar, where Tracey beckoned to a slim, blond boy with a full beard and said, "Bill, this is your man, Jimmy Riley."

The blond kid jumped off his bar chair and pumped Riley's hand enthusiastically. Riley was looking at him thinking, Holy Christ! Don't tell me this little bearded prick is really a detective!

"My father came in The Job the same day as you, Mr. Riley. I hope you remember him. George Moynihan. He retired as a lieutenant out of the Forty-fifth in the Bronx."

"Sure," Riley said, even though he didn't know George Moynihan from Adam. "Sure I remember George, and I think it's wonderful for him to have a fine young son like you to follow in his footsteps."

All the time Riley was thinking, How in Christ's name would anyone expect me to remember some guy in my class in rookie school thirty-three years ago? And the fucking Bronx, how I hated that asshole borough. And now this kid with his goddam beard . . . Jesus help me!

They talked for a few minutes about how New York was changing—to Riley, it only changed for the better, and he loved it more every day of his life—but he sipped the drink they bought him and agreed how tough it was with the spics and blacks overrunning the city. He was quietly nodding his head and agreeing with them, meanwhile silently concluding they were both full of shit. Out of a clear blue sky the little blond, bearded prick said, "You know, Mr. Riley, Johnny and I and a lot of guys in The Job we hang out with always talk about you as a kind of legend, you know, a sort of reverse Frank Serpico."

Riley was beginning to throw out his chest and preen a little when he came to the part about his being a legend. He was even beginning to think the little blond, bearded prick might not be too bad a cop after all, when the last part of the sentence hit him like a shot.

Riley's face struggled to stay straight and only his eyes clouded over so that anyone who knew him would sense that some poor guy was going to get whacked out. He looked at the kid and said, "I don't get you, Bill. What do you mean, a reverse Frank Serpico?"

The kid didn't miss the look on Riley's kisser, but he figured, What the hell, I'm half this guy's age and he won't start anything with a cop, especially in a class joint like this. So he went on, "Please don't get me wrong, Mr. Riley, but you, you know, you have the rep of having made the most money of any cop in New York. And excuse me, sir, I know you paid the penalty for it, but on the opposite side of the coin, you know, Frank Serpico being the most honest cop of all time and bringing integrity back into

The Job and all . . . Well, no offense, but it is a pleasure to meet one of the two most talked-about cops of our time."

As the young detective talked, Riley listened, smiled the little half smile of his, and waited until the kid finished. He then put his drink on the bar and said, "Well, it was nice meeting you, Bill. I have to go back to my party now. Say hello to your father. Don't go down in the muff with that beard of yours or you'll give some broad the crabs, and when you meet the other half of that legend of yours, Frank Serpico, tell him Jimmy Riley says to go fuck himself."

He turned abruptly, leaving the two detectives with their mouths wide open.

When he rejoined Tony and the girls, Tony took one look at him and motioned the girls ahead. Grabbing him tightly by the arm, Tony whispered in his ear, "For the love of Christ, Jimmy, what happened? You're steaming. For Christ's sake, calm down and get that crazy look off your face."

The two girls excused themselves to go to the ladies' room, leaving Jim and Tony alone at the table sipping a little Cordon Bleu brandy.

"All right, Jim, cut the horseshit. Those two young cops really got your goat, didn't they? What the hell happened? They didn't try to shake you, did they?"

"Shake me? For Christ's sake, are you kidding, that's *my* racket! Come on, Tony, let's get rid of these two broads and take a nice long walk. I want to have a long talk with you. I've had something on my mind for quite a while, and I think those two cops triggered it. But first, I really want your opinion."

"Okay, pal." Tony motioned to a waiter nearby and said, "Get George over here."

George the Greek came over to the table in a couple of minutes and said, "What's up, guys?"

"Listen, Georgie, when the two girls we're with come back to the table, give us about five minutes and come over and give me that 'wanted on the telephone' shit. You got it?"

The Greek formed a circle with his index finger and thumb into the okay sign and walked away. Nancy and Marcia came back to the table all sharped up and looking gorgeous. Riley looked at them with an ache in his heart and knew that he and Tony would be crushed when they gave them the air, but what the hell, first things first, and this time the broads had to finish second.

Sure enough, the Greek came to the table and said, "Very, very important telephone call, Mr. Bove. I tried to say that you weren't taking any calls, but they insisted they had to speak to you. Sorry, sir."

Tony excused himself and went out of the dining room to a bank of telephones on the left. About five minutes later he came back with his doomsday face on, shaking his head.

"What's the matter, Tony? You look like the earth's about to open. Bad news on the phone?"

"Would you believe it, Jim? You and I have to meet those Chicago guys in Gallagher's in half an hour—and by ourselves."

"For Christ's sake, you're kidding, Tony. What about the girls?"

Tony looked at the girls almost tearfully and said, "This is really a shame, but you'll just have to forgive the two of us tonight. Something really important came up in our business, these people have to go back to Chicago in the morning and we have to meet them tonight to straighten a problem out."

The two girls were a little taken aback at such an abrupt ending to what had been the start of a very promising night, but they assented gracefully. Tony and Jimmy said their goodbyes, made another date for real soon, put them into a hired car and sent them on their way. They went back to the table to finish their brandy and pay the check. Tony said, "All right, Irish, I've been thinking all day about the nice night I was going to spend with this broad and you go into your act. What the hell happened between you and those two bulls out at the bar?"

"Well, the first guy who came over was a nice enough kid, but he brought me over to his partner at the other end of the bar and he said something I didn't like."

"You mean he insulted you?" asked Tony.

"Not exactly," replied Jimmy.

"Well, what the hell did he say? You came back with the worst-looking Irish kisser I ever saw on anybody; Kevin Barry looked better than you, just before they hung him in Mountjoy Prison."

Jimmy grinned a little sheepishly. "To tell you the truth, he compared me to that prick Frank Serpico."

"How in the name of Christ could he compare you with that guinea bastard?"

"Well, furthermore, it wasn't exactly a flattering comparison. He said Frank Serpico was legendary for being honest, and I was legendary for being dishonest. He didn't say it quite as flat out as that, but that was the gist of it."

"That bearded asshole had some nerve. It's a wonder you didn't give him one of your back-handers."

Jimmy shrugged and said, "Ah, I'm getting too old for that kind of shit. To tell you the truth, after the initial shock of that little prick saying that to me wore off, I started thinking about something. It's what I want to talk to you about."

"What are you going to do, take the veil, become a priest or something? Or maybe you're going to join the Trappists and start making wine instead of drinking the shit."

"Come on, cut it out. Let's get the hell out of here and take a long walk. I've got something on my mind I'd like to get off. You can be the sounding board."

"It better be good, 'cause you just cost me a beautiful piece of ass with one of your goddam Irish moods."

"Save it, Tony, my boy. Save it. You're getting to the age where every piece of ass you lose is one you save."

They paid the check, staked everybody good, shook hands all around, and left the restaurant. It was a lovely spring night. They turned up Park Avenue and Jimmy breathed New York in deeply. No one could believe how beautiful the East Side of New York was on a starry spring night. What a great town! he thought.

Tony was just as wrapped up in the balmy night, and neither of them spoke for a couple of blocks.

Finally Tony broke the ice. "All right, Jim, what's on that scheming, crooked, reverse Frank Serpico mind of yours?"

"To be perfectly honest with you, pal, I've come to the conclusion that I'm finally going to write that book I've been bullshitting about for years."

"Are you serious this time? No shit!"

"Yes, what the hell's the difference? Everyone on the case is either dead or retired and sitting on their fat asses in Florida. Besides, I think it would make a helluva story and maybe release a lot of the shit I've kept inside me all these years."

"I don't see any objection. But what got you started thinking about the book again, that Serpico bullshit tonight in Jimmy Weston's?"

"Exactly. You and I agree he was full of shit. But full of shit or not, he practically became a martyr to some people and at the same time made a ton of cash."

"Absolutely. Didn't you and I always have the idea that that was the prick's original scheme in the first place? Every cop in New York knows he can refuse plainclothes work if he has any scruples about it. All Serpico had to do was say no, I don't want vice-squad work. Every street-smart cop knows that plainclothes is the money route. If he didn't want to make money, why the hell did he take the job in the first place?"

"I've told you my opinion of the guy at least fifty times. I honestly believe he had a master plan. To play honest George and all that shit, then to finally go before an asshole investigative body like the Knapp Commission. Then when he put everybody in the grease, get rich by writing an exposé. Serpico has to be one of the cutest and slickest cops of all time."

Tony laughed and said, "And how about those disguises he wore to catch the big bad bookmakers and numbers runners? What a crock of shit! Every cop and federal agent in the business knows that, unless you catch him dead bank in the act, there's only one way to catch a guy breaking the law, and that's with a stool pigeon. For Christ's sake, imagine dressing like a guinea iceman, walking a big dog and hoping to fall into a floating crap game or a horse room. Can you imagine people swallowing shit like that?"

"Well, they do, Tony, my boy, they sure do. The average John Q. Citizen eats that stuff up. Serpico made himself look like the only honest cop on the New York police force. I felt bad that the dopey bastard got shot, but even then he made his partners look like pieces of shit when he told the story. You and I know the true story. He was sitting outside in the car waiting for his partners to come back with the collar when the stool pigeon told them the only way they could make the 'in' was with someone who could speak Spanish. The dealers were all spics and couldn't speak a word of English. So they get Frank out of the car, he goes up to the apartment the pigeon fingers, knocks on the door, and says in Spanish that he wants a fix. The spic dealer opens the door a little on a latch, recognizes Frank from his beard, and shoots poor Frankie right in the kisser."

"That's right, Jim, and that was tough, but why the hell did they make his partners look so bad afterward? The movie had them looking like real yellow bastards. The truth is that they broke the door down, shot it out with the spics, and killed the guy who shot Frank. What the hell more could you expect from any partners?"

"I guess no one will really ever know what motivated the guy, but life's a funny thing. In some ways his master plan finally worked out. Now they make heroes out of cops who squeal on guys they work with. Now everyone is so afraid of the guy next to him being a rat, the Job is finally turning honest. That is, almost honest. The wise guys never had it so good. Now they work and don't have to pay. They just have to worry about some dopey son of a bitch stumbling into them every once in a while."

"All that is down the river now, Tony. But what do you think, shall I settle down and try to write this goddam book or not?"

"Well, it was a helluva case, Jimmy, and I think it would make a helluva book. If you think you can handle it, why not? Besides, you're getting old, pricko, and if you make enough money maybe you can retire to your place in Florida and swim and play golf to your heart's content. After all, Frankie has a beautiful house in Holland which he got for being so honest. Think what you'll get for being so dishonest?"

"That's a nice thing to say to an old altar boy. Remember I was ten years an altar boy and never stole a candle. I think it was the bad environment I was led into that turned me around. And after all, I was rehabilitated by the great State of New York, wasn't I?" Jimmy laughed and continued. "I'll never forget the first time I met the parole board. Some big, fat, bald-headed prick kept ques-

tioning me about the case and harping on why I didn't cooperate
with the authorities. I insisted I didn't know anything, that I was
framed. He gave me a disgusted look and said, 'Riley, I really
don't believe we can rehabilitate you.'

"I looked this big prick straight in the eye and said, 'Honestly,
sir, the first walk I took around the Dannemora yard I became
completely rehabilitated.'

"The two other commissioners busted out laughing, but the big
fuckin' hatchet man just snarled at me like it wasn't the least bit
funny. Needless to say, I didn't make parole."

They walked up Park Avenue to 86th Street, cut across to Fifth
Avenue, and walked back downtown. They were silent for long
intervals, content with each other's companionship, and finally
reached Jimmy's apartment in the middle Fifties. They went up
for a nightcap and kicked around the whole evening. Tony finally
said, "Look, for no other reason than the fact that you cost me a
gorgeous broad, you might as well write your goddam book. You
have all that shit churning up inside of you, and sooner or later
it's gotta come out. Do it and get it over with."

And that's the way they left off. Riley tossed in bed a little that
night, but when he fell asleep, he was at peace with himself.

The next morning came up raining a hard, spring rain, and
Jimmy Riley sat down at his desk in the living room, looked at
the yellow pad in front of him, and started to write. So began the
sometimes sweet, sometimes sour life of Jimmy Riley...

1

It was one of those mornings in early March when winter seems reluctant to turn into spring. The sky was heavily overcast and it was raw and cold. Jimmy Riley stood assembled with a hundred and ninety-nine other young and apparently healthy guys, waiting for the mayor of the city of New York to swear them in as police officers. They were dressed in their spanking-new blue uniforms, the regalia of New York's Finest. They were paired off in twos, in four orderly lines pretty much according to their respective heights.

Riley was getting cold standing at ease out there amid the brisk, chill winds that were swirling around the front steps of City Hall. He looked up at the sky and saw the flocks of pigeons flying around. He thought about when he was a kid in Brooklyn and how crazy he was about pigeons. How an older guy named Jerry Shea used to let them help fly his pigeons. He remembered them clearly: the tumblers, the tiplets, the homers. And how he always felt sorry for the pigeons they called rats; the pigeons who weren't purebred. He felt badly when Jerry would chase them off the flock with his long bamboo pole with the bandana handkerchief on the end. He marveled how Jerry could spot a rat the minute he landed on the roof where the big coop was. He would whack at them with the pole and they would scurry off into the air, frightened as hell. The poor rats, Riley always thought, what a shame nobody wanted them. And he was sure that the pigeons flying above City Hall today weren't purebreds, that they were rats. If they weren't rats, they would have a nice coop and plenty of feed to come home to.

As Riley looked up at the pigeons on this cold March morning, he wished he were one of them. He wished that he could fly right the hell out of City Hall Park and escape his present trap. Not only was he getting numb from the goddam cold, he felt trapped —trapped and frustrated. He couldn't figure for the life of him how the hell he was standing here waiting to be sworn in as a cop. No way did he want to become a cop. He had filed his application and taken the police tests only to please his father. He grinned a little ruefully. Not only to please him, but because his old man was one tough son of a bitch and would probably have knocked the shit out of him if he disobeyed him. But what the hell else was he going to do? He was married and had a kid, he'd lost a good job because the business closed due to the steel shortage created by the war. Eight torturous months in Todd Shipyards convinced him that he was the world's worst fucking mechanic. He would have killed more shipyard workers than the Jap spies if he'd stayed there. Well, what the hell, he thought. I'm 1-A in the draft and pretty soon maybe I'll get my ass shot off and get out of my misery.

Suddenly there was a rustling and gawking among the lines of the assembled young cops and the audience who were congregated on the perimeter to watch the swearing-in. The Little Flower of New York, Fiorello LaGuardia, was striding up to the lectern on the top steps of City Hall, complete with microphones. He raised his hands to quiet the smattering of applause that greeted him, and in short order administered the oath of office to the young policemen. That finished, he went into a congratulatory speech, welcoming the young rookies into the ranks of New York's Finest. His high-pitched, squeaky voice came over the microphone like a cross between a female impersonator and a crow.

Riley listened with half an ear, wishing the windy little bastard would wind it up so he could go somewhere and get warm again. But the Little Flower loved to talk, and once he got on the subject of the public trust and police corruption, it seemed as endless as a State of the Union message from Franklin D. Roosevelt. Only

Roosevelt was a hundred percent better! Stay clean, young men, stay clean, Fiorello rasped. Keep your hearts and your minds pure. Don't fall into the sinkhole of graft, bribery, and corruption. Beware of crooks and gamblers who try to buy policemen.

What a lot of shit this is, thought Riley. Here's a sanctimonious mayor who just cut a police rookie's salary to one hundred dollars a month and he's up there preaching like a Holy Roller, urging all of us stupid bastards to stay clean. Stay clean and starve, that's what he's really saying.

Riley stood there listening to the mayor's horseshit, cold, unhappy, and completely miserable. He'd always earned his own way ever since he was a kid. He'd never asked anyone for money in his life, and now he was worried to death about how he was going to make it with a wife and kid on the big one hundred a month this fuckin' windy mayor decreed as a salary. Again he looked up at the pigeons and again he wished that he could fly the hell out of his present trap.

Well, all good things have to come to an end, and the mayor finally shut up and the rookies broke ranks. There was a lot of kissing and handshaking going on with the relatives after the ceremony, but Riley didn't know a soul there so he quickly cut out for the subway and home. He was so engrossed in feeling sorry for himself, he almost paid his subway fare, but recovered in time to pass through the exit gate like a real pro. Well, at least my transportation is free, he thought sarcastically. I'll soon figure out whatever the hell else is on the cuff.

Rookie school wasn't all that bad. In spite of himself and the constant doubts and depression about being broke, Jimmy Riley started to enjoy the daily routine. The work in the classrooms was similar to high school, only the curriculum differed. Instead of English, algebra, and history, you received lectures on proper police action, the policeman's responsibility to the public, and most of all, the pitfalls that lay ahead of the unwary young police officer. They didn't dwell on how to avoid getting shot or the shit belted out of you, that seemed too mundane for the instructors. Almost invariably, the lectures seemed to revert to the subject of graft and corruption. The instructors were usually lieutenants in rank; mild-looking and bespectacled and indistinguishable from middle-aged insurance salesmen. They were all so bookish-looking, you would swear that if they ever heard a shot fired they would shit in their pants. There was one thing they all seemed to have in common, a heavy Brooklyn or Bronx accent. Riley had stuttered when he was a young kid, and to conquer it he learned to speak slowly and precisely. When growing up in Irishtown he heard the King's English battered so badly that when he reached the age of reason, he vowed to avoid speaking any semblance of Brooklynese. Consequently, it floored him to hear the "foists" and "toids" roll off the tongues of the learned lieutenants. He soon became quite a card imitating the instructors to the guys after school. Particularly the lecture on graft and bribery and corruption that took place nearly every day. Jimmy had it down pat, and broke the guys up when he did it in a heavy Brooklyn accent.

"Ya see, boys, it's de foist buck dat starts de cancer, den its a deuce, and de foist thing ya know some rotten thieving bookie slips you a hunned, yer foist hunned. It boins a hole in yer pocket and de foist thing ya know, ye're a crooked cop, a member of the bloody gambling conspiracy. What de hell is gonna happen to ya den?"

After Jimmy finished his mimic act, he would proceed to describe what he would do with his first hundred, most of it outrageous. Jimmy was always good for a laugh and got along pretty well. The physical part of the rookie school was right down his alley. He had been a good athlete as a kid and he relished being in shape. He loved the calisthenics, the running, the judo, and the boxing. In the free periods, there was always a touch-football game that was so much fun, Riley even forgot his financial woes and played like he was a teenager again.

The entire routine was geared to prepare you for whatever kind of combat you might meet when you finally hit the streets. The physical instructors were acting sergeants, and to a man, Riley thought, they were full of shit. They screamed at the slightest provocation, and really did a job on some poor rookies who were overweight and out of shape. Riley just kept his mouth shut around these bullshit artists, but really felt sorry for the guys they tortured. What he enjoyed the most was the weekly trips to the shooting range. There the instructors were young sergeants, and they were great. Some guys were timid as hell the first time they handled a gun, but the sergeants were patient and understanding in their training. Jimmy loved to shoot, and after a few trips to the range he began to handle a gun like a young Wyatt Earp. Each trip to the range gave Jimmy more confidence, and when the day finally came that he put three out of six shots right in the center of the target he couldn't remember ever being happier.

But like Tom Brown's school days, rookie school was winding down to an end. The last weeks, all the talk among the guys was of what precinct they would be assigned to. Who had the "rabbi"? Who had the "hook"? The rabbi or the hook being your conveyance to get you assigned to the precinct of your choice, or at least one of the better precincts. Riley remained quiet through all this bullshit because he knew he had a good "hook," his old man.

Then came the day near the end of the learning process, the momentous day.

Classes were over for the day and Jimmy was getting ready to go home. The fatherly lieutenant motioned to him to wait a minute. When everyone left he said, "I have an order here for you to report to the chief inspector's office at headquarters tomorrow at nine A.M. You haven't been fucking around, have you, Riley?"

"Are you kidding, Lieutenant? Of course not."

"Well, you seem like a nice enough kid, but underneath that altar-boy face I think I could be seeing a wise little prick. And you know what happens to wise little pricks in this job. Or do you?"

"Ah, come on, Lieutenant. I thought I was in the running for the mayor's trophy, the rookie gun."

"Just don't try to be a wise guy or you'll get the gun, right up your ass. Now here, James, be there at nine sharp, ya hear, nine sharp. 240 Centre Street. Good luck."

"Thanks a lot, Lieutenant."

Jimmy practically walked on air to the subway and could hardly suppress his excitement when he got home. He decided not to say anything to his wife and not to call his old man until he found out what the order was all about. But he knew he would have to read himself to sleep through a long and fitful night,

wondering what the next day would bring. No one had previously
mentioned a thing to him, not a clue. Just report to the chief's
office at nine o'clock in the morning. In those days that's the way
things were done in the Job. If they had told him to report to
Oshkosh, Wisconsin, the next day, he would have immediately
started to figure how in hell would he get there on time. Blind
obedience to a superior was what was incessantly drummed into
your head. No young cop ever thought of disobeying a superior
officer. Most of the rookies were Irish, Italian, or Jews, and they
had the respect for authority ingrained in them by their parents.
The same respect carried over into the police department, and no
cop ever dreamed of giving any shit to his boss. If he did, the
penalty was usually swift and sure.

Jimmy read for a long time that night, his wife breathing peacefully in a deep sleep next to him. Every so often he would put the
book down and have a wide-awake dream that was unreal. Really
unreal! But finally his eyes drooped, he murmured a silent "Fuck
it," switched the light off, and went to sleep. Like they used to
say when he was a kid in Irishtown, Riley dreamt he was in a
penny-pitching game. He tossed all night. His dreams were of
bull-headed, heavy-fisted Irish sergeants, of cold-eyed, thin-
lipped, scholarly lieutenants—all bawling the shit out of him
wherever he went and whatever he did. When the alarm clock
went off, he shot up in bed like a rocket, and only his wife stirring beside him calmed him and made him realize where he was.
He hopped out of bed, and while soaping himself in the shower
started to think about this day of days. I wonder what the hell they
want to do with me? He soon found out.

Riley's direct orders were to report to a Lieutenant O'Neil, of
the chief inspector's office and to wear civilian clothes. This
morning, he dressed carefully in a nice gray Rogers Peet number,
white button-down shirt, and solid dark blue tie. After several
consultations with his wife Kay and the full-length mirror on his
closet door, he decided he looked the nuts and went off to meet
his fate.

He arrived at police headquarters about a quarter of nine, fifteen minutes early, and was greeted very cordially by a middle-
aged cop. The cop led him into an anteroom, gave him a copy of

Spring 3100 to read, told him to make himself comfortable, that the lieut, and that's what he said, "the lieut," would be in real soon.

Jimmy had read about every word of that magnificent police literary opus, *Spring 3100*, and looking at his watch, seeing it was after ten, began to get restless. Just then the cop receptionist who had greeted him stuck his head in the door and said, "Okay, Riley, you come with me. The Lieut will see you now."

He ushered Jimmy into a big private office and there was the lieut himself—his eminence, Lieutenant Peter O'Neil. He was about six foot two, about two hundred and fifty pounds, with a big bald bullethead. He was in his undershirt, shaving himself over a sink in the office. He half turned, waved to Jimmy, and said, "Sit down, kid. I'll be with you in a minute."

The lieut finished his ablutions and, smelling like a whorehouse, walked over to Jim with his hand extended and said in a surprisingly gentle voice, "How are you, Jimmy? I guess you know by now that I'm Lieutenant Pete O'Neil. But I know all about you, and all I hear is good."

Riley shook hands with his number-one strong grip, acknowledged the compliment with a half smile and a slight bow of the head, meanwhile thinking, This guys knows all about me. For Christ's sake, how would he? But he finally found his voice and, looking the lieut dead in the eye, said, "I'm very pleased to meet you, Lieutenant, and I hope that someday I can justify whatever good you heard about me."

O'Neil smiled, a nice smile, Riley noted, and turned away across the room to a built-in closet and selected a shirt and tie. Jimmy had taken a good long look at his kisser during the amenities, and from the whiskey lines on his face and the bloodshot eyes, he automatically rated him a quart-a-day man. Probably Bells Twelve or Cutty Sark, he thought. Booze was a way of life when Riley was growing up, and at this yet tender stage of his own life he could almost call the shot on how much a guy drank just by looking at his face and eyes. But a beautiful guy, thought Riley. Nice, soft spoken, smells good——a real gentleman after those loudmouth drill instructors and the bullshit, English-wrecking lieutenants that he was used to as superiors in rookie school.

Shirt on, tie adjusted, the lieut put on his suit jacket and walked back over to Jimmy. Riley had been eyeing him through his dress ritual, and as he walked across the room toward him, couldn't take his eyes off the lieut's suit. A great gray sharkskin number, which fitted him like a glove in spite of his heaviness. Jim silently put it in the three-hundred-dollar custom-made class and remembered his mother's words, "Clothes make the man. James, always try to look your best." And if Mother Mame said "Clothes make the man," Lieutenant Peter O'Neil was some man.

The conversation started casually. O'Neil knew Jimmy's father, Mike. "He was a helluva man, Jim. He could fight like a racehorse, hit like a mule."

"I oughta know, Lieutenant, he knocked the shit out of me often enough."

"No kidding, your old man hit you?"

"If you looked cross-eyed, Lieutenant, he'd murder you. One time I'll never forget, I had a little disagreement with my mother, and as was customary, she reported it to my father when he came home from work. He called me on the carpet to explain. Well, during the explanation, I referred to Mother as 'she'—like, 'She wouldn't let me go to Rockaway Beach, I'll never forget it. The old man took one look at me and I knew I was dead. He said, '"She" is the cat. Your mother is "Mother." Go up to your room and wait for me.' That was the death penalty. After about a five-minute workout, my screams for my life brought my mother upstairs and she got him off me and I was saved from certain annihilation."

O'Neil laughed out loud and said, "That's the way all kids should be raised. Get the living shit kicked out of them every month or two and they'd grow up with good manners and into good, decent citizens."

Jimmy shook his head vigorously in agreement, meanwhile thanking his stars that he was still healthy and in one piece as the memories of his father's beatings were revived.

"All right, Jimmy boy, let's get down to brass tacks. I have your folder right here and I've read it. But just to be certain, there's a few things I'd like to go over with you."

"Fine, Lieutenant."

"You've been married a little over two years and have one child, a son, right?"

"Right, Lieutenant."

"You graduated from high school and shortly after that went to sea for a couple of years. Why was that?"

"I couldn't get a job, it was the middle of the Depression."

"How'd you like the life of a merchant seaman, Jimmy?"

"I loved it, Lieutenant."

"I guess it made you grow up in a hurry, didn't it, Jim?"

"It sure did, Lieutenant. It was either grow up quick or get your balls cut off."

"Now listen carefully, Jim. I'm going to offer you a job. It's a job that I want you to give very careful consideration to. I don't want your answer right now. I want you to go home and talk it over with your wife and your father. I like what I see of you. I like your background in your personnel file, and I think you can do a job for me. You might have read a bit about it in the newspapers, but anyway there's a big shake-up going on in the plainclothes squads in the city. As you can see, I head up the chief inspector's office—under the direction of the chief himself, of course. I have to replace my entire squad at the suggestion of the chief and the police commissioner. The mayor's office has recommended that we fill the vacancies with raw rookies right out of the academy. You're the first kid I've interviewed, and maybe the mayor has something, after all. You know, fresh young kids out of rookie school that never had occasion to make friends with gamblers, or politicians interested in gamblers' well-being. You know, as I look at you and think about what a good man your father was, it might not be a bad idea. What do you say, you want to take a shot at being a chief's man?"

Riley sat in stunned silence for about thirty seconds. His face was composed, but his mind was racing. Holy Christ, plainclothes in the chief's office, the five-borough squad. I'll never have another poor day. He gulped, cleared his Adam's apple, which was jumping around his throat like a Ping-Pong ball, and said, calmly as he could, "It sounds very interesting, Lieutenant, and I'm sure I'd love the excitement of it. I am really flattered that you offered me the opportunity. Right now my answer would be yes, of course, but if as you say I can have a day or two, I'd like to talk it over with my wife and family, particularly Big Mike. It would only hurt his feelings if I didn't, and I wouldn't do that for the world. Believe me, I want the job, especially if you feel I can handle it. I just want to clear the air at home, and I'll get back to you in a day or so."

"Fine. Here's my private number. Make sure you call me within three days."

Interview over, Jimmy got up out of his chair, as did the lieutenant. O'Neil put his arm around Jimmy's neck in a nice friendly way, and as he led him to the door he said, "We're going to be all right together, Jim. You're going a long way in The Job."

Jimmy shook hands goodbye, gave profuse thanks, and with his brain whirling, took off for the subway and home. He didn't need the subway, or bus, or plane—he walked on air all the way. Sweet Jesus Christ, you really have been good to your little Irish son. Plainclothes in the chief's office. He remembered what a wise-ass rookie named Doolan had said when they were on a recreation break. They were lounging around in a small group and the conversation swiftly turned to the interminable topic, The Job. Doolan's old man had been a plainclothes cop for years, and Doolan always brought it up like he was a general in the army or the equivalent. Doolan was always bullshitting about having gone to Mount St. Michael's Prep and Fordham University and his sisters who went to Marymount. Pretty good education for four kids on a cop's salary, Riley used to think. One day Doolan explained his version of the plainclothes squads to the other rookies. First, the division men, then the borough men, and then the cream of the crop, the chief inspector's men and the police commissioner's men. The five-borough men, as Doolan called them. Riley remembered Doolan being questioned, "You mean these two squads have jurisdiction over all the squads in all the boroughs, Doolan?"

"Bet your ass, baby, you can bet your sweet ass on it—from Pelham Bay to Sheepshead Bay."

That's all Jimmy thought about on the subway going home— Pelham Bay to Sheepshead Bay. Holy Christ, I'll make a fucking fortune in nothing flat. LaGuardia can stick that hundred a month up the top of his ass. He got off the train at Kings Highway and looked at his watch. Quarter after twelve. He was no kind of daytime drinker, but he decided to stop at Joe Healy's bar for a drink. The bar was almost full when he entered, but the bartender recognized him from coming in with his father, who was a great friend of Joe's, and waved him into an empty spot. Jimmy casually ordered a Cutty Sark and water like a real big shot—he usually ordered nothing but a beer—and coolly surveyed the terrain like the smooth plainclothes bull he was soon to be.

The local bookmaker, Slim Rosen, was at the far end of the bar in business as usual. Every couple of minutes some guy would come up to Slim with a scratch sheet in his hand, whisper in Slim's ear, give him some money, and Slim would write on a small pad, tear off the top sheet, give it to the bettor, and put the carbon copy in a cigar box next to him on the bar. Jimmy liked Slim. Everybody did. He was a big, good-looking Jew with dark curly hair and a great smile. Always ready to buy a drink, always very polite—a real nice guy. Little does big Slim know what I might be doing by next week, Jimmy thought.

He observed the action in a noncommittal way, had another drink, and left the bar to walk on home. If Slim gets away with wide-open shit like this in an asshole spot in Brooklyn, he wondered, how many other bookmakers must there be in the city. And crap games, and blackjack games, and poker games, and roulette wheels. Lovely, lovely, lovely.

Jimmy suppressed his excitement with his wife Kay, only telling her that he was offered a job as a chief's man, which to her was about as obscure as a Greek lesson. He phoned his mother and was told his father would be home for supper, which meant an ironclad six o'clock. He said that he'd be over about eight and to tell Mike not to go for his walk until he got there.

Jimmy arrived at his mother's at eight on the dot, kissed her, and shook hands with his father, who had been reading the evening paper.

"What do you say, Mike, how about a nice walk?"

"Okay, Jim. Something on your mind?"

"We'll talk about it walking, okay, Pop?"

"Sure, Jim. I'll put on a sweater and be with you in a shake."

They walked for about five minutes through the quiet tree-lined streets of Flatbush, exchanging small talk about the Dodgers, the various players, and their pennant chances. Two things the old man lived for, his family and the Brooklyn Dodgers.

"All right, out with it. What's on that scheming mind of yours? I can tell from a mile away you're dying to tell me something."

"You're right, Mike, you're dead right. I was called to headquarters this morning. I didn't want to tell you beforehand 'cause I thought it might be for some sort of reprimand and I didn't want you to kick the shit out of me again. And you know, you're getting old and I might be able to take you."

"That'll be the day, you little prick," he shot back, even though Jimmy loomed five inches over him. "Okay, let's have it."

"Petey O'Neil, a good friend of yours, called me in and wants me to work for him in plainclothes in the chief's office."

"For Christ's sake, you mean the lieutenant Petey O'Neil?"

"Who else?"

"How come he wants the likes of you?"

"It seems that all the plainclothes squads in the city are getting the gate, his included. His Honor, Mayor 'Lu gotz en gul,' has ordered that the two top squads be filled by rookies out of our class. He thinks all the old-timers are too cozy with the wise guys and two-bit politicians and maybe the young guys, you know, new blood, will do a better job enforcing the gambling laws."

"You mean you, in the chief's office, locking up bookies and crap games and whores." He practically spat out "whores."

"That's right, Mike."

"For Jesus' sake, James. As crazy as you are you'll wind up in jail, mixing yourself up with that kind of scum. I told you to be patient. I'll get you into a good precinct, and make a couple of good collars and inside of a couple of years I'll have you in the detective bureau, where good cops belong. I don't want you to mix with that kind of shit. You'll be on the take in nothing flat, and Christ knows what might happen to you."

"Aw, balls, Mike. I've been on my own since I was seventeen and never got into trouble yet. I've been everywhere in this world. I'm big and strong and I can take care of myself. You know how much I respect you and Momma. But for Christ's sake,

I'm getting a big hundred a month and I have a wife and kid to support. How in the name of God do you expect me to do it? I promise you that I'll be very careful, but you know I'm going to grab a few bucks, I'd never shit you."

"Jesus, Jimmy, I'd hate to see you get in trouble. My heart breaks when I hear of some cop being sent to jail and knowing what waits for him in one of those bloody dungeons."

"But look at the percentage, Mike. Very few cops ever went to jail, and plenty of cops got rich in plainclothes. I'm not saying that I want to get rich. I just want to live good and get out of hock, for Christ's sake. I want to buy Kay a couple of dresses, myself some new suits, go out to dinner once in a while, play a decent golf course instead of that eight-hour Dyker Beach track. In other words, stop living like a peasant."

"I know, kid, it's rough, and how that goddam guinea mayor can expect a cop to live on one hundred a month is beyond me. But you're so crazy I hope you don't go off too wild and take a lot of chances. You know, James, I hated to beat you sometimes, but it was always for your own good. I was always sure you would wind up in the Catholic Protectory someday. That's why we moved out of Red Hook and I went into hock up to my ass to buy a house in Flatbush. At least you graduated from a good high school and didn't get into too much trouble where we live now. But, James, the chief's office. It's a great temptation for you. I honestly hate the idea of it, but no matter what the hell I say you'd probably take a whack at the job anyway. So go ahead, take your best shot, but for me and your mother's sake, be careful. Remember, nothing's worth going to prison for."

"I swear to God, Mike, I'll be careful. But I feel a helluva lot better about it with your okay, even if it was only a half-ass okay. And one thing, Mike, if I make any decent scratch, I'll make sure the young kids go to college and that you and Mom are well taken care of."

"Forget about me and your mother. Take care of yourself and your own family. Just stay out of trouble, and if you have a problem along the line, get hold of your old man right away. Okay, I'll call Petey O'Neil in the morning and put the stamp of approval on you. Enough said. Let's start home and have a drink to a good long trip in the chief's office."

Jimmy exulted all the way back home. He would have taken the job anyway, but out of respect he deeply wanted his old man's okay. He loved his mother and father with the fierce, implacable love that springs out of homes where everyone lives on top of one another in almost primitive conditions. The family was welded together by the undying love for Momma, and the fear, respect, and sometimes dubious love for Poppa. One generation removed from the hard life of the peasantry of Ireland. It's funny, Jimmy thought, I guess I'll be asking my old man for his okay on whatever I do until the day he goes to the grave. Jim stole a glance at his old man striding beside him, his forehead wrinkled up in thought. For Christ's sake, he'll never go the grave, not my old man. He's too tough, too strong to die. Jimmy shuddered. Oh, God, don't ever let my father die—and in the name of Jesus, never take my mother. I couldn't bear to think of life without Momma.

Enough of this shit about dying. Jimmy started to think about tomorrow and his phone call to Lieutenant Peter O'Neil. Whooey, Pelham Bay to Sheepshead Bay! Wow!

Rookie school the next morning was alive with rumors of guys getting interviewed for plainclothes jobs. Jimmy kept his mouth shut and just listened. He explained his previous day's absence by saying that he was called downtown to explain a few variances in his personnel file. When the lunch-break whistle sounded, he walked down to a bank of phones at the end of the armory and made the most important call of his young life.

"Hello, Lieutenant O'Neil, chief's office, please."

"Who's calling?"

"Patrolman James Riley."

"Just a minute."

"Hello, Jimmy, how are you? Did you speak to your father and did you give him my best regards?"

"I sure did, Lieutenant, and he sends you his very best. I believe he intends to call you today."

"Well, that's very nice. I'll look forward to speaking to Mike, it's been too long. Well, now, what about you?"

"I'm your man, Lieutenant, if you still want me." Jimmy's heart was in his mouth.

"I sure do, Jimmy. Get your ass over here about ten o'clock tomorrow morning."

"What about rookie school?"

"Your schooldays are over, Jimbo. Just report here dressed like you were the other day. I am putting you on assignment in plainclothes in the chief inspector's office effective as of eight A.M. tomorrow. There will probably be a few other guys you might know here in the office, and we'll spend a few days getting acquainted and giving you the rundown on what's expected of you. Get a good night's sleep, and I'll see you tomorrow morning. So long, Jim."

"Thanks, Lieutenant. See you tomorrow."

Jimmy hung up the receiver in a daze. Holy Christ, no more of this rookie-school crap. No more riding the subways in uniform closing your ears to some half-drunk prick making sneaky wisecracks about cops. He was tempted to knock the living shit out of one of them a couple of times, but the academy instructors continually warned them that things like that would happen, and that rookies were on six months' probation. Keep those rabbit ears closed, only take action if an actual crime is being committed. You're a rookie, a dumb rookie, with brains in your ass, so see no evil and hear no evil and you might survive your six months' probationary period. Well, that shit is over, Jimmy boy, tomorrow starts the glory road. Hallelujah!

Jimmy got off the subway at Canal Street the next morning and New York never looked better. It was a warm, bright spring day, and even the ancient loft buildings around Broome and Lafayette streets looked gorgeous. He entered headquarters and was soon ushered into an anteroom off Lieutenant O'Neil's office. The uniform-cop receptionist told him that this was the plainclothes squad room. It's a good thing the walls can't talk, he thought, as he looked around.

He was surprised to see a couple of other young guys there, whom he made for rookies like himself. They were of rather medium height, and as the school classes were divided according to size, he didn't recognize any of them. The smaller guys were known as Murray's midgets, in honor of the Police Academy's commander, Captain Joseph Murray. The midgets were always subjected to some good-natured ribbing by the bigger guys. "How the fuck did you ever make the height for The Job? Did ya get hit on the head with a hammer after they measured you?" Shit like that, a million small-guy jokes.

Jimmy introduced himself and everyone shook hands all around rather self-consciously. One by one, some other guys showed up and now Jimmy counted eight. A couple of minutes later the lieutenant himself came into the room. He asked for quiet and requested each man to give his name and shield number.

Six Irishmen, one wop, and one Jew. Not a bad ratio, thought Riley.

"Okay, fellows, as you know by now, my name is Lieutenant Peter O'Neil. Welcome to the chief inspector's office. You are on fifteen-day temporary assignments until you finish your probationary period. If you do a good job and stay out of trouble, you will be assigned permanently to this office. You were selected by me and my staff through a screening process all our own. Based on your backgrounds, your families"—he looked hard at Riley— "your I.Q.'s, and last but not least, because none of you look necessarily like a cop. I have assigned four old-timers to work with you for about a month. I will pair you off in partners and have one old-timer work with individual teams to teach you the ropes.

"Now listen, and listen good. For Christ's sake, don't do anything on your own until you get enough experience. Your main objective is to enforce the vice and gambling laws of this city. The chief's office and the police commissioner's office oversee the various division and borough squads throughout the city. Now don't any of you guys try to be a hero. Don't make an arrest on your own until I think you're ready to do so without fucking up. You got that straight? The old-timers will school you for about a month. I don't want you guys to get jammed up in any way, and I'm not kidding. It's a tough world out there in uniform, and it's tougher in plainclothes. And this is the toughest city in the whole fuckin' world. More pimps, degenerates, and wise guys than you'll find in Detroit, L.A., and Chicago combined.

"You got a long way to go in this job, so first you creep, then you crawl, and finally you walk. I know that's the same old shit your father and mother gave you, but it applies one hundred percent in the making of a good plainclothes cop. There isn't any set number of collars you have to make every month like in the division squads. I just want you to make good collars. When you get your feet wet and learn something about this job, you will be assigned every so often to Naval Intelligence down on Church Street to work on undercover details for the navy. This way, you'll be practically draft-proof, you'll be doing something for your country, and you won't have to worry about getting your balls shot off. But if you're not careful and don't watch your step, you might get your balls kicked in or a knife shoved up your ass. Take it nice and slow. Listen to these hairbags who are going to train you, and once again, don't try to be a fuckin' hero. Now has everybody got it straight? Any questions before we break it up?"

Pete's address to the troops was over. There was almost a concerted sigh of relief among the awestruck group of young rookies as Pete loomed over them.

A chunky, dark Irish guy raised his hand, cleared his throat a little, and said, "Fahey, Lieutenant. I wonder if you would make it a little clearer about our draft status. I was wondering why I was picked to work for you. I'm practically set to go into the army."

"Forget the army, kid, your draft board has already been notified that you're an indispensable man. You don't look like too fuckin' much now, but pretty soon I hope you'll prove yourself indispensable."

Fahey reddened a little, but laughed along with the other guys and said, "Thanks a lot, Lieutenant. You sure took a load off my mind. I really appreciate it."

"Okay, men. That's it. Tomorrow morning at nine o'clock, ready to go to work. Wear casual clothes, windbreakers or sport jackets, and get a good night's sleep."

Each guy lined up and shook hands with O'Neil. Jimmy purposely maneuvered to be last in line. He shook hands and O'Neil whispered, "Go across the street to Flanagan's Restaurant on the corner. Wait for me at the bar. Alone, you hear. I'll be there in ten minutes."

Jimmy winked okay, then shook hands with all the guys.

He walked the long way around the block and went into Flanagan's on the corner of Grand and Centre streets. He went up to the bar, ordered a draft beer, and was joined a few minutes later by Lieutenant O'Neil. Sure enough, Pete ordered a double Cutty and water, saying, "Need an eye-opener, Jim. Had a tough one last night." His hands trembled as he raised his drink to salute Jimmy good luck. Jim touched his glass with his beer and silently figured to himself, I've got this prick right, at least a quart-a-day man. After a little small talk, O'Neil said, "Listen, kid, I'm gonna depend on you for a helluva lot. You're the only goddam kid among the whole lot of you who checks out one hundred percent. You got it?"

Riley, smart enough to go along with the act, said, "That's nice of you, Lieutenant."

"Listen, forget the 'lieutenant' horseshit. Call me Pete when we're together. You can save that 'lieutenant' shit for when we're in the company of other bosses, especially the chief himself. You got it?"

"Fine, Pete. Whatever you say."

"Okay then, Jimmy. Who do you want to work with as a partner?"

"Savarese."

"The wop? Why him?"

"He looks like a good kid. He's quiet, he seems to dress nice. You know, kind of my type guy."

"Well, I'm a son of a bitch. You made a good choice, Jim. The kid is a lawyer who couldn't even get a job when he passed the bar, so he took the cops. He had an uncle in The Job, Rocco Maselli, who was a helluva cop. He got shot and killed in a stickup down on Stanton Street quite a few years ago. But not before he killed two of the heist guys and wounded the other. Young Savarese comes pretty well recommended, and I think you two will make a helluva team. Okay, you got him. Now, I gotta run uptown. You go home, go to a movie, do whatever the hell you want. But meet me in Gallagher's restaurant on Fifty-second Street at seven thirty tonight. You got it? You know where it is?"

"Who doesn't know Gallagher's, Pete? I'll be there. Shall I have dinner home, or what?"

"For Christ's sake, of course not. We'll have dinner in Gallagher's, have a good talk, and then I'll show you around a little. Wear your best suit. Look the nuts. Okay, let's get out of here."

O'Neil paid for the drinks, waved to everyone around the bar like an ex-heavyweight champ, and walked outside with Jimmy. When they shook hands goodbye, Jimmy felt the nice smooth feel of something green being pressed into his right hand. He just said goodbye real easy, looked O'Neil square in the eye, and said, "See you tonight, Pete."

Jimmy put his right hand with the money in it deep down in his pants pocket as he turned toward the subway. Nice and deep. He didn't dare take a look until he got on the Canal Street subway platform. He hated to take it out of his pocket. Was it a five? A tenner? Twenty? Jesus, not a fifty? He walked to the front part of the station and surreptitiously lifted the bill out of his pocket and looked at it. Holy Christ, a C-note! One hundred American dollars! You sweetheart, big Petey O'Neil, today you have made me a man. A man of stature, a man of great wealth. See you in Gallagher's, Petey boy.

Gallagher's restaurant on West 52nd Street off Broadway was the "in" steakhouse for the top wise guys and higher-echelon cops during the 1940s. Presided over by Jack Solomon, the urbane, always beautifully dressed owner-host, Gallagher's was famous throughout the country for its fine food and drinks. The steaks were always great, the liquor was always the best, the prices were high—to keep the shit out, as Jack would explain—and the clientele looked as expensive as the tabs they got. There was a famous story often told about Gallagher's and the credibility of its customers. During the oral bookmaking days at the racetrack—before the advent of the pari-mutuel machines—a bettor walked up to the stand of Johnny Ferrone at Saratoga race track. John was a famous bookmaker of his era. The bettor proceeded to give John's clerk a five-thousand dollar bet on a fairly long-priced horse. As was usual, he gave his name and the amount he wanted to bet on the horse. No money. The clerk turned to John and said, "Do you know this guy? He just bet me five thousand on an eight-to-one shot." Johnny Ferrone took a look at the guy and said, "Don't worry about him, he's all right, he eats in Gallagher's every night."

Jimmy arrived in Gallagher's about a quarter after seven and went directly to the bar, which was rectangular and right smack off the entrance to the restaurant. He ordered a Cutty Sark and water. The bartender served him, and Jimmy almost committed his first gaffe. He was about to whip out a ten and put it on the bar like he would in one of the neighborhood joints, when he noticed no money at all on the bar, just tabs in front of the drinkers. You got no class, Riley, you stupid ass, you're in the big time now, act like it. He composed himself, sipped his drink, and looked the bar over pretty good. He liked what he saw. Plenty of white-on-white shirts, plenty of tailor-made suits, and plenty of diamond pinky rings flashing all over the place. Right down your alley, Jimmy boy.

Pete O'Neil arrived about a quarter of eight and got a welcome just short of tumultuous. The maître d' at the rope and Jack Solomon himself gave Pete a big handshake and bear hug. Almost everyone at the bar gave off with "Hiya, Peter," "Whadda you say, Petey boy"—all the high rollers with the pinky rings, almost in unison. Pete waved hello all around and came over to the bar and shook hands with Jimmy. The bartender looked at Jimmy with new respect as he served Pete a drink, and Jimmy knew he was being gunned by every wise guy at the bar. Jimmy thought to himself, this Irish bastard O'Neil set this up for a reason. Every wise guy in the joint now has me pegged as Petey's new boy. Well, if that's the way Petey wants it, then it's okay by me.

Jimmy sipped his drink and stayed nice and cool while Pete chattered away. He was determined to look like he belonged in this world, like he hung out in Gallagher's five nights a week.

They finally sat down to dinner after Jim had met about a dozen guys who came over to Pete ostensibly to shake hands. But Jimmy knew in his heart that the real reason was for Pete to introduce him around. Max, Jackie, Georgie, Tony, Mikie—one name after another. All smooth looking guys. They all looked Jim dead in the eye when he shook hands with them and somehow Jimmy knew he was soon going to be very, very friendly with these guys.

Dinner over, Pete lit up a big cigar and said, "Jimmy, I guess you probably know why we're having dinner together. These guys weren't here by accident tonight, and you know it. So let's cut out the horseshit and get down to the nitty-gritty. Whadda you say?"

"Fine with me, Pete. By the way, thanks for asking me, the dinner was delicious."

"Good, and how was that C-note I slipped you today?"

"Even more delicious, Lieutenant."

"Okay, Jimbo, use it in good health. Tonight I'm going to give you a thousand bucks before we leave here. Don't piss it away and don't do anything flashy with it. Understand? I've got all you goddam young kids wished on me by that dopey guinea mayor of ours, and I'm going half nuts. I have to trust someone immediately, and I picked you. You have a great old man, and if you have half the balls he has, you're going to be all right. I'm not confiding in any of these kids except you. If I ever have to go to jail, I'm not having some punk kid who was planted on me send me there. For all I know, you may be no fucking good, but I have to take a chance on one of you, and what the hell, it might as well be you. At least you check out pretty good."

"Thanks a lot, Lieutenant. You won't be sorry."

"Forget that 'lieutenant' shit, Jimmy. I told you to call me Pete, except on occasions I'm sure you'd recognize. Okay, here we go. As I said earlier, there will be four old-timers attached to the squad for about a month. They'll be there for two reasons. First, to teach you guys how to make a proper pinch. Secondly, and most important, to introduce you to what is known in our trade as the 'cousins.' It's very simple. The cousins are the good guys, the guys who pay us to let them alone. The 'outlaws' are the guys who don't, can't, or won't pay. The outlaws are the guys you fatten up the old batting average with, the guys you pinch. Got it?"

"Sure I got it, Pete. For Christ's sake, I'm a big boy now. I delivered papers to speakeasies when I was a kid. I've been in plenty of horse rooms and crap games. And put your mind at rest, I have absolutely no scruples about gambling, or taking money from gamblers. None, Peter, none. Go to sleep on me. I've been on my own a long time and I think I can handle anything comes my way. You just give me the green light and I'm ready to go."

"Well, you know, Jimmy, most of you kids were raised Catholic, the same as me. I don't want you to get religion all of a sudden, or any shit like that, you get it?" Pete's voice was no longer gentle—it was hard, flat, a little tense. Jimmy sensed that it was murder for him to put all the horseshit right out on the table. He was nervous and beginning to sweat a little. He was also drinking the Scotches like they were water, and Jim was afraid Pete might be getting slightly bombed.

Jimmy decided to relieve the tension by giving Pete a little spritz. "Listen, Pete, I only went to church when my mother or father took me by the hand. Otherwise, I either shot craps or played ball on Sunday, depending on the weather. The main thing is"—and now Jimmy's voice got harsh and tense as he leaned close to Pete—"I don't give a fuck where the money comes from as long as it doesn't come from poor widows and orphans. Just you tell me what to do and where to go. You got your boy. If there is a stool pigeon planted among us, I'll dig him out, leave that shit to me. Another thing, with your permission, of course. We don't need those old-timers a month or two. A couple of weeks will be plenty. You put us kids in there for better or for worse. Just let the older guys show us the way for a short while, and we'll do the rest. After a month or two they'll be getting a taste of the money and they'll be like the Ancient Mariner's albatross, we'll never get rid of them. Please, Pete, have faith in us. Have faith in me. Stay with the young guys and I'll see that no one ever wraps you up."

This was Jimmy's longest speech ever to anyone as exalted as Lieutenant Peter O'Neil and he was a little breathless and nervous when he finished. He sat back in his chair and waited for Pete to reply.

Pete just sat there puffing on his Corona Corona. He sipped his Scotch and looked at Jimmy very carefully, taking him in. His eyes were red from the booze, his belly hung out of his pants a little, but his diamond ring and expensive clothes, his years of authority and being catered to, added up to a still impressive figure. He leaned over and said. "You know, kid, you're hot shit. You're gonna be all right. Come on, let's go. I have an apartment a couple of blocks from here. I keep it for my sweetheart. You and I are going to have a long, long talk."

Pete paid the check, peeling a C-note off a fat roll, and after a chorus of goodbyes from nearly half the joint, he and Jimmy finally left and headed east. Just short of Fifth Avenue, they came to a well-kept three-story brownstone. Pete walked up the front steps with his faithful servant Jimmy Riley behind him, and after fumbling with the lock a couple of minutes, let them both in. Jimmy had been in what he thought were nice apartments before, but this took the cake. The living room was big enough to play a softball game in and was furnished in exquisite taste. Everything was perfect in Jimmy's eyes, from the baby grand piano to the Oriental rug to the solid mahogany bar in the corner of the room.

"How do you like it, Jim?"

Jimmy whistled. "Beautiful, Peter, really beautiful."

"I bought this house for my sweetheart. She'll be in soon, I'm anxious for her to meet you. She runs six hat-check concessions around town, all in top joints. This floor and the one above are ours, and a friend of hers has the downstairs. What the hell, I'm a widower, and I'm too damn old to get married again, so I live here with Rita. I keep a place in Brooklyn where my married daughters can visit me once in a while. That's also my official residence in case they ever investigate me. I pay eighty-five bucks a month in Brooklyn for their benefit. But I'm mostly here with Rita. She does pretty good with her racket and we maneuvered to get this house free and clear, and all in her name. When I go, at least she'll have something to show for putting up with an old pain in the ass like me."

"That's a pretty nice thing to do, Pete, and I bet she's crazy about you."

"I hope so, Jim. But let's have a drink and get down to what the hell we came to the house for. First, here's the thousand bucks for some walking-around money. Remember, no flash. Take care of your wife and don't go further than Rogers Peet for your suits, and don't act like a big shot around your neighborhood. Get it?"

Jimmy put the thousand in his pocket as easy as he used to make a layup shot and said what he hoped was for the last time, "Don't worry about me, Pete. I'm your boy. Let's get down to the real McCoy, okay, Lieutenant?"

Pete made a couple of tall Cutty and waters and put them on a cocktail table flanked by two real-leather easy chairs. He sipped his drink, motioned good luck to Jimmy with a tip of his glass, and said, "Just sit back, Jimmy, and listen carefully. Don't interrupt even if you don't understand everything I say. Relax, sit back, have a nice drink, and shut up. Got it?"

Jimmy nodded yes. He noticed that Pete was now cold sober in contrast to his being a little rocky in Gallagher's. A three-block walk in the fresh air and he was like a new man. What a constitution this prick has, thought Jim. "Go ahead, Lieutenant."

"Well, let's start at the beginning. Every five or ten years some would-be John Q. Reformer of a judge or politican starts an investigation about police corruption. It's like clockwork. In recent years we had that sonofabitch Samuel Seabury, and now we have some shit-kicker named Herlands. Seabury sent a few poor cops off to jail, and maybe Herlands will too. But it's all a lot of shit. Trying to stop gambling is like trying to stop the public from drinking booze. It just won't work. Not in New York City, that's for sure. Everybody—the rich, the middle class, the poor—they all like to drink, fuck, and gamble. Maybe not before I die, but certainly before you die, all this bluenose shit will be legal. At least now you can drink legally, soon you might be able to get laid legally, and sometime in the future you'll be able to make a bet legally away from the racetrack, or go to a crap game or card game just like they are starting to do in Nevada.

"But as for now, gambling and screwing a whore are still illegal. You, my boy, are now a member of the top vice squad in the city, the chief inspector's office. You are charged with enforcing the vice and gambling laws, you understand? But, James, you and I know that these laws are a lot of shit. No one gives a fuck about these so-called illegalities, except to make a headline in the *Daily News* or *Mirror*. The same judges who gave a little bookie ninety days and the same district attorneys who presented the bookie's case are getting laid at Polly Adler's or Peggy Wilde's whorehouse the next night. And they bet the Giants or Dodgers games every day with one of the bigger books. These judges, district attorneys, and politicians are full of shit. Ninety percent of them paid some district leader to get made, and paid plenty. The name of the game is money, Jimbo, money. Show me one sonofabitch who hasn't got his hand out for money, and I'll show you an amputee.

"Take our fuckin' dago mayor. He goes on the radio every Sunday morning and he raves and rants about Frank Erickson and Frank Costello. Meanwhile, he has his main man, Marcantonio, a rabble-rousing spic congressman, landing plane loads and boatloads of Puerto Ricans into New York every hour. Upper Manhattan and the Bronx are beginning to look like downtown San Juan. The poor bastards have no jobs, so they go right on home relief. They got nothing to do but drink and fuck, so in another fifteen or twenty years you'll need to carry a machine gun when you walk around New York just to keep your head on. So I ask you, who's the biggest threat—a dead-honest bookmaker like Frank Erickson, or a morally corrupt prick like Marc who'd sell New York out to make sure he brings in enough spics to assure his political life. They're all the same, Jimmy. The Irish politicians, the Jew politicians, the wop politicians, the colored and the spic politicians—they're all full of shit. They all have their particular touch, and I couldn't give a shit less. I just know where our touches are, and if you use your head and stay clear of trouble, you're going to make a bundle. I got all I need, but while it's still out there to grab, I'll be there to grab it. You understand so far, Jimmy?"

"Sure, Pete. Reminds me of Diogenes."

"Who the fuck is Diogenes?"

"He was an old Greek on a continuous quest for an honest man."

It went right over Pete's head. He said, "No shit. I never heard of him, but speaking of Greeks, they're real high rollers and you'll be meeting the best Greeks in town pretty soon. Especially the big Greek crap-game guys, the baboot guys."

Jimmy kept a straight face and was glad Pete didn't know a high-rolling Greek crap-game guy named Diogenes. Anyway, all American Greeks were named Chris, or George, or even Peter. "Well, go ahead, lieut. I go along one hundred percent with what you're saying, and to say I have no illusions about politicians is the understatement of all time. My uncle Mike ran a big speakeasy and horse room down in Red Hook. His partner was an alderman, and his best customers were lawyers and judges. I am well aware that all politicians and judges are full of shit."

"All right, Jimmy, let's get down to the bare facts. I agree with you about the old-timers I've recruited to break you kids in. Two, three weeks, you give them the air. Stake them good and kiss them off. Any trouble you can't handle, just get back to me. Okay, let's go."

Pete cleared his throat a little, his voice grew husky again, and he seemed a little nervous. Not nervous, Jimmy thought, but a bit leery.

"Come on, Pete. For Christ's sake, give me the straight rundown, it's too fuckin' late now to worry about me."

"I guess you're right, Jimbo, but you better be dead right with me or it's your fuckin' funeral. Okay, here's the layout. The crap games, the roulette wheels, and the fancy top card joints belong to me and the bosses. And never mind who the bosses are. There are two crap games in Brooklyn, one in Queens, four in Manhattan, and two in the Bronx. Staten Island is full of shit-kickers, and whatever you grab out there is all yours. There are two roulette wheels and one chemin de fer game in Manhattan, a high-roller game at the New Yorker Hotel. You and those young kids with you, hands off these games. I'll introduce you personally to a few of the top-notch guys like Frank E., Joe A., and Red and Max. You can grab a few for yourself 'cause these guys are very generous people, but keep those other fuckin' kids off their backs. There'll be plenty of payrolls for you and the other kids. Don't get too hungry, and when you make a pinch, don't knock anybody's balls off. Below you there are the borough and division squads. Try not to hurt them. If you take out a big horse room, even if they are outlaws and not paying, you'll ruin the division guys if you take everybody. Take one, two principals at the most, let it go at that. If you feel you've been screwed, you can always go back to see the guys. For sure, they're not going anywhere. Try not to step on anyone's toes. Keep your hands in your pocket. Don't rap anyone on the chin or kick them in the balls, only in self-defense. These gamblers are one hundred percent peaceful. They're just trying to make a buck like you and me.

"Now this is very important. Once you okay a guy and put him on the payroll, you never pinch him. *Never*, you get it? When you're not honorable about a contract, and that's how we refer to it in The Job—a contract—you soon get to be known as a hunk of shit. And trouble follows shit, just like a toilet flush. Soon the boss of the shoo-flies gets anonymous phone calls and letters, you start to get tailed, and before you know it the heat gets too great and you gotta get the air. And remember, there's plenty of fuckin' air in the Central Park precinct, especially when you're walking a midnight-to-eight in your nice blue uniform. So far so good?"

"Sounds nice, Pete."

"All right, now we get to the whorehouse business. There isn't any money to make here. You get it? I, personally, have never been in a whorehouse. I had my wife for fifteen years, and from then on I had Rita. One good woman was always enough for me. But a lot of heavyweight guys around town are steady customers of Polly Adler, the biggest and the best madam in New York. For Christ's sake, don't bother her. Make sure the kids know that. That goes for Lucille Mallin and Peggy Wilde too. They're both good broads and have lots of friends. All these women run high-class whorehouses at fancy addresses uptown. You or one of the guys want to get laid once in a while, I'll make sure that you meet Polly personally. Like I say, they're all nice broads, and they keep their mouths shut. No money there. Okay? No shakedowns, no bullshit, nothing. If you do want to get laid, that's another story. We're all human and nearly everyone likes a strange piece of ass once in a while, but if you have any brains, let it go at that.

"There are three things that can ruin a young plainclothes cop, and the cause of all three is money. They get a taste of the green and all they want to do is cabaret and drink themselves to death. Then they see so much gambling around them every day that they get fascinated by the racket and start to gamble themselves. Pretty soon, they are way over their heads in debt and they start robbing every poor sonofabitch they can get their hands on to pay their own bookmakers or racetrack tabs. And last, but by far not the least, is that old devil, pussy. You got plenty of cash in your pocket, nice clothes, you're young and not bad looking, and pretty soon you think you're Ramon Navarro or Tyrone Power with the broads. All of a sudden some showgirl or dancer comes along—boom, you fall in love. I've seen it happen a dozen times. And a few times I've seen good cops go hook, line, and sinker over a call girl. Ruined their marriages, fucked themselves up in The Job—all over some fifty-dollar cunt. Believe me, Jimmy, you're a nice kid with a nice appearance, so forget all that shit. Have a fling once in a while, does you good. But hang in there smooth as ice, and get the ice—the moo, kiddo, the money. Is that straight enough?"

Jimmy nodded his head in what was meant to be total agreement with Pete, meanwhile silently hoping he'd end all the moralizing shit and get down to business. The crap games, the wheels, the card joints, who had them? Forget talking about some dopey fuck's weaknesses, he didn't want to hear that shit. He was twenty-four years old, with a nice fresh thousand clams in his kick, and he was ready to conquer the world. At least the gambling world.

He kept his face nice and straight and said, "You're so right, Pete. I hope it never happens to me or any of the other guys. But look, it's after eleven o'clock, and I assume that I have to be in the office at nine tomorrow morning. I still have to go home to Brooklyn, so suppose you clue me in on some of the places and guys you want me to take care of for you. This way, I'll have a better idea of what's in store for me. I also want to make sure that none of the guys in the squad make a mistake right off the bat. We've gone this far, for Christ's sake, get the whole goddam thing off your chest and we'll both feel better about it."

Pete looked at Jimmy for a few minutes without saying a word. He had an amused look on his face. He sipped his Scotch and puffed on his cigar like one of those old Indian chiefs in the cowboy movies who had just finished listening to one of his more insubordinate young braves.

"I have to say it for the tenth time. You are really hot shit, Jimmy. If you had as much balls in a fight as you have sitting opposite me, you'd be a heavyweight contender. This is our first sit-down, our first real meet, and you have me opening up to you like a schoolboy. Okay, call your wife and tell her you're working. Forget about going to Brooklyn tonight. There are two big spare bedrooms upstairs, plenty of clean shirts and underwear, and a toothbrush in the extra bathroom. I'm going to give you the entire rundown—names and all. These are my people, and if you or any of those other kids fuck one of them up, I'll send you to a precinct so far away you'll think you're in Peoria, Illinois. Are you ready for this?"

"Ready and willing, Peter."

And so the whole story of the interrelationship between the cops, the politicians, and the gamblers was unraveled to Jimmy. He sat there nice and calm, occasionally getting up to make drinks for Pete and himself. And brother, he needed a drink. Pete talked steadily for almost three hours. He revealed to Jimmy the names of all the real big shots in the city. All the crap with the Herlands Commission was the same old washed-over horseshit. With the war on and the economy booming, the gambling business was never better. There were day crap games, night crap games, even a game in one of the Republican political clubs that was a big supporter of Marcantonio and La Guardia. And La Guardia was so fucking stupid, he didn't even know about the game.

Pete supplied Jimmy with the names of the guys who ran the big operations and their locations. He again made it emphatic that these belonged to him and the bosses. Jimmy had enough brains not to ask who the bosses were. The emphasis was enough. Pete further assured Jimmy that there would be plenty left over for him and the other guys. Jimmy nodded obediently, like a well-bred cocker spaniel, meanwhile saying to himself, You're fucking well right, Pete, there'll be plenty left over for me and the guys. Watch my smoke when I finally get the green light.

About two in the morning Pete's girl Rita came home. She appeared to be in her forties, tall and thin, and really quite lovely. She gave Pete a big hug and kiss, and Jimmy could tell by the look on Pete's face how proud he was of her. She sat on the floor next to Pete, held his hand, and looked at him like he was Robert Taylor. After some further polite conversation, Jimmy took the hint, said he would find his bedroom, shook hands good night, and went up to bed.

He undressed, washed up, and got into bed, thinking that no way would he ever sleep tonight. But he fell asleep almost immediately. Like Joe E. Lewis used to say, "Nobody sleeps better than the guy whose head lies on a pillow full of hundreds." Jimmy was at peace. In his pants pocket hanging over the chair were ten crisp C-notes. A bigger and better world was just around the corner. Sleep tight tonight, Jimmy baby, many a pitfall may lie ahead, but who gives a fuck as long as the pot of gold is out there.

He woke up at nine o'clock, amazed. He never slept that late. But what the hell, he was in Big Pete's private pad. The memory of last night's fairy tales engulfed him in a wave of happiness, and he was ready for business. He showered, found clean shorts that swam on him, but nailed a beautiful white-on-white shirt that at least fitted him around the neck. He quietly let himself out of the brownstone and walked east to Lexington Avenue, where he found a phone booth.

"Chief's office, please."

"Yessir, just a minute."

"Officer Savarese there, please?"

"Yessir, just a minute."

"Hello, Officer Savarese here. Can I help you?"

"Georgie, this is Jimmy."

"Jimmy, where the hell are you? I called your house and your wife said you were on an assignment with the lieutenant. Were you bullshitting her?"

"No, Georgie, no shit. Look, it's ten o'clock. I'll see you in front of the Paramount in half an hour. You know the Paramount, where your Italian idol, Frank Sinatra, plays. All you wops know where the Paramount is."

"Fuck you, Riley. See you there."

They met and walked up Broadway and went into Lindy's for breakfast. "I hope you have some money, Riley. I've got three singles and forty cents in silver."

"Put your hand under the table, pisano. See, now you've got three hundred and three forty."

Georgie got a little white. "You're kidding me, Jimmy."

"You don't have to look, it's there. A little present to me from the boss and a little walking-around money from me to you. All right?"

"All right! For Christ's sake, I'd strangle some wild animal for three hundred, the shape I'm in. Thanks, Jimmy. I really mean it."

"Look, Georgie boy, from now on we sink or swim together. O'Neil gave me my pick of the guys to be my partner, and I chose you. He singled me out to lay the whole story on and he staked me a G-note up front. We've got one helluva thing going for us, Georgie boy, let's not fuck it up. If we get any kind of a run, we should both get rich. We'll just play it low key for a few weeks, learn as much as we can from those old hairbags assigned to us, and then we'll be on our own. Those guys are supposed to teach us how to make collars, but that's the shit as far as I can see. Their main role is to introduce us to the cousins and to make sure we don't step on anybody's toes. Get it?"

"I got you, Jimmy. Sounds beautiful."

"But we give these old-timers their walking papers in a few weeks. Learn what we can and get rid of them. This is going to be our goddam money, not theirs, and the longer they hang around, the tougher it will be to get rid of them. So pass the word, don't get too chummy with those guys, and after our first squad meeting when we have the wrinkles out of our bellies, we stake them good and chase them. Okay?"

"I'm with you, Jimmy. And, Jimmy, we're going to make a helluva team."

2

THE TRANSITION from civilian to police rookie to top vice squad cop in a few short months was not an easy one. But Jimmy Riley was fortunately blessed with a scheming Irish mind and a conscience that was not inhibited by religious strictures or too strong a sense of morality. He had the good manners and style that came from an upbringing in a staunch Irish Catholic home. But intrinsically, he was a product of the streets. Like all kids from poor homes during the Great Depression, he had worked at various jobs from the time he could remember. He sold newspapers, he delivered orders from the grocer, he shined shoes, he broke his balls digging ditches—he did anything he could to try to give his mother a few bucks a week and leave a buck or two in his pocket. Now, in his own mind, he had finally arrived. The big score was right out there for the taking, and Riley couldn't be happier.

The first day Jimmy and George started to work in the chief's office was a beautiful sunny day in June, a true harbinger of the rich future ahead.

Just as Jimmy Riley guessed, the four old-timers assigned to the rookies were there to make sure they didn't accidentally pinch any cousins. It was pure shit that they were assigned to help show the rookies how to make a proper arrest. However, like the meek and humble, Jimmy and George went along for the ride, keeping their mouths shut but taking everything in and not missing a trick. After the first week Jimmy passed the word to the guys in the squad that he would like to call a meeting in his apartment to compare notes. Everyone agreed, with pleasure.

The night nominated for the meeting, Jimmy's wife Kay laid in a couple of cases of beer and some delicatessen goodies and went to the movies. The squad arrived in pairs, a few minutes apart. After a few beers and a plate of cold cuts, potato salad, and baked beans, the atmosphere started to loosen up. Fahey, the stocky Irish guy from Brooklyn, finally broke the ice.

"Jimmy, for some unknown reason, you seem to be the nominal leader here, and I for one don't give a shit who's the leader. I'd just like to know in what direction we're headed, and exactly what the hell is going on."

"Listen, Tom, I have no desire to be any leader. The only reason I suggested this meeting is because, for Christ's sake, we don't even know one another. I think we should exchange a few ideas, tell each other about where we came from, what's on our minds. We see each other for about an hour in the morning, then we split with our partners. We're a squad, for Christ's sake, not a bunch of strangers!"

"Perfect, Jimmy. Perfect. Everybody agree?"

A chorus. "Everybody agrees."

Jimmy laughed. "All right, here we go. Georgie and I were out all week with two of these hairbags assigned to us. They took us to about fifteen or twenty spots. I got the list in my bedroom drawer. I'll show it to you guys later. Anyway, all these two cunts do is go into a gin mill, drink about five whiskeys apiece, introduce some prick to us as a cousin, and go on to the next joint. Each spot we went to, they would wait until we got back into the car and hand us eighty big dollars. Rapid calculation causes me to believe that that comes to ten bucks a man. Georgie's got the cash. Sixteen hundred we collected so far, right, Georgie?"

"That's right, Jim. Here's the moola, right to the penny." Georgie laid the money out on the coffee table. It was all in tens and twenties and looked like a fortune lying there.

Jimmy said, "Good, Georgie. Okay, who picked up any more cash?"

Friedman the Jew said, "Me and Jackie picked up just over a grand. That right, Jackie?"

Jackie McGrath, a curly-haired, blue-eyed Irish kid, said, "That's right, Sid. And, Jimmy, you couldn't be more right about these old-timers. You gotta wind up some kind of alcoholic working with them. Jesus Christ, I'm not averse to drinking, but a Scotch and water at ten in the morning, not for me, no way. I attempted to drink with them one day and I came home so bombed my wife had to take my clothes off and put me to bed. Fuck these guys. You take Sidney here. This alcoholic Jew nearly got drunk drinking thirty celery tonics."

Everybody laughed. The guys were beginning to really loosen up.

"Okay, two money ports to be heard from, Fahey and Desmond, O'Hara and Ryan."

Fahey stood up. "Fellows, you might not believe this, but I have yet to pick up my first penny. It's mainly because I haven't had a chance to get out with the old-timers, and Dan and I don't want to step on anyone's cock. Dan and I have seen the Dodgers twice this week and we went to the Loew's Met once, all on the tin, by the way." As he finished, he took his police shield from his pocket and kissed it.

Another big laugh.

Jimmy said, "Okay, Tom, we believe you. Now how about you two little midgets, you rob any outlaw dwarf bookmakers?"

Everybody howled as all eyes turned to O'Hara and Ryan. The beer was starting to mellow all the guys.

Bobby O'Hara stood up to his full height, all five feet eight inches of him and a hundred and forty pounds soaking wet.

"Still a wise guy, Riley," he said with a big grin on his face. "I don't think these old-timers think Joey and me are big enough to be real cops. No shit. I see them look at the two of us and shake their hairbag heads. But the two of us are making the best of it and snooping around the city pretty good. While we haven't come up with any cash yet—for the same reason Tommy gave—we came across a few nice things and have something very definite in mind once we get the green light. My cousin Ambrose owned a combination poolroom and bowling alley. I worked there as a kid setting up pins. There was a big bookie working out of there for years, so there's not much I don't know about the gambling racket. I can spot a bookie joint in two minutes. So can Joey, his uncle Ray was a big bookmaker on Broadway. Needing two of these old hairbags to teach us how to lock up a book, for Christ's sake, that's like teaching a baby how to take a piss. We don't need them, and especially the sarcastic looks they give me and Joey 'cause we're so small. If one of them makes another midget wise-crack to me, I'm gonna give him a rap in the fuckin' mouth."

Riley said, "Hey, Bob, way to go. Okay, guys, let's hear it for the featherweight champ."

A big cheer, and Bobby O'Hara sat down with his hands over his head like Billy Graham, the boxing idol of the East Side.

At last, Riley felt in his heart, at last we're starting to know each other, to develop a sense of camaraderie.

Riley raised his can of beer. "Okay, guys, for better or worse we stick together."

Another cheer.

"All right. If all goes well, we'll be toasting each other with champagne next year, or even sooner. Whadda you say, let's whack up this twenty-six hundred. This way everyone will feel a little healthier. We'll appoint Sid the cashier. The Jews are the best at that sort of shit, right, Sid?"

"Fine with me, Jimmy baby. You ignorant Irish are too stupid to know how to count, anyway. Right, wop?" he added, nodding at Georgie.

"Bet your ass, Sid."

The money divided, the air real clear, everybody a little high from the beer and the fresh cash in his pocket, Jimmy Riley decided the time was ripe to stop all the sparring bullshit.

"Listen, guys, this meeting is the best thing that's happened since we all first met. I think we all agree that we go along with the old-timers another week, then kiss them off. They're already starting to act like our bosses, and I'm sure they're sticking plenty of dough in their own kicks that belongs to us. If we have the name, let's play the game and get the dough for ourselves. We all came up the hard way, so it follows that we know the facts of life about gambling. Like Bobby O'Hara just said, we all have some half-ass relative or family friend in the racket. I'm sure we all know how to shoot craps and play cards. If one of us hasn't been to a whorehouse by this stage of his life, tough luck. So from here in, caution is the watchward, and no matter what, we're one for all. It's us against the world. If it's okay with you guys, I'll start greasing the skids with Pete and see that he gives those four old-timers the gate in a week or so. Whadda you say?"

Unanimous vote of confidence.

"Okay then, let's have a nightcap and we'll clean this mess up a little bit. My wife will probably bawl the shit out of me anyway when she comes home, but let's try to make it look a little presentable. I have one further suggestion, that we meet here the same time in about ten days."

Everyone agreed. They hustled about emptying plates into the garbage, and the last beers were consumed amid the greatest conviviality and good humor that Riley could ever hope for. After everyone had said their goodbyes, Riley sat in a lounge chair nursing his last beer. We're going to be a good squad, a good organization, and if there's one stool pigeon among us I'll eat my fucking hat.

Jimmy went to bed jubilant. He felt that he had a full commitment going for him from all the squad members. Again he went over each of them individually, assessing everything they said. He was now convinced he could go to Pete and assure him that all the guys were straight. What a relief! The first thing on the agenda was to call Pete in the morning, even though the next day was Saturday. He had his private New York number and decided he'd meet him for lunch. He soon fell sound asleep, even before his wife came home. The nice deep, peaceful sleep of a guy who feels his troubles are over.

The next morning came.

"Hello, Peter. Did I wake you up?"

"Oh, Jimmy, it's you. No, I'm up. I was just putting the coffee on."

"How about lunch? About one o'clock." It was ten in the morning, and from the sound of Pete's voice last night had been a rocky one. Jimmy gave him three hours' leeway so as not to seem impatient by giving him the big rush.

"Fine, Jim. The same place. See you."

Jimmy hung up. He chuckled to himself. The same good old

Pete; thirty seconds on the telephone in Pete's opinion was thirty seconds too long. Pete's gospel to the Corinthians—the rookies: "Always feel that every phone you speak on is being tapped. Make any phone conversation short and sweet. Mention no names except your own and the person you call, and if you both know each other's voice, no names at all. An old O'Neil adage—the phone is the wise guy's mortal enemy."

Pete was the same way about restaurants. He designated in advance where lunch was to be, or cocktails, or dinner. "The same place" was a fancy little Italian restaurant on East 56th Street, off Lexington Avenue. This was established in Pete's New York apartment a week previous.

Jimmy arrived a few minutes before one, went to the bar and ordered a Bloody Mary. About ten minutes later the lieutenant arrived. There were only about twenty-five people in the place and about half of them came over to shake Pete's hand. Jesus, Jimmy thought, this guy has to shake more hands than Grover Whalen ever did in his heyday.

"How are you, kid? I thought I might take Rita to the ball game today, but I cancelled her out in your favor. You sounded like you had a lot on your mind. Anything wrong?"

"No, Pete. On the contrary, things couldn't be better."

"Sweet Jesus, that's good news. Let me get a couple of Scotches into me so I can feel human again. We'll sit down and talk about it over lunch."

"Fine, Pete. Take your time."

Jimmy nursed his Bloody Mary and was introduced to the owner, Gian, by Pete. He waited at the bar as Pete knocked off three Scotches in a row, meanwhile engaging in some easy banter with Gian. Pete also introduced Jimmy to a few guys who came up to say hello to him. They all looked like they could play the heavy in a gangster movie. Lightweight dark suits, white-on-white shirts, pearl-gray ties, and the inevitable mark of status, the diamond pinky ring. Jimmy chuckled silently to himself. He was always kidding Georgie about the wops. How the only time they went to Confession and Holy Communion was when they went to the electric chair. Anything along those lines got Georgie's goat. George was always bragging about his Italian heritage, about painters like Da Vinci and Michelangelo, musicians like Puccini and Verdi, singers like Caruso and Galli-Curci—all that high-class shit. To George the Irish, until recent years, had no cultural heritage, they were strictly barbarians. He should get a load of these guys, thought Jimmy. But to a man, they were polite and soft-spoken. They seemed pleased to meet Jimmy, and he in turn was glad that these guys were going to be on his side come the revolution. He was also sure that the meet in Gian's restaurant was for the ulterior purpose of meeting the Italian wise guys. Fuck it, he reasoned, if my main man Pete wants to set me up to meet guys this way, he must have the right idea.

The captain showed them to a table in the rear of the restaurant. A bottle of Italian white wine appeared in a bucket of ice right next to the table as soon as they sat down. The waiter popped the cork, poured a little wine in Pete's glass for his approval, and when Pete nodded okay, he filled both glasses and left.

Pete raised his glass and tipped to Jimmy's good luck. "All right, Jimbo, let's have the good news."

"Pete, I thought it important enough to get to you right away. The good news is that you can forget about them planting a stool pigeon among us. At the first squad meeting when you gave your immortal address to the troops, you referred to a screening process all your own, remember? Well, you must have dug up the FBI files on these guys' families or some amazing thing. You won't believe this. Every guy in the squad has an uncle or cousin or some goddam relation who was or is a bookmaker or shylock. The Jewish kid, Friedman, has an uncle who runs a goulash room in the Bronx and is a shylock besides. The only guy who doesn't admit to shady characters in the family is my partner, Georgie, the wop. He's probably related in some way to half the fuckin' guys in this joint but won't admit it."

Pete laughed. "Jesus, that's really funny. Jim, I have to level with you. When I picked these kids I relied on my own intuition. I flew entirely by the seat of my pants. The only one I had a decent line on was you, on account of your old man being in The Job, and being a helluva guy. But, Christ, this is really good news. I don't have to tell you how worried I've been the past few weeks. I have a lot of confidence in your judgment, Jimmy, and if you assure me they're all okay, beautiful."

Jimmy then proceeded to go into detail about the meeting at his house. He told Pete about splitting the ice they collected, and how happy everyone seemed about getting some fresh cash.

"Forget your worries, Pete, all these kids are great. Everything is going to be perfect. There's only one fly in the ointment."

Jimmy looked dead right at Pete. He set himself to spring the *coup de grâce*.

"What's the fly, Jimbo?"

"The old-timers, Pete. Forget about a month, let's get rid of them next week. We need them like we need another dick. If you want all of us to learn how to drink a quart a day, you picked the right guys to teach us. That's about all this supposed instructional shit amounts to. The kids are unhappy about them, and most of all, I am. Please give me your word, Pete. Get rid of them as soon as possible. They're already getting their hooks in pretty good, and the longer we wait, the more they're going to be a pain in the ass. Fire them, Pete. But I don't want any confrontations with these guys. I wouldn't put it past any of them to cause some trouble. I don't know how long you've known these jerks, but three out of four of them are dead lushes, and the sober guy I trust the least. Next week, just transfer them back to where they came from. Tell them to come back and see you for a drink in about a month, that you'll have a nice present for them. By then I'll give you a grand apiece for the four of them. That, plus what they've already scavenged, should make them happy. They'll get over their shock by then, and they'll keep nice and quiet until you give them their present. Take them to dinner, pat them on the ass, and tell them what a good job they did breaking the kids in. Wish them luck, and let's hope they forget about us."

"That won't be hard, Jim. A cinch. I'll take care of it next week, just as you say. But what about the okay spots? You don't know half of them, even a third of them."

"The understatement of the year, Pete. Unless I miss my guess, we don't know ten percent of them. For Christ's sake, how could we? These guys drink most of the day, and bullshit the rest. I've already met a few division and borough guys who can't wait to sit down with me. Relax, leave it to me. Okay, Pete?"

"You're a pisser, Jimmy. All right, go ahead. But for the one hundredth time, stay out of trouble. Case closed. Let's eat, I'm starved."

They left Gian's about three o'clock, Pete going back to Rita and Jimmy to the nearest pay phone.

"Hello. Georgie there? Tell him it's Jimmy."

"Just a minute, please."

"Hi, Jim. What's up?"

"Everything's beautiful, George. How about taking the wives to dinner tonight? Okay, we'll talk about it then. Michael's on Flatbush Avenue. Fine, see you at seven."

And so the plot was laid. In a week the eight rookies had gained their independence. The only one they had to answer to was Pete, and outside of an occasional morning, no one ever even laid eyes on him. If he wanted to communicate with the guys, he called Jimmy for a meet and relayed his instructions. He just made it good and clear whom he and the bosses were interested in. Jimmy knew by heart, but he wanted to make sure all the guys knew. Again, if anyone got on to something really big, lay off unless Pete gave the okay to bust it. It was a very simple program.

The weeks rolled by, and inch by inch the rookies started to get a little hair. Everything fell into place just as Jimmy had anticipated. Each team was delegated to pick up certain sections of the city, and the money began to roll in. As Jimmy had suspected, the eighty bucks a location was a lot of shit.

The first guy Jimmy and George went to see was a big, dark-haired Jew everyone called Gallop. They had met him before, with the veterans in a saloon in Jamaica, Queens. He was delighted to meet the rookies alone, and broke his ass to be nice.

Jimmy said, "Listen, Gallop, I'd like to check the three joints you're paying us for. Via the grapevine, I understand you use lumberyards as a front."

"You heard right, Jim. Fine, let's go. I'm as anxious to show you the joints as you are to see them. All I did the last time I met you guys and Harvey was drink. I was nearly paralyzed when you left."

They drove to the first lumberyard, in a remote section of Queens. They parked the car and went through the front gate with Gallop. They walked down a corridor about thirty feet long and entered the main yard. They took one look and both of them nearly shit in their pants. There must have been two hundred people in the joint. The clerks were on a raised platform taking the action. A loudspeaker was about ten feet back, attached to a wall. Over it flowed all the racing information of the day—post times, late scratches, even running descriptions of the race in progress.

"How do you like it, fellas? Beautiful, right? And, fellas, six years without a pinch."

Jimmy nodded, more in a comatose state than anything else, and said, "It's absolutely gorgeous, Gallop. Let's go see the other yards."

Gallop loaded them back into the car and off they went on their inspection tour. The next two lumberyards were almost identical with the first, though scattered about two miles apart. The same setup, the amount of players about equal.

Gallop proudly explained the technical details of the operation. How the post times, race odds, and running descriptions came directly over a long-distance wire. How he had a guy behind each screen equipped with earphones who relayed the information that came over the wire by a microphone wired to the loudspeakers. He bragged that his guys on the wire were as good as any radio announcers, only sharper, with more brains.

"Whadda you think? Do you like the places, Jimmy?"

"I do have one suggestion, Gallop."

"What's that, Jimmy?" A faint note of alarm crept into Gallop's voice.

"Well, here's what you do, Gallop. You put a ton of horseshit in each yard. Spread it out real good so the players will smell it and maybe even step in it. Then you'll have the closest thing to Aqueduct or Saratoga in the east."

Gallop and Georgie busted out laughing. Gallop a little hesitantly, Jimmy noticed.

"You're not unhappy with the joint, are you, Jim?"

"Gallop, my good man, you were here long before we came around, and hopefully you'll be here long after we're gone. But you can fuck ten dollars a man for each of these joints."

"You gotta be kidding. Your squad gets three hundred a month for each joint, and you and George get a C-note extra for picking me up. That's a nice hat from me to keep a special eye open."

Another swindle by the honest veterans, thought Jimmy. Forget about it.

"That's more like it, Gallop. From now on we're squared away. Give us the G-note direct and we'll see you next month."

That's the way it went all over the city. The rest of the squad caught on pretty fast, and soon with the help of a few pivotal guys, everyone was more or less holding his own in the pickup department. The life dazzled Jimmy. He loved every minute of it. Each day held a new surprise.

About a week after meeting Gallop he really got a surprise. It was the first time he ever saw a real professional crap table. He had always loved to shoot craps. But he had never played except on the sidewalk in Red Hook, against the boys' room wall in high school, or on a blanket on the ships.

Jimmy and George were having dinner in Dinty Moore's on West 45th Street, when Big George McMahon walked over to the table and sat down. Jimmy had seen him at the bar when they came in, having met him that first night with Pete in Gallagher's. He knew he had a real big joint on Columbus Avenue in the Seventies, but he also knew that he was a great friend of Pete's, so he figured hands off. Jimmy introduced him to Georgie and ordered him a drink.

"Jimmy, I'm glad you remembered me from that night with Peter. When the hell are you guys coming up to see me?"

"Anytime you say, George."

"How about tomorrow afternoon about four o'clock?"

"Fine. I wasn't worried about you, George. I figured we'd catch up," Riley said, meanwhile thinking, Here's a guy dying to give us money. I have to have a heart-to-heart talk with Pete and straighten out a few things. Let's not have us poor kids pass up anything through lack of proper communication.

The next day Jimmy and Georgie were right on time, at the bar having a drink with Big George's brother Steve. He informed them right off that he was a police lieutenant in the automobile squad. He fell all over them. He wouldn't let them buy a drink, and kept telling them what great kids they were. Everybody in the city was talking about how nice they conducted themselves, real gentlemen.

Jimmy sipped his Scotch and said, "Thank you, Lieutenant. Honestly, that's really good to hear." Jesus, he thought, this guy's brother is one of the biggest shots in town, and here he makes no bones about telling me he's a lieutenant. Your education continues, James.

Just then Big George walked in and shook hands all around, giving his brother Steve a big bear hug.

"How do you like the restaurant, Jim?"

Jimmy had taken a good look coming in and loved the place. The decor was rich maroon leather, from the banquettes that circled the restaurant to the upholstery on the strong, sturdy chairs surrounding the tables. The tables were draped in immaculate white linen. Rich-looking chandeliers were hung in just the right spots. The bar was a long, old-fashioned mahogany, with a gorgeous antique mirror out of the gay nineties. Great taste to Jimmy's Irish eye.

"I love it, George."

"All right, finish your drink. I'll show you the back room. Steve can stay here with Georgie."

Jimmy followed Big George to the back of the restaurant, figuring he was going to sit down at a rear table. But they kept walking, through a back door into what was evidently the office part of the place. Big George pressed a button, another door opened, Jimmy walked in and almost dropped dead.

The place was jammed with people. The horse room occupied one side of the room, and two blackjack tables and a huge crap table occupied the other. The tables seemed to be going at capacity. Big George shook a few hands around the room, and Jimmy walked over to the crap table. He was completely fascinated. He'd seen a couple in the movies, but this was his first time ever with the real McCoy. He loved it, couldn't take his eyes away from the game. Big George had to grab him by the arm to continue his tour.

"Look around, Jimmy. You can tell, can't you? There's no shit in here. No shit allowed, no how. A customer must wear a jacket and tie at all times. No exceptions. If you don't like it that way, stay the hell out of my place. Ninety-five percent of my customers are legitimate businessmen, and that's the way it stays. I don't want the neighborhood guys, you know, the longshoremen and the truck drivers. They understand, there's no offense. They all bet with Scrapiron Ryan, up on Eighty-fourth Street. By the way, he wants to meet you. I'll arrange it in a day or two. All right, I guess you've seen enough. Let's go."

They went through the door and sat down at a desk in the office. Big George took out a roll that made Jimmy's eyes blink, and counted out twelve one-hundred-dollar bills.

"I'm behind a month's ice. Here's two months'. There's five hundred a month for the squad, and a C-note for you and the wop kid. That's to make sure you take good care of Uncle George. Get it?"

"That's great, George. To tell you the truth, I was a little leery of approaching you, knowing you to be such a good friend of Pete's."

"Don't worry about Peter. I take real good care of him. But that doesn't give me a license not to take care of you kids. I don't want anything from anybody. You're down there to get yours 'cause you deserve it, and I'm here to give it to you. Fuck any free rides, Jimmy. In this racket, if you can't pay, don't play."

They went back to the bar, shook hands goodbye all around, and Jimmy and Georgie got into their car and started downtown.

"How'd it go, Jim?"

Jimmy couldn't help himself laughing as he told Georgie what took place between Big George and himself.

"Can you imagine, Georgie? The first time I ever saw a real live crap table. This is some gorgeous city, Georgie, my little Eyetalian sweetheart. Here I grew up thinking I was a half-ass wise kid. For Christ's sake, I don't know shit from Shinola. But we're getting there, kid. Soon we're going to learn the whole route, walio, the whole route."

Slowly but surely, the whole squad began to learn the whole route. It was the kind of life you dreamed about when you were a kid, especially a poor kid.

The change in all the guys was a gradual one, but certainly unmistakable to anyone with as sharp an eye as Jimmy's. The Howard and Crawford twenty-two-fifty suits and sports jackets soon went to the Salvation Army and were replaced by Rogers Peet and Brooks Brothers. Nobody drank beer anymore, only Scotch whiskey or Canadian Club. The sudden affluence began to show in so many minor and major ways, Jimmy had all he could do to resist a laugh when the squad met for their bimonthly meetings. It was a cardinal rule—unless away on vacation or sick— faithfully to attend the meetings. Not only to cut up the ice everyone collected, but to discuss the various discrepancies that were continually cropping up about the payrolls. They soon learned that wise guys had territorial disputes just as private business and even nations encountered. And it was only a matter of a few months before they outgrew Jimmy's apartment as their rendezvous.

In the sensitive position they were in, it was inevitable that they would meet the general managers of all the big hotels, some of them very fancy and some so-so. About once a week some prominent sucker would get rolled for his wallet or beat for his jewelry by some high-class hooker who patrolled the hotel. The chief's squad generally got the call to make the investigation. Be discreet so the mark's name didn't come out, but try to retrieve his money, credit cards, and jewelry. It was usually a contract to Pete from one of the anonymous bosses. It was via this route that Jimmy met the general manager of a posh Central Park South hotel. He broke his ass to be nice to Jimmy and was delighted to rent him a fancy suite by the month for a modest price. It was under an alias and was kept a well-guarded secret by the guys. It was not only used for the meetings, but also as a convenient place to use in case anyone worked late. Needless to say, it was a perfect place to get laid in case anyone got lucky working the nightclubs.

Every place they frequented—supper clubs, jazz joints, fancy restaurants—the bosses and the help treated them like kings. At the meeting they established codes of behavior concerning the night life. One of the first rules laid down was never to act like a cheap prick. Make sure that you pick up the tab and tip generously. Let the uniform guys and the local squad detectives be on the cuff, that was their privilege in their own domain.

They followed the rules about arrests that Pete laid down to Jimmy. The city was teeming with gambling joints, and it was a simple thing to nail an outlaw. A few bookmakers, a policy guy or two, a couple of hookers, and an occasional card or crap game were sufficient to keep up their batting average. Jimmy soon hooked up with some real smart detectives in the district attorney's, safe and loft, and homicide squads. In return for substantial rewards, he received so much information off their major-crime wiretaps that he and Georgie could have made twenty-five wireroom pinches a month. But they were such lucrative shakedowns, it was almost a sin to arrest any of them. Even the few that had to go to keep their quota of arrests up were always ready to pay a good buck just to get the seized paper work back. This was to prevent their players from putting in a false claim against the book.

There was one thing he found out in very short order. The gambling courts, in spite of all the ice for protection, were a beehive of activity. And nearly all of it larcenous. Pretty nearly everyone was there on a fix. The lawyers and the bondsmen were the most flagrant schemers, but what surprised and even mildly shocked Jimmy were the devious magistrates and judges. But he was shrewd enough to catch on fast, and played the game like a pro. He became a special favorite of the magistrates and judges who slipped him a contract, which, they always intimated, came from the club. At least that's what they'd tell him. Jimmy, this guy has got to go out the window, you don't mind. A little contract from the club, okay. Sure, your Honor, anything you say. And Jimmy would leave a loophole in his testimony that would give the judge just enough room to throw the case out. After the judge dismissed the defendant, he would congratulate Jimmy on a fine piece of police work, saying that it was too bad he didn't have that one vital piece of evidence needed for conviction. Some crock of shit. But whenever Jimmy needed to throw a case, invariably some outlaw he had given a tough complaint to who turned out to have good friends, the contract was always reciprocated.

Life was one big bowl of cherries, and Jimmy loved every minute of it. He loved the night life, the girls, the Garden, Ebbets Field, Yankee Stadium, and especially he loved the money. Everything was falling into place just fine, and so Jimmy was surprised to get a mandatory summons from Pete one afternoon. Outside of a brief hello here and there, he hardly ever saw his eminence.

"What's up, Pete? Everything okay?"

"Couldn't be better, Jim. Tell you why I called you in. I'm going to assign you to the racetrack for a couple of weeks. I'll have a guy there to show you around to make a few bucks. Just look wise and don't arrest anybody even if they make book in front of your nose. It's about time you learned a little something about the racetrack. Start tomorrow and do yourself some good. Take care. See you later."

Jimmy went back to George and told him he was a little puzzled about the racetrack assignment, but orders were orders and tomorrow they would beat the track.

They entered the clubhouse the next day and were greeted by a couple of the division and borough men whom they knew from the courts. They soon learned that all the big bookmakers had men at the track to take off their big customers who were there for a day's outing. They went home that day with pockets full of money, money they never expected to get at a racetrack.

After the last race, going to the parking lot to get their car, Jimmy turned to Georgie and said, "You know, the more I see of this world, the dumber the fuck I have to be. We must have picked up over ten grand today and I always thought that the only bookmaker at the track was New York State itself, the iron horse."

"Jesus, Jimmy, I'm beginning to think there's nothing on the level."

But Jimmy had a rude surprise coming to him. He found to his dismay that all judges weren't dishonest, and his budding career of wealth, health, and happiness was almost nipped in the bud.

His younger sister married a kid in the service and Jimmy threw her a very fancy wedding reception at a smart Booklyn Heights hotel. At the peak of the festivities, Jimmy's new brother-in-law brought him over to meet his uncle—his Honor, Francis X. McMasters, the judge in the family. Jimmy shook his hand enthusiastically, silently figuring it was a real score to have a judge in the family, however remote. But the judge gave him a cold eye and a colder-fish handshake and said, "I understand you're in The Job, Jim. In the chief inspector's office, is that correct?"

"That's right, your Honor."

"What in the name of God is a nice-looking Irish boy from a good family doing in that cesspool?"

Jimmy was startled for a moment, but not losing his aplomb, replied, "I don't get you, your Honor. A cesspool?"

The judge eyed Jimmy carefully from head to toe. The tailor-made suit, the white-on-white shirt, the Countess Mara tie, the hand-stitched cordovan shoes. "Listen, Jimmy, we're at a lovely affair now. Let's all have a good time, and we'll have a drink to the bride and groom." He motioned to a waiter passing by with a tray of drinks. Taking two drinks off the tray, he handed one to Jimmy, tipped his glass, and said, "Good luck to the kids, Jim, they're a beautiful couple. Look, I understand you're a good boy. For the love of God and the sake of your family, be careful and stay out of trouble." He then turned abruptly and joined a group of the groom's relatives on the other side of the room.

Jimmy was a little shaken for a minute or two by the encounter, but he shrugged his shoulders and walked over to his mother, grabbing her by the waist and whirling her around the dance floor. With the band playing, the whiskey flowing, his mother in his arms—the world was beautiful. Be careful. My ass, be careful.

A few months after his sister's wedding, they had a tip on a bookmaking joint in the Williamsburg section of Brooklyn. They checked to make sure that it was an outlaw, and soon had it under surveillance. The action was brisk, and after about a half hour of clocking it they decided to make the pinch. The book was inside a false-front candy store, and within a couple of minutes they threw the place in the air. George stood by the front door and Jimmy grabbed the two sheet writers and announced the place was under arrest. It was a predominantly Jewish neighborhood, and upon hearing the pronouncement of doom all the players started to holler how innocent they were.

The two bookmakers were obviously veteran campaigners. One of them, the older and harder-looking of the two, said, "Where you from, boss?"

"The chief inspector's office, pal."

"Jesus Christ, downtown. Listen, do me a favor and just take me, okay? My friend here has a problem. You won't be sorry."

"All right, pal. Let's go."

There was a big commotion as George let all the players free into the street. They were mostly middle-aged and old Jewish guys, and they fervently thanked Georgie like he was Moses or some kind of messiah.

They drove the prisoner to the nearest precinct house, and as it was Jimmy's pinch, he took him into the back room to get his pedigree.

"You're Jimmy Riley, aren't you?"

Jimmy looked up, a little flattered. "That's right. How do you know my name?"

"I met you outside the Garden with Solly Levy and a bunch of guys a couple of weeks ago. He's my boss."

"Don't tell me you work for Solly. How come this joint isn't on with us?"

"We intended to go on with the downtown squads in another month or two. When we built it up enough to afford you guys."

"For Christ's sake, I must have two hundred slips here, all anywhere from two clams to two hundred. Who are you bullshitting?"

"Honest, Jimmy, it was just a matter of another couple of weeks. Jesus, Jimmy, I got nine convictions. My last sentence was a six months suspended. I'll go to the can if you lock me up."

"Then for Christ's sake, why the fuck did you be a hero and volunteer? Why didn't you give me the other guy?" But Jimmy's sympathies were aroused. He was appalled at the idea of sending a guy to jail for making book. And the guy seemed like a nice sincere fellow.

"The other clerk was only a fill-in for a few days, and his wife just had a baby."

"But look at the stink we raised in the block. For Christ's sake, you'd think we were making a Gestapo raid. Every Jew in Williamsburg knew we were making a pinch."

"I know, Jimmy, I know. You're dead right. But please, let me go and I'll get you a guy to cover you."

"What do you mean, get me a guy?"

"You know, a stiff."

Jimmy had a rule against taking a stiff, but he hated to take a chance on the poor guy going to jail, so he reluctantly agreed. He walked up front to the desk lieutenant, pressed a fifty-dollar bill on him with a handshake, and said, "I'll be right back, Lieutenant."

Jimmy told George to wait and drove back to the scene of the crime with his erstwhile prisoner, and sure enough, Solly Levy was there. Looking a little sheepish.

"How are you, Jimmy?"

"Fuck you, Solly. A cheater here, a cheater there, and how are you, Jimmy? Go fuck yourself."

"All right, Irish, I'm sorry. I'll explain later. Don't get your dumb mick ass in an uproar. I'm tickled to death you didn't book my main man Morris. I'll take good care of you."

"Okay, Sol, let's cut the shit. I need someone to cover me for this. Who've you got?"

Solly motioned across the street to a big Jew who was behind a peddler's pushcart.

"Cherry, come over here."

"Cherry. Where the hell did he get that name, Solly?"

"Don't you see what's on the pushcart? He sells cherries."

Jimmy shook his head in disbelief. Cherry ambled across the street like a worn-out drayhorse. He was big, bovine, raw-boned, and obviously not too bright. Jimmy had instant misgivings.

"Go with this nice man, Cherry, like you did last month. I'll mind your pushcart, and we'll send someone down to get you later."

Jimmy kept looking at the peddler. He turned to Solly and said,

"You sure this guy knows the score, Sol? He looks like one fucking dumb schmuck."

"He's okay, Jim. He's done this for me a couple of times. He's a distant relative of my wife's. I bought him the cherry wagon when he came here from the old country. Go ahead. I'll be in touch and straighten you out real good. I won't forget this, Jimmy. I love you, kid."

Jimmy took Cherry back to the station house and booked him. The lieutenant on the desk almost busted out laughing and even Jimmy had all he could do to keep a straight face during the booking. When that formality was over, the lieutenant said, "Jimmy, I have a suggestion to make. Why don't you take him to afternoon court at Jefferson Market. It's only a few blocks away and you have plenty of time. That way you can avoid the hassle of night court."

"Good idea. Thanks, Lieutenant."

Jimmy and George drove their bucolic bookmaker to the courthouse and Jimmy put him in the bullpen while he went to the court clerk to make out his arrest complaint. The complaint—what bookmakers were usually referred to in the jargon of policemen—was called a nine eighty-six. A violation of Section 986 of the penal code, a violation of the gambling laws, a misdemeanor. Jimmy kidded around with the court clerk and a couple of plainclothes cops who were in the complaint section of the courtroom, and in high humor sat down in the first row of the main courtroom and waited for his case to be called. Suddenly everyone was called to rise by the bailiff's cry and the judge entered and took his seat behind the bench. Jimmy's good cheer instantly deserted him and he experienced a deep feeling of foreboding. The judge was his Honor, Francis X. McMasters.

Cherry's case was soon called. A guard brought him out to be arraigned, and Jimmy stood beside him as the arresting officer. The judge read aloud the complaint which charged Cherry with three separate instances of receiving money and recording horse bets. He then looked the big ox over very carefully and said, "How do you plead to this charge, Mr. Washnofsky"—Cherry's real name—"guilty or not guilty?"

Cherry stood beside Jimmy looking positively stricken, with a puzzled frown on his face, seemingly speechless. The judge posed the question again, very softly—so softly that Jimmy involuntarily shuddered.

"How do you plead, Mr. Washnofsky? Guilty or not guilty?"

Cherry then turned and looked directly at Jimmy. Jimmy was staring straight at the judge, wishing he was dead, but he could feel Cherry's eyes burning a hole in the side of his head.

Again: "Guilty or not guilty, Mr. Washnofsky?"

The lower parts of Jimmy's and Cherry's bodies were concealed by the court stenographer's desk, so Jimmy kicked Cherry in the leg, meanwhile wishing he could kill him.

Cherry winced from the kick and let out a little cry. The courtroom erupted in scattered bursts of laughter. The judge reddened and rapped his gavel. Just then a lawyer friend of Jimmy's who was watching the action from the front of the court stepped up to Cherry's side and said, "I'm sorry I'm a little late, your Honor. I've been retained to handle Mr. Washnofsky. He pleads not guilty, your Honor."

The Honorable Francis X. McMasters' face was almost purple with rage. He surveyed the scene in front of him until he finally got his voice under control and said, "Fine, Counselor. The defendant is released in your custody."

The whole courtroom had been on the verge of collapsing with laughter, particularly when Jimmy kicked Cherry, and only the obvious rage on the judge's face had kept it down to just a few mild titters. Jimmy's most recent best friend in the world, the lawyer for the defense, led Cherry off. Jimmy turned to leave, the weight of the world off his shoulders, when the judge tapped his gavel for silence and said, "There will be a short recess. Just a minute, Officer Riley. In my chambers, if you please." Jimmy nodded his head dumbly and walked to the side of the courtroom and into the judge's chambers like a condemned man going to the electric chair.

The judge was sitting back in a big leather chair, still steaming. He motioned Riley to a nearby sofa and in a harsh, almost strangled voice, said, "You are without a doubt either the nerviest fuck or the dumbest fuck I ever saw for a cop. And believe me, in my time I've seen the nerviest and the dumbest. How in Christ's name could you bring an ignorant immigrant Jew who can barely speak a word of English into my courtroom and try to palm him off as a bookmaker? Now what do you have to say for yourself?"

Like Cherry a few minutes back, Jimmy sat there like a stricken ox, speechless. His always nimble vocal cords absolutely refused to work. He just shook his head.

"Now listen, you. I know what goes on in this city and I know you plainclothes men get away with a lot of shit with some judges. But not with Francis X. McMasters. It's a lucky thing you're in my family, even if it's only through marriage. Don't think the likes of you can kid me. I know who paid for your sister's wedding, and I also know you're not a bad kid, even for a thief. But just try once more to bring a stiff into my court and I'll have you before the district attorney so fast your head will swim. Now, I warned you once to be careful. This is the second and last warning. Now get the hell out of here and never let a thing like this happen again."

Jimmy rose, mumbled a thank-you, and kept walking fast until he got out of the court and into his car, where George was anxiously waiting for him.

"Jesus, Jimmy, what happened? What did the judge say?"

"Georgie, let's go. I'm going to find that fuck Solly Levy and strangle him the minute I can get my hands on him. Could you believe that dumb Jew schmuck he gave me for a stiff?"

"Jimmy, I was dying for you. But honestly, to tell the truth, I almost howled laughing when you kicked that dopey sonofabitch in the leg. Holy Christ, that was funny." Georgie laid his head back against the car seat and really started to howl laughing.

"Laugh. Go ahead, laugh, you dago prick. That fucking judge really reamed my Irish ass out." But the memory of Cherry came back and Jimmy started screaming with laughter along with George.

"Stop the car, we'll get killed laughing like this. Let's go to Quinn's and have a drink so I can get the taste of this afternoon out of mouth."

They were still chuckling about the incident over their third drink when Jimmy said, "You know something, George, seriously, we're taking ourselves too much for granted. Like we got a license to steal. The richer we get, the more complacent we get. From now on, no more stiffs. At the meeting next week I'm going to tell the guys what happened today and hope they'll learn a lesson and agree. No more stiffs."

And so another rule was laid down as Jimmy described his harrowing experience to the squad. Georgie acted out Cherry's part and Jimmy played both himself and the judge. The guys were rolling around the floor laughing as they acted out the whole scene. But in the end they all agreed it could have ended up real bad.

After a little more than a year of nonleadership of his troops, Peter O'Neil and the chief were retired from The Job. The squad held a private dinner for Pete and among other things gave him a solid-gold replica of his lieutenant's shield. Pete made a nice misty-eyed speech in which he thanked everyone for doing such a good job for him, and relieved a lot of tension and high anxiety by assuring the guys that they were going to stay intact under the incoming regime on the specific orders of the mayor.

The new high command took over, and outside of the new lieutenant in charge, things remained pretty much the same. He was a harsh, bluff, ex-detective lieutenant of German extraction. Inevitably, he acquired the nickname Der Führer. He started off making a few bad gambling raids on cousins and seemed like he was going to be a holy terror and a real pain in the pass. The boys got together and finally, by popular acclaim, Jimmy was elected to take him to dinner and discuss the facts of life.

Der Führer and Jimmy had a couple of martinis, a sure ice-breaker, exchanged some small talk, ate a delicious dinner, and then got down to the nitty-gritty.

"Lieutenant, tell me the truth, are you under the impression that this racket's on the level?"

"What do you mean by that, Jimmy?"

"For Christ's sake, Lieutenant, you had the East Side homicide squad for years. You know that there are more bookmakers, numbers guys, and games on the East Side than you can count. And you were supposed to be a real smart detective. Don't tell me you missed a trick."

"Now easy, Jimmy. You know I'm here to protect the chief against any scandal. I refuse to let the city run wild. I don't care, and the chief really doesn't care if you kids make a few bucks. Christ knows, you need it with the pay you get, but I don't want any Monte Carlos, you understand?"

Der Führer even broke down and smiled a little when he finished his speech, so Jimmy decided to throw caution to the winds. He reached into his inside coat pocket and drew out a bulky envelope, filled with cash.

"There won't be any big Monte Carlos, boss, just a kind of junior one. When you get home, count this. If you don't think it's enough, we'll sit down and figure out a few ways to make the cut larger."

Der Führer stuck the envelope in his kick with the smooth motion of a beat cop taking an apple off a fruit stand. "Now remember, Jimmy, not too wild and not too wide open. Okay?"

"Sure, Lieut, you're the boss. If you think something's getting out of hand, you tell me."

By now, well into his second year of newly acquired wealth, Jimmy had bought a home in lower Connecticut, which he loved. He was soon invited to play golf at the local country club, and being personable and a pretty fair player, was put up for membership. He shrugged off his apparent affluence by dropping frequent broad hints that his wife was some sort of heiress. He loved the place, and couldn't wait for the weekends to run up there and play golf and swim with his wife and kids. In due time he became popular in the country club and fit well into the Fairfield County group. He resolved that when the honeymoon was over—when he was bounced out of plainclothes—he would pack The Job in and live in Connecticut.

The weeks turned into months and soon another year passed with everyone in the squad getting healthier, wealthier, and wiser. There was the occasional inevitable argument here and there, which was par for the course among cops. But on the whole, they all liked and respected each other and got along extremely well together.

What with vacations and various emergencies popping up, Jimmy got to work with other guys besides Georgie. Next to

George, the guy he liked most was Jackie McGrath. George was a real home guy who couldn't wait to get back to his wife and kids when the day's work was over. He had bought a place on the extreme end of Long Island and loved to disappear out there for a week at a time. As long as their full quota of pinches were in and all the cabbage was picked up, Jimmy didn't care what he did. By the same token, Jackie's partner, Sid, like nearly all Jews, couldn't see enough of his family. He was forever visiting his or his wife's mother and father, or their sisters and brothers. Consequently, Jackie was left alone a lot. And so Jackie and Jimmy found themselves working together quite a bit, and soon found they had one thing in common—they both loved to live it up. They would go out together at night, finish up whatever they had to do, and head for the Copacabana, Latin Quarter, Club 18, Leon and Eddie's, or any number of East Side smart places where they were well known and well liked. Good-looking and sharply dressed, and their pockets lined with money, they always had plenty of girls giving them the glad eye. The hotel suite was put to frequent use, and the good times rolled.

But as often happens when you think you're sitting on top of the world, boom, you suddenly get knocked on your ass. Jimmy and Jackie went to Harlem one night to discuss a new contract with some black numbers bankers. The meet was in Dickie Wells's restaurant. There were several black racket guys there that they were very friendly with and it soon developed into quite a party. A few gorgeous black chicks joined the table and the wine was flowing real good. Jimmy really dug the black guys' sense of humor and was enjoying himself hugely. The big numbers guy, Johnny Walker, pointed to one of the black beauties and made the age-old feel-like-getting-laid gesture. Jimmy shook his head no. Not that he had anything against spade chicks, he thought they were super, but not tonight. He and Jackie had a date with the two most beautiful dancers in the Latin Quarter. They were to meet them in the Zebra Room on the East Side at one thirty.

Jimmy looked at his watch, saw it was near one o'clock. He caught Jackie's eye, pointed to his watch, and motioned him to get going. They finally said their goodbyes all around and left Dickie's club. Jimmy had driven his car down from Connecticut and Jackie had driven in from Brooklyn. They debated for a minute whether to use Jimmy's car, which was parked just down the block from Dickie's place, but finally decided to drive downtown in separate cars in case they had to split up later. Both in a great mood, with some nice wine in them and the anticipation of the beautiful girls waiting for them, they shook hands goodbye with a mutual "See you in about twenty minutes." That was the longest and toughest twenty minutes of Jackie's young life.

Jackie McGrath was a big, dark-haired Irish kid who had wanted to be a cop from the time he could remember. His father was a cop, his uncle was a police captain, and half of his numerous relations were in The Job. He was about as tall as Jimmy, but while Jimmy was on the rangy side, Jackie was much bigger-boned and huskier. He had sweated out two years as a Port Authority cop working in the Queens Midtown Tunnel before being appointed to The Job. He could barely believe his good fortune after a couple years of inhaling stinking gas fumes. To think he was a plainclothes cop in action all over the city and making this kind of money almost overwhelmed him. And he was very fond of Jimmy, loved to work and play with him. Jimmy had a real easy way about him with all kinds of people, especially girls, that Jackie envied. But he found that he could confide in Jimmy and trust him to keep his mouth shut, even though he was always kidding and fooling around. After he and Jimmy had worked together a few times, and over a bottle of Scotch in the hotel suite, Jackie told Jimmy his most closely guarded secret. He suffered from too rapid ejaculation. He confided that he was a late bloomer, not having gotten laid until he was twenty-five years old, not too unusual for an Irishman. Jimmy heard his story out and promised to try to remedy this horrific situation.

A couple of days later Jimmy told Jackie to meet him at the hotel suite at four in the afternoon and to be alone. When he got there, Jimmy was sitting there like a maharajah, drinking with three beautiful broads. Jackie sat down with them and Jimmy introduced them as Polly's finest stock. In an easy matter-of-fact voice Jimmy said, "Girls, my man Jackie here has a grave problem. He gets off the nut too quick. Now this afternoon is going to be dedicated to slowing down Jackie's come rate. You're all going to have a session with him and the one who keeps Jackie going the longest will get a nice bonus. Okay, Jackie, you got plenty of good Scotch here and three beautiful girls. Take your pick, my good man, and please, take your time."

Well, from that day on, Jackie got a lot surer of himself and better and better in the sack. As he was walking along the Harlem street to his car he couldn't help smiling, thinking of that afternoon and how grateful he was to Jimmy. And now he was on his way to meet Sue Ann, one of the loveliest of the Latin Quarter lovelies. He was about a block from his car when a tall black hustler sidled up to him and said, "Hey, white boy, you want some good lovin' tonight?"

Jackie looked at her, smiled, and said, "How much, baby?"

"You gotta car, honey?"

"Sure, right up the block," he said, pointing to his white-topped, two-door red convertible, parked just short of the far corner.

"Okay, honey, twenty bucks."

Jackie grabbed her by the arm and said, "Fine with me, sugar." This collar was too easy to pass up. He figured he would get her in the car, place her under arrest, and take her to the station house which he knew was only a couple of blocks away. He wouldn't have to arraign her until Monday, he would only keep Jimmy and the girls waiting a few extra minutes, and what the hell, it was one less pinch he would have to make this month. They walked arm in arm up to Jackie's car and as he was unlocking the passenger's side for the hooker to get in, he felt something hard and cold pressed into his back.

"Just freeze, motherfucker. Get out of here, Louise, see you later. All right, white boy, take it nice and easy, you hear. Slide over behind the wheel."

Jackie's blood ran cold. Out of the corner of his eye he got a brief look at them. Three big black dudes, all waving big black guns. He had his own gun in his right-hand coat pocket and his police shield in his left pants pocket. Please God, don't let these bastards search me first or I'll be a goner for sure. But the mouthy black guy just held the door open while Jackie slid in behind the wheel, and motioned to his two pals to get in the back. Jackie knew he was in bad trouble but he was strangely unafraid and remarkably alert. How the fuck am I going to get out of this?

It was tight quarters as the big guy pushed in beside him, and Jackie with his left hand on the door handle on his side, opened it and started to roll back out of the car. In the same motion he drew his gun out of his coat pocket and started to shoot. His first shot hit the big mouthy guy square between the eyes. The two guys in the back were momentarily stunned by this change of events, but got over their consternation quickly and started shooting back and trying to get out the door, which was partially blocked by the dead man. They shot the horn, which started to blow insanely, they hit the windshield, which shattered with a crash. It was pure bedlam. As they tumbled out, Jackie shot the nearest guy in the back of the ear. At the same time, the last guy shot Jackie right in the belly. Jackie staggered back from the force of the bullet, but still got a shot off at the last guy and nailed him in the back. With the shooting, the horn blowing, and the shattering of glass, it was a like a combat zone. Inside of a couple of minutes, the street was alive with radio cars, ambulances, and people. Two big bad black stickup guys were dead, and one was critically wounded. And one big, dark, curly-haired Irish cop who was just on his way to meet a beautiful girl was sitting propped up against the side of his car with his mouth full of blood and a big hole in his belly.

Jimmy was right on time at the Zebra Club and the two girls were there, looking very pretty. Jimmy's date was called the Duchess, a very tall, slim blonde with long legs that started near her shoulders. She was the leader of the Latin Quarter line and she was not only very beautiful, but also extremely funny. Whenever one of Jimmy's pals took a shine to one of the girls in the line, and if she wasn't already spoken for, the Duchess would always arrange a date. This is how Jackie met Sue Ann, and it was developing into quite a romance.

They were soon drinking champagne and listening to the piano and songs of the two guys who worked the room. It looked like the beginning of a very lovely night. About a half hour passed and Jimmy started to get a little apprehensive, especially with Sue

Ann saying every couple of minutes, "Where's Jackie, Jim? What could be keeping him?"

An hour passed and Jimmy really began to worry. The office had a night man on in case of emergency, but he was an elderly, clerical type of guy and Jimmy hated to call him at two thirty in the morning to ask about Jackie's whereabouts. He finally said to himself the hell with it and called.

"Hello, Barney. Jimmy Riley. Anything up?"

"For Christ's sake, where are you, Jimmy? Jackie McGrath got shot about an hour ago up in Harlem. He's being operated on now in Harlem Hospital."

Jimmy was stunned, unbelieving. He struggled to control his voice. "How bad is it, Barney?"

"Pretty bad, Jimmy. In the belly. But I hear he killed two guys and wounded another," he said proudly.

"Thanks, Barney. I'll get right up there."

Jimmy went back to the table, and the Duchess took one look at his ashen face and instantly knew something bad had happened.

"What's up, Jim? Something wrong?"

"Jackie just got shot in the stomach up in Harlem. Jesus Christ, I can't believe it. It seems impossible. I only left him less than an hour ago. Now, for Christ's sake, let's not get hysterical, Sue Ann. Here, Duch, here's fifty dollars. Grab a taxi and the two of you get home. I'll call you when I find out what kind of shape Jackie's in."

Jimmy got up to the hospital about three in the morning, and identifying himself quickly, was led to the floor where Jackie was being operated on. A lot of department brass and a few reporters were already there. Jimmy stayed away from everyone and waited for them to wheel Jackie out of the operating room. After about a half hour of waiting they wheeled Jackie past, and Jimmy's heart sank. Jackie's face was dead white.

While hanging around waiting at the far end of the corridor Jimmy had started a conversation with a nurse and she gave him the name of the doctor who was operating on Jackie. She'd promised to take Jimmy to him when everything quieted down.

The doctor was a tall, handsome mulatto who turned out to be one hell of a guy. He explained to Jimmy that Jackie was shot just once through the belly with a .45-caliber gun, and fortunately the bullet did not hit any vital organs. Still, he was in very bad shape with a big hole in his intestines. If they could control the internal bleeding and if they could overcome the danger of infection, Jackie had a good shot to live. They were loading him up with a new drug called penicillin that they had a lot of confidence in. Jimmy thanked the doctor with all his heart and went off to doze in a chair the nurse provided for him. She promised to wake him when Jackie regained consciousness.

It was seven in the morning when he felt a tap on his shoulder, and the nurse motioned him to follow her. Jimmy took one look at Jackie and his heart nearly broke. He had tubes up his nose and intravenous needles in his arms attached to more tubes hanging from cylinders at the high side of the bed. He looked awful. Jimmy sat by the bed for about an hour, silently cursing the fucks who shot his man, when Jackie suddenly and fuzzily opened his eyes.

Jimmy had a lump in his throat and his eyes were glistening. "How do you feel, you dumb Irish bastard, getting shot up like this?"

A faint, halfhearted smile came over Jackie's face.

"You can't die on me now, you're just beginning to be a good lay, for Christ's sake."

Again the faint smile, this time a little broader. Jackie then put his right hand up and made a circle with his thumb and index finger, the okay signal, and right there Jimmy knew he was going to be all right.

Sure enough, the new wonder drug penicillin worked, Jackie recovered, and in a few months was almost as good as new. The whole squad attended the ceremony when the mayor awarded him the Medal of Honor, the highest award a cop could get. But the real ceremony for Jackie was the party the squad gave him the week he reported back to duty.

It was on a Saturday night and it was at the Club 18. Freddie Lamb, the owner, closed the club to the public that night and the squad took it over. Besides the squad guys and their wives, Jimmy invited all the guys real close to them. Wise guys, bosses, detectives, plainclothesmen—all people they were very friendly with. The place was jammed. Along with the regular floor show featuring Jackie Gleason, Harrington and Hyers, Hazel McNulty and Gaye Lamb, many other fine entertainers did a turn for free. It was agreed by all that it was the most memorable party ever—especially for a guy who just recently got shot in the belly. At the height of the festivities, Jimmy took the mike and called Jackie up and presented him with a beautiful diamond pinky ring—a gift from the squad—and in his presentation speech noted that now Jackie was a real tough guy, not only did he kill a couple guys, but he also wore a diamond pinky ring.

The months rolled by into yet another year, Jackie McGrath healed as good as ever, and despite an occasional hassle from Der Führer, everything was fine. The guys were all maturing into smart plainclothes cops and even smarter businessmen. By this time they all owned their own homes—some even had two homes—and the meetings were similar to those of the Junior Chamber of Commerce. Everyone seemed more concerned with real estate investments, or setting up some relative in the liquor-store or bar-and-grill business, than in the mundane matters of police work.

But there were plenty of things to do to keep Jimmy Riley busy, and from the time he woke up until he went to bed his days were filled with activity. Almost every place he went, it seemed, he met someone who had some sort of "contract" for him, and being an affable and willing guy, he always did his best to comply. He still managed to find time to go to the gym at least twice a week and to play golf weekends in Connecticut, but like all Brooklyn kids he loved the Dodgers and tried to see them whenever possible.

One bright weekday in May he called his father and made a date to meet him outside the press gate at Ebbets Field. The St. Louis Cardinals were in to play the Dodgers, and Whitlow Wyatt was scheduled to pitch against Morton Cooper. He had worked late the previous night, and after checking in by telephone with Georgie and the office, he was in a very cheerful mood in anticipation of the impending pitching duel. He started out for the ball park about noon, as he had a date to meet a guy in Dutch Savarese's bar at one o'clock and game time was at three. His car was in for repair, so he took the BMT subway and got off at Parkside Avenue. He very seldom rode the subway, but he knew that the Parkside Avenue station was only a short distance from Dutch's bar on Flatbush Avenue and Dutch's was only a short walk from Ebbets Field.

He walked up the steps out of the subway and to his surprise and delight saw a few guys with scratch sheets gathered around a short, stocky, dark-haired guy. His antenna quickly shot up. Jimmy was wearing a sport jacket and slacks with an open sport shirt and was confident nobody would mark him for a cop. He pretended not to notice the action and nonchalantly walked across the street to a candy store, bought a scratch sheet, and sat inside sipping a soft drink. Sure enough, two players soon came in with scratch sheets in their hands discussing their forthcoming fortune. Jimmy waited a minute or two and mentioned that he was on his way to the ball game. This immediately opened up the topic of who was favorite in the game and the price on the game.

After the short baseball conversation Jimmy said, "You know, I can't make up my mind in the first at Belmont, and I know for sure I've got the winner in the second. I'd love to make a ten-dollar double before I go to the game. Maybe you guys can give me a winner in the first."

They went hook, line, and sinker for Jimmy's act. In exchange for his winner in the second they gave him their unanimous selection in the first. Like all true horse players, they became the best of friends in five minutes flat. Jimmy explained away his presence in the neighborhood by saying that he had recently moved to Argyle Road, a few blocks from the candy store. He was soon established as a true figure in the sporting world, and the two players took Jimmy across the street to bet the bookmaker. The book gave Jimmy only a passing glance as he bet him five to win on the two horses and a ten-dollar double. He winked at the two players accompanying Jimmy and, with a short nod of the head in Jimmy's direction, said to one of them, in a very low voice that Jimmy barely caught, "Friend of yours?"

"Sure, a real nice guy."

And so in the next hour the real nice guy gave the real friendly bookmaker with the big smile three different bets and never cashed one. Finally giving up any hope of selecting a winner, and with time running short for his appointments, Jimmy walked up to the bookmaker and whispered in his ear, "I'm a cop, pal. Just be nice and quiet and we'll take a little stroll over to the station house on Empire Boulevard, and nobody will even miss you for a little while."

The bookmaker nearly fainted and his big smile grew a little sickly, but he recovered his poise quickly and marched down the block toward Flatbush Avenue in tow with Jimmy like they were old friends.

"Where you from, boss?"

"The chief inspector's office. Nice little thing you have here."

"Are you Jimmy Riley?"

"How'd you guess?"

"Sonafabitch, I knew it when I took that first bet from you. For Christ's sake, I know a million friends of yours. You can't take me."

Jimmy couldn't help admiring this guy's gall. "No shit. Why not? What the hell makes you so sacred? Did it ever occur to you about a minor thing like paying us, you little asshole?"

"I swear to God I was about to get in touch with you. I'm just starting to go good here. I'm only out of the army five months, for Christ's sake. Give me a break."

"Why? Did they find out you were a fucking spy for the enemy?"

"Come on, Jimmy, please. Let's straighten this out. Please. I'll take good care of you."

Jimmy looked at his watch. Almost half past one. He was already late for his meet at Dutch's, and it was fairly important. Further, if he went ahead and booked this guy he might be late meeting his father at Ebbets Field. And Whitlow Wyatt against Morton Cooper, he hated to miss an inning of that. Besides, the guy didn't seem to be a bad kid.

"Okay, what's your name?"

"Harry Gross."

"Tell you what, Harry, go back to work. I'll meet you in

Hughie Casey's restaurant at seven sharp tonight. Be there, or go to the Himalaya Mountains up in Tibet, get it?"

"I'll be there with bells on. Thanks a lot, Jimmy. You won't regret this."

Jimmy often thought about the day of their first meeting and wondered if his life might have turned out differently if he had not had a date to meet his father to see Whitlow Wyatt pitch against Morton Cooper. Suppose he had just pinched Harry, stuck it up his ass, and forgot about him. About the regret part of it, that was another matter. Regrets were never a big part of Jimmy's make-up.

Harry Gross was born a couple of years ahead of Jimmy Riley, to lower-middle-class Jewish parents in the Bensonhurst section of Brooklyn. They were very respectable, religious people who, despite a chronic shortage of money, tried their best to give Harry a good education. But though Harry was more than average smart, high school was as far as they could get him to go. Harry had no illusions about becoming a teacher, a lawyer, or a doctor when he grew up—he was determined to be a wise guy. He was a short, stocky kid, inclined to be a little fat. But he had a great face, with strong, even white teeth and a good head of thick, wavy hair to go with it. If he were six inches taller and forty pounds lighter he would have been handsome enough to be a movie star. And a great movie star he would have been, for he was a consummate actor with a fine sense of humor and immense appeal to the opposite sex. He graduated from high school during the Great Depression and like all kids of that era had a series of minor jobs. During his stint as a soda jerk, he claimed to have laid most of the sweet-toothed young charmers who ventured into his lair. But it wasn't long before the ice cream Casanova started to get into the minor-league rackets.

He had learned how to deal craps at a very early age and soon gained a piece of the action in the local neighborhood games. He finally burst out of the confines of Bensonhurst for good when he hooked up with an old-timer named Sy Gaus. Sy Gaus was one of the greatest flim-flam artists of all time. Even if he tried, he couldn't think straight. It was common knowledge among wise guys that if Sy had a chance to make a score the easy straight way, he would purposely figure a way to go around the block to pull it off. He had every conceivable scheme up his sleeve to clip a sucker, and as fast as he made money he pissed it away on horses.

Sy took Harry under his wing when he started in the phony cloth racket. Harry would carry two suitcases full of expensive imported woolens which Sy would show to the prospective buyers. He would urge the buyer to pick out a particular cloth and then offer to make him a tailor-made suit for a ridiculously low price. He had a list of names of college professors and others high in the academic world. The minds of his clientele were on the ruins of ancient Greece or the Renaissance, certainly not on Sy's sales pitch or they would never have given such an obvious scoundrel an order. Sy would say later, "Those fucking professors dressed so bad. I was doing them a favor making them a new suit."

Only he never made the suits. He just received the money for the cloth they picked and then sent them some shit which was about one-tenth the quality of the original. He would then suggest they use their own tailor. When the poor guardian of academic life realized that he had been swindled he was usually too embarrassed to make a holler.

Sy had met Harry Gross at a crap game, noted his handsome looks, and soon Harry was Harry Coles, draper's assistant, on leave from London's Savile Row. Harry would lug the suitcases full of woolens up and down the stairs and through the musty halls of the academic world until his arms were ready to fall off. When on the rare occasion when Sy shut his mouth and the prospective sucker would direct a question at Harry, he would flash his crinkly, white-toothed grin and reply in a definitive British accent, "By Jove, governor, Mr. Gaus here is really giving you a topping bargain." That was the only line Sy permitted Harry to say.

They usually started their day early so as to finish by one o'clock in the afternoon, in plenty of time for Sy to blow the day's receipts with whatever bookmaker he happened to favor at the time. This was distinctly against Harry's grain, for he loved the other side of the action, the bookmaker's side. He had all he could do to weasel his share of the day's take out of Sy so that he could live, and he would spend his afternoons away from Sy trying to find a bookmaker he could past-post. To past-post a bookmaker, which meant to bet him when you already had the result, was a way of life to hustlers like Harry. There were all sorts of elaborate plots made by past-post artists to beat bookmakers, and a poor honest bookmaker always had to be on his toes to guard against them.

Harry finally realized his dream of dreams one day with a bookie who worked out of a bar on West 33rd Street off Seventh Avenue. The bar was directly opposite the side entrance of the Hotel Pennsylvania, with banks of hotel rooms overlooking it. This gave easy access to the past-post artist who had a co-conspirator on the sidewalk outside the bar. Harry quickly found out that the bookmaker in the bar was not too sharp and reluctantly enlisted his patron of the cloth, Sy Gaus, into his foolproof scheme to get rich quick. Harry rented a room in the Hotel Pennsylvania which overlooked the bar and made a connection with a wire-service outfit to assure him of immediate race results. This could easily be arranged for a modest weekly fee.

Sy soon ingratiated himself with the horde of bettors who hung around the bar, and in a few days became a most welcome customer of the bookmakers. So as not to arouse too much suspicion, they played it cool for a few days and kept their winnings low enough so that even the flamboyant Sy did not attract attention. Sy would leave the bar every half hour or so ostensibly to get some air, but actually to observe his draper's assistant signal him the winner from his rented hotel room five stories above the local action. This was done by a singular method. Harry would get the winner by post-position number via the telephone flash and quickly run to the window overlooking Sy and pull the window shade up and down the required number of times to denote the winner's post position, which was listed on Sy's ever-present scratch sheet. Pull the shade up and down five time, post position five the winner, three times, post position three the winner, and so ad infinitum.

They built the bankroll up to a nice couple of thousand and

were setting up the gullible bookie for the big kill. The day of destiny came, and the third race was set for the score. Sy was to bet five hundred on the first two races and lose as usual, and then bet a thousand on the third race, a guaranteed winner. Sure enough, Harry got the result and rushed over to the window and pulled the shade up and down six times. Sy looked up at Harry and shook his head. Harry looked down at him incredulously and yanked the shade up and down violently six more times. Sy looked up again, shook his head once more, and walked back into the bar. Harry came flying out of the hotel down to the sidewalk outside the bar, and pacing up and down like a madman, trembling with rage and fearing the worst, waited for Sy to come out. A few minutes later, his whole world crashed around him. Sy came out of the bar looking grief-stricken. The doomsday look.

"Now for Christ's sake, don't tell me, please don't tell me. You didn't play number six?"

"Harry, my boy, don't get excited. I hate to tell you this, but knowing what a great handicapper I am, I'm sure you'll forgive me. Well, I was sure you made a mistake, I didn't give the six horse a chance in my figures. I bet the G-note on the favorite, I didn't see how he could lose."

Harry threw up his hands in despair, and grabbing Sy by the arm, walked him up the block out of earshot of the players outside the bar and said, "I oughta kill you, you stupid fucking sonofabitch. Here I give you the winner, the *winner*, and you tell me you didn't make him in your figures. Fuck you and your figures. And your phony cloth and the rest of your horseshit. We're through. Give me what's left of the score and I hope to Christ I never lay eyes on you again."

Poor Harry didn't even get a fair shake on his end, because for every winner Harry signaled, Sy would make a secret bigger bet on the horse he liked in the race. Thus, the two giants of the woolen industry parted. Fortunately, their relationship didn't prove to be all bad for Harry, as he found the sporting life as Sy's companion had enabled him to meet a lot of big shots in the gambling world who got a kick out of Sy. Through one of these connections Harry caught on as a runner for a pretty big Brooklyn bookmaking outfit. He quickly became well liked around the

Flatbush neighborhood which was his designated fief and built up a business of about a thousand a day in small action.

Harry's budding gambling career was soon curtailed by the heavy hand of the military draft and entry into the United States Army. Needless to say, army life was not exactly conducive to Harry's happiness, and favored by a chronic leg condition, he was mustered out in a matter of a few months. Shortly after doing his bit for Uncle Sam, Harry married a nice quiet Jewish girl. Her father was a minor lieutenant in the reigning Jewish Newark mob, presided over by Longy Zwillman and Doc Harris. Harry felt that this betrothal gave him instant status in the underworld, something he craved.

With the proceeds of the wedding gifts and a little boost from the bride's family, Harry set himself up as an independent bookmaker on Parkside Avenue, in the Flatbush section of Brooklyn, right next to the BMT subway station. It was a thriving neighborhood of commuter traffic and busy storekeepers, and Harry soon established a lucrative betting business. But he chafed at the small-time action and hungrily read about big shots like Frank Erickson and Frank Costello and longed for the day he himself would be a big-timer.

The break came in a very unexpected way. Harry had great style and made friends with everyone he did business with, horse business or common everyday business. He kept his car in a gas station run by a fellow named Augie. He and Augie soon became great friends, and Augie relayed any horse customers he could find to Harry. One day a very distinguished, well-dressed Italian gentleman who drove a big Lincoln and who was a customer of Augie's asked Augie to please get a bet in for him. Augie assured him he would and politely asked how much of a bet? Fifty win, fifty place—a good-sized bet for a street bookmaker. Augie took the hundred-dollar bet to Harry a little skeptically, but Harry wrote it up without a qualm. The horse went down. And so did every horse this fine Italian gentleman, whom they soon nicknamed the Count, bet on. He turned out to be a dress manufacturer with a ton of money whose passion in life was betting on horses.

In six months Harry beat the Count for over thirty thousand,

and made such a good friend of him that he would retain him as both friend and customer for years to come. Harry now had a decent bankroll and took his pal Augie out from underneath the trucks at the gas station and put him on the telephone to handle his more exclusive action. Harry manned his post outside the greeting-card place on Parkside Avenue and used Augie and the telephone for the baseball action and the high rollers.

This was the life of Harry Gross the day Jimmy Riley encountered him for the first time. A most memorable meeting.

3

HUGH CASEY was a big, beefy Georgian who was the epitome of the southern "good ol' boy." He was as good-natured as he was large, he loved to cavort around with the guys, and he was a big drinker. Hughie was the great relief pitcher for the Brooklyn Dodgers, and for a few innings he could throw a baseball through the side of an armored tank. He could also throw a curve ball that would break like a golf ball falling off a cocktail table, often to the dismay of the poor guy who was unfortunate enough to be his catcher.

With the tremendous amount of gambling going on during the early 1940s, the security forces of the baseball hierarchy were very meager. It was fairly common for a baseball player to lend his name to a bar or restaurant and no one got too excited about who frequented the places. Casey's restaurant was filled practically every night with fans, bettors, and wise guys, especially after a Dodger home game. Fortunately, every man, woman, and child who lived in Brooklyn was a rabid Dodger fan. Even to think of tampering with a Dodger player was akin to selling secret war plans to the Japs. This act of treason did not prevent a couple of the more amoral wise guys from plotting a betting coup. Because of a few injuries to starting pitchers, the Dodgers' front office announced that they were going to start their ace relief hurler, Hugh Casey, against the incoming Pittsburgh Pirates. The Pirates were loaded with strong hitters, particularly the two Waner brothers, Paul and Lloyd.

The whole place was congratulating Casey the night before the game, wishing him luck on his initial start, particularly two Brownsville bookmakers named Tootsie Greenberg and Herbie Klein. They insinuated themselves next to Casey at the bar, telling him what a great guy and what a great pitcher he was, meanwhile buying him drink after drink. Together with Casey they finally left his place and proceeded to tour a number of Brooklyn night spots. They were faking the drinks, but good old Hughie was belting them down one after the other. They finally drove him home about four in the morning in such bad shape that they actually had to take his clothes off and put him to bed.

The next day, assuming that Casey would have the godfather of all hangovers and in all likelihood be unable to even see home plate, they bet a bankroll on the Pittsburgh Pirates. Hugh Casey, to the eternal chagrin of Tootsie and Herbie and to the cheers of a packed Ebbets Field, shut out Pittsburgh 3–0 on a two-hitter. Such was the physique of Hugh Casey, and he was just as nice and generous as he was strong.

Casey's popular restaurant was located on Flatbush Avenue, a short walk from the ball park. It was softly lit, with a long mahogany bar and a row of roomy booths on either side of the back room. The atmosphere, the whiskey, and the food were all good. When Jimmy Riley arrived the evening after the day ball game, the place was filled. He was in a happy mood, the Dodgers' Whitlow Wyatt had outpitched the Cardinals' Morton Cooper by a score of three to two. It had been one helluva game and he was still exhilarated. Upon entering, he received a barrage of big hellos from the bar, waved to his friends, and sure enough, spotted Harry Gross toward the far end of the bar. He stood drinking there with a friend of Jimmy's, Frank Delfino, a local division plainclothesman.

Jimmy walked directly over to them, saying in an easy voice, "What'd you do, Harry, bring your guinea bodyguard?"

They both laughed. Frankie said, "No, Jimmy. I just showed up to thank you for not pinching Harry, he's a good friend of mine. He's also a real nice kid."

"Sure, Frankie, to you he's a nice kid, he's paying you. To me he's just another hunk of shit, a desperado, an outlaw."

Harry winced a little. "Come on, Jimmy. For Christ's sake, get off my back. I swear. I was just getting ready to put you guys on. Right, Frankie?"

"He was, Jimmy, honest to God."

"Sounds like the Harry and Frankie show, you guys should get your own radio program, like Myrt and Marge. Okay, Frankie, you go in the men's room and take a piss, I want to straighten out with this guy alone."

Frankie walked away from the bar, and Harry reached inside his coat pocket and handed Jimmy a package of money.

Jimmy slipped it into his pants pocket and said, "How much did you give me?"

"Five hundred."

Jimmy took the package out of his pocket and handed it back to Harry, saying, "Stick the five hundred up your ass."

"For Christ's sake, what's wrong with five hundred? What's the matter? Don't get sore."

"Don't get sore, my dick. Since I let you go this afternoon, I've done a little private-eye investigation on you. What the hell do you think, I'm some kind of stupid schoolboy? What about the wire room you have Augie running over the candy store? What about the bunch of runners you have calling in action to him, don't they count? Now come on, do you think I'm some kind of dumb fuck who won't really catch up to your act?"

Harry's face got white and he started to sweat a little. His confidence was oozing and his voice shook. "Jesus Christ, the U.S. Secret Service could certainly use guys like you. One afternoon and you got me dead right. Okay, give me a break. I'll double it, you got a thousand."

"I should quadruple it for you holding out on me about the wire room and runners, you little fuck. But I don't want to embarrass Delfino, and I did hear a few nice things about you, so make it a thousand and consider yourself lucky."

"Beautiful, Jimmy. Thank you. I'll go to the men's room and count out the other five hundred. Be right back."

Frankie came back to join Jimmy at the bar, and Harry shortly rejoined them and pressed the thousand into Jimmy's hand. The opening hostilities over, the ransom money paid, the three of them were soon drinking and laughing together like they had been friends for a million years. The hour getting late, they decided to get a bite to eat at a nearby all-night cafeteria. Frankie dropped them off at the door, pleading that he was tired and had to get up very early the next morning to meet his favorite stool pigeon.

Riley and Gross sat together at a table in the far corner of the cafeteria and ordered bacon and eggs and coffee. They were both still a little high from the whiskey and the conversation was very funny, both of them breaking up as they exchanged some of the funnier things that happened during the course of their work weeks. Harry was even a better storyteller than Jimmy, and he regaled him with some priceless ones about horse players and their habits.

After finishing their meal and sipping their coffee, Harry said, "You know, Jimmy, I've heard an awful lot about you. You may think that I'm bullshitting you, but the truth is I was dying to meet you."

"You were dying to meet me so much that I had to capture you by sheer accident on my way to a ball game. Please, don't give me that shit, Harry. From now on level with me."

"I swear, Jimmy, I'm telling the truth. You can't blame me for ducking the New York squads as long as I could. Who the fuck wants to pay all that money if they can possibly avoid it? I'm only a Johnny-come-lately, the new kid on the block. I just hoped to Christ I could build it up to where I could get a real horse room going and then put you guys on. You understand, don't you, Jim?"

"I guess so. I know what you mean. But you're lucky it was me who nailed you instead of one of the bloodthirsty bastards from the P.C.'s squad or you would have been dead. If she were an outlaw, they wouldn't let their own mother off the hook. Anyway, it's over, ancient history, forget about it. I don't believe in hard feelings. Tell you what, I'll straighten you out next with my guys and the P.C.'s squad, and I promise I won't make the ice too tough."

"You're a sweetheart, Jimmy. You know, you and me could really go places together if we teamed up."

"What do you mean by that?"

"To be honest with you, I've been sizing you up all night, since we met at Casey's. I watched all the wise guys come over to you shaking hands, and Frankie Delfino tells me that you get along great with most of the cops. Frankie says you're a dead-square guy with a contract. What a combination we'd make. With your connections and muscle, and with my knowledge of the book-making racket, the two of us could conquer Brooklyn."

Jimmy looked thoughtfully at Harry and remained silent for a couple of minutes. He took an occasional sip of his coffee. This little Jew boy was something else. He took a good look at him. He was a handsome little bastard, with an infectious laugh and a tremendous sense of humor. Jimmy looked at his watch. Quarter after one.

"Okay, yeah, let's go. You can drive me home, my car is in the shop. Let's forget about talking business for a while, I'm tired. Tell you what, I'll meet you Sunday night for dinner at The Barge in Sheepshead Bay. About eight o'clock. Be alone."

Harry dropped Jimmy off at his house and they shook hands goodnight and parted like old pals. Jimmy lay awake for about an hour, pondering Harry's proposition. Well, let's see what happens. Let the chips fall where they may.

They met at the appointed time at The Barge, a fine old Sheepshead Bay restaurant, and at Jimmy's behest the headwaiter led them to a corner table in a secluded part of the dining room. They each had a couple of drinks to loosen up, and after quite a session of cops-and-robbers and bookmaker talk, Jimmy finally said, "Listen, Harry, I've given a lot of thought to what you mentioned the other night. You remember, about what a dynamite combination the two of us would make. Let's hear what you have in mind."

"Fine, Jimmy, fine. What I have in mind is this," Harry began hesitantly. "Now take this in stride. I have no intention of insulting you or anything close to it, get it? If you don't like my proposition just forget about it. Wash it from your mind. Above all, I want you to be my friend."

"Go ahead, for Christ's sake. I don't get insulted too easily, especially where I can see a buck to be made.

"Well, okay, James, here we go. To tell the God's honest truth,

I'm starting to do pretty good. The street book is growing, and my wire-room business is improving every day. But to tell the real truth, Jimmy, I'm a little scared. Not only of the cops. I'm afraid some mob will move in on me and marry me. You know, either the wops or that tough Jew outfit from Brownsville, Babe and them. Believe me, if they do, I haven't got one fucking guy I can depend on. All I've got around me is a bunch of nice kids who wouldn't hurt a fly. They'd shit if someone slapped them around or pulled a gun on them. And as for that shit, well, that goes for me too. I figure with a guy like you on my side, as my partner, we could branch out and do one helluva number. You know, you being a well-respected cop out of the main New York squad and connected with the top guineas, nobody will bother us if you let them know you're interested in me. The same goes for those Jew shitheels from Brownsville."

Jimmy Riley, ever fascinated by the gambling business listened intently to Harry. His own devious mind was already scheming the endless ramifications of the proposed partnership. He sipped his drink and said, "How far do you want to go? How many spots and runners can we line up? Are there any free-lance guys you got in mind who would go with us right away? And last, but far from least, how about the cabbage? What kind of cash are you talking about? You know, for a bankroll to set this thing up."

Harry, sensing Jimmy was going for his scheme, started to talk excitedly. "Jesus, Jimmy, there's any number of joints looking to go under some guy's wing, especially someone with cash and a little power. Christ, especially if they had an inkling that someone like you was in their corner. I can nail down three or four in a week. I've already got about ten runners calling Augie on a fifty percent sheet. Plus at least twenty-five or thirty regular players. A good nucleus. The joint is starting to coin money. Let's go to the bankroll. I've got about fifty grand I can spare. You put up even-steven, fifty grand, and we'll start off with a bankroll of one hundred big ones. Whadda you say? Sound kosher?"

"The money doesn't present a problem. In fact, I don't see any problem at all. But there are a couple of important, basic things. First, who's going to have control over the bankroll? Second, exactly what is my end going to be? And third, and this is the most important, let's get something straight right out of the gate. If I'm going to put my Irish ass up next to your Jewish ass, just make sure that I get a good count. I like you, like your company, and I'm sure we'll make a good buck together. But if I find you fucking me just once, or lying to me, all bets are off. I'll cleave that curly head right off your fucking shoulders. You got that straight?"

"Jimmy, I swear, that's the least of your worries. As far as the bankroll goes, we'll get a vault in the National City Bank at Flatbush and Church. The manager and I are real tight. He's a nice guy. You and I will have the only keys to the vault and you can check it out anytime you want. As soon as we get rolling we'll each draw a thousand bucks a week. I'll draw an extra thousand for the house and expenses. You know, buying dinner or a drink, whatever. At the end of each month we'll each take a split, meanwhile leaving enough over to beef up the bankroll. There, how about those apples? Does that sound like a fair-and-square proposition to you?"

"Harry, it sounds too good to be true. There's only one flaw, and it worries me. For Christ's sake, I hardly know you. A few days ago I goddam near pinched you, and here I am in Sheepshead Bay having dinner with you and contemplating being your partner. I thought I had some line of shit. You make me look like I'm deaf and dumb, like a guy in the old silent movies. I have to admit that I checked you out pretty thoroughly the last couple of days. Even a couple of the big wops I spoke to had some nice things to say about you. But you have to admit, it's one helluva step for me to take. I hesitate about my name being tossed all over New York as a bookmaker's partner. I've got too good a thing now to blow it, even though I'm tempted at the thought of the score we can make together."

"I swear to God I'll never use your name unless absolutely necessary. Plenty of cops and wise guys are real close friends. The only guy who'll know we're partners would be Augie, my head man. He has a piece of the action, and furthermore, he's one sweetheart of a guy. Come on, Jimmy, come on in with me, we'll knock them dead together."

"How soon do you want an answer?"

"Immediately. Right now."

Jimmy looked hard at him, studying Harry's face for a couple of minutes. Harry's forehead gleamed with sweat, his brown eyes were dancing in his head. Can I really trust this fuck, he thought. He had already checked him out and knew that Harry was a fantastic hustler, his kind of hustler. What the hell, he figured, sooner or later I'm going to get involved in the rackets and I might as well start with this guy. At least I think I can control him. And I won't have any ten partners or shit like that to combat.

"Okay, I'm your man. When do we get the vault and how soon do you want my end of the bankroll?"

Harry let out a low whistle. "Beautiful, Jimmy, really beautiful. I'll start the ball rolling tomorrow and from here on in I'll be in constant touch. Jimmy, you won't regret a thing, kid. We'll make a million dollars together."

We'll make a million dollars together. Screw a million, we'll make five million. Jimmy Riley lay awake that night for a long, long time. He had made the commitment. Was he doing the right thing? Was he jeopardizing his status as a main-office vice cop by joining hands with Harry Gross? But your mind often functions with great clarity when you lie sleepless in bed dissecting your own life and the problems of the world. Being very honest in analyzing himself, he knew that he didn't have too much heart for being a cop. Arresting bookmakers, crap-games, operators, numbers guys, and hookers was not his cup of tea. Perhaps he would have felt better about being a cop if he were a homicide detective or on some major-crime squad. He even doubted that. But one thing he knew for sure, what he was now doing was pure, unadulterated horseshit. Sure, the money, the clothes, the girls, and the night life were all terrific, and he had to admit that he got a feeling of well-being from the recognition he received throughout the city. But deep down in his heart he knew he hated to lock up some poor sucker for any violation of the particular laws he was charged with enforcing. Sometimes he even had a slight pang of conscience about giving a guy a heavy shake for not pinching him, for letting him off the hook. Fortunately, that pang was very rare, for money was the game, Jimmy, he kept reminding himself, and each trip to the safe deposit vault was another step on the stairway to the stars.

Jimmy tacked on another rationale. As the years went by, he found that he enjoyed the company of wise guys. With rare exceptions, he liked wise guys better than cops. At this stage of his life he was in solid with almost every top wise guy in the city, and in some cases top wise guys from all over the country. That went for every ethnic division—Jews, Irish, Italians, and blacks. He was just as much at home in Harlem as he was on Broadway or in Flatbush. He got as big a greeting in Dickie Wells's or Teddy Chambers' Chicken Coop as he got in Gallagher's. He went cabareting at least two or three nights a week at the Copacabana or Latin Quarter, and invariably wound up late at night in some smart East Side supper club in the company of one of the more prominent gamblers or racket guys. These were his kind of people. He wasn't exactly averse to the companionship of so-called legitimate people, he just preferred the company of wise guys. They confided in him and schooled him like he was a younger brother because they trusted him, and he was proud that they trusted him. And so he concluded that deep down, psychologically, he really aspired to be one of them. The proposition from Harry Gross was almost foreordained.

What did he have to lose? Fifty thousand? Fat chance. Besides, he chuckled to himself, look at the fun we're going to have building up this mini-empire of ours. The goddam Job is starting to get boring, anyway. Besides, if all goes well they'll never catch me broke as long as I live. This guy Harry Gross has plenty of brains and moxie, and if he stays on the ball and plays on the level, the sky's the limit. Fuck five million, make it ten million, he thought, never a man to figure too low. With visions of greenbacks dancing in his head, he finally fell asleep. The deep sleep of a guy who at last found his niche.

The endless details of the business arrangement were soon completed, and Jimmy and Harry settled down into extremely good action in short order. Inside a month or two they acquired half a dozen spots in various sections of Brooklyn. Jimmy's role was to make sure that they didn't step on anyone's toes when a spot was added. He checked very discreetly to make certain that the prospective new addition was not in any way connected to a member of the mob. Jimmy had put a good deal of effort into building a friendly relationship with the top mob guys over the three years he had spent in The Job and he was not about to do anything to hurt it. He also refused to kid himself. He knew that he did not have an ounce of muscle among Harry's guys to help him in case of a rumble, so he was smart enough to rely on his own reputation as a nice fellow, quick to do a favor, to keep away any wolves with big eyes. Whenever a possible addition approached Harry to come under his wing, Jimmy would make sure that he checked the main man in the neighborhood to see if he was a free agent. At the same time he checked out the new guy's reputation for honesty and business sense.

When Jimmy was assured that they were not making a move on anybody, and the free agent got good marks for honesty and hustling, they put him on as their spot. The usual arrangement was that the guy who ran the spot received one-third of the profits, and the organization got two-thirds. Jimmy set up the protective devices, and Harry handled all the ice. With the added protection against the law, with no bankroll worries, the new spots prospered and enlarged. Within six months Harry and Jimmy were off and running. Jimmy checked out the bankroll with Harry about once a month and was supremely happy with the way things were going. He was in Harry's company constantly, and it was not long before he had Harry meet him almost everywhere. Consequently, Harry started to meet every top cop in the city, including some very important top brass. They took it for granted that as long as he was around Jimmy, he had to be one hundred percent. Harry, with his flair for clothes, dark good looks, and great sense of humor, soon captivated practically everyone he met, just as he initially captivated Jimmy.

But as Jimmy carried on his multiple duties as vice cop and gambling partner, rumors of imminent changes in The Job began to run wild. He was fully aware that The Job was like a long-dormant volcano. There was always some faint movement present and a violent eruption could take place that would scatter the settlers to the winds. A new mayor, Bill O'Dwyer, had just been elected. With the arrival of a new mayor there invariably would come a new police commissioner. The Job was rampant with speculation as to the identity of the new commissioner. Jimmy's direct boss, the chief inspector, was by all odds the logical candidate for the post. He was extremely capable, dead honest, and a very intelligent administrator who had come up through the rank and file. Among his other accomplishments, he had co-authored a book on criminal investigation which was almost a bible to police departments throughout the world.

During the last couple of years of his reign, the chief and Jimmy had developed a great rapport. He called in Jimmy to see him on certain matters more often than he called in Der Führer. He had one problem, however, and it had become a bit more noticeable in the last year. He drank a little more than he should. There is no race like the Irish as quick to criticize someone who drinks a little too much, possibly because most Irishmen are guilty of the same sin. To a man, Bill O'Dwyer and his inner guard were all heavy drinkers or dues-paying members of Alcoholics Anonymous, consequently very much aware of drinking problems.

The anxiety of waiting for the call that he knew in his heart would never come took its toll on the chief, and he went off on a real beauty of a bender for almost a week. At Jimmy's urging he finally checked into Doctors Hospital on the East Side to dry out. The first day Jimmy was permitted to see the chief, he took one look at him and knew immediately that there was trouble. The chief seemed to have aged twenty years since he had last seen him. Gray, blotchy face, bloodshot eyes, haggard.

The chief tried to appear jaunty. "Hello, Jimmy, my boy. How are you?"

"Fine, Chief. You look great," Jimmy lied.

"Please don't give me that horseshit, Jimmy. I feel terrible and I know I look terrible. Jim, I'm not going to be made police commissioner, I just got the word. They're appointing a guy who's an ex-horseback cop, for Christ's sake. Can you believe that?"

"Come on, Chief, you know the job is yours. Even that big

turkey mayor should have enough brains to appoint you. Christ, there isn't any more qualified guy in the world. You must be kidding, or someone's kidding you."

"Forget about it, Jimmy. I got the official word from one of my few friends left. I put my papers in this morning. I sent for Barney, my chauffeur, and signed whatever was necessary and he took them downtown. Poor Barney, the poor sonofabitch cried."

"Jesus, Chief, this is an awful break. I really feel bad for you. What the hell, with that bunch of vultures around Bill O', I guess you never had a chance. You had too much brains for those shit-heels."

They sat there silently for a few minutes. Jimmy finally summoned his courage and said, "You know, boss, you were some helluva guy, and now that the honeymoon is over I want you to know that we did pretty good under you. We never disgraced you or brought any scandal to the office, just like you asked us the first day you laid down the ground rules, but still, it wasn't too bad a run. Now don't take this wrong, please, but as long as you're on your way out, I know that all the guys would like to do something real nice for you. I mean that sincerely."

"Jim, I know you do, God bless you, and I appreciate it. But forget it, I don't want a dime, just all your prayers and good wishes. I was always honest, and that's the way I want to die. I probably was a damn fool, but what the hell, I raised a good family and they're all doing fine in life. What more can a man ask? But now, Jimmy, if you want to do something for me, you can do it right away."

"Anything you say, Chief."

"Go outside to the nearest liquor store and get me a quart of Cutty Sark. I got the whiskey nerves so bad I'm jumping out of my skin. The only thing that'll calm me down is a stiff drink." Jimmy opened his mouth to say something, but the chief put up his hand. "Look, no fucking medical advice and no lectures. Get me the bottle of Scotch up here as soon as you can. And by the way, I understand you're supposed to be a smart plainclothesman, just make sure you don't get caught smuggling it in."

Jimmy laughed. "I'll be right back, boss, and I promise I won't get nailed."

That was the pattern for the next ten days, while the top brass waited for the chief to be released from the hospital before the changes in The Job could be effected. Jimmy was there every day. He staked all the nurses and attendants real good and consequently he could come and go as he pleased. He always called first to see that the coast was clear, that the chief was not being visited by his wife and family, or by some high-ranking member of the department. He also brought the booze regularly until the chief finally nursed himself off the stuff. The day of judgment finally came.

"I'm being released tomorrow, James. The day after that the new commissioner is to be named. I'm finished then, retired from The Job." The chief didn't sound too bitter, just very, very tired.

"Chief, I'm sorry. You're a great guy, a helluva man."

"But Jimmy, I've got wonderful news for you. I've already given the incoming chief a contract on you, and you alone. I got word to him what a smart plainclothesman I think you are and explained that he would need at least one experienced five-borough man to work along with his new gang. To tell the God's honest truth, he'd never be where he is today if it were not for me, so that's the least he can do for me, to keep you."

"Gee, boss, that's terrific, but I'm not so sure I want to stay under the circumstances. I had a great run with you and the guys in the squad, maybe it's best I leave with the rest of the fellows."

"Now, listen here, Jimmy, don't be a damn fool. Stay on the teat as long as you possibly can. I look back today on all my years in The Job and I wonder whether or not I was a damn fool. I had one ambition in life, to be the police commissioner of New York City. I worked and slaved as a precinct cop, a detective, and a boss to get to the top. I studied for promotion exams until my eyes were ready to fall out. I researched and wrote a fine book on criminal investigation. I've been consulted by the highest-ranking police officials in the world on the best methods of combating crime. And, Jimmy, you know I never took a quarter. Now that the time comes for my reward, when I get one rung from the top of the ladder, what do I get? A kick in the ass. Jesus, for a fucking ex-horseback cop to get the job that rightfully belongs to me, I can't believe it. Well, the hell with all those Irish pricks calling the shots. Jimmy, you do as I say, or I'll come back to haunt you. I know pretty near all about you that there is to know, but you're a good kid and I appreciate the fact that you and the other kids never did a thing to hurt me. So you probably made a few bucks. So what? You go on and make as much as you can without getting into trouble and then look to get into the detective bureau, where a real cop belongs. I'm sure you got the makings of a good detective, just like your old man Mike. Now shake my hand on it, Jimmy, you're going to stay on in the chief's office. That's an order."

Jimmy took the chief's hand and gripped it hard. His eyes were glistening with tears, and he was thinking that here lies one of the best men that ever wore a cop's uniform, dying slowly, not from the booze but from a broken heart. Another great decision by a bullshit politician and his henchmen.

Finally, his voice under control, Jimmy said, "Okay, Chief, you're still the boss. I'll do whatever you say. You know how much I appreciate what you've done, and I promise to do a good job for the new chief. Now you take care of yourself and get well real quick. Tender loving care at home will fix you up. It looks like the Dodgers are going to win the pennant, and I'll personally drive you to every home World Series game. Promise?"

The chief just grinned and grabbed Jimmy and hugged him. Jimmy left the hospital quickly. He knew he wasn't going to see the chief at World Series time, he knew deep down that the next time he'd see him would be at his wake. As he walked to his car, Jimmy couldn't restrain a smile, even though he really loved the old chief. He said he pretty much knew all about me. Holy Christ, if he ever knew *all* about me I would have had to buy him a case of Cutty Sark a day to calm him down. Poor old guy, what a fucking tough break. He thought of his first boss in The Job, the late and lamented Lieutenant Peter O'Neil, and Pete's immortal words, "The booze will get you every time."

Jimmy had a few misgivings about staying on with the incoming squad, but during the interim period he remained quiet about it and acted as if it was a complete surprise to him when the changes were officially announced and he was the only holdover. All of his guys took the news in good spirits and no one betrayed even an ounce of jealousy toward Jimmy about remaining in the office. Of all the guys, it was especially sad saying goodbye to Georgie.

"What do you plan on doing, wop?"

"Jimmy, I swear to God, this thing ending the way it has, it's perfect for me. You'd be surprised how many of the guys are relieved to get out of here with their whole skin intact. You thrive on this kind of shit, so I'm really glad for you. As for my future plans, I've got plenty of dough stashed, and in case you forgot, I'm a member of the bar. Not your kind of bar, you Irish prick, the New York State Bar. I'm going to take my vacation right away and use it to set up a little law office out around Montauk Point near my summer house. I'm going to take Joan and the kids out there to live, and I'm going one hundred percent legitimate. As soon as I feel pretty sure there won't be any repercussions, I'm going to slide out of this job. Someday the shit is going to hit the fan in New York City and I want to be as far away as possible.

And so the initial squad was finally disbanded. They had a big party in the downstairs room at Toots Shor's restaurant, and Jimmy had a strange sensation that all the guys were secretly elated at kissing plainclothes duty goodbye. He was well aware that they all had had a good run, and were all in good financial shape. Most of them planned to stay in The Job, but a couple, like Georgie, were plotting a fast getaway. Parting was sweet sorrow, but life goes on, and after much booze and many, many toasts, the intrepid squad of Peter O'Neil's bright and former rookies finally parted, with only Jimmy Riley left to hold the colors high.

The changing of the guard took about a week to become official, and Jimmy worked night and day running all over the city picking up the money due the squad. He knew most of the new guys either personally or by sight, and they all knew him, so the transition was an easy one. They came practically intact as a squad from South Brooklyn, which was their previous province. The first day they gathered in the chief's plainclothes squad room, they all shook Riley's hand and indicated that they were pleased he was going to remain with them. To a man they were almost totally different from his former comrades, appearing much older and dressed in suits Jimmy wouldn't give to the Salvation Army. The obvious leader of the new mob was a big, beefy, florid-faced gorilla named Len Gordon. Jimmy knew him just casually and the unanimous word he had on him was that he was a no-good prick. Nevertheless, Jimmy had given him and the other new men a lot of thought and resolved to try to forget what he had been warned about them individually; he was going to try to make every effort to get along with them and establish a harmonious relationship.

After a lot of small talk and a short speech by the new lieutenant, a mild-looking, bespectacled type who looked like a law professor, Jimmy gave Lenny Gordon a come-hither wink and got him alone on the side.

"Listen, Lenny, I've got a load of scratch to divide up. Today is the sixth, and I've picked up all the first-of-the-month money. How about we meet somewhere uptown and whack it up?"

"Really! Jeez, that sounds great, Jimmy. When do you want to meet us and where?"

"How about tonight? I hate to have so much cash around, some plainclothes guy is liable to rob me."

Gordon laughed out loud. At least he has a sense of humor, Jimmy thought. Maybe this prick isn't such a bad guy after all.

"How about the St. Moritz Hotel, Suite 2114? By the way, we keep it by the month."

Gordon whistled. "I knew we'd make the big time real soon. You're a beauty, Jimmy."

Jimmy then excused himself and went to the men's room while Gordon gathered his flock together to make sure they were all willing to split up the golden egg that night. While washing his hands he looked in the mirror at himself and thought, For Christ's sake, I've got to dig up some old clothes. These guys look like the greatest collection of shit-kickers I ever saw. And that suit on their peerless leader, Gordon. It had more grease stains on it than a counterman's apron in one of those ptomaine Greek diners. And those two big wops—caps and lumber jackets, for Christ's sake. I have to tell Gordon to make these guys get dressed up in their best twenty-two-fifty Crawford numbers tonight or the manager of the St. Moritz will have a heart attack when they gather in the lobby.

Jimmy went back into the squad room. He sensed a wave of good fellowship emanating from their greetings to him. The old moola, the good old filthy moola, he thought, will make you more friends than you'll ever need.

Gordon winked broadly. "Okay, Jimmy. Eight o'clock all right with you?"

"Perfect, Lenny. I'll be up in the suite and I'll lay in some booze and plenty to eat. We'll have a good meeting. But for Christ's sake, do me a favor. Tell those guys to wear their best suits, and shirts and ties. Get it?"

"Sure, Jimmy. Anything you say."

When they arrived that evening, Jimmy was pleased to see that they were all wearing their First Communion suits and looked fairly respectable. They were properly impressed by the size of the suite and the rich furnishings. After destroying the hors d'oeuvres and sandwiches, and after a few whiskeys apiece loosened them up, the meeting began.

Jimmy had had the money stashed in the valuables vault in the hotel and had removed it shortly before the meeting. When he threw it on the table they were all gathered around. They all blinked a little, even hard-ass Gordon. It was a calculated, theatrical gesture on Jimmy's part, and it had the desired effect.

"There it is, boys. Here's an itemized list to go with it. This is every quarter I picked up and the names of the guys who gave it to me. In other words, the contract guys. Before we get down to cutting it up, I want to make one thing good and clear. We do not fuck, and I emphasize, *do not fuck* with guys who pay us. You're all in the top squad now, and there are a million outlaws out there, so let's make sure we take good care of the guys who take good care of us."

"What if we get a complaint from the boss?" asked one of the big lumberjack wops.

"You stick the complaint up your ass. This isn't the division or half-borough squad. You're in the chief's office, for Christ's sake. We don't pinch anybody who pays us, ever. Now let's divide the cabbage up. It should come out to around five grand a man. Remember, this is only the first-of-the-month payroll, we still have the fifteenth to look forward to. Now let's be honest with each other. I know most of you guys, and you know all about me. Did any of my old squad bother anyone in your backyard who was okay? Answer me, tell the truth."

A muttered assent. It seemed like Jimmy was taking over. He had them all a little cowed, especially with the great big hunk of cash on the table waiting to be cut up. But the leader of the motley crew was not about to let Jimmy usurp his throne so easily. Gordon piped up, "Jimmy, how do we know it is all there? I mean the right count. You know, the right amount of scratch for each spot?"

Jimmy looked the big, beefy prick right in the eye. With all his heart he wished he could punch him in his big, fucking mouth. He said, nice and calm, "I'm not sure you heard me correctly, Gordon. I said it was all there. All carefully itemized, to the penny. Are you insinuating that I'm holding out on you?"

Gordon took one look at Jimmy's face, which was slowly starting to contort. "No, Jimmy. For Christ's sake, no. I didn't mean anything like that. I'm sure me and all the guys couldn't be happier about tonight. I was only figuring that you might have picked up some guys you never did before. Maybe in some places you got the wrong count? It's possible."

"It's possible, Lenny, anything's possible. But from now on we will all pick up the places assigned to us. This way we'll have a double check on everything. But these guys are too honorable to cheat on the ice, go to sleep on it. Okay? Everything clear?"

"Fine, Jimmy." The hostility diminished. Soon everyone had a pocketful of cash and a bellyful of whiskey. All was at peace with the world for the moment, but Jimmy deep down inside felt that sooner or later there had to be a confrontation with some of these guys. Most of them he had already pegged for nitwits, but he pegged Gordon for just what he had been warned he was, a no-good prick.

The squad soon settled down into the customary routine of a five-borough supervisory plainclothes squad. The good fellowship Jimmy had been accustomed to with the kids he broke in with almost completely evaporated. He was assigned a partner who was quite a bit older than he was and much more set in his ways. However, they worked well together and things shortly became comfortable between them. His name was Chick O'Mara. He was a likable Irishman who loved broads, money, and whiskey, in that order. With his multiple enterprises, Jimmy was always very busy, and as soon as their police details were finished he would try to find a way to duck Chick without hurting his feelings. He soon found out that the best way to make Chick happy was to drop him off at a high-class whorehouse where he could fornicate to his heart's content. He always told Chick to hide his shield, money, and gun carefully in case the whorehouse was ever stuck up by some heist guys, something which was fairly prevalent in the whorehouse business.

Sure enough, the day came. Chick was relaxing in a house run by a friend of Jimmy's, a madam named Trudy. It was a sunny afternoon and Chick was sitting on a couch in the living room in his undershirt reading a magazine, at ease with life after having just knocked off a piece with one of Trudy's more succulent dishes, when two guys walked in with guns drawn. Two young kids who looked about twenty-one years old. Chick had stashed his gun, but he still has his police shield and money in his pants pocket, probably out of habit. He took one look and figured to himself, here I go. Trudy, who stupidly answered the doorbell, said to the kids in a pleading voice, "Look, take what you want, but don't hurt any of my customers or my girls, please."

One of the young guys said, "Hey, lady, are you kidding? We're vice cops from the Fifth Division. We're here to arrest all of you." He pulled out his shield and showed it to Trudy.

Chickie boy, who was about to die of a heart attack right there on the sofa, suddenly got his color back. He got up off the couch, took his own shield out, and flashed it at the two kids. He said, "You're going to lock up shit. This woman is helping me on an undercover operation. I'm O'Mara from the chief's office. Where are you from again?"

"We're the new guys from the Fifth Division, Mr. O'Mara. Jesus, now I recognize you, you were pointed out to me in Gamblers Court last week. Holy shit, I never expected to find you here. What's up?"

"Never mind what's up, and never mention that you saw me here. Just forget about pinching this whorehouse or the Fifth Division will become a desert. I'm on a very confidential investigation. Get the kids a drink, Trudy, and introduce them around. If they want to get laid, take care of them."

With that splendid display of bravado, Chick became Prince Valiant to Trudy and her girls. From that day on, their benefactor was their most welcome guest and by far their greatest undercover agent. Chick confided to Jimmy that for him the best was none too good, that Trudy always had her most gorgeous creature waiting whenever he called.

The arrangement with Chick suited Jimmy just fine, as he was spending more and more time with Harry. He preferred not to fraternize with any of the new squad, except Chick occasionally, and tried to keep as low a profile around the squad room as possible. Jimmy couldn't put his finger on it for a couple of months, his reason for disliking most of the new men. One day it finally occurred to him; these guys thought and acted like real cops, like The Job was on the level. They talked about pinching a bookmaker or a numbers guy like he was a bank robber or big-time burglar. Jimmy would listen to their tales of derring-do, how they donned disguises to lock up some poor outlaw who probably was up to his ass in shylock payments. He pretended to think it was great, but inwardly he figured them to be a bunch of horses' asses. They would dress up in longshoremen's outfits and prowl the docks looking for a pinch, or get into some sort of costume they thought would enable them to infiltrate the lower East Side or Greenwich Village to nail some bookmaker.

Jimmy just shook his head at this kind of stupid shit, meanwhile never saying a word to them. With his private cadre of informants, he easily made his quota of pinches and those of his partner, Chick. It was as easy as breaking sticks. Jimmy would rather be seen dead then to don a disguise or even attempt to look like most of the new guys. He was always impeccable in his John Ciano numbers, Countess Mara ties, high shirt collars, and Bob White shoes. This was his uniform, and he wore it proudly. Besides, most of his working days and nights were spent in the better-class restaurants and clubs in town. If he ever showed up in a lumber jacket or pea coat, his real friends would think he had suddenly gone berserk.

All this time the partnership of Harry Gross and Jimmy Riley was flourishing. There was an occasional foray by some would-be tough guy to shake one of the spots, but Jimmy always quickly intervened and straightened out the problem in short order. But they were growing rapidly, and sooner or later, Jimmy reasoned, a major problem would inevitably arise. He constantly worried if they, or he, would be able to cope with it. He had one excellent thing going for him. Through the years he had developed a strong friendship with some very tough guys, real shooters. In return for various favors he did for them, and because they genuinely liked him, they made him promise to call upon them in the event he had some trouble he couldn't handle alone.

But trouble comes in funny ways, and often is upon you before you realize the full impact. As usual, Jimmy stopped in to see Harry and Augie one night at the Dugout, one of their places on Flatbush Avenue. The Dugout was a legitimate restaurant and bar, but it had a huge backyard that Harry had converted into a thriving horse room. Before they had ordered their first drink, Jimmy sensed something heavy troubling Harry and Augie.

"For Christ's sake, what's the matter? You two got kissers on you like a couple of funeral directors. Take the faces off, please, and have a drink. What the hell's wrong, anyway?"

"We've got trouble, Jimmy, real trouble, right outside in the backyard," Harry said in a subdued, worried voice.

"Whadda you mean, we got trouble? Who? Someone breaking our balls? The division?"

"No, nothing like that. No cop trouble. I didn't mention this to you before, so don't get sore. Babe and Georgie from Brownsville asked me to put a guy to work for them, a guy who just came home from Sing Sing and needed a job."

"Babe and Georgie. You knuckled under to those two fucks?" Jimmy started to get enraged. "You stupid bastard. You put one of their guys to work without consulting me?"

Harry cringed. "But, Jimmy, it was only temporary, only as a favor. I thought it was best, and I hate to bother you about every little detail, for Christ's sake. Anyway, his name is Big Seymour and at first he seemed like a nice enough guy."

"Big Seymour, eh? Okay, what did this big prick do to upset

you and Augie so much? You both look as if he kidnapped your kids."

"Almost as bad, Jimmy."

"Will you give it to me? What did he do?"

"Well, we put him on as a clerk for Chet and Little Jimmy for about a week. As you know, the joint in the back is doing real great. After one week as a clerk, he sized up the kind of action we're doing, so he decided to grab the place for himself."

"You gotta be kidding. No shit?"

"Honest to God, Jimmy, no shit. This afternoon he slapped Chet in the mush and chased him and Little Jimmy. He put his own guy in with him as his assistant, a guy named Benny, another half-ass muscle guy. Augie and I tried to reason with him, but he told us to go fuck ourselves, the joint was now his."

"Really? It's his, is it? Just like that, all our hard work and connections go down the drain. Well, we'll soon see about this. Where does this fucking Big Seymour hang out?"

"We never mentioned your name, Jim. But he'll be here tomorrow running the show. Jesus, Jimmy, what the hell are we going to do?"

Jimmy was beside himself, seething, so enraged he could barely speak. "Let's have a drink. You be here tomorrow at the bar with Chet and little Jimmy, ready to work. At twelve noon. Leave it to me, I'll take care of Mr. Big Seymour. That prick will wish he was back in Sing Sing when I get finished with him tomorrow. Okay, here's luck, and fuck Big Seymour and Benny and Babe and Georgie and the rest of those Brownsville bastards. Harry, I swear, if you ever speak to one of those guys again I'll personally break your goddam head."

"Jimmy, I'm really sorry. You're dead right, if you do a favor for those guys it's a sign of weakness."

"Go bet your ass on that, Harry, and never forget it."

Jimmy left Harry and Augie about ten o'clock and went straight home. He was so upset he couldn't even concentrate on the evening paper. He left the house and took a walk around the neighborhood and brooded about Big Seymour until he finally got tired enough to return home and fall asleep around midnight. He slept late the next morning, and called Chick at the office and arranged to meet him later in the day. He had one thing on his mind, Big Seymour. He wasn't exactly sure what lay in store for him with Big Seymour, but he was certain of one thing. Before Big Seymour was going to capture the Dugout, just like that, because he figured that it was a lucrative proposition, he was going to have to kill Jimmy. If he and Harry succumbed to this kind of shit, they could forget about their entire operation. The word would soon spread, and inch by inch the tough guys would muscle in on their spots.

Jimmy dressed carefully before he left the house. He put on heavy shoes, slacks, and a turtleneck sweater. He holstered his snub-nosed .38-caliber detective special on the belt of his slacks underneath the turtleneck. He slipped a small strap-type blackjack with a heavy, compact steel head in his pants pocket. He put a pair of tight pigskin gloves in his other pocket. He casually kissed his wife goodbye and left the house.

He got to the Dugout about noon and briefly nodded to Harry, Chet, and Little Jimmy at the bar. He walked out the back of the restaurant into the yard and casually surveyed the scene. There were about thirty horse players there studying scratch sheets, either alone or exchanging information in groups of three or four. From the brief description Harry had given him he recognized Big Seymour immediately. He was about six foot three, husky, with a large nose and a mop of kinky hair. He was laughing and joking with a short, stocky guy who Jimmy figured was his sidekick, Benny. They looked like they didn't have a care in the world. It was about an hour before the first post, so the horse action was still light. Jimmy slipped on his pigskin gloves and walked directly over to Big Seymour and Benny.

"Hello, pal, are you Seymour?"

"That's me, pal. What can I do for you?"

Jimmy was fascinated by Big Seymour's nose as he stood before him, smiling nice and easy. What a target, he thought, no way I can miss this big prick's schnozz. Jimmy let go. His first punch hit Big Seymour square on the bridge of his nose. Seymour screamed, grabbed his face, reeled back, and fell like a wounded cow. The blood was pouring out of him like a geyser. Benny was so startled he just gasped and stared at Seymour like he was petrified. Jimmy turned and hit Benny over the right eye with a left hook. Benny grabbed his eye and yelled blue murder. Big Seymour was holding his nose and trying to get his feet under him. Jimmy grabbed him by his kinky mop of hair and helped him up. Once up, he hit him as hard as he could on the side of the jaw. Down again went Big Seymour. Benny was holding his eye, crying with pain. The horse players didn't know what the hell was going on, they were scared shitless by all the blood and started to scatter like frightened deer.

Jimmy grabbed Benny by the arm and said, "Stay right next to him," pointing to the stricken Seymour. He took his gun out of his holster. He slapped Seymour on the face with his free hand until he seemed to regain his senses.

"So you two tough guys were going to take this joint over, right?" Jimmy held his gun in the flat of his right hand. He then whacked Big Seymour with the gun as hard as he could on the side of his head.

Seymour crumpled down again, whimpering, "For Christ's sake, who are you? Don't kill me, please. Benny, for Christ's sake tell him who we are."

Jimmy pointed the gun at Benny and then kicked him hard in the shins, and Benny howled again.

"Now listen, you two cunts, shut up your fucking crying and pay attention to what I have to say. May name is Jimmy Riley and I'm from the chief's office. This joint belongs to Harry Gross, who tried to do you a favor. Now once and for all, Harry Gross is my friend, my special friend. The next time you or any of your fucking friends from Brownsville try to pull any more shit like this, or even bother Harry, make sure that you kill Jimmy Riley first. Now get the fuck out of here, and if I ever see either of you on Flatbush Avenue again I'll personally beat the shit out of you."

Benny limped out with his arm around Big Seymour to steady him, and one hand over his eye to try to stop the bleeding. They were both wobbling around like a couple of chickens, and Jimmy couldn't resist a laugh at the sight of the two ex-tough guys. Some of the horse players who were still hanging around fascinated by the slaughter looked at him like he was crazy. Jimmy just waved to them and went from the backyard through the kitchen into the bar. Harry was waiting there with Chet and Little Jimmy.

Harry's face was dead white, but he smiled weakly. "What'd you do to them, for Christ's sake? They looked like they just went through Iwo Jima."

"Fuck them. Get back to work, Chet and Jimmy. From now on I guarantee you won't have any trouble with those guys. That's the end of that. Look, it's too early in the day for me to drink. I'm going home to change my clothes. I have to meet Chick in New York. I'll see you tonight. Make sure if anybody bothers Jimmy or Chet, tell them to see me. Okay, see you tonight."

Jimmy felt great all that day. Like a million dollars. He was proud of himself, the way he handled a potentially very bad situation. He was used to violence in The Job. He had been stabbed once, mugged a few times, and been in countless scrimmages. It was all part of the game. But today he was protecting his own turf. He didn't pull his shield or any cop shit. He didn't ask any questions, he just walked up and whacked the piss out of the two of them. A surprise attack, sure, he chuckled to himself, but it worked. Those two bums won't take another joint over without thinking twice.

That night when he met Harry all the key guys in the organization were there. They shook Jimmy's hand and congratulated him like he had just won the Golden Gloves. A few of them looked at Jimmy in an entirely new light. He was now the enforcer and Harry was the front. A pretty good picture. Not too bad a combination to be with.

It was inevitable that Jimmy became more and more involved with Harry as the months passed by. There were always bits of trouble here and there that required Jimmy's presence to get straightened out, but he usually did so by peaceful means, and the good ship sailed smoothly along. The money was rolling in on both fronts, and even though he was unhappy with the new setup, Jimmy determined to stick it out on the chief's squad as long as he could. He could not seem to get along with the new bunch no matter how hard he tried. Without fail, at least once a month, they would pinch a friend of Jimmy's, a contract, who was also by the ground rules a friend of theirs because they were sharing his money. This would infuriate Jimmy. They would shrug off his rage, saying it was a mistake, or that the lieutenant was with them and insisted on it, or they had a letter complaint on them; always a horseshit excuse. Led by the big shithead, Len Gordon, four of them worked as a team and soon became known and feared around the city as the Four Horsemen.

One of Jimmy's best friends among the racket group in the city was a big man among the wops, one of the biggest, Joe A. He was a smooth, handsome guy who was always dressed as if he just stepped out of a bandbox. He looked more like a collar ad then a tough guy. He was in fact more of a diplomat and go-between for the mob than a muscle guy. He operated a fine Italian restaurant close to Borough Hall in Brooklyn which was a favorite watering place for politicians, judges, district attorneys, and lawyers. He was a very charming guy, and there wasn't anything humanly possible he wouldn't do to help a decent guy who was in a jam. As his connections widened, his strength within the mob grew, and at the time he and Jimmy became friends he was a very powerful guy, right up at the top. Jimmy had met Joe A. right at the start with Pete O'Neil, and a good, deep friendship evolved. There wasn't anything Jimmy would refuse to do for Joe, and vice versa.

Joe had the largest piece of a legendary crap game across the Hudson River in New Jersey, and for years he had Jimmy on a personal payroll, a healthy one, to ensure that no cops bothered his fleet of limousines that whisked the players over the bridge to the game. Because of this piece of business and several others, Jimmy saw Joe frequently. One night he asked Jimmy to keep an eye out for a cop named Nick Scinelli. He was a seasoned veteran who had done a few favors for Joe, and in return Joe had a big politician place him in the chief's squad.

Jimmy was very cordial to Scinelli at first, but cooled on him when he quickly hooked up and became bosom pals with Len Gordon. Scinelli was one of Gordon's Four Horsemen.

One morning, the lieutenant in charge asked Jimmy to report to a certain hospital in Brooklyn where the squad had put in a hot wiretap. Scinelli spoke good Italian, so Jimmy was not too surprised when he got there to see Scinelli with the earphones on, scribbling notes in Italian.

"What's up, Nick?"

"We got a real big one here, Jimmy. I briefed the chief himself on it and he's taken a personal interest in it. Real front-page stuff."

Jimmy looked at Nick and wondered for a minute what the hell he was talking about. He thought he knew when anyone took a piss in Brooklyn. What was so important?

"What the hell in Brooklyn is that big that we haven't got on, Nick?"

"The Italian lottery, Jimmy."

"You mean the lottery with the Italian cities like Milan and Genoa and all that shit?"

"That's correct, Jim."

"A real big one, are you kidding? For years we've done that free as a personal favor to Joe A. and Paddy Diamond. For Christ's sake, you know that lottery supports a lot of the wop old-timers who can barely make a living otherwise. Only the division gets paid, everyone accepts that."

"Listen, Jimmy, forget about Joe and Paddy and feeling sorry for the wop old-timers. This will be some pinch. When the public reads all those Italian names of the guys we pinch, they'll think we broke up the Mafia. I went into the chief myself and told him the information I had. He's hot to make a big splash in the newspapers with it."

"You've gone to the chief? Why, you ass-kissing guinea prick, you're a disgrace to your own kind. Who are you kidding? I happen to know you're Joe's personal contract, and you're going to cross him. You go and fuck yourself with your information. I'm telling Joe A. the minute I leave here, which is right now because I can't stand the stink around here."

"Don't blow this pinch or the chief will have your ass, Jimmy. I never wanted you in on this in the first place."

"Sure you didn't, because you're a two-faced fuck just like your other three pals. Go ahead, pinch the lottery, make a hero plainclothesman out of yourself, you no-good bastard, and I'll personally drag you before Joe A."

Jimmy stormed out of the hospital like a madman. How long could he stand this kind of shit from these treacherous bastards. He called Joe on his private number and was told he was out of town for a week. He called Paddy Diamond and he too was out of town. Finally, he took a shot and called a number where he was supposed to give a prearranged signal in case of a raid. The signal was an old one and he wondered if it would work. He called the number and some cafone answered.

"Hello, whosa dis?"

"Can you possibly get hold of Paddy, it's important."

"No, he'sa not here. I told you. Whosa dis?"

"Could you tell me when you expect him?"

"Whadda ya mean, expecta?"

"I mean when will he be in? Today, tonight, tomorrow—when?"

"I'ma not sure. Whosa dis?"

"For Christ's sake, tell him the painters are coming to get the house ready. Quick. So long."

Scinelli was sitting on the wiretaps where Jimmy called and recognized Jimmy's voice. The same day the Four Horsemen gathered the squad, except Jimmy, and raided the lottery. They hauled in about thirty poor old Italians, missing all the big shots, but they alerted the newspapers before the raid and the pinch was treated like the Lindbergh case for a couple of days. Scinelli and the rest of the Four Horsemen were like heroes around the office for the next few weeks, but the split between Jimmy and them widened like the Grand Canyon. He refused to speak to any of them, only attending the meetings very briefly and even avoiding them if Chick O'Mara could handle their business.

The one thing that kept him alive and in fairly good standing in the office was the quality arrests he made. He and Chick would come up with a sneak crap game, or a roulette wheel on Park Avenue, or something big enough to get a pat on the head from the boss. The other shitheads could never figure out his sources of information. He also made sure that he clipped a few outlaw wire rooms a month plus an outlaw numbers bank or two. This way, nobody in the office bothered him, and that was exactly as he wanted it. Still, the feeling of hostility clung to him like a wet suit, and he knew in his heart that the come-off was bound to take place. The final come-off.

One day in gamblers court in New York he met Lenny Gordon. He hadn't laid eyes on him in weeks and he couldn't care less if he ever did.

Gordon walked over to him and said, "How are you, Jimmy? Can I see you for a few minutes when you finish?"

"Sure, Lenny, in about an hour."

"You want to have lunch together?"

Jimmy would have rather had lunch with a degenerate fuck like Hitler. "No, I'm sorry, Len. I have a date for lunch. Suppose we have coffee down the block?"

"Okay, fine, Jimmy. See you when you finish."

About an hour later Jimmy's case was disposed of, and as he walked out of the courtroom he nodded to Gordon and motioned him to follow. They went across the street to a cafeteria, sat down at a table, and ordered coffee.

"You're getting too fat, Lenny. Plainclothesmen are supposed to have that lean and hungry look, like Cassius."

The literary allusion passed right over the stupid bastard's head. He patted his big belly and let out a forced laugh. "I know, I know, Jimmy. Too much food and too much beer and whiskey. How the hell do you stay in shape?"

"Go to the gym a few days a week, that will help a little. You could also try pushing away from the dinner table too. If you get much heavier you might have a heart attack and never get to enjoy all the money we're stealing. Think about that. Break your ass hustling, and bang, you drop dead and your wife and kids will piss away your hard-earned dough in a couple of years."

"Not my wife. She's tougher with a buck than I am."

"I'll describe that in two words. Im-possible."

They both laughed. They talked idly for a few minutes, and what passed for the social amenities quickly over, they sat sipping their coffee and Jimmy said, "All right, what's on your mind, Lenny?"

"Well, to tell you the truth, I wanted to ask you a couple of questions about Harry Gross."

"Go ahead. Shoot."

"Tell me, Jimmy, what exactly are we getting paid for?"

"You're not kidding me, are you? I have everything listed and itemized, but if you want me to refresh your memory, here goes. Number one, for years you guys were getting paid for the spot on Carroll Street, just above Red Hook. You know, Frankie and Skee's place. Am I right?"

"That's right, Jimmy."

"Did you ever have any trouble with Frankie and Skee?"

"No. Two real nice guys."

"Okay. Now you've got six other spots in Brooklyn and one in New York, plus two phones in the wire room. Everything is perfectly in order, and I'm sure everything is up to date on your list. Now let me ask you a question. What the hell are you worrying about Harry Gross for?"

"Well, some of the guys are a little curious about how close you two are. They think he has more joints than we're getting paid for, and that he's getting away with murder traveling under your wing."

"Is it you, just you, or the other guys who are curious about the relationship between Harry and me? Come on, let's be honest with each other, Lenny. For openers, I don't give one fuck about you and the other guys being curious about Harry and me. He happens to be my friend and I like the guy very much. Every spot he has I take particular pains to list, and the money comes in just like clockwork. I wouldn't let him take the slightest advantage because of our friendship. In fact, he bends over backward to play the game the correct way. What the hell more do you guys want?"

"Well, for instance, I hear he has four phones in the wire room, a real Monte Carlo, and we're only paid for two. For Christ's sake, all I hear in Brooklyn is Harry Gross. The guy must have fifty runners."

Jimmy looked at Gordon, looked at his big, fat, red face and wished he could throw his hot cup of coffee right at it. He was getting livid, but he admonished himself. Keep cool.

Jimmy said very calmly, "Listen, he has two phones, period. Why don't you take my word for it? Christ, you know I've never lied to you. And that's a lot of shit about him having fifty runners."

Jimmy's voice had begun to get a little harsh. Gordon recognized that he was getting hot, losing his temper. He didn't want it to get out of hand. He raised his hand soothingly and said, "Relax, Jimmy. I take your word. Look, I don't want any hard feelings between us. Take it easy, for Christ's sake."

"Take it easy, my ass. You and your three partners seem to take particular pleasure in breaking Jimmy Riley's balls. You all know goddam well I never held out on you or lied to you. What the hell is this continual doubt about me? You never had a pot to piss in when you worked in Brooklyn, you were lucky you made a grand a month. All of a sudden you're rolling in cash, making all kinds of scratch. Well, get this straight. Me and a couple of other key guys broke our nuts organizing this city and you guys fell into a bucket of shit. From the very first day you stepped into the chief's office I made sure that everyone got an even-steven split. Is that correct?"

"I admit that's right. But in all fairness, there are a few things you refuse to go along with, like kicking in out of your share to give the deputy inspector an extra share."

"You're goddam right I won't. You can tell that little Irish prick for me to get from behind the sanctuary of his desk and go out and get a glove and pick up his own money, just like I do, if he wants an extra share. Are you guys serious, a fucking clerical inspector to get two shares? Pig's ass! I wouldn't give that false-face little fuck more than a G-note if I had my way. But you guys are all up the top of his ass, you give him what you want. Count me out."

"Okay, okay, I'm sure he knows where you stand. But to get back to Harry, the guys want to dig a little deeper. You don't mind, do you, Jimmy?"

"You're goddam right, I mind. Now let's clear the air between us. We all have a few particularly close friends in the rackets. Right, it's inevitable, you can't help liking some of the guys who are helping you get rich. Well, to be honest, I have a lot of friends, close friends, and I don't want to see any of them hurt, especially Harry. If you grab an outlaw runner of his and you feel you have to collar him, go ahead. But if you bother him where he is paying, or if anyone else does, they'll answer to me. Now, is that straight?"

"That's fair enough, Jimmy. Let's shake hands on it. No hard feelings?"

"None at all," Jimmy said as he shook Gordon's hand. But as he looked at him, he knew deep down in his heart that the big lying prick and his three confederates had something evil in mind. Well, what the hell am I going to do, he thought. I'll deal with it when the time comes.

The time came quicker than Jimmy expected. He had worked for a few days in a row with Chick O'Mara and they made enough collars to enable them to take it easy for a while. He was at home, nice and relaxed, reading a book. The phone rang.

"Hello, Jimmy. Chick. What's up? What are you doing?"

"I'm reading a book, Chick. You know, a real hard-cover book."

"Yeah? What's it all about?"

"It's all about the most famous whorehouses in ancient Greece. You'd love it, Chick."

Chick laughed. "Even I get tired of whorehouses once in a while. Listen, Jimmy. I've got bad news. I understand Gordon and his three stooges are planning to take Harry's wire room. They drummed up a phony complaint with the deputy, your pal. Is it on Church Avenue, off Flatbush, over a candy store?"

"That's right, Chick. When did you hear this great bit of news?"

"I dropped in the office this morning and McMahon, you know, the new kid, told me he overheard them talking it over with the lieutenant and the deputy. Well, this kid McMahon loves you since you insisted he get a full share right away, and he met you and Harry at the Garden, so he knows you're good friends. Well, anyhow, he heard the whole plot, and when I came in he motioned me into the men's room and laid it out for me."

"When is this raid supposed to happen, Chick?"

"I think today, Jimmy. This afternoon."

"Swell, Chick. I love you. Let's you and I have dinner tonight, somewhere nice, some good French restaurant. First, I'll meet you in Moore's about six o'clock for a drink. Go get laid today.

I'll call Polly for you, maybe she'll get you a one-eyed broad to wink you off. Have a clear head when we meet, we have a lot to talk about."

Jimmy hung up the telephone and looked at his watch. Almost twelve o'clock. He started to put it together; first post was one thirty, they would probably hit the joint around two. He took a shower, shaved, got dressed, kissed his wife goodbye, and took the BMT to Church Avenue. He called Augie, who bossed the wire room, from the corner of Church and Flatbush. He told Augie to be outside on the street in a few minutes to let him into the wire room, as he was calling from a booth on the corner.

Augie was pacing up and down outside the candy store, looking a little nervous. He said, "What's up, Jim? I hope nothing's wrong?"

"Plenty, Augie. I just got a tip that the Four Horsemen are about to raid the joint."

Augie was startled. "Jesus, Jimmy, this is going to be bad. What the hell did we do wrong?"

"Not one fucking thing, Augie, they're just doing it to break my balls. But don't worry, they're not busting shit."

"Jimmy, how can we stop them? I hear those four guys are murder if they get a hard-on for you."

"Just take it nice and easy, Augie. Come on, take me upstairs, I'm going to be right there in the wire room with you when they come in. A one-man welcoming committee."

"Jesus, Jimmy, don't get into any trouble over this. Don't start a war with these guys, it's not worth it. Let me call Harry and maybe he can talk them out of it."

"Fuck Harry. Let's go, Augie. They're not pinching anybody. Now before we go up, you're sure there are only two phones up there?"

"Positive, Jimmy."

Augie let Jimmy into the wire room and the two clerks, Mikie and Blackie, were a little astonished to see him, but they were too busy answering the phones and writing bets to do anything but wave hello to him. Jimmy smiled at them, waved back, and said, "Augie, call Leo downstairs in the candy store and tell him to make himself scarce across the street, near a phone. As soon as he sees those bastards on the block, he's to call us up and give us their every move. Tell him to make sure they don't spot him, and not to leave his place by the phone no matter what. Get it?"

"Okay, Jimmy." Augie called the candy store and gave Leo Jimmy's exact instructions.

Jimmy noticed the two clerks were getting jittery, a little puzzled at what was happening. He said, nice and soft. "Relax, Blackie. Relax, Mikie. Everything is going to turn out just fine. Uncle Jimmy is going to stay right here with you."

Everyone laughed. The phone action started to taper off a bit after the first post at one thirty, and Jimmy and Augie were chatting easily when the call came. Blackie motioned to Augie to pick up his phone.

"Yeah, Leo. Four of them. You're positive one of them is Gordon. Where are they now? They're lowering the fire escape. No shit. Holy Christ, Jimmy, they're coming up the front fire escape, they're coming through the window right there."

Jimmy looked toward the right front window of the loft where Augie pointed and almost simultaneously the window was raised and in came Lenny Gordon, huffing and puffing like a steam engine. Jimmy had assumed a position behind the desks of the two clerks and he was slightly obscured, but he had a clear picture of the entire move. Gordon, once in, helped his buddies in. They brushed their clothes off, and seeing Augie first, then the two clerks, Gordon stepped forward and said, "My, my, what have we got here, boys?"

Jimmy stepped out of the shadows behind the desks. "You've got me here, pricko. Me, Jimmy Riley."

The four of them stopped dead in their tracks, stunned. Gordon was the first one to find his voice. "What the hell are you doing here, Jimmy? We got a letter on this joint. We're here to knock it off."

"If there's a letter on this joint, you probably wrote it yourself, you big prick. And get one thing straight, you're going to knock shit off. You're supposed to be a half-ass telephone man, take a look. You see, there are two phones, both now ringing. One on each desk, two clerks to answer them, and one boss, Augie, whom the four of you all know. Now we get one thousand a month for each phone, two thousand in all. I pick it up and turn it in to the office every first of the month. Each of you get a share of that two grand, and what's more, have gotten it for quite a long time, so forget about this pinch."

"Balls, Jimmy. We're in here now and we're not leaving without busting this fucking joint. So let's be calm about it. We're all cops. You leave here peacefully and we'll give these guys a break in court."

Jimmy was about ten feet from them, in front of Augie, Blackie, and Mikie. The phones were ringing shrilly, nobody daring to answer, the poor horse players probably frantic. Jimmy drew his gun out of his pocket and pointed it at the Four Horsemen, and the cocky looks were instantly replaced by worried ones. He lowered the gun to Gordon's knee level, then swung it a bit left and fired a shot into the baseboard in the far corner of the loft. The pistol shot sounded like a cannon going off in the small loft. The four cops jumped back at the flash, and Augie, Blackie, and Mikie said later that they almost jumped backward over the desks.

Gordon turned dead white. "Are you crazy? For Christ's sake, Jimmy, put that gun away."

"No, you rotten cocksuckers. I got my gun out, you reach for yours, see how much guts you got. But I warn you pricks, as soon as you do I'll blow your legs off."

"For Christ's sake, I can't believe this."

"Well, you better believe it. Now get the fuck out of here and don't ever come back. And one more thing, don't any of you guys ever speak to me again, and make sure you never fuck with me again. I'm goddam sick and tired of trying to be nice to you pieces of shit. You got that straight? Now out."

They all turned to go out the door leading downstairs.

"No, wait a minute. Out, out the way you came in, down the fire escape." Jimmy pointed his gun at them, motioning them toward the front window.

"Aw, come on, Jimmy, give us a break. The neighbors might see us and call the radio cars."

"Good. Maybe you'll get arrested for willfully breaking a contract. Now get the fuck out, down the fire escape."

One by one they climbed out the window and down the fire escape, the way they came in. Jimmy hoped one of them would break a leg on the drop to the street. When they were all out, Jimmy closed the window and turned to Augie, Blackie, and Mikie and began to laugh. Everyone started to howl laughing.

Augie finally wiped his eyes and said, "Jesus, now I've seen everything, Jimmy. When you fired that shot, when I heard the noise, I almost shit. I thought for a minute you shot Gordon."

"I wish I did, that big yellow prick. But listen, let's go. Augie, wrap it up in half an hour. Give everyone the off from here, just in case. I'll stay here with you guys until you warn off all the runners. Give them, and as many players as you can, the alternate number, we'll work out of there tomorrow. Now pay attention. There's bound to be some repercussions over this, but I think I can handle them. Now, Blackie and Mikie, not a word to anyone. Augie, you and Harry meet me tonight at the Hickory House about eight o'clock. Okay, boys, let's start getting ready to wrap it up."

Jimmy met Chick O'Mara in Moore's that same night about six o'clock and related the rather exciting events of the afternoon. He described in detail the way they jumped when he fired the shot, and how he made them go back down the fire escape the way they came in. He had Chick howling, but after he finished laughing and wiping the tears from his eyes, Chick got serious.

"Jimmy, listen to me. These guys are very dangerous bastards. They're not going to take this lying down. They don't have any real balls, but they're sneaky, underhanded cunts, and they'll find a way to get you. I oughta know, I've been with them for years and I've watched some pretty bad shit they've pulled."

"Fuck them, Chick. Tell you what. I don't want them to think that you're too involved with me or they'll include you in my feud. If I lose out, what the hell, I've already had a damn good run. But you're just getting the wrinkles out of your belly, and I don't want to jeopardize your place in the squad. Starting Monday, I'll work with that new kid, McMahon. The lieutenant suggested it anyway, about a week ago. This way, if they throw me into the air you'll be okay. Now don't argue with me. Do as I say. Let's have a drink."

* * *

The months rolled by and Jimmy went along with his new young partner, Bill McMahon, as if there never had been an incident. He completely ignored the Four Horsemen, and almost everyone else in the squad for that matter, only speaking to one of them when necessary. He made his own collars and enough for the new kid to satisfy the top brass. A few of them were more spectacular than the others, and he still received an occasional compliment from the professorial lieutenant. Still, the feeling was always with him that he was on borrowed time, that he was constantly being undermined. He was sure that it was only a matter of time before he would be forced to walk the plank from plainclothes to uniform.

When the denouement came, however, it was from a completely unexpected quarter. It came from the mayor himself, Bill O'Dwyer.

4

THE HONORABLE Bill O'Dwyer, mayor of New York City, was born on July 11, 1890, in Bohola, County Mayo, that hardiest of all Irish counties on the savage west coast. He was the middle son of a large farm family and at an early age showed a sharp aptitude for learning. He excelled in schools, and as was typical of bright young Irish lads of the era, he was soon tapped as material for the priesthood. He was sent off to the University of Salamanca in Spain to continue his theological studies, but his vocation for the priesthood waned and after a couple of years of college he abandoned the heavy studies of religion and philosophy and left for America in 1910.

He was a brawny, tough Irishman, and after a series of rugged jobs such as merchant seaman, longshoreman, and construction worker, he opted to join the New York City police force in 1917. After a couple of years as an ordinary beat patrolman, O'Dwyer evidently cultivated some influential superiors in The Job and soon landed a cushy position as a plainclothesman in Borough Headquarters, located on Poplar Street in downtown Brooklyn. The combined advantages of free time and whatever emoluments a plainclothesman received in those days, long before Jimmy Riley's time, enabled Bill to attend Fordham University Law School at night, and he received his diploma and was admitted to the bar in 1925.

He soon became a fairly prominent and effective lawyer in Brooklyn, and maintained strong ties to both his native Ireland

and the large Brooklyn Irish community by becoming heavily involved in the promoting and importing of Irish Gaelic football teams. Gaelic football was a thunderous sport similar in some respects to karate and American football in equal portions. Bill also was a familiar figure around the Democratic clubhouses of New York, where he curried favor with the Tammany bosses and in 1932 was rewarded with an appointment as a city magistrate.

O'Dwyer was a striking figure of a man, blessed with a deep, cultured voice, laced with enough of a brogue to captivate an audience, particularly an Irish audience. He managed a great press as a magistrate, with a flair for always being on the side of the underdog, the knight on a white charger coming to the aid of the poor, of which there was a plenitude. His vigor, good looks, and Irish charm prevailed, and he was soon nominated for county judge in Brooklyn and was overwhelmingly elected. This was indeed a spectacular rise, from poor Irish farm boy to prominent jurist in less than four decades. But the best was yet to come.

In 1939 the Honorable Bill O'Dwyer shed his black robes and ran for district attorney of Kings County, better known to the outer world as Brooklyn, on the Democratic slate and was duly elected to that high office. Though O'Dwyer often heatedly denied any association with such Tammany figures as Clarence Neal, Mike Kennedy, and Hugo Rogers, it was virtually impossible to get elected even dogcatcher without their endorsement. In his famous acceptance speech upon assuming the mantle of Brooklyn district attorney, O'Dwyer declared in ringing tones, heavily laced with the famous Irish brogue. "Honesty in the public business is essential if democracy is to survive. I believe that the place for all crooks, whether they be pickpockets or politicians, is in jail." Stirring words indeed, but sad to say, many pickpockets do go to jail, but rarely the politician.

At the time of Bill O'Dwyer's elevation to Brooklyn district attorney, Fiorello La Guardia was firmly entrenched as mayor of New York City. Although La Guardia was not particularly smart, he was a very wily politician. He had entered office under the guise of a strong reform movement, but at the same time he built a powerful political machine with some tough Italian enforcers, known as the Ghibbones. They were a good match for the tough

Irish bullyboys of Tammany, and La Guardia saw to it that Italians got their share of the spoils. From all indications La Guardia was an honest man, at least honest as far as career politicians go.

In 1941 Bill O'Dwyer challenged Fiorello La Guardia for the mayoralty of New York City and for the first time tasted defeat. It was a bitter blow to Bill O', his first reversal at the polls, but he brushed it aside and threw himself into the prosecution of a murder-for-hire gang, quickly hailed in the media as Murder, Inc. He soon gained headlines throughout the country as the fearless foe of gangsterism and corruption. The investigation almost concluded, he took a leave of absence from office and entered the United States Army as a colonel. He served with distinction as chief of the War Frauds Commission, investigating crooked war contractors, and after a couple of years he returned to civilian life having reached the rank of brigadier general.

When he entered the army Bill O'Dwyer seems to have made his first error in judgment. He personally appointed a Republican, George Beldock, as the interim district attorney to replace him. Beldock was a relentless, scrupulous man, who quickly became astonished at the loose way the legendary investigation of Murder, Inc. was being conducted. He charged in no uncertain terms that only the underlings were being prosecuted, going to the electric chair, while the top-echelon racket guys who were the real bosses and who ordered the hits were free as the birds flying over Prospect Park. Beldock was outraged to find some files missing on big shots, especially that of Albert Anastasia, a top mobster of the day. He bluntly placed the responsibility for the removal of the files on Jim Moran, then O'Dwyer's chief clerk. In addition, several meetings were proved to have taken place at the home of Frank Costello, a highly placed underworld figure, with Bill O'Dwyer, Hugo Rogers, and other prominent Tammany politicians. O'Dwyer airily brushed them off as part of his ongoing investigation, although he admitted having cocktails and dinner at Costello's home.

Charges flew back and forth on both sides, and Beldock finally convened a grand jury to investigate the allegations of laxity and malfeasance during the Murder, Inc. probe. O'Dwyer refused to repudiate his ties with the Tammany hot shots of City Hall, and further refused to appear before the grand jury. The grand jury findings were implicit. They found that the then district attorney's office of Brooklyn had abandoned the investigation of top waterfront and garment racketeers in spite of strong evidence against them. The failure to prosecute the top mobsters constituted a malfeasance according to the grand jury findings, but nobody was found culpable enough to indict. The grand jury did vote fifty percent in favor of indicting Bill O'Dwyer for criminal contempt, but the number was not sufficient to file a bill.

In spite of this rather shaky track record, Bill O'Dwyer was elected mayor of New York City in 1945. He was aided in his cause by the retirement of La Guardia and a split in the Republican Party. He made another stirring acceptance speech, eloquently promising to continue the reforms ostensibly instituted by his illustrious Italian predecessor. But alas, as our late, great mayor Jimmy Walker once said, "A reformer is a guy who rides through a sewer in a glass-bottomed boat."

If Bill O'Dwyer did not inherit a sewer, it did not take him long to establish the drainage lines and the deep tunnels. Within scarcely a month he made a series of simply incredible appointments. For sheer gall he would take the cake. First, he created a new deputy police commissioner, the seventh, and named his old captain of detectives, Frank Bals, to the post. Bals had been the captain in charge when Abe Reles, "Kid Twist" to the underworld, a top hitter and now turned informer, jumped out of the Half Moon Hotel in Brooklyn without a parachute. With Abe's outdoor aerial act and subsequent demise, the underworld breathed a lot easier. Facing a storm of criticism, Bals had quickly resigned from The Job, and now Bill O' brought him back out of oblivion.

The second and just as incredible appointment was that of Jim Moran as first deputy fire commissioner. The same Moran who had narrowly escaped indictment over the missing Anastasia files and who was bordering on disgrace when Bill O' rewarded him with such a lofty post.

This indeed was the fine state of affairs in City Hall when Jimmy Riley was retained as a holdover in the new chief inspector's squad. And the band played on.

* * *

When in later years Jimmy Riley reflected upon his ouster from plainclothes duty in the chief inspector's office, he attributed it to two significant happenings. According to the basic premise of the law of cause and effect, the cause that triggered his demise was a stormy meeting he had in Brooklyn with Jim Moran, and the one that gave the authorities an effective excuse for his dismissal occurred in the beautiful borough of Queens.

The new mayor, Bill O'Dwyer, had surrounded himself with a rather strange but very influential inner guard. There were four special confidants who wielded the greatest influence, and all had two things in common: they were all Irish and they were all ruthless. Their apparent leader and spokesman was Jim Moran, the former chief clerk and close buddy of O'Dwyer when he was the district attorney of Brooklyn. Jim was a huge, scowling, redhaired Irishman, whom to everyone's surprise O'Dwyer swiftly appointed first deputy fire commissioner. The second was ex-Captain Frank Bals, of Abe Reles' aerial-act fame, an ascetic-looking man who had retired under fire as chief of O'Dwyer's district attorney's detective squad. He was rewarded by Bill O', probably for outstanding heroism under fire, with the newly created post of seventh deputy police commissioner. The third in order of influence was big Joe Boyle, a city detective and a treasured friend, whom Bill O' designated as his personal bodyguard and chauffeur. The fourth was a mild-mannered, easygoing police captain named Bill Whalen, who was probably the nicest guy of all. Another old friend, Bill Whalen was quickly made chief of detectives in The Job, an unprecedented jump in rank. Whalen had a bad booze problem and was constantly either attending Alcoholics Anonymous meetings or dry-out sanitoriums. However diverse the ruling four were physically and personality-wise, they surely had one thing in common, they all loved money.

When elected, Bill O'Dwyer was a widower, and like a lot of Irishmen, somewhat of a recluse. But also in common with a lot of Irishmen, Bill O' was a periodical drinker, one who would stay dry for weeks or even months, then go on a bat for about a week. The ruling four were his drinking companions and backslappers, forever telling him how terrific he was and what a fine mayor he made. They also served the most useful function of getting him off the booze after a five- or six-day bender, and their favorite facility for that was a private hospital on the East Side in the upper Seventies which specialized in the dry-out process. Whatever hold these intrepid four had on our esteemed mayor, it was a powerful one, for in his eyes they could do no wrong.

Not content with the various and plentiful perks that came their way as part of the mayor's inner circle, the four decided to form another five-borough supervisory squad under the aegis of Frank Bals, to be called the seventh deputy commissioner's squad. The city needed another five-borough squad like it needed another set of gambling laws, so it was inevitable that a huge howl of opposition would be raised to the proposal. The present setup of the main-office police commissioner's squad and chief inspector's squad, plus the borough and local division squads, had been in force for many decades, and the gamblers accepted it as a *fait accompli*. To assume the burden of paying ice to another and totally unnecessary top squad was unbearable to the gambling fraternity, and the politicos were deluged with horrified complaints by their gambler friends and contributors, complaints that were certain to reach the ears of the Irish resident landlord, Bill O'Dwyer.

However, plans for the squad moved along and in about a month it took shape, although no definitive course of action was yet established. One day during this period, Jimmy Riley was playing handball at the Knights of Columbus gym near Prospect Park in Brooklyn. After he had finished playing, showered, and dressed, he went to the downstairs bar with a couple of his fellow players to have a few beers. Jim Moran, now the first deputy fire commissioner and still a handball player, was standing at the bar drinking with a few of his satellites. He waved to Jimmy and motioned him aside.

Putting his arm around Jimmy's shoulders like he was his best pal, Moran said, "Jimmy, I'm pleased to see you, you're looking just fine. I'd like to sit down with you real soon, you know, to have a good meeting. I'd also be pleased if you brought along one of the key men from the police commissioner's squad."

Jimmy was surprised and even a little startled at the apparent warmth and cordiality of Moran's greeting. In his five years as a member of the Knights of Columbus, Moran had never even spoken to him once, never gave him a glint of recognition. This was perfectly satisfactory to Jimmy, as Moran had a reputation for being a hard-headed, overbearing, money-hungry sonofabitch who wished he could get his big hooks on a little more than a typewriter, his instrument of work as Bill O'Dwyer's chief clerk.

But Jimmy took the unexpected show of friendship with his usual aplomb and said, "Whenever you say, Commissioner. Can you tell me what you have in mind?"

"That can wait, Jim, we'll get to the point when we meet. Tell me, are you friendly with any particular man in the P.C.'s squad?"

"Yes, Commissioner, I do have a good friend there, a guy named Johnny Crews."

"Jimmy, is he a nice kid, a stand-up guy?"

"I don't think I quite understand you, Commissioner. What exactly have you in mind, some type of investigation?"

"No, no, no, nothing like that at all, Jimmy." Moran was starting to redden, annoyed as Jimmy looked at him innocently with his best altar-boy look.

Mrs. Riley didn't raise a fool for a son, not her Jimmy. He thought to himself, this big Mick is setting me up for something and I'm going to play it straight. The stench of a dead rat was filling his nostrils.

He looked the fire commissioner square in the eye. "Do you mean a young fellow, a guy about my age, whom I'm very friendly with even though we are on supposedly rival squads?"

"You got it right, Jimmy. As long as he can be trusted like you."

"When do you want to set up this meeting, Commissioner?"

"How about next Tuesday night? Right here at the club about seven o'clock. Okay?"

Jimmy thought for a moment. This club was the commissioner's own ball park, his home grounds. He was like a king here, everyone seemed to cater to him. No good. He said, "I'd rather go to Michel's on Flatbush Avenue, it's only a couple of blocks from here and it's nice and quiet there. I'll arrange for a table upstairs, and if he's available I'll bring Johnny Crews along.

If you don't hear from me beforetime, it's a dead date. Okay, Commissioner?"

Moran shook Jimmy's hand. "Fine, see you next Tuesday night at Michel's."

Johnny Crews had been a plainclothesman in the police commissioner's squad for almost as long a time as Jimmy had been a chief's man. He was tall, slim, and handsome, with a quiet, easy way about him that appealed to Jimmy. The police commissioner's squad was much more highly disciplined than the chief's squad, with one sergeant supervising every four men, and two lieutenants over the sergeants, and a deputy inspector and a full inspector in charge of everyone. The men rarely worked in pairs, and were almost always under close supervision. Besides the ordinary pinches, about twice a month they made a spectacular raid, taking out a big horse room, crap game, or roulette wheel. They would pile the principals and players into patrol wagons to the flashing cameras of the press, who were always alerted to record their brave attempts to clean up New York City. The P.C.'s men were invariably on the payrolls of the joints they raided, but would always excuse these violations of contract to the poor unfortunates who paid them by claiming that the raid was on the direct orders of one of their inspectors. This was more or less of a smokescreen to cloak their superiors in honesty, to put them forward as paragons of virtue.

What a crock of shit that was. The bosses took the money their underlings brought in just like everyone else. They sent their kids to fine Catholic prep schools and colleges, and at the drop of a restaurant check, never, God forbid, to reach in and pay it, they would pull pictures of their kids out of their wallets and proudly show off Tommy, Patty, Jack, Nora, and Maureen. They're going to be lawyers or doctors, not a poor cop like me. And I owe it all to Rose, or Nellie, or May. Me, I'm never home, she's the one responsible for the fine kids, God bless her. How many times Jimmy had heard that shit and shaken his poor Irish head.

But Johnny was one of the nicer guys in the plainclothes world. Jimmy had met him in Gamblers Court almost at the inception of their careers and through the years they had struck a strong friendship. They had had a few healthy private transactions together, and by this time Jimmy felt that not only was John dead on the level, but could be trusted completely. It was a simple matter to get hold of John and make sure that he was available for the dinner meeting, but what was really bothering Jimmy was his own squad. At the last squad meeting, which Jimmy reluctantly attended, and only to hand in his own money and to receive his own end, there was a lot of talk of Frank Bals forming a main-office squad, and from the general conversation Jimmy gathered that the Four Horsemen and their cohorts were concerned and even outraged about the idea of some of their power being usurped. He had not paid too much attention to it, and now he felt that he was being put right in the middle of it. What the hell else would Moran want to meet him for? And why all of a sudden acting so friendly? And asking him to bring a trusted P.C.'s man? What else? He wrestled with his conscience for a while, and as much as he hated to do it, he decided to consult Gordon about the meeting with Moran, to get his ideas on what approach to take.

He made it a point to get to work early the next morning and caught Gordon coming out of his pal, the deputy inspector's office.

"Did you make sure you put two sugars in his coffee, Lenny?"

"Come on, Jimmy, knock it off, it's too early in the morning for that shit. Besides, I've got a terrible hangover."

"I hope you weren't out all night throwing your money away on some chorus girls, Lenny."

"Jesus, you're really funny, Jimmy. I think I'll speak to Julie Podell and get you on at the Copa to open the show like one of those horseshit comedians."

"If I make it you'll never get to see me, Lenny. Joe Lopez will never let you past the front rope unless you buy a new suit."

"Okay, Jimmy, forget the jokes. To what do we owe the pleasure of your company this early in the morning? Some broad's husband come home early?"

"Never. Not a clean-living kid like me. Seriously, Lenny, let's you and I take a walk. I think I am the bearer of bad news. I'm really bothered about something that happened yesterday and I think I should talk it over with you, the squad's peerless leader."

Lenny took a long look at Jimmy's face and realized he wasn't kidding. He said, "Let's walk up to Bickford's on Canal Street and get some breakfast. That okay?"

"Perfect, Lenny. Let's go."

They walked up Centre Street to Canal Street like two great friends, chatting amiably about the usual cops-and-robbers gossip, meanwhile secretly hating each other's guts. Not a word was mentioned about any impending trouble until they sat down and ordered breakfast.

"All right, Jimmy, what's on your mind? What is it you think so important that you should discuss it with me?"

"Well, here we go, Lenny, my boy. I was playing handball at the Knights over at Prospect Park yesterday and I ran into Jim Moran at the bar later. Now, understand this, Lenny, think about it. Moran has never even looked at me in the five years I've been in that club, not even the slightest glance. Furthermore, I wouldn't give a shit if the big Mick never said hello to me. Now that Bill O' appointed him first deputy fire commissioner he's the hottest shot in the club, with everyone trying to get up his ass. Last night, out of a clear blue sky, he cuts into me at the bar like I'm his prize nephew, nice as apple pie. Without too much elaboration and detail, to get right to the point, he says straight out that he wants a meet with me and Johnny Crews of the P.C.'s squad. How about those fucking apples?"

Gordon whistled. "Jesus, Jimmy, it's gotta be what we talked about at the last meeting. You know, the new squad Frank Bals has formed."

"Exactly, Lenny. That's all the city needs is another main-office plainclothes squad. You realize that, don't you? What the hell is Bals gonna call it, the seventh deputy commissioner's squad? Isn't that hot shit? Now every deputy commissioner will want to get into the act and have his own squad. The fucking ice will be higher than it is in Alaska. Pretty soon the bookmakers will want to reverse roles, become deputy police commissioners and let the deputies have the books and pay the ice. Incredible."

"You're always on, Jimmy, always being funny, but this time we both know it's no joke. We got to knock Bals's squad out of the box before he gets started or everyone will fold and no one will get paid. What's your plan? What are you going to say to Moran?"

"I'm going to tell him shit. Zero. I'm going to play honest Jimmy Riley, the honest altar boy who never stole a candle. Fuck Moran, and the rest of the Irish Mafia. I'll do my part, don't worry about me. But one thing further, and it's the main thing, you and the top P.C. guys have to knock the legs from under Bals's squad. That should be easy for a heavy hitter like you, Lenny."

Lenny smiled broadly, pleased at the compliment, even though Jimmy meant it sarcastically.

"You're absolutely right, Jimmy. Here's where we'll give Danny the deputy a chance to earn his two shares. He's got the hot line to the chief's ear, and he's also very friendly with Inspector Monahan of the P.C.'s squad, who can get to the commissioner himself. They'll do a number on Bals you won't believe. He won't last a month with that horseshit squad once they put the screws on. Can you imagine, what a lot of nerve those Irish bastards have to start a squad like that in the first place."

"They have some nerve trying to cut in on our racket, right, Lenny?" Jimmy laughed. "And for once I'm on Danny the deputy's side. You couldn't pick a better man to sly rap the Pope, much less Frank Bals, than good old Danny. He'll love this particular job. Okay, Lenny, my man, a temporary truce has been effected between us to slay the giant dragon that is starting to rear its ugly head. When you think of it, those Irish Mafia are all really ugly, not nice and pretty like the chorus boys in our squad."

"Come off it, Jimmy. There's no beauty contest winners among us, including you, even though you think you're the nuts, another Clark Gable."

"Never Clark Gable, Lenny baby. A blond Robert Taylor, perhaps."

"Horseshit, Jimmy. Come on, get serious. No matter what's happened between us, I'm glad you buried the hatchet and came to me. Tell you what. Go ahead, get Johnny Crews, rehearse your act, and just like you said, tell those bastards nothing. I agree a million percent, and I'm sure I speak for the rest of the squad. Let's shake on it. I'll hold my end up just like we said, and you do your act. We'll meet next Wednesday and you can tell me what happened. Okay, let's go back to the office."

The temporary truce firmly in effect, Jimmy sent a message to Johnny Crews that he wanted to meet him privately. They met, Jimmy filled Johnny in on all the details of the Moran encounter and his talk with Gordon, and they laid out their strategy for the Tuesday night meeting. It was agreed that Jimmy was to do most of the talking and John to support him whenever necessary. Jimmy was slyly amused and pleased to see that even quiet, handsome John, with the holy air of a young curate, was outraged at the thought of a new squad coming in on their time-honored territorial rights.

Tuesday night, Jimmy met Johnny at the downstairs bar for a preliminary drink about half an hour before the dinner appointment. They exchanged short bits of conversation for a few minutes, but Jimmy, who was at ease, could sense that Johnny was just a bit uptight, not his usual carefree self.

"John, please excuse my asking you this, but are you a little nervous about this meet?"

"I have to confess, Jimmy, just a little bit. Not scared, just a little shaky. I didn't say a word to any of my bosses about meeting you. As you probably know, the mention of your name is anathema to them. They think you're too chesty for your own good. They don't know the real humble Jimmy Riley."

Jimmy laughed, and it broke the tension a little as Johnny started to laugh too. "It's a goddam good thing they had someone chesty going for them setting up the payrolls five years ago or they'd all be a little poorer today. Right, John?"

"You bet your ass, Jimmy. They never turned down the money you set up. But let's get down to business. To tell the truth, I'm a little leery of the fire commissioner, Moran. I made a few discreet inquiries about him and all the feedback I get is that he's a real hard guy, a tough man."

"Well, John, my boy, we'll soon find out, here's his eminence coming through the front door. Jesus, look who's with him, that broken-nose hairbag lieutenant who used to have the Seventeenth Detective Squad. His name is McGany, I'd heard he went with Bals's squad."

Moran and McGany walked straight to Jimmy at the bar and shook hands enthusiastically. Jimmy introduced Johnny to them and he couldn't miss the sharp appraisal Moran made of him. If it was his looks and the way he was dressed, it had to be a favorable impression, because John had never looked better.

"Do you and the lieutenant care for a drink now, Commissioner, or would you care to go straight upstairs to our table?"

"No, go ahead, finish your drinks, boys. We'll wait until we get to the table."

Jimmy ate in Michel's, a top Brooklyn restaurant, quite often, and the headwaiter greeted his party warmly and sat them at a window table over looking the trolley cars running along beautiful scenic Flatbush Avenue. They had a lot of conversation over drinks and dinner, with the commissioner asking very direct questions about their backgrounds. He was quite impressed when John told him that he was a Fordham University graduate.

Jimmy got a big laugh when the commissioner inquired of his academic credentials and Jimmy answered with a straight face, "U.H.K., Commissioner."

"University of Holy Cross?"

"No, sir, that would be U.H.C. My college was the university of hard knocks."

Big laugh. Oh, the lilt of Irish laughter, thought Jimmy. Oh, the lilt of Irish horseshit is what they should have said.

The laughs, the drinks, and the dinner over, the commissioner didn't waste any time. He got right down to business. He obviously had had a few in him when he arrived, and with the few he had during dinner his voice took on a distinct brogue, like his idol, Bill O'Dwyer.

"Boys, I know you two fine young gentlemen can surely be trusted, so I asked you to meet me tonight to give me a hand with a project of mine. This is very important to me and in some ways to the mayor. As you might know by now, our newly appointed seventh deputy police commissioner, ex-Captain Frank Bals, a fine man, has formed a new main-office squad to help in the supervision of the vice and gambling laws. The good lieutenant here, Jack McGany, whom I'm sure you've heard only good things about, is to be the boss of the squad, under the direction of

Frank himself, of course. It is to be an elite group, only six plain-clothesmen in all, and I'm sure Commissioner Bals and Jack McGany here are more than willing to cooperate with the chief's and P.C.'s squads. Do you get what I mean, Jimmy?"

Jimmy toyed with his after-dinner drink. He looked directly at Moran with a steady gaze, but his mind was racing and his heart pounding. What in the name of Christ is this all about? Here sits the first deputy *fire* commissioner giving me the rundown on the seventh deputy *police* commissioner's squad. Obviously Frank Bals is misnamed, he couldn't have any real balls or he would be sitting at the table opposite John and me discussing the situation. Or is this all bullshit, a façade, is the fire commissioner calling all the shots? Well, my boy, we'll soon find out.

Jimmy sipped his brandy and said, "Exactly what do you mean by cooperating with each other? We're all cops, of course we'll cooperate with Commissioner Bals's squad in every way we can."

"That's my boy, Jimmy. In every way you can. Now you got it, lad. All right, let's get down to the real purpose of why we're having this dinner meeting tonight. The real business."

"Fine. Go ahead, Commissioner."

"First, we want the list of all the spots the chief's and P.C.'s squads have on the payroll, throughout the entire city. Second, how much do they pay, and the main guy to see in each spot."

Jimmy looked at the big red-haired Irish prick. Was he for real? He wants me to serve up on a silver platter what we've been busting our balls for years to accumulate. Fuck him.

Dead straight, all innocent and wide-eyed, Jimmy answered. "I don't think I quite understand what you're getting at Commissioner. What lists? What payrolls? You must have heard wrong, all that's a figment of some asshole's imagination. I think someone in the *fire* department is making unjust accusations against members of the *police* department." Jimmy turned to Johnny Crews. "Right, John?"

"Right. Dead right, Jimmy."

Moran was completely nonplussed by this turn of events, by Jimmy's imperturbable answer. His face got twice as red as usual. He looked at McGany, whose broken nose started to twitch. The Irish brogue was gone now, pure Red Hook Brooklyn took over.

"What the fuck are you telling me? Who are you kiddin'? Whadda you mean, no payrolls, no lists? You think you're bull-shitting somebody, Jimmy? Take another look."

Now it was Jimmy's turn to get strident. He had determined to keep his cool, but this Irish prick was starting to bull him, and that was one thing he wouldn't stand for. Still, he kept his voice soft and low. "Commissioner, as far as you, the fire department, the new seventh deputy police commissioner, Frank Bals, and our detective lieutenant here, Jack McGany, are concerned, there are no fucking lists, no fucking payrolls, no fucking main guys I know. Now get that straight in that fucking hard red head of yours. If you expect me to go out and straighten out that bullshit squad of Frank Bals, you have another guess coming. As far as you're concerned, Commissioner, I, Jamed Edward Riley, am a one hundred percent honest policeman. Furthermore, I have the record to prove it."

"You know something, Riley, you're one hundred percent full of shit. I know all about you, you're on every wise guy's payroll in the city. I've been keeping an eye on you for years in the courts and around the Knights of Columbus. I've watched you, posing around in your custom-made suits and shirts like a lace-curtain-Irish pimp. You never had an ounce of shit in your life, you came from Red Hook like I did, and now everything on your body is tailor-made. One more thing, if I frisked you right now, you'd probably have a couple of grand in your pocket."

"Why don't you try to frisk me, Commissioner?"

"Fuck you."

"And fuck you. But that was a nice compliment about the way I dress. Don't forget I won the Barney's Clothes award last year, three suits for catching a Jew bookmaker up in the Bronx. And don't forget one more thing, I married an heiress, a real Irish heiress."

"Heiress, my ass."

Through all this pleasant bit of byplay, Crews and McGany sat there frozen, absolutely speechless. McGany finally found his tongue. He said in what was supposed to be a conciliatory tone, "Come on, you guys, you're both the same kind. You're both Irish, for Christ's sake. Don't be thick as shit like all the Irish.

We're only here on a peace mission, Jimmy. Really, I think the commissioner was a little too blunt." He turned to Moran. "Jim, you could have laid it out a little more tactfully, you know."

Moran sat back, snapped his fingers at the waiter for another round of drinks. Everybody sat quietly, Jimmy and Moran both smoldering. The round of drinks came. Moran said, "Good luck everybody, and you're going to need it, Riley."

"Is that a threat?"

"Take it any way you want. All I asked for was your coopera- tion and you refused it."

"If my cooperation consists of me putting my head in a fucking noose, I'm not giving it to you or anyone else. I've been hauled before the commissioner of investigations and received a clean bill of health. I've worked for three chiefs, a new Olympic record, and even according to the new chief, who barely knows me, my work has been outstanding. Furthermore, I have two commendations from Commander Kelly of Naval Intelligence for excellent undercover work for him during the war. As far as you're concerned, I'm as honest as Christ himself."

Jimmy shut up finally. He was tempted to go on and tell Moran that there were plenty of skeletons in his closet, like the missing- files episode when he was chief clerk for Bill O'Dwyer during the Murder, Inc. probe, but he bit his tongue and kept quiet.

The hostility hung over the table like the fog over the River Thames on a rainy London night. It was like waiting for a time- bomb to go off. Four big Irishmen at a dinner table in a nice Brooklyn restaurant. With their age differences they could almost have passed for two fathers taking their two sons out to dinner. A nice family reunion.

Everyone simmered down a little as they sipped their drinks. Moran at last broke the silence. "Is that your last word, Jimmy? You still insist you have no lists or payrolls to give us?"

Jimmy took a good look at Moran. What in the name of Christ was the first deputy *fire* commissioner doing dickering for the seventh deputy *police* commissioner. It was readily apparent to him. The trail probably led to His Honor himself. Jesus, he was on shaky grounds having a violent argument with this overbearing fuck. Maybe if Moran hadn't come on so strong, he might have been more conciliatory. After all, Moran was Irish, he must have some good in him. But Jimmy had a rock for a head when it came to guys like Moran.

"I'm sorry we argued, Commissioner, but even if I had a list of payrolls I wouldn't give it to anyone, not even my mother. Take it any way you want, but you're a fireman, a top one, granted, and I'm a cop, bottom of the ladder. As far as you're concerned, Jimmy Riley is as pure as the driven snow, honest as the tick of a grandfather's clock. Case closed."

Moran shoved back from the table, motioned McGany to go with him, and abruptly walked out of the dining room without so much as goodbye.

Jimmy looked at Johnny Crews, who had a worried frown on his face, and laughed. "How could those two Irish pricks leave like that and expect an honest cop like me to pick up this tab?"

The frown disappeared off his face and Johnny roared laughing. "Sometimes I think you're crazy, Jimmy. And Jesus Christ, when you made that speech you were so convincing, even I was beginning to believe you were totally honest. But I hate to admit, you did exactly the right thing. I'm telling you, the man has some goddam nerve, expecting us to hand over the payroll lists just like your wife hands you a shopping list. I think you can figure on a repercussion, don't you think?"

"When it comes I'll handle it. I took one good precaution. He has an asshole buddy named Joe Smith, a fireman, whom he plays handball with. I have this guy Smith bullshitted that I'm an electronic genius. He thinks I can put a wiretap anywhere I want, even though you know I don't even know how to put an electric bulb in the socket. I'll just drop a hint to Smitty that I taped the whole dinner by a secret device, he'll tell Moran, and Moran will shit. Don't worry. I'll lay it on Smitty and he'll run to big Jim like a deer. Moran put him in some kind of action and the guy is finally seeing a little cash. He'll report back to Moran in a flash. Remember one thing, John, Jimmy Riley believes in the law of tit for tat, and the mere thought of this conversation tonight on tape will keep Moran from taking any action against me with Bill O'."

"I hope you're right, Jimmy, and that was good thinking. Now

I hope the next-best honest man to Jimmy Riley, my inspector, Monahan, doesn't ever get wind of this meeting."

"He won't, John, my boy. He won't."

They had another drink for good luck, shook hands and parted. They both felt good, like two secret agents who had just accomplished a successful mission.

A squad meeting was called for the following night, and needless to say, everyone was in attendance, including Dan the deputy, to hear Jimmy Riley's report on the historic summit meeting. Jimmy did the whole number, including Moran's brogue at the beginning of the meeting and his Red Hook snarl at the end, and even his mortal enemies among them broke up laughing. When he finally extracted every laugh he could, like a good ham actor, he turned serious.

"Okay, fellows, I think I did my part about this new cancer in our midst. What's the game plan from here in? As the superior officer here, suppose we hear from you, Danny."

Surprised at the cordiality in Jimmy's tone of voice, and still laughing a little at Jimmy's rendition of the meeting, Danny felt almost fond of him for a brief moment. "You did well, James, very well. That's all we need to do is to expose ourselves to these new interlopers. Bals is an old hairbag and he has surrounded himself with a bunch of old hairbag ex-plainclothesmen and detectives. I had a long talk with the chief the other day and he is strictly against this new Bals squad. In fact, he hates Frank Bals's guts. I called my friend Pat Monahan from the P.C.'s squad this morning and made a date for dinner tomorrow night. I just briefly mentioned Bals's name in passing, and he uttered only two words, 'that sonofabitch,' so I think he'll be on our side. I wouldn't worry about them, they'll never last more than three months. So don't worry about it, fellows, me and Monahan will cool them out. You did good, Jimmy, even for a fresh fuck like you."

Jimmy had a tall Scotch and water in his hand, and he raised it to Danny and said, "Thank you, milord. I have only one life to give to God and Ireland, but my time on earth I will devote to you."

"Still a fucking wise guy, Riley, but even you have some good in you."

"Thank you again, milord."

The meeting broke up amid an air of great camaraderie, everyone determined to unite against the common enemy, Frank Bals's squad.

The weeks rolled around and business went on as usual. Jimmy's time occupied fully between his business with Harry and his plainclothes work. There were recurrent rumors of Bals's squad attempting to establish themselves as a force in the fight against corruption, or better said, the fight to continue corruption, but the squad never got off the ground. O'Dwyer evidently was convinced that another such main-office squad defied tradition, and with the malignant forces of the chief's and P.C.'s superiors constantly sniping and degrading it, the Bals squad was disbanded within less than six months' time of Bill O'Dwyer's election.

There were no regrets at this bit of news throughout The Job or in the gambling world, with the minor exception of the men of Bals's squad, who had no doubt envisioned another Klondike. Tough luck, old fellows, thought Jimmy, when he heard the news. Tough luck, poor chaps.

Whatever concern Jimmy had felt about his violent confrontation with Moran soon abated. He had had a drink the next day with Moran's pal Joe Smith, the fireman, and broadly hinted as to the taping of the dinner meeting by a new secret device, and other tremendous electronic advances that he was capable of instrumenting at will. It was pure horseshit, but Joe Smith took it all in like Jimmy was Thomas Edison or Marconi, and he believed every word.

The safe-and-lock wiretap detectives did all Jimmy's wire work. They did this secretly, and Jimmy rewarded them handsomely, especially when he made a big score off a wire. At first, Jimmy was amazed at their ingenious methods, how they could come up with the correct pairs on a telephone panel in a building several blocks away to tap in on. They would look the area over like KGB agents about to tap the White House, and presto, you were hooked onto your tap of the unfortunate victim. Jimmy was too bright to swallow this charade for long, so he cultivated a guy in the telephone company, an executive, and he gave him the entire rundown. All you ever needed was the desired phone number, the proper equipment to listen and record, and a good connection in the telephone company who would tell you the exact location of the panel pairs to be tapped.

With Frank Bals's ill-fated squad at last folded and out of the way as a threat to the chief inspector's and police commissioner's squads, peace and harmony were restored to the gambling elements of New York City. It was hailed in various high places as a major victory for Jimmy Riley, even if he was not ultimately responsible for their downfall. The mere fact that he had stood his ground against the mighty Jim Moran, close pal of O'Dwyer's, enhanced his reputation throughout the city both among cops and wise guys. However, he brushed aside any talk about it, never reveling in it or discussing it, because he was too cute an Irish boy to want to claim credit for any win over Moran. He realized the extent of Moran's power and his incredible hold over O'Dwyer, and certainly did not want to do anything further to discredit or to antagonize him. He even made a feeble effort to make peace one night in an uptown restaurant when he spotted Moran and a crony at the bar opposite him. He sent them over a drink, and when it was served Moran evidently asked the bartender who was treating, the bartender pointed at Jimmy, Moran almost turned purple and turned the drink upside down, spilling the whiskey all over the bar. The Irish equivalent of "Stick the drink up your ass." This display convinced Jimmy that he had indeed made another mortal enemy, one to add to the growing list.

At this time, Jimmy was not doing well in his battle with Dan the deputy and the Four Horsemen. It seemed that a month never passed that they did not violate one of Jimmy's contracts. Jimmy was in his sixth year of plainclothes work in the chief's office, and had developed such a rapport with most of the guys he personally handled that they were almost like relatives of his. He attended their sons' bar mitzvahs, their daughters' sweet-sixteen parties, the big Italian weddings, almost any event that he deemed important enough that his failure to attend would hurt the guy's feelings. He grew extremely fond of most of the guys he did business with.

The only reason the Four Horsemen pinched a payroll contract was that they were either too stupid or too lazy to go out and dig and lock up an outlaw. Whenever he heard about one of his contracts being pinched he would get apoplectic, homicidal. But the Four Horsemen always had their excuse ready. He cursed and ranted at them to no avail, at least once a month they would commit the same deadly sin. The one thing he was consoled about was that they never touched Harry's spots. Whether it was out of fear, respect, or whatever, he hoped and prayed they never would put him to the test again. The next time it was going to be brutal.

But at least in Harry's area Jimmy had some tranquility, and as conditions worsened between Dan the deputy, the Four Horsemen, and Jimmy, he was slowly coming to the conclusion that his plainclothes life would soon be over. He still loved the glamour of the life—the nightclubs, the ball games, the fights at the Garden, the occasional beautiful showgirl—but lately he sensed that something dire was on the horizon.

The incumbent mayor, though he had his faults and Jimmy did not approve of the people closely allied with him, was an ex-cop, an ex-plainclothesman, and if he was aware of the extent of the gambling operations in his domain he just remained mum or winked at them. The New York papers, particularly the tabloids, the *News* and the *Mirror,* would run an occasional sensational article about a gambling operation, but that would immediately be countered by a big raid by the P.C.'s squad or the Four Horsemen with full press coverage and plenty of photographs of honest horse players or honest crapshooters holding handkerchiefs over their faces while the honest bastions of the law loaded them into paddy wagons.

The reporters who covered the police headquarters were friendly with the main-office plainclothesmen and drank with them in Flanagan's or Carmine's in the neighborhood and would be loath to rock the boat of friendship. In fact, they all patronized the small bookmaker who catered to reporters and cops alike. It was unbelievable, the cops and reporters would be having a drink together, someone would have a tip on a horse, and they would summon the bookie and bet the tip together. As the plainclothes-men made about fifty times more than the reporters, they would always pick up the bar tabs. No one ever questioned their appar-ent affluence, it was simply taken for granted. It was a nice, cozy relationship everyone enjoyed, and Jimmy Riley kept making his visits to the vault every couple of weeks and by this time was so jaded at the sight of money he never bothered to count the bankroll anymore. He only knew that it was getting larger and larger, and though the end was almost certainly near, it would not only be a very comfortable end, but a very promising beginning.

The first tremblings of Jimmy Riley's plainclothes world started in the beautiful borough of Queens. Queens was in most sections an idyllic component of New York City, with wide bou-levards, beautiful wooded areas, and enclaves of luxurious homes and mini-estates. But just like the rest of New York's boroughs it had its share of lower-middle-class and poorer sections of seamy, ancient apartment houses and railroad flats dating from the turn of the century. One of the more populous poorer sections of Queens was Astoria, a multiracial community of blue-collar, hard-work-ing people who always had enough left over from the paycheck to bet numbers and horses all week long and to go drinking on Fri-day and Saturday nights. One of the better-known bookmakers in Astoria was an ex-journeyman prizefighter named Joe Pledge. Joe was a tough Polish guy who enjoyed a good reputation among the denizens of Astoria. Everybody seemed to like Joe except two local division plainclothes cops named Dooley and Destefaro. Joe must have broken a promise or crossed them in some way, be-cause he sure enough got right to the top of their shit list.

There was one cardinal rule that was strictly observed by the plainclothes cops charged with enforcing the vice and gambling laws. This applied right down the line, from the chief's office, the police commissioner's office, down through the borough and local division offices. No matter how much of a hard-on you get for a guy in the gambling business, you never knock him out of the box, never out of business completely. If any plainclothesman wants to accomplish this not very difficult feat, it is a simple procedure, you just arrest the gambler every day. You can sometimes arrest him twice a day if you pinch him early in the afternoon and he makes the five hundred dollars station house bail and resumes his business at his usual post. The gambler is akin to the proverbial sitting duck, as the cops know exactly where he trades and in all likelihood his idiosyncrasies, his work habits, like where he stashes his betting slips, who his runners are, and in most cases who his customers are.

To get even for the alleged affront tendered to them by their well-battered victim, Dooley and Destefaro, those two staunch defenders of law and order, decided to knock Joe Pledge out of business. They followed the simple procedure, they locked Joe up every day for over a week. Joe got the message and acted very predictably—that is, predictably to anyone with a grain of common sense. He had been on his corner for years and years, paying his local ice, and along come two cops who develop a dislike for him and decide to knock him out of business. A definite no-no. Joe started to squawk like a banshee. He threatened to squawk to the mayor, the police commissioner, the district attorney, the newspapers, anyone who would relieve him of his oppression. Common sense dictated that the cops reinstate him to his former status, put him back on the payroll as a bookmaker once again in fine standing. But when things are going too smoothly, the plain-clothes cops sometimes get the idea that they are invincible, that the good ship will never teeter an inch, much less sink.

Joe was crying so loud his laments sooner or later had to be heard. A series of subtle hints began to appear in the columns of some of the more prominent writers on the local Queens newspapers about an impending grand jury investigation into gambling and police corruption. These scary rumors inevitably reached police headquarters in New York City, but if it bothered some of the more nervous types, it did not have any effect at all on Jimmy Riley. He heard about it, and shrugged it off; he had never even heard of Joe Pledge. Let the dumb division bastards who were stupid enough to knock Pledge out of action worry about it, that was their headache.

Besides, Jimmy was well aware of the make-up of the Queens district attorney's office, a den of bandits Jesse James would have been glad to have on his side. Queens Felony Court, where all the

Queens gambling cases were tried, was renamed Queens Friendly
Court by Riley after a couple of experiences with the assistant
district attorneys and magistrates out there. Even if a main-office
cop developed a hard-on for an outlaw bookmaker, generally a
fresh, wise bastard, and threw a real zinger of a complaint at him
with the idea in mind of a conviction, one of the assistants in
cahoots with the judge would get the case dismissed. The dis-
missing of a case never bothered Jimmy, as long as he was declared in with the action ahead of time and received a suitable fee
for his trouble. What used to rile him was when a young assistant
tried to keep the whole pot and toss a case without declaring him
in. Jimmy was smart enough to sense a situation like that immediately, and much to the discomfiture of the budding prosecutor,
would throw in everything but the horse to sink the bookmaker.
Jimmy's tactics did not especially endear him to the Queens
Friendly judiciary and their subalterns, but he couldn't care less.
He made his position very clear: if you want to throw one, make
sure you take care of Jimmy Riley.

Besides, he made very infrequent forays into Queens, but when
he did it was almost always within the confines of a precinct
commanded by a certain Captain Goldberg. Captain Goldberg
was a big, good-looking, red-haired Jew who looked more Irish
than most of the Micks patrolling the beats. He was always posing around the precinct in his sparkling uniform, aware of his
good looks and trying vainly to establish himself as a holy terror
against all forms of vice and gambling. This was a real puzzle to
all the other Jews in The Job, as most of them liked money even
more than the Irish. He would actually raid a candy store trying to
capture a bookmaker, and if he found a punchboard there—a
cardboard device where, if you punched the right number, you
won a big piece of candy—he would make an arrest. A real hero.

Guys like Captain Goldberg sickened Jimmy, and he devised a
plan of attack calculated to shake the shit out of him. He laid in a
few wiretaps in Queens, and when he came across an outlaw he
checked carefully to see if he was operating in Goldberg's precinct. When Jimmy got all set to knock off the wire room he
would wait until he called a friend of his, a cop in Goldberg's
precinct, to confirm that the captain would be on duty the particu-

lar day he brought the prisoners in. Goldberg would go crazy when Jimmy was booking the poor bookmakers at the lieutenant's desk. He would pace up and down like a madman, attempting to grab one of them to murder him if possible, while Jimmy would say, "Captain, please. Those are my prisoners. They're in my charge. Hands off, please."

After the third pinch in one month, a real beauty, three bookmakers who looked like they just escaped from Devil's Island, Goldberg was almost choleric pacing back and forth. The arraignment over and the prisoners consigned to the station house cells to await the ever-ready bondsman, Jimmy asked Captain Goldberg for a private audience in his office. Jimmy sat and talked to the captain with a dead straight face and told him that he positively had to do something about the serious gambling rings that seemed to be thriving in his precinct. He further said that he would have to make a personal report to the chief if this situation continued. Goldberg just stared at Jimmy. He knew in his heart of hearts that Jimmy probably had half of New York City on his payroll, but he couldn't dare open his mouth to malign a chief's man, particularly one who was coming into his precinct every week with a fresh batch of bookmakers. He just sat and listened to Jimmy, his face getting redder and redder until it looked like he was going to have a heart attack. Jimmy would then finish, shake hands with Goldberg like St. Augustine forgiving a desperate sinner, and ask him to do better. When he got back into his car he would describe the look on Goldberg's face to his partner and they would both die laughing.

The laughs throughout The Job got a little fewer as Joe Pledge continued to squawk and even the porous district attorney's office eventually had to pay him some attention. As was certain to follow, the Queens newspapers filtered the sensational charges to the New York City newspapers and in short order there was a general clamor for a grand jury investigation; an investigation no one, particularly the mayor, wanted. Bill O'Dwyer had been in office less than two years, and this was his first bout with a hint of police corruption that might tarnish his regime. His best friends were either cops, ex-cops, or some type of law-enforcement agents. There was no way Bill O'Dwyer was ever going to hurt a cop if he could help it, and he moved swiftly to avert a grand jury investigation by means of which some headline-hungry assistant district attorney might blow things out of proportion. He conferred with the police commissioner and chief inspector and quickly flopped the Astoria division squad into uniform and replaced them with recruits from the Police Academy, similar to La Guardia's move that brought Jimmy Riley to the chief inspector's office.

Through all the travail with Joe Pledge, Jimmy and young Billy McMahon, his new partner, stayed clear of Queens, deciding that discretion was very much the greater part of valor. Jimmy wouldn't put it past one of the young fresh assistants to set up a chief's or P.C.'s man to corral a newspaper headline and show the world how honest they were. Jimmy was very, very careful of his moves during the Joe Pledge investigation and secretly congratulated himself on not knowing the guy. One you missed, Jimmy Boy, one you missed, you lucky bastard.

But as Jimmy was fond of quoting his pal Jersey Ed Murphy, whatever can happen, will happen, and usually for the worst. Sure enough, it happened. Conditions had again worsened between Danny the deputy and Jimmy in spite of their six months' truce during the Bals squad abortion. With the Four Horsemen's continued violations of contracts, and as Jimmy knew, always with the complete confidence and direction of Dan the deputy, the true boss of the squad, he felt a disgust pervade him whenever he met Dan. And Jimmy could not easily disguise his feelings toward Danny, hardly acknowledging him when they met and giving him short, clipped answers to any questions he directed toward Jimmy. The day of reckoning was bound to come.

Jimmy was in the office early one bright late-summer morning. Dan the deputy, he of the clerical skills, round body, and pig Irish face, summoned Jimmy into his office, his sacred portals.

"How are you, Jimmy? Everything all right?"

"You know everything's all right, don't you, Dan? How can there be anything wrong? Certainly there can't be anything worrying you, sitting there behind that nice big desk getting richer each month."

"Always the same remark, always the wise young prick, right,

Riley? Listen, you. I'm trying to be civil to you, so keep that fresh Irish kisser of yours shut for a few minutes, if that's possible. I want to ask you a question, and I'd like the truth. How well do you know Joe Pledge? Level with me."

"In the first place, you get this straight. There's no such thing as leveling with you and your four ass-kissing prize packages out front, so let's forget that shit, you wouldn't know how to level. In the second place, I never laid eyes on Joe Pledge in my entire fucking life. How I missed the screaming sonofabitch I'll never know, but miss him I did. It must be the grace of the Good Lord Jesus rewarding me for being such a decent, honest kid."

"Are you positive, Riley? Don't shit me now with that altar-boy face."

"Honest to God, Danny, on my mother, on my wife and kids."

"Look here, Jimmy, I have a record of all your arrests and it seems that you made quite a few pinches in Queens, and some were in Astoria. I was thinking that maybe you grabbed Pledge at one time or another, or one of his runners, and either shook him for a few or pinched him."

"For Christ's sake, Dan, are you really serious? There must be at least two hundred bookmakers in Queens. There must be thirty in Astoria alone. Sure I made plenty of pinches in Queens, and plenty of shakes, but never Joe Pledge. You know how many guys we have on the payroll out there, you got the list. Where do you think you get those fucking envelopes from every month, the big blue sky?"

"Now I don't want to hear anything like that, Riley. I just called you in here because I heard a very disturbing bit of news. It came back to me from the mayor's office that you were a personal friend of this Joe Pledge."

"That's a lot of pure, unadulterated shit. They've been waiting a long time to get even with me for fucking them around with Bals's squad. And don't forget, you were ready to give me the Medal of Honor for the way I handled that piece of work. And you were as much a beneficiary of the submarine job we did on Bals as I was, or any of the other guys. Listen, you know and I know that they lead the fucking mayor around by the hand when he has his half a load on. For Christ's sake, don't you think I know all about the private hospital on Seventy-third Street where Boyle and Moran and the other guys take that Irish fuck to dry out after one of his six-day benders. When he comes to, he'll believe any shit those guys feed him, and you oughta know how those guys hate me because I refused to make a big payroll for them when Bill O' became the mayor. Fuck them once, and fuck them again, let them go out and get their money the hard way, just like I did."

"In some ways I have to agree with you, Riley. But you know one thing, talking to a smart-ass like you is like talking to a brick wall. You're as thick as shit, Riley, but you're the best cop and the best-informed guy in the squad, that's why you're still around, why you lasted this long. But I can see the handwriting on the wall, kid, your days are numbered. And I must warn you, if Bill O' decides you get the boot there's not a fucking thing I'll try to do to save you."

"Danny, don't bother that chowderhead of yours. You couldn't save a hunk of shit. The only power you have around here is that you're up the top of the chief's ass, and he hasn't got the faintest idea what we're carrying on or even what the hell goes on in the city. If he ever did, if he even had an inkling, he would keel over dead with his rosary beads in his hands. Who in the hell are you trying to shit? Look, his office is two doors away. Let's you and I go in to see him together and have a little heart-to-heart talk."

The deputy inspector's ruddy pig face got ashen, dead white. He shook his head and looked at Riley with hate in his eyes. "Fuck you, Riley. I hope I live to see the day you're strung up by your balls."

"That'll be the day you see that, you little rotten no-good Irish cocksucker. But there's one thing you and the rest of them won't have to worry about. If I go, I won't take anyone with me, even though I'd love to take you, you gutless sonofabitch. But remember this, if I get dumped by the mayor, okay, fair and square. But if you ever try to give me a bad one, I'm warning you straight up, I'll get even. I take an oath to Jesus Christ, I'll get even. And make sure you tell your four rat stooges the same goddam thing. You demanding a double share, you piece of shit, you never took a chance in your entire life. If I had control of this mangy gang, I wouldn't even give you a G-note a month, much less two shares. One last thing, don't ever pull any more of that rank shit on me, like ordering me into this office this morning. When you're cutting up the kind of money we cut up, I'm the guy that ranks, the guy that makes it possible, not sitting on my ass behind a big desk. So stick all that rank jazz up your ass, we're all equal."

Riley turned on his heel and walked out of the deputy inspector's office right through the door of the squad room without looking at anyone, not even his partner, Bill McMahon. He headed down the hall right out of the building and walked uptown all the way to East 14th Street before he finally calmed down. He stared straight ahead without even a glance at anyone coming his way, only occasionally spitting the bile into the gutter that kept rising up into his mouth. Jesus Christ, he thought, what a goddam screwed-up world this is. No matter how hard you try to be nice, you get it stuck into you. There isn't any such thing as a one hundred percent nice guy. His old man Mike used to warn him over and over, "Jimmy, you can't be two percent no good and ninety-eight percent nice guy. If you allow the two percent to creep into you, you might as well go all the way and be a one hundred percent no-good prick." Maybe in your day, Mike, my beloved father, but not nowadays. Jimmy thought of Leo Durocher, the manager of the Brooklyn Dodgers, and his famous axiom, "Nice guys don't win pennants." You're dead right, Leo baby, dead right. The skids are all greased for you, Jimmy, and you know something, deep down in your nice Irish heart you don't give a fuck. You have a vault full of money, a beautiful business going with Harry, and the whole world is out there for you to take a shot at. It will be like getting rid of an albatross to dissociate yourself from those low-life shitheels.

It was a very long day in the young life of Jimmy Riley, but he survived it. Common sense prevailed and urged him to stay on the merry-go-round as long as he could. He continued to operate as usual, steering clear of the office and the enemy as much as possible, only speaking to the lieutenant, Chick, and Bill McMahon, giving everyone else a very wide berth.

The Joe Pledge investigation, starting out with the force of a hurricane, slowly stagnated to a mild summer breeze. It would have died the natural death the Queens district attorney's office had in mind for it, except for an occasional explosive article by one of the New York tabloid's investigative reporters. One article in particular triggered the rapid demise of Jimmy Riley, and it was an obvious plant, a leak from a high-ranking cop to the reporter who wrote the damaging piece.

It was a simple thing for Jimmy to put the whole thing together, the reasons why he was banished. The planted article alluded to a possible strong connection between Joe Pledge and an anonymous well-known New York vice cop who was rumored to own an estate in Connecticut. This was probably all the ammunition the enemy needed to feed to the pipeline of the mayor's inner circle. From what Jimmy learned some time later, the mayor's dry-out squad exulted at this golden opportunity to give him the boot. There ensued a big discussion as to how to improve the New York squad's image, and the purifying agent agreed on was to break Jimmy Riley's sword, rip off his epaulets, and send him back to uniform patrol. The great protector of integrity and vaunted foe of corruption, Bill O'Dwyer, issued these immortal words as the death knell to Jimmy, "I hear that this kid Riley has more money than you can jump over, so let's get rid of him before we have a real problem."

Bang, you're dead. That was the end of the glorious plain-clothes world of Jimmy Riley. When Jimmy later got the rundown on the exact words that the mayor used to expel him, he couldn't help smiling at the crack about the money. But he laughed and figured what the hell, the easily swayed Irish bastard couldn't jump very high anyway, especially with the load he usually had on.

When the final curtain went down, the news was broken very gently. It came on a lovely late-summer afternoon in beautiful Flatbush. Jimmy was playing softball in a schoolyard near his home with a bunch of the guys he grew up with, the usual Saturday afternoon game for a back a man and a keg of beer, when a radio car pulled up to the schoolyard. A young patrolman got out of the car and said, "Who's Jimmy Riley?"

Jimmy, who was playing second base, saw the radio car pull up to a stop and immediately felt a sense of disaster. When he heard the cop call his name he ran over and said, "What's up, officer?"

"Are you Officer James Riley?"

"That's me, kid."

"Okay, Riley, I have an order here for you to report to the chief's office at three o'clock this afternoon. I hate to bother your ball game, but I went to your house first and your wife told me where I could find you. You better get cracking, you don't have a helluva lot of time and this sounds very important. Come on, I'll drive you home."

Jimmy waved a quick goodbye to all his pals, got home, showered, dressed, and drove to police headquarters immediately. The bad-news bunch were all waiting for him, Dan the deputy, the learned-looking lieutenant, two shoo-fly lieutenants Jimmy hardly knew, and two clerical officers, wise guys.

"The chief wants to see you alone," Dan said, scarcely able to conceal a big smile. He ushered him into the chief's private office and said, "Here's Officer Riley, Chief," and made a hasty exit out the door.

The chief was poring through a mass of papers on his desk, and as Jimmy stood there at attention waiting for the chief to address him, he realized that he hardly knew the man. It seemed almost imcomprehensible, here he had worked for him as part of the most prestigious squad in The Job for about two years and he could barely remember seeing him at most three times. What a contrast to his relationship with the former chief. But then too, as he looked the chief over he realized that he was just as much a stranger to the chief as the chief was to him. He knew by reputation that he was a quiet, studious person, an excellent administrator, and a nice, decent man. He was almost totally bald, in his early sixties, with thick, black-rimmed spectacles, and he looked awfully old to Jimmy as he bent over his desk. He looked up and motioned Jimmy to a chair opposite his desk. There was a knock on the door and Dan entered, but the chief put up his hand and said, "Excuse us, Dan. I'd like to speak to Riley alone."

Dan bowed out as obsequiously as the lowest lackey in the king's court.

Riley sat down opposite the chief and waited for the death sentence.

The chief looked up from his desk and said, "Jimmy, I'm afraid I don't know you too well. That is personally, of course. But I'm going through your records and I do think you've done some fine work for me. I can see from your arrest record here in front of me that you've been a pretty good man in the squad, and the lieutenant tells me that you've done excellent work."

"Thank you, Chief."

"However, I'm sorry to say that I have a recommendation from the mayor's office to relieve you of your duties here and place you back on patrol. This is very disturbing to me, but as you know, you can't fight City Hall. But tell me, Jimmy, is there anything you've done that could have caused this directive? Is there anything I should know, anything you want to tell me?"

Jimmy looked the chief right in the eye. Is there anything that could have caused this directive? No, Chief, not what I've done, it's what I haven't done, you poor honest, ignorant dupe. What I haven't done is give the mayor's whores a piece of the action they were too scared to get themselves. What I haven't done is give your ass-kissing pig-faced pal of a deputy my end of his two shares for sitting on his fat Irish ass behind a desk while I go out and take all the chances.

"No, sir. I can't think of anything that I've done wrong. I haven't had any problems either with any collars I've made, the courts, or any superior officers. A good guess is that I've probably been around too long, almost six years. After all, you're my third chief inspector and that must constitute some sort of record. Chief, it's a funny job, sooner or later you're bound to step on somebody's toes, and I guess I stepped on someone who was a friend of the mayor's."

"Well, Riley, I'm honestly sorry to drop you. You seem like a nice sincere young man."

"Thanks again, Chief."

"Jim, have you any preference as to which precinct you would like to be assigned to?"

"Yes, Chief, somewhere near my home. Somewhere in Flatbush, Coney Island, or Boro Park."

"No problem, Jim, I'll take care of that. I want you to keep in touch with me, and if this blows over without any scandal I'll see if I can place you in the Detective Bureau, I think you might make a good one."

"That's very thoughtful of you, Chief. Thanks again." Riley stepped forward, shook hands with the chief, turned and went out the door. The welcoming committee were all in the squad room waiting silently, with mock gloom on their faces. Jimmy stepped by the professorial lieutenant, shook his hand, and said, "Thanks a lot, boss, you're a good guy." He just looked at the others, turned his back on them, and walked out the squad room door for the next to the last time. Fuck them.

He walked out of headquarters and got into his car and drove back to the schoolyard in Flatbush. The game was over, his team had lost. He chipped in his buck and had a couple of nice cold beers. He shrugged off all the questions caused by the radio car urgently rousting him, telling the guys that it was top-secret shit. With a couple of crisp cold beers in his belly he felt strangely exhilarated, high as a kite, free and happy to at last be rid of the plainclothes job, as free and happy as he had been when he first landed it. A strange paradox. He knew deep down that he would make only a token appearance as a beat cop and then pack The Job in. If no one went out of his way to bother him and Harry, they would make millions together. He whistled softly to himself as he put his head back and drank his beer. At the last count, a couple of months ago, they had over a half million in the vault in the bank on Church Avenue. And only God knows how much they had in transit, what the runners and the private players owed.

His ultimate decision finally entrenched in his mind, free and easy, and nice and high from five or six beers, Jimmy said good-bye to his baseball pals and went straight home. This was a night to celebrate. He told Kay to put on her best dress, he called up Nick Venuto, his favorite limousine chauffeur, and proceeded to go on the town, to make the rounds of all his favorite nightclubs. A new life was beckoning somewhere out there, and Jimmy Riley was getting ready for it.

There were no sad goodbyes this time around when Jimmy went to the squad office for the very last time to clean up his files and some unfinished business. Only Chick and young Bill McMahon came up to shake his hand and wish him luck. Jimmy spotted Gordon on the fringe and gave him the eye to meet him outside. He waited on the street for a few minutes, beginning to doubt whether Gordon would come out. Sure enough, after about five minutes he joined Jimmy.

"Whadda you say, Lenny, let's go down the corner to Flanagan's and have a goodbye drink."

"Fine, Jim, whatever you say."

They walked into the bar and Jimmy ordered a Cutty and water and Gordon a beer.

"Listen, Jimmy, believe it or not, I was really sorry you got the gate the other day. Honest, I was shocked when I heard it."

"Lenny, you're full of shit, like always. You don't like me and I don't like you, so let's level with each other and cut out the 'sorry' bullshit."

"You're really murder, Jimmy, but if that's the way you feel, fine with me."

"Good. Just listen to what I have to say, it won't take too long. In spite of our differences, I'm sure you'll find out after I'm gone that I always leveled with you and the other guys. Here's the list of spots I pick up. Do whatever the hell you want with them. The amounts are precisely correct, but there is also a very generous hat for picking up their money and taking particular care of them. For some strange reason, you always doubted me, probably because you guys intrinsically doubt everyone, being such fucking doublecrossers yourselves. But you'll see, my list will check out perfectly. Now in turn, here's what I expect from you guys, and you know who I mean by you guys. According to the ground rules we laid out some time back, I'm supposed to get an even split for six months after I'm flopped. That's supposed to apply to me or any of us who get the ax, right? Am I correct? Well, I'm entitled to that split for the next six months and I want it each and every month, get it? Now, most important of all, I don't want you or any of the other guys breaking Harry Gross's balls just because he's a great friend of mine. Is that clear enough?"

"Sure, Jimmy, sure thing. That's the way we all ruled about the split, you're entitled. And I promise you personally we won't go out of our way to hurt Harry."

"Good enough. Now for Christ's sake I hope someday you guys will realize I've been perfectly honest and aboveboard with you. I'll never understand how you developed such a hard-on for me. Why, you might even get to miss me, most of all that chuckleheaded deputy inspector Danny."

Gordon laughed. "He's not a bad guy. You just don't understand him, never tried to hit it off with him. He's just a little hungry, that's all."

"You're dead right, Lenny, he's a hungry piece of shit. He's brave sitting on his ass behind his desk. I know he put the screws into me, but fuck him. To be honest, I'm glad to get out from under, maybe with me out of the box you'll have complete harmony. So here's goodbye and good luck." Jimmy touched Gordon's glass with his. "Always remember, Lenny, honor thy father and thy mother, and most of all honor Jimmy Riley's last requests." With that, Jimmy turned, walked out of Flanagan's, and never laid eyes on Gordon again for almost three years.

The same night after he bid his fond goodbye to Lenny Gordon, Jimmy did his first tour of uniform patrol in almost six years, since he did a few four-hour ones while in rookie school. The chief had kept his promise, had assigned him to a quiet precinct in east Flatbush where the only ones out after midnight were the milkman, the breadman, and the birds. The second night on patrol he made an arrangement with his mother, who lived a couple of miles from the precinct, to leave her terrace door open, an alarm clock next to the couch out there, and a bed lamp to read by. As soon as the patrol sergeant gave him his first "see," Jimmy would get into his car, which he conveniently parked nearby, and go to his mother's. He would read until he was tired enough to fall asleep. He never needed the alarm clock, because his mother, God bless her, would wake him up in plenty of time and cook a nice hot breakfast for him before he reported back to the station house to conclude his tour.

"Momma, please, you don't have to do this, wake me up and make my breakfast. If you keep this up I won't come here at night, it's an imposition on you."

"Shut up, James. Be quiet. How about you? You're so good to your mother I wouldn't dare think of not doing this for you."

"You're great, Mom, you really are. Gee, it's wonderful to hear you say I'm good to you. I remember when you were going to kill me when I was single and skipped paying you room and board."

"James, you were terrible. But I only got mad 'cause I knew you were making lots of money for a young boy and couldn't give your mother seven dollars a week. You spent all your money on clothes and girls. You never saved a cent."

"What's wrong with that, Momma? But didn't I tell you that I'd be rich someday and fill your apron with hundred-dollar bills, real hundred-dollar bills?"

"You did, James, and you really filled my apron. But I'm always worried about you getting into some kind of trouble, even though I know you're a good boy. All this money, the way you live, where does it all come from?"

"Not from whores and not from dope, Momma. It all comes from nice friendly bookmakers. How many times did you, Pop, and I discuss it, the gambling business? It's a dumb law."

"Well, I hope and pray you don't do anything wrong, James. If you ever got into trouble I'd die."

"Relax, Mom, I'll never get into trouble. I'm too smart."

"That's the real trouble with you, James, you're too damn smart for your own good. And what's this all about, you wearing a uniform? Surely that's a sign of some kind of trouble. I asked your father and he said it's nothing. He said it'll do you good, a taste of the uniform."

"There isn't anything wrong, Mom, I swear. It's just that big bullshit Irish mayor from County Mayo where Poppa and Grandpa came from. The guy you and Pop always loved. He just decided to give me the hook, just like that. I swear to God, Mom, I didn't do a thing wrong."

"If you say so I believe you, James."

"Mom, I have to tell you something. I didn't tell Mike yet or even Kay, but I'm telling you first on account of you make such good bacon and eggs."

"Come on, now, no flattery. What is so important you have to tell me?"

"Mom, I'm quitting, packing The Job in. I'm getting out and going into another business altogether."

"Oh, my God, James, don't quit The Job. What about your pension?"

"Mom, for God's sake, that's twenty-five years from now if I stay in The Job. You must be kidding."

"I'm not kidding. A pension is a wonderful thing, James, especially when you get old. Look at your father, retired now, he gets over four thousand dollars a year."

Jimmy looked at his mother with love in his eyes. How he loved her, what a wonderful lady she was. The old man gets four thousand a year. Christ, I spend that much on singing waiters. I spent over a thousand cabareting with Kay the night I got flopped. How could Momma understand my life?

"Okay, Mom, I have to go, it's been a real tough midnight-to-eight. The breakfast was great, here's fifty dollars for your waitress tip. Give me a kiss and forget about pensions and me getting into trouble. I love you, Mom."

The midnight-to-eight patrols were spent at Jimmy's mother's house and passed pleasurably and swiftly. Next, there was a week of four-to-twelve tours. During this week more wise guys from New York City walked the streets of Flatbush with him than there were housed on one tier of any self-respecting prison. Jimmy could not help wondering when he walked his beat accompanied by a couple of his gorilla friends what would happen if he ran into some kind of bank robbery or ordinary stickup. Whose side would they be on? But he knew that they came to prove their loyalty to him, to show him respect and bolster his morale. It made him feel good that so many guys came to visit and commiserate with him, but he cut them off when too much sympathy came forth. He assured everyone that he was glad the honeymoon was over and that it was time to start a new pursuit.

The eight-to-four daytime tours followed the four-to-midnight, and at the conclusion of the last day tour Jimmy decided to make his move. He asked to see the precinct captain, who was a former plainclothes lieutenant and a good friend of his.

The captain led Jimmy into his office and greeted him warmly, gripping his hand hard. "How are you, Jimmy? You look sharp in your blue uniform. I'm surprised it still fits you after all the years of the good life."

"Thanks, Walter. It's a little tight around my ass, but I managed to stay in fairly good shape. Not easy, with all the booze you get to drink in our racket."

"Truer words were never said. But thank God you're still a young guy, and you got talent. You're going a long way, Jimmy."

"That's what I'm here to see you about, Walter. I sure am going a long way, a long way the hell out of this job."

"Come on, Jim, take it easy, don't let this flop discourage you. I know you're used to excitement and that this precinct is like a morgue, I can understand that. But you made plenty of friends, good friends. You'll be transferred to the Detective Bureau in a few months. If you feel like it, take a couple of weeks off toward your vacation time. Relax, take your wife and the kids up to the country. When you come back you'll have a whole new attitude. You'll feel like a million dollars again."

"Thanks, Walter. I really mean it, you've always been a nice guy, but fuck it. I'm all finished with this shit. There was a time when you could count on guys being honorable in The Job, now you're lucky if half of them are. As far as I can see, it's all downhill. I'm up to my ears in all this backbiting shit, and sure as hell I'm never going to get a detail as long as that Irish prick is the mayor. So, Walter, here goes, I'm going while the going's good."

Riley took his shield off his uniform coat, unbuckled his holster and gun, and laid them on the captain's desk. He said, "I hope the next guy who gets this tin will have as good a time with it as I did. I sincerely mean that, Walter."

"Jimmy, maybe they'll retire your shield. You know, like they retired Babe Ruth's uniform."

They both laughed. "Not a bad idea, Walter."

"Right, Jim, and just by the look on your face I know I can't talk you out of what you're doing, so I won't try. But you forgot one thing."

"What?"

"Your summons book, copper."

"Holy Christ, you're right." He reached into his rear pants

pocket and took out his summons book and placed it on the captain's desk.

The captain opened it and looked at the first page. It was almost black from disuse. "You're some goddam cop, Riley. You never even issued your first summons."

They both laughed uproariously, and it broke the slight tension between them.

"Jimmy, you were always a thousand percent with me when I was a lieutenant in charge of the borough squad, and I don't forget easily. If ever I can do something for you, please don't hesitate to ask me. Now goodbye, and the best of luck. I'm sure you'll succeed in whatever you elect to do."

"Thanks a million, Walter. I appreciate that."

Jimmy shook hands, walked out of the captain's office, waved goodbye to the cops in the station house, and went down the street and got into his car. He took his hat and uniform jacket off and threw them into the back seat. He put his head back for a moment. Holy Christ, he was a civilian. What a relief, he no longer was a cop.

To avoid the inevitable avalanche of phone calls and endless stupid questions, Jimmy went right home the day he quit and phoned a friend of his in Florida and asked him to look for a house he could rent in the Palm Beach area. A few days later he flew down to Florida with Kay and the kids, enrolled his oldest boy in private school, and did nothing but swim and play golf for a month.

Before he left New York he had discussed all his moves with Harry and given him his private phone number in Florida in case of any trouble. During his absence things had run smoothly, and when Harry and Augie picked him up at the airport on his return, Jimmy looked so tanned and fit, Harry said, "You look absolutely great, Jimmy. Whadda you gonna do now, try for a screen test?"

Jimmy laughed, happy as hell to see both of them. "Not with these buck teeth and this broken nose, but maybe I'll get my teeth capped and my nose fixed and take your advice."

"You could play Lawrence Tierney's part as Dillinger with all your experience as a robber. You have to admit, you always were some fucking actor."

"Especially the day I first shook you, you little Jew prick."

They all roared and Jimmy knew that Harry and Augie were as glad to see him as he was to see them. Jesus, it was good to be back in New York, he thought, as he rode along the highway from the airport and looked straight ahead. What a town, my town. God, I love New York.

"Jimmy, have you decided to do something? What are your plans? You can't lay back too long, you have to get some legitimate scam, or else the world will know we're partners, close as we are."

"You're right, Harry, I know I do. I thought a lot about what the hell I would do when I came back from Florida. Tell you what I've got in mind, this will kill you. Let's buy a nightclub. For Christ's sake, we've hung out in enough of them and spent enough to buy the Copa and Latin Quarter combined, so I should know a little about the business. Not a real big joint, Hesh, maybe a medium-size supper club. Somewhere on the East Side in the Fifties, that's the money belt. There's always some place for sale, so we'll all nose around and keep our ears to the ground and we'll come up with something. I'll speak to the division guys, they're all good friends of mine, and they know when someone takes a piss in their ball park."

"A great idea, Jim. I like it already, especially all the nice broads we'll get to meet; and we're bound to get some good horse customers out of the joint. Let's get to work on it right away."

Within two weeks they found just the place that suited them, in the low Fifties between Park and Madison avenues. It was owned by a small-time mobster friend of Jimmy's who had bought it for his sweetheart. He was getting a little old and a little short in the pocket, and though he dearly loved his girlfriend, he couldn't afford to keep her in the style to which she was accustomed and at the same time lose money in a club she did not have the vaguest idea how to operate. A suitable figure was agreed on, and after putting together the necessary camouflage to apply for a liquor license, the deal was consummated. Jimmy put up the cash for the place, using one of their workers, a guy called Sheeny Mike, as a front co-partner. This was to legitimize the financial framework for the holier-than-thou liquor authority.

The introductory session with the liquor board was such a joke to a hip ex-New York vice cop like Jimmy that he almost laughed in their faces. They questioned him as closely as if he were a criminal, and Jimmy knew that most of them would take a hot stove and come back for the smoke. Jimmy had worked the dregs of New York for six solid years and knew that there were more licensed deadfalls, fag joints, and whorehouses than there were in the twin cities of Sodom and Gomorrah. The one thing that made him refrain from telling the liquor-board investigators and commissioners to stop kidding the public and to stick the investigation up their asses was the innate realization that everyone was out to make a buck, himself most of all, so he went along with their act. After about two months of this charade, Jimmy received his liquor license. He had now finally consummated the last of his boyhood dreams; he had been a sailor and a cop, and now he owned his own nightclub.

The club was a little jewel of a place. The wise guy's girl didn't know how to operate a business, but she sure had a great flair for decorating. Everything was in superb taste, and the day Jimmy received his license the club opened for business and was off and running. Jimmy operated the place strictly as a supper club, opening for cocktails at five in the evening and then on into the wee hours of the morning. The division plainclothesmen and the local precinct cops were good friends, or soon became good friends of Jimmy's, and only gave him lots of help, never any bother. He could run as late into the night as he wanted if he had a good crowd.

Jimmy found out one vital thing early in the nightclub business: the more people drank, the later it got, the more they spent. It was not at all unusual for the club to be jammed at eleven o'clock, half full at one o'clock, and then really packed at three in the morning. Jimmy put in a show calculated to appeal to big spenders and knock-around guys, the type that he figured would be his best customers. He had as entertainers a few of the old-timers from the Club 18, which had been torn down, and two really great piano players. His kind of people loved both the at-

mosphere and the entertainment, and it soon became an in place
for New Yorkers with lots of money. Jimmy, always impeccably
dressed in a dinner jacket, worked the floor every night with his
maître d', Dutch Macey, and not even his best friend could buy a
drink at the bar without a necktie and jacket. Everything was
expensive enough to keep the shit out. The prices were high, the
food was excellent, and the drinks were good. The money began
to roll in, not as good as plainclothes, he had to admit, but not too
bad for a legitimate businessman.

While Kay and the kids were living in Florida, Jimmy sold his
house in Brooklyn, sent all the good furniture to Connecticut, and
took a well-appointed three-room suite in a fashionable residential
hotel off Park Avenue, only a few blocks from the club. From this
apartment Jimmy transacted whatever gambling business came up
in the course of a day. Harry had been correct, the nightclub was
greatly enhancing their gambling operations. Harry was in the
club almost every night, and Jimmy made sure that anyone who
resembled a worthwhile bettor received Harry's number at the
office. Jimmy, meanwhile, introduced him to everyone worth
knowing, top wise guys in to pay a courtesy visit to Jimmy and to
catch the show, and best of all, plenty of Wall Street brokers,
lawyers, and top businessmen anxious to have a reliable bookmaker to call. Harry loved the role he was cast in, dressed to kill
every night and perfumed up like a Turkish whorehouse, shaking
hands with top cops and wise guys like a real Sherman Billings-
ley.

There had to be a disappointment or two along the way to mar
Jimmy's advent into this new successful phase of his life, and one
of them really hurt. About two months after he had opened the
club, he sent a message to Chick O'Mara to meet him at his hotel.
At two thirty in the afternoon Jimmy opened the door and greeted
Chick as he stepped off the elevator. They hugged each other, and
Jimmy was really delighted to see him.

"What have I contracted, malaria, the clap, or some obscure
communicable disease, you Irish fuck? Why haven't you been up
to see me?"

"Jimmy, honest to God, we all got strict orders to stay away from your joint. Ordered under pain of death, or an even worse fate, ex-communication from the chief inspector's squad."

"Really? No shit, Chicko? On whose explicit orders, my pal Dan, the pig Irish deputy?"

"Right the first time, Jimbo. What the hell am I going to do? I was really dying to see you and go in and spend a few bucks."

"Forget about it, Chick, forget it, don't get in any jackpot over me. I figured something like that was laid down when you and McMahon never showed in the place. But thank the Good Lord anyway, the club is doing just great without the patronage of the big spenders in the chief's office. Before I'd let them in to mix with my high-class clientele I'd probably have to order new suits for Gordon and his boys so they wouldn't look out of place. Tell me something, Chick, are those animals dressing any better now that they're getting good and rich?"

"Not much better, Jimmy, maybe a little. I think they buy in Moe Levy's now, he gives them the cops' discount. You have to admit, that's a big step up from Crawford's and Howard's."

"Cops' discounts? I can't believe those guys. Well, the hell with those bastards, they'll die with all their money buried in the yard, where I hope it rots. I heard via the grapevine that you were anxious to get hold of me, that's why I sent the message to meet me here. What's on your mind?"

"I hate like hell to tell you this, Jimmy, but I was elected to break the bad news."

"Anything short of a pronouncement of death by the electric chair is good news coming from that office. Come on, for Christ's sake, tell me."

"Well, here goes. Jimmy, they cut you out of your split. I was supposed to bring you a four-month split, remember. I can't really believe you're out of The Job that long. Anyway, the money for your cut was supposed to be put aside every month, at least that's what I thought, so the other night at the meeting I asked them to give it to me so I could bring it to you. They, 'they' meaning Gordon, told me to forget about your cut, that the squad voted you down, no cut whatsoever. I asked for a general vote and Gordon told me to mind my own fucking business, to forget about you."

Jimmy listened, unbelieving. He became incensed, enraged. He got up out of his chair and walked over to the bar at the end of the room and poured himself a glass of Scotch. He couldn't speak for a few minutes, he just took a couple of deep swallows of his drink and paced back and forth until he finally got himself under control.

"You know, Chick, I'll never understand those guys. You know as well as I do that I gave them a hundred percent square shot from the minute you guys took over, and from their first day in the office they've done nothing but fuck me. This is the last straw. I'd love to beat the shit out of Gordon and Danny. Those weasels know goddam well the six-month rule applies to anyone who gets flopped, regardless of who you are. It isn't only the money that drives me crazy, it's the stupidity of those rotten cheapskates. Suppose I had a little stool pigeon in me and tipped over a few hot stoves to the chief or the P.C., or even threatened to, they'd come running to me like scared rabbits. Those stupid bastards would probably screw anyone who had a split coming, not for any reason or certainly not for any noble purpose, just to line their pockets with a few extra thousand that rightfully belongs to another guy. Someday I'll get even with those hungry fucks. Well, the hell with them, Chick. But one last thing, you tell them point blank if they fuck around with any of Harry's joints, I'll put a bullet in that fat prick Gordon's heart. I swear I will."

"Jimmy, take it easy. You know how sorry I am about all this. But honest, there wasn't anything I could do. I'm just hanging in there, just like you told me to. One thing you can almost be sure of, Jimmy, they won't fuck Harry around on account of you. I'm positive of that."

"What makes you so sure?"

"This. Gordon made a big speech about honoring Harry's commitment because of you. He warned everyone not to bother Harry. I'm sure the big prick is scared shitless of you since that incident in the wire room. He told me himself he thought you were crazy."

"Let him try something, he'll find out."

Chick got up to leave and hesitantly stuck out his hand to shake with Jimmy. "Jeez, Jimmy, I hope there's no hard feelings between you and me. Honest, I never had so much fun working with a guy as I did with you."

"Ah, cut it out, Chick. How could I ever get mad at you? There's no way I'd ever blame you for this, I know whose fault it is, you can bet your ass on that. But now that you gave me the bad news and the initial shock is over, you can tell the rest of them that Jimmy Riley says to stick the money up their respective asses. I'll always do all right, and when the honeymoon is over for them and they're out of The Job, those stupid fucks will be looking for jobs as bank guards or Stock Exchange messengers and I'll be a millionaire living on the French Riviera."

That bit of bad news was the last Jimmy heard from the Four Horsemen for some time, and if he never heard another morsel from them, his life would have been perfectly serene. Meanwhile, the supper club was doing fantastic business, and since Jimmy left The Job he decided to raise his salary with Harry to fifteen hundred a week. Every time Jimmy sat Harry down and inquired of their business, Harry would raise his eyebrows ecstatically and reply that it was booming, better than ever. With the money he was earning in the club and his raise in salary with Harry, Jimmy did not have to scale down his way of living. He wasn't making his periodical trips to the bank vault every month, but he consoled himself with the idea that he would make a real healthy visit when he got around to taking a decent split out of the joint bankroll that was steadily increasing and securely lying in the vault he shared with Harry.

Another business opportunity came up for Jimmy from a completely unexpected source. A little Jew bookmaker named Murray was a steady bar customer at the club, one of the great all-time Scotch drinkers. Jimmy used to kid him that he had to be Irish with a name like Murray and the way he could drink. One night Murray confided to Jimmy that he was going a little bad financially, and worse yet, being harassed by the downtown squads. Jimmy suggested a meeting the next day with little Murray and it resulted in the idea of putting a horse room in the club during the day when it was closed to legitimate business. Why waste a perfectly beautiful room during the daytime? This brightened Murray's outlook on life consideraby, and before the week was out the main-office squads gave it the okay and Jimmy and Harry bankrolled the operation. The room was so classy a place to bet horses that the minimum wager accepted was five dollars.

In nothing flat the horse room was a smash, the only trouble being that for the first five or six weeks they could not win a nickel. To Jimmy, this defied Einstein's Law, Newton's Law, and any other law of logic and gravity. If you bet horses, sooner or later you must go. How could they handle a couple of thousand a day in fives and tens and still lose? Jimmy, ever on his mettle as a super-sleuth, set about to solve his most important case. It didn't take too long. He placed his head man in the club, Larry, a very smart wop, in the horse room during the day and had him close out every race a few minutes before the scheduled post time by drawing a red line as the cutoff beneath the last bet on the sheet. This was done over the strong protests of Murray's head man, Louie, who was a thief and naturally had a beautiful thing going for him by slipping in a few late winners. Murray, usually afloat in a sea of Scotch, was unaware and Louie was used to getting away with murder. Jimmy hit Louie one solid whack on the jaw that settled both Louie and all the protests.

Louie faded out of Murray's life lucky he still had his own, and the daytime horse room in the nighttime supper club prospered beyond all expectations. It was like a new toy to Jimmy and he loved it. He had very seldom visited any of his and Harry's horse rooms when he was a cop, only when absolutely necessary. Now that he was an American citizen and civilian again, he was around the horse room at least a couple of hours a day, keeping an eye on things. They gave Murray the usual third, and Jimmy received an extra five hundred a week as the main man in the room. He would have worked it for nothing, he loved the action so much.

There were occasional problems that cropped up every week or so in the mutual enterprise of Jimmy and Harry, but overall, things ran very smoothly. Still, there was one thing that Jimmy was bothered by, that gradually began to gnaw at his mind. Almost a year had rolled by, and now the place was a fixture. Harry was there his usual three or four nights a week, taking bows like a celebrity. This didn't bother Jimmy, it amused him, because he knew Harry lusted to be a big-timer, so good luck to him in his new role. What started to eat Jimmy up was the arrival almost every night of some real high rollers whom Harry would jump up to meet and greet them like they were blood relatives. Jimmy knew them all, if not directly, by reputation. They were blood relatives all right, they would drink your blood. Harry would sit and eat and drink at their table as long as they stayed. Jimmy knew that Harry was in his glory being a big shot. Mixing with top cops and top wise guys like they were his best friends was his idea of paradise. He was much too fond of Harry to criticize him about this display. He was happy for him, glad in most ways he was there to meet the guys who could do him some good.

However, he had grave reservations about a few of the high rollers constantly coming into the club. It soon bothered him enough to take Harry aside and ask, "What the hell are you doing being so chummy with Sam and Meyer Boston? And that blood-sucker, Charley Kay? What the hell is this all about? I hope you have no intentions of dealing to them, they'll take your balls off and hang them out to dry."

"Come on, Jimmy, don't be silly. You think I don't know any better than to deal to them?"

"You better make sure I don't ever hear about it if you do. Look, Harry, our business was built on two-, five- and ten-dollar horse players and fifty- and hundred-dollar sports players. Today we take a little bigger shot, because we can afford to. But always remember, the small guys made us rich, so we'll stay in our own bailiwick. Sure we can take a hundred or two on a horse, or five hundred to a thousand on a game, but stay within our guidelines and we can't miss."

"Jesus Christ, Jimmy, you sound like a schoolteacher. I know what I'm doing, for Christ's sake. Don't start telling me what to do."

Jimmy leaned across the table toward Harry and his eyes were blazing. For the first time in his life he felt like belting Harry, and one look at his face and Harry pulled back. "Now you listen to me, I'm telling you what to do, period. I don't like those fucking vultures, the Bostons and Charley Kay. They will eat you alive. Drink you like a cup of tea. They've forgotten more about the gambling racket than you'll ever know. Furthermore, what are you doing eating a couple of nights a week in Frankie and John-nie's with that asshole Broadway detective, Tommy Bockmann? That guy only uses people. Where was he when you didn't have shit, holes in your pockets?"

Harry's reply was conciliatory, contrite. "Come on, don't get mad, Jim. Tom's a nice guy, you just don't like him. He's got a real problem at home and I put him on for two fifty a week to do a few things for me. You know, a few heavy pick-ups, things like that."

"Here we go again. You put this guy on without consulting me? What the hell is the idea?"

"For Christ's sake, I didn't think it was a big deal, don't get all upset about this guy. You don't happen to like him, and if you don't like a guy he's like the devil to you. Don't worry, I'll do nothing but earn with him. The two fifty a week doesn't mean a thing."

"Look, Harry, I'm a lot freer to get around now that I'm out of The Job. I think we should sit down a little more often and talk things out, and I think I'll get a little more active in the joints. And there's one thing for sure, I don't want you making any big decisions without first consulting me."

"Jesus Christ, Jimmy, I put a detective on for two fifty a week. Is that in your opinion a big decision?"

"It isn't the two fifty, get that straight. That doesn't bother me at all. I just don't like this guy, period. In my book he's a fucking scrounger who'd sell you down the river in a minute flat. Now as long as you're getting balky about this guy, I'm going to take a stand. You get rid of that prick at the first opportunity. Tell him anything, give him Arpège, but get fucking rid of him. You know something, Harry, I don't want to argue with you, 'cause we've never really had the first argument. Just remember one thing, our first argument could be our last argument. We either get along together or I'm through. You try to pull some shit I don't approve of and you can give me my end and go fuck yourself. You under-stand that?"

Harry cringed a little, astonished by Jimmy's vehemence. He could see he was near the boiling point, so he tried to soften him up a bit. "Come on, Jimmy, take it easy, we're too close with each other to beef like this. You know I'd rather die before I'd break up with you. I promise, I'll get rid of Tommy Bockmann first chance I get. One more thing, don't worry about the two Bostons and Charley Kay. I promise I won't do anything with them, I swear to God."

Jimmy looked intently into Harry's face. The brown eyes weren't dancing, they were steady and looked real sincere. He was really crazy about the little Jew bastard and hated to argue with him. They had been through so much shit together and now that it appeared they were on the rise and were really putting together a great operation, ready to make a big score, he knew he had to completely trust him. He believed him.

Jimmy shook Harry's hand and said, "Hesh, I'm sorry I got hot. I apologize. But listen, Harry, everything I point out is for our mutual benefit. You're a big boy now, a real big-timer just like you always wanted to be, but like I said a hundred times before, don't get carried away by these Broadway wise guys. And for Christ's sake, don't fall in love with those wise-ass Broadway detectives, they're all full of shit. Okay, let's have a drink and forget about it. Enough said."

5

THE MONTHS rolled by and business at the supper club, the day-time horse room, and the joint Gross and Riley operation was skyrocketing. Jimmy loved the life he was living, loved his pied-à-terre in New York where he spent weekdays, and his escape hatch to his place in Connecticut where he could walk and play golf and get the whiskey and tobacco fumes out of his head. He only ventured into Brooklyn once a week to see his mother. Harry now took care of all the ice and was constantly in the company of some top cop or other in the city. Jimmy was just as pleased that Harry took over this chore, as he had no desire to run into any of his old squad, and he further felt that this might help to dissociate the idea of their partnership in a few of the more inquisitive minds. There were still some top bosses who insisted that Jimmy, and Jimmy alone, pay them directly. This wasn't too much of an inconvenience, since there were only a few of these contracts, and Jimmy would meet them for a drink and catch up on all the latest developments in The Job.

At the first sign of winter, the first chill winds before a snow-flake fell, Jimmy would rent a house in Palm Beach and send his wife and kids down. The household entourage now included a black maid and a French governess, so Jimmy's wife, Kay, had plenty of time for golf and soon became a pretty fair player. He flew down every other week to spend four or five days playing golf with her and swimming with the kids, finally getting to know them a little bit. They joined a swanky golf club in Palm Beach, and one day when Jimmy and Kay were playing with some friends, they waved a twosome through, Ambassador Kennedy and the Duke of Windsor, with Wally accompanying them along, walking a Scottie dog. The ambassador and the duke thanked them politely and they exchanged the amenities. When they passed out of earshot Jimmy turned to Kay and said, "We've come a long way from Brooklyn, right, sweetheart?" It was an ideal life, the best of everything, a wife and kids to visit and play with in Florida, and a beautiful apartment to come back to and resume the glamorous life in New York City.

Time passed so swiftly that Jimmy found it difficult to believe he had been out of The Job almost two years. He further realized that he did not miss it one goddam bit. He reveled in the nightclub and gambling business, loved every minute of it. Life was rolling along almost too smoothly to last, and sure enough, when the first disquieting rumors started to reach him he refused to believe them. One night a very big bookmaker, a good friend of Jimmy's, came into the club and asked Jimmy over to his table to have a drink. During the course of conversation he mentioned that he laid off a ten-thousand dollar bet on a football game to Harry's office, and when it won the money was a little slow coming up. Jimmy kept a straight face at this startling bit of news, but inwardly was astounded at the size of the bet. He had laid down the law, a thousand-dollar maximum, what the hell was Harry doing taking ten-thousand-dollar hedges?

"What's the matter, Jimmy? Your pal getting a little case of that severe malady, the shorts?"

Jimmy laughed, secretly shaken, and said, "Don't be foolish, Ernie. Harry probably had a ton of money in transit and couldn't get around to you quick enough."

"That's pure horseshit, Jimmy. Like every other bookmaker who amounts to anything, I settle every Tuesday, at the latest Wednesday. Your little friend took over a week to give me my money. I was ready to send someone to go look for him. Jimmy, I love you, kid, you've done a million nice things for me. I know that Harry is a protégé of yours and what you did for him to get him up in the world, so I'm telling you tonight what I think you should know. For one thing, almost every night he hangs out in front of Lindy's with the two Bostons, Charley Kay, and the rest of those cutthroats. If he still has any money left, they'll beat him for it. I only gave him some lay-offs on account of you. And once again, you know what I think of you, so if I were you I'd have a look into Harry's situation."

A broad enough hint, Jimmy thought. Ernie knows that Harry and I are secret partners, there's no bullshitting him, and probably the rest of the world.

"Thanks a lot, Ernie, but I'm dead sure that Harry's all right. For Christ's sake, the joints in Brooklyn are a gold mine, there's no way he could piss through that kind of money."

"Jimmy, now you listen to me, listen to me good. I'm your friend, remember that, and I've been on earth a helluva lot longer than you. I've bumped into Harry a lot since you first introduced us and I always liked the kid. Furthermore, whatever we did together was a million percent until the last few weeks. The last time he gave me some money he looked just a little bit different. You know, he was dressed to the nuts as usual, but his grin seemed a little forced and he looked pale and tired. His face didn't seem to sparkle like it usually does, he seemed worried, tense, like a guy under a lot of stress. Maybe I'm wrong, but you can bet your ass he wasn't the same happy-go-lucky Harry of the last couple of years. Do yourself a favor, Jim, look into it. Okay, I'm talking too much, let's drop the subject and have a drink."

Jimmy sat for a while with Ernie and had a couple of drinks, and though he was smiling and joking on the surface, inside he was churning. He was thinking, I haven't been to that goddam vault to take a good count in over five months. Here I am in the horse room every day like a minor-league Frank Erickson, checking to see that no one beats me out of ten dollars. What a complete asshole. Neglect, sheer neglect, you stupid Irish bastard. I have to get a plan together real quick. First thing tomorrow I'll shoot over to Brooklyn and confront Harry with this bit of great news. Second thing on the agenda, we'll go to the vault on Church Avenue and take a dead count of the bankroll. The last thought gave him a chill down his spine.

Jimmy bowed out of the club early that night and went straight to his hotel, determined to get a good night's sleep. He had laughed and shaken hands with the customers when saying good-night, but as soon as he hit the street for the short walk home, he couldn't shake the sense of impending disaster. He tried to recon-struct the events of the past few months and arrange them in orderly fashion in his mind. He suddenly realized with a sharp impact that he had not seen Harry in almost three weeks, he'd never even been in the club. It further dawned on him that he had not spoken to him on the telephone for over a week, and when he did call it was only a brief how are you, more or less. Why, that little sonofabitch is ducking me and I've been too stupid to see it.

It was a long, long night for Jimmy Riley. He finally read himself to sleep, helped along by a couple of good belts of Cutty Sark to calm his nerves. He called room service for breakfast about nine the next morning and was showered, dressed, and on his way to Brooklyn about an hour later. He never called Harry, Augie, or any wise guy from the hotel phone, so he stopped on Lexington Avenue and called from a drugstore. He dialed Harry at home, his wife answered. He kept his voice nice and gentle. "Hello, sweetheart, this is Jimmy. How are you, how are the kids?"

"Oh, Jimmy, it's you. Everyone is fine. Where have you been? I haven't seen you in ages."

"I know it, kid, and I'm sorry. But we'll get together next week and go out for dinner. Let me speak to Harry, please."

"Gee, don't you know, Jimmy? He's away."

"Away? Where?"

"He mentioned something about Detroit and Chicago. I thought for sure he said he was going with you, on some sort of business, that's why I was surprised to hear your voice."

"No, not me. You must have misunderstood him, you know how fast he talks. Don't worry about it, honey. Augie will know where to get hold of him. It really isn't that important. You sure now, everything's good with you, the kids, everything?"

"Just great, Jimmy. Thanks for calling. See you soon, right?"

"Sure thing. So long, sweetheart."

The plot was beginning to thicken, and so was Jimmy's head. He was starting to get nauseous. What the hell was Harry doing in Detroit and Chicago? That lying little fuck, promising me he would stay away from those high rollers. First the bad news from Ernie, and now this out-of-town shit. And not a phone call to let me know he was going away, in case I needed him. What if one of our real good joints got clipped by the law while he was away and I was in Florida playing golf, who the hell would take care of things? For the love of God, what are we running, some kind of peanut stand? Jimmy went to the drugstore counter and ordered a cup of coffee. He drank it slowly and tried to organize his thoughts, his plan of attack.

Jimmy hailed a taxicab, and gave the driver directions to Church and Flatbush avenues in Brooklyn. It was still not eleven o'clock when he reached there, too early for anyone to be around. He looked over at the National City bank on the corner with a heavy heart. He wasn't ready to investigate it yet. He decided to take a walk along Flatbush Avenue, pausing briefly to take in the lovely architecture of his alma mater, Erasmus Hall. As he looked at Erasmus he thought of all the fun he had there. Dead poor, always broke, but always happy and having a good time. Now, he reflected, maybe I'm on my way to being poor again, but I'm sure as hell not happy about it. Having finished his tour of his boyhood haunts, Jimmy entered the bank and went down the flight of stairs leading to the vaults. He greeted the old bank guard with a big hello and a hearty handshake which contained a ten-dollar bill. When the guard got a sly flash of the ten dollars he almost fell all over Jimmy, and Jimmy secretly smiled and thought that for ten bucks more this guy would give him a cup of nitroglycerin. Jimmy signed his favorite alias, James Redfern, and gave the vault key to the guard, who opened the vault and handed him the closed metal box. Jimmy went into the adjacent private room, the counting room. His hands were trembling as he prepared to open the box. One look at the contents and he immediately knew that something was radically wrong. The box was not nearly as full as usual. It contained bundles of twenty-dollar bills in units of five thousand dollars on the bottom. He rapidly skimmed through the piles, and to his dismay found a lot more thousand-dollar piles than five-thousand-dollar ones. Sixty-two thousand dollars, Holy Christ. Five months ago there had been six hundred and ninety thousand in the same big metal box.

He placed the money back in the box and called his new best friend, the bank guard, who secured it away in the wall of the vaults. He took a walk through the familiar streets of Flatbush for about forty-five minutes and wound up at Leo's candy store, which was their main drop. There were a few of the help around and the guys greeted Jimmy profusely, and he laughed and kidded with them like he didn't have a care in the world. He finally turned to one of the runners and said, "Go upstairs to the wire room and get Augie for me. Tell him I want to see him for a few minutes."

"No good, Jim. He's away for a couple of days."

"Away? For Christ's sake, who's calling the shots in the wire room? Isn't Harry away too?"

"Yeah, Jimmy, they're both away, but I think they went in different directions, not together. Mikie's in charge upstairs while Augie's away, you know that."

"Go up and get him. Tell him to come right down, just for a couple of minutes."

Mikie appeared at Jimmy's side almost immediately and grabbed his hand and shook it enthusiastically, really glad to see him.

"Where've you been, Jim? What's up? You look terrific. Where'd you get the tan?"

"You look terrific too, Mikie, like death warmed over. You'll never lose that horse-room pallor, you'll always look like you're doing life. Why don't you take a vacation like the other two meshuggas and get some sun. Relax. Sun, surf, and swim, the fucking joint will run itself."

"Jeez, Jimmy, I know Harry went out West somewhere a couple of days ago, and Aguie went to Atlanta yesterday to straighten out an office down there that we're dealing to. Augie will be back tonight, that's for sure. I don't know about Harry."

"For Christ's sake, what the hell is going on, Mikie? Chicago, Detroit, Atlanta, what the hell are we doing dealing to these people? Our goddam business is in Brooklyn, maybe a little in Manhattan, but by and large, Brooklyn. Who are these pricks we're dealing to out of town? Are they professionals? Now don't try to shit me, Mike, tell me the truth, and I mean the God's honest truth."

"Jesus, Jimmy, I thought for sure you knew Harry was dealing all over the country. Please, don't blame it on Augie, he was dead set against it. To be perfectly honest, I do think they're pros, and Augie and Harry don't say much, but I think they're kicking our ass in. In fact, I'm pretty sure they're knocking our balls off altogether, just by the way Harry is acting and the way Augie seems so nervous."

Jimmy looked at Mikie. He was ready to explode, but he kept his cool and his voice was as calm and steady as he could keep it. "Okay, Mike, you go back upstairs and go to work. When Augie calls you today, you tell him to come right to the nightclub from the airport. No matter what time he comes in. When you hear from him, you leave a message with Larry if I'm not around. Just make sure that I see Augie tonight. You got that straight?"

"I got it. Jimmy, I hope you're not sore at me and Augie about this out-of-town shit, we're only doing what we're told to do."

"Forget it, Mike. Don't be silly. How the hell could I get sore at you guys? Now you take care, go back to work, and make sure you get Augie to me at the club tonight."

Jimmy shook hands goodbye all around and walked out of Leo's store, headed south on Church Avenue. His head was whirling, he couldn't believe what Mikie had just told him, what he had heard was almost incomprehensible. That lying, fucking Harry. *I promise you, Jimmy, I won't deal to professionals, I swear.* Me believing him, looking into that innocent, conman's face. But it's my own fault, my own goddam fault. What a stupid sonofabitch I am. Stupid, stupid. It was all he kept repeating to himself. He debated whether to grab a cab and go see his mother, but decided that even she couldn't cheer him up today. Besides, one look at the gloom on his face and she would lay down a barrage of questions. Not today, Mom.

He hailed a taxi and told the driver to take him to Manhattan. When he got over the bridge he directed him to the Downtown Athletic Club. He had a good workout, swim, sauna, and massage. He then took a taxi uptown to his hotel. Made himself a stiff double Scotch, and dog-tired, went into a sound sleep for about three hours. He woke up refreshed and extremely alert, just the way he wanted to be when Augie showed up.

The club was about half filled when he arrived about nine o'clock, and he sat with some friends at a corner table in the main room and drank club soda. He was very friendly and at ease at the table, but though he kept a façade of good cheer, his mind kept jumping back to one thing, the amost empty bank vault. About ten thirty his head floor man, Dutch, tapped him on the shoulder and said, "Jimmy, your man Augie's at the bar, waiting for you."

Jimmy excused himself from the table and went out to the far end of the bar to greet Augie. As he approached him, one look at Augie's face was sufficient to confirm his worst fears. Augie's face reminded him of an anti-nuclear-bomb poster, where the father with the doomsday look is clutching his little son to his chest, looking up at a huge mushroom cloud under a stark warning sign: DON'T LET THIS HAPPEN TO OUR CHILDREN.

"How are you, Jim? Something up that's so important you had to see me tonight?"

"I think you know already, Augie. Take your drink and come on up to my office."

Augie gulped down his first drink, ordered another, and with his refill in hand went upstairs with Jimmy.

Jimmy sat behind his desk and motioned Augie to sit in the lounge chair opposite him. Jimmy had a good deal of respect for Augie, knew he was a decent, hardworking, honest guy, and he didn't want to rattle him in any way. But no matter what, one goddam thing for sure, he was going to have Augie tell him the whole truth.

"Now relax, Augie, take it easy. I'm not here to put the D.A. shit on you, but something's going on that I'm not aware of, that I don't know a fucking thing about. But as the bailiff in gambling court says when he swears you in, I want the truth, the whole truth, and nothing but the truth."

The last remark loosened Augie up a little. He grinned, he'd been in gambling court before. He could see Jimmy was a little uptight, but it didn't look like it was directed at him. "Where do you want me to start, Jimmy?"

"We both know where we all started, Augie. You left a good,

moneymaking gas station and I put my money and my ass up for that little, kinky-haired cocksucker. We built a helluva business right there in good old uptown and downtown Brooklyn. But that's beside the point, what the fuck were you doing in Atlanta, and Harry in Detroit and Chicago? Now, Augie, please, answer me these questions and don't bullshit me. You got that dead straight?"

"Jimmy, it had to happen, it couldn't miss, it was bound to happen. Believe me, it's only the past six or eight weeks it all took place. Harry made me promise not to tell you, that we were going to surprise you with all the money we made. He insisted on opening another office, another wire room for the big guys. We called it the western office. From the minute he suggested the idea, I swear to God I was tempted to run right over here and see you. More so, after the first week. But I have to admit, Jim, that little prick has had me mesmerized ever since I left the gas station. I never dreamed we would make the kind of money we made, live the way we do, have it so good. I only thought it would get better and better. I always thought that according to the law of averages, if a guy bet enough, sooner or later he had to go. The percentages are supposedly strictly against the player, that even if he wins at first, eventually he must wind up in the shithouse. But these wise guys we're dealing to in the western office, they're another cup of tea. They're screwing us to death. They bet almost like they had a crystal ball. At first we beat them for a few, then we got buried a little. I wanted to stop, forget about them, but Harry insisted we go further. I told him I wanted your advice, but he screamed at me and told me not to mention a word to you under any circumstances. Jimmy, this is the truth, I swear it is."

Jimmy held up his hands placatingly. "Well, Augie, what the hell are we going to do? The damage is done, let's start fresh. Okay, if you have an idea, let's hear it. How are we for cash? How are the main places doing, the bread-and-butter joints?"

Augie's face was flushed, and Jimmy had a good idea why. There was no way Jimmy was going to tip his mitt about his visit to the vault earlier that day. That was his ace in the hole, for both Augie and Harry.

Augie's voice faltered a little. It was husky, unnatural. "You sure you're ready for the truth, Jimmy?"

"The whole fucking truth, Augie. Start at the beginning, when he first started to deal to the wise guys all over the country. Don't get nervous, don't get excited. I'm not blaming you. But no more horseshit, I want the entire picture, right up until now."

"Well, hold your hat, Jimmy, here goes. We opened the western office about two months ago, at first taking some local big action and then the out-of-town action. Detroit, Chicago, Terre Haute, and Atlanta. The first couple of weeks we won about a hundred, hundred and fifty grand, and I thought to myself, how longhas thhs been going on? We took some lay-offS on horses, Or what was supposeD to be lay-offs, and some baseball action, up to about a thousand a race and five thousand a game. The next few weeks we gave it all back, plus another hundred grand or so of our own cash. That's when I begged Harry to quit."

"Augie, not to interrupt this compelling narrative, but how about all the regular joints, how are they doing? Any problems?"

"No, that's the worst part of it. They're all doing fine. But, Jimmy, here comes the real bad news. I hate to tell you, I swear."

"Let's have it, all of it, for Christ's sake. Most of it is my own goddam fault for being so trusting, so stupid, not watching that con man prick close enough. Go ahead."

"Jimmy, take a good grip on your seat. Last week we lost four hundred and eighty thousand."

"You what? No, say that again."

"Four hundred and eighty grand."

Jimmy whistled softly, shook his head, and sat back in his chair. "Four hundred and eighty fucking grand. The years of hard work and hustle it took us to build a good bankroll, and he wiped it out in nothing flat. I can't believe it. Tell me, did you stop those guys, close the western office? Did you have enough to pay them? How's our reputation, we still own one?"

"Just about, Jimmy, just barely. One more thing, if we have a bad week in the city I'm afraid that we'll have to scrounge around for money. Jimmy, honestly, I feel so bad I could put my head on this desk and cry."

"Listen, Augie, forget about crying and the rest of the 'sorry' shit. There's no sense having any regrets about the past, we'll just have to pick up the pieces and start small again. The way we made all the money in the first place. Don't worry about a bankroll, I'll take care of that."

"But, Jimmy, there's another thing I left out. I think he's into the shylocks pretty good."

"That's his and their fucking headache. As far as I'm concerned, I never okayed one quarter with those animals, and even though plenty of people assume Harry and I are connected, you're the only one that really knows the score, that we're partners. Make sure the western office doesn't open tomorrow, forever for that matter. You go back to Church Avenue to the wire room like nothing happened and take charge again. I'll be over Church Avenue in Leo's every day to get the joints back in shape, to let some of these guys know they got a boss again. When is his nibs coming back?"

"Day after tomorrow."

"Do you know what time his plane gets in?"

"Yeah, about six o'clock. He's going to call me at Leo's sometime in the afternoon and let me know exactly what time so I can pick him up at the airport."

"Okay, you pick him up on schedule. Act like I don't know a thing, like nothing's happened. Just say Jimmy wants to see us to have dinner with him and don't take no for an answer. I don't give a shit what excuse he gives you, make sure you deliver him here. Hand him some bullshit, like there's a new boss giving some of the spots trouble, a real pain in the ass I'm having a problem with. He's been so wrapped up in his high-rolling horseshit world the last couple of months he's forgotten all about cops, and the fact that one murderous cop could knock us out of business. Just make sure you get him here."

"I got you, Jimmy. I'm beginning to feel better already. We never belonged up there in the big leagues anyway, taking five and ten thousand a pop. Personally, I think the little fuck went crazy. We'll do as you say, forget the past and start again the way we got rich in the first place. Don't worry any more about it, I'll deliver him here straight from the plane."

"Atta boy, Augie. Come on, let's go downstairs and have a drink, we both can use one."

Jimmy went to Brooklyn early the next day. He went to the National City Bank, gave the bank guard another ten and he almost flipped, and then emptied the sixty-two thousand out of the vault he and Harry shared and put it with his own money in the vault he shared with his wife Kay. After attending to these financial details, he spent almost the rest of the day closeted with Willie Ricardo, their cashier. He went back over a month's sheets and records of the various spots and was gratified to see that they were all in the black. He spent an hour in the wire room over Leo's with Augie and Mikie clocking the day's action. He was just a bit surprised at the amount of some of the shots they took with private players and their own runners, but overall he was well satisfied that the business was solid and couldn't do anything but win money.

As he went over the figures with Willie and studied the phone action with Augie and Mikie, all he could think about was what a goddam fool Harry was. And he, Jimmy Riley, was twice as stupid for neglecting a gold mine like this. What a dumb bastard he was. How could Harry piss away a moneymaking machine like this to try to be a big-timer, a high roller? But that's life, he thought ruefully, it's like everything else. You never had any money to speak of, suddenly you get lucky and it comes in like an avalanche. The money becomes unreal, and you handle it like Monopoly money, like it's fake. Reality finally sets in when you realize the faucet might get turned off, that you're in danger of going broke.

That thought was really scary, but the one consolation was that, if it had to happen, it was good it did while he was still a young guy. Jimmy had no fear of going broke immediately, far from it. He still had a vault full of his own money and a beautiful home on two gorgeous acres of land in Connecticut, free and clear of mortgages. But that was money he regarded as his wife and kids', to take care of them in case he went to a swift and unjust reward. The kind of life he led, anything could happen.

What bugged him now about Harry pissing away the big bankroll was having to start all over accumulating another one.

He knew it could be done, and a lot quicker with him at the controls. But he had set his original goal at a million dollars, even as short a time ago as last week he had mentally calculated the vault would be at about the million mark by his next visit. He was all set to ask Harry for an okay to invest half of it for them, some in real estate and some in Nevada where a good friend of his, one of the top mob guys, offered him points in one of the projected casinos at twenty thousand a point. From all the talk Jimmy heard, Las Vegas was going to be a real big winner for the wise guys. He was assured that the points would be worth one hundred thousand a rap after a year or two.

The real estate idea was even better. He had become very friendly with a smart real estate guy through playing golf with him at the country club in Connecticut. The guy was right down Jimmy's alley, with plenty of larceny in his heart. He had already set up a blind front for Jimmy to invest in some choice land in the county where he lived, and from all indications the land would quadruple in value in a few years. He had some additional projections for investing in shopping centers for Jimmy and Harry, and other industrial deals that could not seem to miss. Jimmy had romanced the real estate guy to the hilt, inviting him to dinner at his nightclub, having everyone make a big fuss over him when he came in, and putting him next to one of the most beautiful showgirls in town. He really loved Jimmy. Now all the grandiose schemes were temporarily in the shithouse.

But what the hell, he thought, as he worked along with the cashier, clerks, and Augie, at least he had his health and a good business. He laughed like he was the happiest guy in Brooklyn, if not the world. He wore his mask of joviality and good cheer well, even thought his heart was very heavy. At the end of the day's action he took all the key guys to a good Flatbush restaurant and had a great feast of wine, whiskey, steak, and lobster for them. His rapport reestablished and their apprehension allayed, he took a taxi straight home to his New York hotel. He called the nightclub, was assured that everything was fine, and went to bed early with a good book. Tomorrow, James, my boy, is going to be a big day. I wonder how my fucking little friend is going to explain his fling into the big time, why he broke the promises he so sincerely made.

He put his book aside and laid his head back on the propped-up pillows and started to reminisce about Harry, starting from the first day, when he had almost pinched him. What a wonderful relationship they had developed together, what a great business they had built, and best of all, what a great time they had doing it. He had had more fun with Harry than any guy he ever met. Even now, knowing how Harry had demolished them, Jimmy had all he could do to keep from bursting out laughing when he remembered some of the funny things they had done together. Harry was one funny sonofabitch, with a million-dollar sense of humor.

Being very honest with himself, Jimmy had to admit that a lot of their present grief was his own fault.

Augie called from the airport at five thirty the next night. "The plane is on time, Jimmy, we should be in your hotel about seven o'clock."

"Good boy, Augie. Now listen, under no circumstances let him bullshit you out of coming here. Tell him it's a must, absolutely imperative. If he questions you about the western office being closed, tell him I don't know a thing. Act like nothing's up, real calm, but by all means deliver him right straight to the hotel. See you later."

The desk man at the hotel rang Jimmy's suite about a quarter after seven and announced that he had two visitors on the way up. The doorbell rang, Jimmy opened it, and Harry greeted him with a big hug like a long-lost friend, his blood brother, indeed.

"What'll you guys have to drink? Cutty and water okay?"

"Beautiful, Jim, make it a stiff one. I really need a drink. Those airplanes still scare the shit out of me."

Jimmy served the drinks, and after reaching out and tipping glasses good luck with Harry and Augie, said bluntly, "What's all this Detroit and Chicago business, Hesh? What the hell are you doing out there?"

"To be honest, Jimmy, we're getting some lay-offs from a couple of outfits in Detroit and Chicago, and they wanted to meet me and see who they were doing business with. You know, kind of size me up, so I flew out to meet them. Spent a few days with them, had a real good time. You'll love them when you get to meet them."

"What makes you think I want to meet anyone from Detroit or Chicago or Atlanta?" Jimmy's voice got a little belligerent, took on a sharp edge. Harry shook at the sudden change, the slight choking in Jimmy's voice. Five minutes ago he'd hugged and kissed him, two minutes ago he'd handed him the nice tall Scotch in his hand. Now Jimmy was starting to get his maniac look, his eyes narrow, his mouth set tight, and he practically spat out his words. Harry didn't answer, he was temporarily speechless.

Nice and easy, slowly, Jimmy continued, "I said what makes you think I give one good fuck about meeting anyone from Chicago, Detroit, Atlanta, or Shit Creek, for that matter? You heard me correctly, didn't you? Three big cities where you and Augie were gallivanting around instead of minding the store in Brooklyn. Do you by some peculiar twist in your brain figure that you are the Jewish Frank Erickson? Do you aspire to be a national figure in the gambling racket like Frank, or Gil, or Sleep Out Louie? Remember, again I tell you, we got rich in Brooklyn, and now you insist on dealing nationwide. You dumb cocksucker, I told you ice-cold at least ten times to stay away from Broadway, to stop hanging outside Lindy's with those bloodsuckers, and to stay away from that asshole detective Tommy Brockmann. Did I not? Now talk, for Christ's sake, get it off your chest like a man. And don't lie, or I swear to God I'll kill you right here in this hotel room."

Jimmy was shaking with rage. He had not meant to go this far, but the sight of Harry opposite him, the memory of all the broken promises, of a heartsick Augie telling him about the one-week $480,000 loss, and the stark picture of the almost empty bank vault imbedded in his brain almost drove him out of control.

"Jimmy, please calm down, don't get excited. It's not as bad as you think. We'll be all right, you'll see. Don't worry about a thing."

"Don't worry about a thing. You sit there and have the fucking nerve to tell me don't worry about a thing. What about the western office you opened without first discussing it with me? You know goddam well I would never approve of dealing to wise guys. For Christ's sake, don't you know by now that this is a fucking sucker's game. Jesus, Mary, and Joseph, where did the money and all the good living come from, wise guys? You stupid fuck. And I'm twice as stupid for not keeping a closer eye on you, for believing you. Go ahead, keep talking."

Harry was flushed and hesitant, he wished he was in Russia, China, Outer Mongolia, anywhere but opposite the Irish Inquisition, Jimmy. He gulped his drink to steady down. "Honestly, Jim, Augie and I wanted to surprise you. We figured we'd make a fortune with that western office. I had a good man on the wire and Augie supervised it. We didn't get robbed, we just lost our money on the legit, a real run of bad luck."

"How much?"

"Not too bad, about one hundred and fifty grand."

"How much have we left in the bankroll?"

"About four hundred grand, give or take a few," Harry lied in his teeth.

"About four hundred grand, is that it? You know I oughta kick the living shit out of you right here just for lying, you rotten little prick. You know how much there is left in that vault? Have you forgotten with all your lying shit and fucking duplicity that I, Jimmy Riley, have also had a key to the vault from the day we started? Have you forgotten that I put up fifty grand next to yours to get us started, besides my Irish ass?"

Harry's mouth fell open. He collapsed back against the lounge chair he was sitting in and put out his hands as if to ward off a blow. He was sweating. "It's not all that bad, Jim, I have another vault in a New York bank I transferred money to for the sake of convenience."

"How much did you put there? What's left?"

"About two hundred grand."

"Two hundred. I hope this time you're not lying, that it's really there, because I took the sixty-odd grand that was left in the bankroll vault in Brooklyn and transferred it to my own vault. At least we'll have some sort of bankroll to keep going with, I made sure of that. I closed your goddam western office yesterday, you can forget about that fucking fiasco."

"I guess you're right, Jimmy. I'm really sorry about this. I meant no harm, didn't mean to do anything wrong."

"What do you mean, you didn't want to do anything wrong, not to hurt us? You gave me that con man bullshit of yours, made me a dead promise not to deal with those bandits, and then you turned around and double-crossed me. You practically destroyed us, whoring after the big time. I was all set to turn some of our money into good sharp investments that would put us on easy street. This racket can't last forever. Some fucking tough cop gets a hard-on for you or me and we're finished. We started five years ago, remember, you had shit, a corner bookmaker. You got too big for what we built, two Cadillacs, ten pairs of alligator shoes, the works. You couldn't stand being rich, you couldn't pay attention to our business, it was too small-time for you. You had to satisfy your big-time ambitions, be a big shot outside of Lindy's on Broadway. When you were a little Jew kid hustling the street to make a buck, those Broadway guys wouldn't shit on you. But once you made some money you couldn't wait to let them take it away from you. I'd like to go up to Lindy's and grenade those fucking bastards, especially your new asshole buddy Tommy Bockmann. Your Broadway honeymoon is over, Hesh. Back to Brooklyn with the rest of us peasants. Augie goes back bossing the wire room, and you boss the runners and the joints. No one handles the money from now on but me, Jimmy Riley. Willie the cashier will give me a daily report, and I'll have money available here with Larry at the club whenever we need it. You have any objections to what I said?"

"None, Jim. I agree, you're absolutely right. I'll do whatever you say. But there are a couple of things bothering me, things that may cause me a little trouble."

"Like what? Like shylocks?"

"Christ, like I said a million times, you would have made the greatest Secret Service agent of all time. How did you find out about them?"

"A little birdie told me. Once I got wind of your escapades I dug right in and in a day or two learned all I had to know. I could have puked, not only at your bullshit but at myself for neglecting you and the business. Okay, not that it's my problem, but how much do you owe?"

"About fifty grand. I know it's not your responsibility. I took it on my own."

"Bet your sweet ass it's not my responsibility. We'll figure a way to settle with them. Right now I'm not going to lose any sleep over those vultures, and I hope you don't either."

"Anything else, Jimmy? It's been a long day and I'm exhausted. I'd like to leave now and go home and see my wife and kids, I haven't been home in almost a week."

"Okay, Harry, you go ahead, I want to talk a little further with Augie. Whose car did you use to pick him up at the airport, Augie?"

"His maroon Caddy, Jim."

"Good then. Harry, grab your car and go home. Call me here in the morning and we'll make a meet in the New York bank where you said you stashed the two hundred grand. We'll make our plans tomorrow about our business and what you owe the shylocks. Get a good night's sleep, and for Christ's sake, get back to being the old Harry. Keep your nose clean and you'll get even with the world and we'll be back on top in less than a year. No more neglect, no more stupidity on both our parts. Maybe it's a good thing this happened early in the game. We have plenty of good years ahead of us and a helluva business, we'll recuperate. Go ahead. Call me in the morning."

Harry got up and reached over to shake Jimmy's hand, but Jimmy ignored it and waved him away. He pointed to the door. "Go ahead. Out. I'm not ready to forgive and forget right now. See you in the morning."

Jimmy felt his heart constrict and a wave of pity for Harry as he walked out of the apartment. He was hunched over and from the rear he looked like an old man as he slouched silently out through the door. All the laughs, all the jokes, all the fun they had together on the way up; now all pissed down the drain by Harry's insatiable desire to be a big-timer, a real high roller. But the pity lasted for just a fleeting moment. No time for that. He turned to Augie and said, "What do you think, Augie? Did I lean on him too much, was I too hard on him?"

"Not half enough, Jimmy. He's still bullshitting us, right up to the sky."

"You know something, Augie, I'm trying to give him the best of it, but that's exactly the way I feel about him, that he's still bullshitting us. He can't be sincere anymore, you can't believe a goddam thing he tells you. Tell me, how was he when you picked him up at the airport? Was he nervous?"

"He was all smiles at first, but when I told him there was an emergency, that he had to see you right away, he got as nervous as a young racehorse making his first start. No way did he want to face you tonight. I had to convince him that it was a must. He knew before you told him that the western office was closed. He questioned me about it, and I just told him that there was no money to pay if we got killed again. He seemed almost resigned about that—you know, completely subdued, which is not at all like Harry."

"What do you think, Augie? Has he really got that two hundred grand stashed away in the city? I think he's full of shit, that it doesn't exist. There's no way he would borrow from shylocks as long as he had access to cash. He's too smart for anything like that."

"Absolutely right, Jimmy. I think he's got a little getaway cash put aside, and if you want my honest opinion, I think he's going to take it on the lam."

"Jesus, Augie, we're reading each other's minds. That's exactly the feeling I got when he went out the door, that I'd never see him again. At least not around New York, and not for a long time."

"You're right, Jimmy. And he's lying about the shylocks. I think the figure is over a hundred grand, and he still owes some of the out-of-town offices we dealt to. And one more thing, don't forget he was betting himself to try to stem the tide. Can you believe how nuts this guy got?"

"You know, Augie, as I quote our pal Jersey Ed Murphy for the one hundredth time, 'Whatever can happen, will happen, and usually for the worst.' Harry is a classic example of Murphy's law. Listen, let's go over to the club and have a couple of good steaks and a few drinks. That will cheer us up, especially you, the way you love to eat. We'll plan our method of attack from tonight on. If Harry is leveling and joins us, fine, otherwise we'll handle the business together."

The next morning about nine o'clock Jimmy's worst fears were confirmed. The telephone next to his bed rang loud and clear. He sat up in bed, a little startled by the shrillness of the ring, shook the cobwebs out of his head, and reached across the night table, picked up the phone, and said, "Hello, who's this?"

"Jimmy, it's Harry. How do you feel?"

"Not too bad, Hesh, a little hung over. I had quite a few with Augie after you left. We stayed up pretty late. What's up, Harry?"

"Jimmy, I hate to tell you this, but I'm calling you from the airport. Jimmy, I buried myself, I'm taking off. I'm sorry it turned out this way, but I'm broke, the joint is broke, and I can't face the people I owe."

"For Christ's sake, Harry, what good is running away going to do? What about your wife and kids?"

"She'll be okay for a long while. She has the house in Atlantic Beach free and clear and she's put away plenty of cash through the years. She won't starve for a long time. As soon as I get lucky again, maybe I'll send for her."

More bullshit, Jimmy thought. "What about the two hundred grand in the bank vault in New York. More of your horseshit? Were you lying to me about that?"

"Yeah, Jimmy, I was. The only box I had for the joint was the one on Church Avenue which you told me you cleaned out the other day. I'm glad you did or I'd have snatched that and pissed it away."

Jimmy was a little stunned at this piece of news. No two hundred grand. He'd been hoping against hope that it was true. He kept calm. "Where are you headed? Do you have any definite plans?"

"I've arranged to meet some guys down South. I won't tell you where right now, but you're such a Secret Service agent I'm sure you'll soon find out. Jimmy, I wish I were dead. Anyway, I might do some good with these guys and be able to come back and straighten out."

"Harry, I wish you were dead too. And get this straight, once and for all. I don't give a fuck how good you do down South or out West or wherever the hell you go. When you come back, you're not coming back with me. I laid out the ground rules early in the game when we first started out. 'Never try to screw me, you'll never get a second chance.' You did some beauty of a royal number on your friend Jimmy Riley, and you'll never get another crack at him. Just take this bit of advice, forget you ever met Jimmy Riley, 'cause you'll never get another chance to fuck him. So long, Harry."

Jimmy hung up and called room service for his breakfast. When the waiter brought it up he poured himself a cup of coffee. He sipped it slowly and tried to put the whole picture together. Harry was gone, vamoosed, an indisputable fact of life, and now that it was becoming a reality he began to feel happy about it. If he could have conned Harry into meeting him, he might have hurt him, hurt him bad. He was glad he didn't. It was just as well, let him go South or wherever and put the con on some other poor bastards. Jimmy didn't have to shoot him, he was bound to fuck the wrong guy again someday and get cooled out as sure as the stars were in the heavens. What a shame, he thought, a real nice, good-looking guy with everything in the world going for him. Now he's on the lam, bound for nowhere. He's sure to wind up on the balls of his ass, and it serves him right. If only he had always been truthful, a hundred percent on the up and up, they would have made a fortune together, more than they'd ever spend. Jimmy felt a throbbing pain over his left eye when he thought of the bankroll pissed away. And who knows how much more went out the window?

Well, so much for regrets, no time for that shit. Get over to Brooklyn with Augie and start whipping the organization back into shape, it's grown a little lax. This would be some busy week. He smiled when he thought of all the shylocks' anguish when they found out Harry took it on the lam. Too fucking bad. So long, Harry.

6

THE TRANSITION of bosses in the organization took place with a lot less trouble than Jimmy Riley had anticipated. Through the years the key men had become real good friends of his, especially the top bosses like Augie and Mikie, and evidently they had seen so little of Harry during the previous six months that he had become a rapidly eroding memory. Consequently, the news of his departure for places unknown caused only an occasional low whistle and lifting of the eyebrows, just a touch of mild shock. Establishing some sort of diplomatic relations with the shylocks left behind was another cup of tea, a real ball-breaker, and Jimmy had to reach out to his most important connections in the underworld to stave them off.

Like all guys who made a living the hard way, early in life Jimmy had learned it was best to stay out of the clutches of shylocks. Yet in many ways he was sympathetic to them. In his opinion they served a vital function to surprisingly varied segments of the business world, legitimate as well as illegitimate. The only credit reference they demanded was your own good reputation for being honorable, with an occasional assist from a mutual respected friend who in turn vouched for your honor and was held responsible for the debt in case of a welsh. Obviously, anyone who turned to a shylock for a loan had absolutely no chance of borrowing the money from a bank or one of the small finance companies whose interest rates were almost as bad as the shylocks'. Nobody ever had a gun pointed to his head to borrow from a shylock; all the borrower knew was that he needed the money, usually very fast, like the day before, and the shylock was there to give it to him. They didn't want your car, your house, or your wife and kids locked up in the cellar—they just wanted to get paid back at the agreed rates.

When Jimmy took over he was fully aware that in case of any violence there was no way he could handle the shylock enforcers alone, so he took the slight precaution of having two of his tough gorilla friends from the West Side docks close by at all times. At the same time, he moved the headquarters of the business from Leo's candy store on Church Avenue to a large saloon called the Ballfield Tavern, located on Bedford Avenue, one block from Ebbets Field, home of the Brooklyn Dodgers. He did this for two reasons. The main reason was that the wire room operated in a loft above Leo's store, and, being by far the most important and most lucrative operation in the organization, he did not want to jeopardize it in case the police decided to raid their headquarters and by some unlucky chance fall into the wire room. The second reason was the seemingly interminable parade of shylocks. It seemed to Jimmy that Harry had taken a shot at every big loanshark in New York City and environs. He wondered how come they never tripped over each other bringing money to Harry, but upon reflection he found the situation quite understandable. Bookmakers, crap and car game operators, and bettors were the lifeblood of the loanshark business. Until his abrupt financial demise, Harry had enjoyed impeccable credit among the gambling fraternity; paying off the hits against him immediately, never pressing anyone too heavily who owed him money, and with his flair for clothes, his good looks, flashy jewelry, and expensive cars, always flamboyantly living in the grand style. When you added up all of Harry's apparent attributes, plus his winning manner and smooth talk, it was easy to see how these tough Jewish and Italian shylocks fell all over themselves to lend him large amounts of money without asking too many questions. It was this army of angry creditors that Jimmy had to face, and he preferred to face them in the broader confines of the Ballfield Tavern, rather than the narrow aisles of Leo's candy store.

The Ballfield Tavern had a long bar which was heavily frequented before and after the Dodgers home games, and even on off days had a lot of traffic in and out. It was a nice place, and Tony, the owner, was a nice guy. He was a good friend of Jimmy's, so when Jimmy came to him and explained his dilemma he readily agreed to the move and only reluctantly assented to take a modest fee as rent. They set up in the wide back room of the tavern, which originally was partitioned off to serve as a restaurant. The only drawback to that idea was that there was no kitchen to cook food, not even a stove. This unused space was ideal to conduct the daily business, and for the first couple of weeks the tavern served a most useful function as a pleasant bar to have a couple of drinks against and to cool out some of the more belligerent loansharks.

Fortunately, a number of claimants for Harry's curly head knew Jimmy either personally or by reputation. After finally being convinced that Harry was broke, long gone, and highly unlikely to return, they were reluctantly persuaded to arrange some sort of settlement. It was human nature. In the long run, loansharks were exactly the same as banks and the seamier financial lending institutions; half a loaf was only slightly better than none. Jimmy calmed them down at the first meeting, which was always slightly hysterical, and tried to ascertain who their main boss was, who they reported to. He knew that the bosses never went to collect, only the leg-breakers. Once he received this vital bit of intelligence, he reached out for the top guy involved and arranged a sit-down. Through the next couple of weeks Jimmy had more sit-downs than a political candidate on the election trail.

Through his six years in The Job, Jimmy was extremely fortunate to have been in a position to meet the highest-echelon racket guys in New York City and to enjoy their trust and respect. They accepted his version of Harry's moral and financial breakdown, and amicable settlements were quickly reached that were acceptable to both sides. Jimmy agreed to pay one-third of each total loan, with all interest waived. He explained that this sum was Harry's share of the business and that neither he, Augie, nor any of the other bosses were aware of Harry's manipulations. This was readily substantiated by the loansharks, as not even one of them had ever approached Jimmy, Augie, or any of the others to okay the loan and vouch for the repayment. It was incredible that in the space of a couple of months Harry could borrow so much money without so much as an inquiry from one shylock to another. They probably thought they had such a good thing they all kept it to themselves. There was a lot of head-shaking and muttered threats of mayhem, but when all the details were straightened out and the intitial payments made, Jimmy was toasted at Tony's bar like a Count Metternich who had just repaired the international chaos caused by Napoleon Bonaparte. On a later reflection upon his financial acumen and his self-indulgent allusion to Count Metternich, Jimmy thought in how many ways Harry did resemble Napoleon: short, dark-skinned, terribly ambitious, completely venal, out to conquer his own particular world no matter what—a real prick.

With the shylocks at last peacefully put to rest, Jimmy gratefully sent his two West Side bodyguards back to their dock bosses with profuse thanks, and settled down to serious business. He cut back on the size of the bets the wire room could stay with, and established a tighter set of controls throughout each and every spot. But there ws one thing Jimmy soon realized: he could not run a nightclub and at the same time operate a large gambling business. If he ever took a real bad fall he could easily lose his liquor license, and the club had been built up to become a very valuable property. One or the other had to go, and the choice was not a difficult one, as much as he loved the nightclub and the fun he had there. He knew, as he had always known, that the real money was in the gambling business, so he sadly made arrangements to sell the club. A good deal was arranged in quick order by his lawyer and accountant for an amount substantially larger than he had originally paid for the club. He was momentarily staggered when he found out the huge capital gains tax he would have to pay the government when the sale was finalized, but his accountant prevailed upon him to pay the taxes so that the residue could in some measure account for his fancy life-style.

To Jimmy's surprise there was not one word relayed to him from Harry, or of Harry's whereabouts, during the first few months he ran the outfit, and he couldn't have cared less. He worked almost night and day, and crawled into bed dog-tired every night. It killed him to have the shylock payments taking most of the initial profits, but he consoled himself that this too would soon end and if business continued to grow, an era of great prosperity was just around the corner. He had anticipated some flak from one or another of the New York gambling squads about the idea of himself, an ex-cop, running the business, but he was gratified to see that no one bothered him or any of the okay spots. He attributed much of this good fortune to two things.

First, the chief's squad that was in power when he resigned from The Job a couple of years earlier was more or less intact under the same chief. When he met his mortal enemy, Dan the deputy, or one of his other nemeses in the squad at the Garden or Ebbets Field he was smart enough to greet them politely. They naturally assumed that Jimmy had either forgotten or forgiven all past hurts and that the best and safest way to keep the uneasy peace was not to bother any of the gambling places he now controlled, especially as they were getting a healthy slice of ice every month to leave him alone.

The second, and more important reason in Jimmy's eyes, was the assumption that he had a new and exceptionally strong ally. Unfortunately, this assumption would prove to be a grievous error. The esteemed mayor, Bill O'Dwyer, was entering the last year of his term, and as a reward to the political hierarchy who had sponsored and supported him he replaced his benign appointee of three years with a new Irish police commissioner. The new commissioner was a man who had risen through the ranks and who had been a good friend of Jimmy's almost from the day he began his career in plainclothes. Despite the disparity in age and rank, they had many a dinner and drink together, and no holds were barred in the conversations about The Job that inevitably surfaced over a glass or two. Several years earlier there had been a vacancy to be filled as the commander of a borough squad and promotion to the rank of deputy chief, a choice plum. There were three or four candidates vying for the promotion, and his then boss, his old and beloved chief, had asked Jimmy's advice as to the most logical man for the coveted promotion. It was no contest as far as Jimmy was concerned, and word of Jimmy's assistance to his elevation speedily reached the appointee's ears. He invited

Jimmy to dinner, expressed his great appreciation for his help, and vowed that he would never forget it, would always be grateful to him. Through the years they had remained good friends, and when Jimmy left The Job and opened the nightclub the commissioner dropped in a few times to have a drink and reassure him of his undying friendship.

Jimmy knew that it was only logical to assume that after three months of his running the business, it was no longer a secret that Harry was gone and almost forgotten. By now everyone knew that he was at the controls of the small and much-battered mini-empire. He was elated when he heard the news of his old pal, the borough commander, being appointed to the lofty position of police commissioner. What a lucky break, he thought. With the help I'm going to get from New York I should have an all-time great run as long as my man is commissioner and is calling the shots. Subsequent events were to prove him entirely wrong, so completely wrong that no matter how he tried in later years to unravel the reasons why, he could never find a satisfactory answer.

The first signs of impending catastrophe were mild enough not to cause any deep concern, not enough to alarm Jimmy in the slightest. He was sitting in the back room of the Ballfield Tavern about noon with Willie Ricardo, going over the previous day's work sheets, when he received a telephone call.

"Hello, Jimmy, how are you? This is Pete."

"Hey, Pete, how's things?"

"Pretty good, Jimmy, but I think I might have to have the doctor come to the house to have a look at the wife."

"Gee, that's too bad, I'm really sorry. I'll light a candle for her when I go to Mass tomorrow morning. Thanks for calling, Pete. Take it easy, I'm sure everything will turn out all right."

Jimmy hung up the phone and turned around to Willie with a puzzled frown on his face. The conversation he'd just finished was all pure one hundred percent bullshit. It was all a prearranged signal from his man in the police commissioner's squad; he was about to get an unfriendly visit from one of the bosses. "Pete" was the code word for P.C., "the doctor" was the code for one of the top brass, and "the doctor's visit" meant that the danger was imminent. No use worrying and getting everybody panic-stricken, at least he got the courtesy of a phone call for his money.

Jimmy went back to Willie and told him to get lost, they were going to get a visit. He packed him off with all the daily sheets and whatever else incriminating that was lying around. He went out to the front bar, where a few of the runners were having a drink, and told them to finish up and make themselves scarce for the rest of the day. He quietly warned Tommy the bartender to caution the bar customers not to display any scratch sheets, and stationed Sharkey, his former doorman at the club and now his driver and man for all seasons, outside the tavern and told him to tap discreetly on the window when the Cossacks were about to invade. About two o'clock came the anything but discreet tap that almost shattered the window and from inside the tavern sounded like an explosion. Jimmy nodded toward Sharkey through the window and almost laughed out loud. Good old Sharkey, another display of ice-cold courage under fire.

The front door of the Ballfield Tavern opened and in they came, led by the new scourge of the New York City gambling halls, Inspector James Carmody. "Cockeye Jim" to cops everywhere, and "fucking Cockeyed Carmody" to the sporting world and its habitués he so relentlessly pursued. There were five in all, and Riley recognized each of them from his vantage point at the far end of the bar. He had heard a rumor that his friend, the new police commissioner, had recently picked Carmody as one of his top inspectors, but found it impossible to believe. Even as he sipped his drink and casually looked over the invaders it was hard to understand how anyone as hip as the new commissioner could appoint a stupid Irish prick like Carmody to head up his plainclothes squad. The men deployed through the Ballfield Tavern like they were on a scout mission in a recently fallen town in Germany, one of them giving Jimmy a surreptitious wink as he passed him on his way to search the back room. Cockeye Carmody stood erect in the center of the barroom like General George Patton, all he needed was the uniform and the riding crop.

The tavern was clean as a whistle, not even a scratch sheet to be found. The radio blared pure jazz, not even one race result to jar the ears. One of the raiding party, a big Jew named Dorfman, who through the years had had his share of differences with Jimmy, reported back to General Patton Carmody, saying, "Not a thing here, boss. It looks to me like somebody gave them a tip-off."

Carmody's cockeyes blinked behind his steel spectacles, the lenses as thick as the bottoms of Coca-Cola bottles. His face started to get beet red and very stormy-looking. He walked down to the far end of the bar and stopped directly behind Jimmy and said, "You. What's your name?"

Jimmy didn't even turn to look at him. He was about three-quarters turned away from him, talking to a friend of his at the bar. Carmody began to get enraged. He grabbed Jimmy by his coat lapel and turned him face to face.

Jimmy grabbed Carmody by the wrist of the hand that held his lapel. It was thin as a young girl's, surprising to his touch as he looked into Carmody's tough, scowling Irish kisser. "Keep your fucking hands off me or I'll snap your wrist like a chicken bone. Who in the name of Christ do you think you are, grabbing me like that?"

Carmody stepped back, a little astonished at this complete lack of respect for his high office. "I'm Inspector Carmody, of the police commissioner's squad. Who are you?"

"Who am I? My name is Bruce Cabot."

A couple of guys at the bar almost strangled trying to stop laughing at Jimmy's answer. A couple of the cops turned away with a grin on their faces.

"Bruce Cabot, eh? What do you do for a living?"

"I'm a movie actor, Inspector. Mostly in western and gangster pictures."

"You trying to bullshit me or something?" Carmody squinted closely at Jimmy through the bottoms of the Coca-Cola bottles. He was a little uncertain, he hadn't laid eyes on Riley in over four years.

"I tell you what, Inspector, suppose we go to the back room for a couple of minutes and have a private talk. Maybe I can refresh your memory."

Carmody, now unnerved, unsure of himself, nodded his head in the direction of the back room. They walked back and sat down at a table.

"You care for a drink, Inspector?" Nice and soft. Easy does it, Jimmy.

"No. I don't want a drink, not with you. Tell me, you're Jimmy Riley, aren't you?"

"And you're Jimmy Carmody, aren't you? You can save that 'Inspector' shit for some other guy. You won't drink with me now, but you had many a drink with me not too long ago, and you gave me many a contract. Remember four years ago when you were a deputy on the West Side and you gave me a contract on your sweetheart's son who ran a high-class fag joint in the east Fifties. You remember that, don't you, Jimmy Carmody? And remember when her fag son's boyfriend put his head in the oven after a lover's quarrel in the apartment they shared. You begged me to have the detectives in the Seventeenth Squad hush it up so there wouldn't be a scandal. Just make sure my sweetheart's son has no trouble with his high-class restaurant. Too close scrutiny might endanger his liquor license. That's me, Jimmy Riley, the same guy, Inspector Carmody, and from now on, whatever you do, keep your fucking hands off me."

"Yeah, you're Riley, all right. Now I remember you well. You were always a fresh little fuck, and I can see you haven't changed. What the hell are you doing in Harry Gross's joint? We came here to take him out today. Where's all the action, Jimmy? Somebody give you guys the tip-off?"

"Your're right, Inspector, Santa Claus gave us the tip. Seriously, are you going to stand there in front of me and give me that 'honest Irish Inspector' horseshit? What's happened now? Have you got enough money stashed away to suddenly become honest? Do you go to the altar rail every Sunday morning and receive communion like the rest of those bullshit artists? Or maybe now that you've turned honest you'll get promoted real high and retire with a nice big pension. Listen, Carmody, guys like you may bullshit the public, but don't try to bullshit me. You ran the fucking West Side wide open when I was around, and myself and plenty of guys like me gave you a lot of help doing it. And once again, don't forget the help I gave your fag love child when he needed it, when he was really jammed up. Now you know as well as I do there's no more Harry Gross, there's only Jimmy Riley. When you leave here and get in your squad car ask that big schmuck Dorfman what I send over every month, and don't give me that shit you don't get an end. Now you take Dorfman and your boys and get out of here and leave me the fuck alone. Just remember, you and I go way back together and I was always more than decent with you, so you can't have any quarrel with me unless you deliberately look for one. One more thing, I still have a few good friends left who are a little higher than you, and I think they still like me, so you're not going to break my balls like you do the wops and the Jews. Well, I said my piece, Inspector. Anything on your mind?"

Carmody's jaw was rigid and his eyes were blazing behind the Coca-Cola bottles. He shook his head back and forth a few times, started to walk out to the front bar, then stopped and turned. "Okay, Riley, this one is on me, the next time will be another story. The honeymoon is over in New York City for all wise guys as far as Jimmy Carmody goes. From now on we're all going honest."

"The day you all go honest is the day they'll lay me out in Frank Campbell's Funeral Parlor."

"That day may come sooner than you think, as fresh a young fuck as you are."

"You keep taking wise guys' money and locking up the guys who give it to you and you might beat me there. So long, honest Jim."

Jimmy stayed in the back room for a couple of minutes trying to compose himself. Though he had spoken to Carmody in a calm voice, inwardly he was raging. Imagine that Irish shitheel having the nerve to grab me by the coat lapel like I was some kind of hoodlum. The same cockeyed prick who used to practically grovel when he met me, who'd kiss my Irish ass to stay in good with me. The favors I did him, and now he grabs me like some half-ass bum he never saw in his life. *Sic transit gloria.* Alas, poor fallen Roman.

The last thought brought a rueful grin to his face, and he walked from the back room out into the bar. Carmody and the four P.C.'s men were gone. The customers at the bar were very quiet, the tavern was almost hushed. Tommy the bartender looked at Jimmy, and Jimmy gave him a broad wink to break the ice and said, "What the hell do we have here, for Christ's sake, an Irish wake? Give the whole joint a drink, Tom. Everything's okay, no more problems."

"Anything you say, Bruce Cabot."

The place broke up laughing. The customers all started to talk at once as Tommy set up a fresh round of drinks. Sharkey, Jimmy's driver, was the loudest of all as he held court with three or four guys in the middle of the bar. He waved his glass toward Jimmy and said, "I done good, didn't I, Jim? I gave you the signal on those fucking cops just like you said. Right, Jimmy?"

"That's right, Sharkey, but I told you to tap on the window with a coin, not hit it with a baseball bat, for Christ's sake. I thought the whole window was going to cave in. You weren't a little nervous out there, were you, Shark?"

The whole bar erupted with laughter again. Most of the customers in the tavern knew that Shark talked tough but was scared of his own shadow. But even though Jimmy kidded him, he didn't want to take away his hour of glory. "Really, Shark, you did a terrific job out there. You proved you were a real tough guy today."

Sharkey beamed, a few of the guys came over and slapped him on the back, and the Ballfield Tavern at last sat back and relaxed. Some of the customers started to bombard Jimmy with questions, but he fended them off, saying it was a mistake, a routine visit. One thing above all, he didn't want it blown out of proportion so that when it got back to Tony, the owner, it would get him so nervous he'd ask them to move. Jimmy liked the tavern as a headquarters. The bartenders and customers were nice people, the back room was perfect for conducting their business out of the public eye, and best of all, when he had a few spare hours and the Dodgers were at home he only had to walk one block to see his beloved team.

Jimmy stayed at the bar for about an hour and drank a few Cutty Sark and waters. He laughed and joked and seemed serene and happy, but deep inside he was churning, really shaken. He was secretly castigating himself for being such a smart-ass with Cockeye Carmody. Why hadn't I been at least a little humble, a little conciliatory? Why must I always act like a wise bastard when someone comes on with me? One day I'm Count Metternich and the next day I'm the worst asshole diplomat since Joseph Stalin. But there was one thing for sure: Carmody, Dorfman, and those other guys hit the joint loaded for bear. They really meant business, and if they had found anything they would certainly have thrown the whole place in the air. Why in the name of Christ did they get this kind of vicious visit?

As he tried to recall the day's events in orderly fashion, again he wished he hadn't acted so fresh to Carmody. You'd better forget you were ever a cop, Jimmy, and learn how to take a little shit once in a while. Still, the aborted raid kept nagging at him. Why? Why? Why? The P.C.'s were one squad he thought would never hurt him, were in his back pocket, especially with his old friend the new commissioner. And to widen the plot, to send that two-faced cockeyed Irish sonofabitch to bust me. That hatchet-man fuck. Now Jimmy began to feel better about not taking any of his shit. Without a doubt, Carmody was the meanest, rottenest, most underhanded bullshit Irish cop that ever walked. Oh, how I wish I had one more shot in the chief's office. I'd stick it up Carmody's ass so far it would come out his throat. To think of all the nice things I did for that Coca-Cola-eyed rat, and now he tries to put the arm on me, grabbing me by the coat in a bar like some ordinary bum. Hello, Leo Durocher, you're right again about the nice guys.

He could stand at the bar all day and privately lick his wounds, wondering what caused his fall from grace, but that wasn't Jimmy Riley's style. He motioned for Sharkey to get the car and said goodbye all around, shaking hands and taking bows like the local neighborhood fighter who had just won his first start in the Golden Gloves. While toying with the last drink he suddenly decided on a course of action and vowed to get on with it as quickly as possible. He would make it his immediate business to see the new police commissioner face to face, if only for a few minutes; just long enough to straighten out his newfound cockeyed enemy. Certainly the years together and the favors done deserved a few minutes of heart-to-heart talk. He felt it would be foolhardy in his present capacity to send the commissioner a personal message, so he formed a plan to accidentally bump into him on purpose.

The scene he fixed in his mind for this confrontation was the Friday-night fights at Madison Square Garden. The commissioner, a rabid fight fan, attended the card every Friday night and invariably sat in the same loge box officially reserved for him and his entourage by the Garden bosses. Jimmy had spotted him there a couple of times, but made no effort to say hello as he felt it might be an intrusion. Now he had to forget this slight violation of protocol, he had to stop by the box and greet him. He knew that he'd be perceptive enough to determine from the warmth or the coldness of the greeting how matters stood between him and the new commissioner. He was plagued by some nagging doubts, but he dismissed them as a sort of persecution mania brought on by Carmody's raid.

He planned ahead. A week from Friday night, Irish Billy Graham was to fight another outstanding welterweight in the main event. He knew, from previous conversation, that the commissioner was fond of Billy and loved to see him fight. With good luck and no intervening trouble, that would be the night to nail his old friend face to face. If all went well, Jimmy would make a sly date to meet at some obscure place for a quiet dinner where he could clear the air. Perfect.

The night of the Billy Graham fight Jimmy had arranged to get a loge box about two sections beyond the police commissioner's. He planned it so that as he passed him it would seem like sheer accident that they should so unexpectedly meet. He sent the guys he came to the fight with to his reserved box while he stayed on the perimeter of the loge section until just before the semifinal started. He had dead aim on the commissioner for about fifteen minutes and was relieved to see that everyone in the entourage was a friend, or ostensibly a friend, of his.

Just before the semifinal fighters were about to be introduced Jimmy casually sauntered down the loge aisle toward his own box. He timed his pace so that when the animated commissioner turned around to speak to someone behind him he'd be looking directly at Jimmy. The commissioner looked right at him and flushed a little, but Jimmy marched down the few steps to his box, waved to the others in it, and said, "Congratulations, Commissioner, I'm glad you made it. I'm proud of you." He extended his hand to shake, and the commissioner gave him the cold-fish handshake of all time. He just nodded his head and said, "Thanks, Jimmy," and turned away like Jimmy was some kind of communicable disease carrier. He might just as well have hit him with an axe. Jimmy gave the rest of the men in the box a tight smile, walked up the few steps and continued down the aisle to his own box. The guys he came to the fight with took one look at his face and nobody said a word. He sat through a few rounds of the semifinal like a zombie, then excused himself and walked out of the Garden in a trance.

Once out of the Garden he hailed a taxicab and told the driver to take him crosstown to the Copacabana. He snapped out of his coma about ten blocks later. He had taken his share of punches in life—on the jaw, on the head, in the belly, in the balls—but this punch was the worst of all. He had just been totally humiliated, slapped in the face, a direct insult. What the hell is happening in my life, he thought. Here's a guy who was one of my best friends in The Job, like another father to me, and now he turns his back on me like I'm a piece of dogshit.

The whole scenario began to unfold in Jimmy's mind. It was no accident, the visit from the repellent Carmody last week. He's now the boss executioner, and I was the intended victim. These are all calculated moves, and it's only going to get worse. And, James, you can't do a goddam thing about it, so stop worrying. Well, one good thing, Frank Sinatra is working at the Copa tonight and I'll ask Julie Podell to be sure Frank sings "I Guess I'll Have to Change My Plans." You'd better start to change your plans, Jimmy Riley, or change your mouthwash or your deodorant or some fucking thing. The last thought was enough to make Jimmy chuckle in spite of his gloom, and the anticipation of hearing Frank sing started to lift his spirits. By the time he reached the Copa bar he was feeling a hundred percent better, and after the first two Cutty Sark and waters, a thousand percent better. I have only one life, milord, and tonight I offer it up not to Ireland and my crew in Brooklyn, but to whiskey and women, for England in the ominous form of the P.C.'s squad looms darkly on the horizon like the bloody butchers of the valiant men of Mayo.

Jimmy was nursing his third Scotch when one of the restaurant captains came up to him and told him that Joe Lopez, the maître d', wanted to see him downstairs in the main room. Lopez greeted him warmly and ushered him to a ringside table where two of his best friends in the gambling world sat with three beautiful show-girls. They welcomed Jimmy with open arms and quickly estab-lished which one of the girls was his for the night. Frank opened his show with "I Guess I'll Have to Change My Plans," which brought a big grin to Jimmy's face. By the time Frank finished his show—he seemed to sing every one of Jimmy's favorite songs—and a rapport with his beautiful new friend was established, Jimmy was on cloud nine, flying high. The horrific rebuff by the police commissioner a few hours before was washed from his mind, he'd worry about that tomorrow.

The six of them proceeded to cabaret around the better small nightclubs after they left the Copa and wound up on upper Fifth Avenue in Jimmy Carr's, an all-night after-hours private club lo-cated in an elegant three-story brownstone that was the favorite haunt of the money night people. Bobby, the black piano player, was a terrific musician and a great guy. Half of the customers, including Jimmy, thought they were undiscovered stars of the nightclub and musical comedy world and would get up to sing at the slightest urging. Bobby could play any song ever written, and in the early morning hours there were torch songs sung by some of the embryo stars among the clientele that even he had to reach way back to remember. But he had such a great touch he made almost everyone who got up sound good with his subtle, deft artistry on the keys.

Jimmy listened to the songs, sang a couple himself, laughed and carried on like he'd just inherited five million dollars. When he looked at his watch he saw the witching hour was approaching, half past eight in the morning, and said his goodbyes, being very considerate and tender to his new girl friend, promising to call her real soon. He left Jimmy Carr's and decided not to take a taxi back to his apartment but to walk downtown along Fifth Avenue. Jimmy always felt a little strange walking in the fresh morning sunlight, passing people who had all had a good night's sleep; walking their dogs, hurrying to appointments, or just plain going to work. He didn't feel the least bit tired after the strenuous night of cabareting. Instead, he felt exhilarated, strangely anticipatory. Something big is going to happen to me pretty soon, he thought. What the hell's the use worrying about it, they can't send me to the electric chair.

The leaves were just turning on the Central Park side of Fifth Avenue and the foliage in the park was gorgeous. The brisk autumn morning was bright and lovely, and he breathed deeply of the good fall air, clearing his head of the accumulated tobacco and alcohol fumes. How I love New York, he thought, for the thousandth time in his life. He looked up at the tall luxurious apartment houses on his left, with the erect doormen outside, attired perfectly right down to their spanking white gloves. He smiled when he recalled an incident that had happened at the nightclub about a year ago. Some recently acquired friends of his, society guys, came into the club with a nice party. One of the girls with them was a tall, leggy, beautiful redhead. Jimmy sat with them for a drink and she was quick to let him know that she was a divorcée, unattached. As she left the club she shook hands with Jimmy and he felt the sly pressure of a note being slipped into his hand. The note contained her phone number, and out of curiosity Jimmy called her a few days later. They made a date for dinner and she gave Jimmy the address on Fifth Avenue where to pick her up, one of the gracious buildings he was now walking by.

When he arrived, he was announced by the doorman, and brought up to the redhead's floor by a uniformed elevator man. He got off the elevator and was astonished to see that he was in a foyer just off the living room. A butler greeted him, took his coat, and led him through the living room, which was almost the size of some of the basketball courts he played on as a kid. He settled Jimmy in a smaller room containing a bar and made him a Scotch and water. It began to dawn on Jimmy that the *entire floor* of the apartment house belonged to his beautiful redhaired friend with the long legs. She joined Jimmy in a few minutes, asked him if he would like to see the rest of the apartment, and then gave him the grand tour.

When he thought about it now walking down Fifth Avenue he almost laughed remembering how overawed he was. It was a fifteen-room apartment. Fifteen rooms, he had counted every goddam one of them. You thought you lived good, Jimmy Riley. Why, for Christ's sake, you're nothing but an Irish peasant. This is the way you'll live someday, he remembered thinking then, with a butler and a couple of maids and an entire floor to yourself. But that was over a year ago, and since then a lot of his dreams had been shattered and now he was keenly aware that the cops who ran this beautiful New York town were about to screw him pretty good. Well, if it happens it happens, I can't do anything about it.

The next couple of weeks were a pleasant surprise to Jimmy. He went to the Ballfield Tavern headquarters as usual every day and ran his ship of state without one single visit from any of the local or New York gambling squads. He lived day by day with deep premonitions of imminent disaster, but then, as the days rolled by and business boomed, he began to get optimistic again about his chances of survival.

Unfortunately, this self-induced state of euphoria came to an abrupt halt. About three weeks after his Madison Square Garden rebuff by his erstwhile friend, the new police commissioner, he received the fatal phone call.

"Hello, Jimmy. This is your old pal Chicko."

"Chick, my boy, how are you? What's up? Why do I deserve this momentous phone call? Are you about to invite me to the opening of a great New York whorehouse?"

Chick laughed. "You're always onstage, Jimmy. No, nothing like that, I'm sorry to say. No new whorehouses. Look, seriously, I'm not sure what this is all about, but I don't think it's any good. You know me, Jimmy, I'm your friend, I'll never shit you. Something is in the air that stinks."

"Well, for Christ's sake, Chick, let's have it."

"You know the sergeant in the P.C.'s, the guy you had a couple of come-offs with. You know, the big Jew, Dave Dorfman. He got hold of me today and told me he wanted to meet you tonight in Dutch Savarese's joint about eight o'clock. He said it was a must, and he also mentioned something about having a couple of bosses along with him. Sounds a little fishy to me, Jimmy, but I'm just relaying the message. Do what you want."

"Meet him at eight o'clock. Just like that, right? Well, my first impulse is to tell him to go fuck himself, but I can tell from the sound of your voice you're a little worried, so you tell him I'll be there. I wish you would come, I'd love to see you. Besides, you can be my protector in case they decide to give me a beating."

Chick laughed again and sounded a little relieved. "I'll be there, and I promise I won't let anyone hit you. See you at Dutch's around eight. So long, Jimmy."

Jimmy hung up and looked at his watch. Two fifteen. Almost six long hours lay ahead and he wasn't going to start drinking away his troubles, so he told Sharkey to get the car and drive him to New York. He ran a few business errands in New York and then had Sharkey drop him off at the Downtown Athletic Club. He proceeded to have a good workout in the gym, a steam bath, and a massage. He arrived at Dutch Savarese's place promptly at eight o'clock, fresh as a daisy and well prepared to be plucked.

When he arrived there were five of them at the bar, Chick O'Mara, Sergeants Dave Dorfman and Johnny Glynn from the P.C.'s squad, Georgie Knowles, the lieutenant in charge of the local division squad, and Willie Crossin, the boss of the borough squad. Jimmy greeted them all civilly, especially Chick, kidding him about broads, as usual, but there was no one kidding Jimmy Riley, the execution team was there, he could smell them. They had some light conversation over a couple of drinks, Jimmy acting very casual, as cool as Marie Antoinette awaiting the guillotine.

Dorfman, obviously the guy in charge, the take-over guy as always, said, "Let's all go sit at one of the tables in the back where we can have some privacy. Jimmy, we'd like to have a little talk with you. Chick, you don't have to sit in on this if you don't want to."

"That's all right, Dave. Look, I don't know what the hell is going on, but I want everyone here to know Jimmy is a very good friend of mine. If there are no objections, I'd rather sit in on this."

"Whatever you say, Chick."

They all moved to the back of the restaurant to an isolated table and ordered a fresh round of drinks. The waiter brought the drinks in and Jimmy raised his glass to the others. "Good luck, everybody, and from the look on your respective kissers I'm going to need it. Go ahead, give it to me straight. What's up?"

Big Dave Dorfman, the troop leader, cleared his throat, took a swallow of his drink, and said, "You want it dead straight, Jimmy, I'm going to give it to you dead straight. You're through running Harry's business. Through, finished, as of this coming Saturday."

Jimmy looked Dorfman right in the eye. It was Thursday night, for Christ's sake. He's giving me a two-day ultimatum and there's all kinds of money in transit and a million little things to tie up. He kept his emotions in check, spoke in a calm voice.

"Who's responsible for this high-command decision? You?"

"Look, Jimmy, it all boils down to one basic thing. The big boss, and you know who I mean, doesn't want an ex-cop running Harry's business. That's it in a nutshell. Period."

"Okay, if that's the case, the way you people want it, it's fine with me. I'll step down. I'll let Augie run the business. He's completely trustworthy and a capable guy. I'll go and lose myself as the front, but for Christ's sake, don't wrap up all the spots. Those kids who work for us are all nice kids, most of them married with families. Don't put them out on the street."

"No good. I don't think I want Augie running Harry's business. I don't think he's strong enough."

"You? *You* don't think Augie's strong enough? What's all this shit about? And furthermore, what's all this horseshit about 'Harry's business' that you keep repeating? Harry blew this fucking business. He's in New Orleans, or Los Angeles, or Peoria, Illinois, and I couldn't care a good fuck where he is. Just remember one thing, he buried this goddam business, and slowly but surely Augie and I are putting it back on its feet. Think about it, we've never missed a month's ice, have we? In all honesty, answer me that, any one of you sitting here at this table."

A dead silence covered the table like the checkered tablecloth. Jimmy looked around at them, one by one. Knowles and Crossin were very uncomfortable, couldn't look him in the eye. But Dorfman was ice-cold, and so was Glynn, his eyes shaded by dark glasses.

Dorfman spoke again, "Jimmy, to some extent you're right. But let's face it, it *is* Harry's business, we all know that."

"Bullshit, Harry's business. As long as we're on the subject, we might as well let it all hang out. From the beginning, when I was in the chief's office, I put up my money and my Irish ass for Harry when he was a two-bit, shitass bookmaker. Augie helped him get started and left a perfectly good business to join him, and then worked night and day for him. Together we built up a great business and we always paid everybody real good. But that rotten little bastard wanted to be a high roller on his own and in no time at all pissed away a fortune that had taken us years to accumulate. Why, for Christ's sake, we even found out later he put in phony bets to the office and paid himself the money. He also left a trail of loansharks from Brownsville to East Harlem. He fucked us, and then abandoned us and everyone who made him rich. Jesus Christ, Dave, you and John here know that, so does Georgie and Willie. Someone has to run this business, it's too good a thing to throw in the air."

"Someone is, Jimmy."

"Who?"

"Harry. He's back in town. He's sorry about what happened, but he's reformed and ready to go back to work."

Jimmy's mouth fell open, he was dumbfounded. He looked across the table at Chick, who was equally dumbfounded, startled. He took a deep swallow of Scotch. Christ Almighty, if I ever needed a drink, I need one now. He resolved to stay calm. "You can't be serious, you guys, telling me something like this. You mean to say that you're going to put that scheming, crooked little fuck back in action? Can't you see, for the love of God? He's not the same Harry of a few years ago, he's an entirely different guy. Believe me, I think the sonofabitch went crazy on me. We had the world by the nuts and he pissed it all away in a few months. He had to be off his fucking rocker. How can you trust a guy like that, Dave, a guy who double-banks his best friends in the world? Why, for Christ's sake, Dave, if it ever comes to any kind of a clutch, mark my words, he'll bury everybody. It doesn't make an

ounce of sense to bring this goddam gonif back. If that's the way
it is, if he's going to run the outfit again, I'd just as soon close up
the whole shooting match. Fuck everything, if he's back here to
run things it'll all go down the tube in a couple of months anyway. Reformed! Reformed, my ass. He'll never change."

Dorfman had sat drumming his fingers on the table during
Jimmy's plea to the Athenians. His face was cloudy, he was more
than a little vexed. "Listen, Riley, and get this straight. It's not
your decision to put Harry back to run the business. It's mine and
the other bosses' here. He's coming back, you're out, and that's
final."

Jimmy began to boil. He looked across the table at Dorfman,
threw his drink in his face, stood up and lunged over the table at
him. The force of Jimmy's body knocked Dorfman off his chair
and onto his back, and before he could make a move to defend
himself Jimmy was on top of him and had his hands around his
throat trying to strangle him. It happened so suddenly, with the
table going over and the glasses and whiskey sailing through the
air, that the other guys were in a temporary state of shock. A
couple of them fell back on their own asses, and the others
jumped up as the drinks splashed all over. It took them almost a
minute to realize what had happened and to pry Jimmy loose from
Dorfman, whose eyes by that time were rolling back in his head.

When they finally subdued Jimmy and untangled everybody
and some semblance of peace was restored, Jimmy came back to
sanity with Chick sitting on top of him and two of the others
pinning back his arms. He looked up and said, "Okay, okay, get
off me, let my arms go. I'm all right now. Enough is enough."

The two holding his arms let go and Chick got off his stomach
and reached out a hand and helped him to his feet. Everyone was
standing around the table brushing off his clothes. Jimmy looked
at Dorfman, who was about ten feet away with Willie Crossin
between them. Dorfman held a handkerchief over his left eye,
which was bleeding slightly from a small cut. He looked really
shaken up, but Jimmy didn't miss the hate that blazed in his eyes.
He stared bitterly at Jimmy and said, "You better start remembering one thing, Riley, you're not a cop anymore. What's the idea
of pulling that brilliant strong-arm act on me? I'm a fucking po-

lice sergeant. I could put a shot in you for pulling something like this, and I'd probably get a medal for killing a fresh Irish fuck like you."

"Why don't you try it, you big yellow Jew prick. You're an excuse for a police sergeant. You'd take money from a blind man and pinch his newsstand for selling scratch sheets if your cock-eyed Irish boss Carmody told you to. Who the hell do you think you are, telling me that Harry's back and I'm through and that's final? What'd you do, go to the synagogue with Harry and figure you'd reform him, put him back in action, and grab yourself a big piece of the pie? Well, fuck you and Harry Gross. And that goes for all of you here, every goddam one of you. I'm leaving here right now and I'll be back in the Ballfield Tavern tomorrow at twelve noon. You can all take your best goddam shot."

Jimmy turned and walked out of the restaurant onto Flatbush Avenue, his boulevard of broken dreams. Before he got a hundred feet down the avenue Chick caught up to him. He walked beside him for a couple of blocks without saying a word. Then he finally broke the silence. "Jesus, that was a nice scene back there in Dutch's, Jimmy, right out of a Cagney movie. I hope I'm not included in your feud with those other four fucks?"

"Come on, Chick, you know better than that. Of course not. I could kick my ass for going after that big prick like I did, but I blew my top when he gave me that 'final' shit. 'That's final'! Imagine him having the nerve to say a thing like that to me. I should let him cousin up with Harry, he'll have him back behind the wheel of a taxicab like he was before he became a cop. 'I'm a police sergeant.' Did you hear that shit? Somebody had to give that dopey fuck the answers before he took the sergeants test. No way he had the brains to pass."

Chick laughed. "You're a beauty, Jimmy, a real honest-to-God beauty, a real pisser. I used to sometimes think you were crazy when we worked together. Now I'm convinced."

"Ah, maybe you're right, Chick. But look at the way he put it to me, and those other assholes sitting around the table like Holly-wood tough guys. Why, I considered Georgie Knowles and Willie Crossin good friends of mine, and there they were with the two P.C. finks to issue me an ultimatum. Chick, tomorrow you meet those four fucks and tell them that Harry comes back over Jimmy Riley's dead body."

"Jimmy, I'm afraid you're not going to have any choice. Can't you see the handwriting on the wall? For once in your life, don't be as thick as shit. This is the head man's decision, not theirs. They know how friendly you and I are, and that's why I was put in the middle here, like the go-between. It's all over New York City about you running the business. How could anyone miss it, with the bullshit about the shylocks and all? Do you think for a minute the visit you got from Carmody and those guys a couple of weeks ago was an accident? Can't you see, you silly bastard, they don't want to pinch you, it might cause too much of a stink. They just want to get rid of you. A lot of the guys associated with Harry have good friends in The Job, and believe it or not, some of the big bosses still have a high regard for Harry. He must have jerked them off pretty good. Besides, Jimmy, you know nobody wants to miss all that ice every month."

"Chick, everything you're saying sounds logical, but what am I supposed to do, just bow out like Little Lord Fauntleroy and walk away? No good."

"Jimmy, will you listen to me, please? I'm a little older and a helluva lot calmer than you. I know full well they stuck it into you in the chief's office and they're sticking it into you worse now, but take my advice and get the hell out. Grab what you got coming out of the bankroll, set up some kind of weekly payroll from Harry, and forget the rackets for a while. You're a young, good-looking guy, and thank God you still got plenty of money. You'll do good no matter what business you choose. I know you will. Do what I say, Jimmy, please. You know what I think of you, and I don't want to see you get hurt."

"Chick, everything you say sounds great, but I'm far from ready to give in so easily to those bloodsuckers, especially when it looks like they're teaming up with Harry. Besides, if I grab the bankroll, how is the office going to work? And all the spots?"

"Jimmy, this is going to kill you. I have a sneaky idea Dorfman, Crossin, and Knowles are putting up the bankroll for him. I asked them exactly the same question, and they said the bankroll was the least of Harry's headaches, that it was all taken care of.

There's no question you were their major problem. Christ, were they ever right."

"It's hard to believe. As my old pal and fellow sleuth Sherlock Holmes used to say, 'Aha, the plot thickens.' You know something, Chick, you're probably dead right. I smelled a rat the way Dorfman came on so strong, like gangbusters."

"Believe it, Jimmy, you better believe it."

"There's one thing these guys don't fully understand, Chick, and it's crucial. Harry is just not the same Harry. He's not the same funny guy, always with the jokes and laughs, that we all used to be crazy about. He's turned into a real bad guy. He can't tell the truth, you can't rely on him, he'd swindle his own mother if she were alive. Believe me, if the shit ever hits the fan he'll bury anyone to save himself. He's absolutely devoid of a sense of loyalty, without conscience. Christ, who knows better than you what I thought of him and what I did for him? More than I'd do for my own brothers. And what about Augie? Think back what Augie did for him. He worked seven days and seven nights a week. Why? So that little swindling prick could hang around Lindy's on Broadway and piss away all our money. What then? He takes off for parts unknown and leaves us with no money and a million loanshark problems. Now that everything is finally getting halfway straightened out, he contacts his Jew blood brother, Dorfman—who, by the way, he always said he hated—and decides to come back like nothing had ever happened. Is that fair?"

"Jimmy, are you serious? After all your years on earth and especially your years in The Job, are you still expecting anything in this world to be fair?"

"Well, Chick, I think I'm fair."

"In certain ways I agree, Jim, you are fair. But what if you asked some of the guys you shook and robbed, would they consider you fair?"

"If they paid me I never touched them."

"Suppose they couldn't afford to pay you?"

"That was their tough luck."

"Jimmy, you're impossible. Look, we've walked all the way to Newkirk Avenue and we haven't settled one thing. We could argue pro and con like this all night. Tell me, what do you intend to do?"

"Chick, I have a good scheme in mind. You know how much I like you and trust you. And I trust our man Tommy Fahey and Johnny Crews just as much. The best and the only way to handle Harry is to shoot the rat bastard as quick as possible."

"Are you nuts or something? Forget about that, it's too goddam heavy to talk about."

"Far from it, Chick. I was never so positive about somebody as I am about that guy. I'm warning you again, he's turned out bad. Why, for Christ's sake, he knows more about The Job and the guys in it than the head clerk of the department, the guy who keeps the files on everybody. We both got into plainclothes years ago because some headline-hunting politician started an investigation into police corruption. What better target? Luckily, it never got too far off the ground because La Guardia cut it off at the pass to keep his own image. It nearly happened again a few years ago when I got flopped from the chief's office into uniform. You can't forget that, when you lost your best pal. You remember, the Joe Pledge bullshit. The only thing that saved our asses and kept it from being blown out of proportion was your friendly Queens district attorney's office. They were worse than we were. Now, as anyone with a little brains can see, O'Dwyer is rapidly going out of style. He has his load on most of the time, and even his pals in the newspapers are starting to get on his ass. Frank Hogan, like a couple of others, wanted to be mayor so badly they could taste it, and Bill O' screwed them by running again. They all hate his guts and would do anything to discredit him. Believe me, the time is getting ripe for another blow, another scandal, and if they ever grab our friend Harry, it's lights out."

"Jimmy, you can't be serious. Come on, he'll never open up in a million years. I'd bet my life on it."

"Go ahead, bet your life on it. It will be like some of the horses you used to bet on before you took the vow, you'll finish down in the shithouse. Chick, I couldn't be more serious about anything. I just want either you, Tom, or Johnny to drive the car and I'll set him up and hit the little prick. It'll be like a dish of ice cream, and it will be my pleasure."

"What the hell do you want one of us to drive the car for? It should be a snap for you to get a chauffeur."

"For one simple reason. If by some million-to-one shot we get a beef of some kind after we do it, I want a cop driving the car. Not that I expect any beef, I think it will be like taking candy from a baby. I just want the added insurance of one of the three of you as a driver. Why don't you volunteer for this mission? You might go down in history as a folk hero."

"Folk you." They both laughed and Chick continued, "You know something, you're walking my feet off. Let's turn back and have a drink at McGough's. And please, my head's spinning. Let's forget the hit shit for the rest of the night. I promise I'll talk it over with Tom and Johnny and see what they think. You know, none of us like him, and if we agree it's a good idea I'll just tell you we have a meet. If they think the idea is no good, I'll just say the meeting is off. Okay?"

"Fair enough, Chick, but go over what I said to you about O'Dwyer. Tell them to mark my words very carefully and to give it a lot of thought. I don't want any snap decisions, there's plenty of time. There's one more thing. You really think I have to bow out?"

"Positively, there's no other way, especially after that battle scene in Dutch's tonight. Sooner or later the P.C.'s squad will murder you. They'll sic some kids you never heard of on you and they'll knock you right out of the box. Do as I say, grab as much as you can, set up some kind of payroll for yourself, and go legitimate for a while. The business world needs a bright, scheming mind like yours."

"Thanks a lot, pal. I'll put your last remarks on my job résumé. Okay, you get hold of Georgie Knowles and tell him to bring that little fuck around the Ballfield Tavern on Saturday and I'll see what I can work out. One other thing. Keep those two fucks from the P.C.'s squad away from me until this is all settled. Fair enough?"

"Good, Jimmy. Now you're using your head. Here we are, here's McGough's. Let's go in and have a drink, and for Christ's sake, let's talk about broads or baseball, I've had enough action and enough conversation about Harry Gross for one night."

While at McGough's bar with Chick, Jimmy remembered he had to phone Augie and make a date for early the next day. He excused himself from Chick and went to the telephone booth and dialed Augie's home number.

"Hello, Augie, this is Jimmy. I hope I'm not calling too late."

"Not at all, Jim. I'm just sitting here watching my new television set. I stayed up hoping you'd call me, I've got earth-shaking news. Who do you think called me tonight?"

"I'll take one guess, Augie. Harry Gross, and I'm right the first time."

"You're absolutely right. Christ, Jimmy, you could have knocked me over with a feather when I heard his voice. I couldn't believe my own ears, it was like a bad dream. This fucking bum came on with me just like he'd never left, like he was returning from a vacation from Europe or Florida, like he was never on the lam. He sounded just like nothing had happened. He laughed and joked, asked about all the guys, seemed as happy as a clam. I tell you, I'm still in a daze. How'd you find out? Don't tell me he had the nerve to call you?"

"No, nothing like that. I got the news earlier tonight in a scene reminiscent of an Edward G. Robinson movie, co-starring Humphrey Bogart."

"No shit. It wasn't bad, was it, Jimmy? I mean, you know the guys I'm referring to, the guys we talked about who seemed behind him."

"Listen, Aug, let's not go into it on the telephone. You know, 'Loose lips sink ships.' Here's what I want you to do tomorrow. Number one, get hold of Willie the cashier, then the two of you meet me in Leo's candy store at ten thirty tomorrow morning. Number two, tell him to bring all his up-to-date records. And please be there on time. I'll stay in Flatbush at my mother's so I'll be sure to be up early. It's important, Aug. Make sure you dig Willie up tonight and get there early."

"Go to sleep on it, Jimmy. I'll be there on time and I'll have Willie along with me. Jim, I hope this isn't what I think it is, but don't let it get you down. Get a good night's rest. See you tomorrow."

"Thanks, Aug. You're a sweetheart."

Jimmy went back to the bar to rejoin Chick, finished his drink, and said, "Chick, it's almost midnight, I think I'll pack it in. I still have my front-door key, so I think I'll stay at my mother's house. I need a good sleep, it looks like a long day tomorrow. Just one thing before we say goodnight. I want you to meet Tommy and John and give some serious thought to what I said about Harry. We'll all be better off if we send him to a richly deserved reward."

"I promise you, Jimmy, I'll get together with them as soon as possible. What you said makes a lot of sense. Okay, James, go home to Mama, give her my love, and for the last time, take it nice and easy the next couple of days. This could be the best break you ever got in life. Do exactly what I told you to do, Jim, and you'll finish way ahead of the game."

"Thanks a lot, Chickie boy. I really appreciate your sticking up for me tonight, my only friend in the house. So long, pal. Take it easy."

Jimmy drove to his mother's house and let himself in the front door, undressed, and fell asleep on the couch almost immediately.

He was awakened by a tap on the shoulder and looked up into his mother's face. She kissed him tenderly on the lips and said, "Whew, this room smells like a brewery, and you smell like the best customer. Get upstairs to the bathroom and brush your teeth and Listerine your mouth out."

"I'm sorry, Mom. I came in a little late and I didn't want to wake everybody up by running the water in the bathroom. Okay, I'll be right down, showered, shaved, and smelling like a rose. Mom, is my blue suit pressed?"

"You know it is, and a few of your shirts are ironed and hanging in your old closet. Get upstairs."

Jimmy came down about twenty minutes later and grabbed his mother around the waist and kissed her. "How's that, Mom? Do I smell better?"

"A lot better, thank God. Sit over there in the breakfast nook, I'll have your breakfast ready in a couple of minutes. The orange juice is on the table."

Mrs. Riley served her favorite son James a steaming plate of ham and eggs and sat opposite him in the breakfast nook. While he ate she studied him like a museum curator contemplating a new painting. "You know, James, your face is getting a little puffed up, like you're drinking too much. You're not going to get fat and lose your good looks, are you?"

"Never, Mom. Never. You know I'm too vain to get fat."

She got up and reached across and touched her fingers to Jimmy's forehead, pressing them against a little lump there. "Where'd you get this lump on your head? And it's black and blue. Did you get into another fight or something?"

"Mom, are you going crazy, you're looking at me like I'm ten years old. I'm over thirty now, Momma, my fighting days are over."

Jesus, that's where my head must have hit Dorfman over the eye, and like a dope I never even noticed it while shaving.

"Are you sure, James?"

"Honest, Momma, I must have bumped my head getting out of the car last night. Will you please forget my head and stop examining me like a lady doctor. Sit down and drink your coffee. Talk to me. Tell me what's new with you. Have you seen any great movies since I saw you last?"

"Oh, Jim, I saw a great one at the Loew's Met the other day. That girl you went to high school with was wonderful in it."

Jimmy knew the actress she meant, but one of his greatest kicks with his mother was to lead her on in conversations about her movies. Mrs. Riley was a regular Mrs. Malaprop, and would invariably drop a couple of beautiful lines that would cause him inwardly to howl.

"You mean Susan Hayward, Mom? I told you at least fifity times she went to Girls High School near the Botanical Gardens, not Erasmus Hall."

"That's right, you did. Jim, she was absolutely wonderful in this picture. Oh, that poor girl, she got electrocuted in the end."

"What's the name of the picture, Mom?" Jimmy knew, but he waited to hear Mrs. Malaprop's version.

"Let's see, James. I think it was *I Don't Want to Die*. The Hayward girl was magnificent. It was so sad, I cried my eyes out at the end."

"Mom, I think you have the name wrong. The title of the picture is *I Want to Live*."

"What's the difference, it's the same thing. Anyway, the poor girl was electrocuted at the end of the picture."

"No, Mom, she went to the gas chamber. It was based on a famous murder case in California. They send you to the gas chamber out there."

"Well, anyway, she was strapped to the chair. I covered my face, I couldn't look any more at what they were doing to that poor girl."

"Too bad, Mom. I wonder how the poor guy she killed might feel about it."

"Jimmy, that wonderful Hayward girl could never hurt anybody. Let's change the subject, I get the blues just thinking about her in that chair."

They talked together over coffee for another hour, and Jimmy finally had to leave. He kissed his mother goodbye, loving her more than anything in the whole world.

Augie and Willie were waiting for him in the back of Leo's candy store. They both had faces on them like a couple of funeral directors. On the contrary, Jimmy was in exceptionally good spirits, feeling great after the long visit with his mother. All the venom from the night before had left him, and he'd made up his mind to follow Chick's advice and remove himself from the gambling business the best way he could. He shook hands with Willie and Augie and said, "Come on, cheer up. Take the long faces off, the end of the world isn't here."

Willie answered, "I can't believe it, Jimmy, that this little cafone is coming back. You and Augie are finally getting the joint into shape and I can sleep at night knowing I'll have enough cash on hand to pay out the next day in case we get a big hit. The last year with Harry was a nightmare. He was grabbing the cash quicker than we were taking it in. Jimmy, is it really true, like Augie says, that Harry's back and the cops are giving you the gate?"

"You sound like the little kid asking Shoeless Joe Jackson of the White Sox to 'say it ain't so, Joe.' Yes, Willie, I'm afraid it is so. You know the old saying, you can't fight City Hall. And if I stick around, we don't have a chance, we're deadsville. Well, enough of feeling sorry for ourselves, I didn't bring you two in this morning for that. Willie, how much is in the bankroll, cash on hand and the money in transit? What do the runners owe?"

"I can come close, Jimmy, but not one hundred percent on the nose."

"Close is good enough."

"There should be exactly fifty-five grand in the bank vault where you keep it, and we have about thirty grand or so outstanding, all of which is good."

"About how much is left on the shylock payments?"

"Ten thousand. We reduced it fifty thousand."

"Well, that's good news. Okay, Willie, go up to the front of the store, I want to talk to Augie alone."

Willie walked up front and Augie turned to Jimmy and said, "What's on the agenda, Jimmy? What do you intend to do?"

"I'm going to walk out, Aug, or else they're going to knock our brains out. But by all means I want you to stay, and maybe you can keep some kind of check on that bandit. Besides, where else are you going to earn the kind of money you're earning now? What the hell is the use kidding ourselves, Harry won't last a year. He'll put his humble act on for a while and be all business the next few months, but then he'll get the color back in his cheeks and start flying high again. The big-shot complex is in his blood now, he'll never get rid of it. But that's his problem, here's what I want you to do. I want a thousand dollars a week sent up to me in Connecticut, and make sure I don't get passed. Rain or shine, win or lose, I don't want to know a goddam thing, just make sure that G-note gets sent up to me. Now, Aug, you and I will take a walk down the block to our friends at the National City Bank and empty the bankroll money out of the vault. I'm taking fifty grand, my original stake in the business—fifty which should be a million by now if that little fuck had stayed on the level. You take the other five grand for yourself. The outstanding money in transit can be left to serve as a bankroll, plus whatever fresh cash he's getting from his personal Gestapo squad. I'm a sonofabitch if he's using my fifty big ones."

"Sounds good. Whatever you say, Jim. There's only one thing

that's bothering me. How in the hell am I going to handle this guy after what he's done to us?"

"I know how I'd like to handle him, and that might come sooner than you think. You'll just have to conciliate, Augie, go along with the act and roll with the punches. The main thing is to keep the organization intact. You have to admit we have a nice crew, a great bunch of guys. They all have either broads or wives to support, sometimes both, so we have to keep everybody working. Just go along and play it by ear for a while, Aug, and see how it works out. We'll be in constant touch, anyway. As for me and my plans, I'm packing in my New York apartment and going back to Connecticut and get acquainted with my wife and kids. Winter is just around the corner and I'll probably take a house in Palm Beach for four or five months. I'm tired, Augie, I need a good rest. Maybe this could be the best thing ever happened to me."

The hotel operator's wake-up call came at nine the next morning and awakened Jimmy from a sound sleep. He felt fresh and rested. He had only had a couple of drinks and dinner the night before and was home in bed before midnight. He had been tempted to go on the town pretty good, but his better sense dictated that he be fresh and clear-headed on this day of days, to welcome back his former best friend and now his mortal enemy.

While having breakfast he made the decision to move out of his hotel apartment that very day, to leave New York behind for a few months. He would visit the city only if absolutely necessary. He packed his clothes and called his man Sharkey to pick him up at eleven thirty. His rent was on a month-to-month basis, and as it was only the middle of the month and the rent was prepaid, moving out presented no particular problem. He asked one of the hotel owners up for a cup of coffee and thanked him profusely for his kindness during the couple of years he had been their guest. He left envelopes for the two maids who took care of his apartment, the elevator men, telephone operators, and doormen.

When Sharkey came and packed his bags in the car, Jimmy shook hands with several of the help and a couple of the bosses and quickly left. A wave of sadness had engulfed him when he was saying his goodbyes in the lobby, his eyes had filled with tears. What a nice bunch of people, he thought, and how good they were to me the last couple of years. Sure, maybe he was extra generous and always staked everyone pretty good, but he felt their thoughtfulness and sincerity really came from their hearts. But he knew his decision was right, he had to pack up and leave New York for a good long while. If he stayed around he would be like a hanger-on, like an out-of-work actor with a lot of ability and no stage to display his talent.

Sharkey dropped him off at the Ballfield Tavern about half past twelve, and the first one he saw as he entered the bar was Harry, dressed to the teeth, having a drink at the far end of the bar with Augie, Georgie Knowles, the local division lieutenant, and a huge, brutal-looking young plainclothes cop named Flanagan, whom Jimmy had met a couple of times. Jimmy couldn't resist a silent chuckle as he looked at the big animal Harry and Georgie had brought along. They were making sure they had plenty of protection in case of a replay of the brief violence at Dutch's place a couple of nights ago. But Jimmy's mood was one of resignation, he just didn't give a shit. If the powers that be wanted him out so badly, that's the way it was and there wasn't a goddam thing he could do about it.

He walked over to the four of them, everyone visibly a little nervous, Harry's hand shaking as he put his glass on the bar, even though his face wore his familiar false-face smile. Jimmy shook hands with Augie, the lieutenant, and young Flanagan, pointedly ignoring Harry's outstretched hand. He shook his head no to the offer of a drink and said in a clipped, quiet voice, "Too early for me, Georgie. I tell you what, I'd like to get this over with real quick. I want to go in the back with Augie and Harry privately and discuss a couple of personal things that are very important. That okay with you?"

"Sure, Jimmy, that's fine with me. Only no bullshit with your hands, no trouble. You promise?"

"I promise, Georgie. You think I'm sucker enough to start trouble when you have the Irish King Kong along to protect this weasel?"

A little uncertain laugh from Knowles and Flanagan. Harry's face flushed at the "weasel" invective.

Knowles said, "Go ahead, Jimmy, have it out with Harry and we'll wait here and have another couple of drinks. I want to talk to you for a minute when you finish and make a dinner date in a week or so."

"Listen, Georgie, get this straight. I don't care to have dinner with you next week, or the week after, or ever. You already made it clear whose side you're on, so from here on in I consider you an ex-friend of mine. So let's you and I cut out all the friendly horseshit as of right now. Okay, Augie, let's you and I go in the back room with this guy and get our business over with."

Jimmy turned away from the bar abruptly and walked to the back with Augie and Harry following. The three of them sat at a table and Jimmy said, "All right, tell your story, dead on the level. Don't give me any of your lying, double-dealing shit or I swear to God I'll cut your fucking throat no matter who's out there at the bar."

Harry was rattled, but he maintained an air of bravado, apparently secure with his two bodyguards thirty feet away. He said, "Look, Jimmy, I know I was wrong, I did crazy things, but I promise I'll make it up to you. For Christ's sake, your being sore at me is not going to help. Don't worry, I've learned my lesson. This time around I'm going to make it real big, and you'll still be my partner."

"Harry, get this through that fucking crooked head of yours. I don't want to be your partner, or even be associated with you in any way. Think back to the night we shook hands and became partners. I warned you clearly that night, don't ever fuck me 'cause the first time you do will be the last time, you'll never get another chance. I did everything you expected of me and more. What did I get in return? The royal screwing of all time. Ah, but what the hell, that's all ancient history as far as I'm concerned. Every time I think about what we should have today I get sick to my stomach."

"Jimmy, please, don't talk like that. You'll always be with me, I promise you."

"You don't understand, Harry. I don't want to be with you, ever. Not in any way, shape, or form. Forget it, let's get down to the business at hand. Augie and I put the joint back on its feet, and it's not in bad shape. There's approximately thirty thousand in transit coming to the place, and the loansharks you left behind are nearly all paid off. I made a third settlement with them, thinking you were gone forever. Now, I don't know what they'll do, that's your headache. Willie has all the records of what we paid, and the balances. Now for the sixty-four-thousand-dollar question, how about the overall bankroll? How are you going to manage?"

"It's all taken care of, Jimmy. I'll have over a hundred big ones as a starter. That should be plenty."

"I hope this isn't shylock money."

Harry laughed. "Who the hell would loan me, Jimmy? No, I imagine you have an idea where I got it."

"I couldn't give one shit where you got it, and I don't want to know. I left explicit instructions with Augie and Willie. I get sent one thousand dollars a week, and I don't want one payment missed. Is that fair enough?"

"More than fair, Jimmy. I might even do better."

"Forget better, just one grand a week is what I think I deserve. One last thing, don't bother me if you have any problems. Take it up with your friend out at the bar and your blood brother, Dave Dorfman, if you have any trouble. Just make sure you send my money every week, and from now on make believe I'm dead."

"Come on, Jim, you'll always be my friend. Let me tell you where I was the last few months and what I accomplished."

"I don't want to hear one word about your going on the lam, I was only hoping that someday I would get word they found your dead body. Now forget about the 'friend' horseshit. Try to do the right thing for Augie there, he broke his balls for you. If you keep your nose clean, maybe you just might get off again. Okay, Harry, that's all I have to say. Let's go."

Jimmy stood up, shook hands with Augie, and walked through the main bar out the door. On the way out he waved goodbye to Tommy, the bartender, and completely ignored Knowles and his gorilla friend, Flanagan. Sharkey was behind the wheel of the car parked outside the door, and Jimmy got in the back seat and said, "Connecticut, Shark."

As Sharkey headed for the Brooklyn Bridge and the FDR Drive in Manhattan, Jimmy put his head against the seat and strangely enough felt a huge wave of relief settle over him. He was relieved and happy to be through with cops, the gambling racket, and all the additional bullshit that went along with it. In fact, it was very much the same feeling he had experienced a couple of years earlier when he turned in his police shield. Like a big weight was lifted off his shoulders. Like a tight steel band was loosened from around his forehead. As he closed his eyes and stretched his legs out, he started to reminisce about his life up until the present. A wonderful boyhood that was all too short. A couple of years at sea in the merchant marine that soon changed him from a boy into a full-grown man at a tender age. A few years of a lot of fun and a lot of nice girls, and then his marriage and reluctantly joining the police force.

Everything that had happened up until then was only the preliminaries, The Job had to be the main event, phase one in his young life. Then the ride on the magic carpet as a chief inspector's man, culminating in his long, fruitful, and finally aborted relationship with Harry. What good years and good times they were. He thought back to Harry and smiled with the memories of the laughs they had together with the nightclub, the horse room downstairs, the trips they took together. It was one wonderful trip until that dizzy sonofabitch went crazy on him. I guess that had to be phase two in Jimmy Riley's life, he thought. What the hell will I do for an encore? What lies ahead in phase three?

He fell asleep and woke up with Sharkey pulling at his shoulder and telling him they were outside his home in Connecticut.

The first signs of winter came to Connecticut, and Jimmy called his friend in Palm Beach and rented a house for six months. A couple of days before he was to leave he received the long-awaited call from his pal Chick.

"Hello, Jimmy, this is Chick. How's everything in Connecticut?"

"Fine, Chick. I thought you'd died on me. You know, maybe you got shot coming out of a whorehouse."

"No, I was just pretty busy. I'm sorry to say I've got bad news. The meeting is off. It seems every time I call you, Jim, I bring bad news."

"No, that's okay, Chick. Did you explain to those two how I felt about that guy?"

"Exactly the way you laid it out, but they nixed the proposition."

"Okay. What can I say? Listen, I'm going to Florida for a few months. I'll leave a number with Augie where you can reach me in case some emergency comes up. Take care of yourself, Chick. See you real soon after I come back."

"Right. Take care, Jim. Have a good trip."

He hung up the telephone with a strange feeling of disquiet. Those guys were all suckers, they thought the band was never going to stop playing. Someday it would and maybe they'd regret their decision.

The entourage flew into Palm Beach a couple of days later, and Jimmy enrolled his boy in a private grade school and his oldest daughter in nursery school. He and Kay settled down to a good long vacation of reading, swimming, and playing golf. Each week he received his thousand dollars in the form of a bank cashier's check, just as he had arranged with Willie and Augie. He had retained his membership in the fancy country club they had joined the year before, and he soon found a circle of nice guys who liked to play golf and gamble a little money on their game. He played golf mornings, swam in the afternoon with his kids, and dined out frequently with Kay at one of the numerous fine restaurants that Palm Beach was famous for. As an added attraction, once a week they had dinner at the Lake Club, a beautiful gambling casino just outside Palm Beach. After dinner Jimmy would hit the crap table while Kay gambled a little bit at roulette. A little bit was exactly right, because if she lost the fifty dollars Jimmy gave her to play she would almost burst into tears. Jimmy held his own at the crap table, being a wrong bettor by nature and a veteran crap-shooter since the age of eight in Red Hook, Brooklyn. Dinner at the Lake Club was always a night to anticipate, and if it rained during the day and knocked out the golf and swimming, there was a great horse room in downtown Palm Beach where Jimmy loved to spend a few hours. It reminded him of some of the great horse rooms in New York like Big George's, and he always seemed to run into some old friend there with whom to reminisce about the Big City over a tall Cutty Sark and water.

For a while it was an idyllic existence, but as the weeks passed into months in the Florida sunshine, Jimmy slowly but surely started to get itchy, to get ants in his pants. He was elated to be spending so much time with his long-neglected family, and relaxed and happy to be relieved of the constant apprehension of trouble. But he was getting a bit depressed at the rut he was sinking into and knew that it was time to start looking for some sort of action. His two kids wouldn't be finishing their school terms until the end of May, so he left his wife and kids in Florida and flew home the early part of April to get his head together and figure in which direction he should go.

It was pretty much the same life in Connecticut, reading and playing lots of golf, but he established a legitimate payroll for himself that allayed much of his fear of the relentless forces of the Internal Revenue. He managed this by investing a good chunk of money in one of his golfing friends' import and export business. He was still on good terms with the real estate tycoon and bought a few additional pieces of property together with him, property whose value he was assured would skyrocket. His real estate friend kept urging him to throw in with him all the way, all the marbles, but Jimmy felt the real estate business was much too dull and tedious a way to make a living. He had formed this impression from some of the men and women he knew at the country club who made their living in real estate. Ugh, there had to be an easier way.

Augie called Jimmy about twice a month, and lately seemed somewhat distressed, unhappy, far from his usual self. He was never by nature a happy-go-lucky guy, always quiet and a little on the pessimistic side, but from his last few calls Jimmy felt Augie was almost morose. Their luck had changed when Jimmy left, he complained, they couldn't seem to get off. They would win two or three weeks in a row, then lose it all in a few days' bad streak. The outfit was just holding its own, everyone just drawing a week's pay, but not building up the bankroll. At Jimmy's suggestion, Augie and Willie backtracked on Harry every which way to see if he was up to his old tricks, but couldn't find one thing wrong. There was no explanation, they were just in an unbelievable streak of bad luck. No matter how much you have the best of it in the gambling business, you still need your share of good luck. To make matters worse, some new faces were appearing on the vice and gambling plainclothes squads, and a few of them were developing into real ball-breakers. Jimmy mostly listened, occasionally offering some bit of advice, and as much as he would have liked to have dinner with Augie, he assiduously avoided him and everyone else in the outfit. Just make sure you send me that thousand a week, God spare me from all the ongoing headaches.

Jimmy finally started to go to New York one day a week to work out at the athletic club. He would play squash, have a steam bath and massage, then have dinner and play cards until late evening. He would stay overnight at the club, work out the next day and play cards until about dinner time, and then drive up to Connecticut when the traffic eased. He made a number of good friends, several of whom were influential in the business world, and had had a few interesting propositions offered to him, but he couldn't get interested enough to accept even one of them. His family rejoined him the early part of June and for a short while life brightened up considerably, but he was soon chafing at the bit to get seriously involved with something.

One morning he was playing golf with a fairly new member of the country club, a real nice guy, and after they finished he drove Jimmy home and Jimmy invited him in for a drink. They were sitting in the den enjoying a nice tall cold one, when his new friend said, "Jimmy, I only met you for the first time about a month ago, and to be honest, I've become a fan of yours, I really like you. You're a lot of fun to play golf with even if you do go nuts when you miss a shot, and if you don't mind I'd like to talk to you about something you might be interested in."

"Go ahead, Dennis. I'm glad you like me, because a couple of times out there this morning I was ready to kill you. What a partner, you cost me thirty-three bucks."

"I was murder today, I admit, but you weren't exactly Bobby Jones yourself. Anyway, hold the golf shit, this is important, listen to me very carefully. I have a few friends who know you real well, and before I met you I was in your club quite a number of times. A nice place, I really liked it. I also know that you were a vice cop for a long time, but had a pretty good reputation. It follows that you must be sitting on a few bucks. As you know, I'm in the printing business and I do very well. I own my own place and I don't need any partners or any money, but I know you're not doing anything and I have a great idea for you. I have a friend who owns a graphic arts plant. It's very well equipped and this guy Goldman is a crackerjack craftsman, a real top guy. Goldman has had a few bad collection problems and he's a little short of money. Again, he has a nice plant and he does superb work. So good that when I want something out of the ordinary for a special job, I farm out the work to Jack Goldman. Suppose I put you two together. He needs about fifty grand to put him back on his feet. You put the money up strictly as a loan against his equipment, which is worth twice as much. Then I'll set you up as a printing broker, with Goldman doing your work at his cost plus a small profit. You finance the jobs you bring in, the paper, art work, and so on. I guarantee you'll make yourself a ton of money in no time, with all the people you know and the entrées you have. Jimmy, it's a great proposition and you're a natural for this business. Furthermore, there is no way you can get hurt. I know you're a good hustler. Just work hard and you'll make a fortune. Besides, think of it, Jimmy, you'll be legitimate."

"Dennis, whatever caused you to think that in any way I'd be illegitimate?"

Dennis laughed. "Jimmy, I told you I know quite a few guys that know you real good, your reputation precedes you. Besides, I was down in that lovely little room you had below the club a few times trying to pick a winner. That was quite an operation."

"Okay, warden, don't hit me, I'll talk," Jimmy laughed. "When do I meet this starving Michelangelo?"

"How about this coming Monday? I'll make a date for the three of us to have lunch. Any problem about the fifty grand?"

"None at all, Dennis. Drink up, we'll have another to toast my new career."

Dennis put the deal together just as he promised, and Jimmy had his lawyer draw up a contract satisfactory to all parties. He spent a couple of weeks around the plant studying the operation and familiarizing himself with the various terms used in the graphic arts world. Goldman and Dennis both worked with him and taught him the fundamentals of printing. Jimmy absorbed the knowledge and the vernacular of the printing world in about six weeks and set himself up as a printing broker. First he had to sell himself to get the order, then he did as his good friend Dennis had set him up to do. He financed the entire job, paying Goldman up front, and then put a fat profit on for himself. At first he got a few jobs from friends or from buyers recommended by friends, but soon one job ran into the other and he was so busy and making so much money he could hardly believe it.

It was a pretty heady experience, getting off to such a great start in a legitimate enterprise, and before Jimmy knew it he was immersed in the printing world. He even began to frequent the restaurants where the salesmen and buyers were known to drink their lunch. After a few months in the new business he took Goldman, the true resident genius and owner of the graphic arts plant, out to dinner and discussed the possibility of buying half of the business. They had grown fond of one another in their brief tenure, and their relationship appeared to get better each week. Goldman made Jimmy a very fair offer, and they agreed to meet with their respective lawyers the following week.

The sunrise the next day heralded a lovely late-summer day in Connecticut. Jimmy decided not to go to the city, to do some business on the telephone and play golf at the club in the afternoon. After breakfast he walked the couple of miles into town to buy the New York papers. He counted out some change, put it into a tin container on the outside newsstand, and took the *Daily News* and the *New York Times*. He folded them under his arm and walked back to the house. He asked the maid to bring him some fresh coffee in the den and settled down in a lounge chair to read the *News*. The headline on the front page hit him square in the face and he almost jumped out of the chair.

GROSS BOOKIE EMPIRE SMASHED
BY BROOKLYN D. A.'S OFFICE
HINT HUGE POLICE PAYOFFS INVOLVED

Jimmy quickly turned to the inside page for the sordid details and almost got violently ill. It was all over. The wire room in Nassau County had been raided by the local cops in conjunction with the detectives from the Brooklyn district attorney's office. He thought back. Augie had called a couple of weeks ago and told him that they had just missed getting pinched in downtown Brooklyn, where they had moved the wire room from over Leo's candy store. They were lucky enough to get the tip-off in time to vacate. They were getting a lot of heat from the Brooklyn D.A.'s squad and figured if they moved to Nassau County, out of the jurisdiction of New York City, the heat would abate. Jimmy took it for granted they had received the okay from the cops in Nassau County. When he didn't hear anything further, he was sure they had the okay. He read the *Times* version, and it was equally disheartening. They had pinched Mikie, Blackie, and Rocky in the wire room, and had warrants out for Harry and about twenty of the spot operators and runners. All the news that was fit to print was bad.

Jesus Christ, thank God I got out of there before the shit hit the fan. But did I? If everyone stands up I'm okay, but who knows how much balls those guys got? Both papers quoted the district attorney, a twenty-million-dollar empire smashed. The district attorney, a saintly and not too bright Irishman descended from Tammany politicians who had made enough money to send him to good Catholic colleges so he could grow up to have enough clout to get elected to his high office and make a big name for himself catching up with crooked cops. For Christ's sake, that was as hard to do as catching a pigeon in Prospect Park. A special grand jury had already been convened—real bad news, they had plenty of previous information—under the aegis of that staunch foe of bookies and corrupt cops, the defender of one hundred cold-blooded murderers, his Honor, the now virtuous Sam Leibowitz. Jimmy knew through his own political sources that Leibowitz hated Bill O'Dwyer. Indeed, Leibowitz had had his own mayoralty aspirations before Bill O'Dwyer had decided to throw his hat in the ring again. Jimmy got the old familiar chill down his spine, so bad he almost shuddered as he sat in his den and sipped his coffee. This was going to be one bad scene, a great big mess, and a lot of guys were going to get hurt bad. I just hope one of them isn't me.

7

SAMUEL S. LEIBOWITZ was born Samuel Simon Lebeau in the town of Jassy, Rumania, on August 14, 1893. The Lebeau family migrated to America when young Sam was just four years old. Mr. Lebeau did well in America, starting out as an itinerant peddler on the Lower East Side, then graduating into a small-time merchant. For reasons best known to himself, Sam's father changed the family name from Lebeau to Leibowitz. It was often remarked in judicial circles that while he was at it, he might just as well have changed young Samuel Simon Lebeau's name to Simon Legree, a name that would have proved more appropriate to the maniacal Sam in later life.

The family finally settled in the borough of Queens, where young Sam attended public school and proved to be a bright and earnest student. With some financial help from his family and a burning ambition to succeed, young Sam eventually worked his way through Cornell University, where he received his law degree in 1916.

Shortly after graduation he opened a law office in Brooklyn and began the practice of criminal law. The pickings were slim in criminal law in those days, and more seasoned lawyers were quick to refer such ill-paying cases to the up-and-coming young Leibowitz. Sam soon built an enviable reputation for diligence and shrewdness among the habitués of the underworld. He was most adept at winning over juries to gain acquittals with tactics that, while sometimes distressing, were almost always effective.

By the mid-1920s Leibowitz had built a large practice, a criminal clientele that had prospered and become affluent with the advent of the Prohibition era. Alcoholic beverages were banned by the Eighteenth Amendment to the Constitution and given force by the Volstead Act. This was another Draconian measure dreamed up by the legislators to reform the living habits of the American public. Naturally, the American public refused to be reformed, and Prohibition swiftly became the most lawless era in American history. Young Sam's legal practice soared. By now he was a master of courtroom histrionics, with booming voice, scowling face, and derisive gestures at opposing witnesses and prosecutors that often defied the bounds of legal ethics. He was constantly remonstrated with by presiding judges, but he never changed his style. His growing reputation became even more enhanced among the underworld as he beat case after case for its denizens.

Leibowitz soon graduated from paltry criminal cases like grand larceny, bootlegging, and robbery into becoming one of the top defenders of murderers in the entire country. Among his own colleagues, even his most ardent foes, he was known as an incredibly hard worker, a lawyer who really did his homework in preparation of a case. He would immerse himself in the study of medicine, ballistics, or any technological data necessary to confuse the opposition and beguile the jury to gain his client's acquittal. He had one credo, often repeated in later years on the lecture trail: "My job as a criminal lawyer was to sell my client's cause to a jury."

He indeed sold his client's cause to spellbound juries like no other lawyer of his time. Sam slowly but surely built a fantastic record as a lawyer who could get almost any murderer off the hook. He lost but one case in the defense of over a hundred cold-blooded murderers. In later years he claimed he only lost that one because his client had lied to him. As his fame became legendary, Sam Leibowitz prospered beyond his wildest dreams. He built a luxurious brick mansion for his wife and family in the Manhattan Beach section of Brooklyn. Sam loved Brooklyn, and like all true Brooklynites, he also loved the Brooklyn Dodgers.

While Sam Leibowitz soon learned to enjoy the expensive trappings of a successful law practice, he never learned to acquire the slightest amount of humility or personal charm to soften his oppo-

nents' or fellow lawyers' opinion of him. Perhaps it was merely
envy, but to his counterparts in the legal world he seemed to
remain absolutely driven. He was brusque, contemptuous, acidu-
lous—completely devoid of feeling toward anyone he regarded as
an adversary. There were many prominent lawyers of the 1920s
who constantly assailed Sam Leibowitz. They contended that
most of his innumerable victories in his skillful skirmishes with
judges and juries were highly unethical. Sam brushed his critics
aside as he would an errant snowflake from his coat collar. He
reveled in the publicity and criticism, secure in his unlimited tal-
ents as a defender without peer.

Suddenly, in 1925, Sam Leibowitz almost got what some people prayed for, and the members of the legal profession who hated
his guts were jubilant. He was indicted for the serious crime of
subornation of perjury, and the speakeasies surrounding the court-
houses of downtown Brooklyn were crowded with judges and
lawyers toasting his impending demise. The indictment resulted
from Sam's defense of a number of New York City police officers
attached to the vice squad who were accused of shaking down
whorehouses. Leibowitz was indicted for coaching the cops to
give false testimony, for tutoring them to commit perjury in order
to be vindicated. The crime was a felony that could result in a jail
term for Leibowitz and disbarment from the practice of law.

Leibowitz was deeply shocked, panic-stricken. After many
legal machinations, however, the charges were dismissed for lack
of corroboration. Then, to Leibowitz's dismay, the initial ruling
was reversed by the Appellate Division, the charges were reinstated, and Leibowitz was ordered to stand trial. The county judge
who originally dismissed the charges against Leibowitz was
George W. Martin, and it was noted at the time that the dismissal
was indeed under "puzzling circumstances." Eventually, a much
relieved and chastened Leibowitz was returned to grace and the
legal profession by the refusal of the district attorney's office to
prosecute. It was a case that achieved much notoriety, promi-
nently covered by the newspapers of the day, and the puzzling
ending remained inexplicable. Rumor had it that one of the accused vice cops had at first agreed to cooperate with the district
attorney's office in return for leniency, but later recanted. Rumor

notwithstanding, this explanation appeared to be a fairly plausible one in view of Leibowitz's subsequent dim opinion of policemen, especially vice and gambling cops, through the ensuing years.

The onus of criminal prosecution and ultimate disbarment lifted from his sagging shoulders, Sam Leibowitz attained greater fame. He defended Al Capone, the acknowledged leader of the country's underworld, on four separate occasions. He defended Vincent "Mad Dog" Coll, one of the most feared executioners for the mob. He defended Robert Irwin, a psychopath and triple murderer. These were some of the stars in his infamous galaxy of deadly clients. They were all either acquitted or received prison terms. He lost only one to the electric chair, the man who Sam later insisted had lied to him.

Every so often, amid much fanfare, Leibowitz would defend an indigent client without fee. He made certain beforehand that his ace personal investigator, a short Italian named Johnny Terry, assured him the odds in favor of acquittal were great. Sam would inevitably make a tremendous show of the trial, and when the jury returned the desired verdict freeing his client, the newspaper photographers would have a bonanza. He would be sure to be pictured being kissed and hugged by his poor client, revered for his beneficence in defending a poor man or woman without a penny of fee.

In 1935 Sam created a furor among the citizens of the South and eventually of the entire United States by his sensational defense of the Scottsboro Boys. The Scottsboro Boys were nine black youths from Scottsboro, Alabama, who were charged with raping two white prostitutes. Sam, in a compelling legal brief that won him much personal distinction and international acclaim, reversed their conviction in the United States Supreme Court. He convinced that highest of tribunals that it was impossible for a black person to receive a fair and impartial trial in a region where blacks were systematically excluded from serving on juries. This was the specific unwritten law in Alabama and most of the South at that time, and to praise that resounded throughout the civilized world, Leibowitz gained eventual dismissal of all charges against the nine Scottsboro Boys.

This notable victory served to build an aura of ultraliberalism about Sam Leibowitz, which was proved to be almost ludicrous by his startling behavior as a county judge in subsequent years. His flamboyant role as a defender of blacks as innocent victims of society proved more of a publicity stunt than the true motivations of a vehement campaigner for racial justice. Not much later, when he ascended to the bench, Leibowitz came down hard on blacks unfortunate enough to be tried by him. He railed bitterly against welfare recipients, most of whom were black or Hispanic. He claimed most of them were cheats and frauds, chiselers and leeches on society, and urged that they be separated from their children. He expounded shrilly that welfare people were unfit parents and their children were responsible for nearly all of juvenile crime. Take the children away from welfare parents, take them away from the hard-core relief families, he repeatedly urged. A true liberal indeed, Sam Leibowitz.

His fame as a lawyer grew and his personal wealth became sufficient to raise his family in great style and to educate his children at the best universities. But the practice of law had begun to pall. Sam Leibowitz began to lust to become a judge. He did not set his sights on a lower-court judgeship, he had them raised to the important elective office of county judge. County judge was then the highest level of the trial judiciary of Brooklyn.

Having achieved the pinnacle of his goals as a trial lawyer, Leibowitz now determined to be on the prosecutorial side of justice. Perhaps it was the nagging of his own conscience, or his disgust at the lower elements of society he was constantly in touch with as a criminal lawyer. Whatever the reasons his psyche dictated, Leibowitz began to send out trial balloons to the political bosses. What he wanted now most of all was to be a prosecutor —"a crusader against crime," as he constantly repeated to his few friends and members of the press. Not immediately successful in his bid for nomination for office of county judge, Sam tried to enlist the support of prominent Jewish leaders in a vain quest for the Democratic nomination as district attorney of Brooklyn. He cited himself as some sort of Jewish folk hero, and suddenly became involved in Zionist affairs and Jewish charities. This blatant display of instant Jewishness dismayed the prominent leaders of the Jewish community. They denounced Sam as a Johnny-come-lately in Jewish affairs and declared that they had no intention of supporting someone who miraculously became Jewish-conscious when about to seek election to high office.

Frustrated at every turn in his bid for some high elective office in 1935, Sam again attempted in 1939 to run for mayor on an independent ticket against the man whose life he later helped to ruin, Bill O'Dwyer. During the intervening four years Leibowitz had made serious efforts to involve himself more heavily in Jewish circles and helped to mend his rift with Jewish leaders. O'Dwyer feared Sam might create a serious racial issue and damage his own chances for reelection. By now Leibowitz was becoming more than a mere gadfly to the Democratic bosses. The top party boss of Brooklyn, Frank Kelly, offered Leibowitz the nomination for State Supreme Court justice if he would take his hat out of the ring against O'Dwyer. Kelly's offer, when reported back to the reigning State Supreme Court justices, had them up in arms. From all reports, they flatly rejected Leibowitz as a nominee to join their august ranks.

By this time, our man Sam was obsessed with the idea of becoming a judge. He held numerous press conferences extolling the virtue of judges. He told one interviewer, "Of all human functions, there is but one Godlike, to judge." This lofty sentiment seemed to express in a nutshell the philosophy of Samuel Simon Lebeau, better known to fight crowds everywhere as Sam Leibowitz. Subsequent events in his judicial career appeared to substantiate his Godlike image of the eminence of the judiciary.

The Democratic boss, Frank Kelly, after much internecine warfare, finally compromised by awarding Leibowitz the party's nomination for County Court judge in 1940. While temporarily adequate, it wasn't quite what Leibowitz envisioned for himself. He had set more Olympian goals—from district attorney to mayor, from mayor to attorney general, from attorney general to governor. To his undying chagrin, the presidency of the United States was beyond his grasp, he was not a native-born American.

In 1940 Leibowitz was elected to a fourteen-year term on the County Court bench. It appears perfectly obvious in retrospect, just by the record of his constant involvement in controversial issues and his tireless crusades over the next decade, that, in the parlance of baseball, he was merely warming up in the bullpen, getting ready to relieve the starting pitcher. He soon made it quite clear that he wanted to be the next mayor of New York City.

On January 6, 1941, Sam Leibowitz was inducted as a County Court judge. The senior judge, John J. Fitzgerald, quoted Socrates, and Judge Franklin Taylor handed Sam a gavel, his emblem of office, and said, "You have been Samuel Leibowitz, the great lawyer, now you will be Samuel Leibowitz, the great judge." One of his more felicitous biographers, Quentin Reynolds, noted that the two fellow judges, Peter J. Brancato and George W. Martin, also paid their respects. Actually what Judge Martin really had to say was, "Please, just learn to keep your mouth shut and give the lawyers a chance to talk."

Judge Martin disliked Leibowitz intensely. It was the same Judge Martin who had reluctantly dismissed the subornation of perjury charges against Leibowitz which arose from his beleaguered defense of the vice cops charged with whorehouse shakedowns. For a long time the dismissal of the indictment was under a distinct cloud, the aroma from which had reached the noses of the Appellate Division judges who reinstated the indictment. A short time after Leibowitz was elected to the County Court, Judge Martin resigned from the bench to go back into private practice. Not long afterward, ex-Judge Martin appeared on behalf of a client before Judge Leibowitz, the same Leibowitz who was his former colleague and for whom he had previously dismissed a criminal indictment. They locked horns on a point of law, ex-Judge Martin vehemently upholding his theory and Judge Leibowitz in violent disagreement with him. As the argument reached a peak, Leibowitz abruptly halted the trial and ordered the court officers to eject Martin bodily from the courtroom. This sort of conduct by one judge toward a former judge, particularly one who had once apparently attempted to do him a great favor, was a harbinger of what to expect from the "Great Crusader."

Samuel Simon Leibowitz, now entrenched as a Brooklyn County Court judge, in short order became the most highly publicized jurist in the history of New York City. The same man who not too long before had represented every segment of the underworld, who had on four different occasions defended the king of the underworld, Al Capone, now became a terror. He became a harsh, implacable, often hysterical foe of criminals who had the bad luck to be judged by him. There was little mercy in the heart of the man who had once defended and set free the Gigolo Killer, the Mother Honor Slayer, the Mad Dog Killer, and the Breadknife Murderess. He rapidly became the "king of the Crusades." Just as the Holy Roman Church had, he conducted his own Inquisition. But he had another weapon in his arsenal, the grand jury.

Some of his associates on the County Court bench had yet to call their first special grand jury, but Leibowitz appeared to call them at his slightest whim. He would arrange a press conference beforehand so that his name and his aims would constantly recur in the reports of the doings of his special grand juries. He convened special grand juries to investigate the youth courts, bail bondsmen, the State Liquor Authority, the police department, the waterfront rackets, the television industry, the Board of Education, the welfare department, the New York City Department of Investigation, and on and on into the night. He repeatedly extended the life of his special grand juries at his own pleasure—extending some until they were jokingly referred to in the court system as great-grand juries. He extolled his own liberalism, bragging to the press how he had appointed the first black foreman of a grand jury, and then the first foreman of Chinese extraction. The myth of his liberalism was soon shattered, and he was severely criticized by the Bar Association for his appointments of a particular foreman of one of his special grand juries.

Leibowitz, as the presiding judge, had the privilege of recommending one of the chosen panel to be foreman of the special grand jury under his aegis. Leibowitz had been engaging in a furious newspaper battle with the Board of Education. True to form, he impaneled a special grand jury to investigate his allegations of malfeasance. When the jurors were finally chosen, he casually pointed to one of its members and said, "Let the gray-haired man there be the foreman." Shortly afterward, the lawyer representing one of the educators Leibowitz was haranguing was let in on a secret. The gray-haired man Leibowitz had so casually chosen was a close friend and neighbor of his for over twenty years. To make matters worse, Leibowitz knew that he was one of the founders of a powerful taxpayers organization that had a mighty axe to grind against any politicians associated with the Board of Education. This piece of news landed like a bombshell in the press and was greeted with consternation, but good old Sam blustered his way through and again weathered the storm.

Leibowitz maintained strict control over his special grand juries. He insisted on personally trying every indictment that they handed up, an act of prejudice that was looked upon with scorn by his fellow judges. He again looked bad in one of his famous special grand juries, impaneled to investigate, of all great criminals, crooked college basketball players accused of manipulating point spreads. (There was much conjecture here whether good old Sam was protecting the rights of honest bookmakers.) The counsel for two of the defendants accused Leibowitz in open court of altering the minutes of his charge to the special grand jury. He accused Leibowitz of doing this to block a motion to remove himself from the case. The thought of losing the tremendous publicity engendered by the case appalled Leibowitz. But the lawyer, not one to be cowed by the snarler, produced a handwriting expert to verify his accusation, and Leibowitz sheepishly backed off and another judge replaced him.

The enormity of Sam's blatant excesses of authority soon singed the sensitive skins of his fellow judges. Open warfare was declared. His peers charged that he conducted his court with reckless disregard for witnesses and lawyers, as well as the poor defendants. He was compulsive about being in the public eye, meanwhile nurturing his not too secret ambition to become mayor of New York. He maneuvered to grab every important case on the trial calendar, always with the ever-ready assistance of the district attorney's office. Their conviction record soared with Sam sounding the gavel and browbeating the witnesses and lawyers. The harsh sentences he meted out were extraordinary, almost inhuman. In one instance he sentenced a sixteen-year-old kid to twenty to forty years. In another he sentenced a man seventy years old to ten to twenty years. When the aged lawbreaker cried out and protested his age, saying he would never live to finish such a sentence, Leibowitz smilingly replied, "Do as much time as you can."

Leibowitz's bullying tactics and total disregard for the opposition provoked virulent criticism. Unfortunately, his most severe critics were, in the main, afraid to arouse his hostility. Lawyers, who might have to someday appear before him, were terrified of him, as were city officials who might have a skeleton or two in their closet which they feared might be exposed by one of his countless grand juries. One prominent Brooklyn lawyer publicly stated that he wouldn't try a case in front of Leibowitz for twenty-five thousand dollars, a princely sum at the time. Another well-known lawyer quietly passed the word that he could be ready and willing to serve without fee any man, woman, or organization that stood ready to launch formal charges against Leibowitz. The amazing thing was that Leibowitz continued to ride roughshod, capturing the newspaper headlines, and through it all suffered only one mild rebuke by the Brooklyn Bar Association.

But sooner or later even the most high and mighty must take a fall. The most respected of all the judges on the County Court bench in Brooklyn was Judge Nathan Sobel. He was a Hollywood movie judge, tall, dark, and handsome. He was also scholarly, modest, and extremely courteous in his courtroom manner. It was almost impossible to anger Judge Sobel. He conducted his personal and judicial life with an equanimity shared by few men. The easygoing Judge Sobel managed to remain on speaking terms with Leibowitz for a couple of years. He was, in fact, the only County Court judge who maintained even a façade of friendship with headline-hunting Sam. It was only a question of time, however, before the abrasive Leibowitz alienated the mild-mannered Sobel. When he finally did, he so enraged him that in the ensuing clash Sobel slapped Leibowitz across the face.

Leibowitz had just about finished the spectacular Harry Gross episode and was champing at the bit in quest of new headlines. Manna from heaven arrived in the form of the Senate Crime Investigating Committee, the sensational bullshit Washington racket busters headed by Estes Kefauver. At this time, in the wake of Bill O'Dwyer's abdication of the throne, New York City was being run by an interim acting mayor, Vincent Impellitteri. Leibowitz was desperately trying to snare the mayoralty nomination in the upcoming election. Neither the Republicans nor the Democrats wanted any part of him. But Sam refused to believe he wasn't wanted. He tried to form a fusion party with himself as candidate for mayor. This met with very little encouragement. He greeted the Kefauver committee with open arms. They were his equal in seeking headlines; they would crucify anyone they could make the front page with. They used anything—half-truths, sheer innuendo—to gain publicity. And what better game to pursue than Bill O'Dwyer, the recently discredited ex-mayor.

The Kefauver committee dug into O'Dwyer's past from the days when he was the Brooklyn district attorney. They attempted to secure the grand jury minutes of the Murder, Inc. probe. Judge Sobel correctly refused to release the record of the decade-old investigation, citing a specific point of law. In the event that no indictments resulted from secret grand jury proceedings, the minutes were to remain sealed forever.

This precise ruling by Judge Sobel didn't mean a thing to Leibowitz, who violated all judicial protocol. He slyly sent word to Kefauver that his committee could pick up the forbidden records at his Manhattan Beach mansion. On a quiet Friday afternoon, when the courts had closed for the day, he had a couple of his lackeys transport four cartons of the secret information from the dark cellars of the courthouse to the salubrious breezes of Manhattan Beach. He invited the Kefauver committee to lunch the following Sunday afternoon. Reporters, photographers, and television crews had been alerted, and were present at Leibowitz's home in huge numbers. The previously denied records were handed over by Leibowitz to Kefauver with just a bit more pomp and ceremony than Japan's surrender to the United States.

When Judge Sobel got the news on Monday morning, he stormed into Leibowitz's chambers. He was so angry he made no effort to contain his outrage at Leibowitz's unpardonable conduct. Court attendants later reported having heard a shouting match, and when Judge Sobel emerged red-faced and furious, Leibowitz was observed sitting at his desk with his head in his hands, sobbing.

The incident provoked waves of speculation among the reporters who were the courthouse regulars. Judge Sobel was prevailed upon to issue a formal statement to clarify the cause of the violent argument.

Judge Sobel enlightened them. "I informed Judge Leibowitz that the rules of the court must be respected by him as well as all the other judges of the court. I then informed him that not only must he obey that rule, but also that judges of the highest criminal court in the state must conduct themselves with dignity and not engage in and out of court in staging disgusting spectacles. This has been for many months the subject of much controversy between the other judges and Judge Leibowitz. I then left his chambers."

Always the perfect gentleman, Judge Sobel omitted a vital part of the furious argument. It later came out that, as the heated debate reached its height, Leibowitz shouted, "You are an ally of the underworld." That was too much for the universally respected Judge Sobel. He picked up Headline Sam out of his chair and slapped him across the face, and the tough-guy judge, the scourge of Brooklyn, the terror of those who appeared before him, began to cry.

His crocodile tears dried up quickly, and before the end of the week Leibowitz was once again all over the papers with Kefauver's honest crime-busters. One of the committee, the ancient Senator Tobey, broadly suggested that Leibowitz would make a fine mayor of New York City. Senator Tobey was fortunately all alone in his suggestion, however, and as the years rolled by Sam Leibowitz was frustrated at every turn in his mayoralty aspirations.

Neither major political party wanted any truck with Sam, and his attempts to form a fusion candidacy were futile. He never got any further than County Court. He strived to be elevated to the State Supreme Court, to the Appellate Division, anything higher than his present niche. His pleas fell on deaf ears.

His own wife, Belle, tried to heal the breach between Sam and Judge Sobel. She begged Sobel to make peace with her Sam, asking what could be so drastic to cause such a bitter strain. There must be a way to forgive and forget, to renew their uneasy friendship.

"Nat," Belle pleaded, "what happened between you and Sam?"

Sobel told her the whole story. "I could forgive almost anything, but when he called me an ally of the underworld, that was the last straw."

"Oh, Nat, don't be silly," Belle replied. "That's nothing to get excited about. Whenever I argue with Sam he calls me the same thing."

These immortal words by his wife just about sum up Judge Samuel Simon Leibowitz. He was more familiar with the underworld than most people, having defended the bottom and the top rungs of the ladder. He had run the gamut from the sleaziest pickpocket to the reigning king, Al Capone. To listen to him in later life recount his exploits, Diogenes could call off his search, they finally found the first honest man, Sam Leibowitz. He really believed it, or at least he acted like he believed it. With rare exception, if there was an exception, anyone who disagreed with Sam, or God forbid, anyone who stood before him to be judged, was "an ally of the underworld."

8

THE NEWS on television the night after the raid showed pictures of Mikie, Blackie, and Rocky being booked on bookmaking charges. Jimmy was gratified to see that there was no mention of Augie. The newspapers and all the media were playing the raid up to the hilt, and it seemed like every time he turned a page or saw the news on television there was a picture of Leibowitz staring at him. Jimmy sat tight and played it nice and cool over the weekend, just playing golf and going straight home when he finished. He knew that sooner or later Augie would call, so he just sat back and waited to hear from him. The call came early Monday morning.

"Hello, Jim. How are you?"

"I'm fine, kid. Where are you?"

"I'm at a friend's house. The phone is okay."

"Let me have the number. I'll call you back in ten minutes."

Jimmy put the number in his pocket, took a handful of quarters from a glass jar behind the bar, and hopped in his car and drove into town to a gas station owned by a friend of his. There was a public phone outside the station. He put a couple of dollars in quarters on the phone stand and dialed the number Augie had given him.

"Yeah, Augie babe. Christ, am I glad to hear from you. I'm on a public phone, it's okay."

"Good, Jimmy. I guess you know by now what happened? The papers, the television, it's murder."

"Christ, Aug, you can't miss it. It's all over the papers, even the local papers up here. I saw Mikie, Blackie, and the Rock on television the other night. I told you Harry would make us all movie stars. How the hell did they miss you, Augie?"

"So far I'm lucky as hell, Jim. I wasn't in the wire room the day they pinched us. In fact, I haven't been on the phones for weeks. I've been running all over the layout for Harry, paying and collecting, shit like that. Jimmy, as far as I know they don't even have a warrant out for me."

"Jesus, Aug, that's great. Who else did they pinch besides the three movie stars?"

"The world, Jimmy, the fucking entire world. They must of had taps on the wire room and all the spots for a couple of weeks. They know every joint and who the bosses are. They pinched about twenty-five of the guys so far. They picked Harry up yesterday at the Towers Hotel. He'd been staying there the last couple of weeks. He'd had some sort of beef with his wife. I've got Al Newman the bondsman taking them out almost as fast as they're bringing them in. Forget about Mikie and Harry. They set bail on them higher than the roof. Impossible."

"Jesus, that's bad news. Augie, tell me the truth. Does everyone look like they'll stand up?"

"Jimmy, the only one I'm really afraid of is Mikie. Rocky told me he nearly shit in his pants when they crashed in. I got the Rock out yesterday. He gave me the whole rundown. After the three of them were booked, they set bail for Rocky and Blackie at five thousand, and Mikie at fifty. He goddam near started crying, Rocky said, and he looked like he was scared shitless. He took the Rock on the side and told him he's not taking the rap for anybody. Mikie's the only one I'm worried about. If he goes to jail, or is even threatened with jail, sure as Christ he'll blow the whistle."

"Fuck him, let him blow the whistle, the little weasel bastard. What can he get, three or four months, for Christ's sake? What about Harry, how's he taking it?"

"Jimmy, would you believe? They set bail for him at two hundred and fifty thousand, a quarter of a million. This Judge Leibowitz is gotta be whacky or something. You'd think we were a pack of bank robbers or hijackers. Anyway, to get back to Harry, I spoke to Freddie the lawyer and he said Harry seems fine, taking it pretty good. He can't wait to get the latest paper and read about himself."

"Wait until he gets a load of Raymond Street jail for a few weeks. Then we'll see how brave he is. I don't trust that prick anymore, Augie, and you know it. He knows too goddam much about everybody. Now, the million-dollar question. Did my name come up at all?"

"Not a word. So far so good, Jim. I really don't think you have too much to worry about, you've been away from the action a long time."

"I sure as hell hope so. What else, Aug?"

"Oh, I almost forgot. They picked up Willie the cashier yesterday."

"Oh, Christ, Willie's afraid of his own shadow. That little fuck would squeal on his mother if they gave him a little heat. How did they find out about him?"

"It has to be Mikie who gave him up. I understand they're questioning Mike all day long. Jimmy, what do you think? Maybe it would be best if you got lost for a couple of months. These guys Leibowitz and Helfand really mean business. It looks like they don't give a fuck who they hurt. I'd hate to see you get into trouble after the screwing you got from Harry and the cops."

"I'll give it a lot of thought, I promise you, Augie. If I go on the lam you'll know where I am. Now, listen carefully to what I have to say. Don't try to be a hero and stick your neck out too far. Chances are Mikie won't implicate you if he can help it. He knows you're the only one out there who can help him make bail and get him a lawyer. The same thing goes for Willie Ricardo. Play it nice and safe. You know, deep center field. If you need me, by all means call me. Just make sure that you're speaking on an ironclad okay telephone. Give me the number and I'll leave the house and call you exactly as I'm doing now. Take it easy and keep away from everybody. Just give Al Newman the names of the guys you want bailed out and leave him his money with a dead-sure guy. Got that straight? All right, kid, stay loose and don't worry, this bullshit will blow over."

Jimmy hung up, waved to his friend who was pumping gas, got back into his car and drove home. The shit had not only hit the fan this time, it exploded. All he kept seeing in front of him were the faces of Leibowitz and Helfand, the assistant D.A. The enemy has really struck, and they have two formidable generals in these two guys. The enemy also has an excellent plan of attack. Jimmy shook his head. They really have three stand-up guys in custody. If you stripped all three naked you wouldn't find one pair of balls. I can feel it in my bones, this is going to be a real bad scene. I think I'd better get myself a lawyer.

Jimmy went to the phone in the den, out of earshot of Kay. He dialed his friend and golfing partner, John the lawyer, to set up a luncheon meeting. John was a tall, imposing, good-looking Yankee. He possessed all the proper credentials. Excellent family background, Georgetown University, Yale Law School—the works. Best of all, John was very well connected in Connecticut, a state that Jimmy had no intentions of leaving for quite some time.

They arrived within a minute of each other and went to the cocktail lounge to have a drink before lunch. The lounge overlooked a huge waterfall with a group of swans idly swimming on the lake beyond it. Jimmy looked out at the natural beauty of the view and thought what an incredibly beautiful setting he chose to pour out an incredibly ugly story.

They tipped glasses good luck and John said, "All right, Jimmy, take that faraway look off your face and tell me what's on your mind. I know you didn't drag me out here to admire the swans and swoon over the waterfall. Something's troubling you, you look like you just four-putted a green."

"Oh, I'm sorry, John, my mind was wandering. I was thinking what a nice peaceful life those swans have out there. But you're right. I'm still not sure, but I think I'm about to have a headache. If I do, it's going to be a beauty, a real pisser."

"Well, go ahead. Let's have it."

"Okay. Have you read the papers about this gambling mess in Brooklyn? You know, the Harry Gross bookie thing with all the cops and shit."

"Read it? How the hell could anyone miss it? It's on the radio, television, and all over the newspapers. What the hell have you got to do with that?"

"Okay, sit back, John. When I finish you tell me if you want to represent me. I think I'm going to need a lawyer."

For the next half hour Jimmy told John his story. He didn't embellish it, he gave him pretty much the straight facts. He omitted a few of the grimier details, but essentially he gave it to him on the level. He knew from his years of experience that there was no sense bullshitting your lawyer. He ended by telling him of his recent business deals and his future plans. He explained that to all intents and purposes he was finished with the rackets, had been for over a year. He had not seen Harry or any of the guys for the last year or so, and the only link he still retained was the thousand a week which was sent to him. A thousand, he thought ruefully, which he could now forget about forever.

John just sat back and listened, never interrupting once. When Jimmy finally finished his tale of woe, John sipped his second Beefeater martini and waved to the waitress. "Very interesting, Jim. I think we need another drink."

"Whatever you say, lawyer. Tell me, John, are you shocked?"

"I don't shock too easily, Jim. Remember, I was a county prosecutor for years. No, to be honest, I figured you had something going for you long ago. A cop, then all of a sudden an ex-cop. Never looked like you worked too hard. Always the best clothes, plenty of money in your pocket. Then occasionally when I would meet you in New York, the best fight tickets at the Garden, the best seats at the ball game, and the best tables and lots of attention at the restaurants where we met. No, Jimmy, it was obvious you were some kind of wheel. But to be honest, I never gave a shit. You were always a nice guy, a guy who was fun to be with, and that's what's most important to me."

"Then you'll go along with me, represent me?"

"Absolutely."

"That's great, John. I knew you wouldn't fail me. Look, here's a thousand dollars for openers, to make it official. Suppose we finish this last martini and have lunch before we get loaded and take a canoe over the waterfall. You can give me some advice over lunch."

John gave Jimmy some excellent advice over the next few days. He explained that Connecticut and New York had a reciprocal witness agreement; if one state felt that a witness living in the other state was necessary to a grand jury or some kind of trial, a subpoena must be honored. John made it clear that if Jimmy was subpoenaed by Leibowitz's grand jury it would be virtually impossible to avoid extradition to New York. John gave Jimmy his choice of states that he could flee to that had no reciprocal witness agreement with New York. Among these were Florida and Georgia, both states where Jimmy had good friends who would take care of him.

Jimmy gave a lot of thought to taking off for Florida or Georgia. A year or so on the lam and this would blow over. He had plenty of money to get started wherever he settled. Still, the thought of moving his wife and kids depressed him. They loved it here in Connecticut. He loved it too. Besides, he had a good thing going in the printing business, perhaps a partnership with his new friend Jack Goldman. He would blow the whole thing if he left. Again, there was New York. Jimmy Riley's own home town. How could he be happy living in some shit-kicking place where he couldn't jump into New York when the mood seized him? No way. Fuck it. I'll stick around and let the chips fall where they may. Christ, here I am about to run away and they haven't even mentioned my name yet. Talk about balls, maybe I'm losing mine.

It didn't take too long for Jimmy's name to come up in the investigation, but the way it did startled him, shook him up real bad. His older brother, Mick, was a detective assigned to the Manhattan district attorney's office. A quiet, easygoing guy who was a good detective, honest as the day is long, and who wouldn't know how to take a quarter if he fell over it. Mick went to work early one morning and when he arrived at his Manhattan office two men from the Brooklyn district attorney's were waiting for him with a subpoena from Leibowitz's grand jury. Before he fully realized what was happening to him, within two hours he was testifying before the fearsome grand jury. He wasn't advised of his rights to retain counsel or given time to even think, he was just thrown to the wolves.

Through the years Jimmy and Mick had always remained close. It was inevitable that Mick should meet Harry Gross. He had attended a party or two with Harry in Jimmy's company, went to an occasional ball game and once in a while had dinner with the two of them. All perfectly innocent. Before Mick had time to get his bearings in the grand jury room, Helfand had confronted him with the knowledge of a housewarming party a few years previous at Harry's then new home. It had been a terrific party, band and all, and maybe twenty plainclothes cops and bosses were there with their wives. There were also maybe thirty or so wise guys along with their wives. Some stool pigeon had told Helfand of the party and named quite a few policeman guests, including the Riley brothers. Helfand had a list of names who had attended the gala, which he asked Mick to verify. Mick, a true Riley, pleaded loss of memory.

Helfand promptly hauled Mick before the resident tyrant, Leibowitz. The Gauleiter of Brooklyn verbally assailed poor Mick as a monster, demanded he be stripped of his detective's badge, and sentenced him to thirty days in jail for contempt of court. He then adopted the role of benevolent benefactor of the downtrodden. He said, "It's not you we want. We know all about your brother, Jim. I direct you to go up to Connecticut and implore your brother to come down here and tell this grand jury all he knows. He's the big fish, we know you are only a little one."

This was indeed a Hobson's choice for Mick. First Helfand and Leibowitz practically cut his balls off and then they urge him to go up to Connecticut and get his brother to come down and set him free by cooperating with them.

This intermittent fiery and pious denunciation from the bombastic Leibowitz was reported in full open court to the eager press. Within hours reporters from the New York papers were all over the grounds of Jimmy Riley's Connecticut home. In the previous few days before they nailed Mick, there had been sly reports in the papers of a key witness to the probe who was reported missing. It did not require too much imagination for Jimmy to figure out that the key witness was him. Helfand hinted that the much-sought witness was indeed an ex-cop, an ex-plainclothesman, but that rumor had him on the lam in Mexico. The Brooklyn district attorney's office, with the pretense of regard for an individual's constitutional right of privacy, refused to name him outright.

But Jimmy's privacy disappeared quickly. Mick came up to Jimmy's house the next day with his newly retained lawyer, an ex-judge himself, who to Jimmy's disgust spent a good ten minutes posing for the photographers gathered outside the house. Jimmy watched the antics of this asshole through the venetian blinds, and secretly thanked God the house was completely secluded from his neighbors by high old trees on the perimeter of his grounds.

Everyone finally in the house, they shook hands all around and the maid served coffee in the den. Mick's face was a bit strained, but he seemed in good spirits. After a few minutes of small talk, Jimmy said to Mick's lawyer, "Leo, do you mind if Mick and I go off to another room and discuss our matter privately?"

"No, of course not, Jim, go ahead. But remember, I promised Judge Leibowitz that I would bring you back to Brooklyn to help your brother."

"Fuck Judge Leibowitz, Leo, and fuck you too. Don't you dare ever make any promises for me, you got that straight? And don't pull any more of that grandstanding shit you just pulled outside my door. Remember, this is my house, not the fucking Barnum and Bailey Circus."

Leo's mouth fell open. Jimmy jumped out of his chair and motioned with a quick nod of his head for Mick to follow him. They settled in a small room in the rear of the house. Jimmy said, "Mick, you know I feel terrible about this. What the hell happened?"

"Jim, they took me so much by surprise I was completely caught off-guard. They scooped me up at the office about nine o'clock, and I was in front of the grand jury about half past ten. I didn't know either guy who picked me up. One was a young detective, the other was a fat bastard of a half-ass county investigator on their payroll. These two hard-ons just handed me the subpoena and the next thing I knew I was in a car going to Brooklyn. I tried to feel them out, but no dice, they wouldn't even talk to me. I wasn't too worried. I figured, what the hell, I

never did a thing wrong. I assumed they were just going to question me about you. I knew where you were, up here with Kay and
the kids, that all that talk about your being on the lam was a lot of
shit. Then bang, I'm before the grand jury. Christ, you would
have thought I was John Dillinger. They asked me a million questions about you and Harry. I admitted I knew Harry, had met him
through you, because it was plain as day some stool pigeons are
giving them plenty of information. All of a sudden, out of the
blue, they hit me with Harry's housewarming party. I should have
fucked them and said I wasn't there, let them prove it. But Helfand was shooting questions at me so fast I got a little confused.
Then I knew he had some kind of list of who was there and I saw
what I was in for. So I dummied up, said I was a little drunk,
couldn't remember. This guy Helfand then hauls me up before
Leibowitz, and he starts screaming at me like I just blew up the
Brooklyn Bridge. What an arrogant, bloodthirsty sonofabitch he
is, Jimmy. Wait until you have to cross swords with this fuck. I
hope it never comes to pass. What the hell are we going to do,
Jimmy?"

"Mick, you know the answer as well as I do. There's no way I
can go in and cooperate with those rotten bastards, I'd rather die
first. I can't see a way out, you'll just have to go in and take it on
the chin, I'm afraid. Jesus Christ, Mick, I'm sorry as hell about
all this."

"I know you are, Jim, but all this shit isn't your fault. Here you
are, well out of it and happy, and something like this happens. It
was a tough day for the Rileys when that scheming little sonofabitch came into our lives. Well, I hate to lose The Job after all
these years, but what other choice do I have?"

"Fuck The Job, we'll work something out better than that. How
about the thirty days in Raymond Street jail? Can you handle that
okay?"

"Standing on my head, in the corner."

"Good boy, Mick. Now the first thing we do is get rid of this
bullshit Irish ex-judge you got for a lawyer. Where the hell did
you get that windy fuck, anyway? We'll get somebody real good,
like Willie Richter, who's not afraid of that Jew prick Leibowitz.
We'll appeal the contempt sentence. For Christ's sake, this is still

How can Leibowitz get away with shit like
begun to fight, Mick, we'll come out all right.
what's going on in Brooklyn? Is Harry opening
hell is the rat who gave you and me up?"

took his head. "Jimmy, so help me God, ever since
Harry got pinched I laid low, stayed out of sight. I just went to
work and went straight home. I felt it in my bones that this was
going to mushroom into something bad, but to be honest, I was
only worried about you. I never gave the slightest thought to
anything happening to me. I never figured to be mentioned at all.
I completely forgot about that housewarming party. Christ, it had
to be four or five years ago. I haven't even seen Harry in almost
two years. I don't know if Harry's talking, Jim, but you can bet
your ass somebody is. And I hate to say this, but you're way up
high on their shit list from what I gathered. Be prepared to have
your balls broken."

"Mick, my balls have been broken before. Okay, brother, I
guess we got everything straight. Keep your chin up. Let's split
and get back to Leo, he's probably got Kay's ear talked off by
now."

Mick and Jim returned to the den and made it clear to Leo that
Jim wasn't going back to Brooklyn to save anybody. The pomp-
ous horse's ass was already envisioning himself delivering Jimmy
to Leibowitz like a lamb to slaughter, amid the clicking of a
hundred cameras, with himself posturing out front like some kind
of savior. His face fell at the bad news, and he started a righteous
diatribe in an attempt to convince Jimmy of the error of his ways.
Jimmy looked at him ice-cold, and cut him off with a quick wave
of his hand. He saw them both to the door, hugged his brother
Mick goodbye, and turned away with tears brimming his eyes.
Poor Mick, he thought, all this goddam trouble and he never took
a fucking quarter.

The pace picked up very quickly. Mick and Leo returned to
Brooklyn empty-handed, without the prize catch. Leibowitz ex-
coriated Mick before a crowded courtroom of reporters and made
constant references to Jimmy like he was one of his former
clients, Al Capone. This tirade took place before Jimmy was ever

charged, before he had even made one appearance before the special grand jury, all based on hearsay evidence. When he finished blasting the Riley brothers, Leibowitz sentenced Mick to jail and had him stripped of his detective's badge. After seventeen years of being a good cop and surviving a couple of shoot-outs, his whole life went down the drain because he went to a house party with his brother Jim.

Jimmy sat tight the rest of the week. He stayed close to home and read the papers and listened to the news. Each day the Great Crusader managed a new sensation. He brought in one or the other of the top brass in The Job, including Jimmy's ex-pal, the police commissioner. The only honest man in New York was Sam Leibowitz, and he raved and ranted at every witness, spouting all manner of invective at the lowest and highest of police brought before him. The cops who had enough time in to qualify for retirement started running for the hills. Pension papers were thrown in by the score.

According to the Constitution, the law of the land, grand jury proceedings should remain secret until an indictment is obtained. Leibowitz and Helfand flouted this law like it never existed. Every time some unfortunate witness was confronted with a juicy tidbit fed to Helfand by a stool pigeon and showed some signs of balking, Helfand would haul him in front of his pal Leibowitz. The good judge would then make sure that his arena, the courtroom, was filled with members of the press and the so-called secret proceedings would be reported verbatim. The bookmakers and the cops were treated like archvillains, like co-conspirators about to wreck our beloved country. The poor bookies. Only a year or two previous, they were everyone's best friend, some of them making book within a few blocks of the very courthouse where they were now being vilified as traitors.

Jimmy just read, watched the news on television, shook his head and thought what a stupid, fucked-up world we live in.

The fateful summons finally came. A few days after the departure of Mick and Leo the phone rang about ten o'clock in the morning. Jimmy picked it up and a voice said, "Hello. May I speak to Mr. James Riley."

"This is Mr. James Riley. Who's this?"

"Mr. Riley, this is Aaron Koota, an assistant district attorney of Kings County. I'm a special counsel to the rackets grand jury supervised by Judge Leibowitz. I have a warrant for your extradition as a material witness necessary to our investigation."

A nice oily, unctuous voice, very polite, thought Jimmy as he listened. They're always nice and solicitous just before they throw the switch. They'll even blindfold you to ease your way into oblivion.

"And for what reason, Mr. Koota, would you require my presence before your grand jury?" replied Jimmy, just as oily, just as polite.

"Very simple, Mr. Riley. The district attorney feels you might have certain information that might aid our investigation. Would you care to surrender yourself to our office tomorrow?"

"I hope you don't get offended, Mr. Koota, but I'd rather surrender to Joseph Stalin."

A slight, sickly laugh greeted this subtlety. "To be honest with you, Mr. Riley, I don't believe you have a choice. New York State enjoys a reciprocal witness pact with Connecticut, so it would only be a matter of form to extradite you."

"I'll discuss that with my lawyer if you don't mind, Mr. Koota. I'm afraid I have to hang up now, as I think we've both said enough. If you want me, you come and get me. Goodbye, Mr. Koota."

Jimmy hung the phone up. Shit, he thought, here comes the enemy and I haven't the faintest idea of the weapons they possess. He called John the lawyer.

"Hello, John. I just received the death sentence."

"Jimmy. What the hell do you mean?"

"I just had a call from the Brooklyn D.A.'s office, a guy named Aaron Koota. They have a warrant for my extradition. That nervy sonofabitch wanted me to surrender to them tomorrow."

"For Christ's sake, I can't believe those guys in Brooklyn. What did you tell him?"

"He was nice and polite, and I was nice and polite. But I told him no dice, if he wants me, come and get me."

"Good boy, Jim. We'll make them sweat a little and get you proper safeguards as a material witness. Keep your fingers crossed. If we get the right judge in Superior Court in Bridgeport maybe you'll just have to promise to appear when you're needed. They might accept my word as a guarantor of your appearance. But that's not too likely, so don't get your hopes up. Well, Jimmy, I warned you about the statute, you'll probably have to go in."

"I'm well aware, John. I'm satisfied that you've given me excellent advice. Tell you what. Suppose you call this guy Koota and make some sort of arrangement with him. I'm in your hands now. I'll leave it up to you."

"Okay, Jim. I'll call him today. Suppose I stop by the house for a drink about five o'clock and we'll talk things over. See you later, Jim."

They all appeared in Bridgeport the next day, and again it was like a Roman circus. There were about fifty reporters and photographers there, and Koota played his role like a Hollywood actor. He basked in the popping of the flashbulbs, like he was under a barber's sunlamp getting a winter tan. He was short, slight of build, and very gray. He looked like an aging ex-jockey. His manner was smooth, and his voice was just as oily as it was on the telephone.

Jimmy Riley never said a word to anyone. He just stood before the judge while John argued in his behalf. It was all to no avail. The right judge wasn't sitting that day and John lost the argument. Jimmy was handed over to the custody of Koota and two detectives who accompanied him. They were both from the Brooklyn D.A.'s office. One young guy Jimmy didn't know, and one old-timer named Willie Chasen, who was a good friend of Jimmy's. The only sign of recognition that passed between them was an almost imperceptible wink, which from one cop to another meant, Don't worry, I'll do the best I can for you. The conditions were that Jimmy was bound over to Koota for thirty days as a material witness. The hearing finished, he turned, shook hands with John, and said to Koota, "Do you mind if we stop at my house on the way down, Mr. Koota? I'd like to pack some clothes for one thing, and I'd also like to say goodbye to my wife."

"Of course, Jimmy." (Now it was Jimmy, no longer Mr. Riley. What dear friends we'll be.) "Anything you want. Do you care for a bite of lunch before we start out?"

"No, thank you, Mr. Koota. I'll have the maid fix something for us when we get to my house." Fuck this smooth little bastard, let him see how the Connecticut rich live. By the looks of that blue suit and those brown shoes I bet this was his first trip out of Brooklyn.

Jimmy had carefully rehearsed Kay the night before. He explained that it was all a publicity stunt and would soon blow over as the public got tired of reading about Helfand and Leibowitz. He emphasized that the worst that could happen to him was confinement in a hotel room for thirty days as a material witness. She was a strong girl and accepted without question any tale Jimmy wove. Her faith in him was implacable, and he rarely discussed any of his outside affairs with her. He was a good provider, and she and the kids led the good life. To her, he was a proper husband.

There were no hysterics when Jimmy arrived back at the house with Koota, Chasen, and the other young detective. In fact, it was a pleasant couple of hours. The maid prepared lunch for everyone, and Kay got behind the bar in the den and made the drinks while Jimmy went upstairs to pack. He took an additional precaution while he was packing, he took ten one-hundred-dollar bills from a stash he had upstairs and put five C-notes in each shoe. He'd read about the new young rookies in the Brooklyn D.A.'s squad who were assigned to the investigation. They were constantly referred to in the newspapers as the young "Incorruptibles." Incorruptible, my ass, Jimmy would think as he read about them. He thought about when he was a young rookie just assigned to the chief inspector's office. Mayor La Guardia called him an Incorruptible. If this new breed of rookies were the same type of Incorruptibles as Jimmy, then they'd better put an armed guard around the gray brick building in downtown Brooklyn where they worked or the Incorruptibles would walk away with it. He tied his shoes. Hmm, the C-notes felt nice against the soles of his feet, better than Dr. Scholl's footpads any day.

All packed, he went downstairs to the den and joined the group. It was like a friendly little party by now, and when they left for Brooklyn they all kissed Kay goodbye on the cheek like they were taking Jimmy to the ball game.

The ride to downtown Brooklyn took about an hour and a half.
Jimmy sat in the back seat with Koota. They exchanged idle bits
of conversation and Jimmy smiled pleasantly when Koota gushed
about his lovely wife and family. What a nice lady, and what
well-behaved children. Such hospitable people. Jimmy nodded
his head politely, meanwhile thinking they probably gave Joseph
and Mary the same bullshit before they nailed J.C. to the cross.

They pulled up in front of a very fancy Brooklyn Heights hotel
where Koota had a suite reserved for Jimmy and his guard detail.
The hotel brought back some great memories to Jimmy. His sister's wedding, the many dances where he had so many good
times. You can bet your sweet ass these guys will soon have me
dancing, and it won't be the Peabody or the Lindy Hop. Fuck
them.

A new set of bodyguards were awaiting them in the suite. The
new guys looked like they were about eighteen years old. Koota
introduced them. Two nice kids. One Irishman, one Jew. Koota
went to the phone and ordered booze, soda, and ice. Nothing but
the best for you, Jimmy Riley. Cutty Sark okay? I noticed that's
what you served in Connecticut. Perfect, Mr. Koota. While Koota
was busy on the phone, Jimmy caught Willie Chasen's eye and
nodded toward the bathroom. When the bellhop arrived with the
tray of booze, Willie went into the bathroom. Koota busied himself signing the tab and getting the drinks ready, and Jimmy went
to the bathroom door and knocked.

Willie opened the door and stayed back a bit, obscured from
the room beyond. He said, in a very low voice, "Jesus, Jimmy,
I'm sorry about all this."

"Forget it, Willie, I'll be okay. Are these two kids all right?"

"I swear to God I don't know, Jimmy. I hardly speak to these
new kids. Only when necessary."

"Who the hell is screaming to the D.A.?"

"They got plenty of rats, a million of them. Be careful, Jim,
very careful. I'm leaving now. Don't trust this fucking Koota."

"Don't worry. Thanks, Willie."

Jimmy stayed in the bathroom a few minutes, and when he
returned to the living room Koota had the drinks ready for the two

of them and the young Incorruptibles. Willie Chasen and the other young detective had gone.

Drink in hand, Koota said, "Jimmy, that's a beautiful home you have up there in Connecticut. You have a nice family. Your wife is a very gracious woman, and your kids are real nice."

"Thanks, Mr. Koota, I appreciate that. As for the kids, only my big boy was aware of what was going on. It wasn't so much that he seemed well-behaved, he was just scared speechless, scared shitless. For the last week the kids in school have been telling him his father was a big gangster, thanks to all the swell press releases you people in Brooklyn hand out. Can I ask you a question, Mr. Koota?"

Koota, his face having reddened a little at Jimmy's bluntness, nodded. "Go ahead, Jimmy."

"Maybe I'm wrong, but you're a lawyer, and what I have to say has been upsetting me. I have to get it off my chest. Isn't it a basic tenet of law that grand jury testimony remain secret? Isn't that a constitutional guarantee to every United States citizen? Did the United States Constitution get thrown out the window by Leibowitz and you guys in the Brooklyn D.A.'s office? For Christ's sake, you've been leaking the worst kind of garbage to the papers about me for the last couple of weeks. You people didn't know what the hell I even looked like or even where I was. Your boss, that honest descendant of Tammany bosses, McDonald, told the papers I was on the lam in Mexico. All the time I was home sitting in my den where we had lunch today, reading this horseshit. Tell me, what the hell goes on with you guys? You're trying to bury a lot of cops for not upholding the law, meanwhile you're throwing the Constitution in the shithouse, violating every privilege a man has. That's my piece, Mr. Koota. Now it's your turn."

Koota was a little shaken, but he answered very calmly and placatingly. "Jimmy, you're not a lawyer or a district attorney. Sometimes, you have to fight fire with fire to flush out perpetrators of crimes. There's an organized conspiracy between crooked policemen and gamblers that now exists, or did exist. We are determined to get to the bottom of it. We have to use whatever means we feel necessary. Judge Leibowitz is an outstanding judge, a fine human being, and a fair and impartial man. He means to get to the truth and uphold the law the best way he can."

Jimmy put his head back and snorted in derision at Koota's last remark. All this time he was slyly observing the reaction of the two young cops to the dialogue between him and Koota. Jimmy was putting on the act, and to his glee it was going right over Koota's sanctimonious head. Over the years he had found through personal experience that most district attorneys, in fact most lawyers, were complete shitheads. This gray-haired little ex-jockey opposite him was no exception.

He shook his head, looked at Koota, and said, "To be honest, Mr. Koota, we could argue pro and con all night about your tactics and not reach a conclusion. Tell me, man to man, just what the hell do you want from me?"

Koota leaned forward, sipped his drink. Jimmy casually sat back and looked at the two Incorruptibles. Koota said, "Jimmy, we know that you can tell us an awful lot about this conspiracy. You have a lovely wife and family, a nice reputation in your community, and a good business going. We want you to cooperate with us and nail these crooked cops to the wall."

"What makes you think I can help you?"

"Look, let's stop kidding each other. By now we know all about you."

"And what, Mr. Koota, do I get in return for this proposed cooperation?"

"Anything you want, Jimmy."

"Anything I want, Mr. Koota?"

"Anything. Name it."

"Okay, Mr. Koota, I tell you what I want if I cooperate. I want you to get me back on the police force and then get me back in plainclothes in the chief's office. They were by far the best years of my life, and I sure would love another crack at it."

The two Incorruptibles started to laugh. Koota looked at them with a dark face that stopped their laughter in midair. "What the hell is so funny about this guy? Look, Riley" (now it was Riley, no more "Jimmy" baby shit), "we'll see how funny you are when we finish with you. We heard you were a half-ass comedian, but we'll have the last laugh. I'm here trying to be nice to you, to set you straight, and you're acting like a wise guy. We need your cooperation. One way or the other we're going to get it. Is that straight enough for you, Riley?"

Jimmy looked at Koota. He was tempted to tell him to go fuck himself, McDonald, Helfand, and Leibowitz. But he bit his tongue. That was not the way you answered district attorneys who have your balls halfway through the wringer. He put on his apologetic, schoolboy smile. "I'm terribly sorry, Mr. Koota, I didn't mean to annoy you. I guess I'm under too much of a strain, and for some reason I always act like a wise guy when I'm in trouble. Forgive me. You were very nice to me today and I appreciate it."

"Forget about it, Jimmy. Come on, drink up, I have to get home. You two guys clean up and, Jim, you go to bed and get a good night's sleep. Tomorrow is going to be a tough day. Now think about what I said, sleep on it. Forget about helping the guys we have the goods on. We know a lot about you. Those guys stuck it up your ass a few years ago and again last year. You don't owe them a thing. See you tomorrow."

Koota put on his hat and topcoat, shook hands with everyone, and left.

Jimmy sat back with the young Irishman and the young Jew. "How about another drink? I think we all need one after that exchange."

The young Jewish Incorruptible spoke first. "Jesus, Jimmy, that was a real funny line you hit Koota with. You know, about getting you back in the chief's office if you cooperate. I thought he was going to have a stroke." He started to laugh, the Irish Incorruptible started to laugh, and Jimmy started to laugh. For a couple of minutes it was like a Laurel and Hardy movie, the three of them couldn't stop laughing. Finally, they all subsided.

The Irish kid wiped his eyes and said, "That sure was a funny bit. I nearly pissed in my pants at the look on Koota's face. Jeez, Jimmy, we both heard a lot about you, and Morty and I were glad we got the assignment to guard you. Look, Jim, in spite of all the shit you might have read about us, we're still cops. We're not the two worst guys in the world. We both took this job right out of the Police Academy because they promised us gold shields right off the bat. Who the fuck wants to go on patrol in uniform out there in that jungle if they can avoid it? Right?"

"Absolutely right, Ted. Say, can I ask you guys one very important question?"

"Shoot."

"Are you guys really incorruptible, or is that so much bullshit fed to the papers by the district attorney and Leibowitz?"

Morty, the Jewish Incorruptible, answered, "To tell you the truth, Jim, Teddy and I really don't know. We can't answer for the simple reason that no one ever tried to corrupt us. For Christ's sake, we've only been cops about six months, and the last three months we've been here with the D.A."

"Not the best of all possible worlds. Excuse me, Morty, do you mind if I take another piss? My kidneys fill up when I get nervous."

"Go right ahead, Jim, be my guest."

Jimmy went to the bathroom and removed his shoes. He took the five hundred out of each shoe, put four hundred in his shirt pocket, and folded the six hundred with the other money in his pants pocket. He looked himself over in the bathroom mirror, gave himself a big wink, took a deep breath, and returned to the living room.

He sipped his drink and said, "Fellows, if you heard a lot about me I hope it wasn't all bad."

Morty said, "Not at all, Jimmy. On the contrary, it was mostly all good. I have an Uncle Sid in The Job. He thinks the world of you."

"Sid? Not Sid Friedman, for Christ's sake?"

"The one and only, Uncle Sid."

"Christ, I broke in with Sid."

"I know it, Jimmy. He told me all about you."

"Well, in that case, let's cut out any further shit. I'm about to corrupt you two 'Incorruptibles.'" Jimmy took the four hundred-dollar bills out of his shirt pocket. "Here's two hundred apiece. I don't want one thing from you except what you volunteer. Just take the cash and be my friend. Be on the side of the cops where you belong, not with those headline-seeking bloodsuckers who are only out to use you. This so-called big cop investigation is all

a lot of shit they're using to get someplace higher on the public
teat. One guy wants to be Mayor, the other guys some kind of
judge or attorney general. They couldn't give a fuck less about
bookmakers paying cops. They know as well as anybody that it's
been going on for a century, and will go on for another century
until they legalize all the bullshit. Here, stick this money in your
kicks."

They both reached out and grabbed the money like a couple of
kids reaching for their first Hershey bar.

Ted, the Irishman, examined the two C-notes in his hand. "You
know something, Jim? This is the first hundred-dollar bill I ever
saw. No shit. Now I own two of them."

Morty, the Jewish Incorruptible, said, "This calls for a little
celebration, my first score on The Job. Let's have another drink."

They all had another round of drinks and talked freely for the
next couple of hours. Morty and Ted told Jimmy everything they
knew. Mikie was squealing his head off. Eddie, the rat fink who
owned the Dugout, one of their big bookmaking spots, was hollering his head off. Jimmy just shook his head at this news. Eddie
had been a two-bit bartender whom Harry loaned the money to to
buy the restaurant, where he got rich. Now the rat bastard repaid
them by spilling his guts.

Willie Ricardo, the cashier, as predicted, was telling the grand
jury whatever he knew. There were a few guys keeping quiet,
reluctant to talk, but most of them were opening up. As of right
now, the cops were all sitting tight, banding together, nobody
squealing. And now the million-dollar question. What about
Harry Gross? They weren't sure, but so far, nothing. They saw
him in and out of the various D.A.s' offices, but he was still
being held in Raymond Street jail, not having met the very high
bail. He seemed to be standing up so far. But they had seen him a
couple of days ago and he looked pale and drawn, like he was
about to cry. They both agreed with Jimmy that it was inevitable
that he would crack. Give him another few weeks in Raymond
Street jail. That godforsaken shithouse would make Nathan Hale
turn state's evidence. They all had a nightcap and called it a day
the best of friends. Jimmy was elated. From here on in for five

hundred a month apiece, they would keep their eyes and ears wide open and keep him abreast of the latest developments.

Jimmy went to sleep almost immediately. His last thought before he fell off was about the myth of incorruptibility. Somewhere along the line everyone had their price. It was human nature to be at least a little venal in your heart. That's why they invented the Ten Commandments nobody bothered to obey. It was merely ten different ways the average human could become venal. He might skip one or two, but eventually he violated most of them. Jimmy couldn't resist a grin as he was nodding off. He ticked off the Ten Commandments in his head. At least he honored his father and mother.

The next morning his two new pals, Morty and Ted, brought Jimmy to the Brooklyn courthouse. The minute he walked into the lobby of the building he was surrounded by reporters, television cameras, and news photographers. He kept walking straight to the elevator and just smiled and never answered a word to the barrage of questions they put to him. What are you going to tell them, Riley? Were you really Harry Gross's partner, Jimmy? Is it true you're down here to cooperate, Jim?

Mercifully the private elevator came. Morty and Ted at last ushered Jimmy into Julie Helfand's office. The great man was sitting behind a desk talking to Koota and another guy who looked like a young assistant D.A. You usually could tell young D.A.'s from the plainclothesmen, the cops dressed better. Helfand turned to Jimmy and said, "Hello, Riley, we meet again. I haven't seen you in a few years. You look fine."

"Thank you, Mr. Helfand. You look pretty good yourself. Well, here I am. What happens now?"

Helfand addressed the other guys in the office imperiously, like a Mafia boss, "Okay, suppose you all clear out and leave Jimmy and me alone for a while. I'd like to talk to him privately."

They all picked up their belongings and hurriedly exited at this crisp command.

Helfand sat back behind his desk and motioned Jimmy into the chair opposite him. Jimmy sat down and took a good look at him. He hadn't changed much physically. Plenty of hair, a little grayer, hawk nose, stocky build.

"Well, Jimmy, I guess you know better than anybody why we have you here."

"That's easy, Julie. All I have to do is read the newspapers, they report all your doings down to the minutest detail."

"That's a typical Jimmy Riley smart-ass wisecrack. Get wise to yourself, Riley, you're in a lot of goddam trouble. The only way you can save your neck is to go along with me."

"You listen to me, Julie. What the fuck is all the excitement about bookmakers and cops? For Christ's sake, they were under your nose and around your ass for all the ten years we've known each other. What's all the bullshit about? It's certainly nothing new."

"Jimmy, this is a big case. The biggest cop scandal in history. We got the police department by the balls. I could get a judgeship over this, and Judge Leibowitz could become the mayor of New York. He would really clean up New York. There's no way we're going to blow this. You can be a big help to us. You know more than anybody."

Jimmy looked at him incredulously. "Leibowitz clean up New York? Become the goddam mayor? Bullshit, and you know it, Julie. Since when did everyone get so honest? You want me to holler? Okay, I holler on judges, district attorneys, lawyers, politician friends of judges and D.A.s, and a million others besides the poor cops. For Christ's sake, when I finish you'll have to build two new prisons to hold all the guys who ever fucked around. Who are you trying to horseshit? What about Louis Weber? The time he screamed murder that you fucked him. Suppose we tell all we know?"

Helfand's face got beet red at the mention of Louis Weber, the Bolita king, a good-guy Puerto Rican who controlled the Spanish Brooklyn numbers racket. Quite a few years back there were rumors that Helfand had promised Louis a suspended sentence after a bad pinch and instead poor Louis got a year. The argument that later took place could be heard in downtown San Juan, fifteen hundred miles away.

"That Louis Weber thing is a lot of shit, Riley. Nobody proved I had a thing to do with him. You're always the smart prick, right, Riley?"

"That isn't what I mean to be, Julie. What the hell are you trying to prove? You were always a nice guy, as I remember. Are you going to ruin a lot of cops to get ahead in the world? Jesus Christ, you know and I know that until these stupid politicians get together and legalize gambling this kind of shit will always go on."

"Jimmy, I'm not interested in your moralizing about the legality of gambling. All I'm interested in at this point is to obtain indictments against grafting cops. The question is, are you going to help me do it or not?"

"Well, I guess I've said all I have to say, Julie. By the way, I retained Danny Sachs from New York to advise me. I suggest that from now on you speak to him. No hard feelings, Julie."

"Plenty of hard feelings, Riley. Now I'd like you to have a chat with Judge Leibowitz in his chambers. Maybe he can get it into that hard Irish head of yours how deep your ass is in a jam. Maybe you'll change your attitude after you have a little talk with the judge."

"Do whatever the hell you want to do, Julie."

They took the elevator up another couple of floors and walked to Judge Leibowitz's chambers. Helfand and Riley went in alone. There was only a slight air of hostility between them. They both had said what was on their minds, enough was enough. An unspoken truce was declared. They sat silently awaiting the arrival of the Robed Crusader. He came in a couple of minutes later. Helfand jumped up like it was President Truman entering. Jimmy remained seated. Yes, it was Judge Leibowitz, sure enough. He hadn't got any better looking as he got older, but he had got a lot fatter. Jimmy used to see him around the courthouse in his plainclothes days, and he had also seen him at a couple of political dinners. You couldn't miss his grim, scowling face in Mme. Tussaud's Wax Museum.

Leibowitz looked Jimmy over, not saying a word. Jimmy gazed at him steadily, right into his eyes.

"So you're Jimmy Riley, huh?" Nice, friendly, conciliatory tone.

"Yes, Judge, I'm James Riley."

"I've heard a lot about you, Riley. Some of it good, but I'm afraid a whole lot not so good. I hope you came down from Connecticut to cooperate with us in ridding this city of grafting cops and filthy gamblers?"

"I'm not exactly sure how I can help you, your Honor. But you brought me down here, I'm at your disposal."

"Now let's cut out all talk about not knowing how you can help us. You know damn well how you can help this special grand jury and Mr. Helfand here. You're more important to us right now than Harry Gross, and you know it." Leibowitz's face became red and his voice started to rise as he finished his last sentence.

This guy doesn't waste any time, doesn't pull a punch. I guess this product of the Rumanian peasantry is not going to be too kind to this product of the Irish peasantry. Jimmy just looked at him. He wished to God he had his nice .38 detective special in his coat pocket and could pull out and fire about six shots into this scowling horseshit artist. Stay cool, Jimmy, take it nice and easy. As he sat looking at him, he remembered a story that had made the rounds and was told by Johnny Terry, Leibowitz's personal private investigator when Leibowitz was a criminal lawyer. Leibowitz, according to Terry, had a big mirror in his office and he used to stand in front of it by the hour and practice all the theatrical gestures of actors. The arched eyebrows, the vicious snarl, the outstretched hands of outraged innocence, the humble visage—the entire range of human emotions. Tomashefsky, the matinee idol of the Jewish theater, couldn't put on a better act than Sam Leibowitz the lawyer. Now he was Sam Leibowitz the judge, and through the years he'd become a master of every facial and bodily gesture. They were now an intrinsic part of his repertoire. Their effect on witnesses was devastating, and lawyers bitterly claimed they unjustly swayed juries, but the written trial record never showed a vestige of Leibowitz's acting ability.

Jimmy still remained quiet, smoldering. Leibowitz just stared at him. He already had used gestures one and two, now he used number three, the vicious snarl. "What's the matter, Riley? The cat got your tongue?" Eyebrows raised, broad sneer.

"Not at all, Judge." Nice, easy tone—keep your temper in check. "No, not at all. I'm well aware, your Honor, that I don't have to answer any of your or Mr. Helfand's questions without my attorney present. But I did want to be courteous to you people. Now it's obvious to me that that's impossible. But I would like to get matters straight between all of us here right now. I'm a legitimate Connecticut businessman being held in Brooklyn as a material witness. I'm not some cop or bookie you got by the balls, so you both start treating me with respect or I'll walk the fuck right out of Brooklyn. You'll have to chain me to a chair or kill me outright before I answer any questions because of your threats. I don't think either of you has the balls to do that." Jimmy looked at both of them, they seemed a little stunned. "So you can see, your Honor, the cat hasn't got my tongue."

Leibowitz only momentarily lost his aplomb. "We're only telling you for your own good what you're up against, Riley, why you should cooperate."

"You want me to cooperate, that right? The two of you took my brother Mick last week in one hour before the grand jury. You took him completely unawares like a couple of Gestapo agents, without even a chance to collect himself, and then you crucified him. Both of you know good and well he was a hard-working honest detective who never took a quarter. He was as far insulated from the gambling world as the Little Sisters of the Poor. You broke him from The Job and put him in jail for going to a house party with his brother. What about his family? I hope you're both proud of yourselves. That's all I have to say. I'm leaving."

Jimmy got up to go. The two heroes were both red-faced, a little shaken. Helfand rose hesitantly. Leibowitz said, "Sit down, Riley."

"Sit down, my ass. I'm leaving." He started for the door.

"I heard you were an arrogant young prick. I can see now where you got that reputation."

"You have a corner on arrogance, you wrote the book."

"We'll see about that. I've straightened out plenty of fresh wise bastards like you."

"Take your best shot. So long, Judge."

The battle lines were now drawn. Jimmy regretted his outburst against Leibowitz, but he knew deep down it had to happen. During the last couple of weeks he had seethed every time he heard or read his name. Slowly but surely he developed a deep hatred for the hanging judge. He felt a grave sense of outrage at his complete disregard for other people in his quest of the mayoralty, or whatever the hell he aspired to. He could still feel the hot wave of hate that had enveloped him when he came face to face with Leibowitz the first time. It was inevitable, he consoled himself, that sooner or later there had to be a major confrontation between them. Now all pretense was over, they each understood how the other felt.

Still, Jimmy knew he had to put on a contrite act for a while, to con Helfand and mollify Leibowitz a bit. There was a trifle of unfinished business lying in Brooklyn, like sixty thousand dollars in cash lying in a vault in the National City Bank at Church and Flatbush avenues.

Danny Sachs, Jimmy's newly acquired lawyer, was a veteran criminal lawyer who practiced mainly in New York City. He was a bright, trustworthy guy whom Jimmy chose because he rarely tried a case in Brooklyn. For that reason, Jimmy figured that he would not have to play footsie with Leibowitz and Helfand for fear of later retaliation.

Later the same day, Danny, Helfand, and Jimmy had a conference. Danny asked Helfand how he planned to use Jimmy.

"Well, Danny, naturally, we plan to question him before the special grand jury."

"This is what we expected, Julie. Now I hope you understand I want immunity for Jimmy before you put him before any grand jury, especially this one."

"Why should we grant him immunity? If he's an honest businessman like he says, he'll have no problem. I expected him to waive immunity."

"You can't be serious, Julie. I'd deserve to be disbarred if I put him in there without immunity. Now either you grant him immunity, or I'll go up to Superior Court in Connecticut and I'll have him released by tomorrow."

Jimmy just sat there and listened. During their exchange all he could think about was the old Tammany Hall song. One of the great lines in the song was, "Never plead guilty and never waive immunity." He couldn't help grinning.

Helfand held his chin. "I'm not sure Judge Leibowitz will go along with giving Riley immunity."

"Then tell Leibowitz he can kiss Jimmy goodbye as a witness unless he does. And that's final."

The conference over, Jimmy was returned to his hotel. The next few days were spent in the suite with his various guard details. The powers that be were evidently weighing carefully the decision to give Jimmy immunity. Meanwhile, he made himself comfortable and took it nice and easy. He had a swim each morning in the hotel pool, a steam bath and massage, three good meals and a few good drinks every day. All on the tab of New York City. Not altogether bad. He read all day when anyone but his two friendly Incorruptibles were his guards. He was polite and courteous to his other guards, but kept his distance. He felt there had to be one stool pigeon planted among them, and as long as he was lucky enough to find two stand-up kids, leave well enough alone.

The weekend passed and on Monday morning Jimmy was again brought to the courthouse. Danny Sachs was on hand to meet him, as well as a million reporters and photographers. One look at this mob scene and Jimmy thought, Big doings today. My ever-shy prosecutors have orchestrated some kind of outlandish publicity stunt.

The calm, reasoned, scholarly Danny Sachs couldn't afterward believe what had happened in Leibowitz's court. The preliminaries over, Helfand marched Jimmy and Danny before Leibowitz. The courtroom was packed; some spectators, but mostly the press. Leibowitz called the three of them before him.

"I understand, Counselor, that Mr. Riley has refused to testify before the grand jury." He practically spat out the words in a sharp loud voice.

The packed courtroom was eating it up.

"If you please, your Honor, all we're asking for here is a time-honored guarantee of the United States Constitution. I would be a fool if I let my client, Mr. Riley, appear before a grand jury without immunity from any later prosecution as a result of his testimony."

"Counselor, if he's an honest man he'll appear before my grand jury and sign a waiver of immunity." A clear implication right out front that Jimmy Riley was a crook. Cardinal Spellman himself wouldn't go before a Leibowitz grand jury without first being granted immunity.

"I take exception to your remarks, your Honor."

"There'll be none of your exceptions," said his Honor, his face contorted in a snarl. "I'll grant him immunity because I have to." He then pointed an emphatic finger at Jimmy and continued, "But I'm giving you fair warning, young man, you do not have immunity from the crime of perjury when you go before the grand jury. If we catch you in one lie, the prison gates will close on you and maybe never open while you're alive."

Another broad implication, Jimmy thought, staring at the judge. I'm an ex-cop, if I go to the slammer they'll cut my head off. Jimmy looked again at this half-ass raving maniac. This is a judge? Can you believe it? Here we are involved in a gambling investigation, and he's already promising me life imprisonment. Feodor Dostoyevsky, where are you?

"I again take exception to your Honor's remarks. I don't believe these threats to my client are called for, your Honor."

"I already warned you, Counselor. That's enough. Immunity granted, Mr. Helfand. Prepare the necessary papers. Take him away. That's all." Liebowitz got up and strode from the bench, his sagging shoulders shaking with rage.

Danny and Jimmy were alone for a few minutes while Helfand readied up the immunity papers. Jimmy turned to Danny and said, "How about it, Dan? Is he a beauty or is he a beauty?"

"Jim, I've been practicing almost thirty years, and so help me, I've never come across anyone like this guy. I'd heard some pretty wild stories about him, but I thought they were mostly exaggerated. Whew! There's no way this guy can be a Jew, or else I'm going to convert to Baptist. Jews are supposed to have some compassion, this guy seems devoid of it. All I asked for you is a simple matter of law, a constitutional guarantee that any court in the land automatically grants. He made a grandstand play today in front of all those reporters in the courtroom like we were asking for a pardon from the electric chair. Well, let's not worry about him, we have more serious things facing us. Let's get down to facts. Have you ever been before a grand jury before?"

"Once, Dan, as a witness, after I got stabbed up in Harlem. About six, seven years ago."

"Any other time? I mean since you left The Job?"

"No."

"Okay. Jimmy, now listen carefully. I can't go in the grand jury room with you. You're all on your own in there, no lawyer. But remember, I'll be right outside the door in case you get confused or need a breather. 'I have to see my lawyer before I can answer that.' Get it? Plenty of that shit. Now pay attention. Helfand and these guys obviously know a helluva lot about you. Here's the way you answer. 'I'm not quite sure.' 'Could you please repeat that?' 'What day was it?' 'About what time of day?' 'To the best of my recollection.' 'Perhaps I could answer if you refreshed my memory.' Try not to give a direct answer to any question. They're out to cut your balls off, just remember that. Be extremely polite, answer all questions in a calm voice. Remember, this grand jury might later have a shot to vote an indictment against you, so don't lose your head in there. Okay, you got it, Jim? Keep cool, you're a nice young man, not some smart-ass cop or bookie. Put on your best choirboy look. One last thing, Jimmy. Remember that every crime you ever committed is wiped out once you go before the grand jury with immunity. Except the crime of perjury, being caught in a lie. It's a serious offense, Jim, it can get you five years in state prison."

"Don't worry about me, Danny, I won't get rattled. I got away with bullshit on witness stands from the Bronx to Staten Island for over five years."

Julie Helfand led Jimmy into the grand jury room. Jimmy ascended to the witness stand and the foreman of the jury swore him in.

The questions Julie put to Jimmy were simple ones at first. Age, marital status, where born, how long a policeman, where assigned as a policeman, what year he left The Job, what did he do when he first left The Job, where employed now, yearly salary, and whatever other facts justified Jimmy's existence on earth.

Then the questions became a little less tentative, a little more probing. Helfand was a skillful interrogator and Jimmy was a skilled witness. They fenced with each other for over an hour in a lengthy discussion of the gambling laws Jimmy was once charged with enforcing. They got around to gamblers he knew. When he asked Jimmy to pinpoint a certain gambler, Jimmy would ask if Helfand knew his nickname. Did you know Irving Rubinstein? Rocco Fanigletti? Joseph J. O'Keefe? Names like that? What were their nicknames, Mr. Helfand? I hardly knew anyone by his real name. Were they short? Tall? Fat? Thin? Dark-skinned? Fair? What color hair did they have? I'm not sure, Mr. Helfand. Oh, yes, it's possible, Mr. Helfand. If you could give me the date, perhaps it would refresh my memory.

Now exasperation was setting in. "All right, Riley, just why did you associate with gambers when you were a chief inspector's man?"

"Associate with them, Mr. Helfand?"

"You know what I mean. Why were you friendly with them?"

"I guess because a lot of them were really nice guys."

"Why didn't you take more action in enforcing the gambling laws when you were a chief inspector's man?"

"I thought I did. My record in The Job speaks for itself. It was often referred to as being outstanding."

"So outstanding you were dismissed from the chief's office. Why?"

"Only God knows, Mr. Helfand."

"Why did you quit The Job so soon after your dismissal from the chief's office?"

"I guess I was disillusioned. I wanted to take my chances in the outside world, anyway."

"If you wanted, you could have made more gambling arrests, could you not?"

"Probably."

"Why didn't you?"

"As I think about it now, three years removed from The Job, I don't believe I ever took the gambling laws seriously. I think personally that they're a joke. Sooner or later we'll see all gambling legalized. That's the way it should be."

"Please, Riley, we don't need any opinions from you, and no political speeches. Just answer my questions."

"You asked me a question, I thought I answered it. I'm sorry if I offended you, Mr. Helfand."

Jimmy could see exasperation begin to turn into barely restrained rage. Don't get his ass up too much, Jimmy, he's the boss here.

Helfand was spitting out the questions now. "Tell me, Riley, do you know what they call the 'pad'? What it means?"

"What? I don't understand."

"The pad, the pad. You know, the pad."

"Are you referring to what I wore to guard my knees when I played basketball? Kneepads? Is that what you mean, Mr. Helfand?"

"You know that's not what I mean."

"Then I don't understand your question, Mr. Helfand."

Striding back and forth, head shaking. "Do you know what they call the 'ice'?"

"Sure, I know what that is, Mr. Helfand."

"Okay, good. Now go ahead and explain 'ice.'"

"Well, that's like in the wintertime when the water freezes over and turns into ice. You can have a lot of fun skating on it. Is that what you mean, Mr. Helfand?" Aren't you ever the smart-ass, Jimmy, you just couldn't resist that one. He looked out at the jury, two of them were covering their mouths to keep from laughing. My God, a couple of the jurors have a sense of humor.

Helfand was almost speechless. He looked at Jimmy like he wanted to decapitate him. He glared fiercely, his voice bitter. "Do you know a bookmaker named Harry Gross?"

"Yes, I do." Here we go, thought Jimmy. Stay nice and cool, here comes the atomic bomb.

"How long have you known him?"

"We knew each other as kids. We renewed our friendship five or six years ago."

"Were you and Gross partners in a nightclub you opened when you quit The Job?"

"No, sir."

"Are you sure about that?"

"Yes, sir."

"Who was your partner?"

"Mike Aronson."

"You were friendly with Harry Gross when you were a police-man entrusted with enforcing the gambling laws, were you not?"

"Yes, sir."

"You knew he was a bookmaker, a big bookmaker. Yet you were friendly with him?"

"That's right. I told you how I felt about bookmakers, most of them are nice guys. Harry and I knew each other as kids. I'd never lock up a friend."

"And you had a lot of friends, right?"

"I hope so, Mr. Helfand. A man needs friends."

"How did you feel when you locked up other bookmakers who evidently were not your friends?"

Jimmy looked at Helfand. He was no dummy, he'd been around. I'd love to explain to him the meaning of friends, or "cousins," versus the meaning of "outlaws." Christ, would that shake up the group out front.

"How did I feel? What do you mean by that, Mr. Helfand?"

"Did you feel good or bad about locking up certain book-makers?"

"I admit, a little bad. I always felt a little sorry for them."

"Why, then, did you elect to work in the chief's office if it was against your principles to arrest bookmakers and gamblers?"

"Were you ever on foot patrol in Harlem, Mr. Helfand? Or Hell's Kitchen, or Red Hook?"

"Riley, I'll ask the questions, you just answer them."

"I believe my question answered your question."

Helfand was really beginning to blow his cool. He composed himself, took his best shot. "Isn't it true that for a long period of time last year you ran Harry Gross's bookmaking empire?"

There's no question now about Mikie and Willie Ricardo open-ing up. Be careful, Jimmy. "Yes, I did, Mr. Helfand."

"Isn't it true that you and Harry Gross were fifty-fifty partners when you were a cop in the chief inspector's office?"

"No, sir. Just good friends."

"When he left Brooklyn, why were you picked out of a clear blue sky to run Harry's bookmaking business?"

"I agreed to try it for Mike Aronson, my ex-partner in the

nightclub. He was a partner of Harry's in the gambling business. Harry owed him a lot of money when he left town, and Mike asked me to try and recover some of it. I did try until Harry returned and resumed running his business."

"This Mike Aronson you keep referring to. Is this the same Mike Aronson who died a few months ago?"

"That was him, Mr. Helfand. Poor Mike, he was Jewish and they buried him before I had a chance to say a prayer at his wake." Jimmy shook his head mournfully, like he was about to start crying.

Helfand raised his hands, walked back and forth again. He was trying to calm down. He turned to his captive audience, who seemed enthralled by the exchange, even if he wasn't. "Ladies and gentlemen of the grand jury, you're excused for the day. We'll resume tomorrow. Thank you."

Jimmy gave a slight bow in the direction of the jurors and walked out and joined Danny Sachs.

"How did it go, Jimmy?"

"Not too bad, Dan. Pretty good, as a matter of fact. As of now, I'm sure Harry hasn't said a thing. They're fishing around with dribs and drabs of information. They know a little about me, but not too much. Most of the shit I'm sure they can't prove, it's all hearsay. Besides, I have one great ace in the hole. A guy that used to be around us all the time named Mike Aronson. A nice old guy about seventy-five. He used to be a burglar, a fence, anything but work. But he didn't have a felony record, and I had him on the nightclub license to help prove my money to the liquor board. He was always on the fringe with us, just wanted to be in our company. Said it kept him young to be around us. Poor Mike died a few months ago. I plan to lay anything I can on Mike. For sure, no one can hurt him anymore, he's lying up in Valhalla Cemetery. I hope he forgives me for this when I meet up with him down by the River Styx, where all good sinners are supposed to go."

The next few days they let Jimmy cool his heels in the witnesses' anteroom outside the grand jury room. Everyone sat on long benches lining the walls, and he recognized several ex-inspectors who were awaiting their ordeal in the horror chamber. Outside of an occasional sly wink he stayed aloof and read a book while he waited. He couldn't resist a secret smile at the anguished look on the faces of some of the top brass in The Job. One of them, supposedly a real tough guy, was sweating like a bull and looked like he was about to faint any minute. The plainclothesmen present, or by this time, ex-plainclothesmen, with one or two exceptions seemed to be tranquil and chatted amiably among themselves. There was a court officer in constant attendance, a guy who looked to Jimmy like a real fink, and that was another reason Jimmy kept his distance.

The days rolled around until it was Thursday, and still Jimmy waited patiently in the anteroom for his next grand jury appearance. Either they lacked enough ammunition to quiz him about, or they were waging a war of nerves. When he returned to the hotel that night he was gratified to see that he had drawn Morty and Ted as his guard detail. By now they were the best of friends. They greeted each other with big handshakes and Jimmy said, "Ted, do you mind going down to the corner liquor store and getting some booze, ice, and soda? Here's twenty dollars. Christ, I haven't had a drink in three days, I'm dying for one."

A couple of drinks loosened everyone up, and they talked freely about what was going on in the D.A.'s office. By this time, Jimmy trusted them completely. He told them most of what Helfand questioned him about in the grand jury. He convulsed them when he described the look on Helfand's face when he defined the meaning of "pad" and "ice." He gave a great imitation of Helfand strutting up and down while he shot questions at him, and a greater imitation of Helfand's face at some of the answers. A few drinks, and he was getting to be a better actor than Leibowitz.

But even while Jimmy was laughing and kidding with the young Incorruptibles, there was a good-sized pain gnawing at the top of his brain. Ever since he had arrived in Brooklyn as a material witness he had been worried about Helfand asking him about his personal finances. Most of it could easily be explained away, but there was the little matter of the safe deposit box containing sixty thousand dollars. When Helfand got around to that, how in the name of God was he going to explain it? Ever since Harry was raided, he'd stayed clear of Brooklyn for good reason. Now he was here, at their mercy. Sixty thousand dollars. By the looks of things this dilemma of his was going to cost a fortune in legal fees, especially if he was eventually indicted. He needed that money bad. Seizing money was *his* game, he would die if the authorities ever seized it on him.

About the fourth drink, Jimmy said, "I have a proposition for you guys. You two want to make five hundred bucks apiece?"

Morty replied, "Why don't you ask me if I want to bang Marilyn Monroe or Betty Grable? Just tell me what to do. Except I won't kill Leibowitz. Even if I wouldn't let him in my tribe, he's a fellow Jew."

"Okay, here's my plan. Both you guys told me you report to Koota every day. You know, in case I let something slip, some juicy bit of information he might be able to use. Right? Okay, tomorrow morning you report to him that I seem to be getting very jittery. It looks like sitting around all day watching cops go before the grand jury is making me nervous. It wouldn't surprise me if that's their game plan anyway. Now you tell him I paced the floor all night, I didn't sleep at all. You came out to see what was what, and I told you I didn't feel good, I was all upset. Tell him I'm starting to get delusions everyone is squealing, that I'm going to be left holding the bag. Tell him I asked you to get me a doctor to give me a prescription for sleeping pills. You got it. Paint the picture. Jimmy's a nervous wreck."

"That's easy, Jimmy. Can I ask what you have in mind?"

"I'd rather not say, but please do it. Next week I'll hand you guys five hundred apiece. Meanwhile you'll both look like real 'Incorruptibles' to Koota."

Soon after they went to bed that night, Jimmy got an extraordinary break to help along his scheme. They were all asleep when they were awakened by a banging on the door. One of the D.A.'s rookies had a wild look in his eye and was screaming, "Please help me, my witness is killing himself."

They all rushed down the hall and when they got there the other rookie guard had just knocked the bathroom door down. Jimmy followed him into the bathroom, which was covered with blood. The witness had a towel stuffed in his mouth, probably to stifle any screams of pain, and blood was spurting straight up out of his wrists. Jimmy yelled to get a couple of neckties and in a minute or two they put tourniquets on his arms above the elbow and stopped the blood. Jimmy pulled the towel out of the guy's mouth, and nearly jumped out of his skin. It was Willie Ricardo, their cashier. His face was dead white, he was covered with blood, and he looked like he had done a good job, that he was going to die. Jimmy looked at him lying there, the two neckties incongruously tied tight around his arms, and said a silent prayer that he would die. And quickly. One less rat bastard to worry about.

They called an ambulance, and Willie was taken away on a stretcher. They all went back to Jimmy's suite to have a drink. One of Willie's young guards congratulated Jimmy on his quick thinking, and Jimmy modestly thanked him, meanwhile thinking I hope that little prick doesn't make it to the emergency room.

Early the next morning Jimmy called John in Connecticut and asked him to come to Brooklyn. Very important. Call Danny Sachs, tell him you'll be here, not to bother coming to Brooklyn.

They went to the courthouse as usual and Jimmy took his regular seat in the witnesses' anteroom. There was a little buzz of conversation about the previous night's suicide attempt, but Jimmy kept silent. He slowly went into his act. He kept clasping and unclasping his hands, got up and paced around, kept running his hand through his hair—just like the guy in the movies about to crack up, on the edge of a nervous breakdown. A couple of times out of the corner of his eye he spotted Koota casting sneaky glances at him. Finally, Koota came over to him and said in a low voice, "That was a tough situation last night, Riley. I understand from the kids you did a good job."

"I'd rather forget about it, Mr. Koota."

"What's the matter, Riley? You all right? You don't look too good."

"I don't feel too good, Mr. Koota."

"What is it? That thing last night upset you?"

"A lot of things are upsetting me. I feel nervous. I can't seem to sleep nights."

"Well, try to relax, take it easy. By the way, come with me. Your Connecticut lawyer just arrived, he wants to see you."

"Gee, thanks, Mr. Koota."

Koota took Jimmy to an adjoining room and left him with John.

"You okay, Jim? You look a little shook up."

"John, I'm fine. Now listen carefully. I'm going to try to get Helfand to release me in your custody. I think I helped save the life of one of their main witnesses last night and it might benefit me. You just guarantee to return me to them on Monday morning. I'm going to give them a story that I want to get home to talk things over with my wife. I'm getting all nervous watching those cops marching into the grand jury. I'm going to drop a hint that I might cooperate if I have a chance to talk to my wife, to see the kids."

"Are you serious, Jim? That's great. The hell with protecting those guys, you don't owe them a goddam thing."

"John, I love you. You're such a square fucking Yankee. You really should be governor of Connecticut. You run, I'll manage your campaign. For Christ's sake, of course I'm not serious. Please, do as I say. Get me the hell out of their custody for a few days."

"Jimmy, you won't do anything wrong while entrusted to my custody, will you?"

"Me? Do anything wrong? Of course not."

"I wish I believed that. Okay, I'm your lawyer, I'll try to do as you ask."

About an hour later, Jimmy was called to a conference in Helfand's office. John the lawyer had done his bit, and Morty the Incorruptible had done his bit. Helfand congratulated him on his quick action last night with Willie. If he only knew. He even seemed quite sympathetic. He said, "Listen, Jimmy, I know this has been quite an ordeal for you. John here tells me you're very upset about your wife's health. I didn't realize she just had a new baby. Suppose we go up before Judge Leibowitz and I recommend that you be released in your lawyer's custody. I want you to spend the weekend with your family and come back here Monday with John. Get on the bandwagon, Riley, can't you tell by the looks on those cops' faces in the witness room that some of them are starting to crack. Pretty soon they'll all be looking to get out from under. Get smart. Come back here Monday and make a clean breast of things. Then you can go back to your family and your business forever without the threat of a jail sentence over your head."

Jimmy nodded his head humbly. "Just give me a few days with my family to talk things over. I promise I'll be back on Monday with a brand-new attitude."

They all then marched before Leibowitz. The odds were a good five million to one that he had been well briefed beforehand by Koota and Helfand about Jimmy's impending nervous collapse, his anxiety neuroses about his family, and his apparent willingness to cooperate.

The reverential judge still made the grandstand play. The courtroom was no longer an arena, it was St. Peter's Basilica in Rome. He made a quiet speech, and paroled Jimmy in John's custody like he was Jesus Christ pardoning St. Dismas, the Good Thief, on the cross next to him. He forgave him all of his previous mortal sins. The spectators and reporters were overwhelmed with the saintlike judge's magnanimity.

Jimmy just stood there mute, an abject sinner. He privately marveled at Leibowitz's capacity for bullshit. But he just listened, he didn't care if the judge gave the Gettysburg Address, he just wanted out, with no bodyguards on his tail.

They finally released him for the weekend in John's custody.

"Thank God I'm out of here. How'd you come down, John? Did you take the train?"

"No, I have my car. It's parked just a couple of blocks from here."

"Beautiful. I love you, John. Let's go." They got John's car and when they rolled out into Flatbush Avenue, Jimmy said, "Turn right, John. I know a nice place to take you for a couple of drinks and lunch. Christ knows, after listening to Leibowitz I need a drink."

John laughed. "I never saw him so saintly. Jim, wouldn't it be better if we turned left over the bridge and got out of Brooklyn. I think we should stop and eat somewhere on the way home."

"No, John. This is a great seafood place called Oetjen's. You'll love it. It's on Church Avenue, just off Flatbush, about three or four miles from here."

"Whatever you say, Jim."

They parked the car on Church Avenue about thirty feet beyond Oetjen's restaurant, and about two hundred feet beyond the National City Bank. As they got out of the car Jimmy looked diagonally across the street at Leo's candy store, their old headquarters. What memories. He shook his head. It's a good thing *you* can't talk, candy store, or you'd send the whole world to the slammer.

They went to the bar and ordered the official Fairfield County, Connecticut, drink—an extra dry Beefeater martini. Jimmy touched his glass to John's and took a deep swallow. "Gorgeous, really gorgeous. John, will you excuse me a minute. I want to go next door to the bank and close out a checking account Kay and I have there. I won't be five minutes. There's no use keeping any money here. Once I escape from Brooklyn I won't be coming back in a hurry."

"Sure, Jim, go ahead. But don't be too long. I'll hold our second martini till you get back. Hurry up."

Jimmy was out the door, down the block, in the bank, and down into the vault room in Olympic record time. His vault key, which he had secreted in his wallet, was in his hand with a twenty-dollar bill for his old pal, the bank guard. The elderly guard gave a double take when Jimmy greeted him with a handshake, but he felt the nice crisp bill pressed into his hand and with a hearty welcome led Jimmy to his vault.

The money was all there. He smiled as he remembered his old gag when a wise guy would give him a big bundle of cash. He would ask Jimmy if he was going to count it. Jimmy would just pat it and say, "It's all there, I can tell by the weight." He didn't waste any time, the money was all in hundred-dollar bills in packages of five thousand. He divided the packages equally in his pants and coat pockets. It felt real good. The whole deal didn't take more than five or six minutes.

"What took you so long, Jimmy?"

"I'm sorry, John. You know how these bank guys are! They hate to see anyone cancel an account. My checking account, big deal. I also emptied out a safe deposit box we kept there. Took out some insurance papers and a little cash."

"Jesus, Jim, you sure it's okay to do something like that? After all, you are in my custody."

Jimmy laughed. "Come on, warden. For Christ's sake, don't start coming down on me like Leibowitz and Helfand. Whew, this martini tastes delicious. One more, then we'll eat."

"Beautiful, Jim. By the way, are you sure there aren't any more banks you want to visit on your way home?"

"I promise, no more banks. Counselor, you were superb. When we get home to Connecticut I shall reward you with the balance of your fee."

It was a lovely homecoming. You would think Jimmy had been away for a couple of years instead of a couple of weeks. Early the next morning Jimmy drove his wife downtown to the local bank and placed most of the money in a vault she shared with her mother. He breathed a deep sigh of relief.

He had been a shade hesitant about playing golf at the country club after all the publicity, but he was gratified that a lot of the guys either called him to play or to see how he was feeling. The weekend was wonderful, but Sunday night rolled around and Jimmy didn't sleep too well. He dreaded his return to Brooklyn on Monday. He knew deep down that what lay ahead was a real knockdown battle, no holds barred.

He was right. The day started out innocuously enough. John drove him to Brooklyn and they were joined there by Danny Sachs. This was bound to be a two-lawyer, maybe four-lawyer day. Helfand and Koota greeted their arrival like long-lost friends. Do you care for some coffee, gentlemen? Did you have a nice weekend, Jimmy? How is your lovely wife and family? It was in sharp contrast to the animosity of last week. Jimmy just kept a straight face during all this sweetness and sunshine. Smiling, very polite. Oh, yes, Mr. Helfand. Fine, thank you, Mr. Koota. Sent you her regards, by the way. Yes, I did play golf. No, not too well, but I enjoyed being out in the fresh air. John beat the hell out of me. Right, John? John smiled modestly.

The coffee klatsch finished, Helfand arose and said, "Well, gentlemen, if you will excuse me. It's past ten o'clock and I understand the grand jury is waiting. What do you say, Jimmy? Shall we go in and get started?"

"Fine, Mr. Helfand."

Jimmy gave a sly, reassuring wink to John and Danny and walked out with Helfand through the corridors like they were the two best pals ever lived. They entered the grand jury room. Jimmy was sworn in again by the foreman. Helfand took his stance like he was about to square off for the middleweight title.

The first series of questions reestablished Jimmy's identity. The next series were again a little tentative, just a bit probing. Jimmy answered them in the same hesitant, calculating way he had answered questions in his previous appearance. Helfand at first appeared a little surprised at Jimmy's reluctance, and then, true to form, began a slow burn. Jimmy smiled to himself. This guy is beginning to smell I fucked him pretty good with last week's nervous, dying-swan act. Wait until he really gets the bad news!

"Now, Riley, you can still sit there and after six years as a chief inspector's man maintain that you never knew any policemen who took money?"

"Not to the best of my knowledge, Mr. Helfand."

"You mean to say you never knew a top boss in The Job who took any gratuities?"

"What do you mean by gratuities, Mr. Helfand?"

"You know what I mean, Riley. Money, television sets, automobiles—that's gratuities."

"Money, television sets, automobiles. Oh, no, Mr. Helfand."

Helfand started to give the old head shake, his lower lip quivering with rage. Riley sat back and looked at him. War was now officially declared.

"When you ran Harry Gross's empire, do you mean to tell me you never paid any cops to let you operate?"

"Me? Pay cops? Never, Mr. Helfand."

"How could you get away with it without paying cops?"

"Get away with what, Mr. Helfand?"

"You know goddam well—excuse me, ladies and gentlemen—you know good and well what I mean."

"I don't think I understand the question."

"How could you go without paying cops?"

"Go where?"

"Jesus Christ—excuse me, ladies and gentlemen. You know

what I mean. Operate the bookmaking spots without paying cops. Do you understand that?"

"Of, of course, Mr. Helfand. No, I assure you, I never paid any cops. Why should I? They were all my friends."

Helfand walked slowly back and forth, composing himself. Jimmy waited. One "goddam" and one "Jesus Christ," that wasn't too bad, Julie.

"Riley, do you own your own home in Connecticut?"

"No, sir, Mr. Helfand."

"Who owns it?"

"My wife and her parents. The title is all duly recorded in the local town hall."

"Exactly what do you own? In your name?"

"A year-old car, the suit on my back, and a few more home in the upstairs closet."

"Do you have a savings account?"

Here we go, the next half hour is going to be very, very interesting. "No sir, Mr. Helfand."

"Have you a checking account?"

"Yes, sir, Mr. Helfand. A joint checking account at the local town bank."

"How much is in it?"

"About seven, eight hundred dollars."

"Now, Riley, I want you to think hard about my next question before you answer."

"Yes, Mr. Helfand."

"Riley, do you have a safe deposit box in a bank vault? Anywhere?"

"Yes, I do have one, Mr. Helfand."

"Under your own name?"

"No, Mr. Helfand."

"Under an assumed name? A false name?"

"Yes, Mr. Helfand."

A little gasp of surprise from out front. A nodding of heads to one another. Julie Helfand couldn't resist a little smile. Now I got this fresh Irish prick where I want him. Right by his balls. Julie strode up and down in front of Jimmy, nice and easy. Then he turned his back to him and faced the jury.

Jimmy waited for the next question. This guy Helfand is almost as good an actor as Leibowitz. Pretty soon they'll have enough headliners to start another branch of the Yiddish Theater in downtown Brooklyn.

Helfand half-turned to his trapped and helpless prey. Jimmy looked at Julie's prominent beak in profile, and couldn't help thinking of an eagle about to strike his cowering victim.

"What was this assumed, this *false* name you used when you rented the safe deposit box?"

"James Rollins."

Emphatically, hands waving now, almost shouting: "You had this safe deposit box when you were a policeman. Right, Riley?"

"Yes, Mr. Helfand."

"For the last six years, right?"

"About that, I guess."

"Why did you use a false name? If you were the honest man you keep telling the grand jury you are, why the alias?"

"I don't believe there's a law that you must use your right name when renting a safe deposit box. I understand it's a common thing to use another name. It's done all the time."

"Answer the question, Riley. We don't need any speeches, any afterthoughts. I'm sure the members of the grand jury aren't interested in what you think is done all the time."

"I'm sorry, Mr. Helfand."

"All right. Now tell me, where did you keep this safe deposit box under your alias of James Rollins? What bank and what branch?" Helfand was licking his lips. He knew the answer better than Jimmy Riley."

"The National City Bank. Church and Flatbush Avenue branch."

"You have it there at the present time?"

"Yes, sir."

"Tell me, as near as you recall, what's in it?"

"Nothing."

"Nothing?" Incredulously. *"Nothing?"*

"Nothing. It's empty."

"Empty?"

"Yes. Empty."

Helfand's nose started to twitch, he began to smell a rat. The near nervous breakdown was a lot of shit. He'd been had. He walked back and forth for about a minute, like he didn't want to hear the answer to his next question.

"Riley, what day and what month did you last visit the safe deposit box you rented under the false name of James Rollins?"

"Why, Mr. Helfand, this present month. As a matter of fact, it was last Friday."

Helfand nearly jumped out of his shoes. "You what? When?"

"Last Friday, Mr. Helfand."

"Are you telling me that after Judge Leibowitz released you in the custody of your lawyer to visit your family, you went straight to the bank and emptied out your safe deposit box?"

"Why, Mr. Helfand?" Innocently, like a little boy. He couldn't resist adding, "Did I do something wrong, Mr. Helfand?"

Helfand put his hand to his head. He was temporarily shell-shocked. He started walking back and forth again, shaking his head. Out front they were looking intently at Jimmy. Wait'll I tell the wife and the boys at the lodge about this guy. Jimmy felt he could read their minds as he looked out at them.

Julie composed himself, squared his shoulders in his truculent prizefighter's stance. "You say you visited your safe deposit box last Friday. That right, Riley?"

"Yes, Mr. Helfand."

"You emptied it out, right?"

"Yes, Mr. Helfand."

"What was in it?"

"Some insurance papers I needed that my wife asked me to bring up to Connecticut, and a little cash."

"How much cash?"

"Fifteen hundred dollars."

"Fifteen hundred dollars? Are you sure that was all the cash in the box?"

"Positive."

"Why did you empty out the cash ?"

"That's simple. To help pay for my lawyers. My lawyers are here to protect my rights as a citizen. They must be paid."

"I warned you once, Riley. No speeches."

"That isn't a speech, Mr. Helfand. You're a lawyer. You know lawyers cost money."

"Riley, shut up. Shut up."

"I'm sorry, Mr. Helfand."

Helfand shrugged his shoulders and shook his head. He turned to the jury. "Ladies and gentlemen, I believe we'll call a recess now. We'll resume at two o'clock this afternoon. As for you, Riley, I think we'll go up and see what Judge Leibowitz thinks of your conduct. He was generous enough to release you for the weekend to visit your family, and you have the nerve to empty out a safe deposit box."

The next hour could have been staged at nearby Kings County Hospital for the insane. It was pure bedlam. Jimmy rejoined John and Danny outside the grand jury room. Helfand hustled off to confer with his idol, Sam Leibowitz. The two champions of the purer elements of Brooklyn had plenty to confer about.

Jimmy briefed his lawyers on the bitter exchange about the safe deposit box he'd just had with Helfand. Danny laughed out loud, but John, the austere Yankee, was a bit worried. Danny calmed John, assured him it was perfectly all right. He had only been entrusted to return Jimmy to the grand jury this morning, and he did. Right on time. There were no strings attached, no restrictions, let Helfand and Leibowitz drop dead.

The next scene in the continuing melodrama took place shortly. By this time, Helfand had briefed Leibowitz on Jimmy's malfeasance, his temerity in emptying his safe deposit box while on leave from McDonald's dragoons.

The good judge looked almost choleric as he took his seat behind the bar of justice. He did not lose his head all together, for he made sure the reporters were alerted for his upcoming open-court press conference. This one was going to be juicy, a real doozy.

The first one he called before him was John, and he started to berate him in a loud voice. But John was a tough Yankee and he didn't back down an inch. There was a rough exchange. John demanded his right to speak. He was reluctantly granted it. He insisted that there had not been any restrictions put on Riley. John just had to return him Monday, and here he was. Their behavior was exemplary. They went to lunch, had a few drinks before lunch, when Riley excused himself for a few minutes to run next door to the bank to transact some personal business. After lunch they went straight home to Connecticut. What was wrong with that?

As Jimmy sat there listening to John, he knew the only thing wrong with that was that Leibowitz, Helfand, and Koota had been bullshitted. They had been conned out of their shoes. They had fallen for his worried, nervous act. They had been sure he'd come back from his weekend like a good American and fully cooperate and send a thousand guys to jail. Well, shame on you, Leibowitz, Helfand, and Koota. Now I've got the rest of my hard-earned cash put away nice and secure.

Leibowitz was never more bombastic. He ranted about the morning's grand jury proceedings in minute detail. Danny Sachs jumped up a couple of times to try to quell him, to no avail. Danny screamed that Leibowitz was violating Jimmy's constitutional rights, Leibowitz outscreamed Danny. Threatened to hold him in contempt. Leibowitz, in open forum, on his home grounds, was the boss. He bitterly denounced Jimmy. No honest man would keep a safe deposit box under an assumed name. Only a crook would use an alias. Certainly no honest cop would have a safe deposit box. And never, never, under an alias.

Jimmy listened to the tirade with one ear. By now he was used to these guys howling all the time. He looked up at Leibowitz's red face, twisted in an ugly snarl. No honest cop would do this, no honest cop would do that. He smiled inwardly. Who the hell ever said I was honest? You, you alone, my good judge, have a corner on honesty.

The newspapers and television played up Leibowitz's denunciation of Jimmy to the sky. Jimmy's picture was splashed across the evening papers and the television screen like he had just got caught in the act of robbing the National City Bank, instead of merely emptying his own safe deposit vault. He couldn't help laughing a little, despite the avalanche of bad publicity. If they only knew it was sixty grand he lifted, instead of fifteen hundred, the reporters would indeed have had a banner day. Sixty grand would have seemed like a million to most of those guys, who were lucky if they made a couple of hundred a week. It was bad enough as it was, but they could relate to fifteen hundred. Sixty grand would have been another cup of tea. He grinned as he multiplied rapidly in his head—it could have been forty times worse.

The love affair was over. From there on in all pretense of amiability, friendliness, and tender loving care went out the window. Vanished in the night. Evaporated like a water bubble in the sunlight. His three Inquisitors—Leibowitz, Helfand, and Koota—no longer disguised their enmity.

A couple of days after his bitter castigation, Helfand again brought Jimmy before the grand jury. He questioned him relentlessly, inexorably about various meetings, parties, trips he and Harry had taken together; almost every facet of their life. He backtracked again and again trying to confuse Jimmy, but Jimmy stayed cool and answered the way Danny had drilled him. Evade, dodge, swerve, curve—don't give a direct answer unless it's documented.

Jimmy was an apt pupil. I'm not quite sure of that, Mr. Helfand. Can you refresh my memory, please. Have you the exact date? To the best of my recollection. It was quite some time ago, I'm a little hazy about it. Can you pinpoint who else was there?

They went on and on. Helfand spat out the questions and Jimmy kept fencing with him. He rarely gave Helfand a direct, precise answer. As the interrogation continued, Jimmy, like a golfer with lots of practice under his belt, got better, became a more skilled witness. Helfand tried in every way he could to trap Jimmy in a lie, and Jimmy twisted and evaded to avoid the trap.

One thing Jimmy became certain of under Helfand's scathing interrogation: it was apparent that Harry had told them nothing, was standing up like a major. Jimmy became more convinced of it after each grand jury session with Helfand. Jesus, maybe he had Harry wrong after all. Just stand up, Harry, take your medicine. What the hell can they give you? A year? Stand up and these publicity hounds can go fuck themselves.

Another Friday closed out the courthouse week. Jesus, three solid weeks in Brooklyn. Brooklyn was starting to feel like Philadelphia.

The weekend in the hotel suite passed slowly. The following Monday Jimmy was returning to his berth in the witness anteroom. He sat there all morning without being called. He sat and read, scarcely taking his eyes off his book. He went to lunch nearby with his two new pals, Morty and Ted, and returned about one thirty.

He was summoned out of the room by the court officer to see Helfand. Helfand took him to one side. He seemed calm. In a smooth voice he said, "Riley, I'm releasing you as of now as a material witness. I'll tell the two cops guarding you. All you are is a wasted expense to the city. Riley, you lied to me in that grand jury room from the minute I brought you in. The only time you answered truthfully was when it was hard facts, like your age and where you were born. You lied your ass off to me. But I'm warning you, you haven't heard the last of this. You tried to make a fool of me, and someday maybe you'll regret it. Judge Leibowitz and I will get to the bottom of all you grafting cops. Remember, we have the money, the power, and plenty of troops behind us. That's it. Now you can go. Just remember, if I need you as a trial witness, or a trial defendant if I can prove you lied, I want you available. You got that straight?"

Jimmy looked at him. He was tempted to tell him what was on his mind, but he kept his mouth shut. Helfand was right about one thing—they really did have the money, the power, and the troops. No use aggravating him further.

"I'm sorry, Julie, if you feel I wasn't honest with you. I guess that's just the way I'm built, the way my father raised me. I'm also sorry a guy like you, a guy who was always supposed to be a nice guy, is handling a piece of shit like this hatchet job. Whatever damage is done to some of these poor cops will be on your conscience, not on mine. Well, Julie, you give me the okay with these two kids and I'll go back to the hotel and pack my things. I'll say goodbye now, but I can't say I wish you luck."

"I didn't expect you to. How are you going to get back home to Connecticut? Have you got a ride?"

"No, but that's okay. I'll just call the Downtown A.C. to send over a car and chauffeur to drive me home."

Helfand couldn't help smiling. "Riley, I have to admit, you have brass balls. Sheer gall. So long."

"You only live once, Julie. See you around."

They parted without shaking hands. Jimmy joined Marty and Ted in the corridor. He was jubilant. He told them the news and they went and checked with Helfand. They drove Jimmy back to the hotel, where he packed his clothes and called the athletic club to send a car over for him.

Jimmy took them down to the hotel bar for a goodbye drink while he waited for the chauffeur to pick him up. They touched glasses good luck, a little sadly, they all had grown fond of each other.

Jimmy said, "I want you both to know you guys were terrific to me. I don't forget easily, and someday soon, after this mess blows over, I'll make sure the right guys left in The Job know what you did for me. Like I must have repeated a hundred times, the book-making and gambling business will be going on after Leibowitz, Helfand, and Koota are all dead. You guys stay with the white shield, forget trying to buck for detective. Get into plainclothes, where the real cabbage is. When the dust settles after this investigation, there'll be plenty of new inspectors made who'll be looking for young guys they can trust. You can be sure I'll know a few of them and will give you kids the highest marks. I can't compliment you two better than that, and I promise I'll keep my word.

"Now let's get down to our game plan for the next few months. You, Morty, you call me at home if you want me. Memorize my number. I changed my number to a private one because my wife began to get some crackpot calls. When you call, say it's Leo calling, after Leo Durocher, our favorite manager. About the thousand every month, I'll get hold of your Uncle Sid and give it to him. This way we'll never be seen together. I know where to reach him, it's no problem. Let's say I keep you guys on for six months. Look, don't protest, I can afford it. I need you, and you need the money. You've earned it, you got it coming. I hate to admit it, but I still have deep misgivings about Harry. If he only holds still, Leibowitz and Helfand can hold their hands on their asses. But if he blows the whistle, this bullshit is going to mush-room into something real serious. He can hurt an awful lot of people. Okay, here's the ground rules. Call me only if you think it real important. No inconsequential shit. As of now, I figure they know one helluva lot about what went on, but they can't tie it together. The only one left who can do it for them is Harry. The minute you hear he's starting to chirp, give me a call.

"Okay, drink up, here's my chauffeur. So long, you two, and once again, thanks."

It was wonderful to be home. Jimmy was a little gun-shy from all the bad publicity, but after the initial questions about how he'd been treated and quite a bit of good-natured kidding about his hidden millions, things became normal. Slowly but surely the investigation by Leibowitz's special grand jury began to fade into obscurity. All the guys in the organization who'd been pinched were tried in Special Sessions Court away from Leibowitz. Some were acquitted, most of them got off with a fine, and only Blackie and Rocky got three months apiece. Mikie and Willie were severed from the others. Harry still hadn't been tried, was still in Raymond Street in lieu of $250,000 bail.

There was an occasional indictment of some poor unfortunate cop for having been caught in a lie before the grand jury. This served to keep the Sam and Julie Act alive in the papers, but the public's interest began to wane. A new vaudeville act had appeared on the scene. Senator Kefauver formed a committee to investigate organized crime in the big cities throughout the country. They were using every horseshit device possible to gain headlines. The Kefauver committee was due in New York City in the forthcoming year, and there was much speculation about the impact these grass-roots crimebusters would have on the city.

Jimmy took it easy and stayed close to home for a couple of months. He then started to go to New York a few days a week to work with Jack Goldman, the printer. Goldman was as pleasant and helpful as always with Jimmy, never asking him a question about his trouble. They put aside all discussions about the potential partnership. Jimmy preferred to wait until he felt more secure about his future. There was no sense putting up a lot of cash to buy a business and then wind up on a rockpile for a few years.

The blind, naked hate on the faces of Leibowitz and Helfand was a recurring image in Jimmy's mind. He would be laughing, having a drink with a couple of guys or at a big party, when boom, he would suddenly envision one of the snorting dragons. At times he became very withdrawn, very pensive. He kept his fingers crossed when he thought of Harry.

The months rolled by and still Harry stayed tight. Jimmy met with Augie once in a while to catch up on things. Harry's lawyer had put in all kinds of writs of habeas corpus to try to get a reduction of Harry's bail to a nominal amount. Leibowitz and Helfand had blocked every move. There was no way to raise the $250,000 bail. Sooner or later they had to try him. Six months in jail, held in impossibly high bail, with no trial date set. For what? Bookmaking! Christ, you had a better shot in Russia.

Augie had been to see Harry's wife and laid a little money on her. She told Augie that she saw him a few times a week and he seemed to be taking it pretty good. Well, if he stands up he'll come out a hero. One thing for sure, Leibowitz can't try him, it's a misdemeanor, he'll be bound over to a lower court, Special Sessions. Christ, he's got almost six months in already. The time he's doing now will count as part of his sentence. The most they'll ever give him is a year. Stick it out, Harry boy. Do your time, and even I, Jimmy Riley, will forgive a lot of your past sins.

Jimmy was at home, sitting in the den reading. He had just finished a nice dinner, he had had a profitable business day in the city, all was well with the world. The phone rang about eight o'clock.

"Hello, Jimmy, how are you? This is Leo."

"Hey, Leo, how are you, kid? Give me your number, I'll call you right back."

Jimmy got into his car and drove down the road to the public booth at the gas station. His good mood was gone. He had a strong premonition of disaster.

Morty answered on the first ring. "Jimmy boy, I miss you. Jim, I'm afraid I have bad news."

"It figured, kid. Don't worry about it. Go ahead, what's up?"

"Jimmy, they've been marching Harry in and out of Helfand's office the last three days. I got a good look at the two of them together in the hall today. They were kidding and laughing like asshole buddies. The first day Harry came in I heard he looked like a scavanger. Today he had on a white shirt, dark tie, and nice blue suit. He looked like he was ready to go to the Copa. And now for the real bad news. They took him out of Raymond Street jail and put him up in the same hotel where they kept you. Jimmy, he has to be opening up, spilling his guts. Helfand's been going around the last couple of months with a face down to the floor, snapping at everyone. Today he looked as happy as the day he got bar mitzvahed. He was laughing, slapping guys on the back, you know, like one of those Rotarians. It all points to one thing, Jimmy, and I hate to think I'm right."

"I agree, Morty. You're right. No question about it. Jesus Christ, all he had to do was hold out for a few more months. He'd have been a fucking hero. Look, you think you'll get to body-guard him?"

"Positively. We're scheduled to get him two days from now."

"Now listen, Morty, be very careful with this guy. He'll con the living shit out of you. He's funny, likable, a very charming guy. But remember, he's a snake. The little fuck did a million wrong things, but he could've cured them all if he just stood up. Be nice to him, make him your friend, but tell him nothing. If he asks you about me, just say we hardly talked to each other. I mostly stayed in my room and read. Got it? Sound him out a little. Try to see how far he intends to go. Okay, kid, you're a sweetheart. Next time I see your Uncle Sid I'll make sure to tell him his sister produced a helluva kid. Stay in touch."

"That's nice of you to say that. Thanks, Jimmy. Take it easy. I'll be in touch."

Jimmy hung up, hesitated for a minute, and then called Augie at his girl friend's apartment.

"Yeah, Jim. What's up?"

"The end of the world, Augie."

"No shit. He finally caved in?"

"It's not official yet, but all signs point that way. They took him out of Raymond Street. He's in the same hotel I was, with the D.A.'s men. You thinking the same way I am?"

"No question, Jim. What a shame. I figured as long as he went this far he'd stick it out all the way. Well, it's done. What do you intend to do?"

"Just stay loose, I guess. No doubt it'll be all over the papers in a couple of days. Leibowitz and Helfand must have been heart-broken the last couple of months with no publicity. Christ, will they hit the jackpot with this guy. The one thing that really wor-ries me, Augie, is once they start putting this guy's picture in the papers and on television, he'll open up like a stuck pig. He's such a fucking ham actor he'll never shut up. Well, there's nothing we can do about it now. Look, make sure you get hold of Chick right away. Tell him to red-alert everybody. I'll get back to you in a couple of days. If necessary, you drive up here and I'll meet you someplace just as you enter Connecticut. I'm staying out of New York and close to home until I see what's what."

"Good idea, Jim. Okay, kid, so long. And take it easy. I'll be hearing from you."

"Good, Aug. So long, pal."

Jimmy drove home, mixed himself a Cutty Sark and water, sat back in his chair, and contemplated the world and his ultimate fate. His good cheer had deserted him. He was enveloped in gloom, thinking about what lay ahead. He silently cursed Harry. Every rotten, obscene word he could think of he mouthed silently. One thought kept recurring: the sonofabitch couldn't do another few months.

The bad news was verified a couple of days later. The District Attorney, Miles McDonald, called a press conference. A lot of the reporters were surprised to see him, because by this time most of the press thought Julie Helfand was the real D.A., instead of a mere assistant. McDonald had played the entire probe a bit low-key. He had been a warm personal friend of Bill O'Dwyer for years. It could have been that he was embarrassed by the cavalier treatment his old friend had received at the hands of the mayor-hungry Leibowitz. It might also have been embarrassment at the high-handed publicity-seeking antics of Leibowitz and Helfand. Their complete disregard for the constitutional safeguards of wit-nesses, their constant violations of the secrecy of grand jury pro-ceedings, might have been looked on askance by the quiet, mild-mannered McDonald.

This fateful morning, however, McDonald took the spotlight. Flanked by Helfand and Koota, he made his statement to the press. "About a week ago the bail of Harry Gross was reduced to twenty-five thousand dollars. A few days later he pleaded guilty to the charges of bookmaking and conspiracy in Special Sessions Court. He was paroled while awaiting sentence on these charges and is now in the protective custody of the agents of my office."

The gathered reporters started to shout a hundred questions at McDonald.

He waved his arms for quiet.

"Just raise your hands and I will choose one of you at random and answer your questions to the best of my knowledge. Go ahead, you in front with the tortoiseshell glasses."

"When you say you have Gross in protective custody, Mr. District Attorney, would the inference be that he is now a cooperative witness?"

"That is a correct assumption."

That was it. They could have asked the D.A. a million questions but they would have all been redundant. There was only one pertinent fact. Harry Gross was now opening up and implicating a whole lot of cops. The evening papers and the television screen poured out the sad news to a bunch of unhappy guys.

9

THERE WAS much consternation in The Job at McDonald's fateful pronouncement on that raw, cold winter morning. The bleak news was a match for the wretched weather. Since that late-summer day of the Big Brooklyn Bookmaking Raid, when Harry Gross and thirty-five of his satellites were arrested, many plainclothes cops and their bosses had been harassed beyond belief. Along the way a few of them were unhappily caught in lies before the Leibowitz grand jury, mostly about their finances. They were speedily stripped of their police shields, packed off to jail on a lesser plea, or were awaiting trial. Fortunately, they were few, and completely isolated from one another. But as each cop was caught in the web it would send icy chills down the spines of the lucky guys who so far had withstood the onslaught. All they could do was sit back, keep their fingers crossed, and hope and pray Harry wouldn't finger them.

Summer had gently rolled into autumn, and soon the autumn leaves had turned brown. The beautiful tree-lined streets of Flatbush became covered with fallen leaves driven by winter winds. Harry Gross still languished in a drafty cell in forbidding Raymond Street jail, apparently accepting his fate. The apprehensive cops were aware that the D.A.'s office must soon try Harry on the gambling charges. What had happened to him up to now was unprecedented. But then, what Leibowitz, Helfand and company were getting away with was also unprecedented. Harry's basic charge, in spite of all the hurrah, was a simple misdemeanor. The harshest sentence he could conceivably expect was one year in jail, and any time spent in jail prior to trial would count against the final sentence. Also, any prisoner convicted of a misdemeanor was automatically granted a third of his time off for good behavior. These simple mathematics strengthened the anxious cops' hopes as the days went by. All Harry Gross had to do was keep quiet for a few more months and he'd walk out a free man.

None of which deterred the honest minions of the D.A.'s office from daily confronting Harry with dire threats of life imprisonment or exile to Siberia. His crime was soon to be adjudicated in a lower court rather than the lofty edifice where Leibowitz presided. The initial hysterical publicity was dying, and the clamor for the cops' blood had faded. There was no case against the plainclothes cops unless Harry suddenly decided to cooperate with the D.A.'s office. As each day slowly passed, apprehension began to lessen.

Then came McDonald's time bomb. Once it exploded there was nothing to do but to sit back and see how far Harry intended to go. Some of the luckier cops who had their time in had already filed their pension papers and were receiving their monthly remittance. Some of the even luckier ones who had worked in higher-echelon offices like the P.C.'s, chief's, or borough squads and had saved their money had simply turned in their shields and taken off for more distant, safer, and warmer climes. However, there were still many who remained who were extremely vulnerable. Some remained out of personal pride, love for The Job, and convinced of their innocence. But most remained because they were in a state of limbo. This group consisted of guys who were short of the twenty-five-year retirement requisite. Most of them had no money put aside, or if any, not enough to do them much good. In the main, they had been local plainclothesmen, attached to division squads. Whatever money they made, most of them pissed it away on the good life. Cops were so underpaid that at their first taste of easy money they made a new life for themselves and their families. Live for today, don't worry about tomorrow—that was their credo. Now they would have to live by it.

Leibowitz and his henchman went to work with spirited vengeance. Harry became their puppet, their prized pet, and they fed him lumps of sugar and all kinds of goodies as he turned cart-wheels for them. Human rats, like Pavlov's dog, can be conditioned to react predictably.

Harry embroidered his vast knowledge of the inner sanctum of The Job with bits and pieces of information he had picked up through the years of friendly assocation with guys like Jimmy Riley and other plainclothesmen. His imagination ran wild as he was fed all manner of leading questions by the D.A.'s men, who were trying to piece together a lot of scant details they had gathered from previous cooperative witnesses. Everything the crooked little confidence man told them was pure gospel to these saviors of society. They made some superficial checks of certain concrete facts that Harry had somehow managed to store in his screwed-up head, but on the whole, they accepted everything he said as the pure truth. The D.A.'s office was so anxious to believe Harry and crucify every cop they could that they never once doubted the babbling of a half-crazed psycho who couldn't tell the truth to his best friends.

The wheels of justice in downtown Brooklyn turned. The dossier of indictment was reaching its completion. There was immense speculation among the press about the number of defendants who would finally be brought before the Great Crusader to receive their due. The men who at times wore the blue of the Finest now possessed hearts as black as the worst. McDonald, now very much a part of the act with Leibowitz and Helfand, released almost daily statements that fueled the fire for the imminent incineration of the hapless police.

Winter was drawing to a close, the beloved Brooklyn Dodgers were down at their Florida camp in the midst of spring training, everything was coming up roses—except for the poor cops and ex-cops who that day got the worst news of their lives. Their names, age, address, and present status were printed in the morning papers. There were twenty-one policemen indicted on charges of conspiracy. The press seemed disappointed at the meager number. There seemed to be a distinct undercurrent that they expected more. Perhaps twenty-one thousand, the approximate size of the police force at the time.

But McDonald threw them a sop by naming what seemed like a

hundred or more *co-conspirators*. He bravely noted to the press that he had airtight cases only on the unlucky twenty-one. He neglected to add that that was for a jury to decide. He also failed to elucidate the status of the "co-conspirators." It was probably too unwieldy to explain that there were mere unfounded allegations against those named as co-conspirators, not a vestige of concrete evidence. In the opinion of many legal minds, to classify someone as a co-conspirator when there is nothing but hearsay evidence is a distinct form of character assassination against which there is no defense.

According to the rules of the game, once Jimmy Riley had testified before the grand jury with full immunity, he was completely absolved from any prosecution for gambling or other crimes he was questioned about. But the forces of law and order couldn't resist, they named him a co-conspirator for good measure. Jimmy just shook his head when he read his name. It was just a prediction of things to come.

He was a bit surprised and a trifle amused to read his old nemesis, Dan the deputy, named as a co-conspirator. Jimmy was positive that this was an absolute figment of Harry's imagination. There was no way Harry ever met Danny, probably never even laid eyes on him. He'd undoubtedly heard about him through Jimmy, knew Jimmy hated him, so he threw him in the hat. Danny was a behind-the-desk man, too cute Irish to expose himself to any gambler, much less one who had gained the notoriety of Harry Gross.

Harry, to Jimmy's sorrow, named Chick O'Mara, Tommy Fahey, and Johnny Crews. He expected it, but to read their names in the indictment was a body blow. There were several other nice guys named, good friends of Jimmy's, enough to almost make him sick to his stomach. It didn't surprise him to see named the four guys who had engineered Harry's return to grace, led by bold Dave Dorfman. He smiled bitterly when he recalled the wild night in Dutch Savarese's place. How he had warned them about Harry. Implored them to listen, that he wasn't the same Harry anymore —he'd gone bad, he was no good. They were implacable. Look where it got them.

But the greatest surprise was to read that Gordon and two of the other Four Horsemen had been indicted. Why? As far as Jimmy knew, they had kept their promise and stayed far away from Harry. He knew they all hated Harry's guts, if for no other reason than that he was a friend of Jimmy's. Jimmy knew Chick picked up the ice for the squad from Augie every month, he would have nothing to do with Harry. Augie would never implicate anyone. Christ, Augie wasn't even arrested. Jimmy was puzzled, very puzzled, but he shed no tears over these three. He knew deep down in his heart that, one way or the other, they'd created their own jam.

Jimmy stayed in Connecticut, scarcely venturing very far from his own home. He called his friend and business associate in New York, Jack Goldman, and told him he wouldn't be in for a while. As usual, Goldman asked no questions and wished him luck. He had a couple of drinks with John the lawyer, who was outraged at his being named a co-conspirator in the gambling conspiracy indictment. The D.A.'s office was totally wrong. They were probably well aware of it, but they were so high-handed they did whatever they felt like anyway. It's apparent that it was only to smear you some more, and they've already accomplished that by brazenly giving your secret grand jury testimony to the press in open court. Jimmy boy, you've been plenty stigmatized already, by now you must be used to it. Don't worry, Jim, at least they didn't, or shall I say couldn't, indict you.

In spite of John's reassurance, Jimmy was still worried, still constantly blue. Not only for himself, but for his friends. Helfand was demanding and Leibowitz was issuing search warrants for some of the guys' houses, seeking evidence of illicit gifts—television sets, expensive clothes, sterling silver sets—whatever type gift Harry might claim to have laid on them. The media loved it. Search warrants, for Christ's sake, could you believe it? When guys at the golf club or the athletic club used to question Jimmy about what kind of a person Leibowitz really was, Jimmy would grin and kiddingly say, "You got a better shot with Stalin."

A week passed after the bill of indictment was handed down. It was time to get hold of Augie. He reached him at his girl friend's that night and made a date to meet him the next day at a country inn off the Merritt Parkway, just over the Connecticut side of the border.

When they met they greeted each other with a big hug, each eyeing the other to see if there were any apparent effects of the bad news showing on their faces. They each ordered a Cutty and water, touched glasses good luck, and Jimmy said, "Have you heard from anybody? Chick? Tom? Anyone?"

"Not a soul. I've been playing it close, just taking off a few of the big private customers to try to stay alive. I call in the action to Big Max in New York. He's a great guy, Jimmy, he loves you. Most of the customers call direct and I settle with them once a week. I'm on a half-sheet."

"Good boy, Augie, stay in action. Christ knows, you have to live. How's everything in New York? Any slow-up? Are there still some okay phones?"

"Jimmy, like this Brooklyn bullshit never happened. From what I understand, the same thing applies in all the other boroughs."

"Jesus, I'm sure glad to hear that, Augie. Now listen, I wanted you to meet me today 'cause I'm up in the air about a few things. Who gave Chick up? In my heart I don't think Harry ever would."

"Jimmy, please, don't get sentimental about that prick, will you? Sure he did. Or Willie did. A couple of times I was away or busy and I gave Willie the money for Chick and the squad. He wouldn't take it from Harry, he hated him on account of you. What's the difference? They're both stool pigeons, Willie and Harry."

"What about Gordon and the two wops from the Four Horsemen? How come they got indicted?"

"Jimmy, at the time it happened I didn't dare tell you, but now it doesn't matter. One day last summer Gordon and the other two came around the Dugout and wanted to grab Little Jimmy. They gave him the shit, that they had a letter on the joint, a direct order from the boss. Must have a collar to cover the complaint. Anyway, Jimmy got hold of Harry and it was straightened out. He gave them one of the clerks and they moved the pinch a mile away. You see, it had to be the shit or they would have insisted on a pinch back at the Dugout. It was the first time the chief's squad bothered us since you left, so Harry figured what the hell, don't squawk, give them a pinch. Harry staked them pretty good and they gave the clerk an easy one. It was thrown out. We both warned Jimmy and everyone not to breathe one word of it to you. Harry would probably have never met them except for that phony pinch. He knew all about them from the incident in the wire room, but I don't think he ever laid eyes on them before, much less speak to them. And I'm sure he threw their boss in, the deputy, for good measure. I saw his name in the paper as a co-conspirator. Harry just mentioned him for revenge. What the hell is this 'co-conspirator' bullshit, Jimmy? I see you're one of them."

"Nothing, Aug. Just as you say, bullshit. Tell me, how's Chick taking the bad news?"

"Pretty good, I think. I only spoke to him on the phone and he seems okay. He's been through the mill with the grand jury quite a few times, and he seems more nervous about them. He'll be okay. Now, Jimmy, what do you plan to do? Before you give me an answer, I'll tell you what I'd like to see you do. Take off. Go somewhere far away where nobody knows you, until this goddam mess blows over."

"Look, Aug, I know you have my best interests at heart, but I have no intention of going anywhere. I have one thing in mind, one fucking thing I'm living with. Somehow, and just right now I'm not sure how, I'm going to shut that rat bastard's mouth."

"Are you going crazy, Jim? You mean you're going to try to hit him? For Christ's sake, there's a million cops around him all the time."

"No, not a chance, even though I'd love to hit him. I just want to sit him down face to face with me for about half an hour. I'll scare the living shit out of him, you can bet your ass on it."

"How the hell are you going to do that?"

"I'll figure out a way. I'm bound to get some opportunity. I have a scheme or two in mind, one of them will work."

"Jimmy, there's no way I agree with that. All you're looking for is a whole lot of trouble. This Judge Leibowitz and those D.A.'s men really mean business. I never saw so much vindictiveness. They have a hard-on a mile long for O'Dwyer, the police department, and the entire world, from what I can see. They don't seem to care who they hurt, or what methods they use to hurt them. They're going to do a lot of damage to people. I can just picture Harry up there on the witness stand like a half-ass movie actor. Once he gets the limelight, forget about it, he'll never stop fingering people."

"Don't you think I realize that, Augie? But I have to admit, in a lot of ways I do have a guilty conscience. I feel morally responsible for this guy."

"Horseshit, Jimmy. He knew a thousand cops before he ever laid eyes on you. We were going for almost two years before you came on the scene, the day you nailed him. We had everyone on the payroll except the New York squads."

"I know, Aug, I know. But the fact remains, I took him up in the world. I put the sonofabitch in the big time. For Christ's sake, I brought him around and treated him like he was my own brother. He met guys through me who ordinarily wouldn't shit on him. Aug, there's one more thing I want you to do, if you can."

"If it's possible, anything, Jim."

"Remember that Jewish guy I worked with when we first broke in? You know, the big guy, Sid Friedman?"

"Yeah, sure, I remember Sid. Nice guy. What's he doing now?"

"He's a detective up in Ryer Avenue precinct in the Bronx. Get a message to him. Just tell him to have Leo call me soon as possible. Be careful, though. Don't do it on the phone."

"No problem, Jimmy, that's easy. I have a couple of good friends up there who are bound to know him. I'll take care of it."

"Good, Augie. Okay, let's finish this drink and get out of here. You probably have plenty to do. Now, let's understand each other. The next time I call you for a place to meet, we won't have to designate it. This is it. It's nice and quiet, and nobody knows us here."

"Perfect, Jim. Now take it easy, and for Christ's sake, don't do anything rash. I can understand how you feel, but no way this is any of your fault. Forget that 'guilty conscience' shit."

"That's easy to say, Aug, but this guy actually haunts me. Lately, I live with him every day. I wake up with him and at night I go to bed with him. I've got do something about this guy."

"Well, knowing you, you won't change your mind. But Jim, please, be careful. Okay, let's go."

A couple of days later Morty the Incorruptible, alias Leo, called. Jimmy immediately drove to the public phone outside his friend's gas station and called the number Morty had just given him.

"Hey, Morty baby, thanks for calling."

"How does it feel to be a co-conspirator, Jim?"

"A lot better than a regular conspirator, Morty."

Morty laughed. "I see you haven't lost your sense of humor. What's up, Jim? I got an urgent message from Garcia, Big Sid Garcia, to call you right away."

"It isn't too pressing, I just wanted to meet you two guys for a drink. Any time at your convenience, but make sure it's a nice cool place where nobody will recognize us."

"How about the Glen Island Casino? That's not too far from you, and Teddy and I went to hear Tommy Dorsey there last week. It's full of square kids who love to dance. Suppose we make it Friday night about seven o'clock, at the bar."

"That's great. See you there. Thanks, kid."

Jimmy met Morty and Ted at the Glen Island Casino and they were so glad to see each other it was almost emotional. The bar was fairly crowded, which was good, and there were endless tables of groups of guys alone who were eyeing the tables where there were groups of girls alone. Jimmy suppressed a grin. Everyone sniffing around at each other, nobody would ever notice anything out of the ordinary with the summit meeting of the unholy three.

After the initial backslapping and handshaking, they ordered a round of drinks and touched glasses good luck. Jimmy spoke first. "You two guys look terrific. I hope you wound up with some of this gorgeous pussy floating around here when you came up to dance to the syncopathic strains of Tommy Dorsey."

They both laughed. Teddy said, "You know what you warned us fifty times over, Jim. 'Loose lips sink ships.'"

Another big laugh.

"You're right, kid. Christ, I feel like an old man looking at these young chicks and seeing you two guys."

Morty said, "You look like you could take a shot at one of them in a minute, Jim. But let's hear it. You didn't get us up here to discuss girls. What's on your mind?"

"You're right, Leo, I mean Morty. I'm not only happy to see you two, but I've got something I want to talk about that's a little too heavy for the telephone. That's why I wanted to see you in person."

"Go ahead, Jim. You know what we think of you. If we can possibly help you, we will."

Jimmy ordered another round of drinks. He then said, "Before I get into the details, tell me what's happening with all those fearless crimebusters in good old downtown Brooklyn. Suppose you start, Morty. You're the talker, Teddy's the dancer."

Another laugh.

"Jimmy, we've had this rat bastard Harry at least half a dozen times. You are absolutely right, he's got some line of shit. He must have asked us about you fifty times. You know, questioning us, sounding us out. 'Do you think Jimmy is sore at me?' 'I wonder how all this will affect Jimmy? "Boys, no matter what, I'll never hurt Jimmy Riley, he's the best friend I ever had.'"

"Jimmy, it's obvious he's leery as hell about you. A little kid could tell."

"I'm his best friend. That's what he said?"

"He constantly raves about you. But Teddy and I stayed nice and cute. We did exactly as you told us to do. We told him we hardly got to know you, that you stayed to yourself, were very quiet. You know, read a lot, minded your own business, and were very polite. He tried his best to feel us out, but fuck him. Jimmy, I get sick looking at that prick, ratting his balls off against a lot of cops who only did him good."

"I know how you feel about him, Morty, but I want you to go along with this act. Make him think you and Ted are his best friends among all the young cops who guard him. I've got one thing going round and round in my head, and that's to get to see him face to face."

"How the hell are you going to do that, Jimmy? Jesus, they're all over him, guarding him like a hawk. All of us who guard him have to account for every minute we're with that sonofabitch."

"Do you have to keep a log?"

"No, thank God, nothing like that."

"They're too stupid to ask you to do that."

"Still, Jim, they're awfully strict about him."

"I realize that, Morty, but sooner or later the security gets a little lax with witnesses. Harry is a very animated, restless guy. He doesn't read much, he loves broads, and most of all he loves the bright lights. He's a sure pop to con Helfand into letting him bounce around a little. He's been caged up for five or six months, and you can bet your sweet ass he's dying to swing, dying to break loose."

"Jim, I have to agree with you there. Christ, he almost cries about what they did to him in Raymond Street, like it was Devil's Island. He keeps beefing about the terrible conditions there, that he couldn't stand it anymore. Too fucking bad, right, Jim?"

"It figures, knowing Harry. He had to have something to blame for opening up, like how cruel Raymond Street was. He always had an alibi ready whenever he screwed up; it was always some other guy's fault, an unbelievable streak of bad luck, or some kind of horseshit like that. But, Morty, we could talk all night about this guy and arrive right back where we started. One certain, unassailable fact remains—the damage is done. How do we undo it? To be or not to be, that is the question. So, before I get too Shakespearean, I have a diabolical scheme in mind, a proposition for you two."

"Go ahead, Jimmy. So far you've kept your word with us, and we're both on your side. Christ, being around you and then being with him is no contest. If we can somehow help the cops who are indicted without putting our necks out too far in a noose, then we're your guys."

"Beautiful. Now listen carefully. I figure we got a couple of months at most before they put these cops on trial. If the bodyguard cycle remains the same, you two should get to protect him ten or twelve times. Keep your ears and eyes open. Ask a few innocent questions. See how much shit they let him get away with to keep him happy and ready to bury the world. Maybe I can get to meet him when he goes to Atlantic Beach to see his wife and kids. That's if they let him. If so, maybe on the way back to

Brooklyn you can stop for a drink and I'll be accidentally on purpose in the joint you pick. Somehow or other I have to meet this guy head-on. I give you both my word that I'll never physically touch him. I just want to scare the living shit out of him. When I finish talking to him, I promise he'll never give you two up. As a matter of fact, he won't give anybody up."

"Jumping Jesus, Jim, that's asking us to take a big chance."

"What's the big chance? I promise you, don't worry about it, he'll never give you up."

The two young cops and Jimmy argued pro and con about the wisdom of Jimmy's plan for about an hour. They finally capitulated, on two conditions. The proposed meeting with Harry had to appear purely accidental, and there would be no physical violence. The terms agreed on, they ordered a nightcap and got ready to leave. The two Incorruptibles left a thousand dollars apiece richer, and Jimmy left with a little more peace of mind.

The final arrangements were that they were to call Jimmy every ten days or so and give him a rundown on Harry's behavior. How was he reacting to the pressure? Was he nervous, happy, unhappy, scared—or prancing around like the ham actor he always was? They were told to keep drawing Harry out about Jimmy. How did Harry feel about Jimmy? How do you think Jimmy feels about you? When Harry had a couple of drinks and became expansive, keep urging him to tell you about the good times he and Jimmy had when they were rolling high. The trips they took, the night-clubs, the great-looking broads. Were they really that gorgeous, Harry? Keep talking shit like that to this rat bastard. Jimmy wanted the squealing sonofabitch to be full of good memories when they finally met.

The first two calls from Morty were unproductive, a damper on Jimmy's hopes. They were still guarding Harry like he was Fort Knox. He didn't go to see his wife, she had to go see him, with cops always in attendance. Harry was getting very jumpy as the trial date was drawing near, but whenever they brought up Jimmy's name he talked about him like he was his best pal. There's one guy I'll never give up. What a fool I was to break up with Jimmy. Morty said he positively glowed when he reminisced about the good times they had together. The good old days.

So far, so good, Morty—but when the hell am I going to see the guy? There's nothing we can do so far, Jimmy. We are confined to the hotel room with him except when we take him down to see Helfand.

The third call came about a month after the meeting at the Glen Island Casino, and it was all bad news. Morty and Ted had been temporarily relieved from the Harry Gross guard detail. They had been reassigned to an ongoing investigation of some allegedly crooked bail bondsmen. Jesus Christ, of all the bad breaks in the world, this had to be the worst. Alledgely crooked bail bondsmen. That's like an investigation to see if anyone is going to get laid in a whorehouse. They ought to have an investigation to try to find an honest bail bondsman. Next thing you know, they'll have an investigation to see if there are any crooked building inspectors.

This piece of news really gave Jimmy the melancholy blues. The trial date had been definitely set, about five weeks away. Augie came up a few times for dinner but had nothing really important to say. Harry was still held virtually incommunicado, none of the guys had laid eyes on him or heard a word from him. Helfand and Leibowitz were keeping their Benedict Arnold well out of sight of the enemy.

The day of the trial of the infamous twenty-one came, a very warm late-spring morning that promised to be even warmer as the day progressed. For the first time in months Jimmy Riley went to Brooklyn. He left Connecticut very early and parked his car a few blocks from the courthouse. He anticipated a huge crowd of curiosity seekers, and he was correct. The lines were already forming an hour and a half before show time, scheduled for ten o'clock. He had a good friend of many years on tap, a big Irish court officer named Joey Doyle, and he winked at Jimmy to assure him of a seat for the grand spectacle. Jimmy donned a pair of dark glasses, and Joey sat him well back in the court on the extreme right-hand side. He read the morning paper waiting for the proceedings to start, oblivious of the incessant, expectant chatter going on about him.

The defendants finally filed in and took their places in the front of the court. With a few exceptions, Jimmy's heart bled for them.

Helfand made a grand entrance, flanked by Aaron Koota and a young assistant. The major-domo, Leibowitz, was announced by the bailiff and majestically strode to the bench to a buzz of noise from the crowded court. He banged his gavel for quiet and imperiously called the court to order. After a few bitter exchanges between the phalanx of defense lawyers and Helfand, with Leibowitz often getting into the act, they at last started to pick the jury. After much haranguing on both sides, and a few speeches, both teams finally compromised on the first juror. The time had now crawled well past noon and Leibowitz, with a flourish, declared a recess until two o'clock.

Jimmy exited out the rear of the courtroom and stood off to the side talking to Joey Doyle. Suddenly a piercing scream echoed through the corridors of the courthouse. Then a more shrill scream, then another, then what seemed like one continuous scream.

Jimmy said, "Jesus, Joey, what the hell is all the wailing about? For Christ's sake, go across there and see what's up."

Joey Doyle came back in less than a minute. His face was dead white. "Jimmy, I can't believe it. Nick Martino just jumped out the window. Six floors. Holy Christ, poor Nick."

Jimmy's mouth fell open, he could barely speak. "Joey, my God, that's awful. Listen, I'm getting the hell out of here. Get hold of Chick O'Mara and Tommy Fahey and tell them to meet me in Fred Scarmel's place on Montague Street as soon as possible. Thanks a lot, pal."

Jimmy walked over to Fred's place in a daze. Poor Nicky. He went straight to the bar and ordered a Cutty on the rocks. Chick and Tommy came in a few minutes later and motioned the bartender for the same without speaking. There were tears in the eyes of all three of them. They took their drinks and walked to a table in the rear. They sipped their drinks and sat there silently, really shaken.

Chick spoke up. "It was terrible, Jimmy. I was standing right next to him when we left the court. He was very quiet, very tense all morning. It was pretty warm in court and getting hotter as the day went on. The window was wide open. I had turned my back to look for one of the guys, when I heard this lady scream. I turned around and Nicky was gone. The lady was holding her hand across her mouth, pointing to the window. A couple of other women were screaming. I stuck my head out the window and looked down. There was Nicky sprawled face down on the sidewalk. He looked like a big broken doll lying down there. Christ, this is the third guy who dutched out since this shit started. The two captains and now Nicky. They'll have a fatality list to be proud of pretty soon. For what?"

Tommy finally spoke. "In some ways I almost feel it's my fault. I've met Nick a few times before today for a drink and he kept telling me how he dreaded to be confined. He was actually claustrophobic. He had to force himself to get into an elevator, would only get on one when other people were in it. He wouldn't fly in an airplane. He couldn't stay in a room by himself. I noticed when I shook hands with him this morning how tense he looked, like he was going to the chair. But I was so preoccupied sitting there hating Leibowitz and Helfand and daydreaming what I'd like to do to them, I never even looked at Nick. The poor bastard just couldn't stand the thought of going to jail, I guess. I should have kept a closer eye on him, kidded him a little to snap him out of it."

"Christ, Tom, you can't blame yourself for Nick, no more than Chick or I can. There's only one guy at fault, and that's Harry. I hate to say 'I told you so' to you two, but you know what I suggested we do to this prick. Well, it's too late now for that, the cat is out of the bag for sure. Meanwhile, let's get something to eat, you prisoners have to return to the dock."

Chick said, "You're right, Jimmy. At least Nick won't have to listen to Leibowitz and Helfand rant and rave anymore. He'll also be spared the sight of Harry hamming it up on the witness stand. Too bad we can't throw that little fuck out the window."

They ordered lunch, after which they walked back separately to the courthouse. They were greeted with not entirely unexpected news. The trial had been postponed indefinitely.

Jimmy was sad about Nicky as he drove back to Connecticut, but one ray of sunshine kept seeping through his dark mood. The trial was postponed indefinitely. Game called on account of rain. Game called on account of a real nice guy jumping out a sixth-floor window. But that gave him a couple of months' breather to sit Harry down. This time he wouldn't fail.

About a month passed before the D.A.'s office set a new trial date. When Jimmy read the new date he decided it was time to get going, he had two months. He had heard briefly from the two Incorruptibles right after the postponement. They promised to stay in touch, to call every couple of weeks, and he was growing anxious waiting to hear from them. He went about his business, played a lot of golf, but went straight home every afternoon and sat and waited for the call. After about six weeks it came.

"Hello, Jimmy. Leo."

"Hey, how are you, kid? I'm glad to hear from you. Give me your number."

Jimmy took his usual drive to the public phone outside his friend's gas station. His heart was pounding excitedly as he drove, he sensed good news. He called the number Morty gave him.

"Hi, Morty, I thought you'd died. What's up, kid?"

"I have some good news for a change, Jim. We're back in action, back on Harry's case. I'm sorry to say we couldn't find any crooked bail bondsmen."

"No shit. You two are going to make some great goddam plainclothesmen when you get there. Maybe I should speak to McDonald or Helfand and really put you on your mettle, see if you can find two Jews in Brownsville."

"Very funny, Jimmy, you're a real Henny Youngman. But like I said, you Irish comedian, here's the good news. We had the pleasure of guarding the little talkative devil yesterday. It was our first shot at him. I understand from some of the other guys he got real shook up when that cop jumped out the window. One of the guys told me he laid on the bed in the hotel room and cried all day."

"How's he acting now?"

"Like it never happened. He's all over his mourning, that's for sure. He's champing at the bit to get out of the hotel more often. I heard through the grapevine that he and Helfand had a little beef about the heavy confinement. They're starting to loosen up. I understand they're now letting him out for dinner away from the hotel."

"Beautiful. That's a really encouraging sign. Remember what I said, just go along with his act and get very friendly with him. Keep my name up in your conversations with him. I want him to love me when I meet him. Now call me within the next couple of weeks. Make sure it isn't any longer. About the same time of day. Okay, kid. Stay in touch, you're beautiful."

The next call came about ten days later. Jimmy went into his usual routine and called Morty back on the number he left.

"Yeah, kid. How are you?"

"There isn't much new, Jim, except for one thing I thought important enough to call you about. Harry was allowed to go to Manhattan for dinner with one of the other teams. They went to Lindy's, and a couple of guys came over and shook hands with Harry like they were asshole buddies. Harry didn't introduce them to the guys, just went on the side and talked to them a bit."

"I can imagine who they were. Listen carefully. Suppose you and Ted suggest to Harry that you two would love to have dinner with him in the city at some fancy restaurant. Lay it on a little. If he goes for it, be sure to remember on what street you park and the name of the garage. Okay, kid, keep up the good work and stay in constant touch. See you."

On his next call Morty reported that they had only had dinner once outside the hotel suite with Harry, and it was in a small Brooklyn Italian restaurant. But he had been to New York once with one of the other teams. They ate at Jack Dempsey's, on Broadway near 50th Street. Harry had promised Morty and Ted that he'd take them to New York real soon. Morty said that Jimmy's name constantly came up in their talks together. "He sure speaks well of you, Jim. Don't worry about a thing, we'll be having dinner with him in New York next week. He promised to take us to his favorite New York restaurant. A place called Frankie and Johnnie's. Do you know it?"

"Do I know it? Like my own name. That's perfect."

Jimmy drove back home from his favorite telephone booth feeling like a million. At last things were beginning to look up. Frankie and Johnnie's. One of the bosses was a close friend of his, and he would arrange for him to tell him when Harry and the kids were about to leave so he could casually intercept them along the street as they walked toward Broadway. A most fortunate accidental meeting.

Jimmy was on cloud nine with anticipation the next five or six days. He stayed glued to his own home, patiently waiting for the telephone call. His plan of attack was all set. All Harry had to do was to fall for Jimmy's conciliatory act and Jimmy was confident conditions would improve for everybody. Everybody, that is, except for the relentless forces of McDonald's honest crimebusters, who were relishing the approaching police bloodbath.

Morty called about one o'clock in the afternoon. Jimmy was back to him in five minutes flat.

"Yes, my man. What's up?"

"I'm glad I got you this early, Jimmy, I was praying you'd be in. Ted and I have the honor of guarding this guy today. I suggested having dinner in New York tonight, and he said it was a great idea. He's upstairs in the hotel suite now talking to one of the young assistant D.A.s. I stuck my head in the room and said I was going down to the lobby to get some cigarettes. That's where I'm calling you from. We'll probably hit Frankie and Johnnie's about six o'clock and leave about eight. I'll park the car between Sixth and Seventh Avenues, okay? The rest is up to you. If you don't have any message from Leo, then you know where we are."

"That's really great, Morty. I know someday you'll be a great big-league manager. See you tonight."

As Jimmy drove home his mind was racing. His number-one plan now went into high gear. He had plenty of time, so he parked his car outside the garage and walked into town to think things out and make sure his head was on straight. He was a little apprehensive wondering whether he was exposing Morty and Ted too much. But what the hell, he felt in his heart that Harry would be dying to say hello to him and get his reaction, and besides, the two kids had plenty of balls. He had no choice, he had to maneuver Harry into a face-to-face situation.

He went into one of the restaurants in the center of town and stood at the bar and ordered a Cutty and water. He took a few swallows of the drink and went to the phone booth in the back and called his friend Dave Conte, the owner of the Zebra Bar, one of his former hangouts on the East Side. Dave was a great friend of

Jimmy's who would do almost anything he asked. Jimmy had done Dave a big favor concerning some local tough guys who were bothering him a few years ago, and Dave never forgot it.

The phone rang five times. A husky voice finally answered, "Hello, hello."

"Hi, Dave. I'm just calling to see if you are alive or dead. You sound like you're dead, shall I start over again?"

"This has to be Jimmy Riley. How are you, Jimmy boy? What the hell are you doing calling me so early?"

"Early? For Christ's sake, Dave, it's almost two o'clock, you old bastard."

"Two o'clock? In that case I'm glad you woke me up. All right, what's on your mind? Before you tell me, how do you feel?"

"I'm fine, Davey boy, couldn't be better. Dave, you remember that big blond call girl, Betty Baines, I asked you to check out when I called you a few weeks ago?"

"Sure, Jim, it was a cinch. She walked into the joint about a week after you called. She asked all about you, how you were making out. Jim, she's no longer a call girl. She proudly informed me that she's the madam of a very high-class respectable whorehouse on Riverside Drive in the Nineties. I have her number. How's that for quick information? Like I used to tell you a million times, I'd have made a better cop than most of the guys you bring in with you."

"If not a better cop, Davey, certainly a better pimp. If you could dig up murderers and bank robbers like you dig up call girls, maybe I'll recommend you to the new commissioner and you'll get your wish."

"Only on one condition. If he agrees to reinstate you to your former rank and I can become your partner. If that happens, they can stick the nightclub business up their ass, I'll get a helluva lot richer working with you."

"Some case you got getting me reinstated, walio," Jimmy laughed. "Listen, cut the comedy routine, save it for the customers. Dave, get hold of Betty today sometime. Tell her I want to meet her tonight, between nine and ten o'clock. Try to make the meet in your place. If that's not possible, I'll meet her at her place. I'll call you around seven o'clock to check. Make sure I see her, okay, pal?"

"It should be no problem, Jimmy. Just make sure you phone me about seven. See you, kid."

"Thanks, Dave."

Jimmy went back to the bar, finished his drink, and walked back home. If everything broke the way he planned, he should accidentally meet his ex-partner and old pal tonight, and sometime next week, the week before the trial date, they should have a pleasant little sit-down together. He showered and dressed, kissed Kay goodbye, and left for New York.

He arrived in town about six o'clock and parked his car near the end of the block on West 52nd Street between Broadway and Eighth Avenue. He walked back down the street to Gallagher's restaurant. As soon as he entered he received an effusive welcome from Joe Weber, the headwaiter, and Jack Solomon, the owner. They backslapped him all the way to the bar, and while he was savoring his first Cutty Sark and water about ten wise guys came over to shake hands with him. He could barely suppress a big grin. This was the same kind of greeting that good old Petey O'Neil got that first night Jimmy met him in Gallagher's. Jimmy's introduction to the tinseled world of vice and gambling. It made Jimmy feel good all over. He silently toasted the late and often lamented lieutenant. Rest easy, Petey O'Neil, rest easy wherever you are, you were one great guy.

Jimmy drank a couple of Scotches and laughed and kidded with the various guys who came over to say hello, like he didn't have a worry in the world. But one person was on his mind, burning a hole in his brain, Harry Gross.

About seven fifteen he excused himself from the bar and called Frankie and Johnnie's, his heart in his mouth.

"Hello. Mack, please."

"Just a minute. Hello, this is Mack. Who's this?"

"It's Jimmy Riley, Mack. How are you?"

"Jimmy. I can't believe it. I'm fine. How are you? And guess who's here?"

"I've guessed already, Mack. Is he sitting with two young cops?"

"They sure don't look like cops, Jimmy, they look about sixteen years old."

"That's them, two choirboys. How far are they along with their dinner?"

"The waiter was serving their steaks when I was called to the phone. They should be finished in about half an hour."

"Good, Mack. Thanks a million. One thing. Forget I ever called you, okay?"

"Don't worry about a thing, Jim. I forgot your call already. Take care of yourself. Come in soon."

Jimmy then called Dave Conte at the Zebra Bar. The date was on. Betty would meet him in the place about nine.

Jimmy went back to the bar, finished his drink, and paid his tab. He shook hands goodbye all around just like Petey O'Neil taught him, like an ex-heavyweight champ. He walked down Broadway to 45th Street and turned into the block. About three-quarters of the way down the long block he took a vantage point diagonally opposite the entrance to Frankie and Johnnie's and began his vigil.

There was still some daylight left when he spotted Teddy coming out the restaurant. Harry and Morty followed. Jimmy quickly walked across the street to the same side they were approaching on. He stayed obscured in a doorway for a minute, furtively looking up the block. The three of them were walking abreast, very slowly, Harry in the middle, about one hundred feet away. Jimmy walked very casually right toward them. Harry was laughing and gesticulating, probably in the middle of one of his thousand-and-one funny stories. They came together almost abruptly. Harry's face fell, he wasn't quite sure whether to shit or go blind.

Jimmy immediately stuck his hand out and said, "Hey, Hesh, how the hell are you? What are you doing in New York?" Keep it smooth, Jimmy.

Harry's color came back in a rush with Jimmy's unexpectedly warm greeting. "Jimmy, honest to God, I was only just talking about you. Never mind me, what are you doing in New York?"

"I was just going up to meet someone in Frankie and Johnnie's to have a big steak. Hello, fellows. I think I know you two, but I'm sorry, I can't remember your names."

Morty and Ted shook hands with Jimmy and reintroduced themselves. Morty said, "We guarded you a few times when you were in custody, Jim. Don't you remember us?"

"I'd rather forget that goddam Brooklyn, Morty, but now I do remember you guys. How are you and the other kids? Come on, Harry, let's go down the block and have a drink. That okay with you guys?"

Harry said, "Sure, Jimmy, these are two of the nicest and best kids in the D.A.'s office. They'll do anything for me, right, boys?" Harry still had some line of shit, right, boys?

Morty and Teddy nodded a smiling assent.

They walked toward Broadway. Jimmy thought, I'm going to put these two kids in the movies. What a couple of great actors. The four of them went into a seafood restaurant on Broadway at 47th Street. They were ushered to a table in the rear and sat down and ordered a round of drinks. Jimmy was affable, smiling. Harry was talking nervously, a mile a minute, still a trifle suspicious and a little overcome at the cordiality of Jimmy's initial greeting. The two young cops were at the further end of the table opposite each other, and Harry was opposite Jimmy. They all touched glasses good luck. Harry leaned over the table and said in a low voice, "You're not sore at me, are you, Jim?"

Jimmy answered in a low voice, "I don't give a shit about most of those guys, Harry, except for Chick, Tommy, and John."

"I never gave them up, Jim. I swear. It was Willie Ricardo who ratted on them."

"Look, let's not discuss it now in front of these two cops." He switched to his regular voice. "You look pretty good, Harry, considering the ordeal they put you through."

"It was murder, Jimmy, but I'm okay now."

"They're tough customers, Helfand and Leibowitz. But forget about them for a while. Who do you think I have a date with later tonight, Hesh?"

"Who, Jimmy?"

"Your old sweetheart, big Betty. Betty Baines, the blond bombshell."

"Are you serious? Big blond Betty?"

"I swear, Harry, honest to God. She gets more gorgeous as the years go by."

"Christ, Jimmy, was she ever gorgeous. I get a hard-on just thinking about her. God, was she beautiful. And a real nice girl. I used to be crazy about her. If she wasn't a dyed-in-the-wool hooker I'd have kept her when I was doing good."

"She always had a thing for you, Harry. She always liked you. Every time I see her she asks about you."

Harry was salivating, wetting his lips. "She does, Jim? She really does?"

"No shit. And I've got news for you, our friend Betty is no longer a call girl, she is now a very successful madam. Runs a super-duper, high-class whorehouse uptown on Riverside Drive."

Through all this banter Morty and Ted sipped their drinks and kept inscrutable Oriental faces.

"Jimmy, do you think I could get in touch with her?"

"I don't see why not. Look, Harry, if it's okay with these two kids we'll give her place a visit next week. Betty's dying to see you, and we'll get our two friends here a great piece of ass as a reward for being so nice to the two of us. How about it? Okay with you two?"

Morty and Teddy looked at Harry.

Harry said, "Absolutely, Jimmy. Don't worry about a thing, boys, it'll never go further than the four of us. You're with Jimmy and me, you're in good hands."

They had another drink together and finally parted, the best of friends. The date was set for the big bash at Betty's whorehouse. It was made for Wednesday, the following week, the Wednesday preceding the fateful Monday, the date of the Big Trial.

They shook hands goodbye outside the restaurant on Broadway and Jimmy started toward Frankie and Johnnie's like he was going there to eat, but once out of sight he grabbed a taxi and directed the driver to the Zebra Bar. He was excited, happy. More than happy—jubilant. He reached Dave's place on Park Avenue and 56th Street about a quarter to nine. Dave greeted him like he'd just been pardoned from the electric chair. They hadn't seen each other in almost a year, only occasionally speaking on the telephone. After all the hugs and kisses, they sat at a corner table near Willie, the piano player. They ordered a couple of Cutty and waters, and Jimmy gave Willie ten dollars and asked him to play some George Gershwin.

The Scotch tasted sensational, Dave was funnier than usual, and Willie played the ass off Gershwin on the baby grand. Peace, it's wonderful. Jimmy's night of nights soon became complete. Big blond Betty walked in the door, looked the room over for a minute, and walked straight over to Jimmy's table, much to the chagrin of about fifteen guys around the bar, whose eyes almost fell out.

Jimmy gave her a big kiss hello and looked her over. He hadn't seen her in almost two years. She was just a little heavier, but as lovely and sexy-looking as ever. Dave, after giving Betty a big kiss, excused himself and left them alone at the table.

"As always, you look beautiful, Betty."

"Thank you, Jimmy, you look pretty good yourself. You got a little thinner, didn't you, since I last saw you? I hope it wasn't because of worrying about that mess in Brooklyn all you poor guys are involved in."

"No, really, nothing like that. I've just been hanging out in the country, swimming, playing golf, not too much booze, away from the night life. Keeps your weight down, you ought to try the clean life sometime."

"No chance. I have my goals and when I reach them I'm going to pack it in and marry some rich guy."

"Good for you, Betty. How's it going?"

"Terrific, Jim. I've got a great place. How does it look for you?"

"Everything's fine. No problems."

"I'm glad for your sake, Jimmy. Well, here I am. Dave warned me it was very urgent, so I made sure I was here on time."

"I appreciate that, love. But here's what I wanted you here for. I need a favor, a real favor."

"Jimmy, if it's at all possible. I'll do anything you ask. I'll never forget how nice you were to me when I first came to New York. And then how good you were to me when you owned the club. You introduced me to only the best guys, and I made lots of money with them. I'm really glad to see you, Jim, I was worried sick reading about you. Now, come on, what's this big favor you need? I know Davey told you about my new place, he's been up. I want you to come up for a visit, Jim. You'll be on the house, on the whorehouse."

Jimmy's turn to laugh. "I'll be up, Betty, but it won't be on the arm. Beautiful ladies like you have to make a living, don't let anyone go free. Now listen carefully, here's what I want you to do. Remember Harry? Harry Gross?"

"Harry? How can I ever forget him, Jimmy? You put him next to me one night and he didn't leave my apartment for three days. He almost wore me out. I must have gone out and bought him four new shirts and changes of underwear. He'd get up, disappear for a couple of hours, and come right back. When he left finally, he put fifteen hundred dollars under the ashtray on the night table. He was some nice guy, a little too short for me to fall in love with, but I really liked him. I was so sorry to read about him and all the trouble you guys had. What a shame."

"What happens, happens, Betty dear, there's nothing anyone can do about it. Now let's get down to business. I know you have to get back. How many girls do you have working for you?"

"I can arrange as many as you want. But mainly, I have just three or four girls working every night. That is, besides myself, in case of emergency. You should know, Jimmy, there's always some nut who wants to bang the madam."

Jimmy laughed again. "I'd never call a guy a nut who wanted to bang you, Betty. I'd say the guy had exquisite taste, the best. But here's what I want you to do. I have five hundred in my hand under the table, take it. Okay, now next week have three girls there, real knockouts, and you be there in all your glory. Lay in a few bottles of wine and some Scotch. I'm coming up with Harry and a couple of young cops who are bodyguarding him. Now, don't put a face on. Those two kids are a hundred percent, just like we were years ago. Trust me. I'm throwing Harry a little farewell party before he goes away. I can't think of a nicer present for the man who has everything than to give Harry a session with you. Sound okay?"

"Oh, Jimmy, you're so sweet." Betty tucked the five C-notes away in her purse. "What day do you want to come up?"

"How about next Wednesday?"

"Perfect. I'll have three of my best-looking girls there."

"One thing, Betty, and get this straight. No other customers allowed while we're up there. I don't even want the telephone to ring for a couple of hours. Turn your phones down and put all incoming calls on your answering service. Is that okay with you? We'll be there from seven until about nine o'clock."

"Fine, from seven till nine, that'll be perfect. Jimmy, I hate to leave you, but I have to get back to my place. Duty calls. I'll see you next Wednesday, love. Tell Harry I'm looking forward to seeing him. Don't worry about a thing. You'll have a good party, I'll arrange everything."

Jimmy put Betty in a taxi, went back to the table, had a nightcap with Dave, then walked crosstown to his car. He was elated. It was almost too good to be true. Everything had gone according to plan. Driving home to Connecticut, he couldn't help smiling as he reconstructed the night's events. Harry was so anxious to be friendly he'd practically fallen over him when they met. Jimmy was positive Harry wasn't in the least suspicious that their meeting hadn't been purely accidental. They had said goodbye the best of friends, with Harry to call him to verify the date at Betty's house. Jimmy was sure Harry would call. Christ, his tongue was hanging out at the thought of banging big Betty again.

The call came the following Tuesday night. "Hello, Jim. Harry."

"Hi, Harry. What's up?" Very nonchalantly.

"Are we on for tomorrow night?"

"Tomorrow night? Oh, yeah, sure."

"You understand that I'm going to bring those two kids along who were with me last week. Is that okay?"

"The same two I met you with?"

"Yeah. They're two nice kids, you can trust them not to say anything."

That's more than I can say for you, you little rat bastard.

"Okay. Good. I'll make all the arrangements. We'll have a nice party."

"Where do you want us to meet you?"

"How about Riverside Drive and Ninetieth Street about seven o'clock. Betty's on that block."

"Perfect. I'll see you there. I'm really looking forward to it. So long, Jim."

Jimmy hung up the phone. So am I looking forward to it, Harry, my boy. Really looking forward to it.

Jimmy left the house and drove into town and called Betty to tell her the date was on. The next day he left Connecticut about five o'clock and drove to New York. He parked his car on 91st Street between Columbus and Amsterdam avenues. He walked three blocks over to Riverside Drive and stood in a doorway off the corner of 91st Street for about half an hour. Everything looked nice and cool. He scanned the area carefully, and soon became convinced that there were no tails around, no one suspicious. The three of them suddenly appeared on the appointed corner. Morty and Ted were dressed up like they were going to visit royalty instead of Betty Baines's whorehouse. Harry was his usual impeccable self. Jimmy walked down the block and greeted them heartily. They laughed and kidded each other for a couple of minutes and then Jimmy led them into a building right off the corner. The doorman announced them, and Betty was at the door of her apartment waiting for them when they got off the elevator. She wore her hair up in tight little curls and had on a low-cut, long black hostess gown. It displayed her voluptuous figure like she was poured into it. She was pure, unadulterated dynamite.

She threw herself into Harry's arms with a delighted squeal like he was just returning from a tough tour of duty in the French Foreign Legion. There was all kinds of hugging and kissing when they met the other three of Betty's girls. A redhead, a blonde, and a brunette. Beautiful. They all looked like they just got off the plane from Hollywood.

After the near hysteria of the welcome wore off, Betty served them drinks. Jimmy grinned to himself as he slyly observed the look on the faces of Morty and Teddy. They were almost struck dumb, paralyzed. They sat there smiling and nodding, looking at the four gorgeous chicks walking around like gorgeous chicks were just recently invented. Scenes like this are one of the many rewards of a sharp plainclothes cop, my two young friends, it doesn't end up in that Brooklyn bullshit all the time.

They were all soon drinking and laughing and Harry was center-stage, holding court like good old King Henry VIII. He was settled back in a big armchair with his hand on Betty's head, who was sitting on the floor at his feet like he was her hero. He told a few of the Harry and Jimmy stories of bygone days, and he was funnier than ever. Jimmy couldn't help laughing at him. After a couple of drinks Harry got out of his chair, rolled his eyes toward the ceiling, took Betty by the hand, and went off to one of the bedrooms. Morty started to grab one of the girls by the waist and take off to another bedroom, but Jimmy gave him the eye and put his hand out, palm straight up. Stay tight, your turn will come, Uncle Jim will never cheat you out of that beautiful broad. Morty got the message and in turn winked at Ted and gave him the palm-up, stay-tight signal. They all sat and talked for about ten minutes until Harry came out of the bedroom with Betty. He had his socks, pants, and shirt on, collar open. His face was flushed and happy-looking. But who wouldn't be happy after a scene with blond Betty?

Morty and Ted looked at Jimmy and he nodded his head okay. Morty walked over to Jimmy and in a very low voice said, "Where will I stash my gun?"

Jimmy whispered back, "Go to the john, put the bullets in your coat pocket, and stash the gun under the chair cushion, the chair in the corner. Don't let anybody see you stash it."

Teddy went into the bedroom with the blonde and brunette, and Morty went into the other bedroom with the redhead. Harry was standing at the bar in the far corner of the living room talking to Betty as she was making the drinks. Morty came out of the bedroom and surreptitiously slipped his gun under the chair cushion Jimmy had indicated. He went back into the bedroom.

Jimmy walked over to Harry and Betty and took the fresh drink she held out to him. He chatted with the two of them for a couple of minutes, and looking straight into Betty's eyes he said, "Hey, Betty, suppose you go in the bedroom and keep Morty and the redhead company. The other young kid has two girls with him and

Morty is liable to think we're discriminating against him because he's a Jew."

They both laughed, but Betty caught the look in Jimmy's eye and got the message. She left Harry and Jimmy at the bar and went into the bedroom where Morty and the redhead were. The two of them were alone in the living room. Harry stared at Jimmy and he broke into a sickly smile. He didn't like the look on Jimmy's face. He started to become uneasy.

"It's a great party, Jimmy, just like old times. What fun we used to have. Why are you looking at me like that? What's the matter, aren't you going to get laid? I thought you were dying to take a shot at Betty."

"Harry, bring your drink over here. Sit down in that chair," brusquely indicating an armchair. "I didn't come up here to get laid. I'm in no mood for that horseshit. I arranged all this so I could have a little heart-to-heart talk with you. Just like two old pals who haven't seen each other in quite a while."

Jimmy pulled up a chair and sat about three feet in front of Harry. Harry had a very worried look on his face. His brown eyes were dancing the way Jimmy remembered they always danced whenever he got nervous.

"What's this change coming over you, Jim? What's on your mind? You got that maniac look on your face."

"You're fucking well right I have, Harry. Did you ever think for a minute that I was going to forgive you for opening up to the district attorney? Do you think I'm going to let you get away with shit like that?"

"Jimmy, please. For Christ's sake, take it easy. I swear, I never told them a thing about you, about us being hooked up. I never implicated you in any way. Never, honest. What the hell are you getting so excited about?"

"What? What am I getting excited about? Why, you no-good rotten little cocksucker. Those very same cops you're squealing on never did you anything but good. They made you rich, you conniving little fuck. It wasn't their fault you had to be a big shot and piss away all our money. That's right, *our* money. You would never have gotten pinched if you hadn't become a desperado.

Then you couldn't stand the heat for a few more months and keep your mouth shut."

"Jimmy, please, you don't know what it was like in Raymond Street jail. It was murder. The food stunk, you couldn't eat it. There were big rats running around. Brazen, right in your cell. They scared the shit out of me. I was locked up in a cell all day with a big light overhead. They never turned it off, not even late at night. These half-ass drug addicts would scream and moan all night. I couldn't sleep. I never thought they'd let me out of there. I just couldn't stand it anymore. I swear, Jimmy."

"For Christ's sake, common sense would tell you they'd have to let you out, sooner or later. Your own lawyer told you that. You would have come out a hero, instead you came out like the piece of shit you always were. Harry, I've got news for you, you're not taking that witness stand and sending any of my friends to jail. If you do, I make you a solemn promise, I'll blow your fucking head off the first chance I get."

"Jimmy, please. Don't you understand, I have to. They'll crucify me now if I renege on them."

Jimmy went to the bar and made a fresh drink. He was walking angrily up and down. Harry just sat in the armchair, watching him. Immobilized, wishing he were in Alaska. Jimmy strode to the end of the living room, his back to Harry. He put his hand under the chair cushion and removed Morty's gun. He placed his drink on the end table and turned and walked over to Harry with Morty's gun in his right hand. Harry's brown eyes spun around in his head in fright. He opened his mouth like he was about to scream, but no sound came out. Jimmy grabbed his hair in his left hand and jerked his head back. He put the snout of the gun barrel right smack in Harry's open mouth.

"Scream, you fucking rat bum, and I'll blow your brains out. Now I got you dead right. The two cops are in getting laid and you snatched one of their guns, stuck it in your big mouth, and blew your brains out. I'll put this mother in your left hand, your pitching hand. You'll never know what hit you."

Harry's eyes were pleading for mercy. Jimmy disgustedly threw Harry's head back, let go of his hair. He put the gun in his pants pocket.

Harry was the first to speak. "Christ, Jimmy, after all we've been through together, you'd do something like that to me? You would actually kill me?"

"You bet your sweet ass I would, Harry."

"I can't believe it. What exactly do you want me to do? I'll do anything you say."

"Here's what I want you to do. Get amnesia, get lockjaw, get some fucking thing. Only *don't* testify against those cops. Now once and for all, you got that straight? You *don't* testify against any cops."

"All right, Jimmy, I give in. I promise you that I won't testify. I hate that fuck Leibowitz anyway."

"Who the hell doesn't? Now tell me on the level, have I got your promise? No lies, none of your two-faced shit? I want your dead promise."

"You got it, Jimmy. On my wife and kids."

"Case closed, I'm depending on you. Come on, let's have a fresh drink, it sounds like the two kids and the girls are coming out. Act normal, for Christ's sake."

Jimmy slipped the gun back under the chair cushion, went to the bar and made two fresh drinks, and sat down across the room from Harry. Ted and Morty came out of the bedrooms with the four girls looking like they just had a one-way trip to heaven. Jimmy smiled. They probably had a better trip down here than they would in the puritanical precincts of heaven.

Harry sat quietly in his chair, sipping his drink. He was still in a state of mild shock. The two kids sat on the floor, surrounded by the girls, still high as a kite from their flight to the moon. Betty sat next to Harry, holding his hand. She got up and tried to pull him out of his chair to coax him into the bedroom. Harry resisted, and with a weak smile said he didn't feel like any more loving. No wonder.

The party started to break up about nine o'clock. Jimmy took Morty aside for a second and asked him to observe Harry carefully the rest of the night and to make sure he called him the next morning. He wanted to get Harry's reaction. They left Betty's apartment and parted on the sidewalk the best of friends. Harry was still rather subdued, but the two kids were still so high after their whorehouse experience they didn't seem to notice anything wrong. If they did, they both had enough sense to pretend not to.

Jimmy gripped real hard when he shook Harry's hand goodbye and looked straight into his eyes. He turned and walked back to pick up his car. He smiled to himself. Well, it was probably good the goddam gun wasn't loaded. Christ, was I ever tempted to shoot the rat bastard. Now we're in the lap of the gods. We can only sit back and see what happens, how Harry keeps his word. Jimmy was content with himself. He had done the best he could.

The next morning Morty called and Jimmy went to his favorite gas station and called him back. "Hello, kid. How did you finish up? How did it go?"

"Jimmy, I can't thank you enough. I had the best time of my life. Last night I fell in love with two broads at the same time. It was beautiful."

Jimmy laughed. "I know, I know, but forget about broads for a minute. I could tell by the look on your kisser you were in love, but I don't want to know about that. I'm talking about Harry. How did he act on the way home?"

"He was very quiet for a while, Jimmy. I didn't say anything to him. I figured you must have laid the wood on him pretty good. But about half-way back to Brooklyn he loosened up. He told us you proved what a nice guy he always said you were by throwing such a great party. We got back to the hotel around eleven, had one nightcap, and we all went right to bed. We were relieved at nine this morning and I looked in his room and he was still sound asleep. He's okay, don't worry about him."

"Good. Good news. I was a little concerned about him. Thanks a lot, kid. I'll see you real soon."

Jimmy took it nice and easy the next few days. He went to the country club in the morning, played golf, and came home early. His nerves were on edge, he was very jumpy, a little irritable. No matter what he did or how he acted, or what he tried to read, he had only one thing on his mind. The Monday coming up, the day the Big Trial was to start. Would Harry continued to cooperate in open court on the witness stand? Or would he dummy up just like he promised Jimmy he would? These and countless other ramifications kept gnawing at him.

Monday finally came, the day of judgment. A bright, sunny, end-of-summer day. Jimmy stayed home in Connecticut, he didn't plan on going to Brooklyn. He was aware that the first couple of days would be filled with all kinds of motions by the defense lawyers. And then the endless task of picking a jury. He would wait and stay clear of Brooklyn until the actual trial started.

The fateful Monday, Jimmy decided to go to the club and play golf. He played cards afterward and came home about six o'clock. He walked into the den to make a drink. Kay was sitting there, knitting, with a drink next to her.

"Jim, you'll never guess who called you today."

"Look, hon, please, forget the goddam guessing games. Who called? Maybe President Truman?"

"Don't be so damn smart or I won't tell you."

"Please, who?"

"Harry Gross."

"Harry?" Incredulously.

"Harry himself. He couldn't have been sweeter. He spoke to me for about five minutes, wanted to know all about the kids and everything. You know Harry, his usual charming self. He said he'd call you later tonight."

"Christ, the trial started today. I wonder what the hell's on his mind, what he wants to talk to me about."

Jimmy soon found out. The phone rang about seven o'clock. Jimmy picked it up.

"Hello, Jim. Harry."

Jimmy, always on guard that his phone might be tapped, was a bit stunned for a minute. His protective antennae went up, be very careful what you say.

"Yeah, Harry, how are you? What's up?"

"Jimmy, believe it or not, I took off this afternoon. Two of those D.A. kids took me out to see my wife and kids, and while they were sitting in the living room I slipped out the side door, got in my car, and took off. I have plenty of money and my Cadillac. I think I'll go to the West Coast. I have some good friends there, Jimmy, I can't face the idea of the trial. I was there this morning, saw all those cops. You're right, Jimmy, I can't go through with it."

"Harry, where are you calling me from?"

"A Howard Johnson's on the Jersey Turnpike."

"Well, I don't know what the hell to say. I guess you have to do what's best for yourself." Jimmy was fencing. God knows who was listening to them.

"I just called to let you know I'm okay, Jim. No matter what, you'll always be my best friend. You know that."

Listen to this shit. "Okay, Harry, just take care of yourself. Don't do anything foolish. So long."

Jimmy hung up abruptly. No use engaging in a long phone conversation, something incriminating is bound to be dropped. He shook his head. Christ, that crazy sonofabitch took off the day of the Big Trial. A typical Harry Gross solution. Get yourself in a hole a mile over your head and then run away. I'd better make sure to stay up for the eleven o'clock news on television. They'll have to announce sooner or later that their star witness is missing. He has departed for places unknown. I wonder if he called Leibowitz and Helfand to say goodbye. Jimmy doubted it, smilingly.

The news shortly came over radio and television like a cannon shot. The following morning the papers were filled with conjecture concerning Harry's sudden disappearance. Echoes of Abe Reles's sudden demise—he had been the chief informer for the Murder, Inc. probe—were imagined. Did Harry meet with foul play? The D.A. hinted at it. Harry was missing, probably dead. Leibowitz requested additional bodyguards to surround his Manhattan Beach mansion, assassination was in the air. Another bullshit grandstand play.

An all-points bulletin was issued by the New York City Police Department. Pictures of Harry were splashed across the morning papers of the major cities of the country. There were pictures of McDonald and Helfand all over the New York papers. They looked stricken, harassed, shot down. Why not? Their Big Trial was aborted for the second time, the first time by a jump out a sixth-floor window, the second by a jump by a wacky sonofabitch right out of town. The D.A.'s scenario was slowly disintegrating. Their leading man had vanished, their star was gone. Their ambitions to climb up the ranks to the higher public offices of judge, attorney general, or mayor had been yanked out from under them. Panic in the halls of justice.

About noon the day after Harry's call, several reporters appeared on the grounds of Jimmy's house. To keep peace, and to get rid of them, he went to the front door and asked two of them, whom he recognized from his previous Brooklyn grand jury appearances, to come in the house for a drink. He assured them that he knew nothing whatsoever about Harry's sudden flight. He had not seen or heard from Harry for almost a year. Perfectly straight face. Smooth, sincere voice. The reporters believed him, finished their drink, thanked him for his courtesy, and left with the rest of the reporters outside. He hoped the D.A.'s office believed the story when they read it.

At five o'clock an important news bulletin interrupted the regular programming. They had just picked up Harry Gross at the Atlantic City racetrack.

Jimmy just shook his head as he listened. The only foul play Harry met was probably some of the losing horses he bet on. A typical Harry Gross grandstand gesture. The Atlantic City racetrack. For Christ's sake. Where would be the first place the most wanted gambler in the world would be sought? Correct the first time, the racetrack. Jimmy sat back in his chair. I wonder if that psycho sonofabitch will keep his promise?

The next day Harry was returned to New York and kept under lock and key in the hotel suite. Around-the-clock surveillance.

The trial resumed in a couple of days as the color came back into the cheeks of McDonald and Helfand. The second day after the trial resumed, Augie called Jimmy and told him the jury was picked, they were set to start. Harry was due to be the first witness to take the stand.

Jimmy left Connecticut early the next morning and arrived in Brooklyn shortly before nine. He parked his car and walked over to the courthouse. There was a full house of curiosity seekers on line for admittance to the expected fireworks. His old pal, the court officer Joey Doyle, slipped Jimmy into an end seat in the next-to-the-last row of the courtroom. Jimmy wore dark glasses and sat quietly reading a newspaper awaiting the trial to begin.

The cops on trial entered the court through a side entrance with their staff of lawyers. They took their seats at tables arranged inside the knee-high wooden railing separating the main protagonists from the spectators. The jury filed in and took their seats in the jury box to the left of the judge's bench. McDonald, Helfand, and Koota entered the courtroom from a side door at the front. All three of them had big, confident grins on their faces. They exchanged handshakes with the defense lawyers and stood bantering easily with one another as they placed their briefcases and assorted notes on the counsel table reserved for the prosecution. Jimmy observed their actions carefully from his rear seat, and thought if ever three guys looked like the proverbial cat who swallowed the canary, it was these three. Only they never swallowed their pet canary, he was right in the next room ready to take his perch on the witness stand and chirp his little heart out for them. At least, that's what they were fully expecting, judging by their expansive good humor.

The bailiff announced his Honor, Sam Leibowitz, in ringing tones. Big Sam entered the courtroom from his chambers with look number one on his face, from his vast repertoire of looks. Look number one was the pious, solemn look. This was the look he initially affected when he was called on to sit in judgment upon the poor fallen souls who that day sat below his austere gaze humbly awaiting his eventual wrath. Closely observing him, Jimmy thought that Sam must have practiced the number one look an extra fifteen minutes in front of the mirror in his chambers that morning. He looked like a cross between Hillel the Prophet and Pontius Pilate. Alas, what burdens this evil world places on these aging, sagging shoulders. Bullshit, Sam reveled in anticipation of today's unfolding events.

Leibowitz rapped his gavel and the courtroom hushed. He called the court to order, the trial to begin. "Mr. Helfand, will you open for the state, please."

"Thank you, your Honor." Helfand paced back and forth before the all-male jury for a minute without uttering a word, like a boxer waiting for the bell to ring for round one. Then he turned and said, "Gentlemen of the jury, my first witness today will be one Harry Gross. He has been a bookmaker for many years. He was arrested about a year ago and has pleaded guilty to all charges against him. He is presently awaiting sentence on bookmaking and conspiracy charges. Mr. Gross will take the witness stand today and weave an incredible story of a long-standing, ongoing conspiracy between himself, his confederates, and these defendants seated directly opposite you. I say the story is incredible, it is sure to seem incredible to you, but the state will prove that indeed, such a conspiracy existed.

"Gross will tell you today how he started out in life as a small-time bookmaker in Brooklyn and inside of ten years built a gambling empire. The empire, operating without police interference, consisted of twenty-seven horse rooms, eight wire rooms, and four hundred employees."

Helfand punctuated the last sentence with a shout, and the courtroom gasped audibly. Leibowitz rapped his gavel for silence, but Jimmy could see he was loving every minute of it, a broad smile betraying his sentiments. Jimmy sat back low in his seat, feeling a little numb. For Christ's sake, what the hell did Harry tell these guys? What the hell kind of shit did he just hear? Twenty-seven horse rooms, eight wire rooms, four hundred guys working for us? He and Harry never had more than eight places, including his own in New York, and one wire room. And the most guys they ever had working for them was forty or fifty, including outlaw runners.

Helfand was just warming up, his face was flushed and triumphant-looking. He began to enumerate the spots, starting where Harry began his illicit career—Hymie's candy store on Avenue C and McDonald Avenue. Hymie Gravesend, good old Hymie, Harry's first real benefactor. He then ticked off the greeting-card store on Parkside Avenue across from the BMT, Leo's candy store on Church and Flatbush avenues, the Dugout, the Ballfield Tavern, Frankie and Skee in the Italian section of Red Hook, the all-black horse room on Fulton Street and Nostrand Avenue where Patsy and Big Buck, a real nice black guy, operated.

Helfand was blasting out the various spots, one after the other, and as Jimmy sat listening he found himself clicking them off with him. Jimmy had to restrain a laugh. As Helfand was shouting them out, Jimmy was mentally calculating how profitable each one was. Stay cool and just listen, Jimmy, or else someone might read your mind and you'll be up on the stand next to Harry.

Helfand never did get past eight in number, merely tossing off the nineteen figments of Harry's imagination as "innumberable other places." The eight imaginary wire rooms were never spelled out, only the one where the Big Raid took place.

Helfand's opening statement was proving Jimmy's worst fears about Harry opening up. Once he started, he'd never stop. Like Pavlov's dog responding to bells and buzzers, he would respond to anything any of the D.A.s suggested about whoever they might wish to implicate. Harry Gross suffered from a deadly virus which caused a deadlier disease—diarrhea of the mouth.

Helfand postured and continued in loud, clear tones. Jimmy hung on every word from his rear courtroom seat.

"Harry Gross will tell you in his own words how he was allowed to operate this vast bookmaking empire. He was only allowed to operate through the connivance of these defendants and their co-conspirators, these defendants who are sitting before you. And that connivance with these defendants was bought and paid for by Harry Gross. He could not have operated for a day without the okay from these defendants.

"Gross was not the only bookie operating during this period, nor the only bookie whom these defendants were interested in, and I'll prove this. In some instances he was told by the police he couldn't open in a certain locality because another friendly bookie was operating there."

The defense lawyers jumped up as a unit shouting vigorous objections to Helfand's last remarks.

Leibowitz silenced both sides with a rap of his gavel. He and Helfand had probably rehearsed their act more often than the Abbey Players, but he looked down at his protégé, with whom he was as close as Siamese twins, and admonished him sternly. "Mr. Helfand, I order you to confine yourself to the present case, this case alone."

Helfand replied contritely, "I'm sorry, your Honor. Yes, your Honor." He turned again to face the jury, collected his thoughts for a few seconds, pointed a finger at the twelve good men tried and true, and continued, "This wasn't a series of isolated conspiracies, but an overall conspiracy, an overall picture of police corruption. Harry Gross wasn't allowed to open his horse rooms just because the police liked him, but because they had a contract with him for monthly graft payments. This was a contract not drawn by lawyers. It was a contract by mutual understanding, by conversation, by facts and circumstances."

Jimmy sat back listening, enraptured. Julie Helfand was giving a virtuoso performance. Jimmy couldn't believe what he was hearing when he heard what Helfand had to say when he continued. He just shook his head sadly. What a fucking liar Harry was.

"There were terms, real terms, and Gross did not get free rein. He had to submit to these defendants and their co-conspirators. He was forced to give them the names and numbers of his employees. He was further told by the police how many people were permitted in one place at a time, so that no crowds would be attracted."

What a lot of shit, Jimmy thought. Never in a million years would plainclothes cops lay down conditions like Helfand just described. In all his years in plainclothes he never once laid down any set of rules, any conditions, as Helfand put it. Cops universally accepted the gambler's word as to the size of the operation and were paid accordingly. Nineteen out of twenty times the gambler's word was one hundred percent. They were as a group a helluva lot more honorable than most of the so-called legitimate people he knew. As he listened, he resisted another smile. Imagine the cops monitoring the all-black joint on Fulton and Nostrand, or the mob scene in the yard in back of the Dugout. Christ, they'd need an adding machine to count the customers.

Helfand was now strutting back and forth, warming up to his task. He continued the saga of Harry Gross.

"If more people than the police permitted were crowded in a horse room, these defendants called Gross and charged him with violating his contract. Each detail of his operation was watched closely so that nothing went wrong." Then Helfand raised his voice to an almost thunderous pitch and pointed a finger directly at the cops on trial. "That was so nothing went wrong, so they could continue to line their pockets with his dirty money." With that piece of grandiose, bullshit exaggeration, Helfand paused dramatically, lowered his head abjectly, like he was about to say Kaddish for a dear departed friend, turned to face the jury, and said, "Thank you, gentlemen."

The courtroom buzzed in response to Helfand's brilliant, histrionic performance, and Leibowitz once again rapped his gavel for silence. But he was smiling, he looked almost ready to applaud his protégé's hambone act.

Two of the more skilled orators among the defense lawyers were allowed to make speeches in defense of the defendants. They claimed complete innocence, the evidence introduced would be merely hearsay, the words of a convicted criminal trying to save his own skin, and lastly, that the defendants were being victimized by a runaway grand jury. Leibowitz admonished one of them severely for the last remark, but that was that.

"Are you ready to proceed, Mr. Helfand?"

"Yes, your Honor, I am ready."

"Call the first witness for the state, Mr. Helfand."

"Your Honor, my first witness is Harry Gross."

A court officer led Harry out of an adjoining anteroom. Some of the spectators in the rear stood up to get a better view of him, there was a burst of low-pitched sound. That's him, that's Harry. Leibowitz again rapped his gavel to restore quiet in the courtroom.

Harry was all dressed up, like he was going to visit Betty Baines's whorehouse later in the day. His face was pale, drawn-looking, like he just came off a tough night. The bailiff swore him in to tell the truth, the whole truth, so help him God. No one in the courtroom knew better than Jimmy that Harry was psychologically incapable of telling the whole truth, and if he finally did, he would need more than God to help him.

Jimmy watched Harry closely from his rear seat in the courtroom. He was snug and incognito behind his big dark glasses. He sat hunched down, real low, barely able to see over the guy's head in front of him. But the witness stand was raised a couple of feet and he had a clear view of the drama about to take place.

Before Helfand asked Harry the first question, two court officers came up to the witness stand carrying a huge map. Helfand directed them and they climbed a ladder behind Harry's chair and nailed the map to the wall. It was a vivid drawing of the borough of Brooklyn, with a series of bright red squares dotted all over the place. It was a simple matter for Jimmy to perceive that the brilliant red squares indicated the various gambling spots that Harry said he once controlled. It was another dramatic ploy by the prosecution to heighten Harry's testimony.

Helfand began. He started by establishing Harry's identity— age, address, where born, marital status, and whatever else was necessary to prove that he was the real Harry Gross.

Helfand then asked Harry some preliminary questions about his early roots as a bookmaker. Harry, now in the limelight, onstage, began to show less anxiety. He became more expansive, less nervous, as Helfand prodded him on. He explained to the court how he had started in 1940 with Hymie Gravesend out on Avenue C, and how a plainclothes cop, a guy Jimmy never heard of, told him he was a sucker to work without police protection. The cop then set up Hymie and Harry with the various squads. Harry put the onus on this unknown division cop for everything, collecting for all the squads, including the two New York squads—from the chief inspector's office and the police commissioner's office.

Jimmy sat there not believing what he was hearing. Harry never paid those squads in a million years, his story was a pure fabrication.

Helfand fed him the leading questions and Harry eagerly recited his role. He proceeded to paint a picture which was a complete figment of his wild imagination. Harry never had a dime in his pocket to call his own at the time in question. He was strictly a ham-and-egg runner, a lousy street runner, dodging the cops and calling in bets to little Sammy on a half-sheet.

"Mr. Gross, after you paid all your protection money and received the green light from the cops, what did you do then?"

"I rented a garage, cleaned it up and painted it. Then I put some tables and chairs in and a radio to get the race results. A couple of my clerks were stationed behind a counter I had built to take the customers' bets. The radio broadcast scratches, changes in jockeys, and other racing data. The players were made comfortable before and after they bet. In about a month I added a Teleflash news service, which came direct over the telephone. I then attached a loudspeaker to the telephone and the room got actual running descriptions of the races."

"Just like a stock broker's office?" suggested Judge Leibowitz, with a shake of his head, indicating that what he was hearing only happened on the planet Mars, never in Brooklyn.

"A little better than a broker's office," Harry answered proudly, with a smile toward the judge he'd sworn to Jimmy he hated.

Jimmy sat back and shook his head. What a lying fuck this guy is. They never had a Teleflash in any of the okay rooms even when they were going top speed. The Brooklyn cops would never stand for one, not for anybody. Jimmy had taken Harry out to Queens a few times and shown him a couple of layouts like Gallop's lumberyard, complete with Teleflash and house announcer. Harry had almost drooled when he saw those operations. Now he was drawing on what he had learned from Jimmy to embellish his story. Jimmy, for the first time, began to get worried. This prick isn't going to keep his promise to me.

Helfand took a long blackboard pointer in his hand and tapped it harshly to indicate a particular red square on the map of Brooklyn. He posed a question to Harry, when suddenly the map tore loose from the wall and hit Harry smack on top of the head. It was the heavy wood part of the frame that hit him, and Harry winced and let out a little cry of pain. It was a comical bit, and several of the spectators let out an involuntary guffaw. Helfand administered to Harry very solicitously, and Leibowitz rapped his gavel for quiet. The same two clowns came out again and hammered the map up on the wall further to Harry's right, this time almost directly over Leibowitz's head.

Harry had a glass of water to calm his nerves, and Helfand began to question him once more, pointer still in hand. He put the pointer sharply up against the jinxed red square again, and tapping it against the map, waited for his answer. Harry meantime was looking over his shoulder apprehensively at the map, ignoring Helfand, a worried frown on his face. Bang, again the map fell down and hit Leibowitz on the head. Harry jumped right out of the witness chair as the map started to tear off the wall. It was hilarious. Jimmy almost strangled to keep from laughing out loud, but the spectators erupted in gales of laughter.

Leibowitz disentangled himself from the coils of the deadly map, rubbed his head a couple of times, and said, "You see, Mr. Gross, justice is impartial. First the map hits you on the head, then it shows its impartiality and hits me, the judge of the court. Mr. Helfand, please, can we dispense with this map."

Leibowitz got a big laugh with his little joke, and the two half-ass court officer mechanics hauled the ill-fated map away as Helfand glared daggers at them. So much for the prosecution's stage prop number one.

Harry, the danger of falling maps at last removed, was now composed. Helfand resumed. No more of Harry's fanciful gambling history, now he was ready to get down to the main business at hand, the sordid details of the cash payoffs to the cops.

To Jimmy's continuing amazement, Harry again answered like he had been a big wheel ten years before. He glibly reported payoffs to cops and bosses that Jimmy was positive he'd never met. Jimmy knew goddam well he never met them. He almost jumped out of his seat when Harry testified that he'd paid Lieutenant Pete O'Neil from the chief inspector's office on a regular basis. Jimmy's old boss, Pete O'Neil had passed away and gone to his just reward about five or six years ago, the inevitable early victim of too much booze, the high life, and the hypertension that affects almost everyone in the gambling world. A class guy like Pete O'Neil wouldn't walk on the same side of the street with a two-bit runner like Harry in the days Harry was testifying about. Pete wouldn't even piss on him. Jimmy knew for a fact that Harry had never even laid eyes on Petey O'Neil, only knew of him through Jimmy's many fond Petey O'Neil stories. Jimmy began to get a pain deep down in his stomach. This lying, exaggerating little fuck intended to bury everybody, even guys he didn't know.

As the questioning continued and Harry's well-rehearsed answers rolled smoothly from his tongue, one thing heartened Jimmy just a bit, buoyed his hopes. At this phase of the proceedings, Harry had still not mentioned a single one of the defendants as being culpable. He was simply bringing up old-time bullshit about guys who were long retired or dead. He was rehashing a lot of shit about division squads, borough squads, and the two New York squads. But the D.A.s and Leibowitz were savoring it, loving every word, and so were the spectators and the members of the press in the courtroom.

About twelve thirty Leibowitz called a recess for lunch. Everyone back at two o'clock for a resumption of Harry's Odyssey. Harry Gross and good old Homer, the wise and ancient Greek, what marvelous tales they had to tell. Jimmy hoped Homer had been more truthful than Harry was right now.

Jimmy took a little walk, had a sandwich and coffee at a local restaurant, and Joey Doyle slipped him back into his same rear seat about a quarter to two. Shortly after two the court was called to order and Big Sam Leibowitz majestically strode to the bench. He looked serene and happy, like he'd had an excellent lunch. He rapped his gavel for quiet, and Harry took the witness stand ready to resume his web of lies. All during the lunch recess Jimmy had puzzled over Harry's behavior on the stand. Was he or wasn't he going to dummy up? So far his testimony had been innocuous. Inflamatory, yes, detrimental to The Job, yes, but damaging to the cops on trial, no. Up until now, it had only served to build Harry up as a big shot, the role he always loved.

The first few questions Helfand asked Harry as the afternoon session began concerned the definition of the word "cheating." Harry explained, as Helfand drew him out, that "cheating" in the vernacular which cops and gamblers used was a term to describe anyone who ran a book or a game without paying cops. Hence they cheated, were outlaws. Harry further volunteered that it was much easier for everyone concerned to be okay, to pay, rather than cheat. He elucidated that the extra volume of business you were able to do while under the protective wing of the law more than compensated for the ice you paid.

Helfand, moving along now, attempted to show to the jury what a patriotic hero Harry really was, underneath the veneer of flashy clothes, pinky ring, and barbershop facials. He led Harry into the saga of his brief United States Army career, all three months of it, down in the sunny Carolinas. He was no draft dodger, not our Harry, he went into the army like a man, and only a congenital leg defect caused his early discharge and kept him from slaying a thousand Germans. He might have been a Jewish Audie Murphy, only for that bad leg.

That's the leg I'm going to break, Jimmy resolved, as he sat hunched slow in the rear.

Under Helfand's guidance, Harry went on to explain how he left his two mythical horse rooms in charge of a trusted employee and returned from the wars to find the places flourishing. This statement was another product of Harry's imagination, Jimmy well knew. Harry didn't have a pot to piss in when he went in the army, and he didn't have a window to throw it out when he got out of the army.

Now Helfand began to come to more recent times, places of newer vintage.

"Mr. Gross, shortly after you were honorably discharged from the army, you opened a horse room in the Bedford-Stuyvesant section of Brooklyn. Is that correct?"

Harry nodded weakly. "Yes."

Helfand started to get specific, you could see it coming, like an amateur fighter leading with his right. Only Helfand was no amateur, he was a real pro.

"Mr. Gross, what year exactly did you open that horse room in Bedford-Stuyvesant?"

Jimmy leaned forward in his seat, listening intently, waiting for Harry's answer. Christ, he knew personally that it was at least three or four years after Harry got out of the army. He'd been with him when they negotiated for the joint, had got him the okay.

Harry didn't answer. Beads of sweat appeared on his forehead. He began to fidget on the witness stand, clasping and unclasping his hands. Jimmy knew him well, he was beginning to lose his composure, to fall apart. Maybe all the lies he's been telling up there are starting to affect his crooked brain. Harry just kept sitting there, silently, worried-looking, staring at Helfand.

Helfand waited, appeared a little nonplussed. He paused expectantly. You know the answer, Harry boy, give it to your pal, Julie Helfand.

"Now, Harry, take your time. When exactly did you open the horse room in the Bedford-Stuyvesant section? How many of these present defendants were instrumental in arranging your okay?"

Harry just sat there speechless, like he was stricken dumb.

Then he suddenly stood up and shouted, "I refuse to answer any more questions, either now or ever. That's all." With that outburst, he bolted off the witness stand and rushed over to a side window and looked out longingly.

The courtroom almost exploded in a cacophony of sounds. Leibowitz was stunned, for once in his life at a loss for words. He sat on the bench overlooking the court with his mouth open. Helfand stood in front of him rigidly, in a state of mild shock at this unexpected turn of events. He sat down at the counsel table with McDonald and Koota and they talked quietly.

One of the defense lawyers got up to say something. Leibowitz rapped his gavel and restored order. He said to the lawyer, "Are you going to ask for a mistrial, Counselor? I will grant your motion if you do."

Before he could open his mouth, one of the other defense lawyers pulled him down by his coat jacket, stood up, and said, "There are no such intentions by the defense at this time, your Honor."

Christ, what a narrow escape, Jimmy thought. That first dumb lawyer sonofabitch was probably going to ask for a mistrial. That would have been right down the D.A. and Leibowitz 's alley. They'd rev Harry up again, and maybe the next time he would not be so recalcitrant. Give them a couple of weeks, they'd work him over, he'd be a Boy Scout next trip.

Harry still stood staring out the window, his back to everybody.

Jimmy sat back low in his rear seat, loving the whole scene. This was better than a long weekend in Polly Adler's whorehouse. He was thrilled to see the look of shock on the face of Sam Leibowitz. He loved the worried look on the ashen faces of those three fearless crimebusters, Julie, Miles, and Aaron.

Helfand turned to Leibowitz, his ruddy complexion now turned pale, and asked for a short recess. Leibowitz swiftly assented. Helfand then walked over to the star of his show, talked quietly to him for a minute or two, then led him from the window into a side room.

The recess lasted more than an hour, and there was another buzz of excitement as Harry was led back into the courtroom. Leibowitz gave a sharp rap of his gavel and the noise subsided.

Harry again took the witness stand. He looked terrible, awful. His eyes were bloodshot, his face white as a sheet, overall like he just woke up with a bad hangover.

Harry turned toward Leibowitz from the witness stand. "I'm sorry, your Honor, I apologize," he said plaintively, the voice of a martyr about to go to the flames. He pleaded further, "Your Honor, I have to ask for a recess the rest of the day. I have an upset stomach, very upset."

Leibowitz looked down sternly at Harry. He had fully regained his aplomb, his regality. "Mr. Gross, will one day's recess be sufficient? Will you be prepared to come back tomorrow?"

"I believe so. I hope I will, your Honor," Harry answered weakly, perhaps thinking of that snub-nosed .38 piece Jimmy had shoved in his mouth in Betty Baines's whorehouse.

The jurors, mouths agape, had sat there all this time wondering what the hell was going on. Bewildered by Harry's sudden, wacky antics.

Leibowitz then dismissed the jury, warning them not to discuss the episode among themselves in the hotel where they were sequestered for the trial's duration. Jimmy marveled when he heard Sam say this. Could anyone in his right mind honestly believe that these guys on the jury weren't going to discuss today's bizarre incident. Pig's ass, they won't. The jury filed out.

"Now that the jury has retired," Leibowitz asked, "what is the trouble?"

"Your Honor, the witness explained himself," said Helfand. "He has a gall bladder condition and has had it for some time. Because of the excitement of the trial and the crowded courtroom, it has affected his stomach. He assures me that with a good night's rest he will be available to testify tomorrow."

That ended the day's travesty of justice. The court was adjourned until morning, and Jimmy returned to his car and made a fast getaway out of Brooklyn. He was sorely tempted to join Chick, John, and Tommy for a drink at Fred Scarmel's place, but decided it would be too dangerous. If he was ever spotted there with them by one of the innumerable stool pigeons for the D.A., there might be some suspicion regarding his role in Harry's sudden clam-up.

The next morning Jimmy again arrived in Brooklyn early, parked his car, and got to the courtroom about nine o'clock. Today was the big day. The newspapers, radio, and television were having a Roman circus. Harry's blow-up on the witness stand was the main topic of conversation all over the city. The lines of spectators waiting to get into the courtroom stretched down the long corridors for a couple of hundred feet. Jimmy's pal, the court officer Joey Doyle, slipped him into his usual rear seat. He again had on his big dark glasses and sat reading the morning paper, much of which was devoted to Harry and the Big Trial.

The defendants, the defense lawyers, the D.A.s, and finally the jury filed in. The bailiff called the court to order. Big Sam Leibowitz strode to the bench. Jimmy observed that he wore look number three today—the stern, angry, unyielding visage. This was his executioner look. God help Harry. Too bad, he brought all this shit on himself.

Helfand called his star witness, and a court officer brought Harry in from an anteroom and he took the witness stand. He looked worse than he had the day before. Something besides his gall bladder was troubling him.

Helfand took a stance in front of Harry, preparatory to his first question. He looked a bit uncertain, had none of his usual cockiness. He started a question, but Harry put his hand up and said, "I am not going to answer any more questions, Mr. Helfand. Now or ever."

The courtroom buzzed with noise. Jimmy sat hunched back low in his seat and exulted. Atta boy, Harry, fuck these guys. Leibowitz rapped his gavel sharply. The noise quickly subsided. Leibowitz glared at Harry, like he was ready to kill him, and said, "I warn you, Mr. Gross, that for every refusal to answer, I will sentence you to the limit of the law. If you refuse a thousand times I will give you a sentence on each, plus the fine that goes with it. If you have to rot in jail for a hundred years, you will get it."

Harry, defiantly, no longer their trained canary, erupted, "Why don't you explain to the people how you held me in solitary confinement for six months—why don't you explain that, huh? Why did you have me assigned to a cell in solitary the whole twenty-four hours a day with a light twitching in my eyes all the time?"

"Perhaps if you had been kept in solitary this would not have happened."

"You should try it sometime, with the rats running around and the screaming from the drug addicts all night." With that, Harry Gross walked off the witness stand.

Leibowitz got almost choleric. He stood up and shouted to the court officers, "Bring that man back up here."

Harry turned and hollered, "I refuse to take the stand."

"Bring him back and have the gentleman take the stand. By order of the court. Mr. Gross, I will chain you to the stand with handcuffs. You cannot thwart the dignity of the court in that fashion. Twenty months of labor have gone into this case."

The court officers stood beside Harry, petrified. They were obviously frightened of Leibowitz and afraid to use any muscle on Harry before a packed courtroom.

Harry shouted back at Leibowitz, "You took twenty years off my life, you might as well give me the electric chair. I'm only a bookmaker, I'm not a criminal."

The court officers spoke quietly to Harry and returned him to the stand. He went willingly. Jimmy's heart was in his mouth. Was this sonofabitch Harry crazy, or wasn't he? I knew deep down a couple of years ago he was going nuts, and this act today has to prove it.

Helfand and Leibowitz took turns asking Harry questions. He remained mum, tight-lipped, hostile. Then he suddenly ejaculated out of a clear blue sky, "I am in jeopardy, I fear for my life, my family. Go ahead and convict me."

Jimmy's blood ran cold. He gave an involuntary shudder as an icy tremor ran down his spine. He was half tempted to slip out his seat and run like hell all the way to Connecticut.

"You were threatened?" Leibowitz asked. "I thought so. Who threatened you? Who? Face around, Mr. Gross. Sit around straight. You are not at the racetrack now."

"I wish I was at the racetack."

"You know, Mr. Gross, you will simplify this whole proceeding if you tell who threatened you. Now do you want to name them? Name him? You can say yes or no. If you say no, we can go on to something else."

"And need bodyguards the rest of my life? And how about my family?"

"What do you mean you need bodyguards?"

"You should know, you always have about ten bodyguards."

Leibowitz looked like he was going to choke, he hated to hear about the constant police protection he always demanded. It was common knowledge among cops about his constant guard.

Leibowitz turned to the court clerk. "Let the record show that I don't have any bodyguards."

Not in the literal sense, Judge Leibowitz, only the Leibowitz mansion is perpetually surrounded by a police detail. Jimmy knew this to be true.

This last bitter exchange caused Leibowitz momentarily to lose his cool. As a champion of the taxpayers, he hated to be reminded that he might be placing additional burdens on them. Or worse, have cops guarding him who could certainly be put to better use in Brooklyn.

He turned and said, "Mr. McDonald, do you have any information as to threats to this witness?"

McDonald rose and said, "Your Honor, there has been information which has come to my attention, which I was unable to check, that there has been wagering that this man would never testify, and that a substantial sum of money has been paid to him. I understand from fairly reliable sources that the figure is seventy-five thousand dollars. Unfortunately, I have been unable, as I said, to substantiate this information."

Jimmy listened to this crock of horsehit with astonishment. This was the latest pure fabrication by the D.A.'s office. Seventy-five thousand dollars, my ass. Everything Harry had testified to before he dummied up was ninety percent lies. Cops and bosses were marked lousy without a shot to defend themselves. The D.A.'s office didn't give a shit, they just relied on the word of their little psycho canary, and now they were getting exactly what they deserved.

Jimmy was on the edge of his seat. The sooner they got past this threat business, the happier he would be. But Harry seemed strong up there again. Resigned to his fate, but strong. He still had some good in him.

Leibowitz continued, "Mr. Gross, I'll ask you again. Who threatened you?"

"Let's go to lunch."

"I warn you, Mr. Gross, all this sarcasm and smart-aleck retorts are going to cost you dearly."

"Your Honor, how much more trouble can I have than I got?"

With these immortal words, Harry signed off for the day. Leibowitz kept shooting questions at him for about an hour, but Harry just looked at him arrogantly and shook his head to each one. The count finally reached sixty, and even the windbag Leibowitz was running out of gas. He looked at McDonald and Helfand and shook his head.

McDonald rose and addressed the court. "Your Honor, it is utterly futile to proceed. Our other evidence means nothing. I never will say anything with more reluctance. Without Gross's testimony we do not have a case. I move to dismiss the indictment against these defendants and to discharge each of them."

"Motion granted. The charges are dismissed against the defendants."

There was an outburst of jubilation at the defendants' table. The cops and lawyers were hugging and embracing each other in sheer joy.

Harry still was on the witness stand. Leibowitz rapped his gavel for order. He turned to Harry, who sat there mutely, waiting for his ultimate fate. "Step down before the bench, Mr. Gross."

Harry stood before him.

Leibowitz proceeded to give Harry every day and dollar the law allowed on the sixty contempt charges—1,800 days in jail and a $15,000 fine.

"Court dismissed."

Jimmy stood up in the rear of the court, jubilant. Harry stopped and talked to McDonald for a minute, flanked by Joey Doyle and another court officer. They then took him away.

Jimmy got a good look at McDonald and Helfand, arms around each other's shoulders. For Christ's sake, they were crying. Real tears were rolling down their cheeks. What a shame.

When Jimmy arrived at Fred Scarmel's restaurant on Montague Street, Chick, Tommy, and John were there waiting for him. It was the happiest day they had all had together in a long, long time. No Scotch, rye, or gin today. Champagne, French champagne.

The news spread like wildfire around the city, the cops were all acquitted. That night, after four or five hours of food and champagne at Fred's place, they drove out to Queens to Hughie the Irishman's Club. The place was filled with wise guys and cops celebrating the victory. Rose and Dan McCarthy, everyone's favorite entertainers, were at the piano bar and a million old-time songs were sung. Chick sang "Is It True What They Say About Chinese Women?" and Jimmy sang a parody on "Those Wedding Bells Are Breaking Up That Old Gang of Mine." He sang a couple of stanzas in rhyme, starting wtih "Judge Leibowitz is breaking up that old gang of mine."

It was the best cops' party Jimmy had been to since Jackie McGrath got shot. But through all the celebrating and the backslapping Jimmy had an ominous feeling in the pit of his stomach. This thing was far from over. Those guys were a vicious bunch, they weren't going to take this lying down. They were out to get even at any cost. His fears had been confirmed by a conversation he had with Joey Doyle earlier that afternoon at Fred Scarmel's place. He'd asked Joey to meet him there. Jimmy wanted to stake him and thank him for being so considerate of him.

He had walked over to Joey, who was sitting at a table drinking, and sat next to him. "Joe, I almost forgot to ask you. What was that little conversation about between Gross and McDonald before you took him out?"

"Jimmy, you won't believe this. I almost dropped dead at this guy's nerve. He stopped, leaned over to McDonald, and said, 'What makes you think I'd settle for seventy-five thousand dollars? I was already offered a hundred and fifty thousand months ago.'"

"No shit."

"I swear to God, Jim. I'd never lie to you."

Jimmy had just nodded his head at Joey's story.

When they led Harry away, Jimmy's eyes had filled up. He

couldn't help it, he still had a little soft spot in his heart for him. But his remark to McDonald was typical, Harry couldn't resist the impulse to be a big shot. That was the cause of his downfall, their downfall. He still had to be sentenced in the Court of Special Sessions next week on the bookmaking and conspiracy charges. The world hadn't heard the end of Harry Gross, and Jimmy Riley felt that *he* hadn't heard the end of Leibowitz and Helfand.

10

THE NEWSPAPERS and other sectors of the media kept the bizarre doings of the now defunct Big Trial going for three or four days until more lurid events inevitably came along to phase it out. McDonald and Helfand were voluminously quoted in the press as to the questions of bribery and threats that could have caused Harry's abrupt turnabout on the witness stand. There was much wild speculation about his sudden shift from voluble and willing witness to equally sudden silence.

Jimmy Riley sat in his den in Connecticut and read all about it in the daily newspapers. He smiled contentedly, convinced that the D.A.'s office didn't have an inkling of the real cause of Harry's unbelievable collapse. But there was one thing becoming perfectly clear: McDonald and his henchmen were absolutely livid; they were not going to accept this setback lying down.

By now they had developed a deep-rooted hate for the New York City Police Department that often transgressed reasonable behavior. Up until the minute of Harry's clam-up, everything he told them was accepted as pure gospel. The D.A.'s office regularly leaked defamatory grand jury testimony to the press, ignoring the sanctions of secrecy which were constitutionally imposed on such testimony. Gross was a one-way ticket to higher public office, and even with a full-time staff of investigators at their disposal, little was done to check the veracity of Harry's sensational allegations. The cops were crooked. Crooked, period. But then, as Jimmy Riley and almost everyone in the world knew, everyone was a little crooked, everyone had their price—then, now, and forever.

Harry's explosive testimony on the witness stand about the formative years of his gambling career was an absolute fairy tale, without a grain of truth. As Jimmy sat in the courtroom listening, he had marveled at how Harry was fantazing up there on the witness stand, the same as he must have fantasized incredibly in the grand jury room. What troubled Jimmy the most was the eagerness of the D.A.'s office to believe whatever Harry offered that was detrimental to The Job. Every morsel, no matter what he said.

Cops, especially plainclothes cops, were painted in the public eye as a force for evil. Practically any accusation made against cops was accepted as fact. Of course, all judges were honest, all D.A.s were honest, and if you really believed in the fairy godmother, so too were the politicians honest who were responsible for the selection and appointments of the judges and the D.A.s. Each political leader was entitled by fief to appoint a couple of judges, or put them up for elective office. The same applied to the D.A.s and their assistants, most of whom rose through the ranks as loyal members of political clubhouse organizations. There were recurrent rumors and scandals involving huge sums of money paid by prominent lawyers anxious to cap their careers by donning the esteemed robes of the judiciary.

Before the new aborted trial, there had been several vain attempts by the defense attorneys to submit Harry to a sanity test. They argued forcefully and well. They cited repeated instances of his schizophrenic behavior, his apparent irrationality on many occasions. All to no avail. Leibowitz scoffed at these well-founded legal motions and flatly denied them. The last afternoon and following morning of the Big Trial proved that Harry should have been testifying in a straitjacket rather than a well-tailored dark gray suit. Harry's flights of hallucination, his bloated ego, his preening, his big-shot complex, his utter inability to tell the truth —all proved to Jimmy what he had begun to suspect a couple of years previous. Harry was barely skirting the edge of sanity.

The day of Harry's sentencing arrived. The D.A.'s Benedict Arnold had turned against the borough of Brooklyn, his native country. He would now be hung by his traitorous balls. Before the court convened, McDonald quietly let it be known that he planned to spread the entire story, including names and dates, on the court record. Every New York newspaper and wire service assigned extra men to handle the forthcoming 45,000-word exposé. Together with a sizable group of choice spectators, the members of the press waited expectantly to hear the inside story.

Fortunately, for once, cooler heads prevailed. Whoever nipped in the bud this unsavory attempt to violate all individual rights and carry out wholesale character assassinations should have received the golden gavel award. Sure enough, the composer of the entire symphony, the great liberal who orchestrated the beleaguered probe, Sam Leibowtiz, put the damper on McDonald's vituperative plan.

McDonald and Helfand were all set to deliver their unfounded 45,000-word exposé of the police and the O'Dwyer regime. What they were going to read into the record had been principally recited to them by Harry Gross, whose recent maniacal conduct better qualified him for the state hospital for the insane rather than the city jail. They had it laid out on the table before them when they were hurriedly summoned to Leibowitz's chambers, along with their constant companions, the press.

"I am of the firm opinion," said Sam, the champion of the people, "that it would be manifestly unfair and un-American for a name, or names, or incidents, or information which would make it possible to identify anyone of the persons named by Gross when he testified before the grand jury to be made public in the Court of Special Sessions, where such persons would have no opportunity to defend themselves against the charges made by Gross. Such a procedure would violate every elementary rule of civil liberties and due process of law. To thus cause the ruination of any person in this manner would be unconscionable."

But Leibowitz only put the lid on about halfway, and even that must have pained him deeply. The entire exposé should have been unceremoniously scuttled. But McDonald had no intention of keeping the Gross testimony an entire secret. The D.A.'s office wasn't about to cheat the citizenry out of savoring a deliberate, uncorroborated smear of the police. They read nearly all of Harry's fairy tale testimony in open court.

The three sitting judges of Special Sessions Court had before them Harry's entire testimony. They simply allowed the exposé with only the names deleted. It was Officer Blank, Sergeant Blank, Lieutenant Blank, Captain Blank, and, of course, Inspector Blank. Harry's mythical kingdom of thirty-five horse and wire rooms was described in vivid detail. His extensive police connections were expounded upon, and his corrupt tentacles even spread to the inner sanctums of the venerable Ma Bell. Our man Harry Gross never worried about his phones being tapped, he had a corrupt female employee of the telephone company tip him off whenever a legal wiretap was applied for. This phantom telephone-company Mata Hari went out with a phantom lieutenant friend of Harry's, and in the midst of an amorous embrace would reveal the secret wiretap. This included every wiretap in New York City.

Common sense would ask that, if this hallucinatory bullshit about wiretaps were true, how come the D.A.'s office was able to tap Harry's phones for God knows how long before they conducted the Big Raid. Telephone company executives were quick to reply to this flight of fancy, demanding the name of the willowy wench who revealed the wiretap locations. Of course, she was nonexistent.

Through all the long recital of Harry's trip into dreamsville, Harry sat in the defendant's chair awaiting sentence. He seemed calm, composed, and implacable. The entire pre-sentencing charade over, Harry's lawyer was finally allowed the floor to put forth a plea in his behalf. After a few minutes of high praise for Harry's fine family and noting that the charge against him was but a misdemeanor, a victimless crime, his lawyer then described an incident which astonished everyone in the courtroom except the D.A.s. The incident had occurred the day before the Big Trial, and perhaps could explain his irrational subsequent conduct.

He told of how Harry was permitted to visit his wife and children the Sunday before the start of the trial at their home in Atlantic Beach. Harry was accompanied by two police bodyguards. His six-year-old son, a bright kid, had often watched the cops holstering and unholstering their guns. The little boy slyly observed where one of the young cops secreted his revolver, and while Harry was in one room talking to his wife and the cops were in the den watching television, Harry's son climbed up, reached the gun, pointed it at his three-year-old sister's head, and fired it. Fortunately, it narrowly missed her and lodged in the wall next to her head. The explosion of the pistol shot and the two little kids' screams of terror put the house in an uproar. Harry's wife almost had a nervous breakdown on the spot and wept uncontrollably for hours.

This incredible recital caused an audible gasp of shock from the courtroom, including the three judges. They asked McDonald if he was aware of the almost fatal incident, and he glibly confirmed the episode. With a stiff upper lip, he emphasized that the careless bodyguard has been forthwith detached from his impeccable staff. To Siberia, no doubt.

The tiny clucks of sympathy rapidly vanished. The presiding one of the three noble men in black called Harry to the bench before them. He gave a short, stern speech and sentenced Harry Gross to *twelve years* in jail. Harry took it standing up, passively, without changing his expression. The court officers immediately hustled him out of the courtroom, and the members of the press dashed out for the nearest phones.

McDonald and Helfand shook hands, smiling broadly. Justice had been served. It was a mind-boggling sentence. Simple arithmetic could easily sum it up. Big Sam Leibowitz had already given Harry 1,800 days for contempt. That five years, give or take a couple of weeks, plus twelve years equals seventeen years. It would be a correct assumption that Harry would be penniless after serving the better part of this horror. Leibowitz had also tagged him with a $15,000 fine. He had shouted from the bench that Harry would serve a day for every dollar he failed to pay when ready for release from his prior sentences. That would add another forty-one years to his original seventeen, totaling fifty-eight years.

Jimmy shuddered as he read what the kangaroo court, brothers under the skin to the D.A.'s office, meted out as a sentence. This new twelve years added to Leibowitz's sentence could realistically total fifty-eight years. For bookmaking! He sat back, shook his head in pain.

It was early in the day, too early to have a drink, but Jimmy mixed a big Cutty and water, took a couple of deep swallows, and said to himself, What the hell, I did the best I could. What happens, happens.

What had impressed Jimmy the most as he read about the case the day after the three judges doomed Harry and on subsequent days as McDonald lingered in the headlines was the fact that not one reporter or columnist raised the slightest outcry at the severity of the sentence. It appeared they pouted; they had been cheated out of salacious stories, sensational disclosures, foiled along with the D.A. at the chance to take deep drafts of the now freed policemen's blood.

What further amazed him was their complete faith in whatever scandalous news emanated from the gristmill of the D.A.'s towering wrath. A few days after Harry's sentencing and the astonishing quasi-exposé that accompanied it, McDonald and company again captured the headlines. This time it was at the expense of their former boss and beloved colleague, Bill O'Dwyer, the initial target of their probe. O'Dwyer had been driven out of office like the fox he was, by a pack of hounds who put him on the run and finally cornered him. He was now the ambassador to Mexico, a political plum awarded him for valor under fire by his loftier adherents in the Democratic Party. To deduce from this incredible appointment that politicans take care of fellow politicans would be to state a universal truth.

Jimmy Riley had no love for either Bill O'Dwyer or Jim Moran, his chief lieutenant, but he seethed inwardly at the unmerciful smear laid at their doorstep. O'Dwyer was a virtual exile. Moran was free on bail appealing a perjury conviction sustained as a result of an ill-fated appearance before the Kefauver Senate committee. Both were defenseless.

Harry's grand jury testimony was leaked again through the hypocritical justification of a free press reporting the relevant facts. In inch-high headlines, the newspapers reported election campaign gifts by Harry Gross to Jim Moran to help finance O'Dwyer's election to the mayoralty of New York City. This bit of tabloid

information was released directly from the 45,000-word exposé of
Harry's testimony that was supposedly under the cloak of secrecy
ordered by Leibowitz. When asked whether the allegations were
true, McDonald answered tersely, "No comment."

The story beneath the blaring headlines spelled out Harry's testimony concerning Moran and O'Dwyer. It was such a complete
fabrication, so patently false, such pure horseshit, that Jimmy
shook his head in disbelief as he read it. Harry testified that he
gave Jim Moran $5,000 in 1945, and further, that he upped the
ante to $15,000 in 1949. These questions about O'Dwyer's cam-
paign funds had to be deliberate, planned questions, aimed at
discrediting Bill O'Dwyer, and Harry answered them like a well-
trained talking dog, and further elaborated that all the bookies in
town were required to make contributions.

Jimmy positively, absolutely knew that Harry had never even
laid eyes on Jim Moran until 1947 when Jimmy pointed Moran
out to him one night in the lobby of Madison Square Garden. The
only thing Harry knew of Moran was the bad blood that existed
between him and Jimmy over the Bals squad debacle. In 1945,
Harry was just climbing out of the street corner bookie class and
couldn't afford to lay out $5,000 to see FDR rise out of his grave.
In 1949 Harry was on the lam for almost five months, as the
D.A.'s office was well aware. He was so much in hock he was on
the balls of his ass. He couldn't afford to give O'Dwyer $15,
much less $15,000.

Jimmy knew that Moran and O'Dwyer had greased the skids
for his slide clear out of The Job, but he was still outraged at the
callous disregard the press and the D.A.'s office had for the truth.
He sat back and wondered how long and how deep they were
going to dig before they called it a day.

The weeks rolled by and Leibowitz's grand jury, now snidely
referred to as Leibowitz's great-grand jury because it had been
empaneled so long, was extended once more. The three stalwarts
of justice kept sniping away at cop after cop, occasionally releasing sensational tidbits to keep their names on the front pages of
the papers. They had the power of the subpoena and they used it
like a skilled fencer uses his rapier. Venom deftly spewed from
the angry mouths of the demons of the D.A.'s office. Helfand and

Koota, taking turns firing questions in the grand jury room, dissatisfied with a reluctant witness or an aberrant answer, would haul their helpless prey before the Great Crusader. Leibowitz quizzed witness after witness relentlessly. They might as well have had the grand jury doing their number at home plate in Ebbets Field on Opening Day. Amplifiers turned on real loud, to a packed stadium.

Jimmy finally got sick of reading about the antics of all the actors in Brooklyn and Leibowitz's grand jury. The air was again getting chill, snow was on the horizon, he decided to go to Florida for the winter with his wife and family. He wasn't ready to go to work until the grand jury was dissolved, and he didn't see any sense hanging around New York City and Connecticut. All of his friends who had beaten indictments when the Big Trial caved in and about an equal number who had been named co-conspirators were suspended without pay to await a police department trial, another kangaroo court. Jimmy, logically enough, kept his distance from these alleged pariahs, and decided to put another fifteen hundred miles between them. He called his friend in Florida and made arrangements for the same house he had rented the previous couple of years.

A few days before he was to leave, he was sitting reading in the den, content with the world, when the telephone rang.

"Jimmy, that you?" He immediately recognized the voice. "Hey, Chick, sure it's me. How are you, kid? I haven't heard from you since you sang your golden medley with Rose and Dan."

"I know, Jim. I thought it better to pass each other for a while. You know, like we agreed."

"You're right, Chick, but I miss you. What's up?"

"Not too good, Jimmy. I got real bad news today. I'd like to see you. Can we meet tomorrow for lunch? You name the place."

"How about Mike Manuche's about one o'clock?"

"Perfect. See you then."

Mike Manuche's restaurant was located on 52nd Street east of Broadway, just down the block from Gallagher's. Manuche's, like Gallagher's, was famous as a gathering place for celebrities of the sports world and television, but featured as customers more guys who actually played or announced the games than guys who either booked or bet on them. The whiskey and the food were equally good, and Chick and Jimmy loved to eat there.

They arrived almost simultaneously, had one Scotch at the bar, and Gino, the maître d', ushered them to a secluded rear table. When fresh drinks arrived and the waiter left, Jimmy touched Chick's glass good luck and said, "Okay, take that goddam look off your face, you look like the world is going to end any minute. What's up? You got the clap?"

Chick laughed. "No, not the clap, and the world isn't about to end, it just collapsed. Jimmy, I got indicted for perjury. I got the word yesterday."

Jimmy almost dropped his glass in shock. "For Christ's sake, don't say a thing like that. Are you sure? How did it happen?"

"Jim, you remember years ago when we first started working together as partners and you confided in me about the safe deposit box you had in the bank at Flatbush and Church avenues?"

"Jesus, that bank. How could I ever forget it? Until I die I'll never forget the look on Helfand's kisser when I told him I'd just emptied it out when he thought he had me dead right before the grand jury."

Chick laughed out loud. He was brightening up a little, which helped Jimmy's mood.

"Jim, we all nearly died laughing about that when we read about it the next day. That was one funny bit, typical Jimmy Riley. But the worm's turned, nothing's so funny now. Anyway, I opened a box there under a phony name just like you did. When all the trouble started I hot-footed over to the bank and naturally emptied it out and buried the dough in a secure place. When they were questioning me in the grand jury, they finally got down to my finances. They asked if I had a safe deposit box. I never figured that they'd catch up to me, so I told them no. The other day a good friend of mine in the D.A.'s office tipped me that they had caught up to me. They got me ice-cold. Jim, what the hell do I do now?"

"Christ, Chick, I'm sorry to hear this. I don't know what to say. I hate to sound like an 'I told you so' or a past-post guy, but I never would have gone into that murderous grand jury and signed a waiver of immunity if they put a fucking gun to my head. I wouldn't give a shit if I had two weeks to go to be eligible for my pension. I'd still never waive immunity."

"I know, I know, goddam it. When the shit hit the fan, I thought about packing it in and taking off for Florida like some of the guys, but I honestly never thought they would go so far. Would you believe they had me down there to the grand jury on a subpoena last week. I was wondering why they never called me, they just let me sit there and sweat. Jimmy, there must have been fifty people there with subpoenas. Cops' wives, uncles, in-laws, all kinds of relatives. They had one old wop there, I think he was Louis Gangeni's father-in-law, who was a riot. He worked for the city somewhere. You know, the sanitation or the parks department. He said he didn't understand English, so they put an interpreter on him to question him about his healthy bank books. He drove them crazy. He looked like an old iceman. I heard he kept throwing up his hands, pretending the interpreter spoke a different dialect. He kept saying to every question, 'What, whatta you-a say? I no-a understand.' I heard even Leibowitz finally gave up on him. Jim, before they're through they'll have every relative of a cop and every bank record in the city subpoenaed."

"You're right. I can't believe most of this shit I read about. Like it's unreal, like they just don't seem to want to quit. I thought the whole thing would die a natural death when Harry dummied up on them, especially after they buried him to get even. But Christ, now they're getting more vicious than ever."

"You're absolutely right, Jim, and you better watch your own ass. If they ever get wind of the act you pulled with Harry they'll send you to the electric chair. They have a hard-on for you a mile long, and they admit it. So once again, Jimmy, watch your ass."

"Don't worry about me, Chick, let's worry about you. Are you dead sure you're indicted?"

"Positive. From what I hear, they're all set to come out with a big splash in the early edition of the Monday *Daily News*. Everyone in New York reads the first edition of the Monday *News* on Sunday night to get all the late football scores and to see just how all their bets went down the drain. There's a couple of other guys in The Job on the hook with me for the same kind of hidden assets shit."

"Do you know who else? The other guys?"

"No, but I'm sure as hell about myself."

"Okay, here comes our lunch, let's eat. You know, Chick, the condemned man is always supposed to eat a hearty meal. Let's forget about indictments for about half an hour. We'll talk about broads and football for a while. Okay?"

They ate a delicious lunch, chatting away like two guys without a care in the world. Lunch finished, the waiter cleared the table and they ordered coffee and brandy stingers on the rocks. Again they touched glasses good luck and Jimmy said, "Chick, with all my heart I wish you the best of luck. At least you won't have to worry about any more grand jury subpoenas now that you're indicted. They probably had you down last week for exercise, so some bank guy or somebody could look you over and identify you. After they finish with all the bullshit publicity they'll reap from your indictment, they'll probably offer you some kind of deal to cooperate. You know, the old army game. The same deal the cops and D.A.s have been using from the time they first invented cops and D.A.s. First they nail you, then try to make a fink out of you."

"Fuck them, Jimmy. You know me, they can stick their deals up their ass."

"Chick, I have great confidence, implicit faith in you. But remember, much as you like pussy, you'll have to give it up for a couple of years. I hope the thought of that deprivation won't cause you to cooperate with Judge Leibowitz."

Chick laughed, shook his head. "You're right, Jimmy, that's going to really hurt. But one consolation, the good clean life for a couple of years will prolong my sex life a helluva lot when I finally do come home."

"Chick, let's get down to business. I want to ask you a few questions. Have you got any idea who you're going to use to defend you? And are those cheap bastards we used to work with going to help defray your legal expenses and help your family if you go away?"

"I think I'll be okay along those lines. We had a big meeting when all the horseshit started and we all agreed to help whoever got into trouble, so that's pretty well taken care of."

"Good, I'm glad. It's none of my business, so I'll forget about it. All I'm interested in is that you're okay. Make sure you get the best lawyer possible, preferably someone from outside Brooklyn who won't take any shit from that crew. You know that they have ninety percent of the lawyers in Brooklyn bullshitted, scared stiff of them. Please, Chick, take a long look, make a hard decision before you hire a lawyer. One more thing before we leave. I want you to know I feel very badly about this, Chick. If I can do anything, get hold of me right away. I told you I'm off to Florida in a few days. I'll call you when I get there so you'll have my number. I'll be gone three or four months, so chances are I'll be home by the time they put you on trial."

"Thanks, Jimmy. Don't worry about me. Go away and have a good time. I'll be okay."

Jimmy drove back home to Connecticut very carefully, very thoughtfully. Not because of the amount of booze he'd drunk, but because he was extremely upset at hearing Chick's bad news. He had kept on a happy face all day, not wanting to further depress Chick, but inwardly he was shocked. Chick was a nice, decent guy. An easygoing type, friend of everybody, no enemies. He dreaded to think about Chick going upstate to prison, how he would cope with it. Through the years they both were well connected with the top wise guys, so word would surely be sent upstate to keep an eye on Chick, to look out for him so that he wouldn't have any problems. But there was always the risk of some psychotic cop-hater ready to break his balls. Chick was tough, but he was getting a little old. Christ, here I go jumping the gun again, Jimmy thought. Not only do I already have Chick doing hard time in some rough prison, but I have him having trouble with a crazy whackeroo.

He smiled to himself. It's not over yet. They'll have to give Chick a change of venue away from Brooklyn. Or a lesser plea to a misdemeanor. Or even maybe probation or a suspended sentence. He started to cheer up. Jesus, maybe by some miracle Chick might even beat the case.

* * *

On the Monday following his lunch date with Chick, Jimmy sat and read the morning *Daily News* with a heavy heart. Chick's tip-off had been correct, he and two other cops were indicted for perjury. As Jimmy read the bad news he became more aware than ever that any hope of leniency without full cooperation with the D.A.'s office was wishful thinking. Just as Chick had predicted, they really splashed it in banner headlines: THREE GROSS CASE COPS INDICTED. The unfortunates were Chick, a guy named Max Bresloff from the local division, and another young cop Jimmy didn't know.

He knew Bresloff fairly well. He had played cards with him a few times, drank with him a few times, and overall thought he was a pretty nice guy. His heart ached for all three, especially Chick, his good pal, and Bresloff, who always seemed such a nice fellow. The indictments stemmed from some type of concealed assets, personal property or undeclared safe deposit boxes. The charges were tenuous at best, but serious enough to be rated a felony, punishable by five years in state prison.

Perjury. A truly ominous word, enough to send that now familiar chill up Jimmy's spine. He left his chair in the den and went to the wall bookcase in the living room and reached for the king-sized Webster's dictionary. He wanted the definitive meaning indelibly printed in his mind. "Perjury: In law, the willfull teling of a lie while under oath to tell the truth in a matter material to the point of inquiry."

Jimmy put the cumbersome dictionary back in the boockase and returned to the den. He sat back and contemplated all his years of courtroom experience. Who the hell ever told the truth in a court of law? The entire legal system was predicated on evasiveness, cunning, and theatrics. He involuntarily broke into a big grin when he thought of some of the antics and fabrications of lawyers, D.A.s, and judges he had observed throughout his busy career. He'd seen all kinds of cases tossed out of court, all kinds of outrageous lies told in open court. Christ, among most vice and gambling cops it was one big joke. Lawyers he had become intimate with through the years told him unbelievable tales of chicanery in civil and criminal courts. The ones who started as "ambulance chasers" when first out of law school were the funniest of all.

But there it was, in the dictionary and in the penal code: *perjury*. Jesus, what a weapon those vengeance-bent disciples of Captain Javert had at their disposal. Jimmy put his head back and thought about all of his grand jury appearances. They totaled almost fifteen hours in all. He knew the statistics because Danny Sachs had kept a precise record of them for possible future reference. When he was finally dismissed by Helfand, he and Danny had stopped at a nearby bar for a farewell drink and when Dan told him the whole ordeal comprised only fifteen hours he was surprised. It had seemed more like fifty hours.

Jimmy smiled. I wonder how many lies I told Helfand while being questioned in the horror chamber. Let's see, fifteen hours. Conservatively at ten an hour, I probably told him approximately one hundred and fifty lies. He laughed. Christ, if Leibowitz ever catches me in all those lies he'll probably give me seven hundred and fifty years. Even if I got paroled after one hundred years, I'll be too goddam old to have any fun when I get out. Beautiful girls, twelve-year-old Scotch, swinging nightclubs, fancy restaurants, the Garden, Ebbets Field—Christ, I'll be over a hundred and thirty.

Sick and tired of hearing about the almost daily recurrence of bad news flowing out of Brooklyn, Jimmy flew down to Florida with his wife, kids, and the maid in the early part of December. The house was familiar and comfortable and they all loved it. The two older kids were enrolled in private school, and Jimmy's cares were shed and life became happier as the days rolled by. The viselike pressure of the Big Trial was off, he was satisfied in his heart that he had done the best he could. The Big Trial had blown up in smithereens, that was his main concern. However, the recurrent bullshit perjury indictments were like malignant tumors, cropping up every couple of months to his despair. But those cops should have known better than to go into that grand jury room without being well coached. Certainly any cop who potentially could be involved should never have gone in there and signed a waiver of immunity. That had to be the biggest sucker's move of all time.

The Christmas holidays arrived and passed peacefully and happily. But still, a constant pall hung over the head of Jimmy Riley. It was like the approach of a formation of dark, menacing clouds when he was on the golf course. In a few minutes it was going to thunder, flash lightning, and rain like hell, washing out the day. And that was the constant pall around Jimmy, the dark, threatening clouds of the Brooklyn D.A.'s office that could suddenly loom overhead and wash out his life. He kept a cheerful face in front of his family and friends, laughed and kidded, swam and played golf, but the sword was always hanging over his head suspended by a slender hair. He often smiled ruefully, thinking, Here I sit, Damocles Riley.

The days melted into weeks, the weeks into months, and finally the monotony of the climate and the boredom of his daily routine began to get on Jimmy's nerves. He toyed with the idea of permanently residing in Florida, discussed it with Kay, but in the end always rejected it. In his heart Jimmy Riley was a New York guy and would die a New York guy. Besides, in his will he had specified that he be buried out of Frank Campbell's Funeral Home on Madison Avenue. Who the hell would go to his wake in Florida?

The house was rented until May 1, but by the end of March Jimmy had finally had enough of the sun, the ocean, and the golf course. He took the two kids out of school and flew the family back home to their natural habitat. Dark clouds overhead or not, he had to get back into action. He still had plenty of money, but the way he lived and pissed it away, it wouldn't be too long before he might have to curtail his lifestyle. Please, let's not let that happen. Once you get used to the good life, God forbid you might have to cut back, struggle a little. That, Jimmy had no intention of doing. He had plenty of confidence in himself, he had lots of good friends, and with money no problem, he was sure he could get started in a good, lucrative business again.

He could always go back to his friend Jack Goldman, the graphic arts genius, but he dismissed the idea as long as the threat of indictment loomed over him. He'd already had two false starts with Jack and he'd collected all the money coming to him, plus a nice bonus, so Jimmy figured leave well enough alone. He went to the city a couple of times a week, listening to an occasional business proposition, and usually stayed overnight at the Downtown Athletic Club. He would arise early, have a strenuous workout, eat lunch, play cards until early in the evening, then drive back to Connecticut. Life was routine, not too boring, and each week brought him closer to deciding what to do with his life. It was unbelievable how time flew. Pretty soon it would be two years since the Big Raid in Brooklyn, the grand jury, and the angry faces of Leibowitz and Helfand. Two years, Christ, he hated to wish his life away, but he wished it would soon be five years instead of two. After five years, the statute of limitations would end all his troubles.

Jimmy had just finished dinner and was at peace with the world as he sat reading a book in the seclusion of his den. The telephone on the table next to him rang shrilly, startling him, almost causing him to jump out of his chair. He was further shaken when he recognized the voice on the other end of the phone.

"Yes, who's this?"

"Hey, Jim. It's me, Leo. How are you?"

Morty, the ex-Incorruptible. Jimmy hadn't heard from Morty in four or five months. Bad news was in the air, the old familiar chill hit his spine.

"I'm fine, kid. It's good to hear from you. Let's have your number, I'll call you right back."

Jimmy got his car out of the garage and as he drove to the friendly gas station with the public phone booth he knew nothing good awaited him.

"It's me, Morty. What's up?"

"Jimmy, I'm sorry but I always seem to bring you the worst news. But you asked me to call when something earth-shaking happened, and today I heard something I felt you should know."

"Good, Morty, I appreciate it. Okay, my man, what's so important?"

"Jimmy, you know that guy Max Bresloff, the division cop that got indicted for perjury before you went to Florida?"

Jimmy's stomach began to turn. "Sure I know him. What about him?"

"Jim, I hate to tell you this, but he's hollering his fucking head off. I overheard one of the guys in the squad talking about him this afternoon. He said he'd been standing next to Helfand and heard him say, 'Well, we finally got that wise guy sonofabitch Jimmy Riley. Bresloff came across for us. We'll see how arrogant and tough that wise bastard is when we bring him in this time.'"

Jimmy was stunned. "Morty, are you sure?"

"I'm sure Bresloff is opening up, Jimmy. That's positive. The news is all over the office. He's the first cop to break the cops' code of silence. I overheard plenty of other bullshit, but I'm certain about Bresloff. I'm sure it's true."

"All right, kid. Now listen. Hang around the office all day tomorrow and find out as much as you can. Don't be too obvious, but try to learn how they can hurt me and what they have on me and if they intend to indict me. You got it?"

"No problem, Jim."

"What time are you free tomorrow?"

"I'm off work at five o'clock."

"Good. I'll meet you in the same place. We'll dine to the musical tunes of the most danceable of the big hands. About seven o'clock. Okay?"

"Perfect. See you there."

Jimmy got into his car and drove home. He went behind the bar in the den and mixed a Cutty and water. Plenty of Scotch, a little bit of water. He sat back in his big leather lounge chair, sipping his drink. What the hell could Bresloff tell them that could implicate him? He went over their brief association very carefully. He tried to pinpoint the few times they were alone together. Jimmy was certain they couldn't pin any gambling or assault charges on him. That shit went out the window when he received full immunity from the grand jury. The only thing that they could possibly get him on was the fucking charge of perjury. *Perjury.* How he hated the sound of that goddam word.

He was sure he'd never cut up any money with Bresloff when he was in The Job. He'd never paid him a quarter when Harry was on the lam. He just knew him as a pretty nice guy, a couple of card games, a few drinks. That was it. But Jimmy knew Helfand was a very shrewd guy, he was like a bulldog when he sank his teeth into you. Jimmy was also well aware that Helfand hated his guts. Helfand and Leibowitz were in a tie in the Hate Jimmy Riley race, with McDonald a close second. But no matter how he turned and twisted Max Bresloff in his mind he couldn't come up with a logical explanation of Helfand's remark. We finally got that wise guy sonofabitch.

Jimmy didn't give too much credence to Morty's remark about the code of silence. He didn't have much faith in that "cops' code" shit. He was suspicious of a few guys who were important to the investigation, guys he knew surely must have been mentioned by Harry or one of the other stool pigeons. They had just walked away unscathed after their first couple of appearances before the grand jury. A couple of them still remained in The Job, a couple of them just peacefully left The Job and were no longer harassed. Jimmy always felt deep down that there were a couple of undercover rats among the cops. Guys who traded juicy bits of information that the D.A.'s office enlarged through Harry's vivid imagination. In return they were allowed to take the fence. Jimmy, Chick, and Tom had talked about it. But how could you prove it? But one thing remained for sure, the D.A.'s office had a helluva lot of knowledge of the inner mechanisms of The Job. More than could be supplied by Harry Gross or shitheads like Mikie the wire-room boss or Willie the cashier.

Jimmy got up from the chair and went to the bar to make himself another Scotch, then decided against it. This was going to be a long night. I'm going to take a nice long walk and keep my head clear.

When he stepped out of the house he was glad of his decision. It was the most beautiful part of the day, just turning dusk. The late-spring air was fresh and balmy. The scent of fragrant vegetation filled his nose as Jimmy tramped through the woods behind his house until he reached an old back-country road that he knew stretched a couple of miles. The sun was setting in the west midst a burst of brilliant colors. The terrain along the ancient black-topped trail was lovely; the immaculate spacious homes with their long, winding driveways, their landscaped lawns blooming with lilacs, tulips, daffodils. It was Jimmy's favorite part of the countryside, a soothing brisk walk amidst the lovely verdant background that always helped sort out in his mind whatever puzzled him. As the twilight shadows began to deepen, his mood became lighter, cheered by the beauty that surrounded him.

What the hell could they get on him? He had followed his lawyers' game plan to the minutest degree. He always answered as they had coached him—"I'm not exactly sure," "To the best of my recollection," "I couldn't be positive but," "Could you please refresh my memory," "Could you please give me the exact date," "Could you please tell me who else was there and maybe it will refresh my memory"—and enough evasive shit like that until he could have recited it in his sleep. Why would Helfand make that remark about me? Jimmy knew that the D.A.'s office and Leibowitz's grand jury would hit him with an indictment on the slightest shred of evidence they thought could bury him. The rackets grand jury, what a laugh. After two years they'd come up with a couple of numbers banks, about six bookmakers, the imaginary bullshit empire of Harry Gross, and the stunning, incredible, hair-raising evidence that a New York cop was known to take a buck or two from a bookmaker. It was wholly transparent to anyone with half a brain that the name of the game was publicity. The grand jury was a showcase for Leibowitz and the D.A.'s office. Their every move was predicated upon the next day's headlines. When all the horseshit was finally over, the headliners would be rewarded with their cherished judgeships. There wasn't a doubt in Jimmy's mind about that. But as he walked along he smiled, thinking, Sam Leibowitz has as much chance to be mayor of New York City as I have.

His smiled broadened. If I don't get indicted, I'll reestablish my city residence and run against him. Christ, imagine if I was ever elected mayor, his flight of fancy soaring as he breathed deeply of the night air. I'd make Chick the police commissioner, Tommy the chief inspector, and John the assistant chief in charge of all the gambling squads. They'd have to buy their own bank to hold all the money they'd make. He caught himself from laughing out loud, a couple were walking their dog toward him about a hundred feet away. They'd surely think he was some kind of nut when all he was doing was imagining himself another Jimmy Walker.

He finished his walk and picked his way through the woods to his house just as darkness fell. He went to the bar and made himself the nice double Scotch he felt was his reward for his long walk and resolved to push Bresloff and the Brooklyn enemy from his mind until tomorrow. My young good friend, my ex-Incorruptible, Morty, will clue me in on all the imminent trouble awaiting me. Tonight might well be the only serene one I'll have for a long, long time.

Jimmy sat on a stool at the corner of the bar at the Glen Island Casino. He ordered a drink and looked the room over with an amused eye. The music of Glen Gray wasn't scheduled to start for almost two hours but the place was already three-quarters filled with pretty young girls and horny-looking young guys. It was a perfect place to meet. The only thing on the minds of all the young kids nervously sizing each other up was music, dancing, and hopefully, l'amour. He had just finished his first drink when Morty walked in. They shook hands and hugged each other. Jimmy ordered a fresh round of drinks and scrutinized Morty closely as he chatted away. His usual great smile seemed a little forced. He appeared to have aged a bit, there was a worried look about his eyes as they touched glasses good luck.

Jimmy paid the bar tab and motioned to a waiter for a table. He told the waiter where they wanted to sit, way out in right field of the cavernous dining room. The waiter settled them barely within sight of the other people and brought them a fresh round of drinks and the dinner menus.

"Okay, Morty, take off the sad look, wash off the greasepaint, give me the bad news."

"It's all bad, Jimmy, all fucking bad. I hate to tell you. Jimmy, you're dead. Dead."

"From the look on your face, it's you who's dead. I'm breathing, feel my pulse. Come on, please, for Christ's sake. Tell me what you found out or I'll have a heart attack right here at the table."

"Jimmy, you're definitely being indicted. I got the whole story today, right from the feedbox."

"For what?"

"Perjury, first degree, a felony. They're all celebrating in the D.A.'s office. The word went out, they finally nailed the wise-ass Irish bastard. I'm really sorry, Jim. I almost cried when I heard it, honest."

"Perjury? What? How?"

"That guy Bresloff who got indicted for perjury the end of last year for lying about a safe deposit box? Well, the story I got goes this way. They were all set to put him on trial when he and his lawyer walked up to Helfand and McDonald and said, 'What the hell do you want with a small-time division guy like me? Let me out of my rap and I'll deliver you Jimmy Riley. I know how you can get him and convict him. He's the real big shot in this case, and you people know it. Harry Gross wouldn't take a piss without Jimmy Riley first okaying it. And he dealt personally with all the big shots in The Job. You let me go and I promise you I'll hand you Jimmy Riley on a silver platter.'"

Jimmy's mind was bananas as he listened to Morty's bad news. "Did you find out exactly how this rat prick was going to deliver me?"

"Wait'll you hear this. Do you remember an airplane trip to Chicago you guys took to see the second Zale–Graziano fight?"

"Jesus Christ. You're right, sure I remember it. And now I remember Helfand asking me who was on that trip. But shit, he asked me about a few trips and all kinds of parties. Now that I think about it, Bresloff was on that trip. Morty, that was about five years ago. I never gave that trip a second thought, much less remembered Bresloff on the plane. I do remember him in the hotel in Chicago, though. We had some sort of reservation mix-up, and I remember we had a couple of drinks together at the bar until it got straightened out. But that's all I remember about him, that couple of drinks. I don't remember him on the plane going out, and I flew back alone with Billy Graham and Danny Sargone from the docks. Christ, how could they indict me on a piece of shit like this?"

"Jimmy, I warned you a few times. They want a piece of your ass so bad they'll do anything to nail you. One of the guys in the squad told me that Helfand and McDonald were happy as a couple of kids on Halloween about Bresloff opening up."

"Then what the hell is the delay? Why are they waiting to indict me?"

"They just sent one of the older detectives in the squad to check out Bresloff's story in Chicago. You know, the hotel register and the rest of the shit he squealed about. They want it all verified. When he comes back they'll probably tie it all in and present the evidence to Leibowitz's grand jury. Then they'll set it up like they always do, to get the greatest possible publicity. They got good copy in you, Jimmy. You're a big bit with all that big house of yours and country club shit. You're a star."

"Some fucking star, Morty. You mean a falling star. Christ, I can't believe this, what you just told me. That goddam trip was five years ago. They questioned me about it three or four years after we took it. While you're telling me about it, I'm trying to piece it together in my mind. If I recall correctly, when Helfand asked me about it he didn't seem to dwell on it like it was a big deal. It was kind of a routine question. Some stool pigeon laid the trip on him, but it didn't seem that important to him. You know, compared to other things he asked me when he got upset by my answers, he didn't seem to stress the Chicago trip too much. Holy shit, is that goddam trip going to put me in the slammer for five years. Impossible."

"I hope it's impossible for your sake, Jimmy, it would be a goddam shame. Jim, there's something preying on my mind I have to ask you about. I hope you don't hold it against me, but I have to ask you this."

"Don't be silly, Morty. Go ahead, ask me."

"Jimmy, remember the night Teddy, me, and Harry met you and we went up to that gorgeous blond broad's whorehouse? You know, big Betty."

"Not only do I remember, but I'll never forget the blissful look on your Yiddisher kisser when you came over to the bar in the living room after your double-header with Betty and the redhead."

Morty laughed. "I'll never foregt that night as long as I live. I was in a state of sheer ecstasy for a week afterward. What a night.

But, I've been worried about that night ever since. I'm no idiot, Jimmy you know that. I trust you, and I know that you trust me. It was obvious something real heavy took place between you and Harry when Teddy and me were in the bedrooms getting laid. Harry was happy as a clam when we left you two alone, but when we finally came out to have a drink he was almost in shock, subdued. I knew you had just laid into him pretty good, a ten-year-old kid could tell that. All the way back to Brooklyn he was very quiet, too quiet. Then when he blew up on the witness stand I figured it might be as a result of that night. I was sure you were behind it. Now the worse thing is, Jim, and what I'm worried about, the D.A.'s office is almost sure you're the guy who threatened him. They've practically zeroed in on it. They make no bones about it."

Jimmy had been listening patiently. He could understand how the kid might be afraid of being implicated, of losing his job.

"There's nothing to be concerned about, Morty. What can they do? Revive Harry again? They just buried him worse than if they buried him in Holy Cross Cemetery, where a Jew could never rest in peace. He got the kiss of death, he's finished, washed up."

"Suppose somehow they get the story, if he opens up about you after he's away awhile. What the hell will I tell them?"

"Tell them shit, just like I will. If you have to tell them anything, tell them Harry wanted to visit an old girl friend and I happened to be there when you arrived. Your instructions were to be good to him, do anything for him, jerk him off if necessary. Just make sure he would be a happy and cooperative witness when the trial started."

"You make it all sound easy."

"Look, once we were in the apartment he went to another room with her and we sat in the living room and had a couple of drinks. All perfectly innocent. Stop worrying. If it will ease your mind any, Morty, big Betty Baines has left New York for Houston, Texas. My friend Dave Conte, who owns the Zebra Bar, told me some big oil guy came into New York, met Betty, and flipped over her. I hear he took her back to Texas to marry her. Probably to meet his mother first." Jimmy laughed. "Anyway, it couldn't happen to a better broad than Betty. So you see, Morty all your worries are over."

"Jesus, Jimmy that's great news. What a relief. But now you know something, Jim, I feel lousy, depressed. As nervous as I was about getting into a jam and maybe losing my job, I was still going to ask you tonight if you could arrange another rendezvous with Betty. I was dying for another shot at her. Now she's gone, oh, my aching heart."

Jimmy laughed. "You mean your aching dick, Morty. Remember, it's tough to have both—peace of mind in your head and peace of mind in your cock. So kiss your memory of Betty goodbye, forever. And stop worrying about Harry, he'll never squeal on me. Okay, here's the waiter. Let's get something to eat. After dinner I'm leaving you alone here, and if a nice-looking Jewish kid and great dancer like you can't score tonight with one of these great-looking chicks, then shame on you."

They finished dinner and Morty walked Jimmy to the door to say goodbye. He was taking Jimmy's advice, staying around to Peabody and Lindy Hop one of these young chicks into submission to the music of Glen Gray. As they shook hands Morty tried to pull away from the two C-notes Jimmy pressed into his palm. "Come on, Jim, you have your own headaches, you've already done enough for me. Please."

"Morty, take it, for Christ's sake. You've been aces with me and I'll never forget you. Even if it was bad news, you gave me a million-dollar tip-off tonight and I appreciate it. Put one of these C-notes away and take the other one, grab one of these young chicks, and toss your money around like you were a plainclothes lieutenant in the P.C.'s office. That'll soften her up. Money helps to nail a nice girl every time."

Morty laughed, his face beaming, happy again. He looked at Jimmy with a big grin and said, "You are a pisser, Jim, a real beauty. Now before we leave each other, what do you want me to do from here on in?"

"There's only one thing left, to find out about the indictment. If you know for sure that I'm definitely indicted, call me from Tuesday on at the Downtown A.C. You know the number. If they zing me, just call and tell me you can't meet me. You got it? You can't meet me."

"I got you. Jim. Good luck. Take care, pal."

It would be a longer night for Jimmy Riley than ever, and in recent months life had been a series of long nights. When he arrived home Kay asked whether he had had dinner and, as usual, accepted his laconic answer without question. No use worrying her about it. She was knitting, watching television, and Jimmy made himself a drink and pretended to watch it along with her. He kept a façade of calm, his mind everywhere but on the television screen in front of him. His brain was flipping, doing gyrations, spinning like a top. He was trying to arrange his thoughts in orderly fashion, to try to recall the exact grand jury appearance when Helfand questioned him about the tirp to Chicago. It was early in the game, he recalled, the first or second appearance. He was positive he gave Helfand plenty of Danny's expert coaching, the "If I recall properly," "To the best of my recollection" shit. Christ, of all the guys on the trip, Max Bresloff. I can't even remember the rat sonofabitch on the plane going out. I only remember being with him once, at the hotel bar. I'm sure that he didn't return with me. I caught a late plane home with Billy Graham and Danny Sargone. Rae McKinnon, the ballet dancer, met us at the airport and drove us all to New York. In three days in Chicago, I can remember seeing Bresloff only that one time. That could be an expensive couple of drinks. Well, there's one consolation, I'll be playing golf with John tomorrow morning and he might put my head on straight. One more drink and off to bed, this goddam television will drive me crazy.

They finished playing golf the next day a little bit after noon and afer a couple of drinks and lunch in the men's grill they went to shower and change into fresh clothes. Jimmy quietly told John that he had to sit down privately with him for about an hour. Very important. John got the message and followed behind Jimmy in his car to Jimmy's house.

They sat in the den having a drink and Jimmy poured out the entire sorry tale of the night before, only omitting Morty's name. John listened thoughtfully, occasionally nodding his head the way all lawyers do when hearing out a client's troubles. Like the wisest of men hearing the confessions of an errant juvenile.

John sipped his Scotch. "You're sure you only saw this guy once, Jim? In the hotel bar while you waited for your reservations to be straightened out?"

"Positive, John."

"And you're also positive, like Danny and I drilled into you, that you gave it plenty of evasiveness to Helfand in the grand jury? 'I'm not sure,' 'To the best of my recollection'—all that kind of jazz?"

"John, to the best of my knowledge," Jimmy burst out laughing. He recoverd and said, "You see, John, for the rest of my life I'll be answering questions with that kind of shit I started to answer you."

They both howled laughing.

"John, I'm as sure as I can be. But maybe I'm blocking out of my mind some shit I don't want to remember. Of course, only the grand jury minutes will bear me out."

"You're right, Jim. The indictment will have to contain specifics. Helfand's series of questions and your complete answers."

"I figured that. Now, what do you suggest?"

"Here's what we'll do. I'll call Danny on Monday and have him alert a bondsman to be ready to bail you out. Knowing Leibowitz, whom you'll undoubtedly be arraigned before, he'll hold you in as high bail as possible. Do you plan to stay up here until they extradite you?"

"No. Fuck that. I want to keep a low profile, keep as much publicity away from here as I can. They have an automatic extradition at their disposal, anyway. I plan on going to the Downtown Athletic Club on Tuesday like I usually do and stay there the rest of the week. I have a few friends in the D.A.'s office who'll clue me in on the indictment. They all know I'm a member of the D.A.C. and stay there a few nights a week. If they call home, I'll tell Kay where they can reach me. I'm at the club, right, make it easy for them to find me. There's no use trying to duck them, they'll nail me if I go to the Himalayas. I might as well go along with them and try to beat them in court. The indictment has to be a piece of shit, don't you agree?"

"Jimmy, it sounds weak enough, but these guys hold all the cards. You took some calculated risks, so don't depend too much on beating the indictment. Perhaps on appeal, but even that's going to be tough. These judges have a brotherhood when there's a lot of pressure to punish someone. Jim, be prepared, you might have to do a lot of time."

"There's not much I can do about it, John. If I have to, I have to. Okay, let's have one more drink before you go. I'm like a zombie from lack of sleep."

"I could see that all morning. You played like a zombie."

Jimmy laughed. "You weren't exactly Ben Hogan. What was your excuse?"

"You're right, we were both pretty bad out there. Thank God we only lost twenty-eight dollars, the way we played. But here goes, Jim," John touched Jimmy's glass. "Whatever happens, I wish you the best of luck. You know how sorry I am to hear this, but we'll do the best we can to help you beat it."

"That's all I can ask, John."

John called Jimmy on Monday and said that after speaking to Danny he thought it would be a good idea if Jimmy dropped by Danny's office the next morning before he went to the Downtown A.C.

About ten o'clock Tuesday morning Jimmy walked across the street from Grand Central Terminal to Danny's office on East 42nd Street. Danny was concerned as they discussed the impending indictment, but decided to delay any preliminary strategy until he saw what they actually were faced with. He had left the message with the bail bondsman, no problem there. Jimmy shook hands with Danny, left, and caught a taxicab to the club to begin his vigil.

He had lunch, played cards all afternoon, took time out for dinner, played cards until around midnight, and no call came from Morty. The next day he worked out in the morning and around lunchtime resumed exactly the same routine. Still no call from Morty. He had only three suits at the club and about the same amount of changes of linen and socks, so he decided that if he didn't receive Morty's call that day he would invite Kay in to see

Frank Sinatra, who was appearing at the Copacabana, and then go back to Connecticut by chauffeured car.

When he didn't receive a call from Morty by two o'clock he called home and asked Kay to meet him at Joe and Rose's Restaurant on Third Avenue and 46th Street for dinner, and then off to see Sinatra. She was elated.

About three in the afternoon he was in the middle of a gin rummy game when he was paged to the telephone. His heart sank as he excused himself from the table and went to the booth in the bar to take the call.

"Yes, this is Jimmy Riley."

"Hi, Jim. Leo. I can't meet you, kid. I'm terribly sorry. I really mean it, Jim."

"Thanks, kid." Jimmy hung up. Numb. I can't meet you. You're officially indicted.

He played mechanically, his mind barely on the cards. He smiled and kept a straight face; a little quieter than usual, not very funny. He was secretly wondering how to break the news to Kay. What the hell do you tell your wife? I'm sorry, dear, but I just got indicted. Jesus.

The gin game was a nickel a point, three men on a side. A good, fast game. Jimmy's team got off to a bad start, went from bad to worse, and got a triple schneider, the maximum loss. Seventy points at a nickel a point, the scorekeeper on the winning side was chortling with glee, like all good winners. Three hundred and fifty bananas. The winners howl laughing and the losers scream "play cards." They got ready to draw partners for another game when Jimmy was paged to the phone again.

"Hello. Jimmy Riley?"

"Yes, this is Jimmy."

"Jim, this is Larry Calabrese from the Brooklyn D.A.'s office."

"Hey, Larry. How are you?"

"I'm fine, Jim, but I've got bad news for you. I'm downstairs in the lobby. I've got a warrant for your arrest."

Jimmy took a deep breath. At last. "Okay, Larry. Do you mind coming up to the men's bar? I'll buy you a drink. I'm just finishing playing cars, I want to settle up."

"Jimmy, I'm with a young cop and this guy Herb Buckholz,

Helfand's ace investigator. He's murder, this guy, he's no fucking good. Jimmy, I'm warning you, be careful with him. We'll be up in a couple of minutes if he gives the okay."

"I know all about him, Larry. Don't worry, the big fat prick won't bother me. Tell him to come up and have a drink, for Christ's sake. I'm not going to bite him. There's no sense staying down there in the lobby, you'll give the club a bad name."

Larry laughed. "Hold on, Jim, please, just a minute. I'll clear it with Herbie." Pause. "Okay, we'll be right up."

"Thanks, Larry. Just take the elevator to the men's bar, and you'll see a big Irish bartender named Barney. Tell him you're my guests. I'll be right with you, soon as I pay what I owe."

Jimmy walked back to the table. Was this a harbinger of things to come? First, a triple schneider and then an arrest warrant within two minutes of each other. He paid his tab at the table and laughed at all the good-natured ribbing he received about how badly he'd played the last sheet. Like a real shithead. Like his head was in the clouds, on another planet. Jimmy laughed along with them, they didn't know how right they were. He apologized for not being able to continue and contribute to their fortune, explaining he had some unexpected guests at the bar. A euphemism if he had ever heard one.

He spotted Larry and the other two at the bar and went directly to them. He shook hands with Larry, a nice guy and an old friend of his. Larry introduced him to the young cop, a nice-looking, tall, blond kid named Harold Furash, and to Herb Buckholz, a heavy-set, round-faced, surly-looking guy. Buckholz, the relentless civilian D.A.s' investigator. If there's one thing a cop or an ex-cop automatically dislikes, it's a civilian D.A.'s investigator. Like a cat hates a dog, like a wounded jungle animal hates a jackal, like a sheep hates a wolf. Logically, the reverse is also true. Most civilian D.A.s' investigators hate cops.

Larry had ordered drinks from Barney for the three of them and Jimmy ordered a Cutty Sark and water, his first of the day. It tasted delicious. Barney turned away after serving Jimmy and walked toward the center of the bar, leaving the four of them alone at the corner. Buckholz took a paper out of his inside coat pocket and started to read aloud—like he was reciting the pledge of allegiance to the American flag.

"Mr. James Riley, I have in my hand a warrant for your arrest. It is for—"

Jimmy grabbed the paper out of his hand. "For Christ's sake, Buckholz, stop acting like a fucking Keystone Cop. I know you have a warrant. Larry told me on the phone that I'm arrested, that's enough. I'm here in front you. I'm your prisoner, okay. Let's stand here nice and easy and have a drink. This is a private club, my club, so act civilized."

"That's your headache, Riley."

Jimmy started to burn, his face got red. Larry put his arm around Jimmy and said, "Take it easy, Herbie. Jimmy's a nice guy. There's no trouble with him. Relax."

Herbie Buckholz muttered something in a low voice, probably unintelligible.

Jimmy just looked at him, decided to compromise for once, not fly off the handle. "Look, it's after five o'clock and I have a date to meet my wife at Joe and Rose's uptown on Third Avenue. I would appreciate it very much if you drive me up to meet her and I could break the bad news to her over a drink. I'd like to also buy you guys dinner, it's a great restaurant. What do you say?"

Calabrese and young Furash looked at Buckholz. He was Helfand's man, he was calling the shots. Buckholz looked dubious, not quite sure what to say. He finally said, "I'll have to call Mr. Helfand to get the okay. He's in the office waiting to hear if we picked you up. Can I use the phone here?"

"Sure, Herb, right here. Here's my club card, just give the operator the printed number on it and she'll complete your call." Very conciliatory.

"Okay, boys. I'll be right back." Like Humphrey Bogart.

Buckholz went to the phone and Jimmy turned to Larry and the young cop, Furash. "Where did Helfand get this guy, Larry? Out of the fucking zoo?"

"Jimmy, Herbie is dedicated, loyal, and subservient. A former great Boy Scout and now a great civilian investigator. Why, he even found you at the D.A.C."

The three of them laughed, and Jimmy ordered another round

of drinks. Buckholz emerged from the phone booth. Jimmy gave
him his fresh drink and Buckholz said, "Mr. Helfand gave us the
okay. We have to book you at the East Fifty-first Street precinct
no later than nine o'clock. That should give you enough time with
your wife to break the bad news. One more thing, Riley, we have
to put you up for the night in Raymond Street jail in Brooklyn.
Tomorrow you'll be arraigned before Judge Leibowitz. He'll set
your bail. After that it's up to you."

The four of them had one more drink, then left the Downtown
A.C. and drove uptown in an unmarked police cruiser to Joe and
Rose's. It was just about six o'clock when they entered the restaurant. They went straight to the bar and ordered a round of drinks.
Freddie, the owner, came over to shake hands with Jimmy, and
Jimmy introduced him to the three D.A.'s men like they were old
friends of his. Kay arrived a few minutes later. She looked at him
uncertainly, like what the hell was he doing drinking with these
three obvious-looking cops when he had a date to take her later to
see the guy she really loved, Frank Sinatra?

Jimmy ordered a drink for Kay, and after some polite conversation he waved Freddie over and asked him to get his three companions a table in the back and to please put Kay and him in a
booth up front where they could have some privacy. As Jimmy
explained this in a low voice, Freddie looked puzzled, but nodded
his head okay. About ten minutes later he came back to the bar
and announced that the tables were ready. He directed the three
forces of law and order to their table and came back and escorted
Kay and Jimmy to a booth. When Freddie sat them down he
leaned over to Jimmy and said, "Jimmy, what the hell is going
on? Are these guys cops?"

Jimmy put a finger to his lips and said, "It's all right, Fred. I'll
explain later."

Kay and Jimmy sat opposite each other in the booth, fresh
drinks in front of them. She had on her severe, schoolteacher
look. "All right, Jim, if you can't tell Freddie, suppose you tell
me what's going on. These three men are really policemen, aren't
they?"

"You're right, hon, they are cops. At least the two good-looking guys are, Calabrese and Furash. The other guy is a civilian investigator for the D.A.'s office."

"Helfand?" Kay thought Helfand was the D.A.

"Yes, dear, Mr. Julie Helfand. I might as well break the news as long as you're sitting down. Kay, I got indicted by the grand jury in Brooklyn. These three guys had a warrant for my arrest. They picked me up at the D.A.C. late this afternoon and were nice enough to bring me up here when I told them you were on your way in to meet me."

"Oh, Jim, please, you're not indicted? Don't say that." Her face got white under her tan, tears popped into her eyes.

"Now for Christ's sake, Kay, no tears, please. Look, it's a horseshit thing. There's no way they'll ever convict me, I swear. I'll be okay, so please, don't worry about me. There's one more thing. I hate to tell you this, but I have to leave you after we finish dinner. I can't take you to see Frank Sinatra tonight. These three cops are booking me in the East Fifty-first Street precinct, and after that I'll have to spend tonight in jail."

"In jail? What for?"

"I told you, hon, I'm *indicted*. It's the procedure. I have to be arraigned in County Court in Brooklyn tomorrow before Judge Leibowitz. This is all a planned maneuver to get the D.A.'s office a big spread in tomorrow's newspapers. You can bet Helfand will have alerted fifty reporters to greet me in the station house."

"Oh, my God. Jim, are we going to start all over again with the papers. God, the poor two kids in school. I thought we were all finished with this rotten nonsense."

"So did I, kid, but those guys in Brooklyn had other ideas. Now, come on, cheer up. You were always game, let's have a big smile and I'll buy you another drink. That's the girl. After we finish our dinner, you stay here for a while. I'll tell Freddie to call you a limousine to take you home. Under no circumstances do I want you to take the train back to Connecticut. I'll be home tomorrow afternoon. Danny Sachs has Al Newman, the bondsman, on the alert to bail me out. If all goes well I should be out by noon and on my way home. Now, that doesn't sound too bad, does it?"

"Are you sure? You make it sound so simple, but I'm afraid."

"Kay, there's nothing to be afraid of, honestly. I'll be fine. And I'll be home in time for dinner. I promise."

Jimmy gradually calmed Kay, and the tears stopped flowing. About eight fifteen, after the condemned man and his consort ate a hearty meal, Jimmy called Freddie over to the table and explained his dilemma. Freddie was shocked to hear the bad news, but promised that he and his wife Renee would sit with Kay for a while and later call a car and chauffeur to drive her back to Connecticut.

Jimmy rose, leaned across to kiss Kay goodbye, and waved to the three D.A.'s men at the rear table. Time to go, boys. Let's get the show on the road.

In about ten minutes they drove up in front of the East 51st Street station house and got out of the car. As Jimmy had predicted, there was a swarm of reporters and photographers awaiting their arrival. He walked up the station-house steps flanked by Larry Calabrese and Herb Buckholz, who was mugging like he was doing a screen test. It seemed like a million questions were shot at him, and another million flashbulbs popped in his face. But Jimmy held his head high, smiled, not saying a word. They took him in front of the desk lieutenant and booked him. After they had his pedigree, they led him upstairs to the detective squad room to fingerprint him.

Jimmy was good friends with most of the Seventeenth Squad detectives. His old nightclub was located within the precinct and the team on night duty had almost never failed to stop by and have a drink. One after the other they came up to shake hands with him and wish him luck. They looked at Buckholz, who was bossing the operation, like he was a piece of dogshit.

The booking process over, Jimmy again braved a crowd of newsmen as the three D.A.'s men hustled him into the car to drive him across the bridge to Brooklyn and Raymond Street jail. The drive took about an hour, and very little was said on the trip. Jimmy sat in the back of the car with young Furash and they talked a bit about the Dodgers' pennant chances, but the talk soon trailed off into silence. The young cop respected his feelings and made no attempt to continue the conversation.

The car pulled up in front of the dreaded jail in downtown

Brooklyn, and Jimmy was soon admitted. He was exhausted, dog-tired from the strain of the last few days. He shook hands goodbye with Larry and young Furash, thanked them for their courtesy, and pointedly ignored Buckholz, who kept glancing at him with a superior smile on his oafish kisser.

Alone for a minute, Jimmy looked around. So this was Raymond Street, Brooklyn's answer to Devil's Island. A young guard appeared and very politely led him to a single cell on the ground floor. The ceiling light was blazing overhead, but he carefully folded his clothes, stripped down to his shorts, pulled an old army-type blanket over him, and immediately fell into a deep sleep.

A guard woke him up at seven o'clock in the morning as he shoved a tray into his cell containing cereal, bread, and coffee. The guard was very pleasant and considerate, and as Jimmy was finishing his breakfast he tossed a copy of the *Daily News* into his cell and said, "You're going to make some convict, Riley. You slept like you were at the Waldorf. Here, read all about yourself in the paper."

Jimmy grinned at him and thanked him. Jesus, he really had slept well. He felt great. He opened the *News*. The publicity-hungry D.A.'s office had really done a number on him. His picture was on the front page showing him walking up the station-house steps with the three D.A.'s men. The caption above announcing his arrest was in bold headlines. The inside pages gave an account of the chain of events that led to his eventual arrest. All the sensational disclosures and highlights of his grand jury testimony were rehashed in lurid detail. The ill-fated Chicago airplane trip was pictured as nothing less than a Roman holiday, with Harry Gross as the lascivious Nero hosting a three-day debauch. Jimmy couldn't help smiling and shaking his head as he read the account of his arrest. These D.A. guys were real pros, they really knew how to do a job on you.

About eight thirty the nice-guy guard asked Jimmy if he wanted to have a shave before he went to court and led him through a long corridor to the prison barbershop. The inmate barber gave him a nice close shave. While he was working on him Jimmy smiled, thinking he was glad this guy shaving around his Adam's apple with a stiletto-sharp straight razor never ran a bookie joint or a numbers bank he busted.

Buckholz and another young cop picked Jimmy up at the jail about nine thirty. They signed him out and were about to leave the prison when Buckholz took a pair of handcuffs out of his back pocket, told Jimmy to hold his wrists out, and snapped the cuffs on them.

Jimmy's easy good humor of the morning vanished. Could you believe a shithead like this? "What kind of shit is this, Herbie? What the hell goes with you? Do you think for a minute I'm going to try to overpower you and escape? Take these fucking things off."

"Too fucking bad Riley. This is the D.A.'s orders, and I work for the D.A. The cuffs stay on."

"I've met some cunts in my life, Herb, but you take the cake. You're no fucking good."

"That's enough of your shit, Riley. Let's go."

They got into the car parked outside the jail and entered the Criminal Court Building about ten minutes later. As he expected, there was another crowd of reporters and photographers on hand to meet them. Jimmy was embarrassed by the handcuffs on his wrists, but kept a smile on his face and tried to act calm and composed throughout the long press-besieged walk from the courthouse entrance to the elevator leading to Leibowitz's courtroom.

The journey finally ended in an anteroom off the main courtroom where Helfand and Koota were waiting. Helfand nodded his head in the direction of Jimmy's handcuffed wrists, and Buckholz took a key out of his coat pocket and unlocked them. He dismissed Buckholz and the young cop and said, "How are you, Riley? We meet once more." Nice friendly tone, very cordial.

Jimmy rubbed his wrists. "That's right, Mr. Helfand, and I notice you staged it real low key, like I was a cross between Al Capone and Jimmy Cagney."

Helfand laughed. "You brought all this grief on yourself, Riley. You asked for it, and we'll accommodate you. And I see you haven't lost that smart tongue of yours. When will you get over being a fresh guy?"

Jimmy smiled. Stay cool, these suckers have you right by your Irish balls. "I always let my prisoners make a phone call, Mr. Helfand. I saw it done in a gangster movie once and I thought it was a good idea. Now, do you think I can make a phone call, Mr. Helfand?"

Helfand smiled again. "Are you thinking of calling your lawyer, Danny Sachs?"

"That's right, Mr. Helfand."

"He's right outside the door, Riley. I'll send for him. He reached me early this morning and came right over to Brooklyn for his most famous client."

"Thank you, Mr. Helfand, that was nice of you. Could I see him now?"

"Sure." Helfand nodded to Koota, and Koota opened the door, motioned, and Danny walked in. Jimmy was never so glad to see anyone in his life. Danny walked right over to Jimmy, winked reassuringly, and shook hands. He then shook hands with Helfand and Koota. Helfand said very politely, "Dan, before we arraign Jimmy, I have a proposal to make that might be of benefit to him. I'd like to have you bring him into Judge Leibowitz's chambers for an off-the-record talk. It'll be only you, Riley, myself, and the judge. Strictly confidential. What do you say?"

Danny said, "Julie, it's an unusual request, but I'll agree on one condition."

"What? Name it."

"I don't want Jimmy held in any unreasonable bail. If possible, I would like him released on his own recognizance with me responsible for him."

"The judge won't go for that, Dan, but I promise I'll ask for reasonable bail—say twenty-five thousand?"

"Are you serious, Julie? Five thousand is plenty."

"How about fifteen?"

"Okay, Julie. Let's go, Jim, we'll see what the great man has to say to us."

Helfand led them down the hall and they entered a small room where a court officer sat behind a desk. One look at Helfand and his companions caused him to jump to his feet. He opened a door behind his desk and said, "Mr. Helfand is here, your Honor."

"Send him in."

Judge Leibowitz was sitting behind a huge mahogany desk with his beloved black robes on. He wore his kindly yet stern headmaster's face, as if he was about to lecture an unruly pupil. The unruly pupil, James Riley, stood before him with a tight halfsmile on his lips, but murder in his heart so strong he almost became nauseous. He was light-headed with concealed rage.

"Pull a couple of chairs over near my desk, Mr. Helfand, and make Mr. Sachs and Mr. Riley comfortable," said the kindly judge.

Helfand arranged the chairs and they all sat directly in front of the Great Crusader. It was like a panel of *Meet the Press,* with big Sam the moderator. He cleared his throat and said, "Riley, whether you know it or not, we have you dead to right on this indictment." He held up his hand as Danny started to speak. "Please, Mr. Sachs, this is an informal conference, strictly off the record. I just want to impress some plain facts on our young friend here. Riley, we have definite information that you were the bag man for the chief inspector's office and the higher-ups in The Job. You were a big fish, young man, but the bigger fish got away. We know you can identify him and many other big fish. You're not a witness in the grand jury anymore, where you were evasive and refused to incriminate anybody, you're *indicted.* You face five years in prison. *Five years,* do you hear me? I know that you have a nice wife and family, and are a product of a fine mother and father. We don't want to send you away for five years, we want the Big Fish and the ones around the Big Fish."

All through this stirring speech Leibowitz had looked dead straight into Jimmy's eyes. He stopped speaking, and the large room was hushed for a minute, everyone's gaze on Jimmy.

"Can I ask you something, your Honor?"

"Go ahead. Like I said, this is strictly informal."

"Would I be correct in assuming the Big Fish you keep referring to is our ex-mayor, William O'Dwyer?"

Leibowitz flushed a little. "I'd say so."

"Then why do you and the D.A.'s office keep beating around the bush by anonymously referring to the Big Fish? Why not come out in the open and say Bill O'Dwyer, he's our target?"

"We have our reasons."

"Is it that he has diplomatic immunity as ambassador to Mexico?"

"That's not the reason."

"Then why not subpoena him and get it over with?"

"Maybe that's why we have you here."

"Well, if it matters at all, your Honor, and I'm being sincere, I never gave a quarter to Bill O'Dwyer, or Jim Moran, or anyone connected to the mayor's office. And again, sincerely, your Honor, neither did Harry Gross."

"What do you mean by that?"

"Exactly what I said. Gross never gave O'Dwyer or Moran a penny. He never knew either one of them personally. He lied about them the same way he lied about a hundred other things. I have no reason to protect O'Dwyer or Moran. Mr. Helfand knows the story better than I do. They greased the skids under me right out of The Job. Mr. Helfand knows that's the truth. I'd be crazy to protect them at the possible cost of my liberty, but I won't lie about them to save myself."

"What about the other people in high places? You know who I mean. Would you protect them?"

"Your Honor, no offense, but here we go again. Give me a little time to collect myself." Jimmy turned to Danny and said, "Dan, I had a rough night, can't we end this now?" He turned back to Leibowitz and said, "Again, your Honor, no offense, but it's been a long twenty-four hours. I'll be more than glad to talk again to you informally a bit later."

"All right, Riley. Just think it over. You're a fool to go to prison to protect this scum. Get in touch with me when you're ready." He turned to Helfand and said, "Suppose we get ready for his arraignment, Mr. Helfand. I'll be on the bench in fifteen minutes."

Jimmy was glad to see that Leibowitz didn't seem too displeased when they all arose. He had seemed a little gun-shy about Jimmy's pointed questions about O'Dwyer, but the tight grip he now held over Jimmy was bound to make him happy, bound to arouse his aging loins.

Jimmy was arraigned a short time later before a packed court-

room. Standing before the bench flanked by Danny Sachs and
Helfand, he listened intently as Helfand read the indictment.

Helfand kept his promise. He requested $15,000 bail, and Lei-
bowitz quickly assented.

Just as they were about to lead Jimmy out of the courtroom to
an anteroom to await the bail bond to be arranged, good old Sam
couldn't resist a last juicy barb for the benefit of the press. It was
a thinly veiled hint that indicated some mysterious information he
possessed about the archvillain, Jimmy Riley.

"Now, I'm warning you, Riley, before you post bond, make
sure you are here when the district attorney requests your presence. No trips on the banana boat out of the country, and you
know what I mean by the banana boat. You got that? No banana
boats." With that, he quickly left the bench for the sanctity of his
chambers.

The courtroom buzzed.

Jimmy flushed with anger. That rotten sonofabitch, he was referring to a dead legitimate deal Jimmy had had with two Italian
friends of his from East Harlem. They both were tough guys, but
great pals of his. The three of them had bought a refrigerated
trawler and had it under contract to haul bananas from Central
America. They did pretty good and they finally bought Jimmy
out, parted very friendly. Some stool pigeon had given Helfand
the story, but Jimmy had produced cancelled checks to prove the
legitimacy of the deal. Now, by innuendo, Leibowitz deliberately
planted in the minds of the reporters in the courtroom that Jimmy
was part of some clandestine smuggling ring. A cryptic warning.
It was sure to be pictured as sinister in the papers. Jimmy felt
almost helpless as he looked at Danny and Helfand, who turned
his eyes away. Well, that does it, war is declared. Fuck these
Brooklyn bastards. Before I knuckle down to them they'll have to
kill me.

Bail was quickly arranged by Jimmy's pal of many years, Al
Newman. The spring air felt wonderful as he walked with Danny
to a nearby restaurant. They no sooner were seated when several
friends of Jimmy's—a couple of cops, several lawyers, and one
high-ranking judge—came over to his table, shook hands with
him, and wished him luck. The first couple of drinks and the

warm welcome he received soon had Jimmy in a lot better mood. He and Danny discussed Leibowitz's antics and soon both of them were laughing.

"Jimmy," Danny said, "let me explain our present problem, the specifics of your indictment. Jim, in my opinion, legally, it's a real hunk of shit. I mean that honestly. If we could ever expect a fair shake over here in Brooklyn, it would be tossed out before trial. It would be a piece of cake to beat. I have to compliment you, you answered the questions in the grand jury beautifully, just like we drilled it into your thick Irish head. The testimony reads that you admitted you were on the trip but you weren't positive who was with you beside Gross and Vogel. You further said you weren't sure who was on the plane besides them, that there were a number of people. Yes, there were others, but you only were sure about Gross and Vogel, that you three attended the fight together. You also stressed the time element, the lapse of three years, to explain your faulty recollection. The point of law is that you didn't withhold anything willfully, which is perjury, you just didn't recollect. Helfand never prodded your memory with certain names, never pinpointed anyone special for you to deny their presence on the plane. He just accepted what you said, never asked you more than five or six questions about the entire plane trip. Jimmy, you should never have been indicted on something as slender as this, it is obviously sheer vindictiveness."

Jimmy laughed, a little relieved. "Okay, Dan. Can I go now, you just acquitted me."

"I wish you could, Jim, but I honestly can't see how this indictment can stand up. I have one suggestion I want you to think about. We won't need John here. In fact, he called me and said he would rather not come down, he can't spare the time. I want to bring in another lawyer, Eddie Levine, the former head of the Appeals Bureau when O'Dwyer was the D.A. here in Brooklyn. He's pretty expensive, but he's a crackerjack on constitutional law and appeals work. Furthermore, he's a nice guy and completely trustworthy. What do you think?"

"Danny, it's costing me all kinds of money being out of action waiting for the ax to fall. What the hell's the difference if it costs a few more bucks and I beat the case. At least I'll be finally finished with these vultures and able to go back in business again and start earning money."

"Okay, good, Jim. We'll make a date for lunch next week with Eddie Levine. Now remember you're out on bail. Get your ass back to Connecticut and stay out of New York until you go to trial."

The next week Jimmy met Danny for lunch and he brought along Eddie Levine. It was love at first sight. The three of them shared one common emotion, they all despised Leibowitz. Over a couple of drinks and lunch Eddie regaled them with stories about Leibowitz that bordered on the incredible. He told a particular one of how he made Leibowitz back down in abject fright. Eddie was to defend a couple of guys in a college basketball scandal—a real headline maker. In his ranting and raving Leibowitz went far across the borderline of pre-trial prejudice. He recognized this but did not want to be removed as trial judge and lose the resultant publicity. He proceeded to alter the minutes of the case, to doctor them to remove the inflammatory segments. Eddie brought in a handwriting specialist and caught Leibowitz red-handed, a criminal act. Leibowitz backed off, removed himself as trial judge, tacitly admitting his guilt, indeed his crime. But such was his clout in Brooklyn, so in awe or fear of him were his peers, that the charge simply faded away. He never even received a slap on the wrist.

Eddie was a contemporary of Leibowitz and had intimate knowledge of where the skeletons were buried during Leibowitz's career as a lawyer, including the almost fatal slip when he was indicted and barely escaped prison. Jimmy left the two lawyers with renewed confidence in his chances of acquittal, as well as quite a bit less in his cash reserve.

The trial date was set for the early part of summer, only five weeks away. Eddie submitted several motions to have the indictment dismissed before trial as having no substance, but they were all denied.

About two weeks before the trial the three of them had a conference in Danny's office. They kicked around a few points of law and Eddie said, "You know, Dan, I'm a little worried. I was sure Jim would never be brought to trial on such a flimsy indictment."

"I agree, Ed. It has me worried too. One more thing, the D.A.'s office called me again and asked if Jimmy had any intention of cooperating with them. I did just as Jimmy instructed me to do. I told them that he felt there was nothing he could add to his previous grand jury testimony. We maintain that he is perfectly innocent, period."

"Good, Dan. Have you considered a motion for a change of venue—to some place upstate, or way out on Long Island?"

"Certainly I have, Eddie. As venomous as Leibowitz has been to Jim, it would appear on the surface to be easy to get. He'd be sure to get a better break from an outside, impartial judge. But these Brooklyn judges stick together like glue, even if most of them have no use for Leibowitz."

"You're telling me? The motions I submitted were based on solid points of law. The indictment was pure horseshit, but I doubt that they even studied my motions. They just peremptorily denied them."

"I read them, Ed. The arguments were excellent. You're probably right about the judges."

"Dan, I have a better idea. See what you think of it. Suppose we go on trial before Leibowitz as planned. He hates Jimmy's guts, makes no secret of it. Sooner or later, knowing in his heart the indictment is weak, he's going to reach out, step on his own cock—he'll unload on Jim somewhere along the trial with conduct so prejudicial that even if Jimmy is found guilty the verdict is bound to be reversed. The appeals judges upstate are a different breed of cat. Not only will they see the indictment as inadequate, but whatever comments prejudicial to Jimmy's rights big Sam is sure to give us. I feel we could get a complete reversal."

Jimmy sat listening to his two lawyers quietly, but very intently. Through his years of experience he was used to lawyers like Ed and Danny. Discussing his fate like two doctors trying to figure where to start cutting a guy they just anesthetized. He suppressed a grin. Don't ask my opinion. I'm only the guy who's going to rot in jail if your well-laid plans go awry. The best laid plans often go astray—but the lawyers live for another day. Back to the barristers.

"Eddie, that sounds like a helluva good idea. You're right. Leibowitz has been reversed several times upstate. Sooner or later he won't be able to resist, he'll throw a couple of zingers into Jimmy that will annihilate the trial record. The Court of Appeals won't believe it. What do you say, Jim? Sound good to you?"

"Me?" Jimmy laughed. "I thought you two guys forgot about me." They both laughed. "Listen, like I've repeated to you guys a half dozen times, I'm in your hands. Like the priest says when you get married—for better or for worse. Dan, I'll do whatever you and Eddie decide."

"Good. Ed will let the trial date stand as scheduled. Don't worry, Jim. It won't be easy, but eventually we should be able to beat this indictment."

The trial day arrived. A warm, lovely summer day in Brooklyn. Jimmy came in from Connecticut early and arrived at the courthouse a little before nine. A few reporters were already there and attempted to ask him a few questions, but he brushed them off politely, hoped they understood, he had nothing to say. A couple of them shook his hand, wished him luck. A short time later Dan and Eddie arrived.

The three of them took the elevator to the courtroom floor and entered Helfand's office. Helfand and Jimmy's two lawyers shook hands heartily, like opposing football captains just before the first-half kickoff. Jimmy stood to one side, silently. Helfand gave him a slight nod of recognition. Jimmy nodded back, surveying the friendly scene. Well, the game starts soon and these jolly players are only going to use one football—me.

He watched while the opposing captains chatted away like the impending duel was far from a critical one. The whistle blew, get ready. A court clerk stuck his head inside the door and said that the judge was ready, would be on the bench in ten minutes.

The courtroom was filled as the principals walked in. The defendant's table was about twenty feet to the right, below the bench. Jimmy sat in the middle, Danny and Eddie on either side of him. Helfand, Koota, and a young assistant were at a table just to the left of them.

The bailiff called the court to order, the Honorable Samuel Leibowitz strode to the bench. He rapped his gavel to silence the buzz his majestic entrance into the courtroom invariably caused. He stared balefully down at Jimmy. Jimmy stared right back, locked his eyes into Leibowitz's until the judge turned away to the events at hand. Jimmy looked Leibowitz over, recognizing the "Godlike" look he had no doubt practiced before the mirror that morning. Once again, something came into his mind that he had read about the judge. Sam was being interviewed for a magazine article, when, with all the innate modesty at his command, he said to the writer, "Of all human functions, there is but one God-like, to judge." Ethereal, omniscient, somber—yes, Godlike. What better look to wear when judging a disciple of the Devil like Jimmy Riley? We'll see you in hell, you scheming, corrupt, arrogant, lying Irish sonofabitch.

The morning wore on as the tedious process of jury selection seemed endless. Jimmy sat there taking it all in. Danny and Eddie issued sharp challenges to the prospective jurors as they were led in single file, one after the other. He watched Helfand as he cocked his head in the odd way Jimmy remembered from his bouts with him in the grand jury. He listened as Leibowitz admonished prospective jurors that they were not to prejudge Riley, not to be influenced by media publicity generated by the Gross case. This was the quintessence of unadulterated, hypocritical bullshit. After dismembering what ever rights Jimmy ever had, here he was sanctimoniously presenting a façade of protecting them. Leibowitz and the D.A.'s office had made sure every man, woman, and child who could read knew of the liaison between Harry Gross and Jimmy Riley. They had blown up every nuance of testimony—truth, half-truth, or outrageous lie—to the extreme degree necessary to generate the most sensational copy.

Lunch recess mercifully came. The afternoon session resumed an hour later, and the jury was finally chosen. All male. Jimmy could not discern a kind face. They all looked like relatives of Leibowitz—sober, disapproving faces. Not one woman. Were Leibowitz and Helfand afraid that the winsome Gaelic charm of Jimmy Riley might perhaps beguile a frustrated housewife or lonely secretary to forgive him his sins? Vote for acquittal? Ah, you cruel world.

The court broke for the day. The jury was ordered sequestered for the duration of the trial. Full speed ahead tomorrow.

Danny was quiet as Jimmy drove him to New York. He said little, except that he was satisfied with the jury. Their argument was one of strict law. You answered hundreds of questions truthfully for fifteen hours. Why send you to prison because of one question, where at the very most you equivocated, did not lie?

Danny's position made sense. After he left Danny off in New York, Jimmy drove back to Connecticut with a lighter heart than he had had in weeks. When he reached home he assured Kay that there wasn't a thing in the world to worry about, everything was going fine. He had a couple of drinks with her, a good dinner, and took a long walk along his favorite trail. He went to bed early with a good book.

He had arranged to meet Danny early in his office, so the next morning he took the six-fifteen train and was in Grand Central Terminal an hour later. He had some juice and coffee and was in Danny's office before eight. After they had gone over a couple of things, they left the office and took a taxi to Brooklyn. On the way Danny again asked Jimmy whether he felt like taking the witness stand in his own defense. He warned him that he and Eddie felt that Helfand couldn't wait for just that—to get at Jimmy. He has something up his sleeve, I can tell by talking to him. It would be like opening a Pandora's box. A can of worms. Jimmy agreed. He would not take the witness stand.

The trial started promptly at ten o'clock. The courtroom was packed. Julie Helfand opened for the people with his usual panache—smooth, well-modulated voice, convincing finger extended as he emphasized his points. He was good, no doubt about it, Jimmy thought. Too bad he was such a vindictive prick.

Julie finished, sat down easily, and threw his head back, like a matinee idol waiting for the applause to erupt. Danny Sachs took the floor. Immaculate, scholarly, tortoiseshell glasses, quiet, easy voice. Jimmy was proud of him. Dan said there wouldn't be much of a defense, it wasn't necessary. Riley did not commit a crime. He carefully defined the crime of perjury, read the portions

of the grand jury minutes pertinent to the alleged lie, and insisted
that to the best of his recollection Mr. Riley had told the truth.
The plane trip had taken place more than three years prior to the
time he was asked the question concerning it. He was never presented with names to jog his memory, the few questions were
almost cursory ones. Why should Mr. Riley have lied about one
trip when he answered hundreds of questions truthfully? That was
it, short and sweet.

It sounded very logical to Jimmy. At least *he* believed Danny,
he hoped the jury would. Danny came back to the table and joined
Jimmy and Eddie. Jimmy gripped Danny's hand under the table.
You did fine, Dan.

The first witness for the state took the stand, Max Bresloff. He
looked nervous as a cat on a shaky tree with two doberman
pinschers stalking below. He caught Jimmy's eye briefly, flushed
beet red, and quickly averted his face. He looked hopefully at his
new friend, Julie Helfand, who was saving him from doing time
in the slammer at the sacrifice of his manhood. The bright crim-
son flush left Bresloff's sallow cheeks as he recited his story of
the Chicago trip. He named several other guys on the plane, em-
bellished a few highlights of the trip, things Jimmy didn't remember.

It never fails, Jimmy thought, as he listened to Bresloff. When
the law turns a guy into a stool pigeon, invariably his imagination
runs wild. He invents situations to please his benefactors. The
stool pigeon syndrome. Helfand finished on a high note. He
brought out the friendship between Bresloff and Jimmy. Max had
been a real good friend, an intimate, someone who couldn't fail to
remember Jimmy being on the plane. Damon and Pythias.

Danny took over on cross-examination. He trapped Bresloff in
a couple of lies, especially about the return trip, caused him to
recant, admit Jimmy wasn't with him. But Jimmy hardly listened.
His confidence had begun to sag earlier when Bresloff was telling
Helfand what great friends they were. He knew instantly that this
was clever of Helfand and damaging to him. Jimmy shook his
head as he looked at Bresloff. He hardly knew the lying, rat
bastard.

Danny finished and Bresloff was about to leave the witness

stand. Leibowitz had been, for him, almost impassive up to this point. Smiling, sneering, shaking his head once in a while at some of the testimony. As Bresloff arose from his seat Leibowitz snarled and said in brutal tones, "Bresloff, were you one of the crooked cops on the vice squad?"

Bresloff almost dropped dead. He put his hand to his face as if to ward off a blow. What the hell kind of thing is that to say to a cooperative stool pigeon, Judge? I'm on your side, remember? He stood there mute, speechless.

"Were you?" Louder.

"Well, er, yes, your Honor."

Leibowitz then shifted his wrathful gaze from Bresloff to Jimmy Riley and thundered, "Were you one of those crooked, grafting cops, the scum on the vice squad?"

The twelve good men on the jury turned as one body and followed Leibowitz's piercing eyes turned on Jimmy. Bresloff was staring at the side of Leibowitz's head, paralyzed.

Danny stood up, outraged. "Your Honor—"

"Sit down, Counselor, I'm asking this witness a question." He switched his eyes back to Bresloff. "Answer me. Were you one of those crooked, grafting cops on the vice squad?"

Weakly, barely audible, he replied, "Yes, your Honor. I was only obeying orders." With that mealy-mouthed confession, Bresloff slunk off the witness stand like the mangy rat he was, slinking back to his hole in the garbage pile.

The rest of the day was occupied by a parade of witnesses. The first two were bookmaker friends of Jimmy's, the third a retired cop friend of Harry's, a hanger-on, errand-boy type. They all remembered being on the trip with Jimmy, not much else. They had been scooped up in the web when Bresloff started to squeal. Airline tickets and hotel reservations were simple to check. They were almost dying at having to testify against Jimmy, especially the two bookmakers. But Jimmy didn't resent what they were doing, the gun had been placed at their heads when Bresloff opened up. The state, Julie Helfand, wound up with a hotel guy from Chicago and an airline guy. Danny never cross-examined another witness after he finished with Bresloff. His defense rested on the technical definition of perjury.

Court was recessed. Trial to resume tomorrow. The jury was excused, back to the hotel where they were sequestered. Jimmy got out of his chair, about to leave with Eddie and Danny. He was dying, absolutely dying for a nice tall Cutty and water. Plenty of ice.

Leibowitz rapped his gavel for silence. He spat out his next words. "Stand still, Riley. Defendant's bail is revoked for the duration of the trial. I remand him to Raymond Street jail to spend the night until the trial resumes."

Jimmy stood dumbfounded. There goes my ice-cold Cutty and water. Eddie and Danny were equally shocked. Danny found his voice. "Your Honor, my client has appeared when—"

"That's enough, counselor." Leibowitz cut Danny off. He indicated Jimmy to a court officer. "Take him away."

The court officer came over and snapped a pair of handcuffs on Jimmy's wrists. As he was being led away, Jimmy turned to Eddie and Dan and smiled. "If it's so good in America, what the hell am I doing in Russia? See you tomorrow."

Jimmy was led down a long corridor of the courthouse and placed in a large holding cell which was already occupied by about a dozen prisoners. It was about five o'clock when the trial was halted for the day, but still the cell seemed like an oven after the cool courtroom he had just left. A short time later all the cell occupants were marched into a large prison van and transported back to Raymond Street jail. No more police cruisers, personal escorts, VIP treatment. Jimmy Riley was now just another prisoner, another member of the motley crew.

When the prison van reached the jail he was herded out with the other guys, searched, relieved of his valuables, and led to the same ground-floor cell where he spent the first night he was arrested. A huge 500-watt bulb blazed overhead, and the summer heat made the tiny cell like a sweatbox. The air was stifling, the stink overwhelming, a ripe mixture of piss, shit, and corruption.

Jimmy shook his head and smiled as he stripped down to this shorts, stretched out on the narrow cot, and lay his head back on the bulky rubber pillow. There's no place like home. And home this sewer was destined to be for the next few months of his life while Leibowitz sipped his pre-dinner cocktails on the breezy terrace of his oceanside mansion patiently waiting to catch the Big Fish.

The same nice-guy guard was on duty who had taken care of Jimmy on his previous overnight stay, and they greeted each other warmly. He fetched Jimmy an evening newspaper, a glass of milk, and a piece of apple pie. A couple of hours later he stopped by and introduced himself. He said, "Jimmy, I have a lot of friends from my neighborhood in South Brooklyn who know you well, and they speak good of you. My name is Larry Cuccia. There's not a helluva lot I can do for you in here, but whatever is possible I'll do. Most of the hacks are nice guys and you'll be treated good."

"Thanks, Larry, that's nice of you. But I hope I won't be a guest for very long."

"What the hell happened? I thought your trial was still on. No?"

"My old pal Leibowitz revoked my bail for the duration of the trial. We go to the jury tomorrow, and from what I can sense, you'd better not rent my room here to another guy. I can feel it in my bones that I'm already convicted, so I'll see you tomorrow if you're on duty."

"I'm on all week from four to midnight, so I'll be here. Anyway, I wish you luck, Jim. With Leibowitz you'll need it."

"Thanks, Larry. Can I ask you a question?"

"Sure, Jim, go ahead, anything."

"First of all, what causes this murderous stink in here?"

Larry laughed. "You won't even notice it in a couple of weeks, Jim. I'm so used to it that when I hit real fresh air sometimes, like on the beach or the golf course, I even miss the smell. We get drunks, drug addicts, guys who lose control of their bowels, piss in their clothes. It's murder."

Jimmy laughed. "You'll live to be a hundred, Larry. One more question. I know for years they've been talking about condemning this goddam joint. When the hell was it built?"

"I'm going to give you a little bit of history all New Yorkers, especially Brooklynites, oughta be proud about. This sinkhole, this shithouse, was built by the British Army in 1756. Would you believe that, 1756? It was built as a jail for American colonists who rebelled against the English Crown. You know, revolutionaries. They hung a couple of hundred guys here in the old days, right out in the courtyard. They modernized it two or three times, you know, put in flush toilets, electricity, shit like that. But the original buildings—granite walls, stone floors, dungeons—still remain from when the British ruled America."

"How about that, walio? Here I sit, another Irishman winding up a prisoner of the British." They both roared laughing. "One last thing, Larry. This fucking light overhead, when does it go off?"

"Never. It stays on day and night, and I can't help you there, Jim. That's strict orders from the top. You're on the ground-floor tier of Cell Block A. Your neighbors are stool pigeons, potential stool pigeons, material witnesses, and guys whose balls they'd like to break—which means you. You'll get used to it. And there's one good thing about the light being on all night, it scares the rats away from your cell. In case one comes in your cell for a visit, keep a newspaper folded real tight and whack the little son-ofabitch with it. He'll tell his pals and they won't bother you anymore."

"Thanks, Larry, you're a sweetheart. Well, I'm tired. I think these piss fumes are making me sleepy, so I'll see you tomorrow. If you see any rats when you make your rounds, say hello for me."

The next morning they hustled Jimmy and another small corps of guys into a prison van and transported them to Criminal Court. A while later he was unhandcuffed and left into a room where Danny and Eddie were waiting. He badly needed a shave and knew that he smelled worse than a goat. He had washed the best he could in the cell sink, but the crowded van had been like the equator and sweat poured out of him.

They both looked at him like they were going to burst into tears. He raised his hand and said, "Please, no hugs, no kisses, or I'll asphyxiate you stone dead. God knows, I need my lawyers."

They both laughed, lifting the tension. They asked Jimmy about the jail conditions, but he shrugged it off. Before they really had a chance to speak, they were summoned to the courtroom. Jimmy took his place at the defendant's table between Dan and Eddie. Always conscious of his appearance, he knew he looked awful, smelled rank. Christ, Jean Valjean looked better than me after a tough day at the oars.

The jurors came out of an adjoining room and took their places in the jury box. The twelve good men inspected Jimmy closely, and as he looked up at their faces he knew they agreed with his low opinion of his sad physical appearance. Like he just emerged from the drunk tank. He even imagined he detected a slight sniff or two as they glanced in his direction. Helfand, Koota, and a young assistant came out. Dan and Eddie stood up and they shook hands all around. What great pals lawyers always seemed to be. They probably had their own secret password—like the Masons or the Knights of Columbus. Helfand looked at Jimmy sitting there, shook his head as if to say "you poor, dumb sucker."

The courtroom was now almost filled with curious spectators. The Great Crusader was announced by the bailiff, and again he drew an excited buzz of noise as he solemnly strode to the bench in his black robes. Today was his day of days, surely the last day of the trial. His always learned, always paternal charge to the jury was scheduled to be the highlight. He wore his number three look today, the look of severe retribution awaiting the smelly, unshaven enemy of the people he briefly trained his stony gaze on. He rapped his gavel smartly, the courtroom hushed, proceedings began.

Helfand rose and asked permission to bring Max Bresloff back to the stand. His request was speedily granted.

Something's up, it looks like they already had a dress rehearsal.

Bresloff took the stand. His face was dead white. He looked scared shitless. The court clerk swore him in. Helfand stood there with a half smile on his lips. He turned back to Leibowitz and nodded. In walked a court officer with Harry Gross. He stood no farther than three feet from the defendant's table. He had on prison-issue grays. He looked thinner, a whole lot thinner, and pale, sad-looking.

Helfand said in a dramatic voice, "Mr. Bresloff, is this the man who paid the bills for the trip, as you testified previously?"

"It is."

"What's his name?"

The whole fucking world knew his name, for Christ's sake. Helfand, what an actor he was.

"Harry Gross," said Bresloff.

"That's all."

Leibowitz said, "Any questions, Mr. Sachs?"

"No, your Honor."

The court officer came up to Harry to lead him out. Harry turned, looked directly at Jimmy, and winked. Jimmy stared ahead like he never saw him before, but he didn't miss the wink. That fuck Harry has to be bananas.

Both sides rested their case. Eddie stood up and made a motion for dismissal of the indictment on the grounds that the state did not prove a prima facie case. Leibowitz denied it almost as soon as Eddie uttered the last word. Danny addressed the jury and repeatedly hammered home the weak points of the indictment. According to law a crime was not committed. He finished and sat down.

His Honor, Justice Samuel S. Leibowitz, cleared his throat, it was his turn onstage. He smiled like a loving parent at his twelve disciples and began delivering his charge to the jury. He spoke softly, yet resonantly, as he emphasized points of law and highlights of the witnesses' testimony. He elucidated for about fifteen minutes as the courtroom hung on his every word. His rhetoric was splendid.

His voice then picked up, became strident, almost brutal. He turned to Jimmy in the defendant's chair—a grimy ad for a popular shaving cream or a strong antiperspirant, scummy-looking— pointed his finger at him, and said, "Gentlemen of the jury, let us assume he confessed that he was a partner of Gross, that he took bribes from Gross, that he was his pal, his buddy. That he got money from Gross and plane trips and things."

Danny was making guttural noises as he said this. Jimmy felt Eddie's hand reach across under the table to squeeze Danny's arm. As Leibowitz turned back to the jury Eddie whispered, "Keep quiet, Dan. Let him rave."

Leibowitz continued, "Let us assume for sake of argument that all this is so. When Riley testified before the grand jury and did *not* sign a waiver of immunity, the grand jury could not prosecute him, he could not be indicted. He was *free*. He was immune from prosecution even though he gave evidence against himself. That is the *law*. Once they compelled him to testify without signing a waiver of immunity in cases of bribery and gambling and such offenses, Riley was free as a bird. He could not be prosecuted if he told the truth." Leibowitz punctuated the last sentence with a glare at Jimmy. He then seemed to collect himself and gentle his voice. He talked a few minutes more, and at last mercifully ended his charge.

The jury retired to ponder the fate of Jimmy Riley. Eddie arose and for the court record made an objection to the part of Leibowitz's charge concerning the assumed accusations against Jimmy. Helfand's face was beet red. He seemed distressed but remained silent. Sam triumphantly marched off the bench, another theatrical masterpiece added to his bag of vaudeville tricks.

Danny, Eddie, and Jimmy retired to a small adjacent room and were served coffee by a D.A.'s aide. Jimmy couldn't miss the look on Eddie's face. It was shining in sheer jubilation. The room cleared and they were finally alone. Eddie said in a low voice. "Dan, Jim, I knew it had to happen. Leibowitz had to step on his cock like he always does, only this time he was completely out of line. Did you see the look on the faces of Helfand and Koota? There's no way he can bring up Jimmy's failure to sign a waiver of immunity in his jury charge. That's an unqualified constitutional privilege of an American citizen. What a tirade. I can't believe my own ears. He points his finger directly at Jimmy and starts the 'let us assume' bullshit. He uses 'let us assume' to accuse Jimmy of every crime in the world and then tells the jury he got away with it because he wouldn't waive immunity. Now he says, as he points his finger at Jimmy, make sure you convict him of perjury. Oh, my God."

Jimmy was listening carefully. "Look, you guys make it sound all well and good, but what about the jury verdict? You can tell just by looking at me and smelling me that rathole Raymond Street isn't exactly the St. Regis Hotel. I think I'm a sure pop to be convicted. What do you guys think?"

They both were quiet, a little uncomfortable, looked at each other. Danny said, "Jimmy, we took a calculated risk, and like Eddie just explained, we're almost positive we'll get a reversal. The faulty indictment should be enough, but now this diatribe by Leibowitz ices the cake."

"Okay, Dan, then give me an honest answer. How long will this reversal take?"

"At the outside, a year."

"You're kidding. A year? Then for Christ's sake, get me up-state to Sing Sing as soon as you can. Get me out of that shithole in Brooklyn."

"You know we'll do our best, Jim. But honestly, you'd better prepare yourself to stay in Raymond Street for three or four months."

"Three or four months? Why?" Incredulously.

"For the simple reason that they're going to break your balls, do a number on you to try to force you to cooperate."

"Danny, we went all over this with Helfand and Leibowitz when I was first arrested. They're both full of shit. They'll never subpoena Bill O'Dwyer, and how much more time do they expect Jim Moran to get? Christ, haven't they been smeared enough?"

Eddie spoke up. "Jim, I was an assistant district attorney for a long time, and there's one thing I know—keeping your name in the papers is what furthers your career. Look, Dan and I both realize you have a rocky road ahead of you. Rest assured we'll do everything possible to get you out as quickly as we can."

"I know that, Eddie. Don't misunderstand me, I'm not crying. But just thinking about a long summer in Raymond Street is a bitch. I want you guys to try to get me upstate in Sing Sing, where I can breathe fresh air and live like a human being. Okay, that's it, no more bellyaching. Maybe by some miracle I'll even get acquitted."

The miracle never happened. The jury came back in less than two hours. The ultimate, guilty of perjury, first degree. The court-room was again a cacophony of oohs and aahs from the spectators and the bustle of the reporters rushing out of their seats to phone in the good news. Leibowitz, Helfand, and Koota were all smiles, like they had just hung Hitler.

Jimmy had stood there unmoved as the foreman read the verdict. Danny Sachs and Eddie Levine took it hard, appeared more shaken than Jimmy.

Leibowitz smilingly thanked the jury, commending them for doing an outstanding service to the community, and forthwith excused the twelve good citizens of Brooklyn. The jury filed out, and Leibowitz ordered Jimmy and his lawyers to the front of the bench. He could barely conceal his high good humor. He pointed his finger and said, "You, Riley, are remanded to Raymond Street jail to await a probation report and until I see fit to sentence you. I'm sure that in one night you have already found Raymond Street a little different from the green meadows and the golf links of Connecticut. I want you to stay there awhile and think things over a little bit. Mr. McDonald, Mr. Helfand, and I will offer extreme leniency in exchange for exposing the corruption in the police department.

"You can help yourself. You can tell us more than Harry Gross. You can turn state's evidence and blow the lid off the whole sorry mess. The district attorney says that you were Harry Gross's partner. He also has information that you and Harry Gross had a fistfight shortly before the Big Trial of the corrupt policemen. We want to know everything. You'll have plenty of time in Raymond Street to think about it. Take him away."

Leibowitz then abruptly walked off the bench. Jimmy stared at his retreating back. He was tempted to scream every invective he ever learned in the streets of Brooklyn at the sadistic sonofabitch. Eddie tightened his grip on Jimmy's arm and said, "Take it easy, Jim. Our day will come." The court officer came over to handcuff him when Jimmy finished shaking hands with Dan and Eddie. Helfand and Koota came over to say a few words to Dan and Eddie.

Koota turned to Jimmy and said, "Think about what the judge said, Riley."

"Fuck you, Koota."

The court officer led him away. He didn't take him to the holding cell as expected, but stopped at a small room off the corridor. They walked in, and Jimmy was stunned. His father, Big Mike, was standing there, tears streaming down his cheeks. Jimmy couldn't hug him with handcuffs on, so he just nuzzled against him like a puppy dog and in a choked voice managed to say, "Come on, Mike. For Christ's sake, don't cry. You always told me that someday I'd wind up in jail."

Mike laughed a little through his tears. "I'm all right now, Jim. Everything will be all right pretty soon. You're a good boy, Jimmy. Take it on the chin, never give anybody up."

"You raised me, Mike, you know better. Now tell me, what the hell were you doing in court? You know I begged everybody to stay away."

"I had to see you, Jim. I can't believe what these people are doing to everybody. I can't bear the thought of you going to prison. And it's killing your mother, all she does is cry."

"Now look, Mike, we all talked it over. There's nothing I can do about it. My lawyers think the whole thing will be tossed out and it'll only be a matter of a few months, so please stop worrying."

"I promise."

"Good. Now as long as you're here you can do me a big favor. Bring me about six T-shirts and shorts to Raymond Street tomorrow. And Momma knows the closet where I have some short-sleeve shirts and light summer slacks. It would be great if you do that. It's like a steam room there, and I might have a fairly long stay. Would you please do that, Mike?"

"I'll be there tomorrow with everything."

"One more thing, Mike. No visits after tomorrow. No one, please, unless I send a message I want to see you. Okay?"

"Why? I've got plenty of time on my hands. I want to come down and visit you."

"Please, Mike. That joint would depress the Archangel Gabriel, and I don't want it depressing my family. Call Kay and tell her the same. No visits, please. So long, Mike. This officer has been kind enough. I have to go now."

"All right, son. Take care of yourself, keep your chin up. I'll see you tomorrow."

The cool clothes Mike brought the next day were a blessing, and in a few days Jimmy settled down into the routine of city prison. He had a little over four hundred dollars in his pocket when he was remanded, and that served as a bank for him. He had all the street-smarts and determined to make the best of life in this goddam hellhole. His pal, the nice-guy guard Larry Cuccia, was a godsend. He introduced him to all the other hacks on the tier, and despite the restrictions forced on him by the authorities, they treated him well.

The 500-watt bulb still blazed overhead so that, if it weren't for his wristwatch, he'd never know what time of day it was. The only windows were high overhead on the wall opposite his cell, and any glimpse of daylight was blocked out by a tall connecting building separated only by the small hangman's courtyard of Revolutionary days. Jimmy was ordered confined to his cell twenty-three hours a day. He was allowed a daily one-hour walk up and down the tier.

The food, except for the cereal, roll, and coffee at breakfast, was inedible. The hacks brought his meals to his cell since he wasn't allowed to go to the mess hall, but he soon discouraged lunch and dinner.

After about a week, when with Larry's help he had established a rapport with the other hacks, he was able to take a daily shower. This was absolute heaven even when he found himself in the communal shower at the time when the drunks were being hosed down. It unnerved him at first to see them cowering on the floor, screaming for someone to please remove the insects, mice, rats, or whatever they imagined were crawling over their bodies and sucking their blood. It was like showering in an insane asylum, and when he returned to his cell he sometimes debated whether he would swear off drinking when he got out of prison. He would smile, the decision always went in favor on continuing.

And then there were the rats. Larry the hack wasn't kidding. Jimmy was used to rats, they had been commonplace where he grew up. When he was a young kid during the Depression he lived near a vast tract of muddy land on which the government planned to build a huge low-cost housing development. Hundreds of tons of fill were poured into the tract as a base. Truckload after truckload of garbage and assorted debris were dumped, forming a mountain of rubbish. With the rubbish came the rats.

Half the Irish families on the block owned Irish terriers, a fierce strain of dog that was famous among the Irish as a ratter. Jim and his older brother John would take their Irish terrier, Paddy, down to the dump and Paddy would go to work at his chosen profession like a madman. He would scurry into a pile of rubbish, come out with a rat between his jaws, snap its neck with a crunch, and flip it about ten feet in the air. It was child's play for Paddy to nail twenty rats in one outing. Around his own house Jimmy's mother set so many rattraps it was almost as dangerous as walking through a mine field if one of the kids ever had to get up in the middle of the night to relieve himself.

A couple of weeks after he was in residence, Jimmy was propped up on his cot, deeply absorbed in a book, when he heard a rustling noise in his cell. He put the book aside to rest his eyes for a moment. He closed his eyes to soothe them, when he definitely heard a squeaking noise. It was after midnight. Outside his cell it was almost pitch dark. He slowly opened his eyes, focused them on the floor, and there he was—a dark gray, furry rat about eight inches long. Beady red eyes, ears perked out, looking like he wanted to say hello. Jimmy looked down at him and said very softly, "Hello, rat. What's your name? Max?" The rat jumped back out of the cell. Jimmy was now fascinated, a break in the monotony.

A couple of minutes passed. The rat returned with a friend. The friend rat was a bit smaller, dark brown, not quite so red-eyed—a much better-looking rat. They both stared boldly at Jimmy. He looked down at them thoughtfully. Maybe the better-looking one is his girl friend? How the hell do you tell girl rats from boy rats? He had a piece of pound cake on the table next to his cot. He reached for it very slowly, broke off about a quarter of it, and threw it toward the two rats in the corner of the cell. They dashed out like a flash.

Jimmy was intent now on this new drama. He sat propped up, still as possible, to watch the action. A couple of minutes later they came back to the cell door, sneaking, like two cat burglars casing a jewelry store. The bigger, dark gray one darted under the bars and snatched the cake up in his mouth and ran out of the cell to join his girl friend and share the wealth.

Jimmy felt tremendously pleased. He was right, the dark gray

rat was the male, the breadwinner, and he was bringing home the
bacon to share it with dearie. He almost laughed out loud as he
went back to his book. Every day you learn a little more about
life, now I can tell the difference between boy rats and girl rats.
But I was mean, I shouldn't have called the boy rat Max. No
wonder he ran away.

The district attorney's office let Jimmy sit in Raymond Street a
month before they made their first overture. Jimmy was a veteran
trouper by now, coping, adapting himself to the environment like
a grizzly bear to the polar regions. He kept a bowl of water on the
table next to his cot, and when he had read himself out and was
ready for sleep he would soak a handkerchief and cover his eyes
against the glaring overhead light. He slept like a baby. The
blood-curdling howls of the drunks, the withdrawal screams of
the drug addicts, the constant wails that pierced the endless days
and nights with a bedlam of sound rarely bothered him.

If he awoke suddenly he never struggled to go back to sleep.
The light, the omnipresent light was blazing. He would reach for
his book on the table, turn to the page he left off, and read. Six,
seven hours at a stretch. He religiously exercised two half-hour
periods a day in his cell and walked his allotted hour at a brisk
pace.

Once a week he went to the barbershop for a shave or haircut,
always in response to a message from a friendly hack that an old
friend wanted to see him. The heat was on in the streets of
Brooklyn, the judges were getting rough, and more bookmakers
and numbers guys were passing through Raymond Street on their
way to Rikers Island than bathing beauties were going to Coney
Island. The barbershop served as a place to wish each other well,
have a few laughs, and talk of the good old days.

Jimmy learned to live with the smothering heat and the acrid,
piss-laden stink. There were consolations. The daily shower was
a sweet oasis. He lived on cereal and milk and what the wagon
man brought around. Jimmy bribed him to bring him fresh fruit—
apples, oranges, pears, peaches. Larry occasionally smuggled
him in a pepper and sausage hero between the folds of a newspa-

per. By the time Larry got it to him it was soggy and cold, but Jimmy ate it like it was a prime steak at Mike Manuche's.

But through all the coping, adapting, and foraging, the one constant was the fierce, implacable hatred for Leibowitz and the D.A.'s men. He forced himself to sublimate any thoughts of them, for to think of them was to make him almost nauseous with hate. And so, Jimmy Riley's mood was one of seeming complacency, his frame of mind good when the first call to repent came.

He was reading when the hack came to his cell and said, "Jimmy, a Mr. Clark is here to see you in the warden's office." The hack was a nice guy, by now a good friend of Jimmy's.

"Who's Mr. Clark, Allie?

"He's a real important guy, Jim, the chief probation officer for the D.A.'s office. I hear he's right up the top of Leibowitz's ass."

"He is, eh? Well, Allie, no offense to you, but go back and tell that Irish fuck if he wants to see me he can come down here to the fucking Raymond Street Turkish Baths. I'll see him here, not in the warden's air-conditioned office. Then when he sweats his balls off he can go out and cool off at Leibowitz's beach house, where he can tell *him* to go fuck himself. He comes down here, I don't go up there. That's it. Okay, Allie?"

"Jimmy, I think you're wrong. Why don't you go up and see him? Give him a little con, it won't hurt. They'll only break your balls worse."

"Allie, are you serious? I'm in here almost five weeks. Look at me, for Christ's sake, I must have lost fifteen pounds. What the hell worse can happen to me than what they're already doing? Jesus, I look forward to getting a visit from those two rats every night."

Allie laughed. "You're a beauty, Jim. Okay. I'll tell him. If he wants to see you he has to come to your cell. Like the priest does in the movies when the con is going to the electric chair."

Jimmy laughed. "Don't worry, Allie, he won't come down here. He'll shit in his pants at the thought of it, like the rest of them."

That was the end of overture number one.

* * *

Another month rolled smoothly by, and the only good thing that happened in the intervening time was it began to cool off. The same old routine—day after day after day. The conditions of Jimmy's confinement were unyielding. The blinding light overhead, the meals in the cell, the hour-a-day walk along the tier, with only book after book to offer him solace. He assiduously stuck to his daily regimen, and the hacks to a man were very good to him. Any little privilege they could offer him was freely given. He blessed the daily shower, the occasional sandwich they brought to him. He forced himself to try the jail food once, but after one mouthful almost threw up. He laughed about that. It made him think that all those brave guys who went on hunger strikes in jail weren't the martyrs they appeared to be, they were just exceptionally smart guys to avoid eating this unadulterated shit.

Eddie Levine finally came with news. Jimmy's appeal was to be argued in the fall term of the appellate court, five judges on the panel. Eddie assured Jimmy that he would be home by Christmas. There was no way they could miss. They shook hands goodbye. Jimmy, not wanting to appear discouraged, left Eddie with a happy smile on his face. But deep down in his heart he had severe doubts, was very melancholy. When the hack led him back to his cell he thought he might cheer himself up and sing a chorus of "I'll Be Home for Christmas," but he choked on the words. Christmas, it was only the middle of September, Christmas was light-years away. Besides, as Jimmy lay back on his cot and reflected on the pep talk Eddie had just given him, he ruefully remembered that his lawyer wasn't quite precise as to which Christmas he meant. Bad day at Black Rock.

A month after the first overture from the district attorney's office came the second. Allie the hack was on duty again. He came to Jimmy's cell and said, "Jim, Mr. Clark, the chief probation officer, would like to see you in the warden's office. Come on, get your ass upstairs, Jimmy, and see this guy. You won't lose anything."

More out of curiosity and boredom, he decided to see Clark. Allie brought him to another hack, who led him through a series of corridors, gates, and stairs that seemed endless. The warden's office was spacious, well furnished, and air-conditioned. It was like leaving Florida and arriving in Maine within five minutes. The warden was a heavy-set, friendly guy. He introduced him to Clark, an ascetic-looking, tall, very thin Irishman.

The warden said, "I'll leave you two alone. I know you must have a lot to talk about. Before I leave, tell me, Riley, how do you feel you've been treated here?"

Jimmy smiled. "To be honest, Warden, the accommodations leave a little to be desired, but the hacks, er, excuse me, the guards and officers, have treated me courteously and I want you to know I appreciate it."

"I'm glad. Thank you, Riley. See you two later."

Clark sat in the warden's chair behind a large walnut desk. He motioned to Jimmy to sit in the chair directly in front of him. He smiled, one of those brilliant Irish fake smiles, and said, "You look fine, Riley, and I'm pleased to hear you say you've been treated well."

"I don't think you heard me correctly, Mr. Clark. I said that the officers and guards treated me well. For your benefit, and for your bosses' benefit, this fucking prison is a subhuman sewer. You and the likes of you should be ashamed of yourselves to treat men like this. For over two months now you've kept me locked up in a six-by-eight cell twenty-three hours a day. You've had a five-hundred-watt bulb shining in my eyes day and night. The food is such shit you're lucky the rats eat it. I mean the real rats running around down below, not the fucking human rats you try to make out of people."

Clark was abashed at this outburst. He attempted to be conciliatory. He half-smiled. "Come on, Riley. It's not that bad."

"It isn't? Are you serious? I wish you'd try it for a few days. Plus a couple of your pals."

"Jimmy, no prisons are any good. But you can leave here anytime you want. Right now."

"What do you mean by that?"

"Take a look out the window over there."

Jimmy got up and looked out the window next to the desk where Clark sat. It was his first look at the outside world in over two months. He was fascinated, just seeing the sky, the sun, people, traffic. He drank it all in. He had almost forgotten that there was a world out there. It was nice.

Clark stood up behind him and pointed to a car parked on the opposite side of the street. "See that car, Jimmy? Say the word, and that's your vehicle out of here. I came over here in that car. It belongs to the district attorney's office. You go back downstairs, get dressed, and we'll take a ride downtown, where Judge Leibowitz and the district attorney are waiting for us. Get everything off your chest to the judge. He's a fine man, Jimmy. You do that, and I promise he'll reduce your sentence to time served."

Jimmy looked at Clark. Another mealy-mouthed fuck from the Brooklyn court system. None of these guys would know how to make a quarter if they weren't on the public teat.

"Mr. Clark, I don't care if you take this personally or not. You happen to be associated with people whom I consider to have some type of persecution mania. I think if they thought they could get away with physical torture, they'd try it. As much as I despise Harry Gross for breaking down, now I can sympathize with him a little. You people put him in this fucking pigsty under the same conditions you're holding me. You made his bail so high it was impossible. You kept him like a caged animal for over five months and probably offered the carrot to him every few weeks, just like you're now offering me. Why? What for? For Christ's sake, the man was a bookmaker, a fucking bookmaker, not an armed robber, rapist, or murderer. You know what for? Headlines, publicity, that's what for. This bullshit about Bill O'Dwyer. Every goddam one of you worked for him or with him. You broke bread with him and drank whiskey with him. Why didn't they subpoena him when they had the chance? Don't shit Jimmy Riley, Mr. Clark, this investigation was launched to enhance all their careers. They all want to be judges."

"What's the difference, Jimmy? Everyone wants to get ahead. They want you to unfold the whole story of police corruption, tell all you know."

"Christ, is this horseshit story of police corruption intended to last another ten years? They've already smeared The Job beyond redemption. Take a look at the casualty list. Three or four guys committed suicide. Hundreds of guys, plenty of them real great cops, left The Job or were bounced out of it. A lot of the top bosses resigned and left in disgrace. A dozen guys or more are in jail or on their way to jail. And, Mr. Clark, most of this was based on sheer bullshit and innuendo."

Clark said sharply, "Now don't say that. Most of the evidence was based on fact."

"Correction, Mr Clark. Very little fact. Harry Gross was a fucking psychopathic liar, and I'm one guy who positively knows it. Now, let's level with each other. What do you expect from me? Do you people want me to add another dimension to this continuing smear? To add a little more filth for the public to eat up? You got the wrong guy, Mr. Clark. You guys broke poor Harry, and then when he realized the shit he was handing you he collapsed. Then you buried him for life, for Christ's sake. I wouldn't even sit in the same room with the people you're associated with, Mr. Clark, unless I was handcuffed and had no choice. Let them judge me, then look at their own conscience."

Clark's face got white. He bit his lower lip to keep from blowing up. After all, he was on a diplomatic mission. He stood up. "Is that your final answer?"

"It is, Mr. Clark. Go back and tell them, and I mean all of them, they haven't got Harry Gross here, they got Jimmy Riley. And I don't give a fuck if they keep me here the rest of my life. I hate all those rotten bastards so much I'd rather die before I'd go lie for them."

Jimmy stood up. He was seething, almost shaking with rage. Clark looked at him and pushed a buzzer. A hack came in. Jimmy turned without saying a word and walked out of the office with the hack beside him.

The two of them marched back down through all the myriad steps, locks, and gates without exchanging a word. When they reached his cell Jimmy thanked the hack and flopped on his cot. His head was pounding with rage and frustration. How much more of this shit will I be subjected to?

Three weeks had gone by since the tempestuous bout with Chief Probation Officer Clark, personal emissary of Judge Leibowitz. The everyday deadly routine remained the same. The au-

tumn air somehow penetrated the thick granite walls of Raymond
Street jail and even the overpowering stink lifted a little. Jimmy
still treasured the solace of his books, reading constantly. The
hacks would often stop by his cell, especially Larry, and talk
football for a while, which helped break the monotony. He would
still be summoned every few days to the barbershop to say hello
to an old gambling friend who was on his way to the city jail of
Rikers Island. This was always a pleasant interlude, with just a
touch of sadness when they shook hands goodbye.

Some guys brought bad news. Chick, good old Chick, got three
years. He was already settled in state prison. Chick was going to
be all right. The word was sent up, he was already in good hands.
It was still terrible news to bear, a long, long night for Jimmy
Riley.

A hack came to his cell early one morning and said, "Jimmy,
get dressed. Your lawyer, Mr. Sachs, is upstairs in the counsel
room."

Jimmy scrambled up, threw on pants and a shirt in a flash. He
was anxious to see Danny. First time since he was convicted.

Danny greeted Jimmy with a big hug. He looked at him real
close. Danny always had a little tic under his left eye, now it was
a rapid-fire tic.

"Christ, Jimmy, what the hell are these guys doing to you? You
look like a skeleton."

"That's the new look, Danny, the jailbird look. Seriously, considering this shithouse of a jail, everyone treats me good. I just
don't eat very much, no booze, and I do a million sit-ups and
push-ups a day."

"God, Jim, you must have lost thirty pounds at least."

"It won't hurt me, Dan. I'll put it back on. Forget how I look,
when the hell am I getting out of here?"

"Jim, I don't know whether it's good news or bad news, but
you're on for sentencing next week."

"Dan, that's the best news I've heard in months. I'm over three
months in this joint, and to be honest it's really beginning to get
on my nerves. When do I get the bad news?"

"Next Thursday."

"When did you find this out?"

"Yesterday. The D.A.'s office called and told me the date. Jimmy, they also said you refused to answer any questions for the chief probation officer. Is that right?" A worried frown crossed his face.

"Danny, they already have my entire life history from the time I took my first piss. What the hell more do they want? They sent this skinny bullshit mick here about a month ago, and he gave me the usual con about the D.A.'s car waiting outside to carry me to freedom. Even pointed it out from the window of the warden's office. All I had to do was bury the entire world. The same tired old horseshit. Now they're saying I wouldn't talk to them? Fuck them and fuck Leibowitz. Who are they kidding? All he can give me is five years, and you can bet your sweet ass that's what I'm getting. This is just another excuse to make a speech when he sentences me."

"I guess you're right, Jim. I can't believe what I see happening in Brooklyn. It's like another world, another set of laws."

"There's no use moaning about it, Danny. We're here. How's Eddie? How's the appeal going?"

"Jim, Eddie is a master, a genius. I read it three times before he submitted it and I had a couple of good friends, retired judges, read a copy of it. They couldn't believe the indictment, much less what Leibowitz put on the trial record in his jury charge. They all think we have a sure reversal."

Jimmy broke into a big grin, the first good news in a long time. "That's beautiful, Dan, really great. When is he arguing it in appellate court?"

"We're on the November calendar."

"Shall I do one chorus of "I'll Be Home for Christmas'?"

"Jim, please, as confident as we are, don't get your hopes too high. This Appellate Division embraces Brooklyn. That's all I fear. Will we get a fair shake from the brotherhood?"

This morsel of lawyer logic dampened Jimmy's spirits for a minute, but only for a minute. At least he was leaving Raymond Street, one step in the right direction. The up direction. Up the river to Sing Sing.

11

THURSDAY, THE day set for sentencing, had seemed like it would never come. Jimmy had felt like a little kid the week before Christmas. The Big Day would never come. But all Big Days eventually come. The day you're born, the day you're married, the day you die—and for some poor guys the day they receive their first jail sentence. Wednesday night had been a long night, only broken up by a few of the hacks who stopped by his cell to wish him luck and say goodbye. Even his two friendly rats didn't come by to pay a farewell visit. They were heartbroken, he decided, they probably sensed I was about to leave them. Just as well, no tearful goodbyes, no parting chunks of pound cake.

The hack on duty woke him from a sound sleep very early on Thursday morning. He brought to his cell the tan tropical suit he wore when he first took up residence in the Raymond Street Arms Hotel. After he showered he was treated to a nice shave at the barbershop. Suit pressed, fresh underwear and socks, laundered white shirt and brown tie—Jimmy felt like a real sheik again. Spiffy, like the time he wore the first suit of his young life—when he made his First Communion.

As he was tying the knot in his tie he weighed whether he would ever have changed his life if somehow he could revert to the day of his First Communion and begin all over. Never, not in a million years. I'm satisfied. The suit swam on him from all the weight he had lost, but he felt great as he was handcuffed and led into the prison van with a dozen other guys and transported to

Criminal Court. When they reached the courthouse, he was separated from the group and led to a small room where Danny Sachs was waiting for him.

Danny explained away Eddie's absence and assured him that he was certainly eloquent enough to plead for a lenient sentence for Jimmy. Jimmy grinned ruefully as he listened to Danny. Socrates himself, in all his eloquence, at the zenith of his illustrious career, would never move Justice Samuel Leibowitz to leniency. The electric chair was simply out of the question. Thank God for that, Jimmy Riley, you lucky devil.

Jimmy was arraigned before Leibowitz about an hour later. The courtroom was only half full, but the usual gaggle of reporters was on hand, waiting for the final kill. Helfand walked in and took a position on Jimmy's right. Their eyes met and Jimmy sensed a slight shocked look, a look of sympathy as Helfand sized him up. No wonder. Jimmy's face was dead white, and he was thin enough to appear almost skeletal. He looked about one shade better than a Dachau survivor.

Danny made his eloquent speech, short and sweet. He ticked off a number of points that should be considered when meting out Jimmy's sentence. But it was like shoveling shit against the tide.

The look on Leibowitz's face was enough to discourage a young mother pleading for the life of her first-born. He sneered in disbelief, shook his head in apparent disbelief, reveled in total disbelief. Danny finished on a half-hearted note and sat down.

Helfand cleared his throat to address the Roman Senate and amphitheater. Leibowitz smiled benignly. His protégé, his pal, was now on. Any sympathy Helfand might have initially felt at seeing the change three months in Raymond Street had wrought in Jimmy had quickly vanished.

"Your Honor, I urge the maximum sentence for the defendant, James Riley. The district attorney's office has extended the hand of kindness, the olive branch of friendship, the promise of extreme leniency, the exculpation of his crime—without response. Our pleas fell on deaf ears. Riley could tell us of massive protection payments to whole squads of police. He was Gross's godfather, introduced him to the hierarchy of the police department, even ran his empire for six months.

"Riley amassed a fortune for a young man under thirty years of age when he resigned from the police department. He lived a life of luxury on a Connecticut estate. The D.A.'s office knows all this to be factual, still we offered leniency in return for his cooperation. Riley has remained adamant. Your Honor, once more, I urge the maximum sentence be imposed."

Julie, you're a real sweetheart, thought Jimmy Riley, as he looked sideways at him.

Leibowitz looked down at Jimmy. Uh-oh, the denouement is finally at hand. He hadn't even started yet and his face was contorted with anger. Jimmy looked right at him. When they want you, they'll get you. One way or the other, they'll get you. Now big Sam had him. All the shouting back and forth in chambers, his constant threats, Jimmy's defiance—it was all over. Jimmy stood before him in the dock, awaiting his fate. In his heart he had known that someday it would come down to this moment.

It had started with the first time he was brought face to face with him a couple of years ago. Jimmy's warning antennae had gone straight up. He could almost physically feel the malevolence that generated from Leibowitz, like a wild animal quickly senses the first changes in the terrain that indicate the imminence of an earthquake. But Jimmy had no place to scurry to safety then, and surely, there was no place to scurry now. The earth was opening. Get it over with, you big, grandstanding prick. Get it over with.

Leibowitz started softly, but the hatred he held inside for Jimmy rapidly came to the surface. It sounded to Jimmy, standing before him impassively, that in the first few minutes Leibowitz used the word "arrogance" about fifteen times when describing him. Another word rolled off his persistent tongue, "humility," Jimmy Riley had no humility. Imagine that. No humility. No shit.

Jimmy stood there and listened with half an ear to this arrogant, overbearing sonofabitch castigate him for being arrogant and possessing no humility. Leibowitz was the absolute apex of arrogance, had not the faintest idea of the meaning of humility. His definition of arrogance and lack of humility applied to anyone who refused to grovel before him, beg for mercy, plead for his freedom.

Jimmy closed his ears to Leibowitz, blocked him out of his

mind just as he had blocked out the stink putrefaction, and blazing lights of Raymond Street jail. He stood before him physically, not hearing a word of the invective spewed forth from his vengeful lunatic on the bench.

He stood there dreaming of Wolfe Tone, Michael Collins, O'Connell, Parnell—the great patriots of Irish history. Which one of the great ones uttered the immortal words now running around in my brain? "I have only honor and my life, milord, and rather I lose my life than lose my honor." He barely suppressed a grin. Jimmy was proud he was Irish. Proud that his mother and father had implicit faith in him. Do what you think is right, Jim. No recriminations.

Jimmy snapped back to reality. Judge Leibowitz at last began to wind down his stirring address to the New York newspapers. Dear God, this too shall pass.

"Riley, we knew you were the big man, the contact man for the chief inspector's office, for all the New York squads." He shifted his severe gaze away from Jimmy's immobile face. He looked out beyond to the courtroom, to his fans seated there hanging on to every acrid work of condemnation, to his beloved reporters who adored him for his headline value. He pointed his finger at Jimmy and again his voice got brutal. "He's a big fish, but there were higher ones. There was one Big Fish that escaped. Why he escaped we will not discuss at this time. And he is right next to the Kingfish. We won't identify him."

Jimmy listened to this bullshit incredulously. Here we go with the Big Fish who escaped. Why don't you come right out and say Bill O'Dwyer, the ex-mayor of New York City. Why, you fucking, lying scandalmonger, you and your D.A. pals never had the balls to even subpoena him. Only Christ himself knows what he might have on you guys. He was right in your midst, married a beautiful young chick, and got appointed ambassador to Mexico. You couldn't get appointed ambassador to Coney Island.

And now, a new figment of Leibowitz's imagination to titillate the press. The Kingfish, Bill O'Dwyer was the Big Fish who escaped. Now we have a Kingfish, but we won't identify him. Now who in the name of Christ could he be that big Sam won't identify him? Maybe Harry Truman? Maybe Harry Gross told him that he bought Harry Truman's presidential election? A possibility! Perhaps the Kingfish was Winston Churchill? General Eisenhower? J. Edgar Hoover?

By this time every inside guy like Jimmy Riley and the rest of the literate population of Brooklyn who can read the Brooklyn *Daily Eagle* knows that the Big Fish is Bill O'Dwyer. Come on, tell us, Sam, tell your fans out there who the Kingfish is or else you are a sanctimonious lying disgrace to the black robes you wear.

"Riley, have you anything to say before I pronounce sentence upon you?"

I've got plenty to say. One day I'll piss on your grave and that day will be the happiest day of my entire life.

"Nothing? Nothing to say, Riley?" Unctuous, tantalizing.

Jimmy shook his head no. He didn't trust himself to speak. He realized he was being baited, like a trapped, helpless animal. I'm not giving him a chance to add a contempt sentence to what he already has in mind. Fuck you, Sam, take your best shot.

"I sentence you for the crime of perjury, first degree, to five years in the state prison. Take him away."

Jimmy turned, shook hands with Danny, and held his hands out for the court officer to handcuff him. A huge wave of relief swept over him. Thank God that by tomorrow he would be out of Raymond Street jail on his way upstate to Sing Sing. He knew that he had a lot of good friends up there. Sing Sing was right on the banks of the Hudson River. He would breathe fresh air once again, eat decent food, do some type of work, walk in the yard. After three months in the shithouse Raymond Street he felt like he was on his way to heaven.

Early the next morning they moved him to the large holding cell. They led guys in a couple at a time. To Jimmy's delight about the tenth guy they led in was Bobby Tucker, a tough black kid who used to work for them in the black horse room they had at Fulton and Nostrand. They hugged each other, laughing, happy to see a friendly face from the outside.

The words rushed out of Jimmy. "What the hell are you doing here, Bobby? How long you been in? You going upstate? What for, for Christ's sake?"

"I'm here, all right, Jim. I knew you were here, but I was upstairs on the other side. I couldn't reach you. I'm going upstate right next to you, man."

"What the hell did you do?"

"Remember Cheesecake, the big, fat motherfucker? After the horse joint closed down I opened up a card game with Cheesecake. We were doing great for a couple of months and then he tried to screw me out of my end. I went after him. I only wanted to scare the fat bastard, but his ass looked so big when I caught up to him I fired a bullet right up his fat ass. He screamed like I shot him in the fucking heart. Anyway, the cops picked me up. I took a plea, and I got three years."

"Jeez, Bobby, I'm sorry."

"Fuck him. As you always said, you gotta protect your rights. But what about you, Jimmy? What'd you get?"

"Five years, Bobby."

"For this shit? Christ, I'm sorry, Jimmy. You were always a good dude with me and Buck."

They talked about the street and various guys they knew until finally the group in the cell were readied up for the long ride upstate to Sing Sing. Allie the hack was in charge. As they were ready to enter the van they were handcuffed together in pairs. Jimmy winked at Allie, indicated Bobby Tucker, and they were handcuffed together.

It was a large bus-type van, and it was fairly comfortable going during the two-hour trip upstate. Once inside the walls of Sing Sing prison the van stopped outside a red brick building and they were let out to stretch their legs and use the bathroom. They were all unhandcuffed and allowed to walk freely around a yard adjacent to the red brick building.

Jimmy and Bobby had talked and laughed all the way up, making the trip mercifully short. Now that they were there, Jimmy took a good look at his surroundings. The early autumn sky was azure blue, not a cloud in sight. The mild morning air was crystal clear and through the maze of buildings in the vast complex Jimmy could see the striking slate-gray expanse of the Hudson River. He was thrilled. This view sure beat the one at his last hotel.

They were all taken to a small mess hall and fed. Meatballs and spaghetti, Italian bread, tea, and rice pudding. Jimmy ate voraciously, his first good hot meal in months. Bobby Tucker ate like he was in Papa Jack's Soul Food Joint. They were all stripped to their shorts and put through the Bertillon system of identification. Size, weight, color of hair, color of eyes, scars, extremities missing, fingerprints—every conceivable physical detail.

They were putting their clothes back on when a big black guy walked over to Bobby and Jimmy and said, "Bobby, mah eyes maroon?"

Bobby looked right into him, motioned for Jimmy to do the same. For Christ's sake, they really were maroon!

Bobby said, "No, Dickie, no way. Your eyes are brown. Right, Jimmy?"

"That's right, Dickie."

"Thank you, fellers. That motherfucker back in there says mah eyes were maroon. Scared the shit out of me." He walked away.

Jimmy and Bobby looked at each other, walked down to the corner of the yard and nearly died laughing.

The group was then taken to the state shop, clothiers to the prison population. Sing Sing's answer to Brooks Brothers. They were measured and outfitted in prison clothes. Shorts, T-shirts, high-topped shoes, pants, shirts, and mackinaw. Their new prison identification number was stamped on every item. They were relieved of their street clothes and money and given receipts for everything.

They were then led to the reception tier, where they were assigned individual cells. Jimmy was disappointed to learn that they were to spend two weeks there while being indoctrinated, but soon shrugged it off. The cells were roomier and much brighter than Raymond Street. They were on the second tier of the cell block, and Jimmy was making his bed when he heard a lot of loud laughter and good-natured shouting from the floor below. He turned and looked out his cell bars to see what was going on.

There were about twenty-five wild faggots on the floor below, all shapes, sizes, and colors. They were waving and shouting up to the "new mickies" who had just arrived. It was an absolute panic. Some of the repartee back and forth convulsed Jimmy. He was howling. It reminded him of the fag nightclubs in Greenwich Village he used to visit when he was in plainclothes. This bit was funnier. The language was outrageous, and even some of the hacks were doubled up laughing when they finally cleared the welcoming committee away.

This joint isn't going to be monotonous, that's for sure, thought Jimmy, as he lay back on his nice comfortable bed. He was still grinning about the funny bit with the fags, his belly was full, his spirits were high. Even if, God forbid, he had to do a good stretch, this place wasn't too bad at all.

The next surprise was even a more pleasant one. The two convicts who ran the reception tier came up to his cell and introduced themselves. We have the word on you, Jimmy, we'll take good care of you. Anyway you want, anything within reason.

How about a nice blond, six-foot tall showgirl for the afternoon?

A big laugh all around.

We hate to tell you this, Jimmy, but even if we could, you'd have to be third on line.

Another big laugh.

Handsome George and Big Dutch, the two reception clerks. Georgie didn't come by his name without reason. He was handsomer than nine out of ten Hollywood actors—tall, blond hair, great build, blue eyes—a good solid jewel thief who was caught robbing the wrong manager. He never should have had to steal jewels, a hundred rich widows would've given him a truckload to share their beds.

Big Dutch, a dyed-in-the-wool tough guy from Hell's Kitchen on the West Side. In and out of reform school and jail since he was twelve years old. Dutch knew fifty friends of Jimmy's from the West Side.

Relax, Jim, you're in good hands.

Jimmy chafed a little at the continued confinement, but consoled himself that he'd soon be out in the population. It helped that the new group was kept relatively busy during the two-week indoctrination period. The first few days they attended lectures on adapting themselves to a whole new way of life—prison life. The lectures were given by seasoned convicts with the assistance of a prison psychiatrist. They were surprisingly good, straight to the point. But they all boiled down to one thing. Some of you are here for a short time, some for a long time. You'll be treated well, as long as you conform to the rules. Don't fight the system, or it will eat you up for breakfast. They were all inoculated against every possible disease, given extensive written and I.Q. tests, and subjected to psychological profiles.

The mandatory two-week confinement was passing swiftly. Georgie brought Jimmy a table lamp to read by, a priceless luxury. Dutch brought him up meals cooked by Italian guys he knew from the outside. Lasagna, manicotti, sausage and peppers, ziti —he sent half of it to Bobby Tucker, it was so much. He kidded Bobby, who was few cells away, "Keep it up, Bobby. We'll turn you into a paisan yet."

Jimmy was gaining back the lost weight. He looked human again. Too human. He decided to double his sit-up and push-up routines. The nights were cool enough to need blankets when sleeping, and except for the sound of toilets flushing, the nights were peaceful, almost without noise. Each cell was equipped with a pair of earphones for listening to music, news, or football games. Every day some friend, or friend of a friend, would stop on the floor below his cell and say hello or send regards. Jimmy's spirits were buoyed, he was at peace with himself. If you had to go the slammer, Sing Sing was all right.

During the last part of his reception confinement he reflected upon how contented he was. He had begun to accept the fate of a convict and equated Raymond Street jail with what lay in store for him if his appeal was turned down. He hoped for a better way of life in Sing Sing, but after a siege in Raymond Street he had learned to be stoical, to always expect the worst and you won't be disappointed.

Now he had peace and quiet during the long hours of the night, fresh air breezing through his cell as he lay huddled under the blankets, and the salty fragrance of the Hudson River filling his nostrils. No more piss-laden air, no more unendurable, all-pervading stink. What a relief.

The two-week confinement period finally passed and Jimmy was released from reception into the general prison population.

He was reassigned to another cell block, was allowed to take his treasured table lamp, and all was serene with his world. His first day out in the prison yard was like an old-grad reunion. He met guys from East Harlem, Harlem, the East Side, the West Side, Brooklyn, guys whom through the years of his tenure in the chief's office, his nightclub, and the gambling business he had developed a strong friendship with.

In turn his old friends introduced him to a few of the prison heavy-weights like Joe Gray, the labor leader, who turned out to be an old friend of his father, Mike. The first couple of days out in the population he walked the yard with Joe Gray, a witty, intelligent man whose conversation Jimmy enjoyed immensely. Joe assured him that the P.K., the Principal Keeper, the guy who really ran the prison, had already been given the message that Jimmy was to be treated favorably.

Jimmy would have a good job in a day or two, would eat with Joe, Hickey, Richie, and Fred—top guys in the caste system of the prison world.

Jimmy was happy as a clam when he went back to his cell late in the afternoon of his second day out. Sing Sing surpassed his expectations, the guys and the hacks couldn't be nicer. He still worried about the pending appeal, but if it was delayed longer than expected, at least Sing Sing was a decent place to do your time.

He had blocked from his mind all thoughts of home, Kay, and the kids. He had left strict orders. No visits. He read for hours every night, wallowing in the luxury of his table lamp, until he couldn't keep his eyes open any longer. He fell asleep contented, his stomach not empty and growling, but filled with the haute cuisine of Hickey, Italian chef *par excellence*.

After a few days of idleness he awoke one morning with eager anticipation. He was anxious to have a job, be busy, and he felt in his bones that today would be the day he would get an assignment. He marched to the mess hall for breakfast, and when finished, marched back to his cell. All the guys on the tier who had jobs were released from their cells about a half hour later and marched off with their work units.

Jimmy sat propped up on the bed reading, his mind occasionally wandering, daydreaming as to what type of job he would be given. The morning passed and he was marched to the mess hall for the midday meal—the big meal of the day—and again ate like he was going to the chair. He was returned to the cell again and patiently sat back to read until three o'clock, when he was allowed recreation period in the big yard.

About half past two a hack came to his cell and told him the P.K. wanted to see him. The hack unlocked his cell and led him through the countless series of locks, gates, and stairs that seemed to comprise all prisons. Jimmy always marveled how some deviously clever convict ever escaped from one of these joints. He always decided that the escapee would have had to turn into an eel to make it.

The hack finally delivered Jimmy to the P.K.'s office, knocked on the door, and ushered him in. The P.K. dismissed the hack with a curt nod and motioned Jimmy to sit down in a chair opposite his desk. He was a heavy-set Irishman. Thick glasses, graying red hair, and a nice smile. Before he sat behind his desk he shook hands with Jimmy and said, "Well, Jimmy Riley, what the hell is a nice Irish lad like you doing in a place like this?"

Jimmy laughed. "It's a complete misunderstanding, sir. I'm a victim of mistaken identity."

The P.K. laughed, but Jimmy with his sharp eyes noticed it was a forced, worried laugh. Something's up, Jimmy boy, and it's not good.

"Jimmy, as much as I hate to, I must get straight to the point. For one thing, I want you to know that you have good friends here in Sing Sing and good friends on the outside. I'm speaking of Frank and Max, enough said. I made a definite promise to them that I would do my best to take care of you. To make it easy for me to do that, you scored exceptionally well on all the tests we give the new men. I planned to have you teach school here, but the other day Dr. Gluck, the head psychiatrist, requested you to work as a clerk for him in an experimental study he's about to start. This request from Dr. Gluck made it doubly easy for me to uphold my promise to Frank and Max.

"Jimmy, hold tight, here's the bad news. This morning I received a directive from the commissioner of corrections, the top boss, to transfer you as soon as possible to Clinton Prison, in Dannemora, New York. I'm sorry, Jimmy."

Jimmy sat there stunned. Dannemora, Little Siberia, he'd heard a hundred crazy stories about that forbidden wasteland. Here we go, the fine hand of the Brooklyn brotherhood had reached out again. He was tempted to stand up and scream "Those dirty rotten no-good bastards." Big Sam made a sly promise he'd get my head cut off someday, he's sure trying to make good on his promise.

Shaken as he was, Jimmy just shrugged and said, "I understand, sir, and I realize full well where the order came from. It sure didn't begin with the commissioner of corrections." He smiled bitterly. "It's a shame, P.K., too bad. I've been here less than three weeks and everyone's treated me great. I was just beginning to enjoy myself. What's the procedure now?"

"When you go back to your cell you'll find a duffel bag there with some of your belongings in it. Put whatever personal possessions you want to take with you in the bag, and a guard will put you in the solitary area until six o'clock tonight. From here in you are to be held incommunicado. A guard from Dannemora is already here, and you two will catch the seven o'clock sleeper out of the Harmon railroad station, a few miles from here. Jim, these are the prison rules for men about to be 'boated,' so I have to adhere to them. Dannemora isn't as bad as they make it out to be. You have some good friends left, you'll be all right. Good luck, Jimmy."

The P.K. got up, shook hands, walked Jimmy to the door, and that was that. The briefest great friendship on record. As he walked back to his cell with the hack Jimmy's heart grew heavier. When he packed the duffel bag and the hack led him to the solitary confinement area he could barely contain his rage and frustration. He sat back on the bed, never so goddam mad in his life. He felt like banging his head against the bars and screaming blue murder. The worst part of his anger was the sheer helplessness of his situation.

He finally calmed down, resigned himself to the next adventure he faced. What the hell, November was here, the appeal was to be argued in a week or two, the decision expected in early December. Home sweet home and freedom. He relaxed, indulged himself in the verboten reminiscences of home. He dozed off, dreamed of Kay, the kids, Connecticut.

A sharp rap of a nightstick on the cell bars awakened him. An aging hack grunted a hello and handed in a tray of food. Coffee, a bologna sandwich, a piece of cherry pie.

"Eat it, kid. You've got a long trip ahead of you."

"Thank you." He ate it, he was starved.

Jimmy had just finished his snack when the old hack came by and opened his cell. He took him to a small office where his duffel bag lay. He introduced Jimmy to his escort to Dannemora. A big, raw-boned hack named Mr. Dubois. It's all "Mister" from now on, no more familiarity, no more first names.

Jimmy put on his mackinaw and Mr. Dubois handcuffed him. They went outside to a waiting car and were driven to the Harmon railroad station. There was still a little daylight left. They were the only two passengers on the platform. The hack said very little to Jimmy as they waited for the train. He had a strange accent, almost foreign. Jimmy was to learn later that it was a French-Canadian accent. Ninety-eight percent of the Dannemora hacks were of French-Canadian descent.

Mr. Dubois smoked a couple of cigarettes while they waited. He was polite enough, offered Jimmy a cigarette, was surprised to learn Jimmy didn't smoke. Only vice I don't have, Mr. Dubois. I can't understand how I missed that one. A weak attempt at humor. Maybe I can thaw this guy out. Dubois just grunted. End of conversation.

The train arrived and stopped briefly to pick them up. It all seemed prearranged. The conductor led them to a half-filled car and placed them square in the middle, more or less isolated from the rest of the passengers. Eyebrows were raised curiously as Dubois unhandcuffed Jimmy, removed his mackinaw, and replaced the cuffs. By now shit like that rolled right off Jimmy's back. Nothing embarrassed him anymore. He had checked his dignity outside the walls of Raymond Street jail and resolved to keep it in mothballs until he was set free.

The train trip was twelve hours long and it seemed like twelve days. Dubois just smoked cigarette after cigarette, stared ahead, occasionally put his head back to rest but never closed his eyes.

He never unhandcuffed Jimmy. After a few hours on the bumpy train Jimmy had to take a leak and Dubois accompanied him up the aisle to the lavatory. As they walked through the aisle of the swaying train, a little girl about six stood up from her seat and smiled at Jimmy. He was about to pat her on the head affectionately when her mother, a skinny, hatchet-face bitch, reached out and snatched the kid to her side.

The endless journey finally ended. There was a car waiting for them at the Plattsburgh station. The first thing Jimmy felt when he got off the train was the stinging cold. Christ, was it cold. He'd lived on the equator in Raymond Street for so long, his blood had thinned out. He shivered as they walked to the waiting car and his teeth were chattering. He was grateful for the warmth of the car when they took off for Dannemora.

A very curt hello was exchanged between Dubois and the hack driving the car. Jimmy was beginning to get the picture—these taciturn, beefy French-Canadians were men of very few words. The hack driving had a French-sounding name which Jimmy didn't quite catch. Not ten words were exchanged during the whole half-hour drive from the Plattsburgh railroad station to Dannemora prison.

They finally reached Little Siberia. Jimmy had a good view from the car window. Just as he mentally pictured it—like the prisons in a Jimmy Cagney or Humphrey Bogart movie. High walls, high gun towers on top of the high walls. A door opened magically, and the car rolled through and stopped outside what appeared to be an administration building.

Dubois helped Jimmy out of the back seat and unhandcuffed him. Jimmy took a good look around, suppressed a grin. He had suddenly recalled the victory party at Hughie's after the Big Trial collapsed, when he had sung with Rose and Dan "How are things in Dannemora." What a riot he was that night. He tried to recall the next stanza he had improvised, but his brain was becoming numb from the cold. Whew, now he knew how things were in Dannemora. Freezing, icy enough to freeze your balls off.

In 1841 a need to build another prison in upstate New York was established by the state assembly's committee on prisons. Prisons were little more than harsh work camps in these pre–Civil War days when convicts were not allowed to speak to each other and the inmates' labor was supposed to pay for the cost of their maintenance. The site selected for the new project was in Clinton County in the far reaches of the Adirondack Mountains a short distance from the Canadian border.

The main reason this barren outpost was picked was because biological surveys had shown that the area had what appeared to be inexhaustible deposits of iron ore. The track of land selected was seventeen miles west of Plattsburgh. It was reported that the ore could be mined with comparative ease, and that the region also possessed ready access to materials needed for smelting.

There was some opposition and squabbling among the rival political factions of the day, but a year and half after the initial proposal a resolution to build an iron-making penitentiary in Clinton County was passed by the state legislature. Within a year the building of Clinton Prison began, an energetic program of construction and iron-making which admirers predicted would create a new era in the history of penal reform.

In anticipation of the institution's success, citizens named the agglomeration of dwelling houses and log shanties which came to be scattered throughout the woods near the prison "Dannemora" after the world-famous Swedish iron center.

Dannemora was completed in 1845. There were many studies of the new prison in the ensuing years. The previously held concept of prison was that reformation could best be produced by breaking the spirit of a man, subjecting him to hard and humiliating discipline, and literally burying him from the world. The new approach favored an attempt to bring out the best in an inmate through humane treatment and some small extensions of privilege which might help alleviate the isolation and severity of convict life. Dannemora was the first prison to use the sting of the lash sparingly and even allowed inmates chewing tobacco.

There was much public criticism of the comparatively mild treatment of felons in the new prison at Dannemora. It was rebutted in turn by reformers who wanted to use harsh physical punishment only when necessary and who believed rehabilitation to be both possible and important. Their credo was, "Severe treatment has proved that men cannot be driven to the path of virtue."

They urged active employment, a strict but not severe discipline, the right to speak to each other after work hours, and proper food and rest to keep their bodies strong.

Twelve hours a day the convicts worked under this new humanitarian approach to prison life, with only a highly vocal church group enabling them a day of rest on Sunday so as not to tarnish their already blackened souls by working on the Lord's day. Unfortunately, the geological surveys proved inaccurate and the iron ore ran down by 1860. There was much speculation as to whether Dannemora would be abandoned at this time, but the other state facilities at Sing Sing and Auburn were already over-crowded and Dannemora was destined to stay.

Through the years the prison has been modernized and greatly added to. A good deal of minor manufacturing goes on within its confines and no one in the convict population is idle, except the infirm or the unlucky guys in solitary confinement.

Still, it was a grim, forbidding place as Jimmy Riley looked around that bleak November morning. A place that echoed the words of its critics of a century ago—too inaccessible, too exposed to intense cold and snowstorms—to ever be other than a lost cause as a prison.

12

Dubois led Jimmy into a small office inside the reception building. His pedigree was taken once more and he was again fingerprinted. Dubois then led him through the familiar maze of locks and gates to the state shop. A counterpart to the one where he was outfitted in Sing Sing. He again received a new wardrobe, this time made of heavier fabrics. No more T-shirts and shorts—heavy long johns were issued to protect against the icy blasts of the north country. The new clothes felt good, especially the mackinaw, which was much stronger and warmer than the one he had worn up from Sing Sing.

This finished, Dubois finally led him to a cell in B-Block. It was on the fourth tier of a six-tier cell block. Dubois wished him good luck, and Jimmy set about making his bed up, setting up his table lamp, toothbrush, and toilet articles. About eleven o'clock a hack came to his cell with a tray of food and explained that he would see the Principal Keeper the next morning, would only be confined to his cell for a day or two at the most. Good news.

The accommodations were similar to Sing Sing, only it was much colder in the cell. Jimmy had brought along a couple of paperbacks in his duffel bag and was soon transported into another world with his book, tucked comfortably under a couple of blankets.

A convict came up to his cell and introduced himself. Tony Polumbo, from East Harlem. They shook hands through the bars and Tony said, "We got the word this morning, Jimmy. It's all over the joint that you're here. I'm a good friend of Joe B's and Big Paulie from Harlem, and I've been told to take care of you. Anything you want?"

"Gee, Tony, thanks. No, I'm okay, a little tired from sitting up in the train all night, but I'll get a good night's sleep tonight if my nose doesn't freeze off above the covers."

Tony laughed. "Jesus, Jimmy, this is warm. Wait'll another month or two when it really get cold. It goes to thirty, forty below zero sometimes."

"You're kidding me. Thirty, forty below zero?"

"I swear, Jimmy. But you'll get used to it. They say the cold weather is healthier for you."

"How long you been here, Tony?"

"Eight years."

"You must be the healthiest guy on earth."

Tony laughed. "Shit, Jim, eight years around here is nothing. We've got guys here been in this joint forty, forty-five years. They're *really* healthy."

Jimmy shook his head in wonder. "Been here forty, forty-five years? They're still alive? Not entombed here, anything like that?"

Tony laughed again. "I swear. And like I said, it's healthy. How long you got, Jimmy?"

"Five years."

"Don't tell anyone that's all you got, or they'll be jealous of you. Around here five years is like a slap on the wrist."

"Tony, at this point, five years looks like fifty years to me. Tell me, how's the joint here? Good place to do time?"

"Not only good, it's the best place to do time. The P.K.'s half a nut, but the hacks are okay. Nobody bothers you if you mind your own business, they're tough but fair. We have our share of stool pigeons, like all joints, but you'll be tipped off to be wise to them. Outside of the snow and the cold, this joint is okay. When you get out in the main yard you'll get on a good court and be with a good bunch of guys. You can cook out there weekends and some of these old-timers are terrific chefs. Do you ski, Jimmy?"

"Ski? Where the hell do you ski in the can?"

"Wait until the snow hits in a week or two, this joint is like a winter resort. Skiing, tobogganing, ice skating—you won't believe it. Now, okay, Jim, I gotta go. You'll be out of here in a day or two to find out about the joint for yourself. I'll be back later and bring you some tuna fish, sardines, and a can opener for your cell. Take care of your can opener. In this joint a can opener is a man's best friend. I'm one of the tier men in this block. So anything you want, just holler for me. Okay, Jimmy?"

"Thanks, Tony. I really appreciate it."

The day passed quietly, the men marched back to their cells after work and yard period. Only an occasional curious glance came Jimmy's way as they passed his cell. There was no talking allowed after the evening bell rang at seven o'clock, a perfect rule as far as Jimmy was concerned. The excitement of being in a new prison, the warm greeting from Tony, his vivid description of the yard, all helped make Jimmy's first day in Dannemora a pleasant one. About nine o'clock that night he put his book away, switched his reading lamp off, and closed his eyes. He was exhausted. Huddled under three blankets to ward off the chill of the night, he slept his first night in Dannemora like the proverbial log. He never moved until the morning wake-up bell rang piercingly at six o'clock. Time to rise and shine!

He had learned the art of shaving with cold water at Sing Sing, so that when the hack came to take him to see the P.K. he was scrubbed, clean-shaven, and ready for his job interview. The only thing he lacked was a résumé. Again they went down flights of stairs, through long corridors and gates until they reached the Principal Keeper's office. The hack ushered Jimmy in and left. The P.K. was bent over his desk studying some paper work, totally ignoring Jimmy, who stood at attention a couple of feet in front of his desk.

The P.K. looked up and with a wave of his hand motioned Jimmy to a seat. Jimmy studied him, the famous Lloyd La Morte, Principal Keeper and absolute ruler of Dannemora prison. He appeared to be about sixty years old, with steel-gray, crew-cropped hair, thick eyeglasses, big hands, wide shoulders. He didn't seem to be as big and brawny as the other hacks up here Jimmy had seen so far. Maybe after sixty years of life in this godforsaken place the cold weather had shrunk him.

He finally pushed aside his paper work and said, "How are you, Riley? I'm Principal Keeper La Morte."

"I'm fine, thank you, Mr. La Morte."

"How was your trip up, Riley?"

"It was all right, Mr. La Morte. No problems." He had the French-Canadian accent of all time. How was your trip oop? Up was oop on the Canadian border.

"Riley, do you consider yourself a menace to society? A man who should be kept in a maximum security prison and who should not be considered for parole?"

Jimmy sat there momentarily stunned, speechless. Was this crewcut comic making up this horseshit? Or was the Brooklyn brotherhood doing another job on him?

"Of course not, Mr. La Morte."

"I have a confidential report on my desk that says exactly that, just what I asked you. Do you have any fears for your personal safety here, anything that might justify keeping you out of the general prison population?"

"Absolutely not. None at all."

"Riley, let me tell you something. You're the first ex-cop we've had here in Dannemora in over thirty years. Do you realize that?"

"I wasn't aware of that, Mr. La Morte."

"The last ex-cop we had here was when I was only an officer, a young man. He was an ex-police captain from Albany. You know what happened to him?"

"I haven't the slightest idea, Mr. La Morte."

"He was here two months, couldn't handle prison life. He hung himself, Riley, committed suicide." La Morte smacked his lips as he said the last sentence. He was walking around now, pacing back and forth like a caged animal. His eyes were blinking behind his thick glasses, dancing in his head.

Jimmy sat there quietly. What did I do in life to deserve these guys—Leibowitz, La Morte? This guy is half a psycho if ever I laid eyes on one.

"Riley, the administration gave me a hot potato in you, and I don't like it one bit. I don't want ex-cops up here who are liable to get killed or commit suicide. This is my prison and I run it clean as a whistle."

"Mr. La Morte, if you don't mind my saying so, I have no intention of either getting killed or committing suicide. I'm counting heavily on an appeal that my lawyers have submitted to upset my conviction. They assure me it will only be a matter of time before I'm vindicated."

"Riley, every con in this prison has some kind of appeal or writ going for him. I wish you luck, but don't count too much on it. Now where am I going to put you to work where you'll be safe?"

"Mr. La Morte, just put me to work somewhere. Don't worry about me being safe, I can take care of myself."

"How would you like to work in the hospital? Are you turned off by the sight of blood? Does it affect you?"

"That doesn't bother me in the least, Mr. La Morte. I'd love to work in the hospital."

"Well, then, I see here that I have an opening for an assistant surgical nurse. The head man there just went home on parole and his assistant took his place. Now he needs a helper. I can see from your tests in reception in Sing Sing that you're far from stupid, maybe you'll fill the bill."

Jimmy just sat there and nodded. He was elated. The hospital, right down his alley.

"All right, Riley, I'll make the necessary arrangements. You'll be sleeping in a large dormitory with twenty other inmates. Any objection?"

"None at all, Mr. La Morte. I'm looking forward to it."

"Good. Now take care of yourself, Riley. We have Box A right down the road, and about twenty-five percent of our present inmates have been in and out of Box A. Be very careful at all times."

"Excuse me, sir, what's Box A?"

"Box A is the mailing address of the State Hospital for the Criminal Insane. This hospital was established for men who cracked up in prison, couldn't handle prison life. They're sent to Box A up here from every prison in the New York State system. They receive psychiatric counseling in Box A, and if the doctors feel that they've responded to treatment well enough they send them down the road to us, Box B. You get it, Riley? There are a couple of hundred certified psychos out there in the yard, so watch your step."

"Thank you, Mr. La Morte. I'll be careful."

The very same morning, Jimmy was moved to the hospital building. It was a fairly new building and it shone, actually sparkled with cleanliness. The floors were polished to a high gleam, the inmates wore starched whites, the walls, ceilings, and doors were painted with a high gloss. It was impeccable.

Jimmy was led to a dormitory which resembled a small auditorium, only instead of seats it had rows of hospital beds around the perimeter of the room. There were writing desks in the center of the room, easy chairs, sofas, bookcases, and card tables. A couple of guys who were off duty came over, shook hands, and introduced themselves to Jimmy.

They ate at noon in a small dining room, and when everyone returned to the dormitory the rest of the guys said hello to Jimmy and made him feel as if he was accepted. It was a good feeling.

About two o'clock the head operating-room nurse came over to the dormitory to meet Jimmy, his new assistant. He turned out to be another West Side guy. There's a saying that on the West Side you either grow up to be a priest, a cop, or you go to jail. Judging from all the West Side guys Jimmy had met in jail, he figured the jail guys had to outnumber the priests and cops at least five to one. This guy was a real sweetheart.

His name was Richard McLaughlin. And he made it clear, his name was Richard, not Dick or Dickie. Jimmy couldn't help grinning at this—a trait of the Irish. The old Irish referred to their progeny or their relatives as Francis, James, Thomas, Richard, Edward, Michael, John, Patrick—never Frankie, Jim, Tommy, Dick, Eddie, Mike, Jack, or Pat. Richard wore glasses, was medium-sized, compact build, and had a very positive manner. He was doing a big bit. No elaboration, he just had a big bit. He and Jimmy had talked together for only a few minutes before they discovered that they had a couple of dozen mutual friends. They got along together from the opening bell.

The first few days in the operating room were quiet ones, only a couple of minor operations. The civilian nurse on the staff was a nice guy, and the head doctor, while a bit haughty and reserved, was always polite and pleasant. Jimmy observed every detail, completely absorbed. He was more fascinated by the skill of Richard, his new pal, than he was by the doctor. He watched as Richard handed the doctor the instruments, the sponges, the sutures. Would he ever be as capable, as well trained to actually assist at an operation?

Richard taught him slowly, assured him that someday he would be good. He liked the way Jimmy reacted to the sight of blood, how he didn't flinch at the sharp incision into the skin. He had observed Jimmy closely at the operating table, thought it was great that he was so absorbed, so fascinated. Yes, Jim, you have the makings of a good surgical nurse. Jimmy thanked Richard, but made one request. Could he have an additional lesson from a nice shapely, red-haired surgical nurse some long snowy afternoon rather than a short, four-eyed guy like him constantly hovering about? A big laugh.

In response to a message relayed to him, Jimmy at last went out to the main yard on Sunday morning shortly after breakfast. He'd heard about the Dannemora yard before but he could never quite picture it. He couldn't believe his eyes. There was a huge combination baseball and football field on the plat part of the yard, and as his eyes looked up at The Hill his first thought was that it looked exactly like old pictures of the Bonus Army of World War I veterans camped out in Washington, D.C. It was almost the exact replica of a hobo camp.

Jimmy had his hospital whites on under a bulky sweater and mackinaw, so it was easy for the guy who'd sent him the message to spot him. He walked straight up to Jimmy and introduced himself. He was a short, stocky Polack named Little Stanley. And, as Jimmy soon learned, a bank robber and safecracker without a peer in the underworld.

Little Stan was very friendly and outgoing as he walked with Jimmy up The Hill. He explained his reason for sending for him. He had been returned for violation of parole about four months back, but when he was on the street a real good friend of Jimmy's, Jackie Coyle from the safe and loft squad, had done him a big favor. Jackie could have buried Little Stan, but instead gave him a good break. He wouldn't take any money for the favor, he just asked Little Stan to keep an eye out for Jimmy if he ever ran across him in prison. So here he was, keeping an eye out for Jimmy.

They arrived at the court, and Little Stan introduced him to the other tenants—Steve the Beast, his partner on the outside, Louie the Eel, Jake the Jew—all top burglars, locksmiths, and safe-crackers. They welcomed Jimmy with open arms. The court was the Dannemora convicts' private piece of land, their own fief. Jimmy was quickly briefed on the convict law: you never entered another court unless you were specifically invited or were exceptionally good friends with the occupants.

Each court was equipped with makeshift stoves similar to hobo kitchens, but highly efficient for cooking magnificent meals. Saturday and Sunday were the big days, and even at this early hour of the morning fires were smoking all over The Hill, readying up the weekend feast.

Little Stan took Jimmy around to court after court and introduced him to what seemed like a couple of hundred guys. Everyone was polite and cordial, several asking about old friends of theirs from the outside world whom Jimmy knew. Jimmy hoped he was passing inspection, for, he knew, that was what this turn around The Hill was all about. Along the way a few guys hollered hello to him, guys he knew from the street, and grabbed him and shook hands enthusiastically. Again, like old home week.

Four walls do not a prison make. Jimmy wondered who had said that, and he knew it probably did not refer to a prison. But what does make a prison, or what makes prison endurable, is the guys you meet and the friends you make. And in their own way Richard and Little Stan embarked Jimmy on the right track in Dannemora. He adjusted speedily and well.

To Jimmy's delight, a bridge game went on every night in the dormitory. When one of the steady players wasn't available, he was asked to sit in. He wasn't in the same class with most of the guys, but a few of the old-timers who were experts taught him the intricacies of the game. He was a willing pupil, loved the game, and soon improved enough to be an acceptable player.

The operating room on most days was busy. Appendectomies,

gall bladders, kidney stones, even a frontal lobotomy for removal of a brain tumor one day. Richard trained Jimmy step by step until one day on a gall bladder operation he allowed Jimmy to assist the doctor all by himself. He was thrilled when they finished, felt like he had just performed a heart transplant.

He came into the dormitory after this heady effort with some spots of blood on his whites and a surgical mask pulled down across his neck. He walked over to a bunch of the guys who were sitting around after lunch, threw up his hands dramatically, and said, "Operations, operations. I hope these golden hands never fail me. The hands of a great concert pianist, my mother used to tell me. Now they merely belong to a doctor, a great surgeon." The guys roared laughing, then booed him. Jimmy flopped on his bed, feigning exhaustion from the harrowing experience.

The hospital was one funny place to work, but things were not destined to be all that happy in the life of Jimmy Riley. About six weeks after he was in Dannemora, just before the holidays, he received his first Christmas present. A letter from his appeal lawyer, Eddie Levine.

Dear Jim,

I regret to inform you that your appeal for a reversal of your conviction has been denied by the 2nd Appellate Division. The only favorable thing I have to report is that we did get one dissenting opinion, which enables us to go on to the Court of Appeals of the State of New York.

The dissenting opinion found very strongly in our favor and I was extremely disappointed that the other justices did not concur. There was no majority opinion written, just a peremptory denial. In retrospect, I honestly feel that we were up against a stone wall in the 2nd Appellate Division, which is comprised in the main of Brooklyn judges. I urge you not to get discouraged, Jim, but to keep up your hopes and continue the good spirits that your recent letters indicate.

I am positive that we will get an unbiased review in the Court of Appeals in Albany. This court has as its members learned jurists from all sections of New York State. I can't conceive of how the first court could have upheld this indictment, much less the conviction after the appalling charge to the jury by Judge Leibowitz.

After the denial, I made a subsequent motion to go on the spring calendar in Albany, the earliest possible date, and I will write and let you know the date set for the hearing.

Once again, Jim, please don't get discouraged, I'm sure that eventually we will win. My heart goes out to you and your family as the holidays near. Keep your chin up.

With warmest regards,
Eddie

Jimmy read the letter twice to make sure he was seeing correctly. He laid the letter aside, he couldn't believe it. All this tortuous shit—Raymond Street, Sing Sing, Dannemora—it was all one big joke. Something you laugh and kid about when you hit the street. "Ever tell you about the tough five I did?"—meaning five months—the average guy could do it standing on his hands. But now, Jimmy boy, you're looking five *years* in the face—another cup of tea.

The blues lasted a few days before Jimmy finally shook them off. No use going around with a long face, being a pain in the ass and miserable to everybody just because you got some bad news. All these guys in here have crosses on their backs, most worse than yours.

The middle of December had brought the heralded snow. At first came the gentle New England-type snowfalls, tiny flakes falling softly and covering the rough terrain with a pristine coat of lovely, glimmering white. As the weeks went by the snowfalls increased in intensity, the flakes became as large as silver dollars. It was continuous, ceaseless, unending.

Great banks of snow were piled ten feet high against the prison walls, and when the men were lined up to march back to their cells after yard period, aisles were dug clear to allow them to form ranks. The snow on either side of them was always chest high. But Jimmy continued walking with Little Stan every Saturday and Sunday, trudging through the snow and working up an appetite for the feast being prepared on the court for later in the day.

The winter sports carnival began, Dannemora's answer to the Winter Olympics. It was unbelievable, incredible. An outsider wouldn't believe it in a million years. The men worked like beavers setting up the ski jump, the ski run, and the toboggan run. They improvised the lift-off on the ski jump, marked out the trails on the ski run, and built a toboggan course that curved from the top of The Hill near the handball courts, banked high against the prison wall, and came to rest at the end of the football field. It was a remarkable piece of engineering.

The convicts skied with homemade skis, made out of barrel staves and leather thongs. They made death-defying leaps off the ski jump, sailing sixty, seventy feet through the air. Some inexperienced daredevil would take off the ski jump, do a clumsy somersault in the air, and almost land on his head. A spectator would swear they'd be stone dead after they hit the slope. But they would struggle upright with everyone, including themselves, howling, laughing. There were still plenty of casualties, however, and the hospital was teeming with sprains, broken legs, and broken arms. By some miracle, no broken necks.

The toboggan run was the thrill of the year. Because of the prison confines it was naturally shorter than regular courses, but it was a chiller-diller just the same. Some kindly soul had donated a few two-man toboggans to the prison and sooner or later everyone had to take a run. Jimmy took his first trip the day before Christmas.

He almost had a heart attack. He checked his professed atheism as he got into the back of the sled ready for push-off, and said at least ten Hail Marys all the way down the run. The sled careened up the snow bank against the wall and for a brief second he thought they were about to fly over the wall to freedom. What price freedom if you were dead when you finally gained it. He survived the toboggan run but valued his life enough never to attempt the ski jump.

The one thing that amazed Jimmy, something he really appreciated, was that the Dannemora authorities placed no restraints on these winter sports in spite of the danger to life and limb and the growing casualty list. It was a way of letting off steam, keeping the lid on things.

The holidays passed swiftly and mercifully, the winter months were rolling along. The snow continued to fall, a day without new snow was an eventful one. Jimmy spent the winter nice and snug in the hospital. He was happy in the dormitory, got along well with his fellow inmates there, played bridge a couple of hours a day, and read into the night until his eyes were ready to close.

Richard and the doctor continued his schooling in operating-room techniques, and by now he was almost a full-fledged surgical nurse. He chafed sometimes at the isolation from the outside world, at the all-male atmosphere, but he remained contented with his lot, counting the days to spring when his appeal would be heard and he would at last be free.

He hadn't seen Little Stanley in over a month because the yard was declared off limits when the temperature dropped below minus fifteen. This was understandable, as there was extreme danger of almost instant frostbite to any exposed part of your body at these temperatures, and only the heavily equipped work gangs were allowed out.

The waning part of the winter became less severe, milder, the temperature about zero, and Jimmy sent a message early one Saturday to Little Stan that he would see him on the court. He had missed the unvarying good humor and funny stories of Little Stan and was in a great mood as he trudged up The Hill to their court, wondering what was on the menu later in the day. He had almost reached the top when a harsh voice called out to him. "Hey, Riley, hold it, I wanna talk to you." Jimmy stopped and looked around. A mangy-looking convict about his age, a couple of inches shorter than him, with a husky build, flat nose, and very pale blue eyes, walked up to him and said, "You're Riley? Right?"

Jimmy had on all his heavy clothes with a wool cap jammed over his eyes. His own mother would have trouble recognizing him in this outfit. This guy knew goddam well who he was.

"Yeah, I'm Riley. What's up?" He made no effort to shake hands, to be polite. He didn't like the way this asshole had accosted him.

"You know me, don't you, Riley?"

"No, I don't. Why should I know you?"

"My name is Puggy Slagle, Riley. You sure now you don't remember me?"

"Look, Puggy, or whatever your name is. I just told you I don't know you or remember you—I never saw you before in my life."

"You saw me, Riley, you and another bull kicked the shit out of me in the squad room in the East Sixty-seventh Street Precinct one night. You gave me a beatin' I'll never forget."

"What exactly did I give you this beatin' for, the one you're talking about?"

"You picked me up for a heist, you and another detective. Beat the living shit out of me."

"Listen, Puggy, get this straight. I was never a detective, I was a plainclothes cop in the gambling squad. I worked on bookmakers and numbers guys. Working on heist guys wasn't my racket, neither was beating the shit out of a guy in the squad room. Now you got it? I never worked on heists. You got the wrong cop, Puggy."

"Riley, I know it was you, I seen your pitcher in the paper last year. It was you, Riley. And now you're just another con, just like me."

"Listen, you, Puggy, or whoever the fuck you are, I may be just another con, but don't confuse me with the likes of you. For the last time, and get it straight. I never laid eyes on you, and I never beat the shit out of you. That wasn't my racket." While they were talking Jimmy could see the guys from Puggy's court taking in every word. Three real shit-kickers watching their main man put on his bullshit tough-guy act. "Puggy, you got the wrong guy." With that Jimmy turned and walked away, up the Hill.

Puggy said, good and loud, "We'll see about this, Riley."

Jimmy half-turned. "Fuck you, Puggy." He continued walking.

He was a little disturbed by the incident, but quickly shrugged it off. The first sign of hostility in almost nine months. Not too bad a track record for an ex-cop, considering the high-class resorts they had been confining him in. He didn't mention a word of it when he greeted the guys on his court. He just stood around drinking coffee, laughing and kidding back and forth, all glad to see one another after a month's absence from the yard and their beloved court.

Little Stanley and Jimmy went down The Hill to take their usual walk up and down the football field. The work gangs had cleared the perimeter of the field and the ground was just beginning to get soft enough underfoot so that their boots could get good traction. They both loved to walk and sooner or later would get into long discussions about the world in general. Little Stanley was hilarious. Jimmy loved his stories about some of the scores he'd made on the outside and some of the unexpected things that happened along the way. He never worked with a gun. He was a genius with locks and burglar alarms. He would slip a lock out of the front door of a bank on a quiet night, make a wax impression for the keys, and then go back a couple of nights later and clean it out. His exploits and the unforeseen pitfalls were hysterical.

After walking for about an hour Jimmy figured he had to tell Little Stanley about that morning's incident, get Puggy Slagle off his chest. The confrontation still was gnawing at him, still bugged him.

"Stan, you know a guy in here named Puggy Slagle?"

"Puggy? A flat-nosed, husky, wild-eyed prick?"

"That's him."

"Why? What about him?"

Jimmy described the incident.

"Don't pay any attention to that crazy fuck. Puggy's been in and out of Box A a couple of times. He's nutty as a fruitcake. Furthermore, he's from Yorkville, a New York guy, and he hangs around with all shit-kicking hoosiers from up around here. Nobody from New York wants any part of that asshole."

"I figured, just looking at him, that he was some kind of psycho, but I tried to act nice at first. Then I could see he was putting on the act for those shitheel pals of his on the court."

"How'd you end up?" Little Stan was disturbed, Jimmy could tell by his voice. Anxious.

"I emphasized it once again, he had the wrong guy. I finally walked away, and when I was about twenty feet from him, he said, 'We'll see about this, Riley.' I just turned around, looked at him, and told him to go fuck himself."

"Good. Just what you shoulda said to the crazy bastard. Jimmy, you want me to speak to this guy, straighten him out?"

"For Christ's sake, no, Stan. And don't mention it to the other guys. This piece of shit Puggy might think I need help with the likes of him. Forget I told you, and please, not a word about it on the court. Come on, let's go back up The Hill. I'm starved and I'm getting cold."

Jimmy reflected upon the scene with Puggy a few times during the next couple of weeks but finally dismissed it from his mind. The times he thought about it he couldn't help smiling a little. Way back when Chick told him that he'd been indicted, Jimmy worried about how Chick would fare in prison. His main concern was that Chick might run across some psychotic cop-hater. Just my luck I meet a dyed-in-the-wool psycho cop-hater, right out of Box A. Fuck him.

The snow finally came to a halt near the end of March, and by the middle of April the Great Weatherman in the Sky finally sounded the all-clear signal. There was still a chill in the air, but flowers were already blooming in the corners of the yard and on the courts up on The Hill. Dannemora had a cheery, spring look.

Jimmy loved his work in the hospital. The operations still fascinated him, and the weekends in the yard with Little Stan and the other guys were always funny and pleasant. But one thing was uppermost in his mind, the decision from the Court of Appeals. It had been ten days since Eddie argued it before the Court. He had written Jimmy that it couldn't have gone better. The judges had seemed sympathetic and receptive. He was almost certain the conviction would be reversed.

Jimmy's spirits had soared, he would soon be free. He even went so far as to ask Little Stan and the other guys how he could help them when he got out. About a week later, after a quiet day in the hospital, Jimmy was through work early and went back to the dormitory. He was lying on his bed, reading, the only guy in the dorm. A convict messenger, a guy Jimmy knew slightly, walked over to him and said, "Riley, I have a special delivery letter for you. The boss told me to bring it right over."

"Hey, thanks a lot." Jimmy swung his feet off the bed, his heart racing a mile a minute. The envelope bore the return address of

Eddie's law office. He tore the envelope open, his hands were trembling.

Dear Jim,
    It is with the greatest regret that I must inform you that the Court of Appeals has denied our motion and upheld your conviction.
    Jim, I cannot tell you how unhappy both Danny Sachs and I were to hear the bad news. It is almost impossible to understand their decision. It was unanimous, not a dissenting vote.
    It is incomprehensible to me that your conviction was upheld. I regret terribly my recent letter to you in which I so confidently predicted a reversal. How I must have raised your hopes, and now to see them dashed.
    Jim, I can't begin to tell you how sorry I am. There are no more avenues to pursue in face of this unanimous decision. Once again, Jim, keep your chin up.
                                            Warmest regards,
                                            Eddie

Jimmy sat back on the bed, almost in a daze. He swung his feet up and propped the pillows beneath his head. He read the letter again. It was true. The deck was stacked, you poor dumb bastard. It was like going up against a crooked crap table. You never had a chance to win, not one in a million. The whole scenario is unfolding. The relentless vendetta of the Brooklyn brotherhood.

First, a bullshit indictment. Then, a hanging judge. A ball-breaking few months in Raymond Street jail. A quick removal from the comfortable confines and salty air of the Hudson River to the desolate snows of Dannemora. One fucking dissent out of twelve judges. The wheels of justice turn slowly, inexorably. Whoever said that was full of shit. The wheels of justice, Brooklyn justice, turn swiftly, grind your flesh into little bits.

Jimmy walked around the next couple of weeks almost in a trance. He felt sure that he had reached the lowest point in his life. He couldn't seem to shake the blues that had a half-nelson grip on his head. The only one to whom he confided the bad news was Richard, otherwise he kept things to himself. The guys in the dormitory could tell from his face that something was deeply disturbing him, but no one questioned him, everyone just let him alone with his trouble. He declined all offers to play bridge, didn't laugh and joke in his usual way, just lay on his bed when he came in from work and read or stared off into space with his hands behind his head.

He couldn't seem to reconcile himself to the idea of spending five years in Dannemora. With the way things were breaking for him, he held little hope for any kind of parole, at least any hope of an early parole. The words of the P.K. at their first meeting now gained full impact, recurred constantly in his mind. Menace to society; to be confined to a maximum security prison; not to be considered for parole.

Jimmy was fully aware of who was responsible for this murderous shit. What a number they were doing on him, and no chance to defend himself. He lived his waking hours in a state of inner rage and when finally asleep would wake up in the middle of the night, night after night, tempted to scream at the top of his lungs. Now he understood how easy it was for guys to crack up in these joints and wind up down the road in that fucking nuthouse, Box A.

Little Stanley, with no word from Jimmy in weeks and no response to a couple of messages, came up to the hospital on sick call, feigning illness. "What the hell's wrong with you? I hear you're walking around here like a zombie. Why haven't you been out in the yard? The guys are all worried about you."

"Okay, take it easy. Look, I'm glad you came up here, glad to see you. You probably guessed it by now, Stan, but anyway, I got turned down by the Court of Appeals. Blew it all the way, seven to nothing. I'm dead, Stanley, dead as a mackerel."

"Oh, Christ, Jim, I thought it might be that. I'm really sorry for you, but listen, these things happen. You can't hold everything inside yourself and walk around with a long face the rest of your bit. You've got to make the best of it while you're in here. You knew it wasn't going to be any picnic, what you were getting into, so you have to accept this like you've accepted everything else. Come on, cheer up, for Christ's sake. I'll see you Saturday morning, and that's an order. I miss my walking partner, so make sure you're out in the yard good and early."

Little Stan, with his funny stories and great sense of humor, gradually shook Jimmy out of his blue funk and in a few weeks he was almost his old self again. He resumed playing bridge, sent for a couple of college correspondence courses, and buried himself in all kinds of books in his free time. The operating room was as fascinating as ever, even more so as the doctor loosened up and took time to explain some of the procedures to him. He looked forward to the yard on weekends as the nice weather set in, and the guys on the court were a great bunch, wonderful to be with.

Jimmy was walking up The Hill on a Saturday morning a couple of months after he received the bad news, when he heard his name called out. It was Puggy. They were on top of The Hill about halfway between Jimmy's court and the one he assumed was Puggy's. He had seen Puggy a couple of times since their confrontation, but ignored him as if he didn't exist.

Puggy strolled up to him with a lazy, wise-guy strut, accompanied by a tall, lanky, moon-faced hoosier.

"Yeah, Puggy, what's up?" Jimmy stood there easily, figuring that at least he'd acknowledge this whacky bastard. Be polite.

"Riley, this is my friend, Daniel Boone Williams. Daniel's the best rifle shot in the north country. Comes from up here, Malone, New York. He killed three guys over one of those family feuds. Right, Daniel?"

Daniel nodded, like the big dumb ox that he was.

"Hello, Daniel, how are you?" No attempt to shake hands. What's this crazy bastard Puggy telling me this for, introducing this asshole to me? Jimmy tensed, the hair on the nape of his neck raised. This prick is looking for trouble.

"Daniel, Riley's the guy I told you about. The cop who kicked the shit out of me once down in New York City."

"Puggy, I told you twice before, you got the wrong cop. Now do me a big favor, you and your man Daniel here, fuck off. Leave me alone. You got that straight?"

"You talk pretty tough, Riley, but you haven't got your gun and your badge now. Me and Daniel would like to see how tough you are."

Jimmy stood flat-footed, hands by his side. There were crowds of guys scattered all over The Hill, obscuring the three of them from the hacks stationed at opposite ends of The Hill. Puggy was talking loud, getting up his courage. A couple of cons were standing near, listening to every word. No time to take any shit.

"Go ahead, Puggy, see for yourself."

Puggy stood there hesitantly, looked nervously at his man Daniel Boone. He was a couple of feet in front on Jimmy. He pulled his right hand back and stepped forward to throw a punch. Jimmy, anticipating, shifted his weight and whistled a left hook square on Puggy's jaw and he dropped flat on his back. Daniel stood there with his mouth open, startled at this unexpected turn of events. But only for a second. He stepped forward and Jimmy hit him a perfect right on the jaw. Daniel landed hard, smack on his ass.

Jimmy straddled Puggy on the ground and slapped him hard across the face with his open palm and in a hoarse voice said, "You bughouse prick, if you ever talk to me or bother me as long as I'm in this joint I'll cut your fucking head off. The next time I swear I'll put you in the hospital or in your grave. Now lay off me, once and for all."

Jimmy got to his feet and brushed his clothes off. Nobody around them said a word. Puggy lay there on his back, his pale blue eyes seeming to whirl in his head. Daniel Boone Williams, the best rifle shot in the north country, picked himself up and backed away.

Jimmy turned and continued walking like nothing had happened, happy that the hacks hadn't seen the fight. He reached his own court and over a cup of coffee told Little Stan and the other guys about the fight. They were all for going down to Puggy's court and scaring the living shit out of them, but Jimmy prevailed upon them to forget about it. He assured the guys Puggy wouldn't bother him anymore. Neither would Daniel Boone Williams, unless they smuggled him in a hunting rifle.

The encounter served to release a lot of the tension he still held inside himself, and that weekend was the happiest one he had spent in months. On succeeding weekends Jimmy purposely marched past Puggy's court every time he went into the yard and up The Hill, but Puggy never called to him anymore and always averted his glance. The same thing went for Daniel Boone Williams when he ran across him in the yard. No more worries from those two.

Spring rolled into summer, and one day Jimmy looked at the calendar hanging on the wall of the dormitory and realized that he'd been in jail over a year. One entire year. It seemed by now he'd been in Dannemora half his life, and he'd only been here eight months. He received weekly letters from home and knew Kay and the kids were all well, but still he refused to have any visitors. One look at the outside of this place would depress the hell out of anybody. He wrote and said how great it was, perhaps this coming Christmas he would be happy to receive a visit. He smiled. That's the way a convict gets conditioned to think, you plan something a few months in advance as if it was only a matter of a few days.

One day while on his lunch hour Jimmy was listening to the news on the radio in Richard's room. Richard had his own room and bath, a rare privilege given to an inmate holding the esteemed position of head surgical nurse. The news commentator stridently announced that Joe Gray, the famous ex-labor leader, now serving twenty years for extortion, had received numerous visits in Sing Sing from a prominent politician and was the recipient of very favored treatment. What a lot of shit, Jimmy thought. Joe Gray did the same time as everybody else, day by day, and he was the nicest and most respected guy in Sing Sing.

Then the commentator dropped the bombshell. As a result of the scandal, the governor had ordered Joe transferred to Dannemora prison, near the Canadian border. Jimmy proceeded to tell Richard what a great guy Joe was and how nice he had treated him in the short time they spent together in Sing Sing. They sent a guy with a message to Tony Palumbo, the tier man, to be on the lookout for Joe and to make sure he got whatever he needed.

The next day Jimmy received a message from Joe Gray to meet him in the yard the following afternoon. They met and greeted each other with a big hug and walked in the yard for a couple of hours. Jimmy was caught up on all the news of the guys who had befriended him in Sing Sing, and Joe explained how some jealous stool pigeon bastard blew the whistle on the visits from his politi-cian friend, who was a pal from boyhood days.

Jimmy gave Joe the rundown on Dannemora like he had had twenty years in, clueing him in on the Principal Keeper, the hacks, the court system the convicts maintained on The Hill, and the delights of the coming winter. Joe shook his head at what he had to soon expect and thanked Jimmy for the tuna fish, sardines, and can opener, especially the can opener. Tony Palumbo was a nice guy, brought him whatever he needed.

On the surface, Joe seemed to take the transfer in pretty good stride. But Jimmy could see he was upset, and his heart bled for him. He was getting on in years, had been very contented in Sing Sing, and was finally due to meet the parole board early the next year. He confided to Jimmy that that was what bothered him the most, because he still wanted to see a little more of the outside world before he went to his Maker. But Joe was a genuine tough guy who didn't flinch in the face of disaster, and by the third day of walking together he was laughing and kidding with Jimmy like he didn't have a care in the world.

A few days after Joe Gray's arrival in Dannemora, Jimmy was summoned to the P.K.'s office. He was a little puzzled when the hack came for him right out of the blue. As he walked through the corridors he tried to figure out the reason La Morte wanted to see him, thought it might be a delayed reaction from his fight with Puggy, but dismissed that idea as being too old an incident for the P.K. to be asking about it now.

The hack ushered Jimmy into the P.K.'s office and La Morte immediately rose from his desk, walked over to him, and shook hands like he was his best friend. Jimmy was surprised, but pleased at such a warm greeting. He relaxed, things were okay, this half a nut is acting like I'm his dearest pal.

"Well, Riley, you certainly look like Dannemora is agreeing with you. You look twice as good as you did when you first arrived."

"Thank you, Mr. La Morte, but that wouldn't be too hard. I do feel good, though."

"How's everything going in the hospital?"

"I think I'm doing fine, Mr. La Morte. Richard and the doctor have taken a lot of pains training me, and I'm finally getting the hang of being a surgical nurse."

"The doctor has only praise for you, Riley. He says you caught on real quick."

"That's good to hear, sir."

"Now, have you any idea why I sent for you, Riley?"

"No, sir."

"I understand that you're a real close friend of Mr. Joe Gray, our famous new inmate."

"I'm not sure I'm that close, Mr. La Morte. I only met him for the first time in my life in Sing Sing. He was an old friend of my father's many years ago and he was very nice to me the short time I was in Sing Sing. I tried to reciprocate and extend the same courtesy to him when he arrived up here. He's an extremely nice man, Mr. La Morte, a perfect gentleman."

"Riley, I don't give a shit how nice a man he is." La Morte's voice suddenly got harsh, his face began to contort. No more Mr. Nice Guy. He paced back and forth. "Joe Gray is another hot potato these big shots in Albany are handing me. Him and his fucking politician friends."

Jimmy stood in front of La Morte, stunned at his abrupt change of attitude. This guy's half a maniac if ever I saw one. Why in the name of Christ is he telling me all this? Just keep your mouth shut and wait for his next move.

La Morte stopped pacing, his voice became softer, almost apologetic. "Riley, I shouldn't jump on you. Here's why I sent for you. I want you to report to me personally everything Joe Gray does in this prison."

"I don't think I understand, Mr. La Morte."

"Riley, you do like your hospital job, don't you?"

"Yes, sir."

"Did I cooperate with you and give you a nice clean job, a comfortable hospital bed in a dormitory?"

"Yes, sir."

"Now, Riley, listen carefully. I want you to cooperate with me one hundred percent. I know you're a good friend of Joe Gray's, the only inmate he looked up here, the only inmate he's hung out with since he's been here." La Morte's voice became harsh again, louder. "I want you to keep tabs on Gray for me. I want to know who his friends are, if any guards do him favors, who he eats with, everything. I want to know every time Gray takes a piss while he's in my prison."

Jimmy looked at this nut. *What the hell is it about me that every sonofabitch who has me by the balls tries to make a stool pigeon out of me? I no sooner get finished with that power-mad Leibowitz and now I wind up with this psycho bastard.*

"I don't think there's any necessity for that, Mr. La Morte. Joe Gray won't give you an ounce of trouble."

"Riley, I didn't ask for your opinion. I'm just telling you what I want you to do."

"Mr. La Morte, do you know why I was sent to prison, why I'm standing here before you?"

"I don't give a shit why or how you got here, Riley, all I know is that you're here. Right here, a fucking inmate."

Now it was Jimmy's turn to get angry. *Fuck this maniacal bastard.* "Get this straight, Mr. La Morte, I don't report on anybody. Get yourself another boy. Count me out."

"Is that your final answer?"

"Yes, sir."

"Well, *you* get this straight, Riley. You're out of the hospital as of now. You're going to solitary for a few days until I decide what to do with you."

"What for?"

"For insubordination. Then I'm going to put you in one of the shops, where you'd better make sure you watch your ass and your head, 'cause someone might cut you a new asshole or take your head off your shoulders." With that splendid admonition he angrily pushed the buzzer on his desk and a big hack came. He pointed his finger at Jimmy and said, "Take this man up to solitary confinement, Officer."

"Should I get his stuff first, sir?"

"You heard what I said. Take him right up to the solitary confinement block."

Jimmy just stood there mute, lips buttoner tight. *No use aggravating the situation worse than it was. Christ, what a world, I can't even write a letter to my local congressman.*

The big hack marched Jimmy through another series of stairs, corridors, and gates until they reached the Box, as the solitary confinement area was called. There he turned him over to the custody of another hack, who met him with a smile and seemed like a nice guy. He took Jimmy along the tier to an empty cell, opened the cell door, and said, "Here we go, Riley. Anything you want to know, ask me now. You're not allowed to talk in here, not to anyone, unless you get sick. Then, if you know what's good for you, you better be real sick." He winked at Jimmy as he locked the cell door, smiled sympathetically.

"How about a book? Can I read?"

"I'll see if I can find something for you, but you can only read during the day. You're not allowed any lights in here. Take it easy, Riley."

Jimmy sat back on the bed and looked his new quarters over. He decided he liked the dormitory a whole lot better. The cell was clean, the usual bed, flush toilet, and sink. He lay back and propped a pillow beneath his head, contemplating where he had gone wrong in this rotten fucking world to keep meeting up with the likes of Leibowitz and La Morte. He hoped Joe Gray wouldn't hear about the come-off between him and La Morte and get upset about it. He's had enough aggravation the past month. Jimmy consoled himself, there's nothing you can do to combat guys who have dictator complexes and who have the whip hand over you. Lie back and relax, tomorrow will be a better day.

About twenty minutes after he was locked in, a paperback book landed in front of Jimmy's cell. Somebody near him had heard his request to the hack. God bless you, whoever you are. It was a good mystery story and consumed the rest of the day.

A couple of other books arrived to Jimmy's delight. The meals were served through an opening in the cell bars, plain and simple, but not too bad. After a year in prison Jimmy wasn't the slightest bit fussy about food, he ate what was served and was satisfied. It was like a morgue in the Box, as quiet as six o'clock Mass on a winter morning. But you didn't hear the tinkling bells of the priest as he performed the ritual, you heard only slamming metal gates and the rustling of the hack's keys as he walked along the tier every hour to make sure no one escaped. Some chance. The nights weren't too long, as it was still daylight saving time, and Jimmy could turn his pillow to the foot of the bed and read until the last ray of light when darkness fell. He would then do a series of sit-ups and push-ups, wash thoroughly, stretch out and fall into a deep sleep. Jimmy Riley had adapted to the environment, he had finally become a true-blue convict.

The fourth morning of his stay, he was released from solitary. He was led back to the hospital by a hack to get his belongings, and when he arrived Richard greeted him like a long-lost brother. He was allowed to use Richard's room, where he showered, brushed his teeth for about five minutes, and shaved off his newly acquired mini-beard. He finished his ablutions and changed from his hospital whites to regular prison grays.

"What the hell happened to you?" Richard asked.

"I had an argument with that crazy fuck La Morte, and as you can see, he won. He put me in the Box for a few days."

"Jesus, Jimmy, why did he do that?"

"He tried to make a stool pigeon out of me, wanted me to report all Joe Gray's daily activities to him, personally. Imagine that?"

"That no-good sonofabitch. Can you believe this guy? You're being transferred, you know that?"

"I know. But where? Do you know?"

"Yeah, Jim. It hurts to tell you, you're going to the weave shop. The civilian nurse, Armand, he told me."

"Shit. Not the weave shop?"

"That's the bad news, Jimmy. I'm sorry. Here, you take my shiv, you might need it. I'll make another one, don't worry about it. And here's a roll of adhesive tape. Tape the shiv to your chest every morning and cut a small hole in your mattress and bunk it there every night in case they give your cell a toss. You're high on the shit list, so expect a toss every couple of days. They do that to break your chops."

"Thanks, Richard." Jimmy fondled the shiv. It was a half section of a large scissors, honed down to razor sharpness on the flintstone wheel Richard used to sharpen the surgical scalpels. It was a beauty, and as Jimmy taped it to his chest it gave him a good feeling.

He said his sad goodbyes to Richard, the doctor, Mr. Armand, and a few of the guys who were around the dormitory. He packed his belongings in a duffel bag, and the hack took him to an E-Block tier where the guys from the weave ship were put up. That afternoon he went out to the yard and met Joe Gray and Little Stanley. The cause of the argument he had with La Morte and the punishment it resulted in was all over the yard. Joe felt badly about it, but Jimmy reassured him, it had to come. Little Stanley was proud of him for standing up to La Morte, and so were the other guys on the court. A half-dozen guys came over and shook hands with him, not mentioning anything, but Jimmy could see the approval in their eyes. He felt good all over, happy to be out of the Box. He'd stood firm, held his ground with the P.K. Fuck that crazy bastard La Morte, Leibowitz, and the rest of the bounty hunters.

The first couple of days in the weave shop were a nightmare. Jimmy's job was to operate a loom, to weave sheets out of a rough off-white fabric. He was undoubtedly the worst candidate in the world for running a loom. He couldn't even run a vacuum cleaner, much less a loom. He was mired in confusion, sick with helplessness. He had bobbins to change, constantly breaking needles to fix—all seemingly insoluble mysteries to him. If there was ever a new word to be coined to describe Jimmy around machinery it would be "unmechanical." Yessir, Jimmy Riley was simply unmechanical.

There was a young kid from East Harlem named Ricky on the next machine, and he and one of the shop mechanics worked with him for about a week until he finally mastered the subtleties of the loom and became a passable weaver. Certainly a cherished goal in his life.

The shop was huge, with about a hundred machines working, one guy to each machine, and about a dozen inmate mechanics walking around to make speedy repairs to the ancient looms. The weave-shop boss hack sat on a high thronelike chair overseeing the men while another hack patrolled around the rows of machines.

It was a spartan regimen after the easy life in the hospital. The wake-up bell rang at six o'clock and you were expected out of your cell, washed and dressed, by six thirty to march to the giant mess hall for breakfast. You marched back from the mess hall to your cell, stayed there about ten minutes, and then marched off to the weave shop to begin work at eight o'clock. Promptly on the hour a bell rang, the boss hack blew his whistle, and the men started their machines. At ten o'clock a bell rang for coffee break and at ten thirty the bell and whistle signaled work to resume.

The routine was a pain in the ass for a while but Jimmy soon adjusted to it, for no other reason than he knew that he must adjust to it. There was one fly in the ointment, one thing that disturbed him—Puggy Slagle was one of the shop mechanics. He appeared to have the run of the place, but he never spoke a word, never came close to Jimmy's machine. His pal, Daniel Boone Williams, the great white hunter, was another weaver, way back on the far side of the shop. Jimmy occasionally came face to face with him but always ignored the stupid-looking fuck.

The two of them were on Jimmy's mind for a week or so, but he gradually dismissed them as two shitheels not worth worrying about. Leave well enough alone, they don't bother me, I won't bother them. Still, he took the precaution of taping the shiv to his chest every morning, and every once in a while patted his chest.

Three weeks passed and Jimmy began to feel more comfortable at the loom. Maybe he had a secret mechanical talent after all. He became friendly with the kid, Ricky, on the next machine, spent his coffee break with him, and ate next to him in the mess hall. He walked in the yard every afternoon with Little Stanley and spent some time with Joe gray every weekend. Joe had decided to join another court to take the heat off Jimmy with the P.K.

To his dying day Jimmy will never know what really happened. He was japped, taken by a surprise attack. He guessed later that he must have got careless, but for Christ's sake, you can't walk around all your life expecting to get a shiv stuck into you. You'd die a nervous wreck before your time.

It was just after the bell rang to end the coffee break and resume work. Jimmy returned to his loom, started it, and watched for the bobbin to run out of thread so he could replace it with a fresh one. His machine was in the last row, just off a wall, the second from the front end near the boss hack's chair. Ricky had the front machine off the aisle, just to the left of Jimmy. There was a loud commotion a couple of rows ahead, distinct over the hum of the looms. Shouting, arguing—evidently a fight had broken out between two inmates. The bell rang shrilly, all machines stopped, the shouting and yelling were louder up ahead. The hack blew his whistle frantically, scrambled down from his high chair, and ran toward the end of the shop.

Jimmy and Ricky walked around the front to see what was going on. Ricky turned to say something, and suddenly a wild look came over his face and he screamed, "Jimmy, look out!"

Jimmy turned and saw Puggy Slagle about five feet away coming at him with a shiv. He instinctively raised his arm up to his head, and never remembered another thing. Daniel Boone Williams, he learned later, hit him on the back of the head with a length of pipe. He fell forward like he was shot, and Puggy ripped him across the face with his shiv. Daniel Boone dropped the pipe and ran to the rear of the weave shop. Ricky kicked Puggy in the balls, knocked the shiv out of his hand, and sailed it to the back of the shop. Puggy picked himself off Jimmy, doubled up in pain, and hobbled to the rear screaming every curse word he knew around one phrase, "I got him, I got him, I got him."

Someone hollered for the hacks, and in a few minutes a stretcher arrived for Jimmy. His face was covered with blood, he was out, ice cold. They carried him across the yard to the hospital. Ricky was one of the stretcher-bearers and he exhorted the others to run all the way.

Jimmy came to a couple of times for a brief second or two while on the operating table. He'd hear voices, then they'd fade away into blackness, he'd faintly hear them again and then lapse off into another world. They finally shot him up with a strong sedative and he never heard another voice. He was unconscious for two days.

He returned to the world groggily, looked around to get his bearings, realized he was in the hospital. It was daylight outside, the sun pouring through the wide windows. He saw that he had tubes in his arms, recognized the apparatus hanging next to him and knew he was being fed intravenously. His mouth was terribly dry, parched, he was almost dehydrated. There was a pitcher of water and a glass on the table next to his bed—he reached for them and the room whirled around like a top. He felt very weak, dizzy, exhausted. He lay back, closed his eyes, and fell sound asleep again.

He awoke again, this time feeling a little better. There were lights on, it was night outside. He turned his head, it hurt like hell. Richard was sitting next to his bed. Jimmy winked at him.

"Jim, how do you feel? You okay? Can you talk?"

"Richard. Christ, what the hell hit me? Get me some water, please. I'm dying of thirst."

Richard lifted his head slightly and he sipped water noisily through a long straw. Christ, the water tasted good, a little Cutty in it would've tasted better.

"How's that, Jim? You okay now?"

"I guess I'll live, Richard. I was as dizzy as hell when I woke up this afternoon, but now I'm feeling pretty good. What the hell are all these bandages? What happened to my face?"

"You don't know?"

"I only know I got some whack in the back of the head, that's all I remember."

"Jimmy, I hate to tell you this, but that crazy fucking Puggy cut your face."

Jimmy felt the right side of his face, it was one long pad of gauze kept in place by strips of adhesive tape. That rotten sneaky nut bastard, I'll cut his fucking head off when I get out of here.

"You were lucky, Jim, he cut you along the mandible, which is the jaw-bone. I cauterized it until we reached the doctor, who sewed it up. Not too bad, about three and a half inches, seventy-eight stitches. Jesus, you were covered with blood and your face was dead white. I thought he hit your jugular. Anyway, I threw a blanket over you and snatched my shiv back off your chest, so no one knows you were carrying that."

"Jeez, Richard, I forgot about the shiv. Good boy."

"It was easy, Jim. The hacks were scared shitless, they thought you were dead. They were running around all over the place. Anyway, to get back to your face, the doctor says a good plastic surgeon can fix it easy. But wait until you get home, the plastic surgeon that comes in here is a fucking butcher. Meanwhile, you'll look like the Irish Al Capone."

"That's a pleasant thought. What about this cast on my right hand? What happened to that?"

"When that big hoosier fuck hit you with the pipe you evidently had your hand against your head. He fractured your thumb and the knuckle next to it, but it reduced the force of the blow on your head. You're very lucky, Jim, you only got a severe concussion, no fracture of the skull. The doctor and I X-rayed your skull when you were out cold. He was amazed the X-rays didn't show a fracture, you have some fucking hard Irish head."

Jimmy smiled. "You sound just like Judge Leibowitz, that's what he kept telling me."

Richard laughed. "You want to hear the outcome, the pay-off from your getting whacked out?"

"Go ahead, tell me."

"They took Puggy out of here in a straitjacket, stark raving mad. He's back again in Box A. This time for good, I hope. You can forget about getting even with him unless you want to sign yourself into the nuthouse."

"Who hit me with the pipe? Daniel Boone?"

"You guessed it the first time. He went right to the P.K. and asked for protection, the big yellow bastard. The P.K. sent him to the Box."

While Richard and Jimmy were talking the doctor stopped by. He was very concerned, but pleased to see Jimmy alert and speaking rationally. He described Jimmy's injuries, using words like hematoma, subdural hemorrhage, mandible, and other medical terms as if Jimmy was a fellow physician rather than a novice assistant surgical nurse. But he mainly stressed how lucky Jimmy was that his hand had softened the blow from the lead pipe. He smiled and added that he was also lucky to have a hard Irish head. Maybe Judge Leibowitz had been right all along.

Another week passed by and Jimmy was allowed to get out of bed and walk around the hospital ward. Richard and the other guys fed him outrageously, took care of him like a baby, and he was regaining his strength every day.

He was in bed reading one afternoon when the P.K. appeared at his side. Jimmy looked up and said sarcastically, "Well, you almost got your wish, Mr. La Morte."

La Morte looked like he was about to cry. "I didn't really mean what I said, Riley. I was just angry, steamed up at you. I'm sorry you got hit. Who did it, Riley? I want to prosecute these men."

"I haven't the vaguest idea, Mr. La Morte. I was hit from behind and knocked cold. I never saw the guy who cut my face."

"Come on, Riley, I know the inmate Slagle cut you. We had to commit him to Box A. I want to indict him anyway. Now this inmate Daniel Boone Williams, he was mixed up in this in some way. He came to me and requested protection. I know he slugged you but I have no witnesses, nobody saw a thing. I put Williams in the Box. He'll be there a long time. I want you to cooperate with me, Riley, and name these men."

Jimmy had determined to act nice, let bygones be bygones, but the word "cooperate" was by now as irritating as waving a red flag in front of a bull.

"Mr. La Morte, if you use the word 'cooperate' to me again, I'm going to puke all over this bed. Now for Christ's sake, leave me alone with this 'cooperate' bullshit. That goes for as long as I'm in *your* prison. You can just forget that word exists."

"All right, Riley, take it easy, don't get excited. Tell me, do you intend to tell anyone how this all began, how you were transferred out of the hospital to the weave shop?"

Jimmy looked at the P.K. This weak-kneed fuck is afraid I'm going to squeal on him, write to the governor or call my lawyers.

"Mr. La Morte, I told you once, I don't report back to anybody. You did what you felt you had to do, you're the boss here. There's no regrets, no hard feelings. I just want to be left alone and do my bit in peace."

La Morte started to go into his pacing back and forth act. He turned to Jimmy and said, "Would you like to go back to work in the hospital, Riley?"

"No strings attached, Mr. La Morte?"

"No strings, Riley, I give up on you. You can have your old job back when you get better. You want to know something, Riley? I never replaced you."

"Why?"

"I figured after a few days in the Box and a couple of weeks in the weave shop you'd come crawling back to me."

"I guess you figured wrong, Mr. La Morte."

"I guess I did. Maybe you got some good in you, after all, Riley. I'll see you around."

La Morte turned away abruptly and walked out of the ward. Jimmy looked at his retreating back. Christ, it must have killed him to say that. Maybe he's got some good in him, even if he is a nut. I guess if you become the P.K. of a joint like this, you have to sooner or later turn into some kind of nut.

Jimmy recovered rapidly and was just about ready to return to work. His transfer back to the hospital had come through, and he had moved back to the dormitory and his old bed. Richard was just as elated by the good news as Jimmy was. Little Stanley had been up to the hospital to see him, and though at first he was very upset about the condition he was in, he soon had both of them howling laughing at some of his old experiences. Little Stan laughed at his own jokes louder than anyone, and his laughter was infectious.

Little Stanley urged him to go to the yard, the guys on the court and Joe Gray were anxious to see him, but he didn't feel up to the yard just yet. He wasn't ready to face the stares and the inevitable questions. Let the yard wait for a while. Though the stitches were out of his jawbone, the scar was bright red and ugly-looking. The doctor assured him the wound would calm down considerably as the months rolled by, but he was still very conscious of it.

Jimmy decided to take his first walk in the fresh air of the hospital yard. It was small compared to the main yard but ample distance to walk back and forth. The hospital yard lay between the side of the building and the high gray prison wall. He was dressed warmly, for the sharp chill of autumn was in the air. He walked up and back in the yard at a leisurely pace, his legs still a bit weak from his long siege in bed. It felt wonderful to walk alone on this crisp, beautiful day. He was thrilled to be alive. Happy, very happy. He looked about at the high gray walls and reminisced back when he was a little boy and his mother and father took him to see his older brother John graduate from grade school.

How proud he was when John, dressed in blue suit, starched white shirt, and Sacred Heart tie, came onstage to sing "The Dear Little Town in the Old County Down." How clear his sweet boyish tenor rang out in the small auditorium. Could he ever forget the verse?

> Sure if I had the wings of an angel
> Over these prison walls I would fly.
> I would fly to the arms of my darling
> And there I would gladly die.
>
> Way down in the west
> Where the sun comes to rest
> There's a sweet little nest
> It's the place I love best.

Poor John, gone long before his time. Oh, if only I had the wings of an angel, would I ever fly over these prison walls. To home, the kids, the arms of my darling. He grinned. Some angel I'd make. I've got a better chance with the guy down Below and maybe I could get out underneath these prison walls.

He looked up at the blue sky and saw the pigeons flying over the prison. How free they soared against the background of white clouds—over walls, gun towers, all the ugliness of Dannemora. He remembered the cold March day he was sworn into The Job by Mayor LaGuardia on the steps of City Hall. How trapped and frustrated he was that day, and how he wished he was a pigeon and could fly out of the trap he thought The Job would be. And then the dumb bastard of a mayor, who preached against corruption for a half hour that cold March day, soon had him in the city-wide vice squad working for a hundred dollars a month and expected him to be honest.

Jimmy laughed to himself. I wonder if all this was worth the great trip I had. Seven or eight wonderful years. He looked up at the pigeons again—oh, pigeon, if I could only fly out of this trap. All the humiliation, the intimidation, the disfiguration—

being treated like shit from the first day I was pinched. The best years of my life spent in these shithouses—Raymond Street, Dannemora.

Jimmy brushed off the bitterness, thought again of the good days. It was a great trip—the high life, fine clothes, beautiful showgirls, money coming out of every pocket. Would I ever want to turn the clock back to boyhood and begin again? Never. In spite of everything, I had a sweet life. And one day soon Jimmy Riley would be home again and get another crack at life—the sweet life that Jimmy Riley knew.

TOUGH STREETS

The grit, the dirt, the cheap cost of life—the ongoing struggle between the law...and the lawbreakers.

BIG TIME TOMMY SLOANE
James Reardon
_____ 90981-0 $3.95 U.S.   _____ 90982-9 $4.95 Can.

TIGHT CASE
Edward J. Hogan
_____ 91142-4 $3.95 U.S.   _____ 91143-2 $4.95 Can.

RIDE A TIGER
Harold Livingston
_____ 90487-8 $4.95 U.S.   _____ 90488-6 $5.95 Can.

THE RIGHT TO REMAIN SILENT
Charles Brandt
_____ 91381-8 $3.95 U.S.   _____ 91382-6 $4.95 Can.

THE EIGHTH VICTIM
Eugene Izzi
_____ 91218-8 $3.95 U.S.   _____ 91219-6 $4.95 Can.

THE TAKE
Eugene Izzi
_____ 91120-3 $3.50 U.S.   _____ 91121-1 $4.50 Can.

Publishers Book and Audio Mailing Service
P.O. Box 120159, Staten Island, NY 10312-0004

Please send me the book(s) I have checked above. I am enclosing
$ _____ (please add $1.25 for the first book, and $.25 for each
additional book to cover postage and handling. Send check or
money order only—no CODs.)

Name _____

Address _____

City _____ State/Zip _____

Please allow six weeks for delivery. Prices subject to change
without notice.